THE LION'S ROAR

The adventures of Tevye the Milkman continue in *The Lion's Roar*, the third dramatic novel in the *"Tevye in the Promised Land"* Series. While Tevye's granddaughter, Hannie, is finishing her college degree in New York, the love of her life, Avraham "Yair" Stern is purchasing weapons in Poland and training Jewish soldiers for a war against British forces in Palestine. When Perchik is murdered and three Revisionists falsely accused of the crime, brotherly strife in the Holy Land threatens the future of the entire Zionist endeavor. Perchik's wife, and his son, Ben Zion, hide the identity of the true murderers, and the ugly, blood libel leads to the false conviction of Avraham Stavsky. Rabbi Kook's campaign on behalf of the condemned man culminates in his triumphant acquittal. In a gallant bid of rapprochement with Ben Gurion, the efforts of Ze'ev Jabotinsky prove futile. In a more joyous development, Hannie's tumultuous, on and off romance with the volatile Yair finally leads to the *chuppah*. But another Arab uprising leaves Jews slaughtered throughout the country. When Tevye's attempt to assassinate the Grand Mufti fails, he is forced to flee to America, where he raises funds for the *Irgun* underground with the assistance of the notorious Jewish mobsters, Meyer Lansky and Bugsy Siegel. In Jerusalem, under the command of David Raziel, Tevye's son, Tzvi, carries out devastating, reprisal attacks against the Arabs. When the British hang the *Betar* youth, Shlomo Ben Yosef, Jabotinsky's leadership is challenged by Avraham Stern and the young Menachem Begin. Returning to the Holy Land, Tevye captains a boatful of "illegal" *ma'apilim* immigrants to the shores of Palestine, where the il the secret, nighttim h commander, Orde Cha , joins with the *Haganal* b Revolt by unapolo r encampments and enti ı severely curtail Jewish i and outlaw the further sale of land to jews, the *Irgun* retaliates with a series of deadly attacks against British targets. During a mission to blow up the Rex Cinema in Jerusalem, Tevye's daughter is captured and brutally tortured. Willing to die for the cause of freedom, the young girl attempts a daring escape from the Bethlehem Prison for Women, in a symbolic act of defiance that rallies the awakening Nation to rise up in revolt against the British usurpers of the Jewish Homeland.

"All I can say is, Wow! Tzvi Fishman has a way of making the reader feel a part of the drama. In Volume Three of the *Tevye in the Promised Land* Series, *The Lion's Roar*, I felt like I was sitting on the defendant's bench alongside Avraham Stavsky in the famous murder trial that rocked the Jews of Palestine; felt like I was spending the last minutes in Acco Prison with Shlomo Ben Yosef on his way to the gallows; and there I was accompanying Tevye on his way to assassinate the Grand Mufti of Jerusalem, and hanging around with Meyer Lansky in New York to solicit his help in the cause. All from a refreshingly patriotic point of view, from the pen of a proud Zionist and lover of Israel like Fishman."

Baruch Gordon, Founder, Israel National News

"The *Tevye in the Promised Land* Series is a wonderful achievement. For adults and young people alike, these historical novels about the rebirth of the Jewish People in the Land of Israel are powerful tools, inviting people to enjoy once again the almost lost art of reading. The incredible drama of Modern Zionism, along with the towering personalities which dominated the era, their heroism and great ideals, come alive in the pages of this fun-reading saga. If the next two volumes of the series possess the same passion and charm, then Mr. Fishman has created a literary treasure for the Jewish People."

Yisrael Medad, Menachem Begin Heritage Center

"Tzvi Fishman is a splendid writer on any topic he chooses, but on Israel, he is simply brilliant. Attention must be paid to this writer whose prose is direct, passionate and so illuminating. If the philosophy of the political Left in Israel still has a heartbeat, this recount of modern Zionist history will bury it completely."

Jack Engelhard, Bestselling Novelist

"A fun and fascinating way to learn about modern Jewish history. Many people toss around the names of Rabbi Kook, Yosef Trumpledor, Zeev Jabotinsky, Avraham Yair Stern, Uri Zvi Greenberg, and other Zionist figures, without knowing very much about them. In the novels *Arise and Shine!* and its sequel, *The Lion's Roar*, these inspiring, larger-than-life characters come alive in a way you will never forget. *Yasher koach gadol!*"

Rabbi David Samson, Dean of the YTA and Atid High School Institutions in Israel

THE LION'S ROAR

Volume Three of the Series
Tevye in the Promised Land

Tzvi Fishman

AM K'LAVI • Jerusalem

With heartfelt thanks to the Almighty for enabling me to write this book; and to my wife, my children, and my parents for their love, ever-lasting patience, and support.

THE LION'S ROAR
Published by Am K'Lavi, Jerusalem
Distributed by:
Sifriyat Beit-El Publishing Ltd. Jerusalem, Israel
02-6427117
For mail orders: www.beitel.co.il

Cover Art by Anna Kogan - anakogan85@gmail.com
Graphics by Noam Fishman
Computer Typeset by Moshe Kaplan

For more information: www.tzvifishmanbooks.com
ISBN 800-1081004
Printed in Israel

For the millions of Jews who perished in the Holocaust, without ever seeing the Promised Land, and for all of the "Anonymous Soldiers" who fought and sacrificed their lives in the struggle to conquer and rebuild it.

The publication of *Arise and Shine!* was made possible by Mrs. Cherna Moskowitz, a true builder of Israel in our time, and by the Cherna Moskowitz Foundation.

Many of the events in this novel were created around historical events which make up the background canvas for this literary presentation. While inspired by the characters in the Sholom Aleichem stories, "Tevye the Milkman," all of the characters are the invention of the author, and are entirely fictional. Exceptions are the public figures, such as David Ben Gurion and Zev Jabotinsky, who lived at the time, and whose fanciful portraits in the novel have been made a part of the story. To aid the reader, a list of background sources, and a glossary of Yiddish and Hebrew words and expressions can be found at the end of the book.

OLD CITY

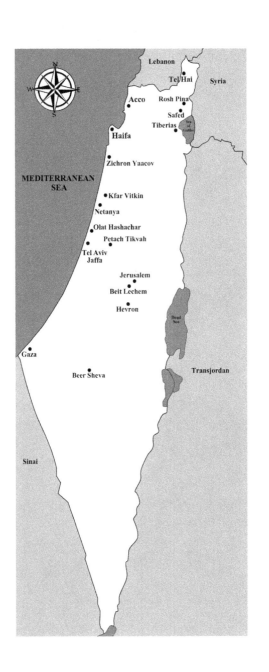

Contents

Chapter 1: *HORN OF THE BEAST* *19*

Chapter 2: *BEYOND THE SEA* *46*

Chapter 3: *THE BURNING BUSH* *55*

Chapter 4: *THE ARONOV MURDER* *68*

Chapter 5: *FROM FLORENCE WITH LOVE* *109*

Chapter 6: *FIRE IN THE LAND* *126*

Chapter 7: *FRIENDS AT LAST* *185*

Chapter 8: *YAIR* *200*

Chapter 9: *IF NOT NOW, WHEN?* *249*

Chapter 10: *VENGEANCE IS MINE* *263*

Chapter 11: *GOD BLESS AMERICA!* *277*

Chapter 12: *ANONYMOUS SOLDIERS* *309*

Chapter 13: *THE SQUEAKY DOOR* *341*

Chapter 14: *HOMEWARD BOUND* *385*

Chapter 15: *WINGATE CRUSHES THE REVOLT* *432*

Chapter 16: *REBELLION AT LAST* *461*

Glossary 510

"The lion has roared, who will not fear?"
Amos, 3:8

THE
LION'S
ROAR

1933

Chapter One
HORN OF THE BEAST

On *Rosh HaShanah* morning, Tevye prayed the *shacharit* prayer in the Ohel Yitzhak Synagogue on HaGai Street, along with other Jews who hadn't fled the Old's City's Western Wall Quarter after the bloody Arab pogroms of 1929. In another half hour, the blasts of the *shofar* would resound in the beautiful house of worship, which had been built by the Jewish Hungarian community in 1875. They called themselves "*Shomrei HaChomot*" – the "Guardians of the Walls" – establishing their homes as close to the Wailing Wall as they could, to make sure that the ancient remnant of the Second Temple remained in Jewish hands, and that the Holy City remained populated by a majority of Jews. But on the first day of the festive holiday, Tevye decided to hear the *shofar* blowing in the *Hurva* Synagogue, located in the upper Jewish Quarter, at the top of the hill. Rabbi Kook was scheduled to arrive there to deliver a New Year's sermon, after he concluded his *shacharit* prayers in his "*Mercaz HaRav Yeshiva*" on the Street of the Prophets. The previous week, posters had been pasted around the city announcing that the Ashkenazi Chief Rabbi would deliver a *Rosh HaShanah* sermon at the *Hurva* Synagogue in the Old City before the sounding of the *shofar*, so a large crowd was expected.

"Let's go, *Abba*," Tevye's nineteen-year-old son, Tzvi, urged. "If we don't get there on time, we won't find any seats."

"So we will stand," Tevye answered. "That's why the Almighty has given us legs. Standing won't be such a tragedy, my son. On this holy day, we stand for six hours in prayer all morning long, so if we must stand for another half-hour in order to hear the great Rabbi Kook, *nisht der suf fun der velt*, it is not the end of the world."

Boaz, Tevye's seventeen-year-old, followed them out of the synagogue, along with some of the other worshippers. Outside, Tevye's wife, Carmel, was waiting, with their daughter, Naomi, both wearing their finest holiday garb. Tevye's daughters Hodel and Ruchel joined the procession, with their teenage children, David, Sarah, Yehoshua, and Ruth. "A real tribe," Tevye mused with great pride. Carmel's younger brother, Nachshon, followed in the rear, his hand gripping the revolver in his jacket pocket. The new *Betar* Youth Movement, which had drawn many young people away from the ranks of the lusterless *Haganah*, provided escort protection for Jews in the Old City, but they didn't have guns to hand out to everyone. In addition, under British Mandate law, the possession of firearms was forbidden. Tevye, who had a gun of his own, didn't ask Nachshon where he acquired his. Not only was the Yemenite youth, Nachshon, his brother-in-law, he was best friends with Tzvi, who also had a rifle or two of his own. If Arabs staged an ambush along the alleyways of the Old City, Tevye's entourage had the means to respond.

Tevye herded his family along the cobblestoned Hevron Street and up through the Arab *casbah*. With his white tallit draped over his shoulders like a cape, he resembled a French general leading his troops. No longer a young chicken at sixty, he still walked with powerful strides – when his back wasn't aching from lugging heavy milk containers all morning long. Arab merchants nodded their heads in respect as he passed. Everyone recognized the Jewish milkman. Why couldn't the sons of Jacob and the sons of Ishmael always live in peace, Tevye wondered, as they had for the past two years? Yet he knew it wasn't meant to be. Long, long ago, the Almighty had given the Promised Land to the Jews, and the Arabs were still driven by an ancient jealousy. *Haval, haval* – what a shame! Especially on *Rosh Hashanah*, when the Jews prayed for the welfare of all mankind, and for the glorious day when the whole world, with one heart, would acknowledge God as their King, may it be soon.

More and more Jews from all over the city filled the narrow streets leading to "*HaRova HaYehudi*" - the Jewish Quarter – to hear Rabbi Kook's sermon. Some were dressed in European suits and hats; others in colorful Oriental robes and turbans; and there were also the Ultra-Orthodox of

Jerusalem, wearing their traditional, striped, ankle-length gowns and round, furry *streimels* squarely on their heads.

Tevye's group reached the Jaffa Gate plaza in time to greet the entourage accompanying the Chief Rabbi. Though the regal-looking sage was approaching his seventies, he walked with a quick and upright gait. A silk, black robe extended down to his shoes. His fur *spodik* hat graced his head like a crown. Seeing Tevye, his eyes sparkled and he nodded his head, even though he was the Chief Rabbi and Tevye was only a milkman. Ever since Tevye had first met the Rabbi in Jaffa, over thirty years before upon Tevye's arrival in the Promised Land, Rabbi Kook's eyes had reached out and captured him. Never in his life had he encountered such eyes! While they glittered with a mystical, dreamy, faraway look, at the same time, the light of his glance penetrated down to your soul, enveloping it with a tangible feeling of kindness and unconditional love. Escorting the Chief Rabbi were his son, Rabbi Tzvi Yehuda Kook, Rabbi Moshe Harlop, the saintly Rabbi Aryeh Levine, and the young and beardless Rabbi Moshe Segal, the famous blower of the *Yom Kippur shofar* at the *Kotel*, which was heard around the world in defiance of British law. The distinguished attorney, Mordechai Eliash, walked at the Rabbi's side. Ruchel's scholarly husband, Nachman, followed the group, along with the tall, red-bearded Hevedke, Hava's husband, may her murder be avenged. Tevye's grandson, Akiva, grasped Hevedke's hand. Yeshiva students, *baal habatim*, and children joined in the festive march. Amongst the entourage, Tevye also recognized a few of the secular leaders of the Zionist Executive in Jerusalem who respected the esteemed Torah scholar for his broad and enlightened world-outlook, which distinguished him from the spiritual leaders of the *Old Yishuv* who stridently opposed anything new. Understanding the deep Biblical roots of Zionism, and recognizing the supreme value of dwelling in the Land of Israel to the individual Jew and to the Jewish Nation as a whole, Rabbi Kook appreciated the secular Zionists for their contribution in helping to restore life to the country's desolate waste-places. While recognizing their shortcomings in Torah observance, Rabbi Kook chose to emphasize the positive achievements of the secular pioneers, and not reject them out of hand, in order to unite the Jewish People in the exalted mission of National Revival. For this, he was chosen Chief Rabbi, along with his Sephardic counterpart, HaRav Yaacov Meir, another wise Torah scholar who saw God's Hand in the return of the scattered exiles to Zion.

The Arab peddlers in the cobblestone Jaffa Gate plaza stopped their doings to watch the Jews stride by in their holiday dress. Even the two British policemen on guard duty, known for their expressionless stares, removed their helmets and bowed in respect as the Chief Rabbi passed by. *Sephardi* Jews rushed forward to kiss the Rabbi's hand. In the crowded procession, Tevye spotted Tzvi's friends, David Raziel, the poet Uri Zvi Greenberg, and the militant writer, Abba Ahimeir, who brazenly called the British "occupiers," and a "foreign regime." Tevye couldn't help but notice the thin, dapperly-dressed young man who was walking beside the outspoken revolutionist. He wore a stylish Fedora hat, and his suit jacket draped over his shoulders like a prayer shawl. His name was Avraham Stern – the Rasputin who had stolen the heart of Tevye's granddaughter, Hannie. Tevye had sent the innocent girl to New York to escape his unbridled advances.

"I'll meet you at the *shul*," Tzvi told his father, as he hurried off to join the Rabbi's procession, enthusiastically shaking the hands of Stern and Ahimeir and walking along at their sides.

"The swastika flag at the German Consulate is an insult to Jerusalem," Ahimeir told the enthusiastic youth, as if he were giving him a command.

"Yes, *Abba*," Tzvi replied, immediately understanding the assignment. Like his friends, he called Ahimeir by his first name, which meant "father," when addressing him, as a sign of loyalty and affection.

Tevye didn't share his son's admiration for the preachers of revolution. Not that he disagreed with their messianic beliefs, but if the boy hung around in their company, he was sure to get himself into trouble. Ahimeir had formed a secret group called the *"Brit HaBirionim,"* named after a radical band of Jews who had rebelled against Rome's ancient conquest of the Land of Israel. "*Birionim*" meant "thugs." Ahimeir had already been arrested for organizing rowdy protests against the British Mandate Authority. The World Zionist Executive and the Jewish Agency, controlled by Chaim Weizmann and David Ben Gurion, were also frequent targets of his scorching pen. Recently, Tzvi had shown his father an editorial Ahimeir published in his ultra-Revisionist "*Hazit Ha'Am*" newspaper, decrying the abandonment of the *Kotel*:

"Everyone, everyone has abandoned the Western Wall. Everyone, except our brave Chief Rabbis and a handful of Israeli youth who refuse to participate in the treachery. Following the exalted example of Moshe Segal, who sounded the shofar at the Wall after the *Yom Kippur* prayers of 1929 - against the wishes of the Mufti, and the British High Commissioner, and against the wishes of the 'new patriarchs' of the Nation, the champions of socialism who view the Jewish community of Palestine as their private *kibbutz*.

"The ancient *Birionim* toppled the golden Roman eagle which hung on the Temple's Wall, for which the Edomite King burned them at the stake. Even after the Gentiles exiled the Jews from their Homeland, for the duration of almost two-thousand years, brave warriors of the holy, remnants of the once great Israelite Kingdom, continued to dwell amidst the ruins of Jerusalem to guard over the Wall. And now the great grandchildren of those *Birionim* are going joyfully to prison, willing to go hungry to defend the honor of Israel.

"Public opinion may not be with us, but for us, the Wall is everything! For us, the stones which comprise the Wall encompass the entire Land of Israel. For us, the Land of Israel is not crop land, not Dead Sea potash, not geographical proximity to Suez. She is first and foremost - the Land of the Wall. Alas, today, material success is placed first, but, for us, the spirituality of the Wall is the basis of everything."

Although Ahimeir's style was too belligerent for Tevye, who felt more at home with the Sholom Aleichem's more humorous way with words, Tevye agreed with Ahimeir's opinions. In fact, if Tevye had the free time, he might have signed on as one of the *Birionim* himself, even if it got him into trouble. For the milkman from Anatevka, the days of bowing down to the *goyim* were over. Where had it gotten the Jews? They had been slaughtered and thrown out of their Biblical Homeland by the Babylonians and Romans, chased out of their villages in Russia and Poland by the Cossacks of the Czar, had their new settlements in Palestine burnt to the ground by the Turks, and now Jewish sons and daughters were ruthlessly slaughtered and raped by the Arabs, while British soldiers and British policemen turned indifferently away. Ahimeir and his comrades spoke the truth, but since the Mandate Authorities were known to send Jews with seditious ideas to prison for months on end, or ban them from the country for defending themselves, as they had done with Ze'ev Jabotinsky, Tevye wasn't thrilled when his son Tzvi ran off to walk proudly alongside the outspoken underground rebels.

A large crowd anxiously awaited the Chief Rabbi's arrival at the magnificently-domed *Hurva* Synagogue in the upper Jewish Quarter, where hundreds of Jewish families still lived in relative safety. In the year 1700, a community of Eastern European Jews, led by Rabbi Yehuda HaHasid, immigrated to the Land of Israel and settled in Jerusalem. They purchased a plot of land in the Old City a few days before the aging Rabbi ascended to Heaven. His followers began to build the synagogue and "Ashkenazi Courtyard," taking building loans at high interest rates from Arab money-lenders. Two decades later, when the Jews couldn't keep up with the ballooning payments, the Arabs destroyed the still-unfinished house of worship. A century later, the renowned Torah leader, the *Gaon of Vilna*, sent his disciples to the Holy Land to settle its desolate borders, warning them that a terrible storm was brewing that would uproot the Jewish communities of Europe. The only refuge was Zion, he told them in a trembling voice, literally envisioning the rampage of murder to come. Arriving in the Holy City, the new pioneers began to pay back all debts, redeem the buildings in the Ashkenazi Courtyard, and rebuild the synagogue, known as the "*Hurva*" - meaning "ruin." Receiving funds from Jewish philanthropists around the world, they succeeded in their goal, naming the magnificent sanctuary *"Beit Yaacov"* in recognition of the Baron James Yaacov de Rothschild, a grand patron of Jewish settlement in *Eretz Yisrael*. Later, during Israel's War of Independence, Jordanian soldiers of the Arab Legion overran the Jewish Quarter and blew up the synagogue, reducing it to heaps of rubble. But I am getting too far ahead in our story.

In 1933, the impressive three-story structure towered over the Old City. From the circular terrace which surrounded the dome, you could see Mount Zion to the west, the City of David to the south, the Temple Mount and the Mount of Olives to the east, and all of the Old City to the north, all the way to Mount Scopus. On a clear day, the mountain range on the eastern side of the Jordan River was visible, a part of Biblical Israel which had originally been awarded to the Jews in the original British Mandate of 1919, then taken away - the first of many subsequent treacheries by the British.

The great hall of the synagogue was filled to overflowing. People pushed to squeeze through the doors. The women headed for the entrance which led to the upper balcony. The pews, the aisles, the open spaces around the *bimah* and in front of the *Aron HaKodesh* housing the Torah scrolls were all crowded with worshippers. Sweating from the heat, Tevye opened his collar. When Rabbi Kook ascended the steps leading to the pulpit, a hush fell over the gathered multitude. Normally on *Rosh HaShanah*, before the sounding of the *shofar*, a great anticipation and tension filled the synagogue, but now, with Rabbi Kook about to speak, the feeling of electricity was as tangible as the light shining down from the arched windows circling the upper balcony. Tevye glanced around at the sea of faces graced with looks of rapture. Avraham Stern, Abba Ahimeir, Uri Zvi Greenberg, and David Raziel, who studied at the Chief Rabbi's yeshiva, gazed intently toward the pulpit, waiting to hear the famous Torah scholar's address. Another youth who studied at the Rabbi's yeshiva stood up from his chair and kindly offered it to Tevye. Finally, the Chief Rabbi began, commencing with a verse from the prophet, Isaiah.

"And it shall come to pass on that day, that a great shofar shall

be blown, and they shall come who were lost in the land of Ashur, and the outcasts in the land of Egypt, and they shall worship the Lord on the Holy Mountain in Jerusalem."

Hearing the Chief Rabbi utter the prophecy, Tevye felt goosebumps break out on his muscular forearms. There could be no doubt that *Hashem's* promise to redeem His People was coming true in their time. The Jews from all over the world who filled the crowded *Hurva* Synagogue were living proof that the long-awaited ingathering of the exiles was already underway.

"In another few moments, we will all pray the holiday *Musaf* prayer, 'Our God and God of our Forefathers, sound the *great shofar* for our freedom....'

"The Prophet spoke of the *'great shofar'* of Redemption, and we pray to sound a *'great shofar'* – specifically a *'great shofar.'*

"There exist different levels of the *shofar* of Redemption. There is the great *shofar*; the regular average *shofar*; and the small *shofar*. In parallel, the laws of *Rosh HaShanah* list three types of *shofars* as well. If possible, a ram's horn should be used. If a ram's horn isn't available, other types of *shofars* are allowed. A *shofar* from a non-*kosher* animal, and a *shofar* taken from an animal that was used in idol worship, are forbidden. If no *kosher shofar* can be found, it is permissible to sound a non-*kosher shofar*, but without reciting a blessing. If one of these were sounded, the commandment of blowing the *shofar* has been fulfilled. These different levels prescribed for *Rosh HaShanah* parallel the different *shofars* of Redemption.

Having heard many Torah lectures from Rabbi Kook, it was obvious to Tevye that on a public occasion like this, he was not giving a dry halachic lesson about *shofar* blowing, simply stating the laws, but rather using the *shofar* to present a far deeper idea. Rabbi Kook continued:

"First, we have to understand the meaning of Redemption. For the Jewish People, Redemption heralds the ending of our exile in foreign lands, and the re-establishment of independent Israelite sovereignty in *Eretz Yisrael*. We are redeemed from subjugation to the nations. Through terrible world conflagrations, international agreements, and the pioneering self-sacrifice of our People, *Hashem* brings us home. Our Sages teach that the Redemption unfolds slowly, '*kimah kimah*,' a little at a time, like the dawning of a new day, gradually, in a developing process which returns the Jewish People to its Land, its Kingdom, and it unique Torah life."

Tevye glanced at Avraham Stern, who stood by the wall at a side of the hall, holding his white Stetson hat by his heart, gazing at the Rabbi in rapture. Maybe, Tevye thought, the tempestuous fellow had some redeeming characteristics after all. If his granddaughter, Hannie, loved him, surely she had a reason.

"What is the essence of the *shofar of Redemption* – what we call the '*shofar of Mashiach*'?" Rabbi Kook asked, speaking loudly so that his voice would carry to the upper balcony where the women sat quietly listening to the cherished Chief Rabbi.

"When we say, 'the *shofar of Mashiach*,' we mean the forces stimulating the Nation of Israel toward rebirth and Redemption. This sounding of the *shofar* gathers the exiles and the scattered outcasts, and brings them back to the Holy Mountain in Jerusalem, where we are gathered today. The righteous souls of the Nation hear the call of this '*great shofar*' and yearn for our full Redemption – which will lead to the Redemption of the world, when all of mankind '*will flock to Jerusalem to learn the ways of the God of Jacob.*'

Once again, Tevye glanced around at the gathered worshippers. All eyes were riveted on Rabbi Kook. He had a way of expressing the deepest spiritual concepts in a way that even a milkman could understand.

"There are other Jews whose religious sensitivities have weakened and who feel distant from exalted religious teachings, but whom nonetheless retain healthy human natures, whose roots also derive from the realm of the holy."

Tevye knew that Rabbi Kook was referring to the secular pioneers.

"And this healthy nature includes the natural desire to be sovereign in one's own Land, to liberate oneself from foreign rule and to live a free life, just like other nations. This natural national desire is exemplified by the normal *shofar* which is commonly found. Although it is a *kosher shofar*, the commandment is more completely fulfilled with the *great shofar*, exemplified by the righteous of the Nation."

Rabbi Kook paused. Suddenly, he looked down at the pulpit and broke into tears. The crowd reacted with stunned silence. Seeing what no one else saw, the Chief Rabbi rested his head in his palm and sobbed. With a deep breath, he regained his composure and continued:

"There is also a third level of the *shofar* of *Mashiach*. This is the non-*kosher shofar*, which is only blown from necessity when no *kosher shofar* is available. When there is an absence of holy exaltation and the yearning for Redemption that stems from it; and if the natural, healthy, yearning for nationalism is also missing; then it is impossible to sound a *kosher shofar of Redemption*, and then the enemies of Israel appear and sound an *impure shofar of Redemption* in our ears. They compel us to hear the sound of the *shofar*. Without giving us respite, they noisily sound a warning siren in our ears, the cries of persecution and oppression, which force us to look toward the Land of Israel for refuge. In this case, the horn of an impure beast becomes the *shofar of Mashiach*. This is the *shofar* of Amalek and of Hitler. They awaken in us the yearning for Redemption. And those who were deaf to the call of the first *shofar*, and to the call of the second, because their ears were sealed – they will hear, against their will, the blast of the forbidden, *impure shofar* – they will be compelled to listen."

Tevye gazed at the listeners. His son's eyes were shining. So were the eyes of Abba Ahimeir, Uri Zvi Greenberg, and Avraham Stern.

"Even these people are considered to have fulfilled the commandment of hearing the *shofar*. However, over this shofar of affliction sounded by *'the enemy of the Jews,'* there is no blessing, for over cursed afflictions we don't recite a blessing."

No one spoke, no one applauded, even the children sat still as Rabbi Kook concluded his sermon.

"We pray that the Holy One Blessed Be He will not compel us to hear the *shofar of the impure beast*. Yet the plain, ordinary *shofar* devoid of religious spirit cannot fully redeem a holy People. Thus we are filled with the prayer: 'Sound the *great shofar* for our freedom,' the *shofar* which derives from the holy depths of the soul of the Israelite Nation, out of the Holy of Holies of our beings – then the Redemption shall be complete."

All of the Jews in the Hurva Synagogue responded with a thunderous, "Amen!"

2.

Not everyone saw the consequences of Hitler's rise to power as clearly as Rabbi Kook. Like the old expression states, most people preferred to keep their heads in the sand. Rabbi Kook wrote letters of warning to Rabbis and Jewish congregations in Europe, but his fervent urgings, calling upon Jews to come to Israel fell on deaf ears, as the prophet Isaiah foresaw: "*Who is blind as he who is perfect, and blind as the Lord's servant? Seeing many things, thou observes not; opening the ears, but he hears not.*" Ze'ev Jabotinsky traveled around Europe, from city to city, but very few adults took his predictions of doom to heart. Only young people still had eyes to see, and ears to hear. Inspired by his message of Jewish pride and bravery, they flocked to join his *Betar* Youth Movement to learn how to march like soldiers.

In Germany, the Weimar Republic had failed to rebuild the defeated country after its losses in World War One. In addition, the worldwide Depression left Germany in economic ruin. Unemployment soared. Widespread frustration and anger gripped the once powerful nation. With his perverted genius, Hitler found someone to blame – the Jews.

When the Nazis became the most powerful party in the Reichstag elections of 1932, the aging Weimar President, Paul von Hindenburg, reluctantly appointed the relentlessly ambitious Hitler as Chancellor of the Reich, planning to strip him of any real power. Hindenburg's old wartime partner, Erich Ludendorff, wrote to the President: "By appointing Hitler to be Chancellor of the Reich you have handed over our sacred German Fatherland to one of the greatest demagogues of all time. I prophesy to you that this evil man will plunge our Reich into the abyss and will inflict immeasurable woe on our nation. Future generations will curse you in your grave for this action."

The eighty-five-year-old Hindenburg answered, "I will make him a postmaster, and he will lick stamps with my portrait pictured on them."

But Hitler had other plans. His murderous purge, "The Night of Long Knives," eliminated all opposition. When Hindenburg died within the year, Hitler became Germany's dictator.

News of the Nazi persecution of German Jewry reached Tevye and Rabbi Kook directly. For several years, in the afternoon, after finishing his milk rounds, Tevye had served Rabbi Kook as a part-time *shamash*, attending to the needs of the round-the-clock guests who visited the Rabbi's residence. After surreptitiously avenging his daughter's rape and murder, Tevye had avoided the Chief Rabbi, fearing that the scholar's piercing gaze would uncover Tevye's private reprisal. While the Reader is, no doubt, curious to learn more about these dramatic events, it would not be appropriate to interrupt our story to recount what was described in cinematic detail in our previous volume, *Arise and Shine!* Likewise, Tevye's eviction from Anatevka, his trek to Palestine with his daughters, and his adventures as a Zionist pioneer before and during World War One, can be found in *Tevye in the Promised Land*, the first volume of this historical-fictional pentalogy. Therefore, as Sholom Aleichem, Tevye's original creator, would say, "To get on with the story...."

After a year, when Rabbi Kook said nothing to Tevye about the unsolved killings, the milkman returned to his afternoon post at the Chief Rabbi's residence, in order to pitch in for his son-in-law, Nachman, who, on the Rabbi's heeding, gave up the hours he spent managing the affairs of the house and yeshiva to devote his time toward the rigorous study required to become a *dayan* in the Jerusalem Rabbinic Court.

One day, not long after the Days of Awe, an agitated, well-dressed, young woman appeared at Rabbi Kook's house wanting to see the Chief Rabbi. Her family name was

Schneider. She spoke a basic Yiddish, with a heavy German accent.

"What would you like to speak to the Rabbi about?" Tevye asked.

"My brother has been arrested and transported out of Jerusalem to a 'holding camp' in Haifa until a ship arrives to take him back to Germany."

"Can I ask why?" Tevye inquired.

"His tourist visa has expired."

Tevye nodded. He had heard of similar cases, but this was the first time that someone had come seeking the help of Rabbi Kook.

Tevye asked her to wait. As usual, when he entered the Rabbi's study, he found the scholar at his desk, writing down detailed explanations of the Torah, or composing a letter. Every day, two dozen epistles arrived for the Chief Rabbi, requesting the Torah scholar's opinion and advice on a myriad of subjects, along with questions in Torah exegesis and law. Hardly sleeping at night, when he finished his midnight prayers and nocturnal study, he dedicated a few hours to his prolific writings on Jewish Law and *Emunah*, the study of Jewish Faith, illuminating the age-old tenets of Judaism in light of the Nation's Revival in *Eretz Yisrael*. His book, *"Orot,"* a deep study of the Nation's rebirth and Redemption, was banned from the Ultra-Orthodox yeshivas of the *Old Yishuv* because of a few sentences praising the young secular pioneers for engaging in exercise and sports to maintain the strong, healthy bodies needed to rebuild the Nation in *Eretz Yisrael*. The bitter controversy, described in the previous volume of this "fictory," pained the deeply-sensitive Rabbi to the core of his being, but he continued to publish his Torah insights, saying that the truths of the times must be told, even if people failed to understand them at first.

When the Rabbi glanced up from his writing, Tevye explained the visitor's concern for her brother.

"Deported back to Germany?" Rabbi Kook said. "How could it be?"

"The British," Tevye answered, as if that one word explained everything.

"Please have her come in," Rabbi Kook told him.

Tevye escorted her into the small room and motioned for her to sit in a chair on the other side of Rabbi Kook's book-cluttered desk. The only other pieces of furniture were two wooden cabinets filled with Talmudic texts. An arched window looked out over the courtyard of the house. Tevye remained standing by the open door. In the name of modesty, whenever a woman came to see Rabbi Kook, someone remained in the room during the meeting. In accordance with the teachings of the Sages of old, the holy scholar avoided looking at women directly. Unaccustomed to be in the presence of so holy a man, the visitor sat stiffly, but Rabbi Kook's immediate reaction of deep concern for her brother assuaged her initial uneasiness.

"Your brother's plight is an outrage," he declared. "God willing, I will speak about the matter personally with the British High Commissioner."

"Thank you, your honor," she said. "My brother isn't the only one facing deportation. Hundreds of Jews have been rounded up to be sent back to Germany."

"Why wasn't I made aware of this?" the Chief Rabbi asked, gazing at Tevye. The milkman could only shrug.

"My family owns a large clothing business in Bonn, and a chain of department stores," the woman explained. "Before Hitler seized power, we never encountered problems with the Germans. The Depression hurt our business, like with everyone else, but we survived. When Hitler began to close Jewish stores and factories, our factories were allowed to continue manufacturing because we employ over ten-thousand Aryans. When my father was told that Jews could no longer work in the factories, he sent my brother to Palestine to see if we could have a better future here. After several weeks in the country, my brother sent for me to join him. Now the British are set to deport him."

"It is like ordering a man who has escaped from a burning house to return to the inferno," Rabbi Kook remarked.

"Yes, I'm afraid so," she agreed. "I am frightened over what will be, for him, for my family, for all of the Jews of Germany."

"Please tell me what is happening there," the Rabbi asked her.

"The Nazis have an anti-Semitic newspaper called *Der Sturmer* which publishes horrible caricatures of Jews. Their articles blame the Jews for all of the country's woes. In Mannheim, Bonn, and other cities, Hitler's Stormtroopers have closed all Jewish businesses. Almost everywhere, they have broken into Jewish homes and beaten people ruthlessly. At first, many Germans opposed the boycott of Jewish businesses imposed by the government, but after sympathizers were arrested, no one dared to speak out in defense of the Jews. Brown-shirted Stormtroopers stand in front of Jewish stores not allowing customers to enter. Who would ever believe that this could happen in a cultured society like Germany? Seemingly overnight, Germans gazed at us with hatred in their eyes. It didn't matter that Jews had fought at their sides in defending the Fatherland in war after war. Suddenly, we were enemies of the Reich. Jewish doctors are banned from working in the public health system, and Jewish attorneys have been banned from practicing in all branches of the German justice system."

Rabbi Kook stood up as he sometimes did when he was troubled. He walked to the window of the small study and gazed outside. "I'm listening," he said.

"The laws prohibiting the hiring of Jews also apply to university professors and high school and elementary school teachers. The witch hunt began at Frankfurt University, a bastion of liberal thinking. When the faculty was declared *judenrein*, none of the famous liberal professors raised a peep in protest in fear of the SS Stormtroopers, who were posted around the campus. At Freiburg University, the famous German philosopher, Heidegger, praised National Socialism and called Hitler 'the savior of the nation.' When he joined the Nazi Party, he was made president of the university. Accepting the appointment, he thanked the Fuhrer, raised his arm in a Nazi salute, and shouted 'Heil Hitler!' In Berlin, the renowned Jewish physicist, Albert Einstein, relinquished his position at the University, and left the country for America."

"Yes, that I know," Rabbi Kook said. "Years ago, I met him when he visited Jerusalem."

The distraught woman continued. "Jews are barred from government service, organized sports, medical schools, the legal profession, and newspaper work. Even the German Chess Association, the League of German Authors, and Cultural clubs have outlawed Jewish membership. Jewish students must carry a special yellow identity card. I can't remember all of the enactments. Jews live in terror, not knowing what will be next."

Rabbi Kook returned to his desk. "Thank you for coming," he said. "May God help His troubled People. I will endeavor to do whatever I can."

3.

Rabbi Kook asked Tevye to join him when he met with the British High Commissioner, the General, Sir Arthur Grenfell Wauchope, in his palatial, three-story mansion in the Armon HaNatziv neighborhood of the city. On official occasions like these, whenever Tevye accompanied the Chief Rabbi, he wore his holiday suit and polished shoes. That way, with his full beard, he looked like a Rabbi, and not like an ordinary milkman. The respected attorney, Mordechai Eliash, completed the small religious entourage. Not only was he familiar with the powers entrusted to the British under their Mandate over Palestine, and with the labyrinth of Turkish and British Colonial Law applying to the territories, he could act as an English translator if needed. Rabbi Kook had learned the language by reviewing the entire Talmud in English while he was in London during the World War, but words escaped him now and then. When he found time, he studied chapters of Mishna with Tevye in English, encouraging him to learn the language as well, not only because of its widespread use in Palestine, but because of the great many Jews in America who spoke neither Yiddish, nor Hebrew.

The impressive mansion was situated on a hill overlooking the mountains of Transjordan to the east. The vast tract of territory, four times the size of the slender strip of land on the west bank of the river, had been originally awarded to the Jews in the aftermath of the "Balfour Declaration." In apportioning this ancient region of Biblical Israel to the boundaries of the "National Jewish Homeland" which England promised to re-establish, exponents of the plan stated that the region was necessary to insure a "proper military frontier for the Jews." *The London Times* explained, "The Jordon River will not do as Palestine's eastern boundary. Our duty as a Mandatory is to make Jewish Palestine not a struggling State, but one that is capable of a vigorous and independent national life." Unfortunately for the Jews, not every member of the British Government shared Lord Balfour's reverence toward the Bible, nor his respect for the Jewish People. Seeking to maintain control over the strategic chunk of territory east of the Jordan River, in the "best interests of the British Empire," the final drafters of the Mandate, which was submitted to the League of Nations for ratification, gave Britain the option of retaining its sovereignty over the vast area. The Zionist Establishment at the time was shocked by this blatant ploy to rob the Jews of two-thirds of their Homeland, but the Britain Government answered all protests by threatening to withdraw England's offer to assist the Jews in establishing their own national entity in Palestine. Faced with the enormous task of coagulating Jews scattered all over the world to a desert wasteland, and not having had practical experience in self-government or warfare for almost two-thousand years, the Zionist Movement's leaders, led by Chaim Weizmann, raised their hands in helpless compliance to the treachery of the British.

Nevertheless, in line with his great love for all people, Rabbi Kook chose to judge the British in a positive light, grateful for their praiseworthy efforts on behalf of the Jewish People, rather than condemning them for their shortcomings. A British soldier escorted them across the mansion's spacious lobby, replete with carpets, stately furniture, and chandeliers, to an open lift operated by cables and a pulley, and manned by a uniformed attendant with white gloves, who slid the wire door closed behind them. They rode up two floors to a rotunda and circular staircase, guarded by another soldier. Another floor up in the tower, an Arab attendant, dressed like a butler, awaited them in the outer waiting room of the High Commissioner's office. Sir Arthur was sitting at his shiny mahogany desk, six times the size of the modest writing table in Rabbi Kook's study. During the first two years of his appointment, the distinguished British war hero had been generally sympathetic to the Zionist cause. Over a thirty year period, Wauchope had led British troops in battle on three continents. After the First World War, he served in Germany as the chief of the British section of the Berlin Control Commission, followed by two years in Northern Ireland. In 1931, he was assigned to be the High Commissioner of Palestine, where he was respected by Jews and Arabs alike, devoting his energies, in an impressive military manner, to improve the roadways, public works, and civil engineering.

Tevye mused that for a war hero, the British official was remarkably thin, with a gaunt face and gray hair, parted to the side in the English fashion. Wearing his highly-decorated General's uniform, he greeted the Chief Rabbi with respectful cordiality, one leader meeting another. Nonetheless, in his royally furnished office overlooking the hills of Judea and the distant mountains of Transjordan, east of the Jordan River, it was obvious, at least at the beginning of the meeting, that he was the supreme authority in Palestine, and that the Rabbi, for all of his spiritual stature, was merely a guest whom the High Commissioner had consented to receive. While they were talking, Tevye counted sixteen medals on the Englishman's chest.

With a slight bow, the High Commissioner nodded and motioned for his guests to sit down in the upholstered armchairs on the other side of the desk.

"Would you care for tea?" he asked in a friendly tone. Before anyone could answer, he turned toward the Arab butler standing by the door. "Reggie, bring us all tea," he requested. Then, turning back to his guests, he explained, "During a piece of nasty hand-to-hand combat in Mesopotamia, I was stabbed in the back. Reggie grabbed me and pulled me away to safety. Ever since, we have been together."

The obsequious Reggie backed out of the room with a bow.

"Before we get down to the matter at hand, let me please extend my most gracious welcome to the Chief Rabbi, who is known to be a true shepherd of the Jewish community and a spiritual leader of impeccable traits. For my part, since my appointment as British High Commissioner, I have striven to advance the Zionist enterprise, to double the immigration from previous years, and to ensure the safety of the Jews of Palestine. Nonetheless, while I am sympathetic to the nationalistic goals of the Jewish People under the British Mandate, I also have the national aspirations of the Arabs to consider, and, of course, the laws of the land, which I have been entrusted to enforce. Concerning the purpose of your visit, I have already met with Mr. Ben Gurion and other officials of the Jewish Agency. We discussed the problem of tourists overstaying their visas, and the question of Jewish immigration to Palestine in its broader scope, and, while we did not agree on all matters, I believe we arrived at a general understanding, satisfactory to both sides."

A smile spread over the mustachioed face of the High Commissioner.

"Indeed, we are grateful for the many fine deeds of the distinguished High Commissioner, which are already too numerous to enumerate," Rabbi Kook began. "May you be blessed for your dedication to the rebuilding of the Jewish Homeland. However, as much as we are indebted to your accomplishments, we are dismayed and distraught about the recent policy of rounding up German Jews and sending them back to Germany. When a man has escaped from the jaws of a lion, how is it possible to send him back to the lion's den?"

The General twitched, not having anticipated a rebuttal.

"With all due respect to the honored Chief Rabbi, I cannot agree with the comparison. Mr. Hitler, for all of his inflammatory rhetoric, does not make a practice of killing Jews."

Sensing the mounting tension in the room, Mordechai Eliash interrupted the exchange. "Having read some of

Hitler's inflammatory writings, I must remind the High Commissioner that where there is smoke there is fire."

"Perhaps," Sir Wauchope conceded. "What will be, will be. I am in charge of the present situation in Palestine, not what may come to pass in Germany in the future. The fact is that from January to June of this year, 5000 Jews holding tourists visas have overstayed their time allotment. During the past two months, another two thousand have remained in the country. When I first arrived in Palestine, the numbers were much smaller, and I was prepared to look the other way. But now, the situation has gotten out of hand. The representatives of the Jewish Agency have also expressed their opposition to this phenomenon."

Assuming the role of a courtroom lawyer, Mordechai Eliash continued to explain their complaint. "As a lawyer who works with the Jewish Agency, I know their position quite well. Their opposition to the phenomenon is not because they don't want these people to stay, but rather because of the Government's threat that the number of Jews who take up residence in Palestine in this manner will cause the Government to count them as a part of the official immigration quota. As a result, fewer immigration certificates will be awarded, and fewer Jews will be allowed to immigrate through the official channels."

"This country is not to become a haven for unemployed Jews," the former general replied in a no-nonsense manner. "The existing immigration quota is based on the country's ability to economically absorb new arrivals."

"Didn't Mr. Ben Gurion tell you that the majority of people who remain in the country beyond the limitations of their visas find work as clerks, merchants, and representatives of foreign businesses, and not as agricultural workers, or builders, or workers in the public sector concerning whom the immigration quota is based?"

"Yes, he informed me of that," the High Commissioner answered with a tone of irritation in his voice. "Presently, the economy in the country is stable, but who knows what the future will bring? Also, you must admit that many Jews find employment traditionally carried out by Arabs. With the swelling increase over the last past few years in Jewish immigration, which I am proud to say that I have enthusiastically supported until now, the Arabs feel economically threatened."

"The truth is exactly the opposite," Eliash countered in his convincing and knowledgeable fashion. "The more Jews that there are in the country, the more the economy prospers, making life better for the Arabs as well. The average Arab merchant and laborer welcomes the boom that the Jews have brought to the country. Arab opposition to Jewish immigration comes not from the peasants and Arab workers, but from the Arab leadership, for political and religious reasons, not because of economic competition."

The ring of the telephone on the High Commissioner's desk interrupted the conversation. Annoyed, he lifted the receiver with an impatient, "To the point!" Cutting the call short, he said, "Later," and hung up the phone. Lifting a smoking pipe from his desk, he banged it against his palm to clean out the tobacco in the bowl. He looked up and smiled in annoyance.

"As someone who has had a great deal of experience in colonies throughout the British Empire, I understand why the local Arab leadership is displeased with the great increase of Jews to the country. It's the old complaint, 'We were here first.'"

"Excuse me, but we were here first," Tevye corrected.

"Yes," the High Commissioner answered. "I have studied ancient history. Nevertheless, putting the Bible aside, Arabs who grew up in Palestine understandably feel that the land belongs to them."

"When it comes to the Jewish People, you cannot put the Bible aside," Rabbi Kook injected.

"Yes, I appreciate that. And so did Lord Balfour. But not every member of the British Parliament agrees. And there are many Jews, including Mr. Weizmann, who feel that ancient Biblical prophecies have no bearing on today's political questions. Besides, the Arabs have their own book which they follow."

"The *Koran* also acknowledges that the Land of Israel belongs to the Jews," Rabbi Kook informed him.

"Perhaps," the Englishman retorted, looking

uncomfortable in his tight-fitting, military collar. "I am not familiar with its contents."

Irritably, he banged the wooden pipe on his desk

"During the last few years, there has been relative peace between the Jewish and Arab communities," he said. "But the situation could erupt at any moment. You must take that factor into consideration when the British Government insists on maintaining current immigration quotas, or on lessening them if need be. I am convinced that new demands to increase Jewish immigration at this time will cause the powder keg to explode. According to the law, the people who overstay their visas are in Palestine illegally. That is the reason they are being deported – in accordance with the law."

"What law are you speaking about?" Rabbi Kook asked.

"The law of the British Mandate Government, which I have been appointed to enforce."

"There is a higher law than British law, which I have been appointed to enforce," Rabbi Kook told him, his eyes shining with an unworldly glow, the fire of the prophets of Israel whose inner beings blazed with the spirit of the Lord.

"What law is that?" the surprised official asked.

"The Law of God. It was He who bequeathed the Land of Israel to the Jewish People, not the British Parliament, and not the League of Nations. All actions taken to deport Jews from this Land, or to limit the immigration of Jews, are immoral and illegal, defying the will of God! They have no basis or substance whatsoever."

Again, Sir Wauchope flinched. For several seconds, he didn't know how to react.

"Allow me to paraphrase the words of the Chief Rabbi in purely political terms," the attorney, Eliash, injected. "Palestine is not a British colony. It is not part of the British Empire. You are in Palestine by the grace of the League of Nations, which assigned you with the Mandate of carrying out the principles set forth in the Balfour Declaration. That Declaration says you are to establish a National Home for the Jewish people in Palestine. The essence of this national revival is Jewish immigration. If your government reneges on its pledge by limiting immigration, and by deporting

Jews back to Europe, you will no longer have any moral or legal right to govern in this Land."

"I am a soldier and a politician, not a theologian," the shaken High Commissioner replied, addressing Eliash without his previous pompous posture. "Politically, I advise you to follow the example of the Jewish Agency and accept the present situation in silence without making demands on the British Government, which finds itself all too often positioned between the hammer and the nail when it comes to its policies in Palestine. To preserve the delicate peace between your people and the Arabs, who are becoming more and more agitated by the growth in Jewish immigration, the Mandate Authority is forced to adopt measures, temporary in nature, limiting the number of Jews in the country. Professor Weizmann and the leaders of the Jewish Agency understand this, why can't you?"

Rabbi Kook rose to his feet in defense of the Jewish People, just as he had during the International Western Wall Commission hearings.

"For whatever it may be worth, allow me to explain something in my capacity as Chief Rabbi, whose appointment was sanctioned by the British Government itself. The blood of mankind was spilled in the World War because the nations involved, descendants of Rome, did not return to the Jewish People the country they stole from us. For almost two-thousand years, these nations, in their arrogance, did not atone for their sin. The Master of the World, the Orchestrator of History, brought about the World War, the Balfour Declaration, and the international agreements which followed in order to bring His Children home. Therefore, the time for silence has ended. We will not allow the theft of our Holy Land to continue. We cannot remain silent while Jews are deported from their Homeland and others are prevented from reaching its shores, while their very existence is threatened by yet another descendent of Amalek. The time has come to cry out: 'Let our People come home!'"

Rabbi Kook's face was on fire. No one dared to utter a word. Reggie stood in the doorway, holding a tray crowded with cups of tea. Sensing the tension, he quietly backed out of the room, accompanied by the sound of tea cups rattling in their saucers. In most uncharacteristic fashion, Rabbi Kook raised his voice in prophetic warning.

"To the people of England, I shout out, 'Beware!' Hitler will not stop with the Jews. If the British Government betrays its promise to help all of the Jewish People to return to their national Homeland, then London will not be spared Hitler's madness. The ground of all Europe shall quake as it never has before, and even more blood will be shed than in the last awful war."

White in the face, the High Commissioner stood up and walked away from his desk, unable to withstand the Rabbi's piercing stare. He gazed at the framed photographs on a wall, pictures of himself in his soldier days, receiving medals for his exemplary service in battle, as if to bolster the wall of confidence which the passionate religious figure had shattered. Noticing the look of worry on Tevye's face, Mordechai Eliash flashed him a reassuring smile. But Rabbi Kook wasn't finished.

"Since we have been awarded the privilege of meeting with the High Commissioner, I would like to mention another equally distressing matter. I hereby most vehemently protest the immoral and illegal policy of immigrant selection carried out by the British, whereby Certificates of Immigration are awarded exclusively to those who possess socialist ideology and strong bodies, suited for agricultural labor, while the old and the frail are overlooked, along with the religious and all those who harbor opposing political beliefs from those held by the leaders of the existing Zionist hierarchy."

"Regarding that matter, you will have to express your displeasure to Mr. Ben Gurion and Professor Weizmann," the High Commissioner replied. "They decide who receives the Certificates, not us."

"Very well. We thank the High Commissioner for having presented us with the opportunity to voice our concerns. I trust that the people awaiting deportation in Haifa will be allowed to remain in the country and become registered citizens, in a gesture of good faith on the part of his

Excellency, in accord with the mission of the Mandate, and as human decency and the law of the Almighty demands."

Concluding the visit, Rabbi Kook bowed his head in parting and strode with his natural regal bearing toward the door.

"Oh, Rabbi," Wauchope said. "If I succeed in doing what you ask, though I cannot promise you, since it is not my decision alone, perhaps you can help me. Your countryman, Mr. Ben Gurion, informed me that his life has been threatened. Though he doesn't personally fear for his safety, and though he rejected my offer to provide him with bodyguards, he has been empowered by the Zionist Congress to determine whether there exists a group of Jewish terrorists within the Zionist Movement. If you should discover anything concerning this suspicion, please forward the information to us. We are acquainted with the opinions of Mr. Ahimeir, and his bellicose society of 'Birionim,' and we are monitoring their activities. I can assure you that Jewish terrorists, of any nature or form, will not advance the Zionist cause. While I am sure that the esteemed Chief Rabbis, you and your Sephardi counterpart, Rabbi Meir, have nothing to do with riffraff of this sort - should any secret, rebellious activities come to your attention, please know that they spell disaster for the future of the *Yishuv* and for constructive British-Jewish relations. Thank you very much for coming and have a good day."

No one shook hands. The visiting entourage walked out of the office. Backing off in fear of the Chief Rabbi, the Arab chamberlain, Reggie, pointed the way to the hallway. Tevye mumbled. When they reached the rotunda leading to the circular stairway, Tevye quipped softly in his finest British accent, "Thank you very much for coming and have a good day."

The attorney, Eliash grinned. "That was a visit that the High Commissioner won't soon forget."

"*Bezrat Hashem*," Rabbi Kook said. "*Bezrat Hashem*. With the help and assistance of God."

Hearing the metal gate of the elevator clang behind them, Tevye sighed. His pride and exaltation over Rabbi Kook's defiant stand was marred by his fatherly worry over his son, who was under the spell of Ahimeir and his band of revolutionaries. While Tevye admired the boy's spirit and readiness to sacrifice himself for the Zionist cause, he didn't want his beloved son, Tzvi, to spend years behind bars in a British prison.

4.

Tzvi gazed up at the hated flag with its bold black swastika, the symbol of Nazi persecution against the Jews. His fifteen-year old sister, Naomi, and Hodel's daughter, Ruth, stood beside him, gazing across the Street of the Prophets at the three-story German Consulate building. Now that the Nazi Party had gained control of the Reichstag, the large red, white, and black banner was raised each morning beside the flag of the German Republic on the third-floor terrace. The sight of the giant swastika waving over Jerusalem aroused the wrath of the Jews of the city, and an appeal to have the flag removed was made to the German Consul, Heinrich Wolff, whose wife was Jewish. Since the order to display the flag had come from the highest echelons in Berlin, the Consul was unwilling to show any sympathy toward the Jews. Nevertheless, it wasn't long before his loyalty to the Aryan people was called into question, because of his Jewish wife, and he was stripped of his position. The Jewish Agency sent a telegram to Germany's President Hindenburg, requesting that the flag not be displayed in Palestine, but the appeal went unanswered.

Two German soldiers stood by the entrance to the building, where they had been posted ever since a mysterious fire had set the first floor of the building aflame on *Lag B'Omer* night when Tzvi and some "*Birionim*" friends decided to have a little fun with the slabs of wood they had collected for their holiday bonfire.

Tevye's spirited *kinder* hurried around the block to an alley which led to the back of the Consulate. Moshe Svorai and Haim Dviri were waiting with a ladder. A few years older than Tzvi, the athletic pair had joined Ahimeir's secret group at its inception. Scrambling up the ladder, they hoisted themselves up to the first balcony. Tzvi followed deftly after them. The muscular Dviri was the strongest of the three. After Svorai lifted Tzvi onto his shoulders, Dviri bent under Svorai's legs and raised the two of them into the air. Tzvi grabbed ahold of the upper balcony railing and shimmied his way up to the circular terrace. Quickly, in broad daylight, he ran around the terrace to the flag pole. The wire attaching the flag to the pole was thicker than he expected, and the flag itself was much bigger up close. The wire-cutter he had with him wasn't strong enough to cut through the wire. Struggling, and nervous to finish the job before he was spotted, he twisted the wire back and forth until its cables snapped. Afraid to take the time to cut the other wire attached to the flag, he yanked the swastika down from the pole with a tug that broke the pole in half. Dragging the giant flag and uncut wire along the terrace, he hurried to the back of the building, where he dropped the flag to the lower balcony, where Svorai and Dviri stood waiting. They threw the booty down to the two girls in the alley, who folded the big flag as best as they could. The boys leaped down to the ground. With his shears, Tzvi cut through the remaining wire with a mighty twist and tug, falling backwards onto his rump.

"*L'Azazel*!" he cursed.

The girls giggled.

Stuffing the prize into a suitcase which Svorai had brought from his home, the young revolutionaries ran off laughing down the alley, scattering in different directions. Dviri returned the ladder to a nearby hardware store. The girls hurried home. Tzvi and Dviri lugged the suitcase to the apartment of Avraham Stern, at the end of Jaffa Road. From there, they were planning to bring it by car to "*Birionim*" headquarters in Tel Aviv. With proud smiles, they opened the suitcase for Stern to see. He stared at the Nazi flag with no expression, not even a grin.

"Well?" Tzvi asked. "What do you have to say? It's the flag from the German Consulate. We tore it down from the building."

"Abba Ahimeir may be pleased," Stern told them. "To me, it's child's play."

Chapter Two
BEYOND THE SEA

"Many are the thoughts in a person's heart, but the counsel of the Lord shall stand."

Tevye's plan backfired. The more his granddaughter, Hannie, was away from Avraham, the more she yearned to be with him. Every time she opened one of his letters, her heart skipped a beat. For over three years, she waited to read one simple sentence, "I want to marry you." Those five words would have brought her back to Jerusalem immediately. But the sentence didn't appear. Avraham wrote about everything under the sun. He sent her poems. He penned passionate letters. He described every little thing he was doing, but those five simple words eluded him, as if they weren't a part of his vocabulary. So she remained in New York, studying at college, never once going out on a date, as if that would be a betrayal of the man she loved.

She lived for his letters. He wrote every day. She cut the stamps off the envelopes and pasted them into an album, even though they hardly varied: a simple sketch of the Tomb of Rachel; or the Tower of David by the Jaffa Gate; the City of Tiberias by the Galilee Sea. Avraham never used the stamps depicting the Dome of the Rock Shrine, believing that the Islamic shrine didn't belong on the Temple Mount in Jerusalem, where the Third Temple was destined to be built. Each day, Hannie waited for the mailman to come. If she had to leave home early to take the elevated train to Upper Broadway, where Barnard College was located, she couldn't wait to return home to discover his letters in the mailbox. During the day, her body was in the classroom, but her heart and mind were in *Eretz Yisrael*, the Land of Israel, dreaming about Avraham, and looking forward to the moment they would be united. She did her best to concentrate on her studies, she passed all her courses, but her thoughts remained far across the sea. When would he write the words she longed to hear? "I want to marry you."

Was it such a difficult sentence? Her aunt, Baylke, encouraged her to meet other men. She had plenty of offers. But she remained true to Avraham. How could she date someone else? She was his. Like they said in America, "Till death do us part."

At first, Avraham was busy with his studies at Hebrew University and with the *Haganah*. He wrote Hannie in Russian and Hebrew, describing his stream of non-stop thoughts, his somber ruminations, fiery passions, and the mundane details of his days. It wasn't long before he grew discouraged with the *Haganah's* policy of restraint and joined the "*Irgun*," the more militant wing of "*Betar*." Later, when he traveled to Florence, his language became punctuated with codes that Hannie had to decipher, hinting at his work for the underground, acquiring "farming equipment" and "new agriculture techniques," which she understood to be rifles and bombs.

"My little Hannie," he wrote from Jerusalem. "My good girl. My Hannila! Finally, a letter from you arrived after a terrible silence of ten days. I was at my wits' end, not knowing what to think. How I wait for you! Nights pass on the roofs of the Old City, guarding over the holy neighborhoods clustered with Jews. Magical nights aglow with starlight and the shimmering rays of the moon. If only you were here with me! How slowly pass the days! Long, hot days, seemingly unending. And horribly lonesome nights! Hannie. How I wait for you! How I want you! And when you come, beware of me!"

His writing was so unbridled, it caused goose bumps to sprout on her flesh. When she read his confessions, it was as if he were with her, kneeling before her, exposing his soul, in a way that he rarely had when they had been together in Jerusalem.

"How hard it is for me," he wrote. "A deep melancholy enshrouds my soul. A despair lacking hope. I ponder, over and over, the same subject, this cursed ruse called life, with its mundane concerns and duties, when my soul yearns to soar. To fly is what I crave, into the heavens, to the silvery stars, to purple vistas, to faraway planets, to turquoise horizons like seas with no end – for this I was born. I dream of you, of the day you will come, and the yearning for you gives me hope for a better life, a verdant green field graced by the sun, symbol of a sparkling future, days filled with joy... Come back to me, Hannila, my hope, my yearning, my completion, my soul, my life!"

His outpourings of loneliness wrenched her heart, but where were the few short words she so longed to hear? If only he would say them, she would rush straight to his arms!

"I am still here, and you are still there," he wrote, back in Jerusalem after three weeks of volunteer guard duty in the Galilee, guarding all night without a rifle, because there were no spare rifles to share. "Without you, everything seems strange and deserted. How painful it is for me to stroll along the streets and alleyways we walked together, when I would stop you for a forbidden hug and drown in the pools of your eyes. The streets of Jerusalem are just as they were, but now they seem empty because you are missing.

"Alone, I walk alone through the deserted streets of the Holy City. Three weeks I was gone, twenty long days, and lengthier nights, with only the moon and stars to light up my darkness. Days and nights of yearning. Nights haunted by sweet memories of you, turned bitter by your absence. I was so alone. It seemed to me that the mountain ranges, as cruel in their silence as corpses, separated me from everything, from the past and from the future, leaving me alone and abandoned, a stranger to everyone and distant from everything. Emptiness, loneliness, and silence. Utter alienation. The only thing near me – death. Only he didn't forget me. Only he awaits me.

"And on clear, bright, and golden days, the heaviness weighs upon my heart, a strangling feeling... and dark, moonless nights, heavy with apprehension, every strange sound of the trees, quivering bushes, harbingers of danger, like black ravens above my head. Not once, climbing the ascent to the hilltop where I would take up my position, on guard without a weapon, I wondered, 'Perhaps this time I won't need to descend. Perhaps this night will be my last.'"

How haunting, how disturbing, how ghoulish, she

thought with a shudder. What a complicated being he was. But she loved him all the same. Even more. If only she could shelter him from his demons, and light up his life with her love.

Surprisingly, Hannie received a letter from Alexandria, where Avraham was visiting a relative.

"On the train ride to Egypt, I gazed out the window and I would pronounce out loud, for the pleasure it brought to my ears, the gentle names of the Hebrew settlements along the way: Beer Yaacov, Rehovot, Yavne – my soul filled with joy to gaze upon the seas of green fields and the blossoming orchards, the slumbering soil reawakening to life as its children return to embrace the Land. And I thought to myself, how happy I would be to sacrifice my life to see all of *Eretz Yisrael* in such a blossoming condition, so that all of *Eretz Yisrael* would become one great orchard, yielding baskets and bushels of fruits to *Am Yisrael*. David Raziel showed me a teaching in the *Gemara* which states that the surest sign of Israel's Redemption is when the trees of *Eretz Yisrael* give forth fruits in abundance. Hannila – it is no longer a dream! It is happening now! And we, the Jews of our generation, are so blessed and privileged to see it come true after the Land's having laid desolate and fallow for nearly two-thousand years!

"*Eretz Yisrael* is so splendid, casting a spell on the soul, like a dream of indescribable enchantment. *Eretz Yisrael* is the Nation's first love, and it will be its last. We love the Land of Israel more than our own lives, more than life itself, and, for it, we are ready to sacrifice ourselves and our beings. If I were a prophet, or a poet, with the highest inspiration I would sing about the future of our Motherland. If I were wealthy, I would give all of my money to our Nation."

"If only he loved me the way he loves the Land of Israel," the young woman brooded.

Living apart on two faraway continents, they could never depend upon the mail. Sometimes, a letter took three weeks to reach its destination. Sometimes four. Some letters were never delivered. For the next two months, he asked her to send her letters to Alexandria, saying he could not live without them.

"My dear, dear, little one," he wrote her. "I don't know why I have not received a letter from you. If I knew that the reason was that you want to end our relationship - that would be more bearable than my worry that something has happened to you, or that you are sick. Tell me that you are well. New York is cold in the winter. Did you buy yourself a warm coat?

"Perhaps, you have you found some other suitor, a fellow nobler than me? That shouldn't be hard for a woman of your charms. I wouldn't blame you at all. Why you took a liking to me in the first place, I cannot fathom, a suffering soul, so bitter and despairing, angry, jealous, selfish, wary of happiness, distrusting of life, plagued by doubts, suspicions, and dark obsessions of death. How fearful I am that you will leave me. And rightly so. How egotistical of me to want you, when I can only offer to drag you down into the abyss of darkness wherein I dwell.

Returning to Jerusalem, Avraham wrote to Hannie about the progress in his studies, and about his growing involvement in national affairs. With each letter, with each passing day and month, the more he bared his stormy emotions and confessed his love, the more she realized that in choosing a life with Avraham, she would have to share him with an even stronger love, even more passionate than the burning ardor he vowed he felt for her - his love for the Jewish Nation.

"My roommate has moved up north for a bout of physical work, which can be a wonderful elixir for the mind as well, so I am left alone, alone again, all alone, yet I am glad to be among those whose lot is a life of depravation and suffering. Happiness, it seems, is not for me. Nor the dull contentment of the herd. My happiness will be in suffering for the Nation, for our own lives pass by and are no more, but the Jewish People live on forever...."

"By the way, I won two awards at the University for my essays on "Middle Age Cults" and on "Shakespearian Tragedy." Teachers have found work for me tutoring other students, and I will be teaching English to a group of twenty-five adults at the YMCA. Can you believe it? I am sure your English is better than mine, now that you are living in New York. Professors here want me to become a part of the Classics faculty at Hebrew University when I finish my studies. I am sure they would think otherwise if they knew of my nationalist leanings, which are far too radical for academics whose main concern in life is belonging to the intellectual circles of the Gentiles, and in safeguarding their monthly salary and future pension. They are certainly not interested in dying penniless as 'Anonymous Soldiers' in the fight for Hebrew independence in our Land. But we, who raise aloft the Redemption of our Nation in our cherished Homeland as the crowning goal of our life's mission, for which we are ready to sacrifice our lives in the face of all opposition; no matter how scorned and misunderstood we may be by brothers who seek personal advancement alone; no matter how hunted we be, we must, without any thought of ourselves, persevere day and night in the battle until we achieve victory, whether through our lives or through our deaths."

Hannie sighed. Even with all of the love she felt for him, how could she ever reach his level of idealism, which recognized no limits or fears?

"Reality is not a given which can't be changed," he wrote. "Through the force of will and steadfast dedication to a goal, reality depends on our deeds. Revolutions don't come about from books resting on library shelves. Books have their place in the battle, and they can inspire a nation, or a deprived and subjugated people, to set off to war, but without rifle and sword, nations do not step aside for other nations to take their place. For the individual, as well as for the nation, to achieve anything in life, you have to yearn for it with all of your spiritual powers, to be ready for every sacrifice, to stand firm in the face of all doubts, all worries, all uncertainties, and all practical considerations which argue against the truth."

While Hannie admired his great patriotism, his pristine aspirations, and his bravery to face the hardships and dangers of rebellion and war, she returned time and again to the same gnawing question – what frightened him so much about marriage? If he didn't want to link his life with hers, why did he tell her about all the details of his daily activities and share all of his thoughts? How could he love her so deeply, yet keep her dangling out of water like a fish on a fisherman's hook?

"Fraternity life on campus draws more and more students to fraternity gatherings and social activities, but I resist their invitations to join, even though it might lighten my loneliness," he told her. "Many people are joining *Betar*, the youth movement which Ze'ev Jabotinsky founded, with the goal of creating a powerful Jewish army worldwide and bringing all Jews home to Israel. But they waste too much time on uniforms and badges, on ceremony and parades, on army discipline and saluting commanders. It seems like child's play to me."

Nevertheless, at the urging of his friend, David Raziel, Stern joined the newest group in town, the "*Irgun*." In a series of letters, he described, in a general way, his induction and training in the nascent underground organization, which aspired to be a more potent fighting force against Arab aggression than the *Haganah*, whose military capability was consistently stymied by the policy of appeasement and concession fostered by the socialist leaders of the *Yishuv*.

"Of course I believe, like the socialists, in the universal dream of equality and justice for all peoples in the brotherhood of man, but we live in a time when the very survival of our Nation is threatened, and therefore, as a Jew, the welfare of my own Jewish family comes first.

"The terrible pogroms which erupted throughout our cherished Land, revealing the true face of the Arabs and the British, came as a cruel catalyst from out of the sky, forcing me to clarify my thinking on the mission of the Jewish People in this world, and on my mission in the rebirth of the Jewish Nation in our Land. Without the exposure to thinkers gifted with understandings far more encompassing than mine, I would have remained a babe lost in the woods. During the week that your grandfather and your family sat *shiva* for your aunt, Hava, may her memory be for a blessing, I met some of the great visionaries of our time, men like Rabbi Kook, Abba Ahimeir, Dr. Yehoshua H. Yevin, the poet Uri Zvi Greenberg, and the young Moshe Segal, all of whom inspired me to explore the startling things they were saying, rather than following after the so-called 'enlightenment' of the false prophets of socialism. Though our communist and socialist brothers are well-meaning people, they, like so many of the professors at the University, in order to be embraced by the family of nations, seek to strip the Jewish People of everything uniquely Jewish, including our own uniquely Israelite Kingdom and Israelite sovereignty over all of our Land."

Hannie read over passages like these again and again, trying to understand the depth of his thinking. Who was this man who had come into her life in such a whirlwind fashion? Avraham was like twenty people in one - philosopher, Zionist, poet, actor, soldier, revolutionary, student of the Classics and Shakespeare, orator, and lost little boy.

"If we want to survive as Jews, we must fight," he wrote. "What is the point in sitting passively, waiting to be annihilated? It is not true that it isn't 'Jewish' to fight. From our very beginnings, we took up the sword when we had to, and though killing is loathsome to our natures, in order to survive, and to rid the world of evil, we must, when necessary, take hold of the weapons of Esau and set forth to battle, while preserving the high moral standards of Yaacov. I heard Rabbi Kook say this himself in a class which I attending with David Raziel and your brother.

"Did I tell you that I started to attend meetings and lectures of the Revisionists? I have not met the movement's founding father, Mr. Jabotinsky, because the British refuse to let him re-enter the country, fearing that his firebrand vision of Zionism and his charismatic personality will lead to a Jewish revolution. I read the articles he publishes with keen interest. Abba Ahimeir is even more uncompromising in his thinking. Once a Labor Zionist, he now views them as traitors to the national struggle for Hebrew sovereignty. He was the first to cry out publicly about the treachery of the British, and he is still a lone wolf in a nation of sheep. How the socialists scream out against him for having the nerve to openly criticize 'our great friends, the British!' Already arrested and beaten by the British police, he still openly declares that British Mandate Authority in Palestine is null and void for having abandoned the foundations of the Balfour Declaration. In conclusion, he cries out, 'Jewish brothers, rebel!' while the Weizmanns and Ben Gurions champion appeasement and concession, condemning all expressions of true Jewish freedom as dangerous zealotry, as if the Maccabees were a gang of immoral thugs for actively resisting the religious and cultural oppression of the Greeks."

The outpouring of Avraham's thinking didn't appear in one letter, but in pieces of budding political exposition. While Hannie read everything that Avraham wrote with great interest, she never imagined the depth of his growing involvement in what was to become a deadly armed revolt against British rule in Palestine. Nor in her wildest imaginations did she picture him as the future leader of the most wanted group of revolutionaries, the "Stern Gang." In her mind, her Avraham was destined to be, if not a respected professor of Classic Literature, then a noted stage actor, and maybe, if he didn't give up his messianic ideas, some kind of political leader. So while she reread each letter several times, carefully trying to understand his beliefs, she was more interested to learn that he had conversed with her grandfather at an evening lecture and accompanied him home, as if they had made peace! She was happy to discover that he would study Torah occasionally with her brother, Moishe, in his yeshiva, along with Tzvi, who, Avraham wrote, looked up to him as a type of older brother, seeking his guidance and advice. It seemed that her family had become his "adopted" family in Jerusalem, increasing her hope that their wedding day was only a matter of time. He even wrote her that he wanted his home to be *kosher*, and that he intended to keep the Fast Days and honor the Sabbath. He informed her that he now prayed in the morning, and that he didn't go to sleep before he studied some chapters of *Tanach*. Though he didn't write the words she longed to hear, she prayed that he was coming closer.

Chapter Three
THE BURNING BUSH

In Jerusalem, Avraham's heart beat rapidly as he hurried along a dark alleyway in an Arab neighborhood of the Western Wall Quarter of the Old City. Sometimes, meeting Hannie in the past, he felt the same excitement, but Hannie was across the sea in New York. He had a new love just as strong as a man's love for a woman. For him, it was even stronger. He was in love with an idea.

An elderly Arab sat in front of the metal door which led to the hidden cave. Avraham dropped a 10 mils coin into his palm and waited for the slow-moving fellow to rise and push the heavy door open with his cane. The holed, copper-nickel coin, was the smallest fraction of the Palestine pound. With fifty mils you could buy two loaves of bread, so the price of admission was a bargain. Candles lit the narrow rock stairway which led to the underground chamber. A sizeable crowd of young people had already gathered. In the candlelight shining off the moist, rocky walls of the cavern, Avraham recognized the faces of Moshe Segal, Tzvi, Nachshon, and Hannie's brother, Moishe. They sat on the ledge of a deep cistern, dating back to the time of the Second Temple. Across the ancient aqueduct, he could make out the huge boulders of the *Kotel* whose foundations extended underground for five-hundred meters from the famous site of prayer known as the Wailing Wall. For most people, visitors to Jerusalem and residents alike, the real length of the Wall, and of the sealed and undiscovered, underground tunnel running alongside it, were two of the Holy City's many secrets.

Edging his way forward, Avraham found an empty spot by his friends. It wasn't hard to imagine that they were surviving soldiers of the Maccabees from the Hasmonean era, more than two-thousand years before. When Uri Zvi Greenberg rose, a hush spread through the subterranean grotto. In the eerie glow of the candlelight, the thin figure of the poet moved to a ledge above his seated listeners. His gaunt, prophet-like face looked scorched by the sun in the golden light around him. Sitting on a rock, he stared toward the massive boulders of the Wall which had withstood conqueror after conqueror, as if to absorb inspiration from its undefeatable stones.

People called him the "Burning Bush." Indeed, for young Avraham, the heralded poet was a guiding light, a volcano of wisdom, a gushing stream of revelation. All of his ardent followers believed that his genius bordered on prophecy. Like Rabbi Kook, he lived suspended between Israel's glorious past and its splendid future, which he portrayed in stirring imagery, making the words of Israel's prophets come alive in the hearts of a young generation yearning for Jewish glory and splendor. For visionaries like Greenberg and Rabbi Kook, the Kingdom of Israel and the Temple were realities, invisible at the moment, but always present in the Jewish People's national psyche and soul, which had been damaged by the trauma of exile, during which the once proud Lions of Judah lost all of their national majesty and pride. Nevertheless, Divinely-inspired leaders like Rabbi Kook and Greenberg taught, the glory of Israel's Kingdom pulsated deep in the essence of every Jew, ready to awaken like a lion from its slumber and roar. "Let it roar!" Avraham thought, anxiously waiting to hear the poet recite his new poem, which Abba Ahimeir had published in his newspaper, and which Avraham knew by heart. How exciting to learn who you really are, and where the Jewish People were headed! How Avraham wished that Hannie could be with him to share his discoveries! At Hebrew University, they learned about everything in the world, except who they really were as Jews. They learned about the statehood of the Romans and Greeks, but nothing about the mighty Israelite Kingdom which was waiting to rise once again like a young lion, like a king returning to his royal throne.

"Good evening, dear friends and comrades," the poet began.

Around Avraham, the eyes of Tzvi and Nachshon shone with a glow as bright and pure as candlelight.

"Please know that Bar Kochva's revolt against Rome was the right course of action, even though it outwardly failed. The Rabbis of the time were divided in their opinions, as Rabbis tend to be. But the greatest Rabbi of the era, Rabbi Akiva, supported Bar Kochva and even carried his weapons when Bar Kochva led the armies of Israel to battle. Often they hid in caves like this. Jerusalem fell, but Rabbi Akiva's cry of '*Shema Yisrael*' echoes throughout all generations. See how the mighty empires and civilizations of the past lay buried in the catacombs of history, while, today, the Nation of Israel rises up from the dust."

How the words of the "Burning Bush" burned in the hearts of his listeners! Inspired by his imagery, the young idealists felt swept away to a totally different reality in which their own Jewish country was possible, if only they had the courage to make it real – as Herzl had stated – "If you will it, it isn't a dream." The Divinely-touched poet instilled in them the confidence that the visions of the Prophets lay only a stretch of the arm away. True, it was hard to imagine their own Jewish State in the Palestine of the moment, when England ruled over the Land, and when the Jews of Europe were impotent to combat the rising wave of persecution threatening their very existence, and when the Jews in the United States were struggling to succeed in their new Diaspora, trying their hardest to be as American as everyone else, and when bitter conflicts divided the Jewish camp in the Jerusalem of the hour, the same "Achilles heel" which had brought the Jews to their downfall in the past.

To Greenberg's uncompromising way of thinking, the self-proclaimed pioneers of the *New Yishuv* were spineless compared to the heroes of our past. He boldly declared that the socialists were like Sanballat and his followers of old, who fought against Nechemiah's attempts to rebuild the walls of Jerusalem. In his poem, "Decay in the House of Israel," he raged against the Zionists who scorned the Torah and Israel's holy roots, chastising them for seeking peace at any price, without demanding revenge for the Jewish blood which bloodied the Land. In his controversial poem, Greenberg called out to tear down the soulless houses which the socialists built on their godless *kibbutzim*. Avraham felt that Rabbi Kook had a more encompassing vision, seeing the shortcomings of the times as the foundation stones of a holier future, just as the Temple was first physically constructed with ordinary stones then later sanctified. So too, Rabbi Kook explained, the Ark of the Covenant was first crafted from wood and gold, and only later was the Torah placed within its chambers. Nonetheless, Avraham Stern, the emerging revolutionary who was to become the "Most Wanted" man in Palestine, with the highest reward on his head, found validity in what Uri Zvi Greenberg wrote in his poem.

"Listen!" the poet said:

"The arms of their ancestors reached out for God
But these have lost God and lost His Heavens.
They offer up no arms in prayer.
Their necks they offer to any Arab
Who flashes a knife. Their lives they offer, out of fear."

The young men and women who were gathered in the ancient cave by the Temple Mount, a new generation of Jews possessed with the spirit of freedom throbbing in their veins, stared at the revered poet as candlelight flickered over their intent faces and sparkling eyes. The bard of rebellion stood up and shouted:

"Rise from the flames!
Become a Burning Bush of wrath right here!
Rise up from the blood!
Be a Pillar of Glory spreading over the Land,
Armed with the sword of lightening and the power of thunder!
Enough sickeningly sweet songs to accompany
The dead victims, while the horizon turned to ruins.

"Tear asunder the godless settlements!
Tear the roofs off the houses.
Scatter them across the seas to the seventy exiles
To Jews deceived by speeches and stories
Heralding the wonders of a Great Society of utopian
kibbutzim.

"Scatter the stench of an ailing
bureaucratic-literary-philosophical Zionism....
They could have heroically attained the dreams of old
To become rulers here, the way all other people rule.
Expunge the stench of their 'reasonableness' so hopefully
offered
By those who pity Arab murderers, but not their own
brothers
Whose blood is shed so near their homes.
They who are willing to be disgraced by any Gentile.
They who are willing to persecute any brother."

Avraham's hands clenched in a fist. Anger seized his heart.
The eyes of Moshe Segal were on fire. Tzvi and Nachshon
looked ready to rise and fight. Walking closer to the group,
the impassioned seer leaned back against the rocks of the
mountain upon which Jerusalem rested. Though he was
only thirty-five, to his listeners, he was like a father. His
profile was razor sharp, with a pointed nose and chin. A
vein bulged out on a broad, intelligent forehead, which was
crowned by a free-flowing bluster of hair. With the large,
all-seeing eyes of an owl, he peered, one by one, into the
souls of the young people around him.

"Who dares reveal the shame?
Who dares to challenge them to conquer, plain and simple,
just like all other peoples on earth?"

"Now in this Land that longs for a new Song of David
For a new conquest, from the Sea to the Mountains of
Moab
No princely offspring of David stride, robed in fire,
Burning with Godly desire for self-rule.
Rather only the incapacitated children of David
Small of mind and poor of understanding
Lacking God and mocking *Malchut*."

Avraham turned toward Moshe Segal who was always
speaking about *Malchut* and the restoration of the ancient
Israelite Kingdom. They young Rabbi's eyes possessed the
same fire as Greenberg's.

"The faith of Sinai, foreigners could not melt its iron.
Even if they burned our bodies around the world.
Yet, here, the Jews rush to rid themselves of their Faith, or
ignore it.
Their hands cut out personages from our national treasure.
No kings, prophets, no zealots of faith, no Sages, no
martyrs.
They came here not to build a State, but only a refuge
That doesn't demand a battle hymn and a sacrificing soul.

"Life is easier without Malchut David, they chanted.
Easier without Sinai, and without a Burning Bush!
Must we fall a third time at the hands of Edom?
At the slaying hands of Arab savages?
Must we fall again without uttering a word of protest?
Must we surrender without even a battle?"
Uri Zvi Greenberg gazed upon Avraham as if from the
depths of the cavernous chamber.

"You who hate this tragedy
You who scorn this great untruth
Remain a rebel, and speak out to those
who are forever loyal to Sinai! Tear asunder! Tear the roofs
off from the houses. And scatter the stench of their
treachery across the many seas."

Later that evening, back in his one-room apartment,
Avraham wrote out the long poem and enclosed it in his
next letter to Hannie. "*Baruch Hashem*," he began. "Blessed
be the Lord for having sent us an angel like Uri Zvi
Greenberg to illuminate our path." Avraham's use of the
expression, "*Baruch Hashem*," which suddenly appeared in
his letters, pleased Hannie immensely. Could it be the
influence of her grandfather, Tevye? Or his religious friend
at the University, David Raziel? Whatever the cause, she
sensed that along with his maturing political views,
Avraham's spiritual world was awakening too, something
which could only deepen their mutual love. Although she
had left the small *moshav* of Olat HaShachar to discover the
bigger world beyond, *Hashem* was always with her, and her
belief in Him could not be uprooted by all of the temptations

of modernism and the seductions of material pleasure abounding all around her in New York.

For Avraham, his experiences were only complete after he shared them with Hannie. Even if she were an ocean away, writing her was like being with her, as if she were still by his side. He wanted her to know everything he was thinking. So he wrote her about everything, not wanting her to miss a moment of his existence, as if life had no meaning without her.

"Your grandfather and I, along with Tzvi, Hevedke, Moishe, Nachman, and Carmel's young brother, Nachshon, a true Nachshon in every cell of his being, ready at the slightest command to leap forward into a raging sea, all of us attended a lecture by Dr. Yehoshua Hershel Yevin, a maximalist like Ahimeir, who takes Jabotinsky's teachings to the upmost extreme. I brought a notebook with me to jot down his words. Fortunately, *Baruch Hashem*, I retain lectures I hear. Surely, there are things I may have altered or paraphrased whenever I lost pace, and I am condensing his exposition because the costs of stamps weighs heavily on my meager budget, but this is the gist of what he told us:

'Fifty additional Jewish settlements in Palestine are not worth the sacrifice and investment if they cannot be defended. There can be no future for our national hopes if Arab riots repeatedly cause a British Commission to be formed with no further action taken. These theatrical comedies invariably decide to retreat from obligations set forth in the Mandate. And there can be no future for our Nation in the Land of Israel if the *Yishuv* depends on British bayonets for protection. Independent Hebrew military strength must be established now, bullet by bullet.

'There is nothing holier than guarding Jewish homes, Jewish lives, and Jewish land. But defense alone, without a strong offence to supplement it, cannot quell aggression. Our Hebrew youth must train and be willing to sacrifice everything – not only life itself, but all of the humanitarian philosophies that demand that we treat our enemies as if they were our brothers. No. We must set out to war to kill the enemy, not to embrace them. Every young man and woman must know that they are contributing their blood toward the magnificent edifice of independent Hebrew might in our Hebrew Homeland. Without this, it will not be rebuilt.'"

The lecture to Avraham was clear and common sense. Yevin's philosophy expressed his feelings completely. It was only a matter of time before he joined the "*Irgun*." He immediately informed Hannie of the news, noting that her brother, Moishe, along with Tzvi and Nachshon had also been inducted into the secret organization. Even Hevedke had volunteered, saying that if Trumpeldor could fight with only one arm, so could he.

By nature, Avraham was not an aficionado of organizations and clubs, preferring to go his own way, rather than follow a group. But after attending many of the *Betar* Movement lectures, he saw no reason not to join its more militant branch. While many students at the University stayed with the *Haganah*, the socialists who had taken control of the organization were, in Avraham's opinion, making the same mistake of fostering fraternal division and internecine strife - the very things which led to the Second Temple's destruction. For them, anyone who opened a small factory, business, or farm on his own, and who didn't embrace socialism by joining their *Histadrut* worker's union, was marked as an enemy of Zionism, to be boycotted and crushed. They employed Bolshevik techniques, pressuring employers to dismiss workers who identified themselves with the *Betar* or Revisionist Movements. Ahimeir, Yevin, and Greenberg all bellicosely proclaimed that number-one socialist objective was to control the *Yishuv* and to create a State more socialist than Jewish, in keeping with their modern Hellenistic beliefs. Instead of fighting the local Arab marauders and the pro-Arab policies of the British Mandate Authority, they turned their formidable energies against Jews who cherished a different vision of Zion and a more assertive brand of Zionism.

The main points of the Revisionists, as established by Ze'ev Jabotinsky, were to establish a Jewish State in the Land of Israel as soon as possible on both banks of the Jordan River; the immediate Aliyah of millions of Jews worldwide, irrespective of their backgrounds and ideologies; and active military readiness, not only for defense, but also for liberation. Avraham explained to Hannie that the name *Betar* was short for '*Brit Trumpeldor*' and that its members were encouraged to adopt the attributes of bravery and self-sacrifice for the Motherland, traits which Yosef Trumpeldor exemplified in his defense of the doomed colony of Tel Hai.

Avraham detailed the chain of events to his sweetheart in New York: "One evening after a *Betar* meeting, David Raziel told me about a new, secret group that was forming, 'a purely apolitical military organization,' he said, also inspired by the teachings of Ze'ev Jabotinsky. For some time, I had noticed people at our meetings dressed in clean khaki shirts and pants that looked sparkling new. Often they left early before the end of the evening. David said that he wasn't free to disclose any more details. First, I had to meet a small committee, and then my suitability would be weighed."

When his no-nonsense friend, Raziel, wasn't studying Torah at Rabbi Kook's Central Universal Yeshiva, he poured through all the books he could find on military history and warfare in the Hebrew University Library. One night, Avraham went to the address Raziel had given him, which turned out to be a basement of a school. Discovering the door closed, when a voice answered his knocking, he uttered the password which Raziel had given him. The door opened and a woman clutching a revolver ushered him into a dark room, which he realized was a kindergarten with small chairs and boxes of toys. In the darkness, he couldn't make out the woman's features. Gruffly, she led Stern toward the end of the room and told him to wait, then returned to her post by the door. A sliver of light appeared from under a doorway. When the door opened, a shaft of light lit the floor and a guard led someone through the semi-darkness to the exit. Immediately, the newcomer was summoned into the inner room, a larger room than the first, though just as dark. A lamp resting on a table shone in Stern's face. Three people sat behind the lamp, but with the blinding light in his eyes, Avraham couldn't make out their faces. The windows of the room were covered with sheets, so the darkness was almost hermetic. The silhouetted man in the middle motioned for Stern to sit and readjusted the lamp so that it shone in his eyes. He was flanked by two other men. "Imagine my surprise," Stern wrote to Hannie, "when I recognized the voice of the dark figure in front of me. It was your grandfather, Tevye!"

"You are Avraham Stern?' he asked, as if they had never met.

"Yes," Stern replied.

"Do you know why you are?" he inquired.

"Vaguely," the young recruit said, playing along as if he didn't know his interrogator.

"Do you know what is expected of you?"

"Not really."

The shadowed figure on Tevye's right continued the clandestined proceedings. After a few seconds, Avraham realized that he was Moshe Rosenberg, a veteran commander of the *Haganah*.

"You have been recommended for the *Etzel*, an acronym for the *Irgun Tzvai Leumi*, the National Military Organization, also known as the *Irgun*," he explained. "We have investigated your credentials and are willing to consider your participation in our activities. First, we need to hear your answers to some questions."

Stern waited silently, wondering why the need for such guarded secrecy.

"Are you aware that you may be engaged in very sensitive and highly dangerous undertakings? Are you prepared to accept rigid military discipline? Finally, do you agree to swear loyalty to our goal of independent Israeli Statehood?'

Without hesitation, the future underground leader answered yes to all of the questions.

"Why do you want to join the *Irgun*?" the interrogator asked.

The budding philosopher began to formulate his answer, but before he began, Tevye added, "Your response needn't be a twenty-page dissertation, Mr. Stern."

"That was a big relief," Stern later wrote to Hannie. "I simply stated that Jews of Palestine were entitled to their own army like every other nation, and that it was the duty of all young people to serve their country and to defend the Hebrew Homeland. 'Very well, Avraham,' your grandfather said. 'You will hear from us shortly. In the meantime, this meeting will remain a secret.'"

"I walked home alone. I think it was the first time that your grandfather addressed me by my first name! How is that for progress? Maybe now he will let me meet with you, but, alas, you are thousands of kilometers away! In the meantime, don't worry about my underground activities. At the moment, there is no danger. I will let you know what develops. How strange and wonderful life can be! And how terrible! What will be, will be."

Hannie waited anxiously for Avraham's next letter. It continued where the previous letter had ended.

"The following week, David Raziel informed me that I had been accepted as a member of the *Irgun*. He told me the time, place, and password of the swearing-in ceremony, and instructed me to wear a clean khaki shirt and slacks, with polished shoes. When I asked for more information about the organization, he said that the less we know individually, the better for everyone. That way, if someone is captured and tortured by the British, he or she can't incriminate other members of the organization, or disclose the range of its activities. The address turned out to be a dentist's office. Among the ten new enlistees were Moishe, Tzvi, Nachshon, and Hevedke. We all shared a small laugh. I didn't know any of the others. A section commander named Yitzhak Ben Ami, whom I knew from *Betar*, conducted the simple ceremony. He was flanked by two uniformed officers. On the table in front of him were a Bible and a gun. 'Gentlemen,' he said. 'You have been accepted into the *Irgun*. We are a voluntary military organization, and you are expected to act like soldiers. You will receive the best training and arms we can provide. For those of you who have served in foreign armies, our means are far more humble. Nonetheless, you are expected to devote all of yourselves to our mission. Know in advance that some of you may be lost in the battle for our cause. The *Irgun* must now become your number-one priority, more important than your life itself. You can still change your decision to enlist. Are there any questions?'

"When no one spoke up, he said, 'Stand at attention! Repeat after me: We swear allegiance to the national army, the *Irgun Tzvai Leumi* in *Eretz Yisrael*. At all times, we are ready to act on behalf of the revival of the Jewish Nation in its Land. To live and to die for it!'"

Reading the words, Hannie felt goosebumps erupt all over her skin.

"We repeated his words," Avraham concluded the letter. "I glanced at Moishe, Tzvi, Nachshon, and Hevedke, who all stood straight at attention, perfect soldiers, their eyes aglow. Hevedke's face was as red as his beard. Moshe, Tzvi, and Nachshon were the proudest soldiers I have ever seen. Then, to my happy surprise, the commander, Ben-Ami, and the two officers present, began to sing my song, 'Anonymous Soldiers.' The *Irgun* has adopted it as their anthem! Do you remember how you wrote down the notes for me when I sang it to you in my room? They seemed surprised when we joined in, already knowing the tune and the words! Then Tzvi told them that I had written the song! Hadn't Raziel told them? Or your grandfather? Maybe the organization is so guarded, no one speaks to anyone else. Or Maybe Ben-Ami was new to his position. Anyway, it broke the solemnity of the ceremony, and we all had a good laugh."

Avraham felt compelled to write something more:

"One more thing, my dearest Hannie. Please forgive me that I accepted the oath, placing the *Irgun* above all other priorities. Though I mouthed the words, in the secret chambers of my heart, no loyalty could be greater than the loyalty I hold for you. In reality, both loyalties are the same, for you and the Organization and the Nation are one, and I am absolutely committed to each with all of my heart and soul, and with all of my life. Come home to me soon. Who knows what the morrow will bring? Who can tell when a bullet may put an end to writing letters? Life is not forever. Come home to me, love of my life, fire of my soul, my hope and my desire. Come home to me soon. Please."

How could Hannie say no? But she was in the middle of her studies. And still, with all of his fervor, he still didn't write the words which would have brought her rushing back to him. Yes, he loved her. Yes, he wanted her. But marriage? He was married to the *Irgun*.

Chapter Four
THE ARONOV MURDER

Though it was Sabbath Eve in Tel Aviv, restaurants and nightclubs were open for business as usual. On HaYarkon Street, Perchik and Sonia Aronov sat dining on the veranda of the seaside, Katie Dan Hotel. The simple, home-style restaurant was a popular eating place for the "elite crowd" of the *"New Yishuv."* Having just returned from an important mission in Germany, Perchik was the star of the evening. In fact, after Abba Ahimeir had penned a scathing attack on the rising Labor Zionist, accusing him of collaborating with the Nazis, Perchik Aronov was the talk of the town. The newspaper, the *"Birionim,"* was the voice of the extreme Revisionist right. Known for his blunt and militant language, Ahimeir termed Aronov, *"Mapai's* communist diplomat crawling on all fours before Hitler." Perchik knew that many of his party colleagues, including Ben Gurion, were also displeased with his trip. But what could he do? He was one of the only Laborites who sensed that a terrible destruction was facing the Jews of Germany. As the new Political Director of the Jewish Agency, he had traveled to Berlin to forge an economic agreement allowing Jews the right to immigrate to Palestine. "The Jewish Nation will not forget your visit to Nazi Germany," the Ahimeir editorial had declared. "The Jewish People will know how to deal appropriately with this treacherous crime."

As the attractive, young Aronov couple waited to pay their bill, another well-wisher approached their table to shake Perchik's hand.

"A superb achievement!" he said with a big, congratulatory smile. "Absolutely historic. You did the right thing."

Perchik thanked him. It was reassuring to know that he had supporters. That was one of the reasons he had taken his wife out to dinner – to get a feeling for public opinion regarding the controversial *"Ha'avara Agreement."*

"Let's go for a quiet walk on the beach," Sonia said. "It's hard to be on a date with a famous politician."

Perchik chuckled. He had worked diligently to get to the top of the Zionist leadership, steering his way cautiously through stormy seas and towering waves, avoiding a collision with the great ocean liners like David Ben Gurion, Chaim Weizmann, Berl Katzenelson, and Moshe Shertok, who could easily sink his ship. While he felt great satisfaction with his success and growing national importance, he longed for a few days of rest, removed the eye of the storm. While many influential *Mapainikim* considered Aronov to be the Party's most articulate visionary, and a prime candidate to lead the Labor Zionist Movement, his longtime mentor, Ben Gurion, was not one of them. He knew that the younger man's outgoing and friendly personality, coupled with his keen intelligence and dedication to the cause, attracted adherents more readily than his own more abrasive and commanding style. And regarding the Jews of Germany, why worry about a doomsday which might never develop? For Ben Gurion, the most important thing at hand was to win control of the World Zionist Congress and defeat the Revisionists, and that couldn't be done by traveling off to Berlin to secure the mass emigration of Jews, whom the British wouldn't let into Palestine in any event.

Perchik and Sonia walked down the steps of the veranda that led to the dark beach. A refreshing sea breeze cooled the summer night. Waves reached the shore and sighed, as if they were exhausted from a long journey. The rumble of the Mediterranean Sea, like a gentle roar, blanketed the sounds of the city behind them. In the distance to the south, the lights of the Jaffa port sparkled like a necklace around the old Ottoman fort on the hill jutting out from the coastline. Perchik held his wife's hand and led her to the beach, heading north, away from the lights of Tel Aviv. They both wanted to be alone, in a secluded place, without all of the responsibility and stormy emotions that came with his job. They strolled by other people on the beach, couples who also wanted to find an island of intimacy in the darkness embracing the shore. Stars filled the sky, but they were too far away to light up the night, and the moon was in hiding. Perchik squeezed his wife's hand, glad to be home after such a long absence. She squeezed his hand in return, not having to speak, letting the wind and sea do the talking for them. Soon, the city of Tel Aviv receded behind them, with all of its buildings and bustle. They passed the last lamp poles until they were completely alone, surrounded only by darkness and the love they felt for one another. Now and again, the dim beam of a car headlight flashed from the shoreline road beyond the sand dunes. Sonia shivered.

"Chilly?" Perchik asked.

"Maybe we should head back," she said. "We're completely alone here."

"That's what makes it so wonderful," he answered.

Behind him, in the distance, two figures walked in their direction. "All the same, let's head back," she repeated.

With a swift motion, he swooped her up in the air. Laughing, he ran further down the beach, carrying her in his arms.

"Put me down!" she exclaimed happily, enjoying the feeling of young romance that the years of their marriage, and the constant tension of his work, had erased. Finally, he set her feet down on the sand. They laughed together. On the hillside, a small Muslim cemetery, no longer used, was the only discernable landmark. In the darkness behind them, she saw the two figures still heading their way. Sonia felt a growing uneasiness.

"You see the North Star at the end of the Big Dipper?" Perchik asked, pointing up at the sky. "Turkey lies in this direction, and Greece straight across the sea. Maybe we can take a trip to Athens one day."

"Let's go back," she urged. "We're far away from everything."

"There's no one here, don't worry."

"Look behind you," she said. "I think those two men have been following us."

Turning, he saw the two dark figures walking at a crisp pace in their direction. Instinctively, Perchik grasped his wife's hand. The silhouetted figures approached and passed them, walking by the water a few meters away. The steady noise of the sea muffled their words, but the excited rhythm of their speech sounded like Arabic. The darkness of night hid their features. One was tall, broad shouldered, with a duck-like walk. The other was shorter and less full-bodied. Both had the gait of young men. Suddenly, they turned and circled back. When they reached the Aronovs, the shorter man stopped and began to relieve himself on the beach, without turning his back to the bewildered couple, as if he wanted to be seen.

"Please, Perchik," Sonia pleaded.

"OK," he said. "We'll head back."

They started walking back toward the city. The sea continued its steady roar. Increasing their pace, the young couple could now see the lights of the buildings along the shoreline. They heard the sound of footsteps coming closer behind them.

"They're following us," Sonia said, glancing back at their stalkers.

"It's all right," Perchik assured her. "We are almost back in the city."

Though Perchik and his wife were walking quite quickly, the two men passed them without saying a word. The shorter one stared back toward Sonia. He said something to his friend, and the two men made an abrupt about face and walked toward the Jews, blocking their path.

"Can you tell me the time?" the taller one asked, speaking Hebrew with an Arab accent.

Sonia squeezed her husband's hand in fright.

"I can't see my watch," Perchik replied.

"I have a flashlight," the young voice said.

The tall man switched on a flashlight and shone it in Perchik's face, making it hard for him to see.

"Why are you bothering us?" Perchik asked in irritation.

"Leave us alone," Sonia said.

"How much for an hour alone with the lady?" the taller man asked, still shining the light in Perchik's eyes.

With a laugh, the shorter man made rude, immodest motions with his hands and body.

"How much?" the man with the flashlight repeated.

"She's my wife," Perchik said angrily.

"I want her," the other man said.

Squeezing Sonia's hand, Perchik stepped forward, as if to pass them. The taller man stepped in his way.

Perchik understood very well what they wanted. Angered, he swung his free hand at the flashlight, but the Arab held on to it firmly. The short Arab suddenly raised a revolver and aimed it at Perchik. The flashlight went dark. Blackness engulfed them.

"Give them money!" Sonia shouted hysterically, thinking that would satisfy them.

Perchick lunged at the weapon, hoping to knock it from the assailant's hand and give his wife an opportunity to remove the small revolver which she carried in her purse. A gunshot sounded over the murmur of the waves, shattering the silence along the dark beach. Perchik grunted and fell on his knees to the sand. Sonia screamed out for help.

The two assailants stepped backward. Holding his belly, Perchik toppled into the sand with a groan.

"Help! Help!" Sonia screamed, dropping down on her knees beside her wounded husband. "Murderers! Murderers!" she shouted.

Amplified by the wind, her shout echoed loudly over the seashore. The two Arabs ran off toward the sloping hillside which hid the shoreline roadway.

"Sonia. Sonia," Perchik whispered.

"They were Jews?" she asked.

"No, Sonia, no," he answered.

He raised himself on an arm and tried to crawl forward. With his other hand, he clutched at his stomach, as if to seal the bleeding wound. Using all of her strength, Sonia raised him to his feet. He wrapped an arm over her shoulder and let her guide him along the beach toward the road. He stumbled forward as best as he could, all the time clutching at his belly. Blood covered his hands. Sonia propped him up, but their progress was terribly slow.

"It will be all right," was all she could say, needing all of her strength to drag him across the stretch of sand toward the dark roadway. Two figures came running their way. "Help! Help!" Sonia called out.

They were Jews. Taking a hold of Perchik between them,

they carried him to the nearest building, the foul-smelling Lebcovitz Tannery. Hysterically, Sonia ran back toward the restaurant.

What happened?" one of the rescuers asked, holding the badly wounded Perchik.

"Later," he managed to answer before losing consciousness.

The other man ran out on the road and stopped a passing car.

Perchik was bleeding profusely. The men carried him to the automobile and lay him on the backseat. "To the hospital, in a hurry," one said. The car sped off. Perchik heard the car's frantic honking and opened his eyes.

"Where's my wife?" he asked.

"You're going to be all right," the driver told him. "What happened?"

"Two Arabs," he managed to answer. "One shot me." Then he passed out again.

Distraught and out of breath, Sonia reached the restaurant. Her wild appearance caused an immediate commotion. Blood covered her hands and dress. Her hair was disheveled. Everyone rose from their seats.

"They shot my husband!" she exclaimed.

Katie Dan, the proprietor of the restaurant, took Sonia's hand and led her into her office, followed by a few customers who knew Aronov personally.

"Where's Perchik?" Katie Dan asked Aronov's trembling wife.

Sonia felt like she must be dreaming. Surely, she was in the midst of a horrible nightmare. She couldn't believe that her husband had been shot.

"We were walking on the beach," she told them. "Two Arabs followed us. One had a gun. He shot my husband."

Perchik was still alive when they reached Tel Aviv's Hadassah Hospital. A blood sample was hurried off to the lab to determine what blood type was needed. A nurse searched for an infusion stand without success. The Jewish doctor in the emergency room saw that the bullet, fired at close range, had punctured Perchik's abdomen near the liver. For the moment, the best he could do was to stop the heavy bleeding and bandage the wound.

Sonia remained at the seaside restaurant, recovering from her shock on the couch in Katie Dan's office. Her trembling had lessened, but finding herself surrounded by policemen, she felt dizzy and confused. The motherly, restaurant owner sat beside her, holding a hand on her knee, to help calm her shattered nerves. Sonia answered a policeman's questions as best as she could. Some people arrived whom she recognized, but she didn't recall their names.

"Do you want me to phone someone for you?" a person asked.

For several seconds, Sonia's mind was a blank. "Yes, please," she finally said. She told them the telephone number of her home. When Ben Zion answered, Katie Dan led Sonia to her desk and handed her the receiver.

"Hello?" Sonia said.

"*Shalom*," Ben Zion replied.

"Ben Zion?"

"Yes."

"Your father was shot. They took him to the hospital."

"Shot by who?" the startled youth asked.

"By two assailants. After we ate dinner. While we were walking on the beach."

"You're in Tel Aviv?"

"Yes."

"They took him to Hadassah Hospital?" Perchik's son inquired.

Sonia didn't know. She looked at a policeman.

"Where is my husband?" she asked.

"Hadassah Hospital," he told her.

Sonia passed on the information to Perchik's oldest son.

Captain Bechor Shitreet, chief investigator for the Mandatory Police Force, entered the room with another officer. The seasoned detective, one of the few Jews who had risen in the ranks, told Sonia that he needed to ask her a few questions. Still disoriented from the shock of what had occurred, she related the events of the evening as best as she could remember.

"Are you sure the two men were Arabs?" he asked when she had finished her tearful account.

"Absolutely," she answered.

Three hours after the shooting, Perchik was still alive. But no blood had arrived to replenish the large quantity he had lost.

"The pain," Perchik muttered.

"I can give you some morphine," the doctor told him.

"Where's my wife? Where's Sonia?" he wanted to know.

"The police are speaking with her," the physician answered.

"The pain," Perchik mumbled again.

"I'll prepare a dose of morphine," the doctor told the badly wounded Aronov as he drifted out of consciousness once again.

Moshe Stillman hurried into the examining room. A friend of Perchik, a fellow *Mapainik*, and representative of the Jewish Agency, he had rushed to the hospital the minute he heard the news. Seeing Perchik's white face, he stopped and stared at the bloodstained sheet. "Perchik! It's Moshe," he said, stepping up to the wounded man's bedside. "For God's sake, what happened?"

Aronov didn't answer.

"He's lost a significant amount of blood," the doctor told him.

Again the door opened and Ben Zion stepped cautiously into the room. The doctor guessed that he was Aronov's son.

"How is he?" the youth asked. His face was almost as pale as his father's.

"He's in and out of consciousness," the doctor informed him.

"Can't you do something?" Stillman inquired.

"A surgeon is on the way," the doctor answered, hurrying out of the room.

Ben Zion stared at his father. The bloody sheet covering his chest moved up and down in a jerky fashion from his uneven breathing. His face looked like a mask of stone. With a shudder, the youth stepped forward and grasped his father's limp hand.

"*Abba*," he said. "It's me. Ben Zion."

His father's hand twitched. Perchik squeezed his son's fingers. His eyes slowly opened and gazed up deliriously at the ceiling.

"It's me, *Abba*," Ben Zion repeated.

Perchik turned his head slightly to look at son. The youth sensed that his father was about to leave him forever. His bloodless lips managed to form a dying smile.

"Ben Zion," he said softly. "A child of Zion. Carry on with my work."

"Who shot you?" the boy asked.

"Two Arabs," his father answered weakly. "They wanted to molest your mother."

Blood trickled from his mouth. Sonia wasn't Ben Zion's mother, but that's what his father liked to call her, so that his son would respect her.

"Where is she?" Perchik asked.

"She's fine," Stillman assured him. "She's being questioned by the police."

Perchik gave Ben Zion's hand a final squeeze. Then his body quaked with a sudden spasm. His eyes closed, but he was still breathing.

The door opened and the doctor reappeared, followed by two orderlies. Quickly, they wheeled the bed out of the room.

"We're taking him to surgery," the doctor said.

Ben Zion gazed at his father's ghostlike expression. "*Abba*," he whispered.

Two policemen appeared in the doorway, but there was no longer someone to question. In the operating room, the surgeon tried his best to save the wounded man, but Aronov had lost so much blood, there was nothing the surgeon could do.

News of the murder hit Tel Aviv like a tidal wave. Everyone who read newspapers had heard of Perchik Aronov, the young, rising-star of the *Mapai* Party, who had recently been appointed to head the Political Division of the Jewish Agency. The lone gunshot on the beach reverberated like a bombshell throughout the *Yishuv*. People crowded around radios to hear details of the shocking crime. Who had killed Aronov? And why? Rumors spread almost as fast as the news, though the bad tidings didn't reach Tevye until the following evening, at the conclusion of the *Shabbat*. He was stunned. The murder of a Jew by an Arab was an almost weekly occurrence, but Perchik, his former son-in-law? Such a good man! True, they had quarreled in the past, but they had also fought side-by-side together as well. Who would want to kill Perchik? Not the Arabs. He tried to be their friend, attempting, with Chaim Weizmann, to reach a cooperation agreement with them. True, not every Arab leader had supported the negotiation, and radical Revisionists had condemned the highly-publicized meeting at the King David Hotel, and even Ben Gurion belittled the unripe initiative, but political assassination – could it be? And what would become of Perchik's son, Ben Zion, Tevye's grandson? Who would look after the boy?

Ben Zion followed his father to the operating room, where he waited outside in the corridor. Doctors came and left, but no one said a word. Finally, a nurse walked out with a lowered head. Another doctor appeared with a defeated expression. Then the doctor from the emergency room left the operating room. Glancing at Ben Zion, he sadly shook his head. "I'm sorry," he said.

When Ben Zion returned to the hospital entrance, he saw Sonia at the other side of the lobby. She was surrounded by a noisy crowd of *Mapai* supporters, some of whom Ben Zion recognized as being from the highest echelons of the party. Groups of policemen and journalists also gathered around her. Ben Zion tried to approach his step-mother, but he was jostled away. The emergency-room doctor had better success. The crowd let him through to the bench where the distraught wife was sitting with her legs tightly crossed. Moshe Stillman sat beside her, holding her hand. When the doleful news was announced, a hush fell over the lobby of the hospital, then pandemonium broke out, like at a political convention when the results of a controversial vote is announced. "The Revisionists killed him!" Stillman shouted. The accusation brought forth a wave of catcalls and curses. "Jabotinsky's henchmen pulled the trigger!" someone else exclaimed. "Revenge! Revenge!" still others yelled. Sonia's body went limp. Her husband's friend turned to hold her.

"Back away!" Stillman yelled at the crowd, comforting the widow in his arms. "Give her space to breathe!"

Ben Zion tried unsuccessfully to get Sonia's attention. Finally, using his shoulder as a wedge, he forced his way through the outer ring of the circle until someone shouted. "It's Aronov's son. Let him through!"

Ben Zion had never felt close to his step-mother. He had never kissed her, turning his face away slightly to let her kiss his cheek whenever she held out her arms to hug him. He didn't intend to hurt her feelings, but he couldn't do something he didn't feel. After all, Hodel was his mother, not Sonia, his father's second wife. Nonetheless, seeing Ben Zion, Sonia lost her composure completely and burst out sobbing. She too, on her part, had no great feeling for the youth, but he was Perchik's oldest son. Seeing him made the loss of her husband all the more poignant. She reached out a hand. Stillman made room for the boy on the bench. The shouting of the crowd continued unabated. Journalists from all of the local newspapers tried to learn whatever information they could from *Mapai* leaders, doctors, and the police.

"Your father was a great man," Sonia said to Ben Zion. "He could have become the leader of the country."

"What do you want me to do?" Ben Zion asked.

"Where are the children?"

"I left them at home."

"Then go home to them. Be with them. I'll come home later."

Ben Zion nodded. As he rose, a journalist pushed his way forward toward Sonia. Ben Zion shoved him away. Policemen appeared beside the murdered man's widow, keeping the mob away.

"Down with the Revisionist murderers!" someone yelled out.

"Jabotinsky will pay for this!" Stillman shouted.

Ben Zion gazed at him in disgust. Stillman had been in the emergency room, standing by his father's bedside when his father had said that the assailants were Arabs. What did Jabotinsky have to do with the murder? Seeing the boy's look of repulsion, the politician turned away. The crowd continued to cry for revenge.

Ben Zion left Sonia with the noisy mob. Why did they have to turn everything into politics? Especially at a time like this. How callous could you be, he wondered? Leaving the hospital, he paused on the sidewalk to get his bearings. It was already late in the evening, and buses had ended their routes. He would have to walk home to be with his half-brother and half-sister. Suddenly, he recalled that he was an *onen*, a mourner before the burial. According to the *halacha*, there were certain religious customs he had to follow. On the other hand, it was *Shabbat* when mourning was not allowed. But since he didn't observe the Sabbath any longer, nor observe the commandments, all of that wasn't an issue. Normally, at the funeral, a son would begin to recite the Mourner's *Kaddish*, but his father had never been a believer, so why should he dishonor his father's memory by adopting a ritual that his father scorned? In addition, if he were to recite the *Kaddish* prayer for the year of mourning, he would have to do so in a *minyan* of ten Jews, and that meant going to a synagogue three times a day, another ritual practice that his father shunned. He thought about all of these things, not because he wanted to uphold Jewish tradition, but because he had been raised in a religious world. Usually, the mourners in the family sat *shiva* for a week. Ben Zion didn't know if non-religious Jews had that custom. He didn't know if the *Chevra Kadisha* Burial Society took care of the funeral, or whether it was the family's responsibility to make arrangements directly with the cemetery. He crossed the street and stood on the corner, not knowing which way was which. From both directions, car headlights and police cars converged on the hospital. His father had tried to make peace with the Arabs, and Arabs had killed him. Should Ben Zion find a gun, go to Jafo, and kill as many Arabs as he could? Vengeance for the sake of vengeance wasn't a concept which his father embraced. Ben Zion stood alone on a street corner, unable to think clearly, still dazed from what had happened. What did he himself believe in, he wondered? On his death bed, his father had instructed him to continue his work for the Nation. But he hated politics. What should he do? Bewildered and without a father, Tevye's grandson felt totally alone in the world.

2.

For the past three months, David Ben Gurion had been traveling throughout the ghettos in Eastern Europe to gather votes for the Labor Party delegation to the upcoming World Zionist Congress. The *Betar* Youth Movement, founded by Ze'ev Jabotinsky, had caught on like fire, calling for a new "army of Zionists who would win back the Jewish Homeland with guns." Though Ben Gurion's speeches often aroused cheers from the crowds who showed up at his appearances, he didn't harbor any illusions. Jabotinsky had already won the hearts of these simple Jews with his more dramatic and eloquent orations. Jabotinsky had his young *Betar* enthusiasts following him wherever he went, creating a strong, military impression which gave hope to the downtrodden Jews. Resorting to scare tactics, Ben Gurion warned that the irresponsible militarism and fantasies of the Revisionists would only awaken the wrath of the *goyim*. Dubbing the head of *Betar* a fascist, Ben Gurion played on their fears of the Nazis, declaring that the fanaticism of "Ze'ev Vladimir Hitler" was even more dangerous to the Jews than his counterpart Adolf.

Nevertheless, as he traveled through town after town in Poland, Lithuania, Estonia, and Latvia, Ben Gurion felt that his efforts to sway voters away from Jabotinsky was reaping reward. In a letter to his wife, Katia, who he had again left alone in their modest Tel Aviv home with the children, he boasted that, "People walk four or five hours to hear me, sometimes in heavy rains. Sometimes, halls are so full that people stand outside by the windows to hear me speak." He said he knew that his long absences were difficult on the family, but if he didn't derail the great gains that Jabotinsky was making, the Revisionists would become the leading force in the Zionist Congress, and all of the socialist edifice which he had built in Palestine, along with the *Histadrut*, would be destroyed in the takeover, along with his dreams for a socialist State founded upon the principles of equality and justice. And if the Revisionists should wrestle the helm of the ship from his grasp, it would all be for naught, he wrote her, for the British would never tolerate the kind of armed militarism with the Revisionists championed.

On that fateful Saturday, when a cloud of civil war began to darken the shores of the Holy Land, Ben Gurion's train arrived in Vilna. At his hotel, a telegram was waiting for him. Though a single sentence in length, its contents had the weight of ten lengthy tomes. "Perchik Aronov has been murdered in Tel Aviv," the telegram stated. Ben Gurion later wrote in his diary: "Receiving the news, I fainted."

Another cable arrived soon afterward. "Apparently, the murderers were Arabs," it read. Startled by the development, Ben Gurion tried to speak with whomever he could on the telephone to find out as many details as possible. As few days later, he wrote to his wife: "Gradually, a terrible suspicion planted itself in my mind. Why should Arabs murder Aronov? He had become a peace monger. Who then had the most to gain from his death? The Revisionists. That much is clear."

Thousands of Jews crowded the Trumpeldor Cemetery in Tel Aviv for the funeral. People from all political parties and ideological persuasions turned out to pay last respects to the young Zionist leader, in an unusual show of unity, as if to say that enemies would not defeat the spirit of Zionism. They made their way to the funeral from all over the country, in spite of the summer heat and humidity. Tevye, Hodel, and Tzvi made the journey from Jerusalem to walk behind Ben Zion, Sonia, and Perchik's two other children, Yisrael and Sharon. Also present were Abba Ahimeir, who had written fierce condemnations of Aronov, castigating him for his secret meetings with the Nazis. A tall young man, Avraham Stavsky, a recent *oleh* who had arrived from Poland three months earlier, came along with Ahimeir, never dreaming that a week later he would be arrested as one of the murderers. Perhaps it was Sonia's loud sobs by the grave which silenced potential rabble rousers. The widow's white handkerchief waved like a miniature flag as she wiped the tears from her cheeks. One of the bearded gravediggers from the *Chevra Kadisha* Burial Society recited some prayers and chanted the somber "*Al Rachamin*" melody. Perhaps because of his grandfather's presence, Ben Zion recited the Mourner's *Kaddish*, though he didn't plan to continue throughout the year. The crowd answered the Aramaic verses with a reverberating "*Amen!*" Sharon clung to her mother. After the burial service, Tevye hugged his grandson and set a small stone on the freshly dug grave. Hearing that the family would not be sitting *shiva*, Tevye and Hodel offered their condolences to Sonia at the gravesite. Shedding tears of her own, Hodel embraced her son, who stood as upright as a statue, mustering as much manly composure as he could, though inside he was gripped by a deep and bitter sadness.

"Come visit us in Jerusalem," she told him. "It's still your home."

"Yes, Mother, I will," he answered, not knowing if he would.

That evening, Sonia received a telephone call from David Ben Gurion.

"Sonia, dear Sonia," he said. "I wish to express my deep condolences. Upon hearing the news, I fainted. The terrible tragedy which has befallen you and your family, and the Jewish People as a whole, is also a shocking loss for me. Your husband was a dear friend and colleague for many years."

"Thank you," she said, skeptical about his sincerity. Once upon a time, Sonia may have been a simple *kibbutz* girl, but after almost twenty years of marriage to a man devoted to politics, she knew that not every politician spoke from his heart. Ever since her husband had stepped out from beneath Ben Gurion's shadow and started building a name for himself in the Labor Party oligarchy, her husband had become anathema to his former boss, who viewed Aronov's political successes as a serious threat to his leadership of the Labor Zionists. When Aronov was appointed to head the Political Department of the Jewish Agency, without any help from Ben Gurion, the Party dictator severed all contact with his once devoted disciple.

"I regret that I was unable to attend the funeral," Ben Gurion told Aronov's widow. "As you probably know, I am in Vilna, preparing the groundwork for the upcoming Zionist Congress, which the Revisionists are trying to wrestle from our grasp. They who so vilified your husband, and who are suspected, I am informed by many people, to be behind his ghastly murder, they and their hooliganism must be stopped. The most fitting monument we can erect on your husband's grave is to foil the ambitions of the Head of *Betar* and crush his army of thugs by publically exposing the type of dangerous fanatics they are, as witnessed by the atmosphere of incitement and hatred which they created, prompting your husband's killers to commit this unforgivable crime."

Sonia held the telephone a little away from her ear as she listened to what seemed to be a carefully formulated speech.

"When the news spreads that the Revisionists have done away with a true Jewish leader like your husband, surely the delegates at the Zionist Congress will desert them, as if they carried the plague, and our cause will triumph. Do you hear me, Sonia? Do you understand what I'm saying?"

"Yes, I hear you. I understand. Many people have already spoken with me about the matter."

"In the memory of your husband, and for the sake of the ideals he fostered, we will continue to pursue his dreams of a safe and utopian society for Jews in the Land of Israel, purified from all dross and extremism."

"That's what my husband would want."

"If you need anything, don't hesitate to call me."

"Thank you, sir," Sonia replied.

"Don't call me, 'sir.' I'm not that old. Call me David."

Sonia remembered the time when she had worked as a housekeeper and nurse maid for the Ben Gurions, when Katia Ben Gurion had first arrived in Palestine with her baby. Her employment hadn't lasted very long. Not liking the way Ben Gurion gazed at the pretty housekeeper, Katia had fired her.

"Very well," she said. "Thank you, David."

"I hope to meet you at the first opportunity, to express my condolences in person. In the meantime, please feel free to request my assistance in at any time. The Party will take care of you, don't worry."

"Thank you, David. You are very kind," she said, wondering exactly what kind of help he had in mind.

The following day, the Jewish newspapers all carried the initial police report verbatim, based on Sonia Aronov's eyewitness account:

"Murder Suspect Number 1 held a flashlight. Male, taller than average, large build, age 30–40, clean-shaven, full face, light-skinned, tough expression, brownish-reddish hair, stands with legs apart, has a duck-like walk. Wearing a dark suit in a European style – black or dark blue – and the stitching may be in a double-breasted style. Collar and long tie. Wearing shoes, speaks Hebrew with some kind of accent.

"Suspect Number 2 shot the gun. Male, short, hulky, fit body, age 30, dark Mediterranean type, long nose, unshaven, tough expression, dark hair, wearing a dark suit in a European style with irregular stripes. Maybe is wearing a gray hat and shoes. He makes expressive movements with his hands."

The police offered a 500 *lira* reward to anyone with information about the suspects. That was the end of the "facts." In the socialist papers, all of the editorials pointed an accusing finger at Jabotinsky and the Revisionists, claiming that their incitement against Aronov had led to his murder.

Ben Zion read through a few of the newspapers. They all carried the same police report. He was stunned. On the night of the murder, his father and Sonia had both stated with certainty that their assailants had been Arabs. But that basic fact was glaringly missing in the police report, which pointed the accusing finger at Jews, who were more likely to wear the dark, European-style suits she described. How could it be? Why the sudden difference? Confused and angered, he showed the newspapers to Sonia.

"You told me on the telephone that the killers were Arabs, yet the police report doesn't say that at all," he said, confronting her.

"At the beginning, right after the shooting, in the shock of what had occurred, I was terribly confused. Who else could it have been but Arabs? Later, I began to remember more clearly," she said.

"You're lying," he said bluntly.

Sonia flinched, as if he had slapped her in the face.

"What a terrible thing to say after what I've been through," she exclaimed, in a voice filled with hurt and indignation.

"Why? Why change the story? What have you to gain?" the youth persisted, certain that she was lying.

"I didn't change the story. It was dark. We could hardly see. One of them shined a flashlight in your father's face. He was blinded by it. Maybe because of our fear, we assumed they were Arabs. Jews have been killed there before. That was the reason I didn't want to walk so far away from the restaurant. But your father wasn't afraid. Then, when the police started asking me a lot of questions, I began to remember what the attackers looked like."

"If it was dark, how could you have noticed so many details, like the pattern of their suits and their facial expressions?"

"It wasn't pitch black," she answered. "Oh, Ben Zion. Have some compassion. I loved your father. He was my whole life. I always tried to help him. And now they've killed him and I'm all alone."

He stared at her coldly. She wanted pity, but he didn't feel any for her. He didn't know why, but she was lying. She sat on her bed, sobbing like a Hollywood actress. In his mind, she was betraying his father.

"The newspapers are saying that the Revisionists are responsible for the murder," he told her. "You know the newspapers are just the mouthpieces of the Labor parties and the communists. You've changed the truth to fit their accusations."

"I didn't change anything," she insisted. "I told the police what I remembered. What difference does it make now who killed your father? He's dead. If this can help advance all the things he believed in, then he would be pleased."

"My father believed in truth, not lies."

"Who's going to look after me and your brother and sister? You? You're still a boy."

"*Abba's* friends? The Party? Did they promise to take care of you?"

"Yes. They promised. Because they value your father and what he believed in more than you do."

"You disgust me," he said, throwing a newspaper at her. He stormed out of the room. Furious, he walked out of the house. He didn't want to live there anymore. He didn't know where he would go, but he couldn't continue to live in the same house with a person like her, even if she was his father's wife. Outside, the night was as dark as the night of the murder. And now, Ben Zion, the son of Perchik Aronov, was free of everything and totally on his own.

3.

As Sholom Aleichem would say, to make a long story short.... The day after the funeral, Moshe Stillman, and a few other influential *Mapai* leaders, sat in the office of Harry Rice, Deputy Inspector General of the Palestine Police, who was in charge of the murder investigation for the Mandate Administration. The British Police had a long score to settle with radical Revisionist, Abba Ahimeir, and his gang of "*Birionim,*" so Rice didn't need to be persuaded by the Labor politicians that the time had come to crush him and his organization.

Ahimeir was Ze'ev Jabotinsky's most radical follower, taking Revisionist ideology to the extreme, far more than "*Rosh Betar*" himself. Editor and publisher of the stridently nationalist newspaper, *Hazit Ha'Am*, his articles were spiced with historical references to armed rebellion against foreign conquerors. His underground group, the "*Brit HaBirionim*" was named after a fierce faction of Jewish rebels who fought against the Roman invaders, and against the Jews who advocated surrendering to Caesar's legions, just before the destruction of the Second Temple. It was the first Jewish organization to call the British Authorities in Palestine a "foreign regime" and to refer to the British Mandate over Palestine as "an illegal occupation." Led by Ahimeir, Uri Zvi Greenberg, and Dr. Yehoshua Yevin, the group had conducted a series of disturbances and civil disobediences against British rule, including a bold rally against the British Under-Secretary-of-State for the Colonies, Drummond Shiels, in Tel Aviv, for which Ahimeir was arrested. Upon his release, as he strode through the prison gate, a young woman wearing a *Betar* uniform held out a bouquet of flowers. Taking them, he said to her loudly, so that the crowd of his followers could hear, "We will triumph with guns, not flowers."

Harry Rice already had a thick file on Ahimeir's doings and writings. Some of the information was gleaned from Jewish informers, whom the British Police planted in groups like *Betar*, suspecting that the organization was engaged in subversive activity. Ahimeir's strident lectures found an eager audience amongst Jewish youth who longed for a more sovereign future, unshackled from the passivity toward the Gentiles that characterized Jewish life in exile. "Don't be cowards!" Ahimeir exhorted. "Be brave and then *Eretz Yisrael* will be yours! A land isn't won like a prize, but rather by strength, sacrifice, and blood. Compromise and surrender will not win independence. Agreements drawn up in secret and signed by the Zionist Executive against the best interests of our Nation will lead us nowhere. Not treasonous treaties, but blood will win the war."

In Ahimeir's worldview, the Labor Zionists, with their sycophantic bowing to the British, were traitors to the Israelite mission, and he took every opportunity he could find, in his articles and lectures, to ridicule and condemn them. Thus the Labor Zionists and the British Mandatory Government seized the Aronov murder as an opportunity to crush the "*Birionim*" and the Revisionists in a single swoop.

On the night of the murder, in the emergency room of Tel Aviv's Hadassah Hospital, the dying Perchik Aronov had informed Moshe Stillman and Ben Zion that an Arab had shot him, but Stillman never mentioned this crucial piece of evidence to the police.

"Firstly, we want to thank the Deputy Inspector General for agreeing to meet with us," Stillman began. "We want you to know that the great majority of the Jewish community is horrified by Aronov's murder, and that we, as representative of the mainstream, will do everything we can to help the police apprehend the murderers within the Revisionist camp. It is clear to us that their incitement against Aronov brought about this crime, and it may very well be that one of their activists fired the bullet. To this end, the Jewish Agency will give a 1000 *lira* reward to anyone who provides information leading to the arrest of the killers."

Harry Rice thanked the contingent for their cooperation and for the extra reward money, which he said was bound to reap results. He was especially pleased to learn that the Jewish Agency had decided to fund a team of top-ranked lawyers to represent Sonia Aronov and lead the prosecution when the murderers were arrested and placed on trial.

The hard-working Tevye wasn't a devotee of newspapers, never having had the time or leisure to read them. But now, because of his close relations with the murdered man and his son, Tevye kept abreast of the investigation through the daily deluge of editorials and reports.

The Leftist press began a systematic onslaught against the Revisionist Movement which continued throughout the investigation, and even after the trial. The non-stop campaign ignited a fraternal war that threatened to shake the foundations of the Jewish community in Palestine. A coalition of socialist and centrist parties, including *Mapai, Poalei Tzion, HaShomer-HaTzair, HaPoel, HeChalutz,* and the General Zionist Party, *Al HaMishmar,* signed a joint petition demanding that the Revisionist Party be banned: "We declare that the moral responsibility for this brutal assassination falls upon the entire Revisionist Movement which has created such murderers. Whoever is concerned with the fate of Zionism must divorce himself from the Revisionists. There must be no dealings with the Revisionists in any shape or form! Let our motto be: 'Expel the Revisionist thugs from Jewish life!'" Jabotinsky was attacked mercilessly in editorial after editorial, winning epithets like "a bloodthirsty beast," and, "the man with the shady past."

In articles published in "*Hazit Ha'Am,*" Uri Zvi Greenberg had also penned harsh criticism against Aronov for his bartering with the Germans. When he heard about the murder, the militant poet was in Poland, on a *Betar*-sponsored tour of lectures around the country. His colorful images of *Eretz Yisrael*, coupled with a vision of proud Jewish soldiers armed with Bibles and guns, excited the imaginations of the young people who packed the halls wherever he appeared. "To Zion!" he called, his eyes aflame with the spirit of freedom. Outside on the Polish street, the pro-Labor, yellow-press newspaper, "*Heint*," accused the Revisionists of Aronov's murder with sensational, eye-catching headlines. Street posters demanded that Jabotinsky sympathizers be ostracized from the Jewish Nation: "Stay away from them! Cast them away! Avoid them like lepers! Despise them like murderers whose hands drip with blood! Make no room for the Revisionist killers in our communities. Like a plague, they must be ousted from our midst before they poison the bodies and minds of our Jewish youth!"

Instead of fueling the civil war that the Labor camp was brewing, Greenberg called upon Jews to unite in mourning, albeit in his stinging style: "A Zionist brother of all of us was murdered in Tel Aviv," he wrote. "All of us, all of us whose final goal in life is Zion, we all are in mourning today under a Zionist flag woven together. The *Histadrut* has lost its most favorite son, and the rest of us have lost a Zionist brother of our own flesh and blood. There can be no party politics at this moment. My brother has been murdered! My own blood has been spilled! And those who are drunk with Jewish blood and dance a drunken *hora* around his still-bleeding corpse, the Ben Gurions and Labor Party newspapers dripping with venom, they disgrace the honor due to the dead and bring a terrible curse and pollution upon our Nation."

With all of the "Aronov Murder" headlines, and with so much reward money being offered for information leading to the arrest of the suspects, the Palestine Police received hundreds of phone calls from the public. To head the investigation team, Harry Rice appointed two Jewish officers, Captain Bechor Shitreet and Yehuda Arazi, who, unbeknownst to his boss, coupled as a soldier for the *Haganah*. Three months later, in Arazi's report to the British

Intelligence Agency in London, he stated that the Mandate Administration in Palestine, prodded by the local Labor parties and the Jewish Agency, deliberately sought to blame the Revisionists for the murder. "It is my impression," he wrote, "that all of the witnesses, beginning with Mrs. Aronov, have attempted to incriminate the suspects at all costs." Lo and behold, after writing his report, Arazi was dismissed from the case.

A clerk in the Jewish Immigration Office informed the *Haganah* that a man resembling the description of one of Aronov's killers had applied for a visa to leave Palestine. His name was Avraham Stavsky, a Revisionist and follower of Abba Ahimeir. Obtaining a passport photograph of Stavsky, a *Haganah* agent showed it to Sonia Aronov, and asked her if he was one of the assailants. She answered, yes, it was the man with the flashlight. The immigration agent told the police, who summoned the murdered man's wife, and showed her ten photographs, asking if one of the killers was among them. The still-distressed widow picked out the photo of Stavsky. Then she asked Shitreet and Arazi if she could give them her account of the murder once again, saying that everything was clearer to her, now that the shock had worn off. In her new version of the shooting, she was absolutely certain that the assailants were Jews. Later, during the trial, it was discovered that the file containing her original testimony at the restaurant, where she had told police officers and the restaurant owner that the assailants were Arabs, had mysteriously vanished.

Stavsky, a twenty-seven-year-old immigrant from Poland had only resided in the country three months. A member of *Betar Youth* in Poland, he had helped Jews fabricate visas to immigrate illegally to Palestine, in defiance of strict British quotas. Hearing Abba Ahimeir speak in Warsaw, he decided to come on *Aliyah* himself. In Israel, Ahimeir, the head of the "*Brit HaBirionim*," took him under his wing, allowing him to share his apartment, where he was arrested by the British Police. Stavsky insisted he was innocent, claiming that he had been in Jerusalem on the night of the murder, but in a line-up of suspects at the police station, Sonia Aronov picked him out as one of the killers. Three days later, twenty more Revisionists were arrested, along with Ahimeir, who was charged with instigating the crime. Relying on the services of a woman of dubious character, the *Haganah* led the police to a third suspect, the supposed "trigger man." Zev Rosenblatt was the leader of a *Betar* group from Kfar Saba. He insisted that he had chaired a *Betar* meeting that evening, and that a dozen witness could substantiate his alibi. Pressured by his superiors in the Mandatory Administration to show that the British Police Department was making progress in solving the world-famous "political assassination" in Palestine, Harry Rice instructed Shitreet to arrest Rosenblatt, even though the Jewish policeman had severe reservations about the suspect's involvement. By this time, Shitreet also harbored doubts about whether he himself should resign from heading the investigation, given the many inconsistences, tenuous conjectures, dubious methods of acquiring evidence, and questionable directives he had to follow.

On the street, tensions became so heated that fistfights broke out in cafes and bars between the socialists and Revisionists. Neighbors stopped speaking with one another, and in institutions controlled by the *Histadrut*, teachers and workers with nationalist leanings were blacklisted and even fired from their jobs.

In Europe, Ben Gurion took advantage of the public anger which the biased media had generated against the Revisionists. Attacking them in every speaking engagement for having instigated the loathsome murder, he concluded that they were guilty even before the trial began. Even when contradictory details appeared in the pro-Revisionist press, he continued his attack. To him, the facts of the case weren't important. The important thing was winning the World Zionist Congress election. In a letter to Katia, he wrote, "I am less interested in whether Stavsky is the murderer than I am in discrediting Jabotinsky completely."

Following Ben Gurion's lead, the leading Leftist newspapers in Palestine, *"Dvar"* and *"HaAretz,"* waged daily attacks on the Revisionists, as if guilty verdicts had already been decreed by the High Criminal Court of Palestine. Even the more politically-balanced, *"Doar*

HaYom," published the fabricated reports and rumors
released by the British Mandatory Authority and Jewish
Agency. Since those tabloids enjoyed, by far, the greatest
circulation in the *Yishuv*, the general public was exposed to
a prolonged anti-Revisionist campaign during the Aronov
investigation and trial. The weekly newspaper, *"Hazit
HaAm,"* published by Abba Ahimeir and Yehoshua Yevin,
put out "EXTRA" issues on the newsstands they supplied,
in order to present the real facts of the case, but the fiercely
nationalist newspaper attracted a much smaller readership
than the Leftist dailies. In addition, with his co-editor,
Ahimeir, languishing in prison, Yevin found himself hard
pressed to answer all of the lies and distortions published in
the Labor press. To counter the avalanche of misinformation
and slander, a young Revisionist named Benzion Netanyahu
appeared out of the blue-and-white skies of Zionism to put
his finger in the dam. A student of Jewish History and
Hebrew Literature under the tutelage of Professor Joseph
Klausner, the only teacher at Hebrew University not afraid
to express his nationalistic beliefs, Netanyahu decided to
raise the funds to write and publish a daily Rightest
newspaper which would present the Revisionist side of the
story to the widest readership possible. Already, the young
academic was editor of the widely-circulated, Revisionist
monthly newsletter, *"Betar."* Encouraged by his ardently
Zionistic father, Rabbi Natan Mileikovsky, the first Rabbi to
publically oppose the blood libel surrounding Aronov's
murder, Netanyahu gathered other writers around him and
channeled all of his energies into the journalistic endeavor.
With the support of Jabotinsky, and the backing of Professor
Klausner, the stalwart Netanyahu (who was later to father
two famous sons) published the first issue of *"HaYarden"* the
day after the Aronov trial began. He himself wrote several
articles each day under different pen names, filling the
newspaper with fascinating articles about Jewish History,
Hebrew Literature, and the geography of *Eretz Yisrael*, along
with a day-to-day account of the trial and the background
stories surrounding it. Editorials and essays expounded
Revisionist philosophy, including Jabotinsky's "Iron Wall"
policy, which advocated a clear division between Jews and

Arabs of Palestine, either through an effective British police force, or preferably, through a Jewish army. While Jabotinsky believed that the Jews and Arabs could share Palestine, as long as a Jewish majority prevailed, Netanyahu favored transferring the Arabs to countries of their own. "The vast majority of Arabs would choose to exterminate us if they had the chance," he wrote. "The penchant for conflict is an essential trait of the Arab. In his essence, he holds an animosity toward the Jews. His personality won't allow him to compromise. It doesn't matter what kind of resistance he will meet, or what price he will pay. His lives in a state of perpetual war."

The Rightest newspaper caught on quickly, awakening the national pride of the silent masses and triggering a wave of support for the three imprisoned Jews who were facing a sentence of death by hanging. In spite of expensive fines and two, month-long shutdowns by the British Police on charges of subversion against the regime, the newspaper became a powerful national educator and a beacon of justice in a Land divided by senseless hatred and a cancerous cavern of distrust.

4.

With trembling fingers, Mrs. Ita Stavsky, mother of murder suspect, Avraham Stavsky, opened the letter from her imprisoned son. Like the good boy that he was, he told her not to worry, assuring her of his innocence. The distraught mother could hardly read his words through her tears. What could she do to help, she wondered? She was so far away in Brest? One thing was certain. She had to meet with Mr. Jabotinsky, the Zionist leader whom her son so admired.

That very same day, she hurried to the local *Betar Youth Movement* office in Brest, and asked to see the head of the chapter, twenty-year-old Menachem Begin. In the past, the two families had been neighbors, and Mrs. Stavsky had bounced little Menachem on her knees. She couldn't relate to him in a formal manner, the way other people did. In her eyes, he was anything but a fearsome soldier. His neatly-ironed *Betar* uniform seemed two sizes too big for his frail-looking frame. With his large glasses and pale, scholarly appearance, you would have expected to find him studying Talmudic tomes in one of the local yeshivas, as a natural continuation to his early years in *Talmud Torah*. Only his piercing black eyes gave a clue that his burning love for the Jewish People and Zion would find expression, not as a Rabbi, but as Jabotinsky's successor, and as the leader of the militant underground organization, the "*Etzel*," which adopted the nickname, the "*Irgun*."

Menachem was happy to see her. Naturally, he knew all about the Aronov murder. Immediately, he agreed to travel with her to Warsaw to introduce her to "*Rosh Betar*." Ze'ev Jabotinsky, the founder of *Betar*, and the charismatic leader of the Revisionist Movement, was, to Begin, far more than a modern-day Herzl. He was a prophet whose words were as holy as Torah. Ever since the university student from Brest first heard Jabotinsky speak, in a small, provincial theater overflowing with people, he knew he had found his mentor. There were no empty seats in the hall. The packed gallery looked like it was about to collapse. The teenage Begin squeezed into the orchestra pit, just below the stage. As Jabotinsky began to speak, the young man felt himself lifted up, borne aloft, and born anew. More than won over, the serious-looking idealist became consecrated to the Zionist mission which Jabotinsky portrayed with the brushstrokes of a master artist. The Jewish People had a Homeland, he said. Not Russia. Not Poland. Not British Palestine. *Eretz Yisrael* – the Land of Israel. The Jewish People didn't have to be eternally bullied. They could forge their own destiny. Rise from the dust, My Nation! Arise and Shine! Let the lion of Judah rise up and roar! Either the inferno of Nazi hatred awaited them, or the pride of being a free people in their own Hebrew Homeland, as in the days of their glorious past. Arise, My Nation! Arise!

In Warsaw, Jabotinsky kept abreast of the Aronov murder investigation as best as he could. Relying on his *Betar* followers in *Eretz Yisrael*, and Jewish officers within the Palestine Police Force who harbored secret allegiance to the Revisionist cause, he readily understood that the hate-filled witch hunt was not merely directed against the Revisionist Movement, but that he himself was the target of the pernicious blood libel which Ben Gurion and the Labor Zionists were spreading across the world. Now, wherever he spoke in his tireless mission to alert the Jewish People to the dangers of Hitler's Third Reich, instead of the cheers and applause which had customarily greeted his speeches before Aronov's murder, boos and curses followed him wherever he appeared. Incited by the ocean of lies which covered the front pages of the Leftist press, Jews tried to prevent him from appearing in their towns. Ruffians threw rocks at his car and eggs upon his arrival, shouting out, "Villain!" "Murderer!" "Fascist Scum!" If not for his bodyguard of *Betar* cadets, he could easily have been murdered himself.

The Zionist visionary had spent the last five years of his life fostering a revised understanding of Zionism which rejected the path of concession and appeasement which the socialists had adopted. Convinced of the innocence of Stavsky, Rosenblatt, and Ahimeir, the Revisionist leader called upon his followers to remain "calm and steadfast" in the face of the cancerous blood libel. "I bow my head in silence before the victim of this dastardly assassination," he wrote. "Aronov was a man who served his People with honor. He was fair and upright in debate. I refuse to believe that Jews have committed this foul and cursed murder, which has spawned an atmosphere of hatred and violence in *Eretz Yisrael*. But to Revisionists all over the world I say – we shall not surrender and collapse under the barrage of hatred leveled against us. We shall not alter our conduct one bit. We shall not concede even one inch in our battle against a Zionist movement which seeks the good of the Party over the greater good of the Nation as a whole. Those who denigrate us so violently, and slander our names, claim to do so in the name of Justice, but their real goal is as plain as a bright Mediterranean day - to gain control over the World Zionist Movement and the *Yishuv* in Palestine, in order to impose their beliefs, and their beliefs alone, over Jewish life in the Holy Land. But I can assure you, as sure as the sun will rise in the morning, the instigators of this blood libel will not succeed!"

Jabotinsky had only his pen and the truth of his words to defend himself, and the Revisionist Movement, from the onslaught waged daily against them. "It is common knowledge," he wrote, "that scores of Jews have been murdered by Arabs in *Eretz Yisrael*. Therefore, it would have been natural to look for the murderers of Aronov amongst the Arabs. Yet the suspicions and accusation of the Labor camp immediately fell upon the Revisionists, in an unprecedented campaign of slander and falsehood, condemning, far in advance of the trial, the three men who sit in prison, thereby making an objective verdict impossible for any court of law."

In another article, he wrote: "There are two principles sacred to all civilized humanity. If a man claims that he is innocent, then he is considered innocent until a court declares him guilty; and secondly, if a person is guilty of a crime, his guilt does not cast guilt over the community to which he belongs. Both of these rules should be especially sacrosanct to the Jewish People, who have suffered more than any other People from the violation of these very principles."

Then Jabotinsky turned his literary searchlight on the Jewish public in Palestine, which was allowing itself to be duped by a blood libel against Jews, propagated not by Gentiles, as it had been in the past, but by Jews themselves!

"I accuse a large section of Jewry of violating these two principles. They see a young Jew in Palestine swearing his innocence, fighting for his very life and honor, and though they have not heard any proof against him, they already declare him a murderer and shove him gleefully toward the gallows. In addition, they condemn the entire Revisionist Movement, with tens of thousands of members, and hundreds of thousands of sympathizers, with moral involvement in this heinous crime. And they conduct this vendetta with the obvious motive of political gain. With the weight of a lifetime of self-sacrifice in service of the Jewish Nation, I send my cold and bitter contempt to this unworthy section of *Am Yisrael*.

"I know that the vast majority of our People are ashamed and disgusted by this blood-libel crusade being waged by

Jews against Jews, but I warn them that in their timid silence, they themselves are contributing to the destruction of our public life and unity. By their silence, they are abetting the enemies of Jewry and true Zionism, allowing them to divert the Aronov investigation away from the murder itself in order to discredit the proud and strident voice of a great and growing portion of world Jewry."

Along for his great concern for the welfare of the imprisoned suspects, and his deep chagrin over the senseless hatred which had pitted brother against brother in the Jewish Homeland, Jabotinsky worried about the future of the Zionist enterprise if command of the ship fell into the hands of Ben Gurion, who accused Jabotinsky personally for Aronov's murder.

"Stavsky is a loyal pupil of his master, Ze'ev Jabotinsky,"" Ben Gurion wrote. "He stands in attention, awaiting the supreme and exclusive orders of '*Rosh Betar*.' While the head of an organization cannot know in advance what his followers may do at any given moment, in his capacity as supreme mentor and commander of his troops, Jabotinsky bears the general responsibility for the actions and deeds of all of his *Betarim*."

Arriving in Warsaw, Menachem Begin and Mrs. Ita Stavsky found their way to the modest Krakowsky Hotel, where Jabotinsky had taken a room during his campaign tour before the upcoming World Zionist Congress elections. Hearing that the two visitors had arrived, he immediately hurried to the lobby to greet them. Stavsky's mother tried to kiss the hand of the man who steadfastly defended the innocence of her son, but Jabotinsky wouldn't allow it – instead he bowed and kissed her hand, out of respect for her suffering.

"I am honored to meet the mother who has raised such a fine young man, so dedicated to the Zionist cause," he told her.

"My *Abrasha* is a pure soul," the mother attested, unable to hold back her tears. "He could never, never, do such a thing."

Hoping to set her mind at ease, in a warm and confident tone, Jabotinsky told her not to worry.

"The case will probably never reach court," he assured her. "And if there is a trial, we will hire the best attorney. Please don't fear. We will return your *Abrasha* to you. I give you my word."

All the while, Menechem Begin stood in rigid attention, like a beginning recruit in front of his commander. Jabotinsky's secretary, Joseph Schechtman, who would later write a definitive biography about *"Rosh Betar's"* turmoil-filled life, spoke up, saying, "Your son's accusers will pay dearly for this horrible slander."

"The Jewish Agency has already hired four of the best Jewish lawyers in Palestine to conduct the prosecution," Jabotinsky told Mrs. Stavsky. "We have contacted one of England's top lawyers to represent your son and his comrades. To help prepare our defense, I have asked him to come here to Warsaw before traveling on the Jerusalem. A kindhearted Zionist from South Africa, Mr. Michael Haskel, has agreed to contribute toward the considerable costs of the defense, and we shall ask the general public to donate whatever further funds are needed."

Turning to the young *Betar* activist from Brest, Jabotinsky told him, "Mr. Begin, please stand at ease." The humble disciple remained standing as straight as a rifle. He could hardly breathe. For him, no one on earth possessed a greater passion and dedication to the Jewish Nation. For him, standing in the same room as *"Rosh Betar"* was like being in the presence of God.

Mrs. Stavsky opened her traveling bag and tearfully handed Jabotinsky a small stack of envelopes, letters that her son had sent to her since his arrival in Palestine. "If you read my son's letters, you will see what a fine person he is. He could never have done such a thing. Never."

Jabotinsky promised to read them immediately. Graciously, he excused himself, saying he was going to write an article about her son, based on the letters. Indeed, the very next day, the article, entitled, "Letters to Mother," appeared in the press. Before returning to his room, *"Rosh Betar"* asked his secretary to arrange a meal for the hungry and weary travelers. Then, turning to his dedicated young follower from Brest, he asked, "Mr. Begin, are you a university student?"

"Yes, sir," the young man replied, thrilled at being addressed by the Movement's founder and chief commander.

"Have you chosen a field of endeavor?"

"Yes, sir. Law, sir. Like you."

"Very good," Jabotinsky replied, sensing the youth's leadership potential. "If you like, I will inform you when the lawyer from England will be in Warsaw so that you can join our discussions. It might be very educational for you, both legally, and in broadening your understanding of the underlying quarrels which are threatening to undermine the success of the Zionist enterprise from within, at a time when the monster from Berlin is threatening to destroy our Nation from without."

Menachem Begin smiled from ear to ear. His serious expression gave way to the unabashed joy of a boy. Nothing could have made him happier than the invitation from his mentor.

The lawyer, Horace Samuel, called Jabotinsky, "Commander." Before embarking on his law career, he had served under "Jabo" in the Hebrew Brigade. A staunch Zionist, Samuel had won renown in England as a brilliant criminal lawyer, but meeting with *"Rosh Betar"* in Warsaw, he listened to Jabotinsky's summary of the Aronov case like a law student before his teacher, just like the young and unassuming Menachem Begin, who also attended the pre-trial strategy talks in the simple Warsaw hotel.

"Certainly," Jabotinsky began, "our foremost mission is to prove the innocence of the three imprisoned suspects. Saving their lives is our supreme concern. In addition, the entire Revisionist Movement is on trial. Because I believe in the absolute correctness of our cause, the future of the Zionist enterprise depends upon our success in exposing this ignominious blood libel for what it is, and in exposing the base motives of those who stand behind it. Make no mistake, gentlemen, the ruthlessness of our opponents is no less than the ruthlessness of the Bolsheviks, whom they admire, and in whose shadow they were raised. For them, no tactic is taboo in obtaining their goal of establishing absolute control over the Jewish settlement of Palestine, including sending three innocent Jews to the gallows. While I am not a fervent practitioner of Judaism, the moral tenets of the Torah have always been my guiding light. No doubt, the leaders of the Labor Movement and the *Mapai* Party believe in the righteousness of their methods, and though they are fond of quoting verses from the Prophets, they don't believe in them. As Avraham said to Avimelech, *"There is no fear of God in this place."* Not believing in a Higher Power, they will stop at nothing to achieve their goals. If they succeed in using Aronov's blood to crush the growing support for the Revisionist platform, the Jewish People will be left, after all of the Jewish Agency's concessions to the Arabs and the British, with, at best, a truncated *Eretz Yisrael*, populated by the immigration of the selected few, the followers of *Mapai*, while the Nazi's march the vast majority of Jews to their graves."

While the attorney and Menachem Began focused on every word, Jabotinsky's secretary took notes at a furious pace, trying to transcribe every word.

"Today, the lives of five-hundred-thousand German Jews are in extreme peril. They have nowhere to flee. No one wants them. In his cold pragmatism, Ben Gurion wants only young and able socialists. Unwilling to fight the British on the issue of open immigration, the Jewish Agency grants the limited visas at their disposal only to those who, in their worldview, will be productive workers for the socialist cooperative in Palestine. When we demand unlimited immigration to all Jews, they claim that the *Yishuv* would collapse under the impossible economic burden, covering up their fear that the masses would rally to the Revisionist platform, not theirs.

"The world understands the danger which the Jews of Germany are facing with Hitler's rise to power, and many countries have rallied behind our call for an international boycott of German goods, in order to stop the Nazi beast from growing. Nonetheless, the Labor Zionists are against this strategic boycott, downplaying the immediate danger, and wanting Germany to be a partner in trade in order to economically strengthen the *Yishuv*. And so, Perchik Aronov travels to Berlin to negotiate with Joseph Goebbels, truly believing in the worthwhileness of bartering Jewish lives for the economic benefit of both Germany and the Jews of Palestine – trusting the promises of the Germans, just as the Jewish Agency trusts the promises of the British. For Revisionists, and for writers like Abba Ahimeir, this "Pact with the Devil" is a betrayal of world Jewry. In defying the international economic boycott of Germany, and fostering trade with them, their proposed *Ha'avara* transfer agreement will only strengthen the Nazis. While a small quota of German Jews may be saved, how many millions will perish under the steel treads of Hitler's tanks?"

The attorney, Samuel, interrupted Jabotinsky's background summary of the case. "I read Ahimeir's condemnation of Aronov, and some of his other undeniably abrasive articles. While he doesn't specify murder or violence, there is certainly a tone of incitement in his words."

Jabotinsky nodded his head in agreement. "I personally am not a *Hasid* of Ahimeir. However, as you very well know, incitement without a call for violence against an individual or group is not the kind of incitement that can stand up in a murder trial."

"If it's a fair trial," Samuel noted.

"Yes, you are quite right. Unfortunately, given the lynch atmosphere which the Leftist press in Palestine has brewed, and given the anathema of the British Mandate Authority toward me and the Revisionists for challenging their pro-Arab, pro-imperialistic policies, a fair trial doesn't seem possible. On the other hand, the British tend to have a schizophrenic approach to politics and justice. While the British Administration in Palestine, and the Palestine Police, are corrupt to the core, the British judicial system prides itself on upholding the principles of liberty and justice. If you, as counselor for the defense, succeed in exposing the legal uncertainties and weaknesses of the prosecution, and shed reasonable question on the truth of the witnesses and the supposed 'facts' surrounding the murder, it will be hard for a British court, even in Palestine, to render a prejudiced and unjust verdict, especially in light of the great international attention focused on the case. As far as Ahimeir is concerned, the British Administration in Palestine would enjoy nothing more than sending him to prison for life, but, while I myself do not agree with his radical and caustic tone of writing, and some of his extreme ideas, I am certain that his style is largely poetic, employing literary exaggeration to draw attention to his opinions. He adopts the maximalist point-of-view in order to emphasize the shortcomings of opposing viewpoints, especially those of the socialists and communists, and the British Palestine Administration itself. He himself is not a violent person, and he would never commission anyone to do something which he himself would not agree to do. When you investigate his activities as the head of the "*Birionim*," you will discover that while they engage in acts of civil disobedience, violence is not a part of their modus operandi. So, while Ahimeir's bark can sound like a bulldog's, his bite is more like a puppy's. As for Stavsky, his ill luck was that he was lodging at the Ahimeir home when the police came looking for Ahimeir. As far as I know, outside of the questionable veracity of Mrs. Aronov's testimony, which seems to change with each passing day, the police have no factual evidence whatsoever to support a conviction."

"Who then is the murderer?" the lawyer asked.

"I am sure you will discover that for yourself during your investigation. Perhaps, to clear away some of the umbrage in the forest, allow me, as a student of law, a student of human nature, and a student of the political quagmire in Palestine, to share my hunches with you."

Jabotinsky glanced at Begin, who hadn't uttered a word since the meeting began.

"Are you all right, Menachem?" he asked.

"Yes, sir," was the devotee's curt answer.

"Please feel free to speak your mind," the *Betar* leader told him.

"Perhaps when I understand the overall picture," the young man replied.

"I would like to hear your thoughts up till now."

"Well, sir. To tell you the truth, sir. I find it difficult to believe that Jews could act this way to fellow Jews, if indeed they know that the three suspects are innocent."

"Yes, I agree," Jabotinsky concurred. "It is most distressing. But you can take it from an old war horse like me who has received many blows in battle – many of them from these same self-proclaimed champions of justice – the blindness of ambition and the craving for power can turn an upright man into an advocate for the Devil. To quote a verse from the Prophet Isaiah, '*Your destroyers and those who bring about your ruin come forth from within you.*' Remember, it was Yosef's brothers who threw him into a pit filled with scorpions and deadly snakes. Unfortunately, our brothers have not progressed substantially since then. But it is a fundamental principle of *Betar*, which must never be betrayed, that even if we are attacked in a villainous blood libel like this, we are never to raise up our arms against fellow Jews. The Second Temple and Commonwealth were destroyed by senseless hatred and fraternal strife, and we must never, never, never allow ourselves to be dragged into civil war. No matter the cost. Is that understood?"

The young *Betar* officer felt Jabotinsky's probing stare search through the inner recesses of his soul.

"Yes, *Rosh Betar*," Begin answered.

"We must fight for our principles with all of our resources, and with all of our strength," the Revisionist leader explained. "But never by resorting to violence against Jews. If enemies from within send bullies to beat us, yes, in defense, we will return their blows in kind, without hesitation or weakness, but we will never willfully shed the blood of our brothers, no matter how mistaken or evil their actions may be. Don't ever forget these words."

"Yes, sir, Commander, sir, I never will," Begin said, feeling his body tremble. Not only Begin, but Samuel, and Jabotinsky's secretary and friend, Schechtman, sensed that the admonition was more than a teaching. It contained the weight of a commander passing on his sword to his successor, as if Jabotinsky knew with his uncanny insight that the serious young disciple before him would one day take his place as the leader of *Betar*.

"In my opinion," Jabotinsky said, returning to the murder

case, "The Aronov woman cannot be considered a suspect." He stood up from his chair and began to pace back and forth like a lawyer addressing the court. "I have heard no rumors that she or her husband were involved in the sort of romantic triangle that could lead to a jealously killing. The fact that she had a revolver in her purse indicates that she or her husband felt threatened, but their fear most likely was the precaution many Jews feel in Palestine in light of the constant Arab hostility. However, the fact that she altered her original testimony, asserting that the two men who stalked her husband and her on the beach were Jews, and not Arabs, as she had previously claimed, destroys her reliability as a witness, and shows that she is a morally weak individual, no doubt worried over her future. Who knows what promises she received from the leaders of *Mapai* in agreeing to play along with their malodorous scheme. Needless to say, any line of defense must totally crush her credibility, since she remains the only eyewitness to the murder."

Horace Samuel listened with rapt attention. Writing at a furious pace, Schechtman transcribed Jabotinsky's summary of the case.

"As for the Revisionists, logic says they are innocent of the crime," Jabotinsky continued, clarifying the picture with his keen, analytical mind. "Viewing the case in the most objective manner, as if I were not involved, there are many reasons to discount the theory that the Revisionists planned and carried out the murder. First, they had no understandable motive. Such a despicable act could bring them no gain, and only ruin the Revisionist Movement. We are already witnessing this as thousands of our former supporters have disassociated themselves from our cause in light of the ongoing witch hunt. No Jew could be expected to condone political assassination, and such an action would obviously be fatal to the Revisionist banner, alienating all segments of the Nation. Furthermore, in his dealings with the Germans, Aronov was merely a representative of the Jewish Agency, and his death would not prevent an agreement from being signed with the Germans. While Ahimeir condemned Aronov's actions in the most strident fashion, he did so on his own, not as the spokesman for *Betar*. The Revisionist Movement has never fostered ideological assassination, in any shape or form. Furthermore, the *Mapai* leader who led a constant attack against the Revisionists, portraying them as a danger to Zionism and to the welfare of world Jewry, was David Ben Gurion, not Aronov. Thus, the assassination of Aronov would in no way lessen the fierceness of Ben Gurion's campaign against the Revisionists and serve no purpose whatsoever in altering the militant *Betar* image which Ben Gurion has purposefully manufactured to scare people away from our cause. It should be noted that in most cases of political assassination which are motivated by ideological reasons, the assassins don't deny their actions when arrested, as have Stavsky, Ahimeir, and Rosenblatt – rather they proudly proclaim the righteousness of their deed. Furthermore, it should be pointed out that the suspects attended the funeral, along with leading Revisionists and officers of *Betar*, uniformed and carrying the *Betar* flag, in a sincere expression of shared sorrow and solidarity with the *Yishuv*."

"You haven't left me a whole lot of work to do," Horace Samuel said with a smile. Jabotinsky ignored the compliment, as was his wont, lest the tentacles of hubris trap him in its net.

"Don't worry," Jabotinsky assured him. "You have months of work ahead of you, filling in all the details. To answer the question – who killed Aronov, there are two other possibilities to consider. First, the British. Officials from the Office of the High Commissioner were the last people to meet with Aronov on the Friday afternoon of the murder. This presented them with the opportunity to follow him afterwards. As Mrs. Aronov has testified, no one knew of their plans for that evening, not even she herself. It seems that Aronov, in the late afternoon, decided to leave Jerusalem and travel to Tel Aviv, where he chose to dine, against his wife's wishes, at the beachfront restaurant. His spontaneous behavior completely refutes the theory that the Revisionists carefully plotted out the murder in advance. This also means that the British could not have planned the time and place of his murder in advance, but they could have followed Aronov after their meeting. As for their possible motive – putting the blame on the Revisionists, as they are doing today, is an effective way of destroying the Movement which most opposes their imperialistic and pro-Arab policies in Palestine. With the Revisionists out of the way, Weizmann, with his slavish idolization of the *goyim*, and Ben Gurion, with his persistent kowtowing, would be their puppets, abetting their goal of keeping Palestine under British control. However, while I doubt that the British instigated the murder, their complicity in framing the suspects is an angle that should be exploited. Anything the defense can do to embarrass the British Government in the eyes of the world will put pressure on the British Administration in Palestine to flee from their involvement in what must be portrayed as the new Dreyfus Affair."

Menachem Begin sat awestruck. He knew that his Commander had studied law, but, given his non-stop work in promoting the Revisionist platform, Jabotinsky found no time to practice it. Among other things, the display of legal and political understanding taught Begin the importance of doing one's homework as thoroughly as possible before setting out to achieve a goal.

"What about Ben Gurion himself?" Samuel asked. "Over the last few years, Aronov became his most serious competitor for the leadership of the Zionist Executive and threatened to topple his control of *Mapai*?"

Menachem Begin harbored the same suspicion. He waited for *"Rosh Betar"* to answer. Jabotinsky paused before offering a reply. Samuel seized the moment to add another point for consideration.

"Last year, I met with Aronov. In the course of our conversation, he stated that he had come to the absolute conclusion that under the British rule of Palestine, there was no possibility of achieving a Jewish majority in the country, and that only a putsch against the British could alter the situation. Stressing that he hadn't become a Revisionist in any shape or form, he insisted that a Jewish State could not rise without a transition period of revolutionary rule by a Jewish minority. He told me that he had written his opinion to Chaim Weizmann. Since both Weizmann and Ben Gurion are vehemently opposed to trying to establish a Jewish State through forceful means, Aronov's radicalism, combined with his meteoric rise in Labor Movement, made him a clear rival and threat to both of them.

"If I could inject a point or two," Schechtman said.

"By all means," Jabotinsky agreed.

"At a Mapai Labor Council meeting at the beginning of the year, Ben Gurion condemned Aronov for fostering a too conciliatory policy toward the British Palestine Administration. To Ben Gurion's credit, he favored a more demanding approach, but Aronov retorted that if the Zionist movement adopted a militant posture with the British ruling authorities, the Mandate's attitude toward the Jews would become even colder than it was, and consequently, Arab political influence would increase within the British Administration, jeopardizing Jewish interests and rights in Palestine.

"Then, just a few months ago, Aronov organized what the Jewish Agency called 'an historic event' at the King David Hotel. Aronov was joined by his good friend and political ally, Chaim Weizmann, whom Ben Gurion despises. They met with prominent Arab leaders of Transjordan to promote cooperative undertakings. Aronov believed that by developing an accord with the Arab sheikhs of Transjordan, political relations with the Arab leaders of Mandatory Palestine could be improved. Ben Gurion, who was not invited to the conference, was not at all pleased with discussions that could lead to two future States in *Eretz Israel*. Aronov's initiative in the matter, without asking for Ben Gurion's consent, is said to have made the little man furious."

Jabotinsky nodded. "Ben Gurion's involvement in Aronov's murder is a logical possibility," he said. "But, personally, I cannot accept it. As lawyer for the defense, Mr. Samuel, it is your obligation to take such a possibility into consideration, but I, perhaps out of personal weakness, refuse to believe that Ben Gurion would order his followers to carry out political murder, or hire Arabs to do so. Not because I think he is a saint, but because the slightest mishap in such a plan would mean the end of his career. Granted, it is Ben Gurion who has orchestrated this blood libel from the start, but I have to rule out his involvement in the murder itself. However, there is room to explore the possibility that the *Mapai* leadership, as a whole, stands behind the killing, for the same reason the British may have had – to steer the blame for the dastardly murder on us and thereby bring about our political destruction."

"To summarize?" Schechtman asked, as if he were already editing a future biography.

Jabotinsky stood pensively, staring out into space, like the captain of a ship gazing out from the bow. "To summarize, I think that the strongest possibility is Mrs. Aronov's initial claim that two Arabs committed the murder. The only other eyewitness was Aronov himself. Perhaps, before dying, he told someone what happened – the two Jews who carried him to a car, the driver, a doctor or nurse at the hospital. Perhaps, the police have this information and are covering it up, in order to guard their great fiction. While I doubt whether our friends can receive a fair trial, I remember from my survey of legal texts before the *Haganah* trial after the pogrom of 1920, that the laws of *Eretz Yisrael* require at least two witnesses to hand down a murder conviction. As long as Mrs. Aronov remains the only witness, this important technicality can prevent a disastrous injustice from transpiring. Good luck, Mr. Samuel. The lives of three innocent Jews, and the future of the Jewish People, depend on your skills. May the God of Israel be with you."

Chapter Five
FROM FLORENCE WITH LOVE

Reading Avraham's letter on the subway ride to Barnard College, Hannie was bewildered until she realized that "farming" was a code word for his underground activities. When she reached the campus of the all-women's college on Upper Broadway, she sat on a bench surrounded by pigeons and read the mysterious epistle again.

"Hannila, Hannila, Hannila," her ever-dramatic boyfriend began. "What a fool I was for writing you so bluntly about current events. Thinking of you, I am drunk with love, but that doesn't excuse me for speaking too freely about matters whose exaltedness lies in their secrecy. Please destroy the last letters I wrote you. David R. has warned me. The British intercept letters at the post office before they are mailed. They can open them, read the contents, and reseal the envelope, as if it was never touched. But not to share my life with you is also impossible, so what shall we do? My Hannila, my Hannila. How can I not confess to you all of my thoughts and all of my doings? Yet, I must be reticent to protect others who could be hurt by the disclosure of matters which must, like budding love, be guarded. In our national cause, silence is a supreme and necessary virtue. But to reveal nothing to the love of my life and my soul's completion, this too is impossible. So I will heed the advice of our exalted Sages, the guardians of the Hidden Mysteries, who revealed small glimpses of the Torah's secrets, while leaving the breadth and depth of the matters untold.

"King Solomon wrote the '*Song of Songs*' in the form of a parable, so I shall pen parables and metaphors too! It turns out that the induction ceremony which I wrote to you about is all a big joke! The *Irgun* is really an organization of farmers! An army of farmers rebuilding the Promised Land! First, before you can grow produce and fruit, you must study how to cultivate the soil. You have to learn how to plow and sow, to water and weed. You have to learn how to use a pick-axe, a shovel, a spade, a hoe, a rake, and all the tools of the trade. How do you grip the tool's handle? How do you aim your tool at the right angle? How do you ride a horse and yoke a mule to a wagon? Of course, you can't learn how to be a farmer in the city – you have to find open land where you bother no one, and where no one bothers you. And then, when the time of learning is over, you are sent out to the fields, a trained farmer ready to work wherever you are needed, for the noble goal of restoring the Land. Do you follow me? Are you proud of your Avraham, the farmer? I am learning all of these things in a special farmer-training course, offered by the *Irgun*. When the course is completed, in addition to becoming a farmer myself, I will be able to teach others how to become farmers, and one day, they will become farmers and teachers too. Soon, we will be an army of farmers, marching proudly over the width and breadth of our country, shovels and hoes resting on our shoulders like rifles, an army of trained soldier-farmers dedicated to the reclamation of the reborn Hebrew Nation in its Land!"

Beyond the sea in New York, Hannie's hands trembled as she read Avraham's letter. "Teach me, too!" she felt like shouting, inspired by the passion in his words. "I want to be a farmer too!"

"Needless to say, my dear Hannila," the encoded epistle continued, "farming tools don't grow on trees. They can be made, or they can be bought. If you know of anyone in New York who has an access to farming tools, or the money to buy them, his contribution and assistance will make him a farmer as well in our holy endeavor. My main occupation in the near future may not be farming itself, but in the acquisition of the required tools of our trade."

Hannie noted that his metaphor of "farming" was quickly forgotten in the turbulent sea of ideas and emotions which engulfed him. In a postscript he wrote:

"While it is difficult to part from a letter written by a loved one, my letters to you, for whatever their sentimental value, are surely not gold. Posterity won't suffer if two or three letters of Avraham Stern disappear from the world. I don't consider myself so important that these personal epistles be saved. Therefore, in any letter that I mentioned names in connection with the *Irgun*, please abide by my request. Don't let this matter be a cause of alarm. At this point, since my friends and I haven't done anything, there is no reason to think that anyone is interested in our activities. As I wrote, it is a time of preparation and learning. But there are people, even people who call themselves Jews, who would inform on their brothers in order to further their own personal gain. Let these few words suffice."

The Reader may wonder – why interrupt the story of Perchik Aronov's murder with the trans-Atlantic romance between Tevye's granddaughter and the rogue who refused to marry her? The reason is that the rogue in question is not any simple fly-by-night character, but the future leader of the "Stern Gang," which was to lead the battle against the British in paving the way for Jewish independence in the Land of Israel, a drama awaiting portraying in the next two volumes of the "Tevye in the Promised Land" series. After all, what better way to reveal the inner character of a man than through the ups and downs of a stormy and ardent romance?

His letters didn't always speak about "farming." Avraham informed her that he also had the opportunity to put his writing talents to use.

"I also write now and then for our Organization's newsletter, so I have a chance to use my literary talents as well. A publication of this sort can be a powerful means of educating the youth of our Nation. In answer to an article in the newspaper, *HaAretz*, written by a liberal professor at Hebrew University, favoring appeasement and compromise in response to Arab belligerence, a policy which, in his twisted way of thinking, would make us *'a light to the nations'* in championing the 'absolute universal value of peace,' I wrote the following: 'Only the weak-hearted and those of Lilliputian vision will champion appeasement and surrender in the face of the growing Arab militarism. In contrast, we who yearn to see all of the Hebrew Nation, with all of its millions, living and flourishing in our full and rightful borders, and not in some truncated and indefensible strip of *kibbutzim* hugging the Mediterranean shoreline, for those of us who demand what is rightfully ours, and who are willing to sacrifice ourselves and fight for its attainment, we must stand strong, day and night until victory, on behalf of all of our Nation, in all of their Diasporas, for they shall soon be coming!'

"What do you think, Hannila? Was I too assertive in my response? The pacifist faculty at the University, who pride themselves on being Universalists, look with anathema and scorn at strident Hebrew Nationalism. If I ever hoped to be offered a teaching position in the Classics Department, I cannot expect the University board to employ a person with nationalist views and affiliations. But, my darling, I cannot censor my beliefs for money. I will not abandon the political struggle we face. It is the foundation of my being, the core of my soul. Let me die a thousand deaths as an 'Anonymous Soldier' rather than live a long life as a famous and respectable professor."

Month after month, Avraham sent Hannie several letters each week. More and more, he mentioned the times he spent with her family.

"I attended another *Betar* lecture with Moishe, Tzvi, and Nachshon. Only you were missing, and so for me, though I was with others, I was alone. Yes, there were women there, in case you are wondering. But don't worry. I don't speak with them. How can I? My loyalty to you is greater than any other allegiance. No other woman, nor any mortal, can ever interfere. Only the cruel joker called death.

"Believe it or not, after all that I said about the University being a fortress of liberal philosophy, a professor from the University gave the lecture we attended. His name is Joseph Klausner, and he is an incredible man, a brave man, the only professor I know who isn't afraid to express the ideas of Hebrew Nationalism, though he is scorned by his colleagues who denigrate every positive mention of our Biblical heritage, and who equate the Bible with primitivism and regression, portraying proud Jewish nationalism as unenlightened chauvinism and fascism. Listen to his words and be proud, my Hannila. Don't let the glitter of New York blind you to the real things in life. Don't forget our little country in all of the vastness around you. Don't try to be a new kind of Jew in America, the assimilated Jew of the great United States, the melting pot where Jews and Jewish ways will surely melt into oblivion. Listen to the words of this brave professor, and remember that I, a humble student of history, await to reunite with you in the Land of our Forefathers, and in the city of our God.

"From our past, my cherished Hannie, we learn about the present. These are Joseph Klausner's words:

'Bar Kochva rebelled against mighty Rome. For three years, the Jews struggled and fought. They lost a half a million people in the Great Revolt. Yet they kept on rebelling, again and again. It is the proud spirit of Bar Kochva and Rabbi Akiva, which the stubborn Jews took with them into exile, which has sustained us throughout the centuries, despite all attempts to wipe us out. The conquered and defeated Bar Kochva is as dear to us as the conquering and victorious Yehuda the Maccabee. The spirit of Bar Kochva calls out to you - young Jews, be strong! Don't succumb to spiritual or physical laziness, to compromise, or defeatism. Don't abandon your people to shame and degradation. Freedom is acquired through blood. A homeland is won through sacrifice. And even the vanquished, in the battle for honor and liberty, are the conquerors. Be heroes! Remember Bar Kochva! Remember the resistance at Betar and be heroes like them!'"

Hannie was in a quandary. Maybe, she ruminated, growing more anxious with the arrival of each new letter, maybe the time had come to return to Jerusalem. America was indeed a melting pot. If not for Avraham's letters, and her heart's fierce attachment to him, maybe she too would have melted like her aunt Baylke, Pedhotzer, and their son, George, who acted more American than Jewish. For them, Zion was a type of ancient symbol that had no concrete bearing on their lives. Yes, they had family in the Holy Land whom they cared and worried about, and that connected them to Palestine in some personal manner, but for them, Zion was nothing more than that. At the conclusion of the *Pesach Seder*, if they reached that far in the *Haggadah*, they recited the sentence, "Next year in Jerusalem," but no one really meant it. They had already discovered their Promised

Land. Hannie couldn't blame them. America was a magical place – not that the streets were paved in gold for everyone, but everyone could hope and dream that they too would go from rags to riches, like so many American immigrants who had found fortune and fame. But because Avraham lived and breathed the Land of Israel, Hannie lived and breathed the Land of Israel too. Because Avraham's soul was bound up with the rebirth of the Jewish Nation in its own Jewish Land, unwilling and unable to be a minority in someone else's country, her soul was bound up with the demand for full Hebrew Nationhood as well.

But if she returned, what would become of her decision not see him again unless he proposed? What would become of her honor? Should she let honor stand in the way of love? It seemed that even her grandfather was ready to put honor aside. Tevye had written her a letter, mentioning his friendship with Avraham, and even praising him for his virtues. His change of heart was a miracle of the Holy Land – that was the only way to explain it. Still, she couldn't make up her mind. What about her college degree? She still had another year to complete. True, she could continue at Hebrew University, so that wasn't a reason to stay in America. As her grandfather was fond of saying, *"Many are the thoughts in a man's heart, but the counsel of God shall come to pass."* That is exactly what happened. Fate decided for her. Avraham wrote that he had been awarded a scholarship to finish his degree in Classic Literature in Florence, where he would have to live for a year!

"There is also the possibility that I can also earn a doctorate degree in Florence by writing a thesis, which shouldn't take very long – perhaps a few extra months or half of a year. Since I am basically penniless in Jerusalem, the offer is very attractive. If you were here, I would never consider leaving you, but since you are presently far away, and since even Anonymous Soldiers have to eat, acquiring the academic degrees will secure the path to a respectable teaching position, and perhaps a professorship of my own. Professor Stern, do you believe it? This would insure me a monthly salary, not like the acting profession, which is perhaps the least stable trade, a vagabond existence, never knowing when work and a paycheck will arrive. What do you think, my dear Hannila? Your opinion means everything to me."

What did she think? On the one hand, she was heartbroken. Another year-and-a-half without being together? The thought made her weep. But he sounded happy. If further study was what he wanted, how could she prevent him from attaining a solid and noble profession? How could she deny him the opportunity to advance? Returning to Jerusalem would spoil all that. And if, with God's help, the day would come when they would have a family, then a professorship would make him a provider, something which was important to every married man, and especially to Avraham, who disliked relying on charity and loans. In addition, she was glad to hear that his anathema toward becoming a university professor had passed, and that his dream of acting had given way to a more mature understanding of reality. So, she wrote him back, agreeing that the scholarship was a wonderful opportunity that he shouldn't pass up, saying that she was very proud of him, and that, anyway, she still had another year of her own college studies in New York before they could be together.

Thus, for the whole next year, Avraham's letters arrived from Florence.

"How painful it was for me to leave the cherished Land," he wrote. "Though Italy is a relatively short boat ride across the Mediterranean, it seems so far away. The greatest blessing a Jew can have is to come to the Land of Israel. I pray with all my heart that God will bring me back soon. As the Psalmist laments: '*How can we sing the Lord's song in a foreign land? If I ever forget you, O Jerusalem, withered be my right hand! May my tongue cleave to my palate, if I ever think not of you, if I ever not set Jerusalem above my highest joy!*' Who can tell what lurks around each corner? We should never take things for granted. Life is so fragile. But I am optimistic. In fact, since coming to know so many idealistic people during the last few years in Jerusalem, by some mysterious osmosis I have absorbed their steadfast beliefs, and the outlook of gloom which haunted me in the past has taken a place backstage. Now my credo is: *'Be strong and of good courage.'* Everything will turn out for the best.

"Yes, my young Hannila, be pleased. You might say that I have been graced with faith. So be it! Weren't the great Jewish heroes of old champions of unshakable belief? Who had more faith than Nachshon who plunged fearlessly into the raging sea? Or the shepherd boy, David, who defied the mighty Goliath with only a slingshot in hand? Or Yehuda the Maccabee who dared to challenge the legions of Greece? Their faith is the heritage of the Jews. It streams through our veins.

"One evening, when I stopped by your home to visit Moishe and Tzvi, Nachman told us a Hasidic fable about a peasant who dreamed of a treasure hidden under a bridge in Vienna. Journeying there, he discovered that the treasure was actually buried under the floor of his home! It turns out that sometimes you have to go a long way out of the way to discover the treasure that was really inside of you all the time. Perhaps, it is in Florence that I shall discover the path to my true inner self.

"What does God expect from His creations? What does the Creator of Heaven and Earth want from Avraham Stern? To study Classic Literature? To write a doctorate thesis on Eros, the Greek god of love? I think not, my dear Hannie. I think not. Many others can do that. What then is my destiny? That is the question!"

Maybe, Hannie thought, New York was her Vienna, for it was in New York that she discovered, beyond all further doubt, that her destiny was to be united with Avraham's, wherever destiny would lead them.

"Florence is, without question, a beautiful city," Avraham mused. "In a way, with its brick-colored roofs, its religious shrines, its mountainous backdrop, and breathtaking sunsets, it reminds me of Jerusalem. The difference is that when I gaze upon the vistas of Jerusalem my heart beats as if I am on the way to see a lover, while when I climb a hillside to gaze at a panorama of Florence, I see a panorama of aesthetic beauty which pleases my mind, leaving my heart and soul untouched. Yet, I am generally happy here, and only feel sadness because I am not at home in the Land of Israel, which I miss with the same fierce longing with which I miss you.

"I am beginning my studies and frequent the university's library to do research on my thesis. Since my skills in Greek, Italian, Latin, and English have greatly improved during my studies in Jerusalem, there is a sea of books in which I can drown. I must admit, Hannila, my precious one, my heart's true and only desire, that I feel a bit awkward, even embarrassed to have chosen Eros, the god of love, as the subject of my doctorate. While the world at large is enamored with passion, and economies are built on it, wars are fought in its name, and men driven mad in its pursuit, how insignificant it seems when compared with the rebuilding of the Jewish People in *Eretz Yisrael*. After all, pleasure is an egotistical pursuit. And the love between a man and a woman, for all of its grandeur, is dwarfed by the love of *Am Yisrael* for its Land.

"Nevertheless, I would be lying if I said that I am not enjoying the cultural life of the city, the concerts and symphonies, the dance performances and theater. However, as *Kohelet* proclaims: '*Vanity of vanities, all is vanity.*' The pleasure is all superficial. The satisfaction is fleeting. Aesthetics captures the senses and the mind, but not the Jewish soul. Additionally, how can I revel in the pleasures of the Arts when my friends in Israel are spending their nights guarding the streets and villages of a Promised Land which eagerly awaits for her exiled children to come home?

"On Sundays, I wander through the city's museums because, on that day, the entrance is free, and my pockets are habitually empty. Talk about a poor, starving student! But I am happy, and if you were here with me, I would have everything!

"And now, a great discovery and confession! You, more than anyone, even more than myself, perhaps have known it all along. I can hardly describe the moment, walking through the Gallery of the Academy, suddenly it stands before you, Michelangelo's supreme masterpiece – the statue of King David, a work of such splendid art and craftsmanship, it is surely graced with the Divine. I speak not about the statue's glaring immodesty, which, in my eye, has no bearing on the work itself, and is more a concession to the popular style and hedonistic culture of the time; I speak of the essence of David himself, which we are forced to confront, when we gaze at the towering marble figure. What is the essence of this Jewish youth with the slingshot slung over his shoulder? What does he see when he stares so seriously, so confidently, so contemptuously at Goliath? What is the secret of David, the shepherd boy, the warrior, the passionate lover, the Psalmist, the *'sweet singer of Israel,'* the conqueror of Jerusalem, the messianic king? So many seemingly contradictory characteristics, all of towering dimension, like the statue itself, contained in one man! Looking at Michelangelo's sculpture of David, I saw myself. In miniature of course. And for the first time in my life, I realized that all of the contradictory passions and talents that I feel, some for good and others for bad, they all have their place, and their time, and their purpose. Just as David stands proudly, in a calm and confident pose, as he sets forth on his national mission, so must I be calm and confident that the Sculptor of all sculptors has sculpted me (in a work still in progress) with everything that I need, as a son of David, to continue the work of nation-building which David began."

Sometimes, Avraham wrote letters of a less philosophical nature, describing for Hannie his daily life. Monday, he wrote, was his favorite day of the week.

"On Monday, the newspapers from Palestine are delivered. What incomparable pleasure to hear news about the Homeland! I read all of the newspapers from beginning to end! Each day, not an hour passes when I don't think about Israel. This constant yearning is no mere longing for a place far away. In my soul, I am there every moment!"

He said he felt proud to be experiencing the same longings for *Eretz Yisrael* that Rabbi Kook had felt during his year in England, where he had been stranded during the World War. To strengthen his friend overseas, David Raziel had sent Avraham some of Rabbi Kook's writings from a journal the Rabbi had kept during his forced exile from the Land.

"Though I am like a wanderer in the exile," Rabbi Kook wrote, "filled with angst in a foreign land, the kindness of

God will not abandon me, and in my longing for the Holy Land, the dew from the Land of Life will strengthen me with blessing and preserve me in my painful exile until Salvation will come, when *Hashem* brings me back to *Eretz Yisrael* to serve Him in completeness, in truth, in humility and reverence, with strength and love. The air of *Eretz Yisrael* accompanies me, thank God, even in my exile. How pleasant is the light of the Torah in the Land of Life, *Eretz Yisrael*, the Land which Hashem watches over, the Land where the holiness of the Divine Presence is revealed. How magnificent and beautiful and pleasant is our Land! Who will grant me the wings of a dove that I may speedily fly away to her courtyards? My heart yearns to unite with its exaltedness, its pastures of faith, its holiness, its joy, its inner serenity, its Heavenly attachment, its truth. Have compassion on me, *Hashem*, God of Mercy and Forgiveness, and allow me to merit to return to the Land in perfect repentance, to the Land which You desire, to witness the joy of Your People and to join in their praises of You. Have mercy and save me, the God who grants Salvation."

Along with his letters, Avraham sent her poems which he wrote. He said that he found time to write even though he was busy with his studies, and with organizing a Zionist club for young people, where he lectured twice a week, always on the lookout for Jewish souls who longed for a more meaningful Jewish life than being good Italian citizens in Italy. He jokingly said that there were as many churches in Florence as there were olive trees in Palestine. Statues of the Christian messiah filled the museums. Perhaps, this is what led him to ruminate on the coming of the Jewish *Mashiach*, who, he said, in a stark, symbolic poem, would be born in a British prison.

My brother, do you know where the *Mashiach* will be
born?
He will be born on a floor of a prison
Upon which a prostitute has vomited and where lies the
dung of a thief,
A vandal and old murderer who raped his little daughter.
He will be greeted by the warm knees of his exiled mother,

Who was raped by a clan of bloodthirsty and murderous
Arabs from Hevron.
Yea, their seed is the seed of horses and their flesh is the
flesh of mules.
He does not have any notion of time, of hours, nor the
moment.
Like the pendulum of a clock, the guard patrols the
corridor,
Back and forth, back and forth, back and forth.
And the *Mashiach* knows that this will be the time of
Redemption,
When the echoing steps of the prison guard will stop and
sound no more.
The shadows which crawl on the wall like a pack of
spiders
Who have woven a dark web of despair
To snare the golden bee – the Hope – that brought
The honey of consolation to the bee-hive-shaped heart of
the *Mashiach*.
The silent orphan quivers in a corner and sobs
When suddenly a ray of light, like a silver sword, cuts the
window's bars
And banishes the spider-like shadows to a dark and
distant corner.
And the *Mashiach* knows that the way to Redemption is by
the sword.
Or, in the morning, the light of dawn drips into the
dungeon and fills
The floor with pools of red blood.
And the *Mashiach* knows that there are two paths to
Redemption,
By blood and by the sword.

After the poem, Avraham added something that she had
suspected all along. Deciphering his coded language, she
understood that during his time in Italy he would be
procuring arms to carry on the struggle for independence
back home:

"It appears, at the request of the *Irgun*, that during my stay
in Italy, in addition to advancing my studies in the Classics,

I will also be learning as much as I can about 'agriculture,' the knowledge of which can be put to good use when I return home to Israel. As you know from your farming work in Olat HaShachar, agricultural methods in Palestine are still quiet primitive. The secret of our success is our love for our holy soil, which, like a rich fertilizer, brings the Land's hidden treasures to life. Now that her children are returning to her borders, the Land of Israel is giving forth its fruits in abundance, for the first time in two-thousand years. Our love for the Land is like the first rains, awakening the long dormant soil. While the country's long list of foreign conquerors tried to bring back the fertile gardens and groves of the past, all of them failed. Only its returning exiles succeeded. Like a living mother, the Land gives suck to her true children alone, proof that the Land of Israel is ours. But love alone isn't enough. We need new techniques in agronomy, and the latest equipment. Why use a rusty old pickaxe when you can use a drill? Why use a horse and plow when you can sit in a tractor? Why swing a sledgehammer for hours on end when a small, properly-planted explosion can do the job in a second, if you know what I mean. While Italy itself is still rather backward in the field of agriculture, still relying on the hard work of laborers and peasants, the modern age has arrived, and new techniques and new tools can be acquired. Maybe this endeavor will bring me to Sicily, famous for its vineyards and wine, and other unique talents about which we, in the *Irgun*, can learn, ha ha ha, I say with a chuckle, sending a wink to the prettiest girl in the world. *Ciao*, my *bambina*. *Ti amo da impazzire*. I love you madly."

Hannie still blushed whenever he wrote so boldly. Then he added in coded language:

"Which reminds me – did you ask around to see if there are people of means in New York who can help us in our agricultural endeavor? Of course, we would prefer that all of the Jews of America would come home to Israel themselves, but, in the meantime, they can help with their money and by supplying us with the tools of our trade. Modern farming equipment is quite expensive, and we lack the financial means to make the large purchases necessary for the success of the project. Perhaps your grandfather would be willing to travel to New York as a *shaliach* on behalf of the cause in order to raise the required funds. His English has quite improved. I am sure he would enjoy visiting you and Baylke, whom he hasn't seen for over twenty years. In addition, he still seems to be mourning for Hava, and the reunion with Baylke, and the change of scenery might get him out of his depression. While my greatest joy would be to be with you again and to continue where we left off, as if this cruel interval never existed, I cannot come to America for the time being, since my *mazel* has brought me here to Italy. Once again, *ciao!*"

Hannie had something new to think about. Her grandfather in New York? What a funny idea. But, then again, there were a lot of religious Jews in New York City. Why not? She mentioned the idea to Baylke, thinking that her husband and his "business partners" in the Jewish Mafia might want to help fellow Jews in Palestine, in their fight against the *goyim* to establish a Jewish State, but Baylke's original enthusiasm vanished after speaking with Pedhotzer. He said that it wasn't the right time. America was struggling through a devastating economic depression, businesses and banks had collapsed, employees laid off, and hundreds of thousands of people couldn't find work. No one, he said, was going to hand out money to a *schnorrer* from Palestine. Hannie didn't knew if that assessment was the objective truth, or whether Pedhotzer simply didn't want his "milkman of a father-in-law" in New York, pestering her husband's rich friends, who didn't seem to be adversely affected by the Great Depression at all. Hannie knew how Baylke's snobbish husband had treated Tevye in the past. Not wanting to cause any friction between Pedhotzer and her aunt, Hannie didn't pursue the matter, telling Avraham that, because of the Depression, the time wasn't ripe for a fundraising trip to New York. Avraham answered that money wasn't the only thing that was needed – a freighter filled with "farming equipment" would be a *m'chaya!* But when Hannie brought up the matter again with her aunt, Baylke turned a cold shoulder.

"Not now," she said. "Period."

When Hannie informed Avraham, he didn't press the issue. Instead, he sent her excerpts from a poem he was writing for "our brave Jewish mothers who must be as heroic as their sons in our struggle for liberation." Hannie realized that his thoughts were centering less and less on Classic Literature and Eros, and more and more on armed revolution and valleys filled with shadows of death.

> You are mothers of life, mothers of death.
> You love and you hate.
> In days of war and nights of apprehension
> You share our danger.
> The stronger the enemy, the stronger your sword.
> You are Yehudit, Yael, and Sarah.
> Mother of life and mother of death.
> You are with us, like a zealous God."

A short poem about war, recalling the "*Shema*," terrified her in its chilling coldness. What did the poem mean? What was Avraham thinking? Hannie was afraid to ask.

> "Listen revenger to the voice of your God.
> Smash the enemy's head with a mighty hand.
> And may His Word be upon your heart.
> Sanctify the weapons of war!
> Each day when you sit in your house
> And when you walk in fields of terror,
> When you lie down, and when you awake,
> Sanctify the weapons of war!
> And if an enemy should be a Jew
> The son of your mother, the blood of her blood.
> And if your parents are among your enemies,
> Sanctify the weapons of war!

When Hitler became the Chancellor of Germany, Avraham wrote Hannie about his premonitions and fears.

"Having read his autobiography, '*Mein Kampf*,' I can assure you that he is a most deranged and dangerous individual, motivated by delusions of grandeur and possessed by an obsessive hatred against the Jews. We have to do everything in our power to bring the Jews in Germany to *Eretz Yisrael* without the slightest delay. Jabotinsky feels

the same way. Even before Hitler's rise to power, Uri Zvi
Greenberg warned in his poems that the soil of Europe
would become a fiery graveyard for the Jews. How can I sit
calmly in a library, reading *The Iliad* and *The Odyssey*,
Homer's epic poems, when our People are on the brink of
mass destruction? Jabotinsky and Greenberg cry out but no
one listens. I have heard Rabbi Kook utter the same
frightening words. The Jews don't want to believe it, but
those who think they have already discovered Jerusalem in
Berlin and Vienna will be uprooted by a satanic whirlwind
of volcanic fury, if they don't escape now. Prayers won't
save them – only guns. Yes, my dearest, Hannie. Only guns.
Not Jewish farmers with scythes and pitchforks, but Jewish
soldiers with rifles and grenades."

His words left her trembling. What could she do, a young
college student in New York?

Then, in a letter that she was expecting, having already
heard the distressing news, he wrote about Perchik.

"What a shock it was to read in Monday's newspapers
about Perchik Aronov! Have you heard? Did Hodel tell you
that he was murdered? Did you read about it in the
newspapers in New York? I never met him, but I have heard
about him from your family, and, of course, from time to
time, I read about his work with the Labor Party.
Apparently, in Israel, the murder is the talk of the town. The
Laborites accuse the Revisionists of carrying out the
assassination, while the Revisionists claim that the Left is
waging a witch hunt and blood libel against them. The
journalist, Abba Ahimeir, whom I know very well, is one of
the accused. While his writings can be very militant, and his
beliefs, in the eyes of the moderates, very extreme, on a
personal level, he is not violent at all. What disturbs me the
most is that the blood libel is not like the blood libels of the
past, when the Gentiles invented fictions as an excuse to kill
Jews. Today, in the Land of Israel itself, the blood libel
comes from Jews themselves, slander and hatred directed
against fellow Jews! May God have mercy."

Hannie had already heard the terrible news in a telegram
from Tevye, and she had read a small article in *The New York
Times*. While Perchik wasn't considered a part of the family,

he was, after all, Hodel's first husband, and Ben Zion's father. Hannie was Ben Zion's cousin, and Tevye was the young man's grandfather, so, of course, for the family, it wasn't just another incident of a Jew being murdered in Palestine. Beyond her concern for her cousin, Ben Zion, who had lost his father, Hannie was worried, like Avraham, about the climate of fraternal hatred in Palestine. Jews killing Jews – how could it be, she wondered?

Chapter Six
FIRE IN THE LAND

Rabbi Kook sat alone in his small study, writing a poem. In addition to an almost unending stream of essays and letters, the great Torah scholar would often jot down his thoughts in the form of poetry. His rich and flowing Hebrew read like masterpieces of literature, winning him the admiration of the finest secular writers of the time. Just as the Israelite Nation had to be born anew, and just as the desolate Land had to be cultivated, he believed the secret treasures of the Hebrew language must also undergo a renaissance as the Hebrew Nation returned to its roots.

I am bound to the world.
All beings, all people are my friends.
Many parts of my soul are intertwined with them.
But how can I share my light with them?
Whatever I see only shrouds my vision,
Dulls my light.
Great is my pain and my anguish.
O, my God, be a help in my time of trouble.
Grant me the graces of expression.
Grant me language and the gift of lucid speech.
Then I shall declare before the multitudes
My fragments of Your Truth, O, my God.

For several years now, ever since the ghastly pogroms throughout the country, a profound mourning plagued the Chief Rabbi's innermost being, robbing him of the total joy with which he had always served God. Outwardly, in his dealings with everyone he met, he appeared full of optimism, unshakable faith, and *simcha*, but in the deepest recesses of his soul, a shadow darkened his inner light. Along with this hidden spiritual pain, a slow and insidious cancer had taken root in his abdomen, the knowledge of which he shared with his physician alone, not wanting to distress his wife and the beloved devotees who gathered around him. Outwardly, with a superhuman will nourished from his unflinching faith in God, he made himself appear strong for the Nation, not letting people see the pain that was racking his body.

The Aronov murder made his inner suffering even greater. His psyche and soul were burdened with his absolute conviction that the suspects had not committed the horrible crime. Like the High Priest in Temple times, Rabbi Kook's being was bound up with the soul of the Nation, and the soul of every Jew. The death of each and every person affected him deeply, as if a son or daughter had died. In addition to the profound loss he felt over the murdered man himself, Perchik Aronov had left behind parents and a family for whom Rabbi Kook felt deep sorrow. Also, the killing of the dedicated Zionist contained foreboding symbolism for the Zionist cause, which was being poisoned by the brotherly hatred surrounding the case, one camp pitted against the other, alarmingly recalling the senseless hatred which had led to the destruction of Jerusalem and the Second Temple.

But as long as the police investigation and trial were continuing, he didn't give public expression to his belief in the innocence of the three men who had been accused of the crime. He himself prayed privately for their acquittal, and he instructed the students in his yeshiva to recite *Tehillim* daily on their behalf, but not wanting to obstruct the progress of the ongoing case, and not wanting to influence the decision of the judges, he remained silent, ignoring the appeals requesting him to take a public stand. He hoped that justice would win out through the work of the justice system itself, without outside interference, firmly believing in the essential goodness of man.

One day, Nachman entered the Chief Rabbi's study with a letter from the imprisoned Abba Ahimeir.

"Read it to me," Rabbi Kook said, setting his pen down on his writing table. Nachman started to read:

From Prison Cell #6 in the City of Yafo

To the Chief Ashkenazi Rabbi of *Eretz Yisrael*, Rabbi Avraham Kook:

If the honored Rabbi were only a giant in Torah, the greatest
Torah Scholar of our generation, like the Prophet Samuel in his
time, I would not have written him. However, in addition to his
stature in Torah, he is also great in deed. Who more than I
remembers the Rabbi's towering defense of our rights to the holy
Kotel? And this is the reason that a holy Angel stands over my
shoulder and exhorts me, "Write to him!" Still my pen hesitated
until the father of Avraham Stavsky visited the honored Rabbi
and informed me about the great distress the Rabbi suffers over
the blood libel which has brought three innocent men to trial.

For over half a year, this injustice has darkened the lives of
three Jews, the sacrificial sheep of this blood libel, and we are
like three innocent Dreyfuses, and like Menachem Mendel Beilis,
who was accused of ritual murder - but this is not Paris, nor
Kiev, but rather Tel Aviv and Jerusalem. We ask ourselves,
"Why is the Nation silent?" I, the elder of the three, remember
the silence surrounding the Beilis blood libel. In our case, all
Jews, except for the communist and socialist "Reds", believe in
our innocence. Naively, they all wait for a just trial from the
Gentile court!

I needn't inform you, most honored Rabbi, that the "Red
Jews" amongst us have made a covenant with the British police
(the same police force that betrayed the Jews of Hevron, Safed...)
in fabricating this blood libel.

As the holiday of Purim approaches, I remind the honored
Rabbi of Mordechai's words to Esther, "*If you remain silent at
this time, then relief and salvation will come to the Jews from
somewhere else.*"

As Nachman read the epistle, he balked at the
not-so-subtle hints of criticism directed at Rabbi Kook.

"Please go on," the Rabbi requested. Tevye's son-in-law
continued to read, fearing that the tone might become even
more acerbic:

We three victims of this blood libel are certain that justice will
be brought to light, for the following reasons: first, we have an
excellent lawyer, Mr. Horace Samuel; second, from his exile in
Paris, the "Shepherd of Israel," Ze'ev Jabotinsky, is watching
over the proceedings; third, we are innocent; and fourth, the
Angel which guards over our Nation, will not allow judgment

to be perverted, nor allow that such a terrible tragedy besmirch the People of God.

But you Jews who are certain of our innocence, and who remain hiding in your homes, how will you be able to look us in the eye? Will the leaders of the generation not be called to account for this shame? In the Beilis Trial, the Rabbi of Moscow, Rabbi Mazeh, of blessed memory, rose up in fearless opposition to the corrupt judicial system of the uncircumcised Philistines, in order to defend the honor of Israel. Will the Torah leaders today not follow his lead and rise up in the defense of justice? Rabbi Mazeh, of blessed memory, didn't keep silent. Will Rabbi Kook?

I am certain that the most honored Rabbi asks himself, 'What can I do? What I do?' Yet, how can I, a prisoner, give advice? I can only offer the advice of the Prophet of old, "*Sanctify a fast, call a solemn assembly, gather the people, assemble the elders...*" in order to cancel the evil decree.

Written and signed in tears. One of your myriad of admirers.

Abba Ahimeir

Rabbi Kook nodded his head. "His admonition is most justified and eloquently stated. The Torah commands us, '*Justice, justice, you shall pursue, that you may live and inherit the Land which the Lord your God gives you.*' Justice must be one of the foundations of our resettlement in the Land of Israel. The Prophet Isaiah declared, '*Zion shall be redeemed with justice, and her returning exiles with righteousness.*' But as *Kohelet* reminds us, there is, '*A time to keep silent, and a time to speak.*' In the meantime, may the Holy One of Israel shine His Countenance upon them and grant them peace."

2.

Who can know what the future will bring? As a young religious boy growing up with his divorced mother in Olat HaShachar, Ben Zion never dreamed that he would give up the Torah and become a socialist like his father. And after he had reunited with his father, he never dreamed that a bullet fired on a beach in Tel Aviv would take the man called Perchik Aronov away from him forever. Nor could he know, as he battled the waves in the choppy sea off the coastline near Kfar Vatkin, just north of Netanya, that his recent enrollment in the *Haganah* officer's training course would bring him to be, years later, the *Haganah's* Tel Aviv commander when the freighter, *Altalena*, reached the very same coastline years later, loaded with enough weapons and ammunition to insure Israel's victory in the War of Independence. The secluded *Mapai* village of Kfar Viktin, set in a wooded area not far from the beach, was the perfect location for the *Haganah* course, which was designed to prepare officers for the coming wave of secret immigration from Nazi Germany. The day-and-night swimming exercises had improved Ben Zion's stamina greatly. He could now swim a good distance with one arm, while rescuing someone with the other. Many of the illegal *ma'apilim* immigrants never learned how to swim. The expression, *ma'apilim*, meant "those who climb mountains." Indeed, the seaborne undertaking was a challenging journey. Since British surveillance had to be avoided, the clandestine transport ships loaded with illegal immigrants couldn't dock at any known ports. They had to approach the coastline during the night, anchoring a hundred meters or more offshore from some remote beach where a *Haganah* welcoming team would be waiting. When rough seas made the use of rowboats too dangerous to ferry the refugees to the beach, long ropes were stretched from ship to shore as lifelines which the immigrants could grasp. But strong waves could easily lift the voyage-weary newcomers into the stormy sea. Therefore, in addition to expertise and stamina in swimming, rescue methods and basic first aid techniques had to be mastered. If the *Ha'avara* agreement which Ben Zion's father had initiated with the Germans came to pass, facilitating the transfer of German Jews and goods to Palestine, in exchange for open trade between Germany and the *Yishuv*, not only would thousands of new immigrants be coming, but the monies made available through the sale of Jewish exports to Germany would replenish the coffers of the *Yishuv*, allowing for increased land purchase and settlement. The Revisionists could squawk as much as they pleased against cooperation with the Nazis – in Ben Zion's eyes, his father was a hero. Perchik Aronov's bold efforts on behalf of the Nation would save countless Jewish lives and further the prosperity of the *Yishuv*. Though the gunshot on the beach had ended his father's mission, Ben Zion was determined to continue on in his footsteps, not as a politician, but as a military commander, first in the Haganah, and then in the official army of the future Jewish State.

After completing their swimming exercises and beach calisthenics, the group of six officer trainees ran back to the small stone house that served as their barracks on the *moshav*. Kinneret, one of the two female *Haganah* volunteers was waiting with two large pitchers of lemonade and biscuits. Her tanned, athletic body filled out her shorts and kaki button-down shirt in all the right places. She flashed Ben Zion a special smile.

"Where's Sharona?" Mailer asked, collapsing onto his cot.

"She's doing the laundry," Kinneret answered.

The two girls lived with families on the *moshav*. In addition to basic firearm training, the energetic girls learned first aid and did most of the cooking and cleaning for the men. Mailer, who probably had seen every movie that had come to Tel Aviv, had fallen hopelessly in love with the blond-haired Sharona, who turned away all of his advances. Perhaps because he hadn't chased after the shiny-eyed Kinneret from the beginning, Ben Zion won out in the competition for her. Since his father's murder, a brooding, melancholy mood had clung to him like a shroud. He wasn't interested in girls. He put all of his energy into the training, wanting to forget everything else. But everyone knew he was the son of Perchik Aronov, and maybe that's what made him different in the pretty girl's eyes. She wanted to mother him. After a few weeks, he surrendered, losing his innocence in a corn field on a dark moonless night.

"The Revisionists have hired a fancy lawyer from London to defend your father's killers," Harry Freeman informed Ben Zion. With his broken leg in a cast, Freeman sat in a chair, reading a newspaper.

"Immediately upon his arrival in Tel Aviv,'" he quoted, broadcasting the report out loud in a serious baritone voice, as if he were an announcer on the radio, "the dapperly-attired attorney, Mr. Horace Samuel, declared that he would petition the High Criminal Court of Palestine to move the trial to London, saying, 'In a most strident and prejudiced manner, the local media has already judged my clients and found them guilty, making it impossible for them to receive a fair trial in Palestine.'"

"Even in England, they'd be sent to the gallows," the tall and broad-shouldered Stein commented, grabbing a handful of fresh biscuits.

"Revisionist killers," Mailer remarked.

Ben Zion gulped down the glass of lemonade that Kinneret had prepared. "You are convicting them even before the trial begins," he said.

"Are you defending them?" Mailer asked.

"No, but...."

"Of course, they're guilty," Freeman declared. "Why even bother with a trial? Your mother identified them. That's all the proof you need."

"She isn't my mother," Ben Zion said softly.

"Your step-mother, so what? What difference does it make?"

Ben Zion didn't answer. He didn't like talking about the case. He didn't want to think about the trial. He had signed up for the *Haganah* officer's course to leave lies and politics behind. His father's last words still echoed in his ears and haunted his dreams. To silence his troubled conscience, he had convinced himself that if Arabs had committed the murder, it was the Revisionists who had paid them to carry out the nefarious deed.

"You only prove the lawyer's contention by determining their guilt from the start," Kinneret told them in a scolding voice. "They maintain they are innocent. They're entitled to a fair trial like everyone else. One of the pillars of law is that a person is innocent until proven guilty. And leave Ben Zion alone."

"Ooooooo," Mailer teased. "Be careful fellows. Don't get Kinneret angry."

"If it wasn't them, some other Revisionists killed Aronov," Stein observed. "That's as obvious as day. Ahimeir, Jabotinsky, and Adolf Hitler, they are all the same. Fascists like them only care about power."

"I'm going outside to wash off the salt water," Ben Zion said. Without another word, he walked out of the room.

Kinneret glared at the others. "Why do you always have to talk about his father's murder? You know that it hurts him."

"What can we do? Stick our heads in the sand. It's the talk of the town."

"You can have a little consideration," she retorted.

"Are we to blame that Aronov was his father?" Mailer asked.

"You're terrible," Kinneret told him.

"Go soothe his wounds," Stein said chidingly. "He only plays the lost soul to get your attention."

Piqued, the girl lifted a pitcher of lemonade and splashed its contents on Stein. "Cool off, big guy," she said, hurrying out of the room, followed by the laughter and catcalls of the *Haganah* trainees.

Outside, as Ben Zion headed for the small bathhouse, he was surprised to see his father's Mapai colleague, Moshe Stillman, walking his way.

"Hello, Ben Zion!" the usually taciturn man called out with a robust greeting, as if the youth was an old, lost friend. He grasped Ben Zion's hand and gave it a shake. Then he hugged the *Haganah* recruit in a bear hug. Ben Zion was taken aback by the outpouring of friendship. Besides their encounter in the hospital, he had met Stillman several times before, when the *Mapai* Party strongman had come to their home to meet with his father, but on those occasions Stillman had acted businesslike and cold, not paying attention to him.

"How's the officer?" he asked.

"Not an officer yet," Ben Zion replied.

"You will be soon, and with the help of a good word here and there to some of my friends in the *Haganah* hierarchy, I'm sure you'll become a lieutenant in no time."

"I appreciate it, Mr. Stillman, but I'd just as soon work my way up the ladder like everyone else."

"Nonsense. There's nothing the matter with *protectia*. It's like gasoline in a car. Especially in this country. Without help from friends, you can't get anywhere."

Ben Zion's glance took in Kinneret as she strode out of the barracks. Seeing him engaged in a conversation with Stillman, she stopped on the path. Ben Zion motioned with his hand that he would meet her later.

"Your girlfriend?" Stillman asked.

"I'm in the competition," Ben Zion replied.

"Excellent. She's a pretty girl."

When Ben Zion didn't answer, you could hear the birds chirping in the tall eucalyptus trees along the pathway.

"Are your quarters all right?" Stillman asked. "If you like, I can ask one of my *Mapai* buddies on the *moshav* to invite you to stay with them."

"Thank you for the offer, but I prefer bunking down with the other officer candidates."

"Like a real soldier."

"I suppose," Ben Zion answered, wondering when the unctuous Stillman was going to stop beating around the bush and get down to the point of his unexpected visit.

"I spoke to Sonia recently. She's worried about you. She says you haven't contacted her since the murder."

"That's the way it is in the army."

"This isn't an easy time for her. You can't imagine the pressure she's under as the investigation continues. To me, she's a real hero. Your father would be very proud of her. Everything she's doing is for him - to further the things he believed in."

"I'm sorry, but I have to get going," Ben Zion said curtly. "They keep us on a tight schedule."

"I'll take the blame if you're late."

"So long, Mr. Stillman," Ben Zion said.

"Just one more thing," the politician added, now with a dead serious expression, his blue eyes as cold as tundra lakes. "The Revisionists have hired a very experienced lawyer from London. He has started his own investigation, and he may try to speak with you. It won't be hard for him to discover that we were the last people to be with your father before he died. He'll want to know if he said anything regarding the shooting. If he speaks with me, I will tell him no, that he was unconscious the whole time we were with him in the emergency room. As far as I am concerned, anything he said was spoken out of delirium and can't be taken seriously. Whoever pulled the trigger, the Revisionists are to blame for his murder. Ahimeir and his friends must be convicted - for the sake of your father and for the banner of Labor Zionism which he championed, and for the sake of the German Jews we can rescue if the Party remains strong, unhampered by the fanaticism of Jabotinsky and his army of hoodlums, ruthless inciters who hounded your father to his death. And for your own sake as well. For your future in the *Haganah* and your future in the Party. I promise you that we will look after you, and after your brother and sister."

Ben Zion could feel his knees trembling. Stillman tried to smile, but anxiety filled his face. He could feel the boy's hatred of him.

"I trust I have made myself clear," Stillman added.

"Good day, Mr. Stillman," Ben Zion said. Turning away, he headed off toward the shower.

3.

All that Horace Samuel needed to fit the image of Sherlock Holmes were a checkered "deerstalker" cap and a curved smoking pipe. As a boy in England, he read all of the stories and books he could find about the famous, fictional detective. Serving in the Hebrew Brigade under Jabotinsky's command, during his free time, he would pull a battered copy of "The Hound of the Baskervilles" out of his backpack and dive back into the Sir Arthur Conan Doyle adventure. In fact, it was Samuel's enthusiasm for the detective stories which inspired Jabotinsky to translate the stories into Hebrew, in order to encourage the young Jews of Palestine to learn their mother tongue. While Samuel didn't go around with a magnifying glass in his overcoat pocket, he conducted his investigations with a pinpoint attention to detail. Keen intuition wasn't enough to win cases in court. A verdict could stand or fall on the hair's-breath difference between one testimony and the next. In the Aronov murder trial, proving to the judge the political righteousness of the Revisionists wouldn't free the prisoners. His job was to shatter the prosecution's case by exposing the unreliability and discrepancies of its witnesses, and by substantiating the alibis of the defendants. After speaking with Jabotinsky in Warsaw, long before meeting the accused and doing the long hours of footwork needed to put the pieces of the puzzle together, the experienced bannister felt that the police account of the murder was as fanciful as Sir Arthur's imaginative whodunits.

His suspicious found substantiation almost immediately when he read Yehuda Arazi's preliminary report to Captain Harry Rice, Deputy Inspector General of the Palestine Police, three months into the investigation. Feeling that the facts of the murder were being manipulated by the British Police in favor of the prosecution and its team of Jewish Agency lawyers, Police Investigator Arazi sent a copy of the document to the British Intelligence Agency in London. The accusing report found its way into the hands of one of Samuel's friends, a Revisionist sympathizer, who worked as an attorney for England's famous Scotland Yard.

First and foremost, Arazi's report questioned the reliability of the prosecution's main and only witness to the murder, Mrs. Sonia Aronov, who identified Avraham Stavsky in a line-up of suspects as the man who had held the flashlight, and Tzvi Rosenblatt as the man who fired the gun. In connection with her testimony, Chief Police Investigator Arazi wrote the following:

"Minutes after the murder, upon returning to the seaside restaurant where she had dined with her husband, Mrs. Aronov detailed the crime before the policeman, Lieutenant Shmuel Streimester. She told him that the murderers were Arabs. Sargent David Friedman, Mr. Sammy Koprestein, and Mrs. Katie Dan were witnesses to their discussion. While still at the restaurant, Streimester reported this testimony by telephone to Jaffa Police Headquarters, to Officer Roger Stafford, that Perchik Aronov had been shot by Arabs on the beach in Tel Aviv. This eyewitness account was recorded in the police station ledger. Streimester reported this information to Police Headquarters in the presence of Mrs. Aronov."

The report continued:

"Shortly after the shooting, in the Katie Dan Restaurant,

Mrs. Aronov told a representative of the Jewish Agency, Mr. Yeshua Gordon, in the presence of Mr. Benady Gott, that she was one-hundred-percent certain that the assailants were Arabs.

"When Mrs. Aronov was brought that evening to the murder site, she said that the man with the gun stood to her husband's left side, that the gun was a "Browning" revolver, and that she heard it cocked twice. At the hospital, it was discovered that the bullet entered from the right side of the deceased and lodged in his left, in contradiction to her testimony. Also, the bullet was from a Russian "Negen" revolver and not from a "Browning." Furthermore, it is impossible to cock the automatic "Negen" and the firearm has no mechanism which sounds like the cocking of a revolver. All of this stands in contrast to her testimony.

"It is not clear why Mrs. Aronov left her husband on the beach with the two men who came along to help, preferring to return to the Katie Dan Restaurant to seek aid. She could have asked one of the men to do this for her, since it is not the nature of a wife to leave her husband when he is wounded and bleeding.

"Mrs. Aronov related that right after the shooting, she shouted at her husband: "Jews killed you." And that her husband answered, "No, Sonia, no, Sonia." During her investigation, she explained her husband's words as meaning, "Don't yell this out now. Tell it to the police and the court." This explanation is most bizarre to me. Does Mrs. Aronov really think that her badly wounded husband was thinking about the police investigation and trial at this moment?

"During her initial testimony that evening to the police, Mrs. Aronov didn't mention the presence of any other witnesses to the crime. Only after several weeks, did she suddenly remember descriptions of people who had been on the beach during her walk with her husband."

For Samuels, the glaring unreliability of the prosecution's star witness, the murdered man's wife, was enough to have the case against the suspects dismissed before ever reaching a trial, but given the charged political atmosphere surrounding the murder, the lawyer read on, elated that such a treasure had fallen into his hands. The boldly expressed reservations of a chief investigator were not something to be taken lightly. During his career, Samuel had encountered very few public servants who were prepared to uphold the banner of truth against a conspiracy of falsehood backed by the authorities, especially when it could cost a police officer his job, or even worse. Arazi went on to report another glaring wrongdoing concerning the testimony of the footprint trackers who had made a sweeping search of the beach and surrounding area:

"Another important witness is the '*gashash*' (footprint tracker), Ibrahim Abu Rejid. Following Mrs. Aronov testimony that the assailants had fled in the direction of the nearby hillside, he conducted a search of the location, including the adjacent orchard and roadside. After a week, he stated that Avraham Stavsky's shoe-prints on the beach matched a trail which he found leading to the hillside and the road. He stated that on the hillside, Stavsky's footprints were joined by those of a dog's and a woman's. In connection with this testimony, I interrogated the three police officers who surveyed the hillside and orchard leading to the road that night after the murder. Two rode on horseback and the other, Officer Feldman, on foot, accompanied by a dog. Feldman maintains that these are the footprints which the '*gashash*' discovered leading to the road. When Stavsky was arrested days later, he was brought to the beach and hillside to take part in a reenactment of the crime. If the tracker found footprints on the beach and hillside matching Stavsky's, they are the footprints made during the reenactment and not on the night on the murder.

"The second '*gashash*' in the case, Abu Roz, is a false witness completely. I heard his original testimony regarding Tzvi Rosenblatt's footprints, in the presence of Chief Investigator Shitreet after 'Suspect Number 2' was arrested. He stated that the shoe prints he found had metal plates at the tip on the shoe and at the heel, along with straps on the sides. I myself brought Rosenblatt's shoes from Kfar Saba to police headquarters. They had metal plates on the heels, but no metal at the top of the sole, and no straps. An hour later, I overheard an officer in the pre-trial interrogating room tell the tracker, Abu Roz, not to mention the metal plates on the soles of the shoes and not the signs of straps, saying that he had obviously made a mistake since Roseblatt's shoes lacked both. Another officer was less blunt. He told Roz that if he mentioned his first report when the case came to trial, 'it will be the last report you make.' Indeed, during his subsequent interrogation before the investigation judge, Roz did not mention the inconsistencies between his testimony and his initial report."

Arazi wrote that in interrogating the murder suspects in jail, he found them to be telling the truth. Stavsky's claim that he had been in Jerusalem on the night of the murder, where he had stayed for the duration of *Shabbat*, and Rosenblatt's alibi of having been at a *Betar* meeting in Kfar Saba the entire evening, were collaborated by witnesses whom he had interrogated, in opposition to the "dubious recollections" of predominantly *Mapai* Party witnesses for the prosecution, who maintained that they saw the suspects in Tel Aviv on the night of the murder. Another glaring point, he noted, was that Rosenblatt in no way matched Mrs. Aronov description of the man who had fired the gun. "In my opinion," Arazi concluded, "Mrs. Aronov and other witnesses for the prosecution, tried, with willful and malicious intention, to convict the suspects through any means, and that a guiding hand lay behind their testimony to patch-over holes in the case for the prosecution."

When Arazi met with Horace Samuel before the trial, he told the defense attorney that during the course of his investigation, whenever he expressed his doubts concerning the guilt of the suspects, and about the veracity of the evidence against them, he was told by his superiors not to undermine the foundations of the case which the prosecution was constructing.

"When I told Captain Rice that the accusation of murder against the suspects lacked foundation, he told me to wait and let the investigation develop before jumping to conclusions, and that we would judge the matter then. After I submitted my preliminary findings, I received an order to report to Haifa where I would be assigned to a new assignment. In Haifa, days passed without any word from the local police commander. When I called Rice, wanting to get to work, his deputy, in an angry tone of voice, told me to be patient. Defying regulations, I returned to my office in Jerusalem. When I arrived, my deputy informed me that an Arab in the Jerusalem Prison, Abdul Megid, had confessed to being Aronov's murderer, along with a friend, Issa Darwish. Of course, I was astounded and happy to hear about this startling development. The Arab's description of what happened that night on the beach closely resembled Mrs. Aronov's version of the event. My deputy said that people in high places were putting pressure on the Arab to retract his confession. When he refused, shiekhs from Jaffa were brought to his cell to convince him to withdraw his confession, which is exactly what he did. In a subsequent interrogation, the Arab stated that Stavsky and Rosenblatt had spoken to him in prison and offered him money to falsely confess to the murder in which he was not involved."

Immediately, Horace Samuel demanded to be shown the Arab's initial confession, but the judges on the investigation committee denied his request, insisting that the Arab prisoner's tale had absolutely no substance in fact.

To Samuels, it was clear that the three suspects had been framed. Any honest judge would never have allowed the case to reach court. But given the bias of the local media, the manipulations of the police and prosecution, and the backing of the Mandate Authority and Jewish Agency, it wasn't clear to him how he could convince the judges at the actual trial that his clients were innocent. "Now is the time for some deep puffs on a pipe," Samuel reflected, wondering what Sherlock Holmes would do in such a corrupt and morally impoverished situation.

4.

A wad of spit splattered over his face. A punch to his belly doubled Abdul Mejid over in pain. Then his brother raised him up against the prison cell wall and spit in his face again. This time, repulsed by the wretched odor, Mejid couldn't contain the surge of nausea rising in his throat. With a choking cough, he vomited up his breakfast.

"Dog!" his brother, Hamin Mejid, said in disgust.

Choking for breath, Abdul continued to vomit out air. Never overfed in prison, his stomach didn't have much to throw up. Across the barren cell in the Arab wing of the Jaffa Prison, Subaki Sablowi stood up from his mat on the concrete floor.

"Why do you have to beat him up in the cell?" he asked Hamin.

"If it wasn't for him, I wouldn't be here," the hot-tempered Hamin answered.

Abdul Mejid collapsed to the floor. Day after day, several times a day, his older and much stronger brother abused him. The seventeen-year old Arab youth from Jaffa could no longer bear his brother's unceasing anger. How he longed to be free, to see the ocean again, bath in its cooling waters, and return to his work as a bicycle and car mechanic in his uncle's garage by the port.

"Guard! Guard!" Hamin yelled out.

"Why are you so angry at him?" Sablowi asked.

"That's my business," the gruff inmate replied.

An Arab prison guard appeared outside the cell. "What's the raucous?" he wanted to know.

"The dog threw up," Hamin told him. "If I don't have a cigarette, I'm going to be sick to."

"Beating on your brother again?" the guard asked him

"Tell the warden to put me in another cell before I kill him."

The guard unlocked the cell door with his key. Hamin removed a cigarette from the pack he kept in his pocket. Putting the cigarette in his mouth, he held out his hands for the guard to handcuff him so he could leave the cell. The guard lit a match and held it up to the cigarette. Locking the cell door, he led Hamin down the corridor toward the smoking room.

"Guard! Guard! How about cleaning up the vomit?!" Sablowi called after him.

"You clean it up," the guard answered.

Abdul Megid breathed heavily as he sat slumped on the floor, dragging himself away from the vomit.

"Why is your bother so angry with you?" his distraught

cellmate asked. Convicted for selling land he didn't own, Sablowi had shared the jail cell with the warring brothers for three weeks.

His spirit totally broken, Abdul leaned against the stone wall, and sighed. He was afraid that his brother would kill him. At his wit's end, he told Sablowi the story.

"Eight years ago," he began, "one of my older brothers was murdered in revenge for having mistreated a young girl. The police arrested one of her brothers, and he was found guilty and sentenced to life in jail. Last year, I learned that he wasn't my brother's real murderer. Another one of her brothers committed the crime, a barber named Lufti. With the help of a friend, I killed him outside of his barber shop. The police arrested me and my older brother, Hamin. I confessed and told the police that my brother was innocent, and that my partner was my buddy, Issa Darwish. When Issa was interrogated, he denied being involved. Because there was no other evidence against him, the police let him go. They refused to free my brother, Hamin. He's has gone crazy thinking he will have to spend the rest of his life in prison for a crime he didn't commit."

"I can understand his anger," Sablowi said. "Who wants to be locked up in a crap hole like this?"

"The barber wasn't the only guy we killed," Megid continued. "Did you hear about the Jew who was murdered six months ago walking on the beach in Tel Aviv with his wife?"

"Aronov?" Sablowi asked in surprised. Anyone who read newspapers knew about the famous murder.

"Yeah. Aronov. It was my friend Darwish who shot him. We were together that night."

Sablowi moved closer, amazed at what he was hearing. He was afraid that Hamin Mejid would return and interrupt the rest of the story.

"Wow. You are really some tough guy," he said, flattering Abdul to encourage him to tell more.

"Darwish wanted to go to the beach that night to look for a prostitute," the young killer explained. "You can find them there, Jewish women, near the Moslem Cemetery. We spotted Aronov and his wife walking along the beach.

Neither of us knew who he was. Darwish liked the looks of the woman. He wanted to check her out for a better look, so we followed them. Darwish got all excited. He's that way. The only thing he talks about is women. He even peed in the ocean to attract her attention. He told me he wanted her, so I stopped them and asked for the time. Aronov said it was too dark to read his watch so I turned on the flashlight I had. Aronov didn't like it when I shined it in his face. Darwish pulled out his gun to scare the guy away so he could rape the woman. He didn't plan on killing him, but when the Jew got nervous, Darwish shot him. We ran off in the darkness before anyone else saw us."

Sablowi was thinking so fast, his eyes darted back and forth, in a race against time. He knew a lot of money was being offered for information about the murder. If he could get his hands on it, he could pay back the money he had stolen in the land swindle and free himself from jail.

"Listen," he said in an excited whisper. "If you want to keep your brother from killing you, go to the warden and tell him about Aronov and your friend. You didn't shoot him, so you have nothing to worry about. You're already doing a life sentence for one murder, so there's no point in them charging you for killing the Jew, and since you're only seventeen, they can't send you to the gallows. Tell the warden that I encouraged you to confess, and get him to promise to reduce your sentence if you agree to testify. When the police learn that Darwish killed Aronov, they will charge him with killing the barber as well, and your brother will be freed. That's how you can get him out of jail, and help yourself too."

Abdul Mejid had never been a good student in school. Dropping out before high school, he learned that his wisdom was concentrated in his hands, not in his head. What his cellmate proposed made sense, but he didn't have time to think it over further – his brother was on his way back to the cell.

To make sure that he received the promised reward for information about the Aronov case, during his free time in the prison yard, Sablowi told a guard that he had to speak to the warden immediately about the Aronov murder. When he met with the stern British official, before he related Mejid's account of the murder, he reminded the warden about the rewards being offered by the Jewish Agency and the British Police. Warden Johnson kept a bored and annoyed expression on his face to hide his true emotions. He promised to get Sablowi the reward money if his information proved valuable to the case. The land swindler repeated the story. Realizing that he had a live bombshell in his hands, the warden summoned Abdul Mejid to his office, telling him that he wanted to hear everything he knew about Aronov's killing.

"I want two things before I tell you," Mejid told him.

"What are they?"

"I want my brother freed because he had nothing to do with the murder of the barber, Lufti. And, for helping you in the Aronov case, I want you to reduce my time in prison and not charge me for killing the Jew, which I didn't."

"I am only the warden of this prison, not a judge or the Attorney General," the Englishman answered in fluent Arabic. "But you can trust me. If it turns out that your information is real, then I will do everything I can to see that your brother goes free immediately, and that you receive a reduced sentence. Not to mention the money being offered by the police."

Satisfied, Mejid told him the story.

After hearing the dramatic account, Warden Johnson phoned Harry Rice, Deputy Inspector General of the Palestine Police, who was stunned to learn about Mejid's unexpected confession. Rice knew that the Jews accused of the murder were innocent, but he never expected the real killers to come forward and confess on their own. Returning the receiver of the telephone to its cradle, Rice sat aghast, staring down at his cluttered desk, wondering what to do. He knew that the case against the three Revisionists was bursting with holes, and that Horace Samuel was certain to attack the prosecution mercilessly, bringing all of its evidence into question, but Mejid's confession threatened to abrogate all charges against the accused. A sudden turnabout like this would mark a great victory for the Revisionists, bringing a horrible stain upon the motives of the Mandatory Government, not to mention the personal embarrassment it would cause him. No doubt he would lose his job. The unexpected disclosure would have to be covered up hermetically, or discredited, or denied.

The next morning, Rice drove to the Jaffa Prison with Head Police Investigator, Captain Bechor Shitreet, to hear Mejid describe the murder again. To make a long story short, the powers that be in the British Mandate Government decided that, in the best interests of Her Majesty's Empire, Mejid's confession should be suppressed. In the meantime, one of the Jewish prison guards leaked the sensational story to a Revisionist friend. The same day, Abba Ahimier's newspaper, "*Hazit Ha'Am*", ran a special edition, declaring that Aronov's true murderers had been discovered!

"ARAB CONVICT TELLS ALL!" the headline read. The lead editorial called upon all Revisionists and sympathizers to keep calm, for the sake of the unity of the *Yishuv*, proclaiming that the full truth would come to light, and that victory would shine in the camp of the pure and the just. Like in the days of Mordechai and Esther in Shushan, the crestfallen followers of Ze'ev Jabotinsky now raised their heads high in triumph and joy. In contrast, a feeling of doom descended over the socialist camp, as if some devastating tragedy had transpired. The Leftist newspapers were silent, hoping that the bad news would go away. Two days later, their rebuttals appeared on the newsstands: "Revisionists Ploy Exposed!" and, "Pop Goes the Balloon! Mejid Denies the Story!" and, "Stavsky and Rosenblum Bribed the Arab to Confess!"

When the police couldn't convince Mejid to retract his confession, they explained to a delegation of sheikhs from Jaffa why it was important to the Arab cause that the young Muslim prisoner alter his story. After a three-hour powwow in Mejid's cell, the Arab leaders convinced Mejid to follow the advice of the police and vow that the whole story was fabricated. The judge leading the investigation rejected Horace Samuel's demands to be shown Mejid's original signed confession. After several appeals to the High Criminal Court, the defense attorney was finally allowed to meet the seventeen-year-old murderer in prison, who now told a different story – Stavsky and Rosenblum had met him in the prison and offered him money to take the blame for the Aronov murder, assuring him that since he was already convicted for murdering a Jaffa barber, he couldn't be punished further. Sonia Aronov was summoned to identify Mejid and Darwish. Dressed in her finest clothes, and looking like a Hollywood actress, the now poised and confident widow shook her head and said that she had never seen either of them in her life. When the trial commenced, the court refused to accept Mejid's confession to the prison warden, ruling the Arab youth to be an unreliable witness who had been bribed by the accused. Even when the widely-respected attorney, Dr. Mordechai Eliash, the court-appointed attorney for Mejid in the barber murder case, presented an affidavit to the court, stating that Mejid - after his retraction to the police - had repeated to him his initial confession that he and Darwish had indeed murdered Perchik Aronov, the court refused to accept it as evidence. Nonetheless, the repercussions of the Arab's confession wouldn't die down, putting a large question mark on the objectivity of the entire proceedings – a question mark which Samuel exploited by repeatedly reminding the court and the press of, what he called, "the most transparent miscarriage of justice, and insidious manipulation of evidence, which I have ever encountered in my many years as a member of the Bar Council of England and Wales."

5.

During the month-long trial in Jerusalem, which began a full year after the murder itself, people flocked to the city to attend the sessions taking place in the High Court of Justice located in the Russian Compound, as if it were one of the Festival pilgrimages of old. Every day, the visitor's gallery was full. Journalists abounded. Tevye attended several sessions, along with Tzvi, Nachshon, Nachman, and Hevedke. The poet, Uri Zvi Greenberg rarely missed a day, and Moshe Segal followed the proceedings with great interest, occasionally bursting out in protest, when he sensed a prosecution witness was lying. Every day, *Maipainiks* squeezed their way into the hall to grab as many seats as they could. The one face that was never seen was the murdered man's son, Ben Zion.

Crowds stood outside the courthouse, waiting to hear the latest developments. The restaurants and cafes on Jaffa Road, a minute walk from the Russian Compound, hummed with noisy chatter. It seemed that everyone in the city was talking about the long-awaited trial, and about the fierce and ugly rivalry that had erupted between Labor Party supporters and Revisionists. Every day, in one place or another, a fistfight broke out.

At the outset of the trial, Ze'ev Jabotinsky paid for a small advertisement in all of the local newspapers, in support of the accused: "To the three innocent children of my heart - the Nation will not slumber or sleep until you are freed! Tel Hai!"

From windows overlooking the street, adventuresome *Betar* activists blasted out the "*Betar* Song" which Jabotinsky had composed:

Betar

From the pit of decay and dust
With blood and sweat
A generation will arise for us
Proud, generous and fierce.
Conquered Betar, Yodefet, and Masada
Will arise in strength and majesty.

Hadar

A Jew even in poverty is a prince
Though a slave or a beggar
You were created the son of a King
Crowned with David's diadem
In light and darkness
The crown of majesty and striving.

Tagar
Despite every oppressor and enemy
Whether you rise or fall
With the torch of revolt
Carry the fire to ignite a blaze – do not fear!
Because silence is despicable.
We shall give up blood and soul
For the sake of the hidden glory
To die or conquer the mount.
Yodefet, Masada, Betar!

Jewish organizations and Zionist groups throughout the Diaspora anxiously followed the daily news reports from the Jerusalem. The Jewish community in London was particularly apprehensive. Jewish liberals and assimilationists, along with the Labor Zionists, wanted the prosecution to win at all costs, hoping that a conviction would blacken the image of the militant Revisionist Movement and lead to its political demise. To the average English Jew who wanted to fit in with the Englishmen, the Revisionists were too noisy, too Jewish, and too strident in their goals. The liberal Jews felt embarrassed by the demands of Ze'ev Jabotinsky, Abba Ahimeir, and Uri Zvi Greenberg for an all-Jewish army, for an independent Jewish State on both sides of the Jordon River, and for the renewal of the Kingdom of David with the ancient Temple rebuilt in the middle of Jerusalem. Extremists like them, they fervently believed, were dangerous to world Jewry. But no one followed the case with more nervous interest than David Ben Gurion, who received a telephone report every day. The day before the court case began, he phoned Sonia Aronov and encouraged her to be strong throughout the trial, in order to lead the Nation to victory over the fanatics who scorned her husband's beliefs, and who sought, in committing the pernicious murder, to extinguish his life endeavor.

"I regret that I cannot be in Jerusalem with you, to provide whatever support I might," he told her. "Unfortunately, I must be overseas until the Zionist Congress is finished, and then, if things go well, I hope to be appointed the head of the Zionist Executive, which sits in London. Since the position may require me to be in England for quite some time, I will need people in Palestine who can insure that my policies at the *Histadrut* are carried out. So, please, have no fears regarding your future. I am sure I can find you a good position in one of our departments.

"That's very thoughtful of you, Ben Gurion," Sonia answered.

"Call me David, please," he said. "I don't have to tell you ever time we speak on the phone. The name Ben Gurion is fine for newspaper articles, but not for close friends. After the trial is over, perhaps you can come to London for a rest and vacation, and we can discuss what job would fit you best. I will arrange a plane ticket for you and a hotel near mine."

"That's all very kind of you... David. You are such a wonderful man."

"In that you are mistaken. Your husband was a wonderful man, far more virtuous than I am. For many years, he was a friend and trusted colleague. Offering my help at this time is the least I can do for his grief-stricken widow."

In Poland, as the general elections of the World Zionist Organization neared, and Ben Gurion prepared the groundwork for the approaching World Zionist Congress convention in Prague, he spoke to large crowds night after night, relentlessly attacking the Revisionists, certain that by linking them to Aronov's murder, he would win votes for his own *Mapai* delegation. His strategy paid off handsomely. In the general elections before the convention, Labor Zionism received forty-four percent of the total world vote, as compared to a mere sixteen percent for the Revisionists. Wooing the support of a few small parties, Ben Gurion commanded a majority in the powerful World Zionist Organization.

Now, the Labor leader moved to take control of the World Zionist Congress itself. In the past, all parties were afforded representation on the Presidium, which determined the issues to be discussed at the convention, and the list and order of speakers. Ben Gurion demanded that the tradition be altered, saying, "There is at this respected democratic convention, a fascist party beside which the Labor Party of *Eretz Yisrael* is not willing to sit on the Presidium. From the ranks of this party, three of their members are currently charged with the murder of one of our comrades." The motion banning subversive groups passed by a tiny margin, effectively excluding the Revisionists from playing at major role at the Congress.

Jabotinsky reacted with fire. "The shameful action of the Eighteenth Zionist Congress will not be forgotten. The Revisionist Party has been pronounced unworthy of representation on the Presidium because of a yet unproved connection with the Aronov murder. This blood libel is a deliberate, organized, and venomous insult designed to discredit a party whose membership numbers in the hundreds of thousands."

Jabotinsky demanded that the threat of Nazi Germany to world Jewry be discussed at the Congress, along with the world boycott of German goods, which he fostered. Not having a place on the Presidium, his demands were set aside by Ben Gurion, who maintained that an open struggle against Nazi Germany would create an immediate threat to the Jews of Germany, who were in the most vulnerable position. Jabotinsky also demanded that the issue of the Aronov trial be removed from the agenda, saying that the matter belonged to the jurisdiction of a court of law and not to the Zionist Congress. But Ben Gurion also managed to push this demand aside. At the first session of the Actions Committee, a commission was appointed "to weed out from the world Zionist organism tendencies that are contrary to the fundamental principles of Jewish ethics, which constitute a danger to the rebuilding of *Eretz Yisrael*." The commission was empowered to "eradicate from the Zionist movement any elements who are guilty of, or responsible for, such tendencies" – meaning the Revisionists.

Stepping up to the rostrum to address the huge crowd at the opening of the Congress, Ben Gurion had to wait several minutes for the thunderous applause to lessen. Dressed in a wrinkled suit, the dwarf-like figure didn't look like a man who could command the leadership of the elegantly dressed members of the Executive Committee sitting on the stage.

His hair looked unkempt, and his white shirt was opened at the collar in typical pioneer fashion. He gave the impression that if he had a tie, he had thrown it into a garbage can on the way to the convention. Who would have believed that this strange-looking creature, the same scrawny youth who had stepped ashore at the port of Jaffa some thirty years before, was about to achieve his dream of becoming the leader of world Zionism? Wouldn't Rivka, the love of his life, be proud!

"May it be known to one and all at this esteemed convention," he shouted. "There will be no negotiation or concession with those who don't accept the majority platform. If they threaten to walk out of the Congress, so be it! Let them go! If any Mussolini threatens to break up the Congress with his gang of hooligans, we, the true defenders of Zion, we know how to respond!"

By the end of the Congress, Ben Gurion was not only the head of the powerful Jewish labor union in *Eretz Yisrael*, the *Histadrut*, and head of the *Mapai* Party, he was voted head of the Zionist Executive of the World Zionist Organization, making him the most influential Zionist in the world. Equally important to him, he succeeded in pushing Ze'ev Jabotinsky to the sidelines.

Jabotinsky could only respond at a press conference held outside the convention hall.

"This Congress and its leaders have failed to do everything they should have done," he declared. "This farce of a democratic convention has humiliated the Jewish Nation before the arrogance of the Third Reich. The Congress shattered the united front of the boycott movement against Germany. It failed to unmask the anti-Zionist essence of the British Mandatory Government in Palestine, which hides its true intentions under a cloak of verbal sympathy to our cause. But, worst of all, this Congress, and its leadership, added more fuel to the inferno of internecine hatred which it created in the Land of Israel, interfering in legal proceedings outside of its jurisdiction, and pushing three innocent Jews toward the gallows, in order to hijack the Zionist Movement from the masses of simple Jews who prefer the proud and truly Jewish Zionism of the Revisionist

Movement, a Zionism untarnished by an sycophantic adherence to other isms and foreign creeds."

6.

Four judges were to decide the fate of the accused: two British judges, an Arab, and a Jew. When the moment arrived for the defense to present its case after the prosecution had summarized the long list of evidence it would submit to the court to prove the guilt of the accused, Horace Samuel attempted, in his opening remarks, to undermine the prosecution's most central assertion – that the murder was a political assassination, motivated by the Revisionist's desire for political gain.

"The court is invited to note," Samuel stated in his very precise and perfectly accented English, "that in cases of political assassination, the assassin customarily receives the cheers of his party or movement. This was not a possibility in the case before us. It would be impossible for a political assassination to win the approval of the Revisionist Movement, or the approval of its leader, who condemns fraternal violence at every opportunity. In addition, in the wake of the universal condemnation that such an act deserves, the Revisionist Party could expect no political gain at all for carrying out such a despicable crime. A political assassination of this nature could only bring the Revisionists harm, by alienating public opinion from their policies – something that has come to pass already, before anyone has been proven guilty, due to the accusations leveled against the suspects by the prosecution and the members of the *Mapai* Party, to which the deceased belonged. Where then is the political gain that the prosecution cites as the motive for the murder?

"Furthermore, a political assassination is the product of careful planning and execution. In our case, the murdered man had only been two days in the country after returning from abroad. No one knew that he would decide to go for a walk on the beach with his wife, nor that he would leave Jerusalem that afternoon for Tel Aviv, or that the couple would dine at the Katie Dan Restaurant – all of these decisions were spontaneous, ruling out the normal methodology of political assassination which knows in advance the place and time of the attack. In addition, political assassinations are carried out in great secrecy, with the assassin doing everything possible to remain unseen and unknown. Yet in the Aronov murder, the assailants revealed themselves to their victims several times during the course of their stroll, circling the couple. One even drew attention to himself by relieving himself in their sight, while the other stood directly facing them when he approached. This is not the method of political assassination. A political assassin who knew the identity of his target would have shot him from the rear. In addition, the gun would have been already cocked, avoiding the unnecessary delay which Mrs. Aronov describes taking place just before the shot was fired. Therefore, given all of these factors, and the actions and sexual gestures of the assailants, which Mrs. Aronov describes in her testimony, we are led to the conclusion that the murder was sexually motivated. The very site of the murder, on a desolate strip of the beach near the old Muslim Cemetery, a place known for illicit sexual activity, lends further credence to this theory, as does the confession of the imprisoned youth, Abdul Mejid, convicted of murder in a different crime, who gave eyewitness evidence which this court will not accept, for reasons I am unable to fathom, that the person who accompanied him that night on the beach, Issa Darwish, desired to have sexual relations with Mrs. Aronov. He is the real murderer, not the men wrongly accused before this court."

Without rising to his feet, one of the defense lawyers interrupted Samuel's remarks. "Objection!" he called out. "Certainly the esteemed barrister for the defense knows that the fairytale surrounding Abdul Mejid has been rejected as evidence by the court, since it has no basis in fact. We demand that the defense lawyer's remarks be stricken from the record."

"Objection sustained," a British judge said. Turning to Horace Samuel, he added. "The defense attorney will refrain from any further mention of Mejid's specious testimony. Please continue with your opening remarks."

Like a fine stage performer, Samuel turned toward the courtroom audience and spread out his hands with an expression that said, "Look how they are manipulating the trial already." Then, turning back toward the judges, he continued:

"All of these points, coupled with Mrs Aronov's initial assertion that their stalkers were Arabs, which she repeated several times to the police ,and her same-night request to be shown photos of Arabs whom she could identify, impel us to discount the prosecution's only eyewitness to the crime, and their claim that Revisionists murdered Perchik Aronov."

"Hip hip, hurray!" Moshe Segal called out in awkward English. "Hip hip, hurray!"

The head judge raised his gavel and banged it on the table before him. "I won't allow this courtroom to turn into a circus!" he shouted.

One of the defendants, Abba Ahimeir, jumped to his feet. "This isn't a trial! It's a witch hunt!" he yelled.

Again the gavel sounded. "One more outburst and the courtroom will be cleared!" the judge threatened.

Horace Samuel held up a hand and the catcalls from the Revisionists in the audience subsided.

At the beginning of the trial, the four Jewish Agency lawyers who led the prosecution team sat with smug expressions on their faces. Whenever Samuel exposed a weakness in their case, or succeeded in discrediting the testimony of a witness, they made scoffing expressions, as if the matter had no bearing on the trial's outcome. But after the first few days in court, their confident airs transformed into looks of worry. Samuel took his time in substantiating the alibis of Stavsky and Rosenblatt, who maintained that they had not been in Tel Aviv at the time of the murder. Samuel told the court that Stavsky was vacationing in Jerusalem and he presented solid witnesses who detailed Stavsky's activities from the afternoon of the day of the murder till late at night. On Friday morning, Stavsky had appeared at the Aliyah Department and the British Consulate to arrange for a visa. He purchased a book at Steimatzky's Bookstore. He had coffee and cake with two young women from Brisk. Afterwards, in the afternoon, he bought socks and returned to his room in the Turgeman Hotel. In the evening, at the time of the murder, he dined for several hours in the HaSharon Restaurant, and five witnesses testified that they had seen him there. The owner of the Turgeman Hotel testified that Stavsky had spent the night in the hotel and had eaten breakfast in the hotel's dining room in the morning.

Samuel pointed out that Stavsky and Rosenblatt had never met, and on the day of the murder, there had been no communication between them. Neither of them had any way of knowing Aronov's plans, which were spontaneously formulated, moment to moment, up to Aronov's decision to travel to Tel Aviv and to dine with his wife at the Katie Dan Restaurant. Not even Sonia Aronov knew that her husband would take her for a nighttime stroll along the beach. Sonia Aronov was the only person who placed Stravsky at the scene of the murder. Three additional witnesses claimed that they saw him in Tel Aviv on Saturday evening and Sunday morning, but, under Samuel's questioning, their testimony fell apart like a house made out of playing cards. The woman who claimed to have seen Stavsky in a café on *Shabbat* was embarrassed to learn that he had indeed frequented the place, but a day later, on Sunday, when he had returned to Tel Aviv to attend Aronov's funeral. As for Rosenblatt, more than a dozen witnesses testified that he had been present all evening at a *Betar* meeting in Kfar Saba. Needless to say, the seemingly watertight alibis of Stavsky and Rosenblatt left the impression that the eyewitness testimony of Mrs. Aronov, who claimed that Stavsky and Rosenblatt were the murderers, was either a case of mistaken identity or an outright lie.

The defense lawyer was caught by surprise when the prosecution introduced a long essay which Abba Ahimeir on the subject of political assassination, called, "The Scroll of the Sicarii." The prosecuting attorney reminded the court that Ahimeir's radical group, the *"Brit HaBirionim"* was named after a fierce faction of Jewish rebels who fought against the Romans, and against the Jews who advocated surrendering to them, just before the destruction of the

Second Temple. "It should also be noted," he said, "that Ahimeir's underground organization commonly refers to the British Authorities in Palestine as a 'foreign regime,' and dubs the British Mandate over Palestine 'an illegal occupation.'"

The prosecution claimed that Stavsky, "Ahimeir's disciple," who was boarding at Ahimeir's home at the time of the murder, had simply "carried out the theories of political murder and terrorism expounded upon in this frightening thesis."

Horace Samuel requested an adjournment to look over the manuscript, reminding the judges that according to the accepted practice in English criminal law, the defense was to be informed in advance about the existence of documents which would be offered as evidence. Winning the court's assent, an adjournment was announced, and Horace Samuel sat down in an adjoining room to read the unquestionably controversial treatise, which contained a plethora of statements which seemed to condone and even laud political assassination.

"A Sicarii war of terror against an existing regime is waged by anonymous heroes. In the main, no organization stands behind them. A state of mind possesses them, inspiring them to strike out lethally, and to accept the possibility of their own downfall as well. Often, they pay with their own lives as a result of their deeds. How happy was Charlotte Corday as she mounted the gallows after striking down Marat, and how forlorn was Dora Kaplan when she failed to put an end to Lenin's life."

Samuel's took a deep breath and read on.

"Belonging to the Sicarri enables a person to be transformed from an unknown being into a hero. With one successful stab of her knife, Corday became as important in history as great generals. To achieve this, one is only required to practice and take sure aim at the target. The deed of the Sicarri does not require prowess nor talent, nor spiritual exertion, for what anguish is there in suffering for a few hours on a crucifix, followed by death, compared to the unending suffering, day to day, for years without end, under the oppression of a foreign regime? The Sicarri sacrifices himself for the sake of a better future for his People. What a glorious, altruistic deed! He leaves the world knowing that life will be better for others, though he himself will not reap the harvest.'"

Samuel reminded himself that a charge of incitement to murder could only be considered relevant if the incitement under question specifically called for an act of violence against a definite individual or group. Nonetheless, coupled with Ahimeir's strident newspaper articles condemning Aronov for his dealings with the Nazis, his having penned a treatise which seemed to glorify political assassination was not going to win Ahimeir any points as a pacifist.

When the court was called back into session, Samuel gave Abba Ahimeir a questioning look.

"I wrote it ten years ago and never published it," the leader of *"HaBirionim"* explained to the lawyer in a quick and low voice, as the gavel sounded and everyone rose, anticipating the return of the judges. "I wrote it in response to the unsuccessful attempt to assassinate Mussolini. I never meant it as a practical manual, nor ever preached the doctrines in the treatise. Stavsky and Rosenblatt never saw it, and I never discussed such matters with them."

Often, a defense attorney's posture, facial expressions, erudition, and certainty of tone, can carry as much weight as pages of unshakable testimony. Knowing this, Samuel had mastered the art of public speaking. In a cool, calm, and very British manner, without showing any sign of worry whatsoever, he proceeded to remove all of the poisonous sting from the very problematic treatise called the "The Scroll of the Sicarii." In fact, the man who loved the stories of Sherlock Holmes seemed almost amused as he rebutted the prosecution's claim that the treatise, discovered in Ahimeir's home and penned in his handwriting, proved that the Revisionist extremist was the ideological mastermind behind the Aronov murder.

"I must say, I am rather surprised that the respected lawyers of the prosecution would deem fit to present Mr. Ahimeir's dust-filled and never-published notebook as evidence of his guilt in Mr. Aronov's murder. The treatise never saw the light of day, Mr. Ahimeir never discussed its contents with either Avraham Stavsky or Tzvi Rosenblatt, nor was he won't to discuss its themes in the many lectures which he delivered around the country. The writer, who has a Doctorate in History, wrote the treatise as a history of political assassination, and as a philosophical examination of its origins and consequences. He wrote it ten years ago, in the wake of a failed attempt in Italy to assassinate the dictator, Mussolini. Ahimeir dedicates the study to two women, Charlotte Corday, who assassinated Jean-Paul Moret while he was taking a bath during the French Revolution, for which she went to the guillotine; and to Dora Kaplan, who attempted to assassinate Lenin, for which she was shot by a firing squad four days later. While the scholarly paper covers many periods, nowhere in the treatise is there a mention of Palestine today, nor of the British Mandate Government, nor the *Mapai* Party, the Jewish Agency, or Perchik Aronov. It is nothing more than a historical survey with philosophic overtones, which the writer, a noted journalist and newspaper editor, never attempted to publish. In no way, shape, or form is it a practical handbook of terror, as the prosecution would like this court, and the public, to believe."

In the course of the world-famous trial, the murder charge against Abba Ahimeir was dismissed in the absence of any concrete evidence connecting him to the crime. But to Ahimeir's surprise, the British did not release him from jail. Rather, the police kept him in prison, charging him with membership in a clandestine organization and sedition against the British Mandatory Government. Citing the "Scroll of the Sicarii" as evidence in the subsequent, "Trial of the *Birionim*," the court sentenced him to 21 months of hard labor.

On a Friday morning in the month of May, over thirty journalists from around the world attended the concluding session of the Aronov trial to hear Horace Samuel's summation. At the beginning of his remarks, he demanded that Stavsky and Rosenblatt be exonerated by the court and set free, due to the total lack of reliable evidence. Samuel repeated his assertion that the murder had not been a political assassination at all, but rather a sexually-motivated crime committed by two Arabs. Samuel reminded the judges of Sonia Aronov's own testimony regarding the sexual actions and gestures of the assailants, and that she had initially testified to nine different people that Arabs had shot her husband. Furthermore, he advised that the Arab who had confessed to the murder, Abdul Mejid, be brought to trial, along with his accomplice, Issa Darwish. Ignoring another objection from the prosecution, he reminded the judges of Mejid's initial confession, before pressure was applied on him to retract the truth of his words. When Samuel held up Barrister Mordechai Eliash's sworn affidavit, which stated that Abdul Mejid had repeated his original confession to him, after his retraction to the police, the Revisionists in the audience and their sympathizers raised a loud raucous. Supporters of the Mapai Party countered with outbursts of their own. It took the head judge five minutes before he succeeded in restoring order.

Samuel continued his summation in an attack designed, not only for the ears of the judges, but for readers of the articles which the journalists in the packed courtroom would send to newspapers throughout the world. "I implore this honored court of law, and the respected judges who preside over the integrity and objectivity of this trial, to pay heed to the very non-objective way the police investigation was conducted, how important documents disappeared, how vital confessions and testimonies were denied or suppressed, and how state witnesses, like the footprint trackers, were pressured to alter their testimonies to match the needs of the prosecution. In my opinion, and it is difficult to think otherwise, Aronov's murder has been politicized by the British Mandatory Government, and by the British Police Administration, for their own political reasons, and that the police team involved in the investigation was pressured to manipulate its findings in a non-objective manner to substantiate the goals and interests of the Government, just as the initial report of police investigator, Yehuda Arazi, infers, so that a guilty verdict would be handed down against the accused."

His words aroused murmurs throughout the courtroom.

This time, all four of the judges had to bang their gavels to silence the uproar.

"In all of my years on the Bar of England, I have never encountered such a prejudiced state investigation," Samuel declared. "Furthermore, the leaders of the *Mapai* Party, and the widely-read Hebrew press, controlled by the political Left, judged the accused to be responsible for the murder, well before the trial begin, creating a volatile and prejudiced atmosphere designed to pressure the court to reach a verdict of guilty. The claim that the Revisionist Movement, and the "*Birionim*" group headed by Abba Ahimeir, masterminded the murder remains a totally illogical science fiction. Until today, the prosecution has failed to show how the Revisionist Movement derived any benefit at all from the despicable crime. Furthermore, this court already cleared Ahimeir of all involvement in the case. No one knew in advance where Aronov would be on the evening of the murder, so pre-planning of the crime was impossible. And the police failed to bring any evidence whatsoever to prove that Stavsky and Rosenblatt had been in contact with one another at any time in their lives. What kind of assassination team is this?"

Pacing in front of the hall while he spoke, Samuel now stopped in front of Sonia Aronov and faced her directly.

"The only witness to the crime was Aronov's wife, whose testimony is so filled with blatant discrepancies that it should have never been seriously considered by the court, on top of the fact that she initially testified, over and over, in front of nine different witnesses, that the assailants were Arabs, not Jews."

The defense lawyer's eyes locked with the eyes of the prosecution's star witness. The attractive woman sat, looking perfectly at ease, in a stylish, yet modest, two-piece suit, with her hair combed in the flat, rather mannish style of the day. Samuel was impressed – she didn't flinch a millimeter. Like a skilled actress, she returned the lawyer's accusing gaze without even blinking.

Taking another few steps, Samuel stood by the table where the defendants were sitting. Turning to the journalists and visitors in the courtroom, he concluded his remarks.

"I declare, on my good name and reputation as a British barrister, and as a member of the British Legal Society for twenty years, that, for the past twelve months, the lives of these two men have been transformed into hell as the innocent victims of a massive and well-oiled blood libel, undertaken by powerful political forces who have tried to influence the decision of this court. In the name of justice, the time has come to free them."

At the end of the Aronov trial, Tzvi Rosenblatt was freed for a lack of substantial evidence. Then Avraham Stavsky's verdict was read:

"A majority of the court finds that Avraham Stavsky took part, with forethought and willful intent, in the premeditated murder of Perchik Aronov, by following him, waiting for him, stopping him, and directing a flashlight upon him, and by being present during the commission of an offense contrary to the law. The accused defendant, Avraham Stavsky, is sentenced to death by hanging, according to the statutes of the court."

Pandemonium broke out in the courtroom. Horace Samuel stood stunned. The lawyers for the prosecution grinned happily at their victory. People rushed forward to shake their hands and pat them on the back. Sonia Aronov sat in her seat with a small, Mona Lisa smile on her lips. Jewish Agency administrator, Moshe Stillman, walked over to her joyfully and held out a congratulating hand. Helping her to her feet, he gave Perchik Aronov's widow a triumphant embrace.

Hearing the verdict, Stavsky jumped to his feet and shouted, "I am not guilty!"

Stavsky's mother, who had come from Poland to be near her son during the trial, burst into tears. "He is innocent! He is innocent!" she cried out in Yiddish.

One of the British judges banged his gavel to restore order. Moshe Valero, the lone Jewish judge, lowered his head in shame. Only he, out of the four judges, had voted for Stavsky's acquittal.

Given the opportunity to make a final statement to the court, an impassioned Stavsky declared: "I committed no crime. I will fight against this unjust verdict until the end. I swear that I am not connected to the crime in any way. On the night in question, I slept in the Turgeman Hotel in Jerusalem. The injustice against me is the workings and provocation of the *Mapai* Party and the Mandate Administration, who sought my conviction, only because I am connected to *Betar*. Until my last ounce of strength, I will fight for a retrial. I am innocent, and you, the judges, you will be responsible for my life, and for the suffering of my parents. And all of the witnesses who lied on the witness stand, their children will learn of their shame. I will appeal this evil decision, and I declare to those who condemned me, that I am confident that the British High Court of Appeals will teach you what justice is. You haven't condemned me - you have blackened the name of the entire British nation. You do not have the power to condemn me, just as a dark cloud cannot extinguish the light of the sun. My innocence remains unsoiled by your verdict. And my innocence will be proved!"

For several moments, only the sobs of Stavsky's mother sounded in the stilled courtroom. Police guards approached Stavsky to lead him away, but his mother ran forward and clung to him, crying hysterically. Finally, police succeeded in forcefully extracting him from her grip.

Stavsky held up his handcuffed hands for everyone to see.

"I am innocent!" he screamed as policemen led him out of the courtroom. "I am innocent!!"

In the jail of the Russian Compound, police guards led Stavsky to the barren dungeon corridor reserved for dangerous criminals. The prisoner was told to strip and put on the red prison uniform worn by convicts sentenced to death. A guard opened a steel door and shoved the doomed prisoner into a solitary cell. Above Stavsky's head, through the bars of the small window by the ceiling, the afternoon sun was descending. Sabbath was on the way.

7.

In the kitchen of Rabbi Kook's house, a two-minute walk from the Russian Compound, the always industrious *Rebbetzin* readied the food she had cooked for *Shabbat*.

Dressed in his long satin coat and furry *Shabbos Sputnik,* Rabbi Kook sat with his head bowed, a hand covering his anguished expression as Nachman read the sole dissenting opinion of Moshe Valero, the trial's only Jewish judge.

"After a thorough review of this trial, I find the defendants innocent. My conclusion is based on the following points:

1) The assailants showed themselves to the victim and his wife several times. One exposed himself immodestly and made sexual gestures before the shooting. 2) The crime occurred in a place and at a time when people are known to frequent the area for immoral purposes. 3) The initial description of the assailants given by Mrs. Aronov is unlike the appearances of Stavsky and Rosenblatt. 4) Mrs. Aronov was mistaken, for whatever reason, in her initial testimony regarding the nationality of the accused, insisting they were Arabs. 5) The alibis of the accused were reasonably substantiated. 6) The Prosecution could not provide any proof that Stavsky and Rosenblatt were in connection with each other. 7) The Prosecution failed to prove the professed motive of political gain. In light of these findings, and a general review of the case, I come to the followings conclusions: 1) the crime was not political, but rather a crime based on sexual motives. 2) Neither of the accused had any connection whatsoever with the murder. Therefore, I find them free of any guilt, and I declare them innocent."

Rabbi Kook looked up and nodded. Earlier, in the course of the trial, he had learned about the confession of Abdul Mejid after the Chief Police Investigator, Bechor Shitreet, revealed the matter in a private meeting with Rabbi Yaacov Meir, the Chief Sefardi Rabbi, informing him of Stavsky's innocence. In addition, the attorney, Dr. Mordechai Eliash, Rabbi Kook's close friend, had informed the Rabbi that Mejid had repeated his confession to him. Moreover, Rabbi Kook's devoted student, the saintly Rabbi Aryeh Levine, had visited Stavsky several times in prison, and he was convinced of his innocence.

"There is a time to keep silent, and a time to speak," Rabbi Kook said, quoting King Solomon's words in *"Kohelet,"* the "Book of Ecclesiastes." He lifted the quill pen on his desk. Setting a piece of paper in front of him, he wrote out a public

proclamation that was to be immediately signed by as many Rabbis as possible:

To The Yishuv

We, the undersigned, find ourselves in a situation requiring us to awaken the hearts of all Jews, and of all moral human beings. At this moment, in Jerusalem, there is a terrible danger that innocent blood will be shed, God forbid, if we do not stand up, all of us as one person, with a spirit of holiness, righteousness, and honor, to defend the innocent victim and save him from destruction. We must not be silent, and thus be guilty of spilling Avraham Stavsky's blood.

We, the undersigned, can all testify before God and man, with a pure conscience, that Avraham Stavsky is innocent of Perchik Aronov's murder. We know that the truth rests with the one judge who opposed the verdict, and we recognize the verdict as a decision to send an innocent man to the gallows.

We may not remain silent! Any Jew or Gentile who has a spark of God in his heart must protest this transgression of spilling innocent and righteous blood. We must do whatever we can to reverse this injustice and save the guiltless victim, Avraham Stavsky, restoring his righteousness and freedom without delay. We hereby proclaim, with a clear conscience, that Avraham Stavsky is innocent and had nothing to do with the murder!

Rabbi Kook signed his name and handed the page to his son, Rabbi Tzvi Yehuda.

"When you have obtained the signatures of as many Rabbis as you can within the next few days, this proclamation is to be posted all over the country," he said, "And please arrange that it be sent abroad in translation."

Then he opened a desk draw and pulled out a telegram form. Once again, his pen darted over the page. "Not only are Ahimeir and Rosenblatt innocent of spilling Perchik Aronov's blood. The righteous Avraham Stavsky is also innocent. You must fight with all of your strength and means for the victory of justice!"

Signing his name, he handed the telegram to Nachman.

"To whom shall I send it?" he asked.

"To every Jew in the world," Rabbi Kook answered. "Immediately after *Shabbat!*"

On *Shabbat*, a large crowd gathered at the Great Synagogue in the Zichron Moshe neighborhood to hear Rabbi Kook speak. He began by praising the late Perchik Aronov as a man who was dedicated to the rebirth of the Jewish People in Zion, for his contributions toward the settlement of the Land, and for his work promoting *Aliyah*, declaring that his death was a tragic loss for the Nation. Then, in what was to become a day-and-night campaign to free Avraham Stavsky, he raised his voice in emotion:

"We vehemently protest against all those who seek to stamp upon our forehead the mark of Cain by claiming that a Jew shed Aronov's blood. This is not true. It is out of the question. If Avraham Stavsky's sentence is carried out and he is executed, then all of us, all of the Jews who dwell in the Holy Land, will be guilty of transgressing the Torah prohibition of, '*Do not slay the innocent and the righteous.*'"

A *Haredi* Jew stood up and addressed the Chief Rabbi. "Why are you so sure that Stavsky is innocent? The court found him guilty."

Rabbi Kook stepped in front of the tall *Aron HaKodesh* which housed the Torah scrolls of the *shul*. "In this holy place," Rabbi Kook answered, "next to the holy Torah scrolls, I declare that to the best of my knowledge, and in a clear conscience, that our brother, Avraham Stavsky, is totally innocent. In the name of this entire holy congregation, I call for Stavsky's release and full freedom."

After the Sabbath, in the course of the next few days, twenty leading Rabbis also signed on the proclamation which Rabbi Kook had penned. His house became the headquarters of a round-the-clock campaign to free the convicted man from the hangman's noose. The Chief Rabbi instructed all congregations, yeshivas, and God fearing Jews, to recite Psalms on behalf of the man unjustly sentenced to death. On the days when the Torah was read in synagogue, Rabbi Kook made a point to offer a public blessing for the health and wellbeing of Avraham, the son of Aharon, adding a prayer for his speedy release from prison. He personally spoke with friends he had made in London when the First World War had stranded him in Europe, beseeching them to meet with the leaders of Parliament and to do everything possible to advance Horace Samuel's request that the British High Court of Appeals agree to review the decision of the High Criminal Court.

Samuel also threatened to bring the case to the Legal Committee of the King's Office in London, which would reopen the trial to the general public in England. The respected English barrister knew that the British Parliament did not want to appear anti-Semitic, and that England wanted to preserve its long-standing image as the world's most adamant upholder of justice. The British Government was already under an earthquake of public pressure, mounted by the many Jews sympathetic to Ze'ev Jabotinsky, who was working day and night to free Stavsky and bring the great injustice to light. In a telegram to Stavsky from Paris, the maligned Revisionist leader wrote: "The Jewish People, the Revisionist Movement, and all of *Betar*, bow to the fortitude you have demonstrated. We are certain that now also, your courage will not fail you. We shall continue our struggle to victory and you shall be freed!"

As deeply as the verdict against Stavsky pained Jabotinsky, he was equally pained and depressed by the great jubilation of the political Left over Stavsky's conviction. After reading through a pile of newspaper reports from Palestine, he wrote to his secretary, Joseph Schechtman: "How joyful they are over the news that a Jew is going to be hanged! A reporter describes the scene by the Edison Theater in Jerusalem where groups of *Histadrut* workers are shaking hands and dancing and wishing each other '*mazel tov!*' over the good news. In Tel Aviv, *Histadrut* workers marched through the streets singing and shouting, 'Death to Stavsky!' Good God, what happened to this segment of the Jewish People? Are their minds so completely poisoned that they rejoice at the prospect of a Jew being hanged? And how are we, all of us, going to live with them in the same country in the future?"

Employing his considerable literary gifts, Jabotinsky placed articles defending Stavsky in every newspaper he could. In an article called, "The Jackals and the Clams," he wrote:

"The jackals are those queer beings, who, though Jewish, go to sleep, hopefully dreaming that other Jews will be executed. They dream of this even though they are aware of the innocence of the accused. But even more curious are the clams. Forgive me, gentlemen of the *Yishuv*, for saying this about you, but a lowly and unscrupulous conspiracy against an innocent Jew is being enacted before your eyes, a conspiracy against justice and Jewish pride. Not even in the Dreyfus and Beilis cases of blood libel was the insolence so brazen. Only clams could permit this to go unchallenged. Any other self-respecting public would rise up in defense of the innocent. But the clams keep mum."

Jabotinsky ordered his followers to establish "Stavsky Defense Committees" all over the world. He convinced several prominent British leaders to pressure the Secretary of State for the Colonies to make sure that, "England wouldn't let itself be dragged into committing judicial murder by sanctioning the actions of the Mandate Government in Palestine."

Now that the universally respected Rabbi Kook, the Chief Rabbi of the Holy Land, had put his considerable moral and spiritual standing behind Avraham Stavsky, the increasing public calls, in England and abroad, for an unprejudiced hearing before the British High Court of Appeals could not be ignored.

8.

Ben Zion Aronov tossed from side to side on his cot, but the frightening dream wouldn't go away. Charlie Chaplin was directing a prison movie, but the movie wasn't funny. Tension surrounded the set. Sonia Perchik stood beside the famous Hollywood movie director. Holding a bullhorn to his mouth, he shouted instructions to an actor in a red prison uniform, as he stood poised to transverse a high platform toward a gallows and dangling hangman's noose. Underneath the platform was a stormy sea. British policemen yelled at the prisoner. Ben Zion felt his heart beating in fear. When the picture jumped to a close-up of the terrified prisoner, Ben Zion recognized his own face. He was the doomed prisoner on the platform, walking toward the gallows! Waves swirled in the noisy waters below his feet. Sonia Aronov smiled proudly. "Keep walking! Keep walking!" the director yelled, his angry face looking nothing like the amusing Charlie Chaplin, whose movies Ben Zion had seen at the Mugrabi Theater in Tel Aviv. When Ben Zion crossed the gangplank and reached the gallows, a hooded executioner stepped forward and placed the noose around his neck, fastening it with sudden tight jerk. The executioner pulled off his mask and smiled. It was Moshe Stillman, his father's friend. Ben Zion heard the sound of a drum roll, then a trap door opened beneath him, and he fell...."

With a scream, Ben Zion fell off the cot to the floor. His body trembled. But he was still alive. Sweating, he gazed about in the darkness, recognizing the barracks. It was a nightmare, he realized. Just a crazy nightmare. Other soldiers slept on their cots in the small room, exhausted from a long day's training. Putting on his shoes, the troubled son of Perchik Aronov slipped on his shirt and headed outside. The only sound in the dark *moshav* came from crickets in the bushes. Not wanting to go back to sleep, he lit up a cigarette. The image of the gallows haunted his mind. He started walking across the grass in the direction of the cool breeze from the ocean which made the tip of his cigarette glow.

News of Stavsky's conviction had made all of his buddies happy, but Ben Zion couldn't share in their triumph. A heaviness gripped his heart. Somber thoughts plagued him throughout the day, distracting him from his training. He couldn't reveal his ruminations to his commander or friends. He didn't want his girlfriend to know. He hadn't spoken to his mother, or grandfather, or cousins, since his father's funeral. He no longer had a Rabbi he could talk to. No longer did he feel any connection to God. What if Stavsky were innocent? What if the death sentence came to pass? How could he let an innocent man be executed? But if he revealed what he knew, what would become of his father's *Mapai* Party, the Jewish Agency, and all of the ideals which his father cherished – they would all be destroyed. How could he shatter his father's work and dreams?

He walked and walked, alone in the night, not knowing where he was going, until he found himself on a sand dune overlooking the dark, roaring sea. Across the black expanse, Hitler and the Nazis threatened the Jews of Germany and Europe. In Palestine, an ugly struggle pitting Jew against Jew for control over the *Yishuv* threatened all hopes for a better future. A thousand thoughts raced in his head. He let the wind and momentum carry his steps down the sand dune to the beach, where he had spent months practicing rescue drills. He slipped off his shoes, and his trousers, and his shirt. He wasn't trying to kill himself. He just wanted to drown out the obsessive thoughts in his brain. The waves were high and relentless, but he had confidence in his swimming. The cool water was like an elixir of life, awakening him from his nightmare, sweeping away his troubles and worries. With strong strokes, he swam further from shore, diving under the waves as they crashed over his head, surfacing to gasp more air, feeling all of the tension and turmoil seep out of his body.

A fisherman walking along the beach before sunrise discovered Ben Zion's body lying in the sand. Quickly, he raised the youth's legs to his chest and pumped. A gush of seawater steamed out of his mouth. The fisherman slapped the unconscious youth on the back until he coughed up another gusher of water. His body was lifeless, but his heart was still beating.

Hours later, Ben Zion lay in the same emergency room where his father had uttered his last dying words. A doctor had pumped all of the water out of his stomach and lungs, but there was nothing else he could do. He had no way of knowing the extent of the damage. Hodel sat by her unconscious son's bedside reading *Tehillim*. Tevye prayed in the hallway. Receiving a telephone call from Kfar Vatkin, they had left Jerusalem immediately for Tel Aviv, taking a taxi to arrive as fast as they could. Seeing Sonia Perchik hurrying through the hospital lobby toward the emergency room, Tevye nodded without ceasing his prayers. Her high heels clicked noisily in the corridor. Hodel stopped praying when the stylishly-dressed woman entered the room.

"How is he?" Perchik's second wife asked, her face tense with worry.

The boy's mother gave her a cool, hostile glance.

"The doctors aren't sure," Hodel replied curtly, not volunteering any other information.

"I'll ask them myself," Sonia said, maintaining her composure.

Piqued by the ice-cold reception, Sonia strode out of the room. Tevye continued to pray, not looking up from the book of Psalms which he grasped in his hands.

"You despise me, don't you?" Sonia asked, confronting him.

Tevye glanced up, torn by mixed emotions. He recalled his arguments with Perchik way back in Anatevka, when he had invited the cocky, headstrong lad to tutor his daughters. He remembered their arguments on the communist *kibbutz* when Tevye had first arrived in Palestine. He remembered their fistfight, and how Perchik had rescued him from the Turks, and how they had fought, side-by-side, in the Hebrew Brigade. It was Perchik who persuaded him to travel to Tel Hai to help rescue Josef Trumpeldor and the brave settlers under siege. He and his new wife Sonia had reacted with joy when Ben Zion had abandoned the Torah. The youth's grandfather gazed up at Sonia Perchik without standing.

"Your husband, for all of his heretical beliefs, was an honorable man," he said. "But you? It doesn't pay a Jew to sell his soul for the whole world, but for a job with the *Histadrut*?"

Tevye stared at her with a look of pity and disgust. He turned his head and spit on the floor. The flustered woman shivered and hurried away toward the hospital exit, the clicking of her high heels echoing in the corridor long after she couldn't be seen.

9.

Outraged by Rabbi Kook's highly-publicized campaign to free Avraham Stavsky, the *Mapai* Party came out in full force against the Chief Rabbi. He was condemned in their newspapers for overstepping his bounds, interfering with justice, and championing the Revisionist cause. On the street, *Histadrut* workers scrawled graffiti over Rabbi Kook's proclamations demanding Stavsky's freedom: "Shame on the Rabbis who aid murderers!" "Rabbi Kook Joins the *Birionim*!" Curses were painted on a wall of his house, and vandals threw rocks at the windows. The Torah sage bore the humiliation in silence. In response, he issued another street proclamation calling on all political parties and groups to gird themselves with moderation in the wake of the trial's conclusion, and to refrain from igniting the flames of fraternal hatred, in the hope that true justice would soon shine over the Nation in Zion. Ever since his arrival in *Eretz Yisrael*, in the face of fierce opposition from the Ultra-Orthodox community, Rabbi Kook had striven to find merit in the praiseworthy deeds of the secular pioneers, in their dedication to rebuilding the Nation and settling the Land. Now their entire camp turned against him, negating all of his efforts to unite the Jewish community in the spirit of brotherly love and peace. The acclaimed poet, Haim Bialik, met with Rabbi Kook, hoping to persuade him to keep out of the controversy, but after hearing the Rabbi's reasoning and seeing the fire ablaze in his eyes, he himself became an advocate of Stavsky's innocence. "Rabbi Kook acts as if he himself were standing under the shadow of the gallows," the poet wrote after the meeting.

Worried by a growing wave of public disdain toward the verdict of the court, the British Administration summoned the Chief Rabbi to Police Headquarters. In the past, on his visits to the Russian Compound, officials of all ranks, whether British, Arab, or Jews, would greet the Chief Rabbi with bows of respect, but now his reception was as cool as the dungeon cells in the adjacent prison where Stavsky sat in isolation, awaiting his fate.

Police Deputy General, Harry Rice, was pointedly cold. "How can a respected spiritual leader of the Jewish community in Palestine take a public stand against a British court enforced with upholding the law of the land, thereby casting a dark shadow over its supreme authority?"

"There is only one Supreme Authority, the Creator of Heaven and Earth," Rabbi Kook answered. "He is King of the Universe and Judge of all mankind. Nevertheless, when the Almighty decreed that the people of Sodom be destroyed, our forefather, Abraham, opposed the decision, pleading stubbornly before the Almighty to alter the harsh decree, lest the light of God's justice be tarnished in the eyes of the world. *'Shall the Judge of the entire world not do justice?'* he asked. If Abraham could disagree with a decree of the Master of the Universe, whose Kingship lasts forever, then certainly I am permitted to find fault with judges of flesh and blood, who are here today and gone tomorrow."

The more vehemently Rabbi Kook pushed for Stavsky's exoneration, the opposition became more hostile. A group of leading *Mapai* leaders including Berl Katzenelson, Moshe Stillman, Yitzhak Ben Zvi, and his wife, Rachel Yanait, came to visit the Chief Rabbi to protest his activities on behalf of the convicted murderer. In line with his custom of not looking at women directly, the holy sage glanced to the side when he responded to her statements. He had welcomed Mr. and Mrs. Ben Zvi in his home on several occasions, and until the Aronov trial, the couple held the Rabbi in great respect. While not always agreeing with his beliefs, they felt awed by his unique blend of holiness and vast erudition. As easily as he could speak about Torah, he could speak with great knowledge about psychology, history, philosophy, literature, and art.

Yitzhak Ben Zvi began the conversation in a friendly tone.

"We all want to thank your honor, the Chief Rabbi of *Eretz Yisrael*, for finding the time to meet with us. I think you know everyone, so introductions are not necessary."

"I have never met the Chief Rabbi," Moshe Stillman said. He took a step forward as if to approach Rabbi Kook and shake his hand, but noticing the Rabbi's stiff bearing and his unwillingness to even glance in his direction, Stillman froze. Suddenly, he felt that if Rabbi Kook were to look at him, he would see all of his sins, including the fact that he had heard the dying Aronov say that Arabs had shot him - crucial information that he never revealed to the police. Noticing Rabbi Kook's uncharacteristic coldness toward

Stillman, Ben Zvi recalled how the Chief Rabbi had refused to shake hands with acting British High Commissioner, Harry Charles Luke, for having encouraged the 1920 Arab pogroms against the Jews of Palestine. On Rabbi Kook's part, the moment Stillman had entered his study, he had received a spiritual warning which caused his soul to shudder. Though the ways of *shalom*, and the love of all people, were foundations of the Torah, the Chief Rabbi's finely-tuned radar reacted to Stillman's presence with a flashing red light.

Ben Zvi's wife, Rachel, also sensed the unusual chill. Like an experienced party hostess, she made some small talk to cover up the awkward moment.

"I hope that the *Rebbetzin* is feeling well," she said, referring to Rabbi Kook's wife.

"Yes, thank you," Rabbi Kook said, motioning his guests to sit in the chairs that Nachman had been prepared for them.

"The Rabbi is making headlines these days," Ketzenelson said with a smile.

Rabbi Kook spoke softly:

"Since it has fallen to my lot to have been appointed Chief Rabbi, along with my colleague, the Sephardi Chief Rabbi, the prince of Torah, Rabbi Yaacov Meir, may he be blessed with long days, it is my duty to see that the light of Torah shines, not only in the halls of our holy *yeshivot*, may they flourish all over the Land, but also in the many diverse facets of our national revival, may it grow and flourish, whether it be in the observance of agricultural laws, in the strict adherence to our unique dietary laws, or in the upholding of justice in the courts of the Land, so that the life of *Am Yisrael* in *Eretz Yisrael* be a true beacon of moral light to all of the nations."

"Amen," Rachel Yanait responded.

"Amen," Katzenelson agreed.

"I am glad to see that the Chief Rabbi has not lost the fighting spirit that he displayed when battling for our rights to pray at the *Kotel*," Ben Zvi said, having accompanied the Chief Rabbi on several meetings with British Administration leaders.

"It was the Jewish People who taught the world the supreme value of justice, and it is our task to upraise its banner whenever it be threatened," the Rabbi answered.

"Isn't interfering in the decisions of a court of law a threat to the institution of justice?" Moshe Stillman asked bluntly, piqued by the stony reception he had received, and not willing to let Ben Zvi's respect and reverence for the Rabbi dull the purpose of their visit.

"Indeed. Doesn't the Mishna in *Pirkei Avot* teach that a person must accept the decisions of the judges?"Berl Katzenelson added.

"And that a person is to accept their rulings even if they say that right is left, and left is right?" Rachel Yanait observed.

Rabbi Kook smiled. "I am happy to see that the Torah is being studied, not only by yeshiva students, but also by the leaders of the Zionist Labor Movement," he quipped with a small smile.

His remark somewhat eased the tension in the room, but the air of confrontation could be seen in the stiff smiles and rigid postures of the visitors.

"The Torah itself describes a situation where the heads of the Sanhedrin err in rendering a decision which leads the congregation astray," Rabbi Kook responded. "When a court of law renders a wrong decision, it demands public rectification."

Katzenelson glanced at the framed pictures, hanging side-by-side on the wall, of the *Gaon of Vilna* and the *Baal HaTanya*, the two famous spiritual leaders of the warring *Misnaged* and *Hasidic* movements of yore.

"Just as the honored *Rav* emphasizes the supreme value unity of the Jewish People in his sermons, and by placing together the two pictures on the wall of Rabbis who didn't always see eye-to-eye, shouldn't the *Rav* be concerned with the unity of the Jewish People now, after the court has made its decision in the Aronov trial, and work toward decreasing the division and hostility between the two warring camps?"

"You are right in saying that the unity of the Jewish People must always be our guiding concern, but we cannot sanction the spilling of innocent blood in its name."

"Did you ever meet Perchik Aronov?" Stillman asked, choosing not to refer to the Rabbi by any title of respect.

"Yes, I did," Rabbi Kook answered. "He visited me here, last year, before a cursed evildoer put an end to his life."

"If you believe that the murderer is an evildoer, why do you exert so much effort to set him free?" Stillman queried accusingly.

The Ben Zvi's glanced sternly at the Jewish Agency official, uncomfortable with his hostile approach.

"Avraham Stavsky is not the murderer. I pray day and night that the real killers be brought to justice."

"The court has already determined the identity of the murderer, whether people agree with its verdict or not," Ketzenelson injected.

"Gentlemen," Rabbi Kook said in a patient, but final tone. "I will not change my belief that Jewish hands did not spill the blood of Perchik Aronov. It is everyone's obligation, and your duty as well, to do everything possible to free an innocent man who sits in prison awaiting salvation, or the hangman's noose, God forbid."

"What stubbornness!" Stillman barked. "We are wasting our time!"

Red in the face, he rose and strode out of the room, first turning right, then turning left, looking for the way out of the house. His colleagues sat in stunned silence, embarrassed by such a crass breach of etiquette.

"I apologize to the Rabbi for our colleague's unseemly behavior," Ben Zvi said in embarrassment. "Mr. Stillman worked side-by-side with Perchik Aronov at the Jewish Agency. Please forgive him."

The Chief Rabbi was silent.

"How can the *Rav* be so certain that Stavsky is innocent," Rachel Yanait asked in a respectful tone, really wanting to know.

"The Chief Rabbi's unconditional love for all Jews is known to everyone," Ketzenelson added before Rabbi Kook could answer. "But his belief in the righteousness and purity of every Jewish heart cannot be the basis for freeing a person who was convicted by three judges after a long and thorough investigation and trial."

Yitzhak Ben Zvi felt true admiration toward Rabbi Kook, whom he considered to be a uniquely brilliant and holy human being. Not wanting to damage their friendly relations, he continued to address him in a respectful voice.

"Perhaps the honored Rabbi doesn't know that the Revisionists viewed Aronov as an enemy. Their newspaper condemned him in the most vile manner, accusing him of making a pact with the devil, and with limiting the immigration of Jews to card-carrying socialists, to the exclusion of everyone else."

"If the Rabbi knew all of the details of the case, I am sure he would feel otherwise," Ketzenelson asserted.

The light of Rabbi Kook's holiness still graced his face. Even though a painful cancer was slowly eating away at his life, a glow of kindness and love radiated from his being.

"I understand that the loss of Mr. Aronov has been very painful to you all, and to his family, and to your Party," he said. "His murder pains me deeply as well. But our pain cannot blind our eyes to justice. The *Shulchan Aruch* details the laws of criminal justice in a very thorough manner. Daily editorials which appear in a Labor Party newspaper cannot take the place of reliable witnesses, and a man may not be executed just because his friends wrote angry and venomous articles about him."

"Sonia Aronov was an eyewitness to the crime," Rachel Ben Zvi noted.

"Sonia Aronov originally testified that Arabs killed her husband. Then, for some unknown reason, she changed her testimony and identified Stavsky and Rosenblatt. A witness of this sort cannot be considered reliable. Especially when no one else witnessed the murder. According to our holy Torah, at least two witnesses are required in cases of capital punishment. I have been following the case very closely from its very beginning. I am familiar with the arguments of both the prosecution and the defense, and I have heard from the most reliable authorities, intimately involved with the proceedings, that Avraham Stavsky is not the murderer."

Realizing that Rabbi Kook was far more familiar with the details of the Aronov case than they thought, the delegation kept silent. Ketzenelson decided to try a different approach.

"The respected Chief Rabbi has endeavored for over two decades to be a friend to all camps in the *Yishuv*, and to bring the pioneers closer to Judaism, always choosing the path of peace, in a way that has made the Rabbi respected and revered, even amongst those who don't follow the commandments of the Torah. But now, in taking sides in this controversy, and defending a convicted murderer in so earnest a fashion, as if the Revisionists who support him are close to your heart, you have given the secular community a reason to move even farther away from the Torah. I remember the Rabbi's tour of the *moshavim* in the north, and your visit to Kinneret, and how you inspired us to follow the rules of *kashrut* and to honor the *Shabbat*. I am sorry to say that all of the good relations which you have established will be destroyed if you persist in your public campaign to free the convicted prisoner."

Yitzhak Ben Zvi and his wife sat silently, waiting for Rabbi Kook to respond to a bitter reality which threatened his life's work of bringing the Jewish People closer to God and the Torah. Berl Katzenelson sat poised at the edge of his chair. Rabbi Kook nodded. All of a sudden, he looked tired and ailing, as if oppressed with an onerous burden.

"If I need to be in opposition to all the world, due to the passion I feel for the deep truths implanted in my soul, which cannot tolerate any trace of falsehood, so be it. I cannot be what I am not. I must always strive to reveal and express the fundamental truths hidden in my spirit. The Torah commands us not to stand idly by when a fellow Jew is in danger. Therefore, in spite of your arguments, I appeal to you to do everything you can to save the life of Avraham Stavsky."

The meeting was over.

While the country's socialists and communists vilified Rabbi Kook's efforts to save Avraham Stavsky from the gallows, the prisoner himself was filled with gratitude. In order to express his feelings personally, he sent a letter in Yiddish to the Rabbi, which Stavsky dictated to his fellow inmate, Abba Ahimeir, who had been convicted of treason against the British. Convicted of a crime he didn't commit,

Stavsky asked the far more erudite writer to enhance his simple prose.

"To the honored Chief Rabbi:

"Behold, I am a simple Jew. I wonder – what is my merit that our generation's greatest Torah scholar, *HaRav* Kook, is so preoccupied with my fate? I do not know why the Almighty has chosen me to be the scapegoat for the entire Jewish Nation. We of flesh and blood cannot comprehend the ways of God. I promise, your honor, that I will endure my sufferings with love. I merely ask that the spiritual leader of the Jewish People forget me not in his prayers. I believe in the power of your prayers in the war against the Satan in the world above, and against his counterpart in this world. Your authority can influence many people in official places to help erase that guilt which has been cast upon my name.

"I have one more request of the Rabbi – that he bless my parents. I know that I do not fulfill my obligations towards the Master of the World. However, I have always fulfilled the *mitzvah* of honoring one's parents, through good times and bad. My afflictions are bearable because I know that a person of Rabbi Kook's personage and stature has a place for me in his mind and his soul when he communes in prayer with his Maker. May the Lord guard over our People.

"Signed with tears – Avraham Stavsky."

At the same time that Rabbi Kook strove to promote Stavsky's innocence, he concerned himself with the fortune of Abba Ahimeir, who, although cleared of all charges in the Aronov murder, still remained behind bars on a new charge of sedition against the British Government. While other members of the "*Birionim*" organization were also accused, the court had released them from custody until the start of their trial. Only Ahimeir remained in the Jerusalem Prison, in a cell not far from Stavsky's. Finding his situation intolerable, Ahimeir wrote a letter to the prison warden:

"I am writing to the honored warden, even though I know that the substance of this letter is not under his jurisdiction. My hope is that the warden will forward the matter to the proper government agency.

"I am sure that you know that all charges have been

dropped against me in connection with the murder of Perchik Aronov. While my release from incarceration should have taken no longer than an hour, behold, after days without end, I am still imprisoned. Today my lawyer informed me that the authorities refuse to release me until I am brought to trial on different charges, even though others accused in the same matter have been released on bail.

"Since my just rights have been denied me, I have no recourse other than to begin a hunger strike. Though my health is suffering after a year of imprisonment in the Aronov case, I am forced to take this measure. It pains me that the Government of Palestine chooses not to learn the ways of justice from the free and democratic nations of the world, but rather from Hitler's Germany and Stalin's Russia, which also keep innocent people in jail.

"Therefore, as of the writing of this letter, I, the undersigned, Dr. Abba Ahimeir, has embarked on a hunger strike. I shall be very grateful to the warden if he could do whatever possible to make sure that this letter reaches the proper destination."

Two days later, standing below the window in his cell so he could hear the exclamations of encouragement from passersby on the street, Ahimeir turned at the unmistakable sound of the jailor's key in the lock of the metal door. A look of surprise flashed over his face as Bechor Shitreet entered his cell. He wore the kaki uniform of the Mandate Police Force, with short pants, knee-length, high black socks, and the domed hat inherited from the days of the Turkish police in Palestine. Sporting the epaulettes of a lieutenant, the high-ranking Jewish policemen faced the gaunt prisoner as he sat down on his cot.

"To what do I owe the dubious privilege of a visit from the Chief Investigator of the British Police?" Ahimeir asked in a cynical tone, clearly unenthused by the Jewish officer's visit. "Has Gestapo Captain Rice sent you to convince me to cease my hunger strike? Did he tell you to speak in Yiddish so that I would think that you really care about the plight of a fellow Jewish *lansman*?"

"I came to tell you that during the course of the trial, I became convinced that Stavsky was innocent. At first, I believed he was guilty, and so I put all of my energy into the investigation, but when the pieces of the puzzle didn't come together, and when Abdul Mejid confessed, I understood that Stavsky was not connected to the crime."

"Why come here to tell me all this?" Ahimeir asked. "What gain is there in it? From the moment of his arrest, I knew that Stavsky was innocent. I am not in need of the private, heart-wrenching confession of a government officer to convince me that my good friend is not guilty. If your conscience weighs heavily on your soul, then go and make a public proclamation that Avraham Stavsky is innocent!"

Shitreet paused before answering the prisoner's acerbic remarks. While he hadn't expected Ahimeir to embrace him with love, he had hoped for a less hostile reaction.

"You should know, Ahimeir, that over the course of the investigation, I had the chance to study your character. You have a fondness for criticizing everything not to your fancy and for belittling everything which does not live up to your absolute demands for the truth, as you choose to define it. If I were to make a public proclamation at this time, it could only hurt Stavsky by forcing the powers-that-be to cling to their previous conclusions in order to defend the honor and righteousness of British rule in Palestine. Furthermore, do you expect me to expose the lies and corrupt dealings which have marked British Administration's handling of this case from the very beginning and jeopardize the good names and livelihood of police officers who have been pressured to twist the facts surrounding the investigation?"

"While I don't expect moral considerations of justice and truth to enter the decisions and actions of Ben Gurion and the other leaders of the *Mapai* Party, I certainly expect a person in your position to stand up for the truth. You are not willing to jeopardize the futures of your fellow policemen, but you are willing to jeopardize Stavsky's life?"

"I assure you that I have revealed my feelings regarding Stavsky's innocence to people of authority whose influence is far greater than mine."

"If you are referring to your confession to Rabbi Yaacov Meir, I know about that, and, indeed, the merit of your action will stand in your behalf when you appear before the

Supreme Judge in the High Court in Heaven. While, I do not deny the praiseworthiness of that deed, it is not enough. Unlike your co-investigator, Yehuda Azari, who chose to reveal the falsehoods surrounding the investigation from the very beginning, and who lost his position because of it, along with other Jewish officers who lost their jobs for refusing to cooperate with the blood libel against fellow Jews, you have waited with sealed lips until now, when Stavsky faces the gallows, and still you have not made a public confession, whether because of your convoluted reasoning that it would bring about a counter reaction and sabotage the success of his appeal, or because you too are concerned about your future in the hierarchy of the Labor Party. No matter. As you see by my hunger strike, I am prepared to die for the truth. Not like you, Officer Shitreet."

Red in the face, the policeman held out an envelope. "This is from Rabbi Kook," he said. With a snap of his wrist, he threw the letter on the cot. Then he walked out of the cell.

Rabbi Kook was pained to hear about Ahimeir's hunger strike. Immediately, he wrote to the prisoner, asking him to stop: "Even though I am very grieved over your prolonged suffering in prison, I cannot allow, under any circumstances, that you resort to a hunger strike which stands in flagrant contradiction to our duty to safeguard our health...."

Moved by the Chief Rabbi's personal concern for his wellbeing, Ahimeir began to eat once again.

10.

Inspired by Rabbi Kook's undaunted stand on behalf of the doomed prisoner, many people, far and wide, came out in Stavsky's defense. In the stubborn way of a "Jewish Mamma" of old, Stavsky's mother knocked on every door she could. Day after day, the distraught woman traveled to Rachel's Tomb to recite Psalms and plead for mercy on her son's behalf. She traveled to the Tomb of the Patriarchs in Hevron, praying that the merit of the Patriarchs and Matriarchs of the Nation would bring her son's innocence to light. Her prayers made as much of a commotion in Heaven as Rabbi Kook's efforts were causing on earth.

The appeal hearing lasted a week. On the day of the decision, Rabbi Kook fasted and recited *Tehillim* in the study hall of his yeshiva. He told his students to open the ark which housed the Torah scrolls and recite the prayer, "*Avinu Malkanu*," recited on Fast Days and the Days of Awe. He told his son, Tzvi Yehuda, "My body is here in the yeshiva, but my heart and soul are in the courtroom." Stavsky's mother woke her family early in the morning and hurried them off to the courthouse, promising that they would return home with "Avrasha."

The convicted man's supporters packed the large hall. Tevye, Hevedke, Nachman, and Tzvi were all present, along with Uri Zvi Greenberg, Moshe Segal, and the secret leaders of the *Irgun*. Joining them were people who had changed their mind about Stavsky's guilt during the course of the trial, especially after Rabbi Kook had declared his absolute belief in the convicted man's innocence. As everyone waited with racing heartbeats, the three British judges rendered a unanimous decision, read out by the head of the High Court of Appeals, Judge MacDonald:

"I cannot find any reason to criticize the conclusion of the High Criminal Court in their acceptance of Mrs. Sonia Aronov's testimony...."

Immediately, a murmur of dissatisfaction swept through the hall.

"If this trial had taken place in England, it would have ended without any appeal, and the conviction would have stood final."

Again, the crowd expressed its loud disapproval.

"We're finished," Stavsky father told his wife in Yiddish. She squeezed his hand and gazed up toward Heaven.

"However," Judge MacDonald continued, "the legislators of the laws of Palestine enacted a ruling that, in criminal cases, a person cannot be convicted of a serious crime on the testimony of only one witness."

A spontaneous roar exploded in the gallery. Realizing that Stavsky was exonerated, shouts of joy resounded throughout the courtroom. At the moment, it didn't matter to anyone that the defense had won the appeal only because of a legal technicality, and that in the eyes of the judges,

Stavsky had been involved in the murder – he was free! With a cry of joy, Stavsky's mother leaned forward and grasped her son's head in her two loving hands.

"My Avrasha!" she cried.

The pounding of a gavel restored a bit of order.

"Therefore," MacDonald concluded. "Since we did not find any substantial supporting evidence which could strengthen Mrs. Aronov's testimony as a lone witness, we are forced to cancel the decision of the High Criminal Court and to annul the conviction. The defendant shall be freed immediately."

The Chief Judge banged his gavel on the table, the judges rose to exit the courtroom, and the happy crowd in the visitor's gallery rushed forward to congratulate Stavsky and his smiling attorney, Horace Samuel. More than a year after he had met with Ze'ev Jabotinsky in Warsaw, it turned out that "Jabo" had analyzed the case correctly, down to its very end. Interestingly, the origin of the law lay in the Torah, which declared that a person could not be convicted of murder through the testimony of a single witness. This was one of the reasons why Rabbi Kook refused to even consider a guilty verdict.

Bechor Shitreet joined the mob of well-wishers, a happy smile on his face. He too wanted to give Stavsky a hug. Catching a glimpse of the Jewish police investigator who had hidden the truth throughout the case, Stavsky turned his back. Tevye, Nachman, and Hevedke surged forward, pushing Shitreet away from the country's new hero. With a sense of relief and satisfaction, Horace Samuel packed his files into his briefcase. True, the Appeals Court had exonerated his client on what seemed to be a mere legality, but the implications were much broader. Now that Stavsky wouldn't be executed, the decision for acquittal saved the face of the British Mandatory Government and the Palestine Police, avoiding the need to expose the corruption surrounding the case. Samuel also understood that the judges had found themselves a clever way of defending the High Criminal Court's basic findings, thus preserving the dark stain of murder which had been attached to the Revisionist Movement. The victorious lawyer nodded cordially toward the Jewish Agency attorneys who had led the prosecution. Though they had suffered a bitter defeat, the Appeal Court's decision allowed the *Mapai* Party to maintain that Stavsky remained guilty of Aronov's murder, and that an arcane and primitive loophole had set him free. In fact, those were Ben Gurion's very words:

"Sonia Aronov identified the man who had participated in the murder. According to English law, this would have been enough to convict him. But the law in *Eretz Yisrael* demands two witnesses. For my part, I have no doubt at all who murdered Perchik Aronov."

In the courtroom, Tevye bent down and placed his head between Stavsky's legs. With a grunt, he straightened his back, lifting the free man into the air high above the jubilant crowd.

"Long live Rabbi Kook!" Stavsky cried out.

"Long live Rabbi Kook!"

Chapter Seven
FRIENDS AT LAST

The famous English playwright, William Shakespeare, wrote an anti-Semitic play called, *The Merchant of Venice*, featuring the evil character, Shylock. Nonetheless, he wrote many other plays on universal themes, having nothing to do with Jews, and these can be rightly enjoyed for their literary brilliance. No man, except for rare exceptions, can be considered all good or all bad. It is not an exaggeration to say that Rabbi Kook was all goodness. In contrast, Adolf Hitler was the personification of evil. In the case of David Ben Gurion good and bad co-existed together. In Shakespeare's classic play, *Julius Caesar*, Antony comes to eulogize the assassinated emperor:

> "Friends, Romans, countrymen, lend me your ears.
> I have come to bury Caesar, not to praise him.
> The evil that men do lives after them.
> The good is oft interred with their bones.
> So let it be with Caesar."

In the literary history which you are reading, with its fictional Tevye and fictional Perchik Aronov, I have not set out to bury the fictional Ben Gurion which I have created, nor to praise him. While it is true that the evil that men do lives after them, while the good is often interred with their bones, it is also true that the good that men do lives after them, while the evil is often interred with their bones. So let it be with Ben Gurion. Therefore, in this chapter centered about a fictional Ben Gurion, allow me to present both the good side and the bad in the literary portrait we have created, as several of his real-life biographers have done. People have strengths and weaknesses, good sides and bad, so let it be with Ben Gurion.

And now, to get on with our story....

Upon hearing the news that Stavsky had been freed, Ze'ev

Jabotinsky immediately sent him a telegram: "Please know that your suffering was not in vain. Your tortures will purify the hearts of all Zionists and Zionism, and lead the way to a nobler Hebrew State!"

To Rabbi Kook, the Revisionist leader wrote: "The Nation and its youth will never forget your outcry which has revealed anew the strength of Jewish tradition."

In the "*HaYarden*" newspaper, Jabotinsky published a passionate appeal, urging his followers not to adopt the tactics of those who had waged a relentless witch-hunt against them all during the Aronov murder investigation and trial: "We call upon all of the supporters of the Revisionist Movement and *Betar* not to respond to provocation, whether verbal or physical. The actions of the Left have generated a terrible bitterness throughout world Jewry. Their own actions will lead the Left to its downfall. Let them do what they will. Remain strong in spirit and truth will triumph in the end."

While Ben Gurion wasn't pleased with the decision of the High Court of Appeals to set Stavsky free, the murder of Perchik Aronov, and the blood libel surrounding it, had helped propel him to the leadership of the World Zionism Organization. But Ze'ev Jabotinsky and his Revisionist Movement would not go away. They still buzzed about, like mosquitoes on a pleasant summer night, not letting Ben Gurion enjoy his prestigious triumphs. In the backlash of Stavsky's acquittal, people who had abandoned the Revisionists during the trial, now returned in increasing numbers, while the *Mapai* Party found itself scorned by the general public for the hatred and discord it had fostered for political gain. While Ben Gurion and the Labor Movement in Palestine continued to maintain in every forum that Stavsky and his Revisionist friends were the murderous culprits, the ordinary man in the street no longer swallowed the foul-smelling, overcooked tale, what Tevye referred to as "*lokshen*."

Sensing that his control of the *Yishuv* was weakening. Ben Gurion ordered the *Histadrut* to wage a series of work strikes to remind the Jews of Palestine who ran the country. The Revisionists, who had their own work unions, crossed the picket lines, defying the striking *Histadrut* bullies. *Betarim* and *Haganah* soldiers who had undergone military training for years without seeing action, now found an outlet for their frustrations. Instead of fighting the Arabs or the British, they fought each other. Every day, fist fights and brawls broke out on the streets of the Holy Land. While slandering the Revisionists for their "fascist-like militarism," the *Histadrut* pressured employers to only hire workers who carried membership cards of the *Mapai* Party, which had never abandoned its Bolshevist roots and strongman tactics. Tensions soared, and Jewish blood stained the cafe tables and sidewalks of Jaffa Street and Rothschild Boulevard. Though Ben Gurion was far away in London, the intrinsic goodness of his soul caused him to shiver when he read the daily reports from Palestine. How could it be that while Nazis were beating up Jews in Berlin, Jews were beating up fellow Jews in the Land of Israel? When Pinhas Rutenberg inquired whether Ben Gurion would agree to meet with Ze'ev Jabotinsky secretly, in the hope of extinguishing the inferno of fraternal strife which was threatening the stability and growth of the *Yishuv*, Ben Gurion took a deep breath and agreed. The serious-faced Rutenberg, a longtime Zionist activist, former *Haganah* commander, and founder of the Palestine Electric Company, was the perfect matchmaker, trusted by both men.

Historians are divided in their opinions why Ben Gurion consented to meet with an opponent he so obsessively hated, whom he called, "The Fuhrer, Ze'ev Vladimir Hitler," and the, "Duce Jabotinsky." Suffice it to say, in this crucial time of Jewish history, his great love for the Jewish People and the Zionist cause enabled him to rise above personal and Party concerns. An entry in his diary, written just days before the historical meeting, sheds light on his thinking. "Hitler's rise to power places the entire Jewish People in jeopardy. What will be our strength in Palestine on the awful judgment day, when the great catastrophe bursts upon the world? Perhaps only four or five years stand between us and that terrible moment. During this period, we must double our number in Palestine, for the size of the

Jewish community will determine our fate in that decisive hour."

At the time, Ben Gurion was living in London, where the Zionist Executive was headquartered. Though he drew from a generous expense account to fill his small hotel room with books, sometimes reading two a day, for his own family needs, he made due with his modest *Histadrut* salary. His wife, Katia, in Palestine with the children, pleaded with him to take an additional salary as head of the Zionist Executive, but he persistently refused. To make ends meet, Katia moved into one part of their small Tel Aviv home with the children, and rented two rooms to tourists. Not telling her husband, she also found part-time work as a nurse in the nearby first-aid station on the beach.

Jabotinsky had taken up residence in Paris, setting up the "Revisionist World Union Headquarters" in a rather rundown, but spacious, three-story building on a quiet street in the Latin Quarter of the city. From its offices, he directed the World *Betar* Movement, which was rapidly growing in size now that the blood libel surrounding the Aronov murder had been exposed as a *Mapai* Party invention. In addition, the threat of Nazi Germany which loomed over Eastern Europe attracted tens of thousands of young Jews to *Betar* with its strident military message of Jewish pride and action. Though the Revisionist Movement had been castigated and ostracized by the recent Zionist Congress, Jabotinsky, with his undying spirit, used the setback as a springboard for increased activity. All of the burning issues that the socialists and liberals refused to tackle, the World Revisionist Union raised up in their stead. First and foremost, they strove to unite world Jewry in the campaign against the Third Reich, and to transfer the Jews of the Diaspora to the Jewish Homeland without limiting their efforts to British quotas. Jabotinsky wanted to instill a new spirit into the Zionist Movement, to rescue it from the smoke-filled halls of Zionist Congresses and Conventions, in order to create a dynamic, messianic migration of Jews to Zion. To accomplish this, he was prepared to meet privately with Ben Gurion in London. Both Zionist leaders agreed to heed Rutenberg's advice not to mention the past. The focus was to be on the future.

The truth is, both battle-scarred warriors harbored a secret respect for each other, the way two champion prizefighters respect the talents and strengths of their opponent. Though Jabotinsky had long been Ben Gurion's arch nemesis in the political arena, and while Ben Gurion had been Jabotinsky's greatest ideological rival, the two men shared a towering concern for the Jewish People. While Ben Gurion also had a towering concern for Ben Gurion, at this crucial hour, he proved his greatness by putting his own personal ego aside.

After a few private meetings in Rutenberg's small hotel room, the two Zionist visionaries realized that their differences could be set aside in view of their common overall goal and the dangers facing world Jewry. Why then did their alliance and truce not last? As both Sholom Aleichm and Tevye would say, "*Many are the plans in a man's heart, but it is the counsel of Hashem which stands.*"

This is what happened....

Jabotinsky arrived first for their initial meeting and chatted with Rutenberg until Ben Gurion knocked on the door of the hotel room.

"I am sure that introductions aren't needed," Rutenberg said before leaving them alone.

Dressed in his usual business suit and tie, Jabotinsky peered at Ben Gurion through the thick, circular frames of his eyeglasses. Never a stickler for formal attire, Ben Gurion wore baggy khaki pants and a white shirt open at the collar, as if he had just been strolling along Herzl Street in Tel Aviv. A vein pulsed on his broad forehead, betraying his tension over the top secret encounter.

"*Shalom,*" the *Mapai* leader said without smiling.

Jabotinsky stood up and extended his hand. "*Shalom,*" he replied.

For an awkward moment, his hand hung in the air. "Don't you want to give me your hand in a gesture of peace?" he asked.

Taken aback by his bluntness, Ben Gurion held out his arm. Their handshake said much more than their many subsequent conversations. The touch of their flesh, just seconds long, triumphed over political differences, party rivalries, and personal pains.

Jabotinsky smiled. "If we can bring it about that our handshake puts an end to the internecine turmoil in *Eretz Yisrael*, then our mutual friend, Rutenberg, will have brought about a miracle."

"You have aged," Ben Gurion noted, remembering "Jabo" from their days in the Hebrew Brigade.

"And your hair has whitened," Jabotinsky said.

"The little of it that I have left," Ben Gurion quipped. "A Rabbi once told me that my hair fell out because I didn't wear a skullcap."

"If that were the case, I would be bald as well."

Their simple batter broke the tension that had gripped the room. Ben Gurion's uneasiness stemmed, not from meeting a hated opponent whom he had vilified at every opportunity, but from the knowledge that such a meeting would surely arouse the opposition and wrath of his colleagues, threatening both his reputation and his leadership of *Mapai*. In contrast, Jabotinsky's tension stemmed from his hopes that their gesture toward peace would succeed, for the betterment of the Nation. By nature, insults directed his way did not weaken or sully his spirit. What mattered was the future of the Jewish People, not what people said about him, however stinging their curses might be.

"Our friend has left us some coffee," Jabotinsky remarked, motioning to a coffee pot and cups on a dresser.

"Perhaps later," Ben Gurion said. Walking to the window, he gazed out at the city of London. "I hate being away from Israel," he noted.

"Unfortunately, I am used to life in foreign places. As you know, the British won't let me enter Palestine."

"I had nothing to do with that," Ben Gurion replied quickly. "In fact, I signed a petition against it."

Adhering to the one condition which Rutenberg had set for meeting, Jabotinsky chose not to answer, not wanting past conflicts to close the door on a more promising future. "My exile is by far the greatest tragedy of my life," he reflected. "Like Cain, I must wander the globe, like a stranger without a home."

The Revisionist leader poured himself a cup of coffee and sat in one of the two chairs in the small and Spartan hotel room.

"However, I am not one to indulge in self-pity," he continued. "In fact, of late, I have discovered a new happiness. I have fallen in love. Yes, I have fallen in love with my new office in Paris."

Ben Gurion turned away from the window and listened to the sincere and openhearted confession.

"All of my life, I detested offices," Jabotinsky explained. "I disliked being caged in an office, like a young boy who dreads the hours he is forced to sit in a classroom. Now, I eagerly rush off to work each morning, like a pious Jew on his way to *shul*. I sit at my desk, and run up and down the three flights of stairs to visit my co-workers on other floors, enjoying every minute. If you visit Paris, don't go to the Louvre. Come and see us at Rue Pontoise."

"I have always appreciated the style, if not the content of your words," Ben Gurion said, sitting in the chair opposite *"Rosh Betar."*

Jabotinsky nodded his head at the compliment. "Sometimes I dream of finding a country house in Switzerland and writing novels. But, in these times, who can afford such indulgences?"

"My most favorite times have been spent doing agricultural work in the fields of the Galilee," Ben Gurion confided. "But, since others were more physically equipped for such labor, I decided to do whatever I could to enhance the fruits of their pioneering endeavor by establishing an organization of workers which would lead to Jewish economic independence."

"Workers unions have value, indeed, but, in my opinion, they should not preclude individual enterprise. When you canonize the worker as the crown of Creation, as the hero of progress and the sole hope for humanity, and view everyone else as an enemy of the State, you have established a background for violence. Though I have been labeled 'bourgeoisie' in my support of free capital enterprise, you must remember that all of the lofty principles of freedom, equality, and brotherhood were first promulgated by the bourgeoisie. Instead of castigating the capitalist, and looking upon him as an enemy, the proletariat should realize that every new factory and business expands the work place and creates more jobs for Jewish labor. The *Yishuv* is still in its infant stage, and if we want to bring millions of Jews to Zion, it is only through free capital investment and enterprise that we can provide work for them all. This, I believe, is readily understandable. The problem arises, if I may speak in a straightforward manner, when the Revisionist platform is seen as attracting young workers away from the ranks of Labor Zionism. But, certainly, in the broad borders of *Eretz Yisrael,* on both side of the Jordan River, which, I believe, we both want to our People to settle, as befitting our moral, historic, and political right, there is room for both socialists and capitalists, without violence and bloodshed. We must always remember that the strategy of the British Empire is to divide the natives and conquer. Why should we help them?"

Ben Gurion rose and walked to the dresser to pour himself a cup of coffee. As he later wrote in his diary, he was fascinated by Jabotinsky. He respected the depth of his thinking and his ability to focus on the root of the issue and not be distracted by its branches. In addition, he had always admired his unwillingness to bow down to the *goyim.* At the same time, Jabotinsky possessed a nobility and knightly refinement, which Ben Gurion knew that he himself lacked. While the Revisionist leader knew how to pen a barb as stinging as Shakespeare himself, he would do so only sparingly, in self-defense, and against his will, clearly anguished by the wars between Jews.

"Of course, I don't expect you to become a despicable bourgeoisie like I am," Jabotinsky joked. "Nor do I expect you to agree on everything I say. On the contrary, I look forward to hearing the famous Ben Gurion directness."

The younger man accepted the remark as a compliment. While Jabotinsky was only six years older, the distinction lent him the standing of 'the elder statesman" of the two.

"If we intend to be open and direct in our discussion," the

Labor leader replied, "I want to warn you at the very outset that any agreements which we may be able to reach in this hotel room, for the sake of restoring peace in the *Yishuv*, may be impossible to carry out in on the streets of Tel Aviv and Jerusalem. While the allegiance of your followers stems from their reverence for you as '*Rosh Betar*', the loyalty of my followers, if they are at all loyal, stems from fear. They think that I am crazy and emotionally unstable, and perhaps rightly so."

"Didn't Weizmann say. 'You don't have to be crazy to be a Zionist, but it certainly helps'?"

"Weizmann utters a lot of dribble, especially to the British, with his groveling airs. As for the members of *Mapai*, each one believes he would make a better leader of the Party than I am. So, whatever understandings we can achieve here in London, are very likely to fall on deaf ears at home. I can offer you well-meaning intentions, but no guarantees."

Thus their discussions began. Rutenberg later commented that they resembled skilled boxers in the very first round of a championship prizefight, circling cautiously to test the strengths and weaknesses of their opponent. Leaving the hotel, they walked together to the nearby Metro station. Both men glanced around, sharing the same concern. What would happen if someone recognized them and saw them walking along the street together, like the best of friends? Such a sensational scoop could send shockwaves throughout the Jewish world! Suddenly, Jabotinsky faced Ben Gurion and asked, "Why didn't you extend your hand in greeting when we met in the hotel room?"

Ben Gurion paused before answering, taken aback by the tone of sincerity in the voice of the rival whom he had slandered and besmirched without compassion.

"Perhaps I was embarrassed. While our hopes are focused on the future, the past is hard to forget," he replied, choosing not to delve deeper into the matter.

"I am prepared to put the past behind us," Jabotinsky responded in his noble manner. Once again, he extended his hand. This time, Ben Gurion grasped it without hesitation. That evening, he wrote in his diary, "Miraculously, no one saw us together, shaking hands."

Day after day, for almost a month, the two men met in Rutenberg's hotel room, or in their own respective hotels. In the course of their marathon meetings, they exchanged views on everything under the Mediterranean sun. Occasionally, they ventured out to a restaurant for a meal, during which their conversation centered on history and literature, subjects which both men relished. The *Mapai* leader, who was an avarice reader, confessed that he literally suffered if he didn't read a book each day. How pleased he was to discover that *"Rosh Betar"* was familiar with almost every work of history he mentioned! Like himself, Jabotinsky had a voracious appetite for books. Each new title which Jabotinsky recommended, Ben Gurion rushed to buy. In a diary entry, Ben Gurion wrote, "The curious fellow is the most erudite and knowledgeable man I have ever encountered in my life."

It soon became apparent that their views were not unbridgeable. Regarding relations with England, over the years Ben Gurion had lessened his great expectations regarding London's sincerity in helping the Jews to establish a National Homeland in Palestine. Nevertheless, while he shared Jabotinsky's dreams for a independent future for the Jews in what Ben Gurion termed, *"Medinat Yisrael,"* by nature he was a realist, appreciating the value of pragmatism. In contrast, *"Rosh Betar"* was possessed with the soul of a dreamer, accepting the present, imperfect state of affairs, only when coerced by powers beyond his control.

"At first I detested Weizmann's obsequious, bend-the-knees approach to diplomacy," Ben Gurion confessed. "I hate going to cocktails parties and laughing at all the silly chatter, while the Nazis grow stronger each day. The vital question is, can we open the gates of immigration through diplomacy or through force? I don't believe we will gain the sympathy of the world by violently demonstrating outside the British Parliament, or by blowing up the London Bridge. The English are civilized people. Just as Balfour was persuaded to assist in the past, I believe we can find the right way to persuade his successors today. First, we have to fill the Land with Jews and build an independent Jewish economy. Once we have a stronger foundation, we can demand our own State. Besides, when it comes to creating our own government, we have a lot to learn from England's tradition of democracy, education, and justice."

Jabotinsky's attitude toward the British was far more reserved. While he previously believed that England offered the best possible partnership in establishing a Jewish State, he now seriously doubted that the British Empire, with its imperialistic goals and pro-Arab leanings, could be a partner at all. And though Ben Gurion might respect the British justice system, Jabotinsky and his Revisionist friends had spent enough time in British prisons to form a very different opinion. But heeding Rutenberg's advice, the unjustly slandered Revisionist leader didn't mention the Aronov affair, nor the judicial corruption surrounding the investigation and trial.

"It is no secret that a growing number of Revisionists have become disillusioned with the British Mandate and advocate a parting of the ways," he told the Labor Movement leader. "Every day, I must stand up to growing impatience and pressure coming from the more militant wing of the Movement. Certainly, in our dealings with England, we have reached a dangerous crossroads. It is now clear to me that the London Government, and especially the Foreign Office, know of the anti-Zionist policies fostered by the Mandate Authority in Palestine and stand in complete sympathy with its pro-Arab agenda. *'The voice is the voice of Jacob, but the hands are the hands of Esau.'* In my opinion, England's presence in Palestine is now a hindrance to our cause and a menace to the future of the *Yishuv.* On the other hand, I am not opposed to one last experiment to see if the marriage can last, provided that we adopt a more aggressive posture in our dealings with the British. If they don't view our demands sympathetically, we will find another partner."

"Who?" Ben Gurion asked.

"Perhaps America."

"I have spent time in America, and as the expression goes, *'gornisht helfn.'* Don't count on help from there. What comforts me is your understanding that at the present time, we cannot survive *b'Aretz* on our own, against the Arab threat which surrounds us."

"At this time, yes," Jabotinsky agreed. "But through mass immigration and our own Jewish army, I am convinced that our divorce from Lady England will soon come, whether we take the initiative, or whether it is forced upon us by the demands and vicissitudes of history."

Regarding the Nazi threat, Jabotinsky wanted Jews around the world to demonstrate publically, to openly petition their governments to join an international economic boycott of Germany, and to put pressure on England to allow the mass immigration of Jews to Palestine. In contrast, Ben Gurion believed that quiet diplomacy would be more effective, worrying that open protest would bring Hitler to unleash his SS squads against German Jews in an even more frightening fashion.

Another two obstacles which stood in the way of a reconciliation between the two Zionist leaders were the World Zionist Organization and the Zionist Executive. For all practical purposes, Ben Gurion had succeeding in ostracizing Jabotinsky from both. In no uncertain terms, Jabotinsky informed his new friend that if existing attitudes and policies were not altered, he would continue to put all of his energies into establishing a new international Zionist organization of his own under the Revisionist banner. However, he added, if Ben Gurion lessened his resistance to the world economic boycott of Germany and to Jabotinsky's "Petition Plan" of hounding foreign governments to pressure Britain to do away with Jewish immigration quotas to Palestine, then he would be flexible in matters concerning the Jewish Agency and the WZO. After long hours of negotiation, they drew up a tentative sketch, stating that the "Petition Plan" would be carried out by the World Zionist Organization, and that all parties would be represented on the Zionist Executive. In concession to Ben Gurion, Jabotinsky agreed that there would be one single labor union, the *Histadrut*, representing the workers in Palestine, with the establishment of a National Arbitration Board to decide on all labor disputes.

As if they were still soldiers in the Hebrew Brigade, after

an all-night session battling out the precise wording, the tired warriors signed their names on a truce which proclaimed:

"In the name of putting an immediate end to the internecine strife between Jews in Palestine, without infringing upon freedom of discussion and criticism within the Zionist Movement, all parties undertake to refrain from all forms of party warfare which are outside the norms of political, ideological discussion, and which are not in conformity with the moral principles of Zionism and civilized conduct. All acts of terror or violence, in any shape or form, are forbidden, as well as slander, libel, and insult to individuals or groups. Violations of these prohibitions will be punished through fines and expulsion from the World Zionist Organization."

Clasping each other around the shoulder, the two exhausted but euphoric Jews could have been mistaken for drunkards as they left the hotel at dawn on that sunny morning in the usually damp and foggy London. Returning to his hotel room, Ben Gurion noted in his diary: "I don't know if all of our comrades will welcome this agreement. It is hard to believe that it can be implemented. It is too good to be true."

Later in the day, after catching up on sleep, Ben Gurion wrote to his new Zionist partner, addressing him as "my colleague and friend."

"Whether our agreement will come to pass or not," he stated, "nothing will change the fact that both of us met and, in the course of many hours, forgot everything which had occurred in the past, out of our joint concern for the Zionist Movement and our mutual trust and respect. This joint effort will never be rooted out of my heart. Whatever may happen in the future, my hand will always be extended to you in times of friendship and stress, in spite of all Party opposition."

Jabotinsky wrote back the same day: "My dear friend, Ben Gurion, I am moved in the depths of my being to hear, after so many years (and what years!), expressions like 'colleague and friend' coming from your lips. I grasp your hand in true friendship."

The day after the signing, Ben Gurion wrote to the *Mapai* leadership in Palestine, informing them of the milestone event. "Surely," he noted in his diary, "they will stone me for the sin of meeting with Jabotinsky."

News of the truce appeared in the press before Ben Gurion's letter arrived. Berl Katzenelson, a close friend and confidant (if the ever-suspicious Ben Gurion could be said to have one) telephoned, reporting that the party was in shock and panic. "You must return home immediately!" he told him.

Far away in London, Ben Gurion grieved that his comrades didn't understand the value of the proposed peace between the two warring groups. A flood of angry telegrams filled his mailbox at the hotel's reception desk. It seemed that no one favored the reconciliation. Moshe Stillman termed it "treachery." Yitzhak Ben Zvi confessed that he had "severe reservations." Beyond a long list of ideological objections in "accepting a pact with the devil," as the Party newspaper reported, Ben Gurion sensed that private concerns were also at stake. Even though a merger of the two Parties was never considered or discussed, any major step toward cooperation would mean that jobs and executive positions would have to be shared as well. Up till the London agreement, *Mapai* and *Histadrut* leaders, with Ben Gurion himself at the forefront, had dreamed of keeping the pie all to themselves. They believed, and Ben Gurion had hammered the illusion into their ears in speech after speech, that the Zionist Executive and the *Yishuv* were their exclusive possessions, and that the Revisionists could go to hell. Now, suddenly, all that had changed. Suddenly, Ben Gurion was willing to share the grand socialist enterprise called Palestine with the same people he had only yesterday dubbed fascists and Nazis.

Jabotinsky had his own battles to face. While his hold over the Revisionists was much stronger than Ben Gurion's always-contested leadership over the Labor Zionists, just several months later, at the Revisionist World Conference, one of his most devoted young disciples, Menachem Begin, rejected the peace pact, declaring, "You may have forgotten that Ben Gurion once called you Vladimir Hitler, but we have a better memory!" Nevertheless, a large majority of Revisionists voted to ratify the agreement.

Returning to Palestine, Ben Gurion was met with vituperative opposition from the *Histadrut's* rank and file, and from his *Mapai* Party. Caricatures of a large-headed Ben Gurion hugging a Jabotinsky with a devil's tail appeared in the Leftist press and on the streets. Ben Gurion's closest colleagues begged him to annul his signature on the pact. Determined to prevail, and risking his political future, the wobbling Labor leader demanded that a referendum be held. After weeks of fist fights and broken windows within the Labor camp itself, an emergency vote was held. Eleven thousand supported the rapprochement, sixteen thousand remained adamantly against.

"You have sinned against the *Yishuv*!" Ben Gurion cried out to the crowd after the result was announced, but to no avail. Putting his reputation on the line, he had fought for peace and ignominiously lost the battle.

A saddened Jabotinsky read the results of the vote in a telegram. But his emotions were mixed. In a letter to Ben Gurion, he wrote: "On learning that the agreement had been rejected, some inner weakness whispered to me, 'Thank God.' And I wondered if perhaps you also felt the same way at the moment. I can't explain why."

Chapter Eight
YAIR

Tzvi handed his father the note that Hannie had asked him to deliver.

"I have gone to Warsaw to meet Avraham," his granddaughter's handwriting read. "I hope to be a married woman when I return to Jerusalem. Pray for me. Love, Hannie."

"She hopes to be a married woman when she returns to Jerusalem," Tevye repeated aloud. "And I hope to be as wealthy as the Rothschilds! What do you say about that?"

Tzvi frowned, knowing that his father disapproved of the match.

"She's a big girl," Tzvi replied. "If that what she wants, why not? Avraham Stern is a *tzaddik*. For years she's waited to marry him without dating anyone else."

"I sent her to America to forget Avraham Stern."

"What's the matter with him?" his son asked.

Tevye sat down in a chair with a groan. Lately, for some reason which he didn't understand, whenever something happened that bothered him, he felt a sharp pain in his lower back.

"I may not be the greatest husband to your mother, or to my first wife, Golda, may she rest in peace, but at least, after finishing my milk rounds, I returned home like a husband should. If your cousin Hannie marries Mr. Stern, she will spend the rest of her life gazing out the window, waiting for him to come home."

"Is it a sin to be an idealist? Didn't you yourself teach us that in this generation, when the Jewish Nation is returning to life in the Land of Israel, no one can live for himself? What comes first is the good of the Nation."

Tevye banged a fist on the table. "Maybe I said it. I say a lot of foolish things. It sounds like something I heard from Rabbi Kook, may his memory be for a blessing. As a general rule, no doubt what he said is true. But not when it comes to my granddaughter!"

Again, Tevye banged his fist on the table, as if that could change her decision. Tzvi shook his head.

"Times have changed, *Abba*," he said. "Young people have minds of their own."

"Nothing has changed," Tevye retorted. "Nothing is knew under the sun. Long ago there were fools who didn't listen to their elders, and the same is true today. Do you think my parents wanted me to marry my Golda, even though she was an angel? No. They had chosen someone else. Did I listen to them? No. And did my daughters want me to remarry after my Golda left this world for the next? Of course they didn't. If I had listened to them, I never would have had a son like you who tells me that times have changed."

"So why be angry at Hannie? She wants Avraham, just like you wanted the women you married. Let her marry whoever she wants."

"Mr. Stern doesn't want her for a wife."

"He's sent for her," Tzvi protested.

"Yes, he's sent for her, but not to be his wife."

Tevye sighed. Maybe he was wrong. Maybe the match was *bershert* – made in Heaven. To whom could he go for advice? Hadn't the Hasidic master, *Rebbe* Nachman of Breslov, taught that a Jew without a Rabbi resembles a monkey pretending to be a man. "*Oy me, Oy mi*," Tevye thought. Rabbi Kook's death had left a gaping hole in his life. Not only in his life, but a darkness had fallen over the entire *Yishuv*, like when a candle goes out in a room that had been illuminated by its light. It seemed that the Stavsky affair had drained the spiritual giant of his Heavenly strength. Not because of the effort he had put into the struggle to free the unjustly accused man, but because of the senseless hatred between brothers which had surrounded the blood libel, polluting the atmosphere in the Holy Land and defiling the Land itself. Nachman, who served as the Rabbi's *shamash*, said that a profound melancholy had seized the Chief Rabbi when the socialist pioneers and their leaders had turned so wrathfully against him for coming to Stavsky's defense, even though Rabbi Kook loved them like children and had always striven to judge them in a favorable light, emphasizing their willingness to sacrifice for the Nation, and the invaluable role they played in the supreme *mitzvah* of settling and rebuilding the Land. Soon after the shameful affair had ended, the festering wound in his stomach which had refused to heal after the pogroms in Jerusalem, Hevron, and Safed, turned into a cancer which ravaged his body.

When Nachman informed his father-in-law that the end was near, Tevye summoned his courage and went to pay a farewell visit at a convalescing home in the Kiryat Moshe neighborhood at the outskirts of the city. Tevye had confronted death many times in his life; he has been with his mother and father until their dying breaths, and he had gently lowered his dear Golda's eyelids so she could rest in peace when the Angel of Death took her away from this world to a more perfect one, but somehow Rabbi Kook was different.

The great Sage lay in bed, propped up with pillows. He wore a dark bathrobe. Blankets covered his legs. His face wasn't the face that Tevye knew and loved. The Chief Rabbi still possessed a royal bearing, but now his noble visage was the portrait of a king exhausted from war. His face was gaunt, pale, and ravaged from suffering. His hair and beard were untypically unkempt, with his black skullcap at the back of his head. Nachman accompanied Tevye into the room and told the Rabbi that he had a visitor, then left them alone. Rabbi Kook opened his eyes, but they lacked their usual luster. Too weak to smile, he raised a hand off the bed.

"Ah, Tevye," he said. "Welcome, my good friend. May your coming be for a blessing."

"We are all disturbed by the Rabbi's weakness and pray for his speeded recovery," Tevye replied.

The dying man spoke in a whisper. Tevye sat in the chair by the bed and bent close to hear. Alas, he reflected, the Tablets of Torah are broken. But their glow still graced the Rabbi's countenance. At times, he addressed his visitor, while at other moments he seemed to be praying, as if he were alone, in some far, distant place.

"What is the great pain that I suffer, you wonder? What is

the source of the infirmity which causes me such great physical and spiritual torment, which has made me like a stranger to brothers and ostracized by fellow Jews? It is due to my inexpressible chagrin at the lack of Heavenly reverence in this exalted generation, to the forgetting of Hashem's Name, the God of Israel. And most especially since this terrible forgetfulness is occurring at the time of the great revival of our Nation. My soul screams within me. My spirit is as restless as a wounded lion. 'Woe to the children who have forgotten their Father.' And the Heavens declare, 'Woe to the Father whose children have forgotten Him.' My darling son, Ephraim, has strayed, and when I think of him, my inward parts are tortured with malaise."

A rattling cough shook Rabbi Kook's body. He waited for the searing pain to subside, then continued. Tevye held his breath.

"I suffer anguish over the neglect of the holy. My soul quakes when I see how the craving for the secular, in ideologies and in deeds, is spreading in the world, capturing hearts and souls and enjoying free expression, while holy aspirations and ideals are seemingly buried under boulders which can't be raised. No one protects our holy treasures; no one explains their exalted meanings to children whose minds have been polluted by foreign, impure wells in the darkness of exile; no one speaks in the language of the generation in order to endear our People to the splendor of holiness and to the glory of our Nation's sacred ways. Over this, I am ill. Over the estrangement from the holy, my whole being shudders. I suffer sufferings of love for my People, which I am prepared to bear, for the sake of our holy Torah and for the sake of Jerusalem, may all of the Nation be cleansed."

Summoning strength, the Chief Rabbi reached out for Tevye's hand.

"Nonetheless, dear Tevye, a mighty certainty increases to grow inside of me that all of the happenings of our times, all of them are manifestations of *Hashem's* glory, hidden in mysteries, and everything will shine forth like a dawning sun to illuminate the Nation in all of its holy splendor. A generation will yet arise and sing to beauty and to life, and it shall discover unending delight from the dew of Heaven. And a People returned to life will hear the treasure of life's secrets from the horizons of the Carmel and the Sharon. A holy light will shine forth and all existence will whisper, the Redemption has come."

Nachman reappeared in the doorway, accompanied by the Rabbi's son. Quietly, they approached the bed. Seeing his son, a flicker of a smile appeared on the Rabbi's lips. Turning his head, his eyes stared up at the ceiling. He let go of Tevye's hand.

"Expanses, expanses, my soul craves Divine expanses," he whispered. "Confine me not in cages of substance or of spirit. I am lovesick. I thirst, I thirst for God. More than the deer for the water streams. Alas, who can describe my pain? The pain of seeking expression. How can I utter the great truth that fills my whole heart? Who will disclose to the world the light stored within my soul? I am bound to the world and to life. All creatures are my brothers. But how can I share with them my light? Whatever I say only dulls my vision. Great is my pain and great is my anguish. O, my God, my God, be a help in my trouble. Find for me the graces of expression. Grant me language and the gift of words. Then I shall declare before the multitudes my fragments of your truth, O my God."

Rabbi Kook's eyes closed. His breath came slowly.

"Father, can I bring you some water," his son asked in a quiet voice.

The Rabbi didn't respond. The Tablets were broken but the pieces still shone. Once again, he opened his eyes.

"O God, help your people," he prayed. "Fill their hearts with the awe of Your Majesty. Strengthen them with Your love. Guide them to follow You with fervor. Kindle in their hearts the light of the Torah. Return them to the pleasant inheritance You have bequeathed to them. Speedily, my God, speedily, soon."

Now that that Rabbi Kook was gone, where could Tevye seek wisdom and advice?

Before the Arab riots of 1929 had forced many Jews to evacuate their homes in the Old City, Baba Shmuel had been a client on Tevye's milk route. Born in Morocco, the holy

Kabbalist wore a long *djellaba* robe with a hood. On the street, he would keep his gaze lowered, never looking beyond the meter directly in front of him. He said that holy sages like Rabbi Yaacov Abuhatzeira could see things that other people couldn't because they didn't look at the things which other people looked upon. Known for his great humbleness, he made his livelihood writing *mezuzot*. Newlyweds often visited him, believing that the parchments he wrote brought blessing to the home.

"If a husband and women let anger into their home, then all of the *mezuzot* in the world won't protect them," Baba Shmuel was wont to tell them.

People suffering from all kinds of problems brought their *mezuzot* to the Rabbi for his inspection. Gazing at the Hebrew letters of the "*Shema*" which were written on the parchment, he suggested ways they could mend their ways and turn misfortune into a blessing. Stories about him, and the amazing miracles which graced the lives of his visitors, were famous all over the city. Once, out of the blue, when Tevye handed him a container of milk, he asked the milkman if he knew a man named Stein.

"The owner of the milk company where I get my milk is named Stein," Tevye answered.

"Please tell him in my name that if he continues adding extra water to the milk he sells, then he should inform his clients and demand a lesser price."

"What?" Tevye mumbled, lost for words.

"And tell him that if he stops this practice immediately and donates the sum he has profited from this deception to a community charity fund, then his daughter will begin speaking again."

Tevye was tongue-tied. Indeed, he had heard from fellow milkmen that Stein's daughter had been stricken with some mysterious muteness.

"If I tell him that, he'll refuse to do business with me," Tevye said.

"On the contrary. If you tell him in my name, and if he makes sincere *tshuva* by repenting over his wrongdoing, then, when the Master of the World heals his daughter, he will offer you a managerial job in his company."

When Tevye relayed the Rabbi's message, Stein repented in his heart and ceased deceiving his customers. Just as Baba Shmuel had suggested, he donated a large sum to the Diskin Orphanage. Lo and behold, his daughter began to speak again! Grateful to Tevye for his part in the miracle, Stein offered the milkman a job with the firm. Tevye sold his milk route and became a district manager of the company in Jerusalem.

After the Arab uprising of 1929 ("*Tarpat*"), Baba Shmuel moved to a small apartment in the neighborhood of Bulcharim. "Ah, Tevye," he said, with his almost toothless smile when his former milkman appeared at his door. "What brings you to Bulcharim?"

"Doesn't the Rabbi know?"

"I know very little. Sometimes I am shown things, that's all."

"My granddaughter, Hannie, thinks she has found her *bershirt*."

"*Mazel tov!*" the Rabbi said. "What is his name?"

"Avraham Stern," Tevye replied.

The Rabbi closed his eyes in deep concentration.

"Oh," he exclaimed in a tone of surprise. "Yair!"

"Her suiter's name is Avraham."

"Yes, I know. Yair Avraham Stern."

Tevye himself didn't know that Stern had adopted the code name Yair for his underground missions.

"He is the *gilgul* of Eleazar Ben Yair," the Kabbalist said.

"Who?" Tevye asked, not recalling the name. The word, *gilgul*, meant reincarnation, which was a basic Kabbalistic belief. The famous mystic, the *Arizal*, who had lived in Safed four-hundred years before under Ottoman rule, had revealed that for errant souls to be purified, in addition to their period of cleansing in the Afterworld, they had to return to this world in a reincarnated form, sometimes again in again, in different bodies and epochs, until their "*tikun*" or rectification was complete.

"The young man is none other than Eleazar Ben Yair," Baba Shmuel explained. "He was a leader of the Sicarri during the Great Revolt against Rome. An uncompromising idealist and patriot, he led his followers in a fierce rebellion against the armies of Rome, and against the Jewish aristocracy who were willing to surrender to foreign rule, as long as they could keep their prestigious standing. When the armies of Titus destroyed Jerusalem, Eleazar Ben Yair escaped from the city and conquered the fortress on Masada which the Romans had captured. With his nine hundred followers, Yair defended the stronghold for three years during a relentless Roman siege. Finally, with no more food or supplies, the staunch and uncompromising commander convinced his comrades to commit mass suicide, rather than be captured and tortured by the Romans. That is the reason why Masada has become a symbol of Jewish bravery and defiance."

A perplexed look spread over Tevye's face.

"You should feel proud to have such a *hatan* in your family," the Rabbi said.

"If he was such a great hero, why did he have to come back to this world in another reincarnation?" Tevye asked, wanting to be absolutely sure of the groom's credentials before he agreed to the match.

"Perhaps because he committed suicide," the Rabbi replied. "Given the circumstances, we admire his courage and his concern for his comrades, and we admire his spirit of freedom, his self-sacrifice for the honor of the Israelite Nation, and his devotion to God. Nevertheless, being killed by a Gentile, for example, is considered a more sanctified death, as in the case of the righteous martyrs of Lod."

"Being killed by a Gentile? What does that mean?"

Baba Shmuel didn't answer.

"Does Avraham Stern have to be killed by a Gentile in order to complete his *tikun*?" Tevye asked.

"Perhaps," the Kabbalist replied.

"Then why should my granddaughter marry him?"

"To be married to such a man, and to play a part in the war he is yet to fight, is an incomparable honor."

"What war?" Tevye asked.

"The war that Yair didn't finish."

"The war against Rome?"

"Against their descendants who now rule in our Land."

In a way, Tevye was sorry he had asked the Rabbi's

advice. Mystical matters like reincarnations were over the
milkman's head. Even if he no longer delivered fresh milk
house-to-house with his donkey and cart, he was still a
simple Jew. And even though he was an "honorary
commander" of the secret *Irgun* underground, what war was
the Rabbi talking about? Against the Arabs? Against the
British? Could it be that his granddaughter's future husband
was going to be the leader of the war of Jewish
independence that he always spoke about? To that
fantastical prospect, Tevye could only think of one word –
"*gevalt.*"

Reeling from the staggering revelation, Tevye went to the
city library and asked for a history book about Rome's
conquest of Jerusalem. The librarian brought him a
thousand-page tome in English called, *The Complete Works of
Josephus*, and told him to look at the chapter, *The Jewish War*.
While the Old City milkman had learned to understand and
speak a respectable English, no one could mistake his
mastery of the language for Winston Churchill's. He knew
that the author of the volume, Josephus Flavius, was a
Jewish soldier called Josef ben Matitiyahu who had deserted
to the camp of the Romans. Winning the favor of Vespasian
and Titus with his literary skills, he became the official
chronicler of their battles against Israel, recording the
capture and destruction of Jerusalem. How much of the
account was true, and how much was fiction, who could
tell? Tevye had learned from the journalists of his own day
not to believe everything he read. For instance, in the
Aronov murder case, the Leftist newspaper accounts of the
happenings were dramatically different than those which
appeared in the Rightist tabloids, "*Hazit HaAm*" and
"*HaYarden.*" Obviously, journalism was not the art of
objective reporting, but rather, journalists were the
mouthpieces for the political parties which published the
newspapers for which they worked. At least, that was the
situation in Palestine. No wonder the Jewish traitor,
Josephus, who was employed by the imperial family, spoke
disparagingly of the Zealots and Sicarri rebels who terrified
the legions of Rome. But, to the credit of Josephus, even
though he received a monthly stipend while writing his

historical opus in a magnificent villa in Rome, in his account of the fall of Masada, Eleazar Ben Yair, and the courageous Jewish defenders of the famous mountaintop citadel, were portrayed as valiant and tragic heroes.

Sitting down a long table in the library, Tevye began to read the chapter which described the fall of Masada, plowing through the literary English like a farmer tilling a dry and rocky field with a rusted plow. The Jewish soldier-turned-Roman-historian claimed to have heard the detailed account from two elderly women who chose to conceal themselves in a cavern, rather than the share the fate of the other nine-hundred-and-sixty souls, who chose suicide rather than capture at the hands of the merciless Romans.

Reading Yair's dramatic speech to his comrades, as they faced their last stand, barricaded in the Masada fortress, with raging fires surrounding the mountain plateau, and Roman troops prepared for a final, devastating assault on the stronghold, Tevye could very well picture Avraham Stern delivering the rallying words with a towering passion, infused with the spirit of God:

Then the Roman commander, Silva, deemed it best to burn down the wooden wall guarding the entrance to the fortress at the peak, so he gave an order that the soldiers should throw a great number of burning torches upon it. When it was set on fire, its dryness made the fire burst into a mighty flame. Now, at the very beginning of this conflagration, a north wind proved terrible to the Romans, for by bringing the flame downward, the fire endangered the Romans, and they were almost in despair of success, fearing their catapults and war machines would be burnt. But all of a sudden, the wind changed toward the south, as if by Divine Providence, and blew strongly the opposite way, carrying the flame and driving it against the fortress's outer wall of defense, which was now on fire through its entire thickness. So the Romans, having been granted assistance from Above, returned to their camp with joy, and resolved to attack their enemy the very next day. That night, they doubled the number of guards on watch, lest any of the Jews should run away.

However, Eleazar ben Yair did not once think of fleeing, nor would he permit anyone else to do so. When he saw their wall burned down by the fire, and could devise no other way of escaping, he set before their eyes what the Romans would do to them, their children, and their wives, if the Romans got them into their power. To avoid that certain and horrible fate, he proposed that they all slay themselves together, encouraging them to take this course of action by the following speech:

"Since we, long ago, my generous friends, resolved never to be servants to the Romans, nor to any other being than to God himself, who alone is the true and just Lord of mankind, the time is now come that obliges us to make our resolution true in practice. We were the very first to revolt against them, and we are the last who fight against them; and I cannot but esteem it a favor that God hath granted us, that it is still in our power to die bravely, and in a state of freedom, which hath not been the case of others, who were conquered, enslaved and killed.

"Those that are already dead in the war, we should esteem them blessed, for they are dead in defending, and not in betraying their liberty. But as to the multitude of those that are now enslaved under the Romans, who does not pity their condition? And who would not make haste to die, before he would suffer the same miseries with them? Some of them have been put upon the rack, and tortured with fire and whippings, and so died. Some have been half devoured by wild beasts, and yet have been preserved alive to be devoured by other beasts a second time, in order to afford laughter and sport to our enemies.

"And where is now that great city, the metropolis of the Jewish Nation, Jerusalem, which was fortified by so many walls round about, which had so many fortresses and large towers to defend it, which could hardly contain the weapons prepared for the war, and which had so many ten thousands of men to fight for it? Where is this city that was believed to have God Himself inhabiting therein? It is now demolished to the very foundations, while nothing remains but the camp of those who have destroyed it, foreigners who dwell upon its ruins; and some unfortunate old men who also lie upon the ashes of the Temple, and a few women preserved alive by the enemy, for our bitter shame and reproach. Now who is there that envisions these things in his mind, and yet is able to bear the sight of the sun?

Who is there so unmanly, and so desirous of living, as not to act out of freedom while he is still alive?

"It is very plain that we shall be taken within a day's time; but it is still a praiseworthy thing to die in a glorious manner, together with our dearest friends. This is what our enemies themselves cannot by any means hinder, although they be very desirous to take us alive. Nor can we propose to continue to fight them and beat them. Let our wives die before they are abused, and our children before they have tasted slavery; and after we have slain our loved ones, let us bestow that glorious benefit upon one another mutually, and preserve ourselves in freedom, as an excellent funeral monument for us. But first let us destroy our money and the fortress by fire; for I am well assured that this will be a great grief to the Romans, that they shall not be able to seize our bodies, and shall not avail of our wealth also; and let us spare nothing but our provisions; for they will be a testimonial when we are dead that we were not subdued for want of necessaries, but that, according to our original resolution, we have preferred death before slavery. Therefore, let us die before we become slaves under our enemies, and let us go out of the world, together with our children and our wives, in a state of freedom, with the praises of God on our lips!"

2.

A twenty-three-year-old woman stood alone on the bow of the ship as it rose over a wave and sped forward into the black, windy night, on its way through the Mediterranean Sea toward Italy. The foreboding roar of the sea enhanced her feeling that she had set out on a dangerous and unpredictable voyage - as dangerous and unpredictable as the man she was traveling to see, the man she loved, the man with whom she yearned to spend her life, even though she had never been able to understand him or really know who he was.

The truth was, Avraham hadn't mentioned marriage in his letter. But why else would he ask her to join him in Warsaw? His family lived in nearby in Soblek, so she could easily meet his parents during the trip. He knew her condition about meeting him – if he didn't want to marry her, she didn't want to see him again.

While she wouldn't admit it, her decision to go had been brought to a boil by another letter he had sent.

"You must know from the newspapers about the frightening situation of the Jews in Poland. In the light of the growing danger, I have decided that it is my duty as a Zionist to save a Jewish soul by 'marrying' a woman fictitiously, so that she will be able to escape the country. I will not do so if you object, but it seems to be that saving a life must outweigh any personal feeling or interest. You should know that marriages of this sort are quite prevalent here for two important reasons. First, by 'marrying' a man from *Eretz Yisrael*, a Polish woman can receive a visa to Palestine without the long wait and great difficulty involved in receiving an official certificate of immigration, and secondly, the women are willing to pay a considerable fee, which can be used to purchase more 'farming equipment.' The scheme is a marriage of convenience for the benefit of everyone involved, and divorces are easy to arrange after the visa has been granted. Since I have become a *shadchan* of sorts, matching Polish women with the men from Israel, I might as well perform the same kindness myself for one of our poor sisters."

While Hannie respected his idealism, and valued his total dedication to the Zionist cause, she didn't fancy the idea that Avraham was spending his days interviewing damsels in distress who wanted to escape from Poland. And though she tried to share his selfless devotion to *Am Yisrael*, Tevye's granddaughter lost sleep at night, ruminating over the possibility that he would marry someone else. What if she didn't agree to divorce him?! And what if his "fictitious" young wife was beautiful, and cultured, more free-spirited than she was, and not the granddaughter of a guardian of the Torah like Tevye, who had broken Avraham's hand for having had the brazen *chutzpah* to touch her?

The chill of the night, the dark restless ocean, and her bleak and somber thoughts, caused Hannie to shiver. Did he love her? Hannie didn't know. He said that he did, but she wasn't sure. Avraham was unknowable. One moment he laughed at a Charlie Chaplin movie like everyone else, then his eyes left the screen and he was suddenly somewhere else, no longer in the cinema, no longer at her side, even though he held her hand, his heart and mind were off on a some faraway journey, or fighting some war, or hiding from the police in a damp and rat-filled basement. He lived in many different worlds at once, this world and the next, the present, the past, and the future. Hannie never knew where he was when he drifted away into one of his trances. And then, the next moment, he was back, laughing, smiling, and charming everyone around him. In a way she couldn't fathom, he was different from normal people, existing on some different plane, as if there were many different Avrahams to his being - the witty scholar, the passionate lover, the caring Avraham, the frightening Avraham, the uncontrollable Avraham, the introspective Avraham, and the little boy. She felt so simple in comparison, far beneath his level, not a genuine match, nor his other half at all. In fact, she didn't understand why he bothered with her – she was so different. He was so exalted and she was so plain. He could have ended their connection long ago, yet he had continued to write to her for the past four years, telling her what he was doing, sharing all of his feelings and thoughts, his dreams and his doubts, his yearnings and his fears.

When the High Criminal Court in Palestine decreed that Avraham Stavsky be executed by hanging, Avraham had written:

"The anguish of the verdict weighs down on us with a terrible heaviness, and we hope, with all of the Nation, that his innocence will come to light. The pain knows no boundary – not because he received a death sentence, but because there are thousands of lowly creatures who congratulate one another and dance over their victory, precisely at a time when European Jewry is so threatened. Very, very shortly, the *Yishuv*, and all the Israelite Nation, will wake up and be forced to face the death sentence which Germany has prepared for it. In these moments, it is very difficult for me to remain in Florence and continue my research of Greek Literature."

Two months passed without receiving another letter. Then an enveloped arrived with Polish stamps and a postmark from Warsaw.

"Yes, I am in Warsaw," he wrote. "The nature of my new work makes it impossible to explain everything in a letter. I left Florence without finishing my studies. What can I do? Life often controls our destinies more than we control life. But I am very happy that I am engaged in work that will benefit others, for the sake of our cherished, holy, and beloved Homeland, which we love with the last breath of our lives."

"Here is a poem I wrote in a Florence café before leaving the city. What do you think of it?" he asked.

> I know that a day or night will come
> When I shall fall alone,
> Dying in the field of battle
> And around me beasts of prey,
> Wilderness, death, sweltering heat.
> How sweet to die in the field of battle,
> How pleasant the heat of the desert,
> When my eyes facing the shadow of death
> Will see the torches of victory.

What did she think of it? His images frightened her. He wrote about dying in battle with the certainty of a prophet who knows what the future will bring. A similar poem arrived from Warsaw where he was, "buying more farming equipment, which we will use to insure our future in the Land."

> Yes I am a poet and fighter too!
> Today I write with the pen
> Tomorrow with the sword.
> Today I'll write in ink
> Tomorrow I'll write in blood.
> Today on paper, tomorrow on flesh.
> Heaven has blessed me with book and with sword.
> Inscribed is my fate: soldier and bard.
> In fiery flames and purple blood
> The vision is woven
> Of he who fights for his liberty.
> On battle's eve
> Throughout the camp the anthem rings.
> Grim is the fight to the finish.

If she could be his shelter from the stormy winds and raging wars in his mind, that was all that she wanted. She would be there when he needed her. She was ready to be his wife, just to be his wife, without demanding anything more.

3.

After a howling, three-day sea voyage with stops in Alexandria and Tunis, the shipped docked at Rome. Hannie didn't waste time on sightseeing. She took a train to Milan, then boarded an express to Vienna, where she changed trains for Warsaw. The money for the trip came from her earnings as a seamstress upon her return to Jerusalem. After graduating from Columbia University with a general Liberal Arts degree, she remained in New York another year to earn a degree in Education. But when she arrived home, sharing an apartment on Jaffa Street with two other young women, she couldn't find a job as a teacher. The Gymnasium High School in Tel Aviv offered her a position, but after living in New York for such a long time, Hannie wanted to be closer to her family in Jerusalem. So she went back to her old job with a dressmaker, where she was put in charge of the wedding-dress department! Fashioning gowns for brides-to-be was an enjoyable occupation, but, day after day, Hannie kept wondering when her time would come for her to stand under the *chuppah*, attired like a queen, at her own wedding. Just in case Avraham decided to marry her in Warsaw, Hannie chose a bridal style she liked and sewed herself a gown whose bulky folds took up most of a suitcase. Filling the remaining space with clothes that were suitable for Poland's colder weather, she decided to take along another suitcase filled with towels, bedsheets, tablecloths, sewing fabric, Sabbath candlesticks, a set of cutlery, and other small household items customarily included in a dowry, to help the newlyweds get started in their new home, in the event that Avraham had to remain in Europe before returning to *Eretz Yisrael*.

The train ride was long and tiring. As usual, all along the way, on the ship, at the port in Rome, in train stations, and on the train, men of all shapes and sizes attempted to strike up a conversation with the pretty young woman, but Hannie cut short all of their advances with curt replies and a stone-like expression, even turning her back rudely to let it be known that she wasn't available. On the ride to Vienna, a well-dressed, mustachioed man sitting opposite her kept flashing friendly smiles which Hannie ignored. She straightened her back and drew her legs closer to her seat, not wanting their knees to touch as the train swayed back and forth along the tracks. Closing her eyes, she pretended to sleep. Finally, after a pronounced silence, he offered to treat her to dinner in the train's dining cabin. Without bothering to answer, Hannie stood up and moved to a different seat, next to a woman wearing a coat with a thick fur collar, and holding a small, obedient poodle in her lap.

For most of the ride, she sat rigidly in her seat, reading from the book she had compiled of Avraham's poems. Copying them from his letters, she had them typeset and printed in a small printing shop on Jaffa Street. Wanting the book to look special, she had it bounded with an expensive leather cover, as a surprise wedding present. For a whole week she pondered over a suitable title, which she had the bookbinder engrave on the cover - "Anonymous Soldiers and other Poems of Redemption." Though she knew them all by heart, she read them once again to help pass the time, and to let everyone know that she was a busy person with no time for frivolous chatter.

A cold and foreign land passed by outside the train window while she read yet another poem obsessed with premonitions of martyrdom and death:

> Behold, I swear an oath of faith
> To the Homeland, to the Nation, to freedom.
> I swear to sacrifice my thoughts, my life,
> To enlist, and to fight, and to be killed!
>
> Not to flee, not to betray, not to abandon,
> Whether in the underground, the dungeon, or at the front.
> I swear to safeguard the holy mission all of my life
> For the sake of the Nation's future.
>
> With my blood I will defend the Land of Israel.

With my life – the life of the Hebrew Nation.
To sanctify its name amongst the nations,
Allow me, O Guardian of Israel, thus increase my task!

And in troubled times, if I betray my brothers,
If I forget and betray my covenant,
Like a leper, like a living corpse let me be,
And cursed in my death I shall be!

And behold, I swear an oath of faith
To the Homeland, to the Nation, to Freedom.
I swear to sacrifice my thoughts, my life,
To enlist, and to fight, and to be killed!

Once again, Hannie trembled, wondering what kind of husband Avraham could possibly be, already married to a mission that excluded all other things, even his own life and being.

"Maybe you've changed you mind?" a voice inquired.

It belonged to the wealthy-looking creature with the moustache.

"The dining car is still open," he said.

"No is no," she answered.

"A person has to eat," he continued. "Having traveled this line in the past, I can vouch for the excellence of the cuisine."

"Please leave me alone," Hannie said tartly.

The Jewish lady passenger sitting beside her gave the intruder a curious look.

"Are you traveling to Warsaw like I am?" he asked.

"To meet my fiancé," she answered.

"Your fiancé? Now that's a lucky man indeed. Perhaps I will challenge him to a dual! With pistols at ten paces."

"He's a soldier and a very good shot," Hannie told him.

The lady beside her leaned over and whispered in her ear. "Why don't you dine with him? He looks rich."

Hannie stood up. Holding the book of poems and taking her traveling bag down from the overhead rack, she strode away down the aisle, calling out, "Conductor! Conductor!"

The rich man chuckled, watching the young woman yank at the sliding cabin door and walk off into the next compartment.

Though Hannie had only been a little girl when the Cossacks expelled the Jews from Anatevka, she recalled how their wagon had stopped at the crossroads outside of the village, and the decision her *Zaide* had made to set off for the Promised Land. She remembered the long journey and the broad expanses, verdant forests, rushing rivers, and towering mountains which characterized the landscapes of Poland, Austria, and Italy, so very different from the Biblical landscapes of *Eretz Yisrael*, with its sand dunes, stark deserts, and arid plains. The excitement she felt now as the train rushed along the tracks emanated not from the ever-changing views outside the windows, nor from any feeling of nostalgia for the "old country," but only from the ever-nearing prospect of seeing Avraham at the train station in Warsaw, standing out from the crowd in his tailored suit and dapper hat. If he reached out to embrace her, would she resist? Could she? After waiting for more than four years?

But, lo and behold, in the middle of the night, when the train's whistled blasted, and the brakes screeched over the tracks, and the steam of the locomotive wafted like a cloud in the dark Warsaw station, when the smoke cleared away from the train and Hannie stepped down to the platform, Avraham was nowhere to be seen in the crowd. Surely, Hannie thought, he was waiting in the station, drinking a cup of coffee in an all-night café. With a fast-beating heart, she inched forward, her progress slowed by the line of descending passengers. On the platform, people rushed forward to greet family and friends, but Avraham wasn't among them. Hannie gazed right and left, waiting to glimpse the stylish hat he always wore, but all the hats she saw belonged to other faces. Happy people jostled her this way and that, but no one rushed forward to hug her. Was he late? Had he forgotten the date of her arrival? Had something happened to him? Hannie's heart suddenly ached with a terrible fright. Had he changed his mind? Had he married some young Polish woman, not to get her an immigration certificate, but for real?

Gradually, the platform emptied in the vaulted station. Save for occasional hisses of steam, the quiet trains seemed to be sleeping. Who could imagine that in another few years, train cars overloaded with frightened Jews would wheel off down the tracks of this civilized metropolis, heading toward Hitler's diabolical slaughterhouses? By the baggage car, Hannie found one of her suitcases, but the large piece of luggage filled with her dowry was nowhere to be found. Flustered, she hurried over to a porter.

"One of my suitcases is missing," she told him in Russian. He shook his head, not understanding.

"I don't speak Polish," she said in English.

The man shook his head again with a frown. Lifting her one suitcase onto a pushcart, he motioned for her to follow. Exasperated, and fighting back her tears, Hannie followed him into the large rotunda of the station, the largest hall she had seen in her life. At a window marked INFORMATION, she explained to the clerk that one of her suitcases had been stolen or lost. Puffing on a foul-smelling cigarette, he instructed her to return in the morning when the Lost and Found Office would open. Feeling lost herself in a strange and foreign city, Hannie asked where she could find the nearest hotel. There were two, the clerk replied, almost directly across the street. Handing the porter a coin, she lugged her large suitcase to the smaller hotel. She took a room for the rest of the night, which she spent crying, too heartbroken to sleep. In the morning, she returned to the Lost and Found window in the now crowded train station, leaving her name and travel information with a different clerk who told her to come back in a few days to see if the missing baggage had been discovered. Then, feeling completely disoriented by her surroundings, and still wiping back tears, she went to search for Avraham, according to the address he had written on his letters. A taxi driver took her to 32 Vareska Street, apartment number 9. Climbing up the stairwell, she came to a door with a small sign that matched the sender's name on his envelopes: "Soresky." A young girl answered her knock.

"Avraham Stern?" Hannie asked, showing her the envelope of a letter.

A mature, woman's voice called out in Polish from within the apartment.

"Who is it?"

"A lady looking for Avraham Stern," the girl answered.

"Take him upstairs."

"Do you speak Yiddish?" Hannie asked the girl.

"Yes," she replied.

"I come from the *Eretz Yisrael*," Hannie told her.

The girl smiled. "We want to move there," she said.

"Avraham lives here?" Hannie asked.

"He boards with another family upstairs on the top floor," the girl answered, leading Hannie up another flight of stairs.

He lived with a family named Chanowitz. Only the mother was at home, a plump *balabusta* in her sixties, dressed in a house robe, apron, and slippers. When she heard that Hannie came from "*Eretz HaKodesh*," she immediately sat the distressed and weary traveler in the small kitchen, set a generous chunk of homemade *mandlbroyt* on a plate, and began to boil water for tea.

"*Es and gedenk*," she said. "Eat and remember to thank God."

Not having eaten anything for hours, and not knowing where else she would find something *kosher*, Hannie treated herself to a bite.

"It's delicious," she said.

"Most of the women Avraham meets here are Polish, hoping to go to *Eretz Yisrael*. What brings you in the other direction?" she asked.

"We're old friends," Hannie replied, piqued to hear about the other women in Avraham's life, even though she knew it was official Zionist business.

Mrs. Chanowitz said that Avraham had gone off to *shul* like he did every morning. Sometimes he came back right away; sometimes he didn't come home until late at night. Sometimes, the next day.

"He says he sells books, but if he sells books, then I'm the star dancer in the Polish ballet. Where are you staying in Warsaw? With family? In a hotel? Don't bother to waste your money. You can stay here with us. Our children are all married and flown away the coop. Would that the Master of the World take us all away to the Land of Israel before the dogs go wild. My husband is a Rabbi and a teacher. On his salary, how we survive is a miracle. Avraham is a smart boy.

At night, he sits and talks with my husband. They learn Torah together. A *baal tshuva mamash*! When he got here, he acted like half a *shaygetz*, but now he eats kosher, keeps *Shabbos*, and puts on *tefillin*. Instead of finding make-believe husbands for women to marry so they can go to Israel, he needs to find an *eshes chayil* himself who will keep him from falling off the end of the planet. Maybe it's you?"

Hannie immediately recognized the flamboyant knock on the door. As she stood up from her chair, her whole body trembled. When Avraham saw her standing behind Mrs. Chanowitz, his mouth opened wide in surprise. Though over four years had passed, he hadn't changed a bit. The same keen grey eyes, the same thin lips, still wearing a suit and tie with a kerchief in the lapel, and holding a white Stetson hat in his hands. He could have been an actor in a Hollywood movie.

"Hannie!" he muttered in surprise. "When did you get here?"

Mrs. Chanowitz gazed back and forth between them, trying to understand the sudden electricity in the air. Avraham eyes lit up like a leopard's in the dark. He looked like he wanted to pounce forward, but his landlady blocked his path. Unable to contain her emotions, Hannie burst into tears. She collapsed back down in the chair, her body heaving with sobs. Avraham stood trembling, at a loss for words.

"Why weren't you at the train station?" Tevye's heart-broken granddaughter cried.

"Good God," he stammered. "I must have forgotten. I'm sorry. I've been so busy. Hannila, forgive me," he pleaded.

He stepped forward to embrace her, but Mrs. Chanowitz stood in his way, as if she were shielding a daughter.

"I must have mixed up the dates," he said. "What a fool I am."

"You didn't come because you don't care," Hannie accused, unable to stop crying.

"No, no, that's not true," he said, flustered. Then, facing his landlady, he tried to explain. "I invited her to come to Warsaw. We've known each other for years. I forgot the date she was coming, that's all. It isn't the end of the world. Hannie, stop crying, please."

His plea went unheeded. Mrs. Chanowitz put a comforting hand on the sobbing girl's shoulder. "It's a misunderstanding that's all," she said. "*In a sheynem epl gefint men a mol a vorem,*" she told her in Yiddish, comforting her. "In a beautiful apple, sometimes you find a worm. Avraham is a good boy. He isn't a *shikker*. He doesn't drink, and he doesn't run around with other girls. You've found yourself a *mentch*, so there's no reason to *plotz*. He's here now and that's all that matters."

Hannie's sobs turned to calmer sniffles. Mrs. Chanowitz flashed her male boarder a disapproving look. Avraham reached into his inside jacket pocket, pulled out an envelope, and extracted a handful of tickets, which he set on the table for Hannie to see.

"Look. I purchased tickets for concerts and plays for the next two weeks. I am so happy you are here! It's a dream come true. Please, Hannila. Stop crying. Let's take a walk outside. I'll show you around. Warsaw is a grand city. There's so much to see and do."

Leading her downstairs, Avraham stopped in the hallway and grabbed her like a lion that hasn't eaten for weeks. She pushed him away, but her strength was no match for his.

"How I've missed you!" he said, leaning forward to give her a kiss.

"No!" Hannie protested, shaking her head back and forth, feeling that in another moment, all her resistance would collapse. She wanted to hold him as much as he longed to hold her, but she first wanted to hear him propose. "No more kisses!" she exclaimed.

"Please, Hannie. If I don't kiss you, I'll die!"

Someone coughed in the corridor. "Don't die in the hallway," a voice said in Yiddish. Avraham stiffened and let her go. The trim-bearded Rabbi Chanowitz stood gazing at them.

Avraham laughed awkwardly. "Rabbi Chanowitz!" he exclaimed. "Good morning! We were just on the way outside. Hannie has come all the way from *Eretz Yisrael*."

Giving her a push, he led her toward the stairs. The Rabbi backed out of their way.

"We will speak about this later," he said as they passed him.

When Avraham and Hannie reached the sidewalk, Avraham couldn't contain a little chuckle and either could she. Soon, they were laughing hysterically, releasing their pent-up emotions, as if the encounter in the stairwell was the funniest thing that ever happened on earth.

"Can you ever forgive me?" he asked.

"I forgive you," she said.

He held out his hand and she took it. Like young lovers, they walked down the street, surrounded by busy Warsaw. The life of the city sped by, but they were elsewhere, in their own different world. Spotting a floral shop, Avraham hurried inside and returned with a bouquet of roses which he gallantly handed to her with a theatrical bow.

"A toast!" Avraham exclaimed with his most winning smile, as they relaxed in a sidewalk café. The food wasn't *kosher*, and the wine wasn't *kosher*, so they ordered two beers. "To the most wonderful two weeks in the world!"

"Why only two weeks?" Hannie asked.

"Not long enough? Then let it be three!"

"Why not a lifetime?" she asked, still holding the chilly glass poised in the air.

Avraham kept smiling but didn't alter his words. "How is your grandfather, Tevye?" he asked, changing the subject.

Hannie didn't want to talk small talk. She hadn't journey thousands of miles to talk about the price of eggs and the weather. But with customers sitting at the tables around them, it wasn't the time and the place to reveal the turbulent emotions she felt in her heart.

"I don't see him so often," she answered. "Sometimes, I visit the family for a meal on *Shabbat*. *Saba* likes to steer the conversation to politics, and Tzvi likes to argue with him. My grandfather speaks about Ze'ev Jabotinsky the way he used to talk about *Moshe Rabainu*. Tzvi doesn't share his enthusiasm. He thinks that Jabotinsky is too enamored with the British, just the way Weizmann and Ben Gurion are."

"Your cousin is right," Avraham said. "A lot of people

admire Jabotinsky for his posture of standing up to the *goyim*, but, in my opinion, he isn't so different from all of the other parlor-room Zionists in London who cling to the illusion that the British are our friends. Jabotinsky is a great patriot, to be sure, but his strategy of negotiating with the British, demanding a Jewish Army for Palestine to protect us from the Arabs, is fundamentally flawed. As long as a Jewish fighting force is beholden to British authority, the moment the British decide to take away our weapons, the Jewish brigades will collapse. Instead of relying on the British, we have to rely on ourselves. A Jewish underground is what we need. Once we begin, the masses will follow."

Then, for the first time, he inducting her into a part of his life which he had hitherto kept secret. Speaking quietly and leaning forward so that only she could hear, he told her about the "*Irgun*," and about some of the people involved with him, without mentioning names. Her pulse was still beating rapidly from being together with him once again, and he was leaning so close to her, it was hard for her to concentrate on his words. His assignment, he confided, was to acquire weapons in Poland and Finland by raising money from wealthy Jews, and to purchase rifles and guns from private gun dealers, and from the Polish Government. He arranged the transport of the "farming equipment" on cargo ships traveling to Palestine with new immigrants- "*olim*" - with the help of sympathetic Jews in the shipping industry. The suitcases filled with weapons were mixed in with the luggage of the *olim*, and when the boats reached Jaffa and Haifa, Jewish officials connected with the *Irgun* made sure that the specially-marked suitcases were loaded onto the truck which carried the baggage of the new arrivals to the "*Beit Olim*" absorption center, where the immigrants were temporarily quartered. An *Irgun* agent made sure the suitcases carrying the weapons were delivered to the organization's secret weapons caches around the country.

Avraham told Hannie that in Warsaw he posed as a publisher of detective stories, using the pseudonym, Haggai Artzi, selling detective magazines which he translated into Polish and Yiddish.

"In my dealings on behalf of the *Irgun*, I use the code name, Yair," he said.

Hannie felt privileged to share this secret side of his life, as if he were breaking down a wall that had stood between them. She told him about her lost or stolen suitcase, not revealing that it contained a wedding gown and the small *"nedunia"* dowry she had brought along for their new home. She decided to let him propose in his own way, when he felt the time was right. Surely, she surmised, he wanted to surprise her in some theatrical way, on a rowboat in the middle of a river, or in a poem that he would read on stage in some smoky cabaret, and she didn't want to spoil his plan. Or perhaps Avraham would propose on the way to visit his parents. In any event, the suitcase filled with the wedding *nedunia* was never found.

Avraham wanted to rent a small hotel room for the both of them during her stay, but Hannie adamantly refused. She even refused to let him enter the hotel room she had taken by the train station. Finally, they agreed that he would continue to sleep at the Chanowitz residence, while she lodged downstairs in the Soresky apartment, where Mrs. Chanowitz's daughter lived with her husband and children. Rabbi Chanowitz gave Avraham a good scolding for his unseemly behavior with Hannie in the hallway of the building, explaining to him the *"niddah"* laws of ritual purity, but as much as Avraham was determined to keep *kosher* and observe the Sabbath, the rule prohibiting an unmarried man and woman to kiss seemed like an ordeal beyond his endurance. While he understood that God hadd chosen the Jewish People to be His special holy Nation, a man was not made out of tablets of stone. Given the overpowering emotions he felt, the "hands-off" policy didn't enhance his growing endearment to Judaism. But, to please Hannie, and recalling Tevye's warning when the iron-hand milkman had crushed the bones in his fingers, Avraham did his best to respect her wishes and the fences of Jewish law, though it would not be truthful to say that he always succeeded.

Avraham took Hannie on a trolley-car ride along the broad boulevards of the city, and on a leisurely boat ride along the

Vistula River. While Warsaw boasted many elegant palaces
and stately buildings, and the river was wider than all of the
rivers in Zion combined, Hannie felt disconnected from
everything around her, save Avraham. Everything in Poland
seemed so Gentile and foreign. She had experienced the
same feeling of strangeness and not belonging during her
years in America. Even though New York City abounded
with exciting events and dazzling sights, and even though
there were neighborhoods crowded with Jews, like in
Warsaw, the broad avenues of Manhattan and its towering
skyscrapers weren't a part of her soul. In comparison, the
simple, dirt streets of Olat HaShachar, and the massive stone
walls of the Old City in Jerusalem, were a part of her.
Avraham, she knew, felt the same way, but, for the time
being, he had to be in Poland, he insisted, even though he
yearned to return to the sun-drenched fields of Israel with
its never-ending galaxies of stars.

They attended two Chopin concerts, a play in Yiddish by
Sholom Aleichem, and a play in Russian by Chekov. He
took her to the Warsaw Ballet, to a famous cabaret, and they
spent a day at the zoo. Walking through the Jewish ghetto
on a Sunday morning, Hannie was startled to discover such
a thriving religious community. Streets after streets were
clustered with Hasidic and Haredi Jews, *kosher* shops, and
signs in Yiddish.

"There are more Jews here than in all of *Eretz Yisrael*," she
noted in surprise. "Why don't they all come to Israel?"

"First of all, they can't. The British grant us a limited
amount of immigration certificates each year, and the Jewish
Agency makes sure that very few religious Jews get on the
list. But even if they had the chance, most of the
Ultra-Orthodox wouldn't come as long as the *Mashiach*
hasn't arrived. They believe that it's his job to return the
Jews to Zion, not the Jewish Agency's. To them, Herzl, and
Jabotinsky, and Ben Gurion are all agents of the devil. They
want the Redemption to be complete from the start, without
having to roll up their cuffs and get their shoes dirty
plowing fields and draining swamps. But I am very afraid,
my dear, sweet Hannie, that if the world doesn't stop the
Nazi menace now, the Jews in this ghetto won't be around

when the *Mashiach* finally shows up to bring them all home to Israel. The only thing he will find will be their skeletons and charred corpses."

Avraham bought her some delicious-smelling cakes in a *kosher* bakery. Outside the shop, while church bells tolled in the distance throughout the city, they sat on a bench in a ghetto park, surrounded by scores of young, idle Jews.

"They have no work and no prospects," Avraham told her. "Many are university graduates who can't find employment. Government positions are closed to them. Of the three-and-a-half million Jews in Poland, a third live below the poverty line. Unless we can get them to *Eretz Yisrael*, they are sure to perish."

"Surely, God will answer our prayers," Hannie said.

A faraway stare gripped Avraham's face, the same ice-cold stare which had frightened Hannie in the past, as if he were gazing at the Angel of Death.

"Uri Zvi Greenberg says that we must pray with rifles," he told her. "But I say that we will pray with rifles, machine guns, and bombs."

Hannie shuddered.

As Sunday church bells continued to sound throughout Warsaw, Avraham read her parts of a poem, written by Uri Zvi Greenberg, called, "In the Kingdom of the Cross," prophesizing a terrible destruction to come. The poem was a ghoulish depiction of a Europe filled with anguish and death. Jewish corpses hung from trees, called grief-trees, while bodies of Jews were piled high in forests and villages called "griefwood," and rivers flowed with Jewish blood until their banks turned crimson. The poet, Avraham said, blamed Christianity's age-old hatred of the Jews for the unprecedented holocaust he saw approaching on the blackening horizon.

The lamb lies down with outstretched neck in the griefwood.
Wounded, split open, I spit blood on the crucifixes in Europe.
Quiver, you young and old, with brains scattered in the griefwood!

For two-thousand years a silence has burned under these
trees,
A poison that gathers in the caverns and festers—and I do
not know
What all this means: two-thousand years of blood, of
silence,
Yet not one mouth has cleansed the poisoned spit from its
tongue.
Each murder at the hands of the Heathen is recorded in
books.
Only the reaction is missing, our response to these deaths.
The grief-trees grows so tall, and the tree-tops writhe in
anguish,
And the dripping blood of corpses is like dew within the
sea.
Mighty Europe! Kingdom of the cross!

Jews that hang on crosses come to me in dreams.
I see their wild heads protruding from the windows of
their houses.
They cannot even see the threat that crouches all around
them.
A black prophecy pours a deadly vile in your sleep.
Cathedral bells have robbed you of your ability to know
when it begins.

I speak to you a prophecy, the Black Prophecy.
Yet you will not perceive the horror in your bodies.
The mindless talk will continue from your burning lips.
Jews! Jews!
As poison gas begins to seep into their temples
And suddenly the icons scream in Yiddish.
What can we do, this terrorized Nation of Jews
When the Church of Rome towers over our heads
And we are forced to hear bells ring by day and by night
On our black Sabbaths and black Holy Days?
What a curse to live out each day as we live now.
Any moment a fire will burst out under our feet
From under the houses.
What can we do, this terrorized Nation of Jews?

Our wives and children lamenting: alas for our lives!
And a bloody tint spreads across roof and window pane.
How horrifying to grow up for nothing.
Like a rock in the street, except bodies are not rocks.
Bodies are made of flesh and blood and bone.
And they feel the slice of a knife.
We are impotent, Father, to climb up the tower
And tear down the bells that are driving us mad.
To pull down the cross that stabs our sanguine skies.
So let us descend to the depths, Father,
And dig under the earth, beneath all the foundations.
And let our pools of poisoned blood seep into the
planet....
Ten will remain, ten wounded Jews, the bloody survivors
To prove that our Nation existed in this Christian land of
pain.

Avraham's grey-blue eyes whitened like frost as he stared into the distance, as if he were watching the ghetto in flames. Hannie turned away, frightened when this trance-like state possessed him. Then he blinked and returned to the here and now of the life-filled ghetto.

"In Jerusalem, Uri Zvi Greenberg told me that as a youth, he and his family survived a pogrom, miraculously escaping from a band of murderous Polish soldiers. That event convinced him that the Jews of Christian Europe were doomed to a dreadful fate. Life for the Jews in Warsaw may seem calm at the moment, but with spreading fires of Nazism heading this way, this place will turn into a raging inferno. That's what Greenberg predicted ten years ago, and it is coming true. The Jews here are doomed unless we can find the way to bring them to *Eretz Yisrael*."

And the church bells of Warsaw continued to ring and ring and ring.... And the church bells of Warsaw continued to ring and ring and ring....

4.

Two weeks passed quickly. Avraham spent his free moments with Hannie, showing her a good time around the city, resigned to the fact that she refused to be alone with him in a room, lest his passion get out of hand. Occasionally, he would go off to work for a few hours, leaving her with the Chanowitz family. She didn't talk about marriage, and neither did he. That was best, she decided, enjoying their time together, thrilled with the way he smiled at her, his eyes sparkling with joy, making her feel that it wouldn't be long before he proposed.

All in all, she was happy she had journeyed to Poland to see him - until the afternoon when he returned to the Chanowitz flat when only she was at home. Like a caged lion, he paced from room to room.

"What's the matter?" she asked.

Suddenly, he faced her and said, "We have to end our relationship. There is no future for us."

Hannie stood stunned. Her heart stopped to beat.

"I am not meant to be a husband," he said. "A dreadful war is brewing, our Nation is threatened like it has never been before, and there are so few soldiers to take up arms against a sea of troubles. It isn't fair to you. You deserve better. A normal home, a normal life, with a man upon whom you can count. You deserve children. A family. This week, I have to travel to Finland. Next week, who knows? There is absolutely no way that we can continue. From this moment on, you are free. I am sorry if I misled you. I too had hopes. But it cannot be. It cannot be."

Hannie collapsed into a chair and burst into tears. Like an insane person tormented with despair, Avraham banged his head again and again against a wall. With a wail, he rushed to the door and left the apartment. Hannie wept hysterically. She wanted to die. Why go on living? What good was life if she couldn't be with the man whom she loved?

The Chanowitzes tried to console her, but her broken heart would not heal. Why hadn't she listened to her grandfather? Why had she deceived herself all of these years? She packed her things into her suitcase. No wonder that her other suitcase, with her wedding gown and dowry, had vanished. Just like her hopes. Avraham reappeared to accompany her to the train station. They barely exchanged a word. He looked uncomfortable, guilty, as if he were leading an innocent man to the gallows. In the taxi, he handed her a novel of Dostoyevsky.

"To read on the way."

The book was called, *Notes from the Underground*.

"Thank you," she said.

"Here are some cookies and pastries from the *kosher* bakery to eat on the way," he added, handing her a small, bulging bag.

"Will you write me?" she asked.

"No," he replied.

A long silence separated them like the ocean which was about to come between them once again.

"I printed all the poems that you sent me and made a book out of them. I left it with Mrs. Chanowitz."

Avraham didn't answer. When they left the taxi, Hannie noticed tears in his eyes. Without speaking, he carried her suitcase.

"You don't have to," she told him. "I can manage."

"I want to," he insisted.

On the platform of the station, when the train whistle blew, he didn't try to hug her. "Goodbye, Hannila," was all that he said.

She couldn't speak. Silent tears rolled down her cheeks. Turning, she hurried to board the train. Climbing the short steps, she paused and turned back. Like always, as he stood on the platform, surrounded by a rush of passengers, Avraham stuck out like the leading man in a movie, dressed to kill in his fitted suit and tie, a portrait of elegant solitude, from his Stetson hat to his polished shoes.

The shrill whistle blew again loudly. Hannie turned away and boarded the train. When she glanced out a window, Avraham had vanished, taking with him her love, her life, and her dreams.

5.

In the darkened room, Hannie stared down at the Bible and revolver which rested on the blue-and-white, Magen David flag on the table. She knew, from his voice, that one of the silhouetted figures seated before her was David

Raziel, even though the darkness camouflaged his features, and the spotlight shining in her eyes blinded her. She didn't recognize the other two men. Raziel had persuaded her to join the secret organization, hoping that the intensive physical training would rescue her from her depression. The fiery Raziel learned with her brother, Moishe, at the *Mercaz HaRav* Yeshiva when he had free time from his duties in the "*Etzel*," another name for the "*Irgun*" underground. He was also a close friend of "Yair," who continued to send her letters. He wrote without the passion that had once graced his correspondence, and without any poems, but still, even the mundane matters he recorded about his life in Warsaw were a connection. Often he included a page filled with codes that he asked her to deliver to Raziel, who knew all about her broken heart from Moishe.

"Stand at attention!" Raziel commanded. "Repeat after me."

Hannie already knew the oath from one of Avraham's letters describing his induction, along with Moishe, Tzvi, Nachshon, and Hevedke, into the secret fighting force. She repeated the words:

"I swear allegiance to the national army, the '*Irgun*,' the '*Irgun Tzva Leumi*' in *Eretz Yisrael*. At all times, I am ready to act, at any time, on behalf of the revival of the Jewish Nation in its Land. To live and to die for it!"

Then the three men started to sing the *Irgun's* anthem, "Anonymous Soldiers," which Avraham had composed. Hannie had written down the notes of the tune for him when he had first sung it to her in his apartment, years before in Jerusalem.

Anonymous soldiers, we are here without uniforms
Fear and the shadow of death surround us.
We have all enlisted for life.
Only death will release us from our duty.
On the red days of pogroms and blood,
On the dark nights of despair,
In cities and towns we will raise our flag
Emblazoned with defense and conquest!
We were not drafted with force, like so many slaves

To spill our blood on foreign lands.
Our desire is to be free men forever.
Our dream is to die for our Nation.
On the red days of pogroms and blood,
On the dark nights of despair,
In cities and towns we will raise our flag
Emblazoned with defense and conquest!

Hannie sung along with the others. Fighting was not a part of her nature, but, just as Avraham, and her grandfather, repeated over and over - in this generation, no Jew could live for himself. Maybe, she thought, when Avraham discovered that she had joined the organization, he would understand that she was ready for the life of self-sacrifice and hardship which he demanded of himself, a life she was prepared to endure as his wife.

The next evening, Raziel came to the Jerusalem apartment which she shared with two young women.

"Pack clothes for a few days, along with your field uniform. Tomorrow morning, at seven o'clock, we will meet at the Jerusalem bus station," he said.

"To go where?" she asked, startled.

"You'll find out," he replied curtly.

"What about my work?" she asked.

"Your brother will inform your employer tomorrow that you had to leave town on an urgent matter."

"I could get fired," she protested.

"Have you forgot the oath so quickly?" he asked.

"No, but...."

"It's an order," he said. Then he left without disclosing anything more.

The next day, they rode on a bus to Tel Aviv without speaking. Hannie gazed out the window, trying to enjoy the scenery as Raziel sat studying a *sefer*.

"What are you reading?" she asked.

"Rabbi Kook's book, *Orot*."

"Teach me something."

"Rabbi Kook's Hebrew is often difficult to understand," he said. Flipping pages backward from the spot he had reached, he read out a passage as the bus made the winding descent toward the coast:

"When we look back at the first generations which are described in the Torah, the Prophets, and the Scriptures, generations which were involved in war, we see that the valiant men of these times are the same great figures whom we cherish for their holy stature. The state of the world at that time, of which war was such a necessary feature, caused the appearance of these specials souls, whose inner sensitivity was so completely whole."

Raziel looked up from the book. "Do you follow the meaning?" he asked her.

"I think I understand. Because of the times and the wars in Biblical days, the heroes of Israel had to be holy people and soldiers at the same time."

"Exactly," he said with a smile of approval, knowing that his friend's attraction to the young woman wasn't only because she was pretty. People like Moses, and Joshua, and David, weren't only holy and righteous individuals, whenever necessary, they led the Nation to war." He continued to read:

"In their inner cognizance, their war of survival, the survival of the Nation, was a battle of God. They were bold in spirit, and they knew how to choose good and deviate from evil in the deep darkness of their times. *'Though I walk through the valley of the shadow of death, I will fear no evil.'*"

The scholar-soldier looked up, and Hannie nodded her head.

"Rabbi Kook goes on to explain that when we meditate on these holy heroes of our past, longing to emulate their bravery, and the powerful life force which shone in all aspects of their personalities, from this contemplation and yearning, our own powers are charged, and our valor is refined, not with a lust for killing, but with a longing to uproot evil and establish God's justice in the world. Today, when this process occurs in our hearts, then those same mighty souls are awakened, like in the days of our glorious past."

"Like the men of the *Irgun*" she noted.

"And the women," he said with a grin.

"The Anonymous Soldiers," she added in almost a whisper, reclining back in her seat, thinking how much the essay fitted Avraham, and David Raziel, and many other brave and idealistic people whom she had come to know.

Arriving in Tel Aviv, they hopped onto a local bus headed for Jaffa. Hannie wanted to telephone the dress shop to verify that Moishe had spoken to her boss, but Raziel said that they didn't have time, and public phones were few and far between. Jews and Arabs crowded the wobbly vehicle. Overhead, just under the luggage racks, were the usual, bold graphic advertisements for Jaffa Oranges, Eagle Beer, Cook's Nile and Palestine Tours, and British Fertilizers. Gazing out the window, Hannie saw the places that had once seemed so new and exciting to her during her first daring outings to the city when she was still a sheltered teenager from the *moshav*, Olat HaShachar. Now, after her years in New York, Tel Aviv was like a miniature toy village in the Fifth-Avenue, store display window of FAO Schwartz. But if she had to go on living without Avraham, she was glad to be in *Eretz Yisrael*, and not in New York, even though every street and corner reminded her of the strolls she had taken with the man she couldn't remove from her mind, no matter how hard she tried.

After a short ride, Hannie followed her commander out of the bus when it stopped at the noisy Jaffa port. It seemed like every truck and car horn in the country were honking. An Arab policeman on a bicycle blew a whistle and waved a white-gloved hand, trying to untangle a traffic jam. In the distance, along the beach, a caravan of camels carried shipping crates toward Tel Aviv. The Torah recounts that when Rebecca first saw Isaac, she was so startled, she fell off the camel she was riding. That was her feeling now. To Hannie's great surprise, at the entranceway to the port, by the gate, stood Avraham, a suitcase at his side, looking as poised and dapper as usual. Her heart plummeted. Her legs trembled. Obviously, by the look on his face, her appearance surprised him too. Both of them stood off-balance and unnerved by the unexpected *shidduch*. David Raziel, the matchmaker, made a grand show of smiles and chatter, hoping to soften the shockwaves that gripped the air between the former passionate sweethearts.

"Avraham! Welcome home! Meet our new recruit!" Raziel said, laughingly. "Oh, but, now I remember. You two have already met!"

Hannie realized that David had planned the surprise rendezvous, thinking to rekindle the flame he sensed still glowed in the both of them. With an awkward smile, Avraham asked how she was, and how her family was faring. Hannie felt so embarrassed, she wanted to run away as fast as she could. She answered his questions curtly. Avraham turned to his friend with an angry look and started speaking about business, but Hannie felt too distracted to concentrate on his words. With a storm of thoughts and emotions flooding her head, she followed the two friends as they walked side-by-side to a bus waiting to load passengers to Tel Aviv. When Avraham glanced back at her in the middle of their conversation without a smile on his face, Hannie thought she would die.

"Why did you do this?" Stern asked Raziel quietly with stiffened lips.

"You know why," his friend answered.

Raziel had written Stern a no-nonsense letter, describing Hannie's depression, stating that it was Avraham's duty to marry the girl. "*Is it right that he deal with our sister as with a harlot?*" he quoted, citing a Biblical verse about Jacob's daughter, Dina, who was mistreated by the prince of Shechem. In addition to his passion for the military, Raziel was a *Talmid Chacham*, steeped in Torah, as his letter clearly showed:

"You have strung her along for years, playing with her emotions, all for your own egotistical pleasure. I strongly suggest, my dear friend (and you know that I greatly value our friendship, and that I am writing this rebuke out of love), that you step down from your high horse and behave like a normal human being on earth, and not like some Greek poet warrior who is holier than all the rest of us. I love our Nation no less than you do, and I am prepared to give my life for the liberation of our beloved Land, turning nights into days, and days into nights, but still I married, just as we

are commanded to by our Maker, *'Be fruitful and multiply!'*
Who are you to put yourself above the orders of our King?
As the Prophet, Isaiah, said when he rebuked Hezekiah for
refusing to marry, *'You must do your duty, and the Lord will do
what pleases Him.'* Act like a man, most noble Yair! Marry the
girl! Have children! That is how we rebuild our Nation in
our Land. Not only with 'farming equipment!' So important
is the *mitzvah* of marrying, the Torah decrees that a groom
in his first year of marriage isn't drafted into the army, so
that he can be at home to make his wife happy. The time is
long overdue, my dear friend, to embrace this holy
commandment, which is far more exalted than any
command which I, or our commanders, in the *Irgun* can give
you. As our Sages have taught us, 'A man without a wife
lives without joy, without blessing, and without good
fortune.' And, as it says in the very beginning of the Torah,
'It is not good that the man should be alone.' Remember the
exoneration of the great Rabbi, Hillel the Elder, who said
long ago, 'If I am not for myself, who will be for me? If I am
only for myself, who am I? If not now, when?' Put aside
your excuses and your excessive concerns about hurting
Hannie. She is a grown woman. She can decide for herself.
As a member of the Organization, she knows the meaning
of the path we have chosen. All of our holy heroes of old
married. Can it be that Avraham Stern is holier and more
exalted than them all? Please, my dear friend, don't be angry
with my words. They come from a comrade-in-arms who
has your best interests, and the best interests of our Nation,
at heart. Peace be upon Israel. Blessings from Jerusalem.
Your friend in life and in death, David Raziel."

After Avraham received the letter in Warsaw, out of anger,
he didn't correspond with Raziel for two weeks. When he
finally did write, he spoke only about the "farming"
business, not mentioning the letter about Hannie and
marriage. Though he knew that his friend's words were
grounded in truth and friendship, he felt wounded. He felt
trapped. He felt unjustly accused. After all, his decision not
to marry was for Hannie's sake – not for his.

Now, in Jaffa, as they walked away from the noisy and
bustling port, Avraham's anger arose once again. Writing a

private letter was one thing, but arranging a surprise encounter in public with Hannie was something very different. His pulse raced and all of the powerful emotions which he had buried suddenly awakened, confounding his thinking.

"Both of you are to report to Itzhak Ben Ami in Olat HaShachar," Raziel told them, in the tone of their commander, after they had boarded a local city bus. "He will explain the mission. There's a bus heading north in half an hour from the Central Bus Station."

Hannie wondered whether she was dreaming. Yesterday, she didn't know when she would see Avraham again, and here he was, standing by her side on the crowded bus as it headed for Tel Aviv. They had to report together to Olat HaShachar, the very *moshav* where Hannie had spent her youth. If it wasn't a dream, it was a miracle! Then, suddenly at the first bus stop, Raziel said a happy goodbye and hopped off the bus, leaving them all alone to fend for themselves. Hannie felt sure that everyone on the bus could hear her heart beating.

"It seems we've been ambushed," Avraham said.

"I didn't know anything about this," Hannie replied.

"Neither did I."

Avraham's expressive face reverted to stone. Hannie had an impulse to get off the bus and run. But they had an assignment, and deep down in her heart, she felt ecstatically happy to see him. But a terrible fear kept her inner joy hidden, lest he hurt her once again.

While waiting at the Central Bus Station, he turned to her and said, "My decision still stands, and for all the same reasons. You deserve a normal husband. I am not capable of marrying."

Again, Hannie thought she would die, or at least pass out from the pain and humiliation. But she held herself together as strongly as she could, wanting to show him that she too, like the Matriarchs of the Nation, had the inner valor to endure all hardships and tests.

"As a member of the Organization, I am not afraid of a life of sacrifice," she said.

Avraham stared at her with a look of confusion and retreated back into his cave of silence.

"Should I call you Yair or Avraham?" she asked.

"Call me Yair," he said.

When they boarded the bus heading north, Hannie chose a seat by the window, where there was an empty seat by her side, but Avraham continued to walk up the aisle. An older woman carrying two bulging sacks sat down beside her.

"I hope I don't get sick," the lady said. "Sometimes I feel sick on bus rides."

Hannie turned away and stared out the window, not focusing on anything she saw outside. Tears rolled down her cheeks. How much disappointment and heartbreak could a person withstand? Why was she being punished this way? Was it because in succumbing to his embraces at the very beginning, she had transgressed the holy tenets of the Torah?

"Do you speak Russian," the lady beside her asked.

"Yes," Hannie replied softly.

"I hope the Arabs don't shoot at us. Last week, they shot at a bus on this route. By a miracle, no one was hurt. But last month, along the same route, their shots killed two Jews. May *Hashem* have mercy upon us."

"Amen," Hannie said.

As the bus left the city behind, Avraham too sat gazing out the window, unable to focus on the landscapes he so loved, and to which he longed to return each time he had to journey away from the Land. What was happening, he wondered? What was this roller coaster of feelings spinning around inside his head? If he didn't love Hannie, why did he feel so excited, now that they were back together, traveling in the same bus? Was it excitement at being finally at home, or because he truly loved the girl? The fact that he was heading toward the *moshav*, Olat HaShachar, wasn't a surprise. After the Arab pogroms in 1929, Carmel's father, Elisha, his sons, Ariel and Nachshon, and a handful of stalwart families, had returned to rebuild the ransacked and evacuated colony. For the past year, the isolated settlement had provided a home for an *Irgun* training center. Barracks had been erected for trainees, and a firing range had been fashioned in a remote location, between the rolling sand dunes by the ocean, where the sound of gunfire was drowned out by the surf and the wind. In a corner of the agricultural settlement, by a guard tower surrounded by a fence, an underground "shelter" had been built which housed a secret lab where the science of explosives was taught by Dmitri, a former demolition engineer in the Russian army. A shipment of rifles from Finland was due to arrive in Haifa in another two days, and Avraham's job was to make sure the crates of "farming equipment" found their way safely to Olat HaShachar, where a storage room had been dug out under the stone house of the colony's smithy.

Suddenly, the bus slowed and came to a halt. Passengers rose from their seats to get off the bus at the Herzliya station. Avraham lost sight of Hannie. What if she had left the bus? Quickly he stood up and shoved his way forward, worried that he would lose her. In the shoving, he found himself standing by her aisle. She looked up at him with a questioning look, unaccustomed to seeing him so flustered.

"I have a proposal to make," he said, feeling the words burst from his throat beyond his control. "Even though it won't be good for you, and you will surely refuse...."

Embarrassed, and stripped of his normal coolness, Avraham switched from Hebrew to Russian so the other passengers would not understand. "I have decided that we should get married."

Hannie gazed at him in wonder. Trembling with emotion, he burst into tears. "I can't live without you," he said.

"*Mazel tov!*" the elderly Russian woman sitting beside Hannie exclaimed. "*Mazel tov!* They're getting married!"

"*Mazel tov! Mazel tov!*" passengers around them called out.

Hannie sat in stunned silence.

"Aren't you happy?" Avraham asked.

"I don't have any more strength to be happy or sad," she replied, unable to believe that he had finally proposed.

With a groan, the lady rose to her feet. "*Mazel tov!*" she exclaimed once again. "Sit down next to your bride!"

Smiling and crying with happiness, Avraham sat down next to Hannie and took off his hat. Like a shy, little boy, he smiled at her through his tears.

"*Az dos harts is ful, geyen di oygn iber*," the lady with the bundles said to Hannie in Yiddish. "When the heart is full, the eyes overflow with tears."

Hannie couldn't believe it was real.

6.

They decided to hold the wedding in Olat HaShachar. When her shock had worn off, Hannie became, if not the happiest, then surely, one of the happiest women in the world. Immediately, she set to work on a new wedding gown to replace the dress which had been lost with her suitcase on the train to Warsaw. It didn't even bother her when Avraham had to leave the country a few days later, to return to Europe on business. His stops in Athens, Warsaw, and Bucharest would take two months, he told her, agreeing that she could already set a date for the wedding as soon as he returned. During his few days *b'Aretz*, he repeated his reservations about the marriage, assuring her that he would make a terrible husband, but he didn't retract his proposal, and by now, she had learned to ignore his hesitations and doubts and self-critical proclamations.

"Don't blame me if you are disappointed in the future," he said. "I have so little to give, and you want to receive so much. But I promise to do my best."

In addition, he told her that in their home, they would honor the *Shabbat*, light Sabbath candles and keep *kosher*. He wrote a letter to Tevye, telling him that he wanted to marry his granddaughter, in a way which sounded as if he were asking for the grandfather's permission to wed the orphaned girl. In closing, he asked Tevye to forward his respects to Nachman and Ruchel, "who raised Hannie to be the special, unique treasure she is." He also sent Hannie's photograph to his parents in Poland, informing them of the approaching wedding and urging them to apply for immigrant visas now, before it was too late.

On a pleasant, late-winter, Friday afternoon, everyone in the Olat HaShachar *moshav* gathered in the spacious yard behind the town hall for the wedding. The day was blessed with a brisk breeze from the ocean which blew away the humidity which frequently hung over the Mediterranean coastline. Tevye bought a suit for the joyous occasion. Carmel wore a pretty new dress. Her father, Elisha stood by her on the lawn, wearing the traditional Yemenite garb which he donned on the holidays. The right sleeve of garment hung loosely by his side, a reminder of the Talmud's teaching that the Land of Israel was acquired through suffering. Elisha's sons, Ariel and Nachshon, stood by his side, dressed in khaki-colored pants and open white shirts, with rifles slung over their shoulders. Hannie's brother, Moishe, couldn't have been happier as he stood on the back porch of the building, gazing over the crowd and the girls his age to see if he could find a bride for himself. While a Torah scholar had to guard his eyes and keep his thoughts holy, how could a man find a wife if he didn't keep a look-out for a possible mate? The other young people in the family, David, Sarah, Yehoshua, Naomi, Boaz, Ruth, and Akiva, wandered about the lawn. Hannie's aunt Hodel was present, and, of course, her aunt Ruchel, who had raised her as if she were her own daughter. And what better Rabbi could there be to perform the marriage ceremony than Nachman, her adopted father for as long as Hannie could remember? That whole week, Nachman had sat with the groom-to-be, teaching him all of the laws a *hatan* needs to know before his wedding. Tevye's manly, twenty-two-year old son, Tzvi, stood at the far end of the yard, holding a rifle like a guard. Behind him, *dunams* of sunflowers stretched out to the north, like a field of happy faces, glittering in the sun as they swayed back and forth in the refreshing winds from the ocean.

Hevedke stood amongst the group of Avraham's friends who had come to the wedding to share in the joyous occasion. The one-armed scholar had, like Elisha, also experienced firsthand the trials in settling the Land. The past year, he had spent several months in Olat HaShachar, learning how to make land mines and bombs. He had already given an arm for the country. If someone had to perform the risky work of preparing explosives, why not him? Moving to Jerusalem with all the other evacuees after the riots in Hevron, the pious convert couldn't find work as a *melamed* of young children with so many other Torah scholars in the Holy City. One day in the Arab Quarter of the Old City, watching a glassblower perform the delicate art of his trade, Hevedke decided to become a glassblower too! Using a vice as a second hand, he learned how to create all kinds of delicate figures which he sold to the tourist shops in the city. With the very same working table and vice, a sanding machine and a hand drill, he also learned how to hollow out and polish *shofars*, which were in great demand overseas. Graduating the course in explosives, he was now learning all about detonators, looking forward to the time when he could personally avenge his wife's rape and murder, and the slaughter that Arabs had inflicted on the Jews of Hevron.

Standing beside the tall, red-bearded Hevedke was the most famous shofar blower in the world, Moshe Segal, the young, strident Rabbi whose shofar blasts at the *Kotel* at the conclusion of *Yom Kippur* prayers, in defiance of British law, had been like a call, alerting the Land's foreign occupiers that the young lion cub of Judah had awoken after ages of slumber. For him, the time had come for the lion to reclaim its lair which has been plundered by thieves. Though every year on *Yom Kippur*, the British police kept a close watch on Segal, some daring Jew managed to follow in his footsteps and sound the horn of freedom at the Wall, as if to declare that God, and God alone, reigned over the Children of Israel – not the British.

Hannie recognized some of Avraham's friends, but other faces were new to her, probably people he knew in the *Irgun,* or from *Betar*, men like David Raziel, Avraham Tehomi, Yirmiyahu Halperin, Moshe Rosenberg, Itzhak Ben-Ami, Abba Ahimeir, Yehezkel Altman, Benjamin Zeroni, Yaacov Eliav, and the famous poet, Uri Zvi Greenberg. It was the last time such a group of underground freedom-fighters would appear in public together. A smiling fiddler and a happy-eyed fellow with a clarinet played festive wedding tunes. The *chuppah* wedding canopy stood waiting out on lawn, decorated with grape vines. Tables draped with white tablecloths and flower bouquets waited for guests to be seated, but where was the groom? It was nearly three o'clock and the sun had starting its descent toward the horizon. *Shabbat* would begin in less than two hours, and guests who wouldn't be spending the holy Sabbath day on the *moshav* had to start the drive back to Tel Aviv.

Hannie could feel her heart palpitating with that old "Avraham" fear. No. No. It couldn't be. Avraham wouldn't do such a thing. He couldn't. After all of his promises about how hard he would try, how could he not show up at their wedding? How could he do such a thing in front of so many guests? And after so much preparation. As she waited out on the lawn, she felt strangled by her gown's high collar. With the sun in her face, in the afternoon heat, in front of so many people, Hannie felt she was going to faint.

"Where the hell is the *shvitzer*?" Tevye growled with growing impatience.

Carmel, his wife, tugged at her husband's sleeve. "*Savlanut*," she said calmly. "Be patient."

"Patient? He's two hours late!"

Carmel left her husband and hurried to catch the bride just as she wobbled and swooned. Ruchel appeared at the same moment to grasp Hannie from the other direction. "Everything is all right," Ruchel said. "Let's get out of the sun and sit on the porch."

"Where is he?" Tevye asked Nachman with an angry and worried look on his face.

"Don't worry," Nachman answered in his always calm and optimistic voice. "He'll be here."

Tevye answered him in Yiddish. "When hair grows on the palm of my hand."

Elisha walked over to Nachman. With only one arm, he couldn't work in the fields, so he had been appointed general manager of the colony. "Maybe we should take down the *chuppah*," he said, "and start preparing for *Shabbat*."

Just when the situation seemed hopeless, salvation arrived! On the dirt road just beyond the backyard, a small herd of cattle lumbered by on the way back to their stalls after an afternoon in the colony's pastures. A cloud of dust rose in the air around them, blocking out the sun. When the dust cleared, a figure appeared in the sunflower field, running towards the yard. It was Avraham! Breaking off a few golden flowers, he burst out from the yellow-green field and sprinted across the lawn. All the guests cheered at the groom's dramatic appearance.

Tevye glanced up to Heaven. "Why did I agree to this marriage?" he asked. Whether it was real, or whether he simply imagined it, his dearly-departed Golda appeared at his side.

"Don't worry, my husband," she said in Hebrew, in a serene, faith-filled voice. "Everything is for the best."

"For great Sages like Rabbi Akiva and Nahum Eish Gamzu, everything is for the best, but I am only a milkman," he told her.

"You were a milkman," she reminded him. "Now you are the manager of a successful milk company. Believe me, it wasn't easy for me to arrange such a big promotion, so don't sell yourself short."

Beside Golda, his daughter, Tzeitl, and her husband, Motel, were holding hands and smiling. Bat Sheva and his beautiful Shprintza were present as well, both of them looking like angels. The light around Hava, dear Hava, was the brightest of all. And wasn't that Hillel with his fiddle?

Hannie remained seated on the porch of the town house, not believing her tear-filled eyes. Smiling broadly, and out of breath, Avraham jumped up the steps and presented the bouquet of freshly picked flowers to his bewildered bride. The round faces of the sunflowers seemed to be smiling too. Brushing the dust off his rented tuxedo, he looked around at the crowd and said, "I hope I'm not late." Then he bent down to Hannie.

"Please don't be angry with me," he said. "I had to do guard duty in Jaffa for a friend, and I couldn't abandon my post until the Arabs finished their Friday prayers."

Rabbi Nachman signaled the musicians to strike up a lively wedding tune. Taking charge of the ceremony, he told Tevye to take Hannie's hand and lead her toward the climactic moment she had been waiting for, and praying for, and dreaming about, for the past five years. Then, he instructed the best man, David Raziel, to escort the smiling groom to the wedding canopy out on the lawn. The guests crowded around the traditional *chuppah* as the wedding procession began. As she walked across the yard in her wedding gown, clutching her *Zaide's* hand, Hannie glanced back, as if to make sure that Avraham was still there. Standing next to her under the wedding canopy, he flashed her one of his Cheshire cat grins and whispered, "Don't ever say that I didn't warn you."

His foreboding remark didn't darken her spirits. She had heard his somber warnings so often before. For the moment, her joy was complete. Just a few years later, when his premonitions turned real, and he was hounded day and night by the British Police, living in fields and basements, and never coming home, she didn't regret her decision. She was his from the time of Creation.

Tevye, the grandfather of the bride, was awarded the honor of reciting the final blessing. Gazing at the grinning groom, he recalled the wise words of King Solomon: *"A time to weep and a time to laugh; a time to mourn and a time to dance; a time to cast away stones and a time to gather stones together."*

Grasping the goblet of wine, he pronounced the sacred blessing:

"Blessed art Thou, O Lord, King of the Universe, who hast created groom and bride, joy and happiness, delight and cheer, love and harmony, peace and companionship...."

From out of the blue, a photographer appeared with a large, box-like camera and took a picture, capturing the happy moment.

"Lord our God, may there soon be heard in the cities of Judea, in the streets of Jerusalem...."

Now everyone began singing the rest of the blessing with him.

"The sound of joy and gladness, the sound of joyous wedding celebrations, the sound of young people feasting and singing. Blessed art Thou, O Lord, who makes the groom to rejoice with the bride."

Avraham grinned. Finally, he could embrace Hannie without the fear that her grandfather would break his hands.

"Mazel tov! Mazel tov!" everyone shouted.

"L'Chaim! L'Chaim! To Life!"

1937

Chapter Nine
IF NOT NOW, WHEN?

That morning, the crowing of roosters didn't wake Tevye. Four gunshots shattered the morning silence. Opening his eyes, he quietly thanked God for restoring his soul, which at night, the Rabbis taught, went for a recharge in Heaven. Judging from the light in the room, it was around six o'clock in the morning. All of his life, the former milkman had risen before dawn to pray the early morning *vatikan* prayer, but now that he was a district manager of the milk company which served the religious neighborhoods of Jerusalem, he allowed himself an extra hour of sleep. With a groan, he threw off his blanket and sat up in bed.

"What is it?" his wife, Carmel, asked.

"Gunshots," her husband answered.

Once upon a time, when he was younger, the wash basin and "*natlah*" which he used to wash his hands in the morning would be waiting on the floor, at the head of the bed, but now, after a lifetime of hauling heavy containers of milk, he kept them on a small stool, so he wouldn't have to bend over to the floor and suffer any unnecessary pains in his back.

"What are you going to do?" his wife asked, sitting up in her bed.

"Probably nothing," he answered. "The Arabs don't wait around for '*mazel tovs*' after they kill Jews."

Just in case, as he dressed, he slipped his *Irgun* revolver out from under the mattress, and stuck it into his pants beneath his shirt and vest.

Footsteps sounded in the salon, and the door of the flat slammed closed. No doubt, his son, Tzvi, was already on his way to find out what happened.

Down on HaGai Street, Jews still adorned with prayer shawls and *tefillin* were hurrying away from the *Kotel*.

"What happened?" Tevye asked, stopping a familiar face.

"Arabs shot a father and son on their way to the *Kotel*," he answered, continuing briskly on toward the Damascus Gate.

Along the main cobblestone alley in the Western Wall Quarter, the merchants who hadn't yet fled from the neighborhood were beginning to open their shops and set up the stalls which would soon be filled with fresh fruits and vegetables. At this hour, Hershel, the Old City milkman, was probably making his morning deliveries to the brave families who still lived in the northern neighborhood near *Shar Shechem*. After the pogrom of 1929, most Jews had either abandoned Hevron Street, or been evacuated by the British, on the pretense that the mighty British Empire couldn't defend them against bloodthirsty Arab mobs. Stores in the Jewish business district surrounding King David Street were now sealed, and a Jew was hardly seen in the once-thriving Quarter. Arab squatters had entered the abandoned Jewish homes on Habad and Medan Streets, and the way to the Western Wall, once crowded with worshippers, remained deserted, even on the Sabbath and holidays.

What an outrage, Tevye thought! The Arab uprising which had continued unabated throughout the year had induced hundreds of Jewish families to evacuate the Quarter. Jews were afraid to walk to the *Kotel* without being escorted by *Betar* guards. But even the *Betarim* didn't stop Arabs from staging ambushes along the alleyways leading to the holy Wall. The guards were also stabbed and shot in the back, along with Rabbis, yeshiva students, women and children.

"When would it end?" Tevye wondered. When would the Jews finally stand up and respond? Why bother with all the secret *Irgun* recruitment and training if not to strike back at the enemy and teach the murderers a lesson?

Indeed, Tevye reflected, it hadn't been a good year for the Jews, but, then again, when had it ever been a good year? In 1917, when Britain had ousted the Turks from the country, that had been a cause for celebration, but then it turned out that British rule over the Land was even worse for the Jews than the centuries of Turkish sovereignty. Time and again, Arabs slaughtered Jews, and the British Mandate Administration did nothing to prevent the atrocities. The

Mandate Government even encouraged the sons of Ishmael in their rampages and blood fests! And the Jews, like stubborn mules, or like chickens without their heads, remained terrified of the Gentiles, just as they had been for almost two-thousand years of exile in foreign lands.

As Tevye hurried along toward the scene of the shooting, Jews rushed by in the opposite direction, their faces distraught with worry. No one bothered to call out the usual *"boker tovs."*

The Arab uprising of 1936 had erupted in Tel Aviv with the murder of nine Jews by a wild horde of knife-wielding marauders. Over fifty Jews were wounded. British police imposed a curfew, but the rioting continued. On the outskirts of Tel Aviv, Jews were murdered in their homes, stores were looted, and factories set ablaze. Hundreds of Jews abandoned the neighborhood, seeking shelter in the center of the city. Around the country, telephone lines were cut, railroad tracks and bridges were blown up, and Jews were ambushed while driving in their cars. Jewish crops and orchards were burnt to the ground. In the Galilee, settlements were attacked on a daily basis. A family of four Jews from America was murdered in Safed; a car filled with Jews was bombed in Haifa; a child was killed and ten people wounded when Arabs fired from a train window along Herzl Street in Tel Aviv; two young Jewish nurses were butchered on their way to work in the government hospital in Jaffa; a Hebrew University professor was murdered in his home in Jerusalem; and four Jewish laborers were murdered in Kfar Saba. Jewish children were slaughtered in schools and orphanages. Hospitals, ambulances, and old-age homes were attacked. Who could remember all of the massacres? There were funerals every day. Very often, victims were hacked to pieces. Jewish women were tortured and raped. In November of 1937, at a clandestine *Irgun* meeting which Tevye had attended, David Raziel read out a Jewish Agency report which summarized the violence that year: 90 Jews killed and over 400 wounded; 1500 bombs exploded; 400 buses and trains attacked; 10,000 acres of crops destroyed; 200,000 trees uprooted or set on fire; 350 houses torched. And all the while, the British Government allowed the violence to continue. A High Arab Committee was established in Shechem, headed by the Grand Mufti of Jerusalem, Haj Amin al-Husseini, a friend of the Nazis. The High Arab Committee organized a general countrywide strike, declared a boycott against Jewish produce and products, and announced that the violence against Jews would continue until Jewish immigration and the sale of land to Jews were halted. Conceding to Arab demands, the British reduced Jewish immigration to a trickle. Jews lacking official visas were rounded up by British soldiers and expelled from the country. The sale of land to Jews was banned. And the leaders of the Zionist establishment reacted like lambs, bleating in protest, but doing next to nothing to halt the slaughter. Even after their demands were met, the Arabs intensified their wave of terror. Seeing the lackadaisical response of the Mandate Authority, the "sons of Ishmael" understood that the British were on their side. On the outskirts of Jerusalem, five Jewish workers, hired by the Jewish National Fund to pave a new road leading to a proposed settlement site, were gunned down and killed. Though all five were members of the *Haganah*, the military defense organization didn't strike back. The official Jewish leadership continued to hope that a policy of restraint would win political gains, but the weakness of the Jews only convinced the British Mandate Authority that any agreements concerning Palestine were more prudently made with the Arabs, the more powerful force in the region.

Tevye was breathing heavily by the time he reached the scene of the shooting at the bottom of Hevron Street, not far from the *Ohel Yitzhak* Synagogue and the passageway which led to the *Kotel*. The father lay sprawled on his back, staring lifelessly up toward the sky. Beside him, his young son lay motionless in a pool of blood. Jews with prayer shawls draped over their shoulders stared at the bodies and hurried away as British policemen ordered them to go about their business. Tevye's oldest son, Tzvi, stepped past one of the "Bobbies" and picked up the cloth bag holding the murdered Jew's *tefillin*. A tall, uniformed Englishman poked at him with his club.

"I told you Yids to clear the area!" he barked.

Tzvi was twenty-three. People said he looked like his father - without Tevye's large, bushy beard, of course. They shared the same broad forehead with three veins protruding slightly in the middle, in the shape of the Hebrew letter, *Shin*. The youth was trim and muscular, with his mother's dark, Yemenite complexion. Watching the boy gaze at the Englishman with hate-filled eyes, Tevye knew what he was thinking - an agent of the British Government was an enemy, no less than the Arabs who murdered Jews.

"Get moving," the policeman ordered again, giving Tzvi another poke with his club. Noticing his father, he walked away to join Tevye by the arched passageway leading to the *Kotel*.

"More *havlaga*?" the hot-blooded youth asked in disgust.

Havlaga was the term used to describe the policy of appeasement that the official Zionist establishment had adopted in response to Arab violence. No matter how many innocent Jews were murdered, no matter how many Jewish women were raped, the response was always the same – *havlaga* – restraint. The *Haganah* could defend settlements, but nothing more. No response. No revenge. Nothing. If attackers fled beyond the settlement's borders, *Haganah* guards had orders to stop without further pursuit. Though reprisal attacks on Arab villages were often proposed and debated, the motions were invariably overruled.

Chaim Weizmann, the venerable Zionist statesman in London, was the foremost champion of *havlaga*, and Ben Gurion, for all of his strident posturing, had adopted the policy as well, turning the *Haganah* into an ineffective defensive force which the Arabs regarded with disdain. Jewish Agency leaders claimed that only quiet diplomacy and parlor-room negotiation with the British would win better protection for the embattled Jews of Palestine. To their way of thinking, if the Jews were to be granted some future form of Statehood, they had to show the world that they were a moral people – not primitive tribesmen like the Arabs who lived by their swords. Political gain could only be achieved by winning the sympathy of the *goyim*, they steadfastly proclaimed. Tzvi was fed up with that, and so was his father.

Even the far-more militant Ze'ev Jabotinsky, leader of the Revisionists and the *Betar* Youth Movement, and spiritual father of its military arm, the *"Etzel,"* code-named, the *"Irgun,"* still favored *havlaga,* clinging to the hope and belief that the civilized English nation would one day honor its noble promise to assist the Jewish People in establishing a national Jewish Homeland in Palestine. Tevye stared at the two murdered Jews on the street, gunned down on their way to pray at the *Kotel* in the Old City of Jerusalem. The Balfour Declaration had been formulated more than twenty years before. For what? Not only had Arab savagery continued unchallenged over the years, Jewish immigration to the country had been almost shut down by the British, at a time when the growing Nazi menace in Germany threatened to eradicate millions of Jews.

Tevye wasn't the only Jew who was fed up with the situation. The secret *Irgun* organization had been founded by frustrated Revisionists, in response to the impotency of the *Haganah*, but they too waited for Jabotinsky's go-ahead before implementing a course of militant counterattacks designed to deter the Arabs from their wanton slaughter of Jews. For three years, the clandestine group had trained new recruits in weaponry and warfare, ready to act when the order came – but the order never arrived. In the meantime, more and more Jewish gravestones rose up on the altar of *havlaga*.

"It's a *chillul Hashem*," Tzvi said. "Every time a Jew is murdered in the Land of Israel, it is a desecration of God, causing the Gentiles to believe that they are more powerful than the Almighty who promised us this Land. Ben Gurion may think that the world will take pity on us when our corpses pile up to the sky, but no one gives a damn when a Jew is murdered. Allowing ourselves to be Jewish martyrs won't get us anywhere. We have to be Jewish fighters if we want to survive in this Land."

Tevye nodded. His son was right. He himself had felt that way for years, but who was he to argue with a famous Zionist leader like Ze'ev Jabotinsky, and with the local leaders of the *Irgun* who insisted that the Jews couldn't fight back until the differing camps in the Zionist Movement were united. "The *Moshiach* will come before Ben Gurion and Jabotinsky make peace," Tevye noted. To his way of thinking, getting hit over the head with the club of a British policeman was no different than getting hit over the head with the club of a Cossack in Anatevka. When it happened in the Land which the Almighty had promised to the Jews, it was even worse. And when the sons of Ishmael slit Jewish necks day and night, and the sons of Abraham didn't fight back, that made Tevye's blood boil like soup left too long on the stove.

"Where is Nachshon?" Tevye asked, inquiring about his wife's youngest brother.

"He went to Olat HaShachar for a few days to visit his father," Tzvi informed him.

"Tell him I want to speak with him," Tevye said. "Just the three of us."

Tzvi could tell from his father's expression that he had finally made up his mind. More than once, he had urged his father to let him and his friends revenge the wave of killings all over the country. But his father had said no. They had to wait for instructions from the people who knew more about politics and military matters than they did. The *Etzel-Irgun* was a military organization, not a gang of vigilantes. But Tevye was tired of the endless procrastination. He was tired of talk. Uri Zvi Greenberg wrote inspiring poems of Redemption, and Abba Ahimeir published powerful diatribes against the British, and everyone liked to sing the *Betar* Song and the *Irgun* anthem, "Anonymous Soldiers," but that didn't prevent Jews from getting slaughtered. Tevye didn't need to read revolutionary literature, or hear militant songs, or learn to march like a soldier to understand what action had to be taken. The Master of the Universe had given the Land of Israel to the Jews – not to the Arabs, and not to the British. To his way of thinking, it was as simple as that.

"Should I tell Raziel?" Tzvi asked.

"No," his father answered. David Raziel, the young, religious head of the Jerusalem *Irgun* chapter, and a family friend, was itching to abandon the policy of *havlaga*. But he was as faithful to Jabotinsky as the rest. "Perhaps I will speak to him alone," Tevye said.

"What about Yair?"

"He can't help us now," Tevye replied. "Yair" – meaning "to shine" - was the code name of Avraham Stern. A short time after his wedding, the passionate lover of Zion returned to Poland to finalize a deal for the purchase and shipment of weapons, and to further his Don Quixote scheme of mustering a Jewish army of forty-thousand youths who would sail to Palestine and liberate the Jewish Homeland from the British.

By now, a large crowd of Jews had gathered at the scene of the shooting, and more British policemen had arrived to keep order. A few angry youths threw some stones at the soldiers, prompting one to fire his rifle in the air. The shot echoed through the arched passageway where Tevye and his son were standing.

"Disperse! Evacuate the area!" the British "peacekeepers" shouted, raising their clubs and pointing their bayonets at the Jews, as if they were the perpetrators of the crime.

Members of the *Chevre Kadisha* Burial Society pushed through the crowd to reach the victims.

"What are you thinking about?" Tzvi asked his father.

"The best way to kill a snake is by chopping off its head," Tevye answered.

"The Grand Mufti of Jerusalem?"

As was his wont, his father answered with a saying of the Sages.

"If not now, when?" he said.

2.

Nachshon was the same age as Tzvi. Perhaps because both of the young men had been born and raised in the Promised Land, and not in foreign lands amongst the Gentiles, they had no innate fear of the Arabs nor the British, the offspring of Ishmael and Esau. In their minds, the time of Esau's ascendency had come to an end with the return of the Children of Israel to their Biblical Homeland. Instead of bowing down to foreign rulers, the time had arrived for the offspring of Jacob to ascend and rule in their place. That's what was written in the Torah; and that's what they were prepared to do now, by adopting the ways and weapons of Ishmael and Esau in the battle to defeat them and to purge them from the Land.

Because Nachshon was the younger brother of Carmel, he was Tevye's brother-in-law, and Tzvi's uncle as well. More importantly to matters at hand, he could fire a rifle from a galloping horse more accurately than most soldiers could shoot while standing firmly on the ground. With his dark Yemenite features and his fluent Arabic, he could also pass for an Arab and spy on the mansion of the Grand Mufti of Jerusalem, Haj Amin el-Husseini.

To Tevye, the red-haired Husseini was the devil on Earth. His demonic and carefully orchestrated incitement of the masses had sparked the Arab riots of 1920 and 1929, leading to the slaughter of nearly 200 Jews, including Tevye's dear friend, Hillel, and the rape and murder of Tevye's daughter, Hava, in Hevron. The small intelligence department of the *Irgun* had intercepted correspondence between the Mufti and contacts in fascist Italy and Nazi Germany, requesting their support in his goal to wipe out the "Jewish invaders of Palestine." In Husseini's most recent *jihad* against the Jews, he had enlisted the support of Fawzi-el-Kaukji, a mercenary Iraqi officer, who came to Palestine with hundreds of savage recruits from Syria and Iraq.

Husseini spent his days secluded in the walled enclave and mansion which he had built for himself in the scarcely populated Sheikh Jarrah neighborhood of Jerusalem. The small fortress was situated between the road leading up to the Hebrew University on Mount Scopus and the tomb of Shimon the Pious, who had served as Jewish High Priest in the time of the Second Temple in Jerusalem, two-thousand years before Husseini was born, and seven-hundred years before the religion of Islam was established in Mecca. Dressed as an Arab selling grapes, Nachshon spent days across the road from the mansion, observing the comings and goings of the Mufti and the visitors whom he received around the clock. Early on Friday mornings, he would customarily be driven to the Temple Mount for meetings with religious leaders and sheikhs from around the country before the mass weekly prayer in the Mosque of Omar, during which he would deliver a fiery sermon to the gathered thousands, inciting them to increase the ongoing violence against the Jews, who, he maintained, were scheming to attack and conquer the Temple Mount.

Supplied with the surveillance data which Nachshon collected, Tevye planned the assassination for a Friday morning. Tzvi wanted to be the gunman, but his father said no.

"You have your whole life ahead of you," Tevye told him. "You can do many things to help the Jews. I have one foot in the grave already. If something goes wrong with the operation, better that I be the one to suffer the consequences, not you."

Tevye's son-in-law, Hevedke, prepared the land mine which Tzvi and Nachshon planted the night before along the road to the south, in order to prevent cars from reaching the site of the attack. Husseini heard the powerful blast, which woke up with half of Jerusalem, as he was preparing to leave his mansion early in the morning. Thinking it was another attack against some Jewish target, he smiled, joked with his bodyguards, left the house under their watchful eyes, and got into the back seat of his four-door Rover. Seeing Husseini's car and an escort car drive out from the enclave, Hevedke's son, Akiva, fired two signal shots in the air from his outpost in the neighboring woods. Cautiously, Husseini's driver took his foot off the gas pedal and pressed lightly on the brake, but the roadway was clear in front of them.

"Probably a victory celebration," guessed one of the bodyguards.

Husseini laughed in the back seat and told them to drive on.

A short distance away, around a narrow bend in the road, Tevye and Tzvi stood waiting behind the wagon they had overturned to look like an accident. When the lead car appeared, the driver honked and slowed to a full stop. He cursed in annoyance as an elderly Jew with a full beard, wearing work clothes and a vest, hurried toward the car with his hands raised in the air for help.

"What is it?" Husseini asked.

"A rotten Jew," the driver answered. "His wagon's turned over."

"Drive around it," Husseini ordered.

"I can't," the driver answered. "It's blocking the road."

The driver rolled down his window as the out-of-breath Jew reached the car. "Move your damn wagon from the road!" the Arab shouted.

Without answering, Tevye pulled a revolver from his belt and, with a steady hand, squeezed the trigger. The gunshot resounded throughout the neighborhood. Dogs pointed their ears. Chickens jumped in the air and crowed. The driver of the car slumped over the steering wheel with a gaping bullet hole in his forehead. Before the startled bodyguard in the front seat could draw his gun, Tevye shot him in the face. The roar of the gunshot echoed in the car. Blood splashed over Tevye's outstretched hand. As the driver and bodyguard in the escort car jumped out from the vehicle, drawing their weapons, Nachshon stepped out from behind a tree on the embankment bordering the road. Dressed as an Arab, he aimed his "Washington" automatic rifle and fired single shots with deadly accuracy. Both Arabs fell dead to the ground. Back at the car, Tevye pointed his revolver at the Grand Mufti who was shaking with fear in the rear seat.

"No, no, please, no," he begged.

"Tell it to the virgins," Tevye said and squeezed the trigger, but nothing happened. The trigger was jammed! He tried to fire again, but the mechanism remained stuck in its place. Hearing sirens in the distance, Tevye pulled back the hammer of the gun, but it still wouldn't fire.

"Let's go!" Tzvi yelled at him.

"*Gevalt*," Tevye thought. Too bad he didn't have the time to strangle the devil with his bare hands and watch him die a slow death. "The next time, we'll get you," he told the speechless Grand Mufti. Then he hurried away from the car back to the wagon. The police sirens sounded more loudly, indicating that the police were quickly approaching. Tzvi raised the motorcycle which was lying on the ground, hidden under the wagon. As he started the engine, his father climbed on behind him.

"Hold on," Tzvi told him, speeding away down an old dirt road that led toward the Mount of Olives and the Old City.

As the first police car appeared, Nachshon aimed the Tommy gun and fired a string of shots which shattered the windshield and drilled holes through the two British policemen inside. Then he ran down from the embankment to the wagon, untied the reins of the jittery horse, jumped on its back and galloped off, disappearing down the dirt road in the cloud of dust left behind by the motorcycle.

The Grand Mufti sat trembling in the back seat of his car in a puddle of urine. One thought, and one thought alone, filled his terrified mind. How was he going to sneak out of the country before the Jews tried to kill him again?

3.

Tevye had already made travel plans to leave the country. Quickly, he finished dressing in his bedroom while everyone waited to say goodbye to him in the salon of his home – his son, Tzvi; his wife, Carmel; his twin eighteen-year-olds, Boaz and Naomi; his son-in-law, Hevedke; his daughters, Hodel and Ruchel, and Ruchel's husband, Nachman. And David Raziel.

When the bedroom door opened, and Tevye appeared as clean-shaven as a baby, everyone received the shock of their lives. Carmel's mouth hung open. Tzvi laughed. Boaz and Naomi were flabbergasted, unable to believe that the dapper gentleman standing in front of them was their father, attired in the latest New York-style, double-breasted, square-shouldered, blue suit with wide lapels, white shirt and tie, grey Fedora hat, and two-tone shoes.

"It's the perfect disguise," David Raziel commented with a broad grin.

The branch commander of the Jerusalem *Irgun* had purchased the new wardrobe for Tevye in Tel Aviv. Raising a large box camera, he stepped close to Tevye and snapped a photograph of his clean-shaven face with a loud "poof" of the flash.

"I'll have the picture pasted in your passport," he said. "We'll meet at the Jaffa Gate in three hours, at noon. You will spend *Shabbat* in Olat HaShachar and sail to Italy in another two days."

"Yes, sir," Tevye said, giving the young commander a salute.

"*Abba*, you shaved off your beard!" Naomi, his daughter, uttered in disbelief.

Tevye smiled sheepishly and gazed at his wife.

"How do I look?" he asked.

Carmel was speechless.

"While the Torah forbids a man to shave off his beard with a razor," Ruchel's husband, Rabbi Nachman, explained, "in a case where a person's life is at stake, it is permitted."

What could he do, he thought with a sigh? Until the police stopped looking for Tevye, the milkman, he had no choice. They were probably already circulating a drawing of him from the Mufti's description.

"It was the hardest thing I ever did in my life," Tevye admitted. "My hand shook the whole time. From now on, I'll use an electric shaver."

"You look twenty years younger," Ruchel said.

"Like a movie star," Hodel added.

"The clothes fit you perfectly," Hevedke remarked.

"*Nu*, Carmel?" Tevye asked his wife.

"You look very elegant," she said softly.

"Doesn't it make my nose look bigger?" he asked.

"So what?" Hodel said. "You're handsome just the same."

"To tell the truth, without my beard, I feel like a plucked chicken," Tevye confessed.

"Twelve o'clock," Raziel repeated. Then, with a military about-face, he turned away and walked to the door.

"You're going to Italy?" Ruchel asked.

"On the way to New York," Tevye replied. "Baylke's husband has agreed to introduce me to some rich and influential people who can help us with our cause."

Indeed, Baylke's generally good-for-nothing husband, Pedhotzer, had mentioned a few names: Meyer Lansky and Bugsy Segal, among them. In addition, Tevye hoped that a letter of recommendation which he had received from the famous Rabbi Kook several years earlier would help open doors in his mission to raise money and buy weapons for the *Irgun*.

"You'll be staying with Baylke?" Hodel asked.

"It's about time, isn't it?" her father answered. "I haven't seen your older sister in almost thirty years."

"How long will you be gone?" Carmel wanted to know.

"Many are the plans in a man's heart..." her husband replied, quoting the Psalmist's expression without adding the rest, which everyone knew by heart.

Tevye raised a hand to his baby-smooth chin, wondering what his dear Golda must be thinking in Heaven. "Are you sure I look all right?" he asked. "I feel like a fool in this outfit."

"You look like a different person," Naomi said, still amazed at the sight of her father.

"Like a New York gangster," Boaz quipped.

"Like million dollars," Tzvi assured him.

Sighing, Tevye spoke in Yiddish, the *mame loshn* language you could always rely on to coin the right phrase. "As the expression goes," he said. "You can change a man's hat, but you can't change his head."

"Go in *shalom*, and come back in *shalom*," Nachman said. "May the God of our Forefathers, Abraham, Isaac, and Jacob, grant you success and watch over you on your journey."

Everyone answered, "*Amen!*"

Chapter Ten
VENGEANCE IS MINE

After the abortive attack on the Grand Mufti, which left four Arab bodyguards and two British policemen dead, Hevedke took the revolver that had jammed to the secret *Irgun* gun workshop in the backroom of his glassblowing shop for the young weapons wizard, Yaacov Eliav, to repair. Tevye spent *Shabbat* in the Olat HaShachar colony, where he had lived before moving to Jerusalem. The following morning, David Raziel drove him to the port city of Haifa. Wearing a Mafia-style trench coat, the stylishly-dressed traveler did his best to flash a calm smile as he handed his passport to the British official at the Passport Security Station. The Englishman studied the clean-shaven face in the photograph and glanced up at the clean-shaven Jew standing in front of him. Without returning Tevye's smile, he stamped the passport and scribbled the date on an empty page. "Next," he said, returning the small booklet to Tevye's visibly trembling hand – the same hand that had calmly attempted to assassinate the Grand Mufti just a few days before. Why was he so nervous now? When he pointed the revolver at the enemy of the Jews, Tevye felt confident that he was purging the world of evil, but facing the passport inspector, he wasn't at all certain that his disguise would work. The British official looked at Tevye questioningly as his twitching hand returned the passport to the inner pocket of his suit jacket.

"I guess old age is catching up with me," Tevye said, explaining the tremor. Then, with a polite tip of his Fedora, he lifted his suitcase from the floor and walked on toward the corridor leading to the dock.

Back in Jerusalem, in the wee hours of the morning, Tevye's eighteen-year-old twins, Boaz and Naomi, crouched down in a dark alley by Jaffa Road. Hearing Akiva's shrill, all-clear whistle, Boaz picked up the wide brush and pail of glue at his feet. Hurrying to a street billboard on Jaffa Road,

he smeared a brush-full of glue over a poster advertising a
new Charlie Chaplin movie called, *Modern Times*. Running
back to the alley, he nodded at his sister. Hearing the whistle
sound again, the tall girl ran to the billboard and stuck a
poster over the fresh glue. Catching a glimpse of Hevedke's
sixteen-year-old son, Akiva, keeping look-out from the dark
entrance of an alley across the street, Naomi ran back to
Boaz, and they hurried off toward the next billboard. Before
leaving for Poland, "Yair" had convinced David Raziel that
reprisals should be preceded or followed by a public
statement from the *Irgun*, explaining the ideological basis
behind their actions, so that they wouldn't be viewed as
wanton revenge. Both of them had worked out the wording
for the first poster which would appear on the streets
whenever the decision was made to ignore the Jewish
Agency's long-standing policy of *havlaga* and strike back at
the enemy:

**"The *Irgun Tzva Leumi* in the Land of Israel, known as
the *Etzel*, has been established because we believe that a
Hebrew State will not be created without the initiative of
Jewish military force. The Jewish Agency and the *Haganah*
foster the policy of *"Havlaga,"* appeasement and
subjugation to Arab aggression and foreign rule over our
Homeland. The *Etzel* has been forced by political reality to
take up arms for the defense of the Jewish People and for
the liberation of our Land. It is the goal of the *Etzel* to
restore full Jewish independence throughout the historical
borders of our Homeland. Only victory or death shall
release us from our duty!"**

2.

In his glassblowing and *shofar* workshop, red-bearded
Hevedke tightened a ten-centimeter connecting pipe, called
a "plumber's fitting," into the vice on his work table,
preparing one of the four *mufa* grenades that would be used
that afternoon to blow up the "International Café" on Jaffa
Road. Situated adjacent to the National Arab Bus Company,
the sidewalk café was frequented by the Arab gang leaders
who had been waging attacks on the Jews of Jerusalem.

Sitting beside Hevedke, twenty-year-old Yaacov Eliav carefully worked on the fuses. Both of the bomb makers had studied the delicate trade with Dmitri, a former demolition expert in the Russia army. Eliav had enhanced his knowledge by taking chemistry courses at Hebrew University. Even though he was young, because of his many skills, nerves of iron, and burning desire to defend the honor of his embattled People, he had been put in command of "Group 81" in Jerusalem. During his *Irgun* training, his favorite weapons were the pistol, the sawed-off rifle, the "Washington" submachine gun, and grenades, because they could all be easily hidden under one's clothing and drawn out swiftly, in order to hit and destroy the target at close range. From Dimitri he had learned the science of explosives, detonators, fuses, land mines, and bombs. After mastering the basics, a God-given talent led him to discover deadly innovations that would terrify the British for the coming ten years.

In addition to the fierce Jewish pride that streamed through his veins, Eliav was motivated by a lasting childhood memory. When he was twelve-years old, a truck arrived on the street outside of his home in Tel Aviv and unloaded a group of women and children, evacuees from the pogrom in Hevron. One of the women, Mrs. Lazarowsky, was a friend of the family. His parents invited her to live with them until she could find permanent quarters. For days, with a terrified look in her eyes, she recounted the horrors she had witnessed. Listening to her words, young Yaacov trembled with rage and with a burning passion for revenge.

"The massacre began on *Shabbat*," she said. "When the Jews realized what lay ahead, a delegation rushed to the Hevron police station, but the Chief of Police dismissed their alarm. I heard a sheikh screaming in the street: 'Kill the Jews! Drink their blood! Today is the day of Islam! The *Koran* commands death to the infidels. Jewish maidens are waiting for you!'

"We thought our home in the Jewish Compound by the medical clinic and bank was safe, but the marauders broke down the front door. When Mr. Slonim fired his pistol, an

Arab smashed an iron bar on his head. Two yeshiva students were killed on the stairs. With swords and axes, the Arabs slaughtered women and children. They stabbed my brother. Israel Kaplansky was stabbed and shot. With sabers, they dismembered the elderly Rabbi Orlinsky and his wife. Rabbi Drabkin's stomach was split open. With their hands, the savages ripped out his organs. I saw them stab Rabbi Ben-Gerson with daggers. Yeshiva students lay in pools of blood. They killed my second brother, Bezalel, and his young daughter. Outside the window, I saw one of the Heikal boys bravely fighting off a mob of Arabs with his fists until he was bludgeoned from behind and hacked into pieces while two British policemen on horseback looked on. In the Slonim house alone, the Arabs slaughtered twenty-four Jews and wounded fourteen. After there were no more Jews to kill, they stole everything in sight. Longtime Arab friends of Slonim joined the wild horde. I escaped by hiding behind a pile of bodies. After the beasts left, I walked through the blood-filled rooms and corridors of the building. I came upon Rabbi Grudzinsky, his left eye gouged out and his brain dangling out from his shattered skull. Young women lay raped and naked in puddles of blood. And the British did nothing to stop it."

Standing in a corner of the salon in Tel Aviv, listening to the woman's account of the massacre, the twelve-year-old Yaacov vowed that he would revenge the atrocity. Images of the pogrom remained ever-engraved in his mind. Hardly a day passed when he didn't remember that the blood of the slaughtered remained unavenged.

Now, a young man of twenty, Eliav watched carefully as the one-armed Hevedke, himself a survivor of the massacre in Hevron, screwed a metal stopper into the end of the thick pipe. He had already drilled a hole in stopper where the fuse would be inserted. Removing the pipe from the vice, he flipped the pipe over, then refastened it between the iron brackets. The former school *melamed* inserted a narrow envelope of dynamite into the pipe. Yaacov handed him the detonator and safety fuse coated with gunpowder, and the one-armed glassblower slid them into place. After cleaning the threads of a stopper of any trace of dynamite, to prevent any sudden explosion when the stopper was set into place, Hevedke pushed the fuse through the opening with a long sewing needle and gently screwed the stopper into the end of the pipe. Eliav had determined the exact length of the fuse so it would explode four feet from the ground when it was dropped down on the sidewalk cafe from the adjoining rooftop. With a small artist's brush, he mixed a pinch of inflammable potassium chlorate and sugar, dabbing the mixture on the tip of the fuse, which he covered with waterproof paper to prevent the explosive material from getting wet. After preparing four grenades, the underground bomb-squad set them inside a large shoe box, into the four compartments they had fashioned inside. In the empty spaces between the compartments, Hevedke gently dropped nails to heighten the shrapnel effect of the explosion. Then all of the fuses were fastened together and tied to the main fuse extending outside the box.

Eliav placed their creation in a bag and shook Hevedke's hand.

"*Hatzlacha*," Hevedke wished him. "May your mission be a resounding success."

The pun brought a grin to the bomb-maker's serious expression.

As Eliav left the Old City, Tzvi was waiting to meet him by the Jaffa Gate, dressed in the black garb of a Hasidic Jew, complete with a false beard and side-curls. Yaacov walked by, without acknowledging him, as if they weren't together. They had simulated the operation a few days before, dressed up as plumbers with tool boxes, which they carried up to the roof of the building which overlooked the Arab tea-house cafe.

In the vicinity of the Russian Compound, a group of British policemen mulled along Jaffa Road, enjoying the few minutes remaining until they had to report to Police Headquarters to begin their shifts. Seeing them at a distance, Yaacov thought that the police had learned of their plan, but when they began walking up the small incline leading to the government enclave, he assured himself that everything was *biseder* - OK. Proceeding as planned, he strolled by the Central Post Office, the Generali Building, and the

Anglo-Palestine Bank until he reached a crowd of Arabs loitering by the popular outdoor hangout. Making sure that no one had followed them, Tzvi kept lookout as Yaacov walked nonchalantly into the three-story office building, carrying the bulky bag as if he were delivering a parcel. Climbing the stairs, he was pleased to see that the door to the roof, whose lock he had broken, was still open. Walking across the roof, he bent down by the low railing which overlooked the tables below on the sidewalk. Arabs sat on stools drinking Turkish coffee and puffing on tobacco-filled *nagilehs*, whose pungent aroma wafted up to the roof. Hearing footsteps, he turned to welcome his Hasidic partner.

"The coast is clear," Tzvi said, kneeling down by the railing.

"Is there some kind of blessing for this?" Yaacov asked.

"We say it three times a day," Tzvi informed him. "Blessed art Thou, O Lord, who smashes enemies and causes evildoers to fall."

"What a fine blessing!" Tzvi's fearless new friend replied.

Yaacov raised the box for Tzvi to light the fuse. A flame shot up with a snake-like hiss, but the young bomber gripped the box with steady hands, setting it on the railing for two seconds before dropping it toward the busy café below. Running back through the door to the roof, the two *Etzel* commandoes began hurrying down the stairs. Their noisy footsteps were silenced by a thunderous explosion which shook the entire building.

Pandemonium broke out on all of the floors. Hysterical workers ran out of their offices toward the stairwell. The bombers joined the crowd and escaped from the building unnoticed. Havoc reigned on the street. Police ran to the scene. Sirens blared. Two Arabs died in the blast. Another five were badly wounded. Damage to the café was extensive. Within an hour, a curfew had been imposed on the city. Clearly panicked, the British began to arrest known Revisionists, but the "Anonymous Soldiers" of the Jewish Underground continued their clandestine activities with no interference.

David Raziel and commanders of the *Irgun* were jubilant,

but they weren't ready to rest on their laurels. Two other operations were on the way, to give the impression that the *Etzel* was a large and well-trained force. Simultaneous strikes were planned for Friday afternoon in Jerusalem after Muslim prayers on the Temple Mount. The *Irgun-Etzel* Intelligence Squad knew that Arab gang leaders and their disciples met regularly in the Old City to plan further attacks against Jews. "Baghdad Nights Restaurant" was the name of their favorite rendezvous spot. Coming up with an idea for a new kind of a time bomb, Eliav created an electric detonating circuit, connecting a battery with a clock, which would close the circuit at the desired time. Replacing the glass cover of the clock with plastic, he drilled a small hole and inserted a screw to be touched by the hour hand of the clock. He connected the other end of the screw to the battery and detonator. This time, he decided not to involve Hevedke in the bomb's construction because of the great deftness involved. When the deadly device was finished, Eliav secured it into a crate and waited for Nachshon to arrive. Arab merchants purchased goods in the trade market located outside of the Old City. Arab porters loaded the merchandise on their backs and lugged the goods to shops inside the walls. That bit of common knowledge was the key to the plan. The dark-complexioned Nachshon showed up on time, dressed like an Arab porter, with a sleeveless shirt, baggy pants and sandals. In the manner of *sabalim*, the muscular youth slipped a thick, protective mat over his shoulders, then bent over as Yaacov hoisted the bulky crate onto his back. Before sending the "Arab porter" on his way, Yaacov tied a sack of knives and forks to the crate, to make the explosion more deadly. Then Yaacov triggered the timer. In practice runs, they knew the exact time it would take to carry the crate to the outdoor café at the corner of David and HaShalshelet Streets, near the Arab vegetable market. Arriving at the crowded and noisy restaurant, Nachshon rested by an alley wall, letting the crate slip slowly to the ground. In Friday's after-prayer festivity, no one paid attention as the porter slipped away, leaving the crate by a cafe wall. The deafening explosion echoed throughout the Old City. Ten Arabs were killed and thirty wounded. It took the police hours to clean up the devastated area. Blood remained splattered on the *Irgun* posters which Boaz and Naomi had plastered the night before on the walls of the neighborhood. Panic gripped the Arabs in the Old City. Instead of dead and wounded Jews, the bodies of mutilated Arabs were carried to the ambulances waiting at the top of David Street. Stores closed and Arabs fled from the Old City in all directions.

A half-hour later at the Jerusalem Bus Station, draped in a long *kaftan* and with a *keffiyeh* covering his head, Tzvi shoved his way onto a jam-packed bus to Hevron. The plan was to arrive early and board the bus before it filled with passengers, so he could disembark immediately while it was still in the station, but the pandemonium on the street slowed up his progress. He held a large straw basket to his chest, praying that the bomb inside wouldn't explode in the jostle. A small Arab throw rug covered the bomb, and a bag filled with *Irgun* flyers rested on the rug. Purposefully, Hevedke had fashioned a simple time bomb without shrapnel, and with just enough TNT to make a loud noise and cause damage to the immediate area, but not to blow up the entire bus with all of its passengers. The goal was to teach a lesson, not to kill as many people as possible. No number of dead bodies could bring his wife back to life, with the other seventy Jews who had been massacred in the decade-old pogrom in Hevron.

Seeing an empty space on the overhead rack, Tzvi lifted the basket over his head and secured it between two other large packages.

"*Ana asef. Ana asef,*" he apologized in Arabic, in a low gruff voice, as he tried to push his way back toward the door of the bus. "Sorry, sorry," he repeated, but with the mass of boarding passengers pushing in the other direction, his progress was completely thwarted. He even lost ground in the battle.

"*Ana asef.* Sorry, sorry," he said hoarsely, afraid that his Hebrew accent would give him away. Arabs cursed at him angrily. Everyone wanted to find a seat. Sweat broke out on his forehead. The bomb was scheduled to explode in another two minutes. Realizing that any forward progress was impossible, he let the momentum of the boarding passengers push him backwards toward the rear exit, where a barricade of Arabs were sitting on the two steps in front of the door, blocking the only other exit.

Desperate, he reached for the door, but none of the passengers agreed to budge.

"It's locked," someone said.

With a pounding heart, he made a decision. Quickly, he rejoined the flow of bodies pushing toward the rear of the bus. At the very end of the aisle, he dropped to his knees as if he were praying. Holding his hands on his head, he bent as low to the floor as he could. "May the killers of my sister, Hava, be avenged," he silently prayed. Even though he knew what was coming, he felt his soul leave his body as the dynamite blast roared through the bus, knocking out windows and blowing walls into the air. The next thing he knew, he lay on the ground of the bus station, surrounded by wild screams and blood. Realizing that he was alive, he dizzily rose to his feet. The explosion had split the flimsy bus in half. Passengers staggered about as if they were drunk. Bodies lay on the ground. Feeling his head, he realized he had lost his *keffiyeh*. Unsteady on his feet, and hearing a loud whistle in his ears, he wobbled away from the mayhem as the *Irgun's* white flyers floated high in the air and drifted back toward the earth like snow. The message was written in Arabic:

PEOPLE OF HEVRON

In the year *Tarpat*, Arab savages murdered and maimed the Jews of Hevron, raping women and torturing children. The British, who did nothing to prevent the massacre, evacuated the Jewish survivors, ending the Jewish presence in the City of our Forefathers, where Jews had lived for thousands of years. You may have forgotten the merciless savagery, but the fighters of the *Etzel* have not. Until now, in the name of peace, we have patiently withstood never-ending violence against us. No Jew ever instigated an attack against an Arab, unless in self-defense. But again and again, Arab leaders have incited riots and acts of wanton brutality and murder against us. No more will the Jews of the Holy Land turn the other cheek. The long arm of the

Jewish Underground will strike whenever and wherever we choose. No Arab bus, train, street, store, or home, is safe in our just struggle to liberate our Promised Land from foreign thieves and murderers. *"Vengeance and recompense are mine."*

3.

Responding to the wave of attacks, the British Police rounded up Revisionist activists and sympathizers and incarcerated them in the Acco Prison. While the common man in the street supported the reprisal attacks of the modern-day Maccabees, those raised on socialist ideologies sided with the Labor Party's condemnation of the "reckless hoodlums in our midst whose actions endanger the whole *Yishuv.*" After the bold reprisal attacks, Leftist newspapers published scorching rebukes. An editorial in the *Jewish Chronicle* stated:

"It is one thing to defend oneself when attacked, but another to strike coldly at innocents in the street. Actions of this sort place Jews on the moral level of the terrorist Arab killers, and they threaten to discredit all of the Jews in the country. They are loathsome to all Jewish sentiment and teaching. The sooner the perpetrators are apprehended and punished, the better for everyone."

The socialist newspaper, *HaPoel HaTzair*, had this to say: "Woe it is, when Jews lower themselves and copy the inhuman deeds of Arab terrorists. Senseless killings of this sort are antithetical to the Jewish way of life, and they sabotage the best interests of the *Yishuv*. We have not returned to the Holy Land to turn into vicious killers."

In a full-page, public notice in the *Palestine Post*, the Jewish Agency declared:

"The Jewish Agency absolutely opposes all reprisal attacks against innocent people. Every act of revenge merely increases Arab terror and puts a horrible stain on the Jewish community of Palestine. The Jewish Agency is certain that the upstanding and justice-loving people of the Jewish Settlement in Palestine will protest in one united voice against these shameful deeds and will take every measure possible to wipe out this scourge of evil from our midst."

Ben Gurion wrote: "These Jewish gangsters imitate all the methods of the Nazis. They are deadly enemies. When you converse with them, you must always remember that you are speaking to an enemy lacking any moral conscience. This does not mean that there should be no contact between us. For the sake of peace, I would even agree to meet with the Grand Mufti, but when I speak with them, I know with whom I am dealing."

To all of the defamation, David Raziel was fond of saying, "They can kiss my you know what!" To his way of thinking, the *Mapai* Party and its leaders were more interested in their positions of power than in the wellbeing of the Jews. Raziel didn't care if he had to spend his nights, a refugee from his home, sleeping in damp basements with rats nibbling at his shoes. If the Arabs made life hell for the Jews, he would turn their life into hell as well. The more the Left protested, the more "bouquets" he ordered planted in Arab neighborhoods to make them terrified of the Land's true landlords.

For many young people, the secret underground organization held a fanciful "Robin Hood" charm. Troubled by the report that some of its workers had sworn allegiance to the ranks of the *Irgun*, the *Histadrut* Worker's Union responded with an announcement in the newspaper *Davar*:

"The seductively sweet proclamations that promise freedom and Redemption, whose honey-covered words are like the temptations of the snake, will not lure the *Histadrut* laborer away from his task. The true goal of these supposed soldiers for freedom is not against external enemies, but rather against our youth, to destroy them by luring them away from the Worker's Union, to weaken the power of the workers and seize for themselves the reins of the *Yishuv*. Their bonfires blaze with the fire of national suicide. But a united voice will answer them with a resounding 'no,' and the banner of the workers will remain uplifted, leading the nation on the true path of freedom."

Members of the *Irgun* felt hunted, not only by the Arabs and the British, but by the socialist majority who held the Revisionists and *Betarim* in contempt, even more than they had in the past, now that the dynamic actions of the *Irgun* had captured the imagination of the public.

To make matters worse, Jabotinsky himself harbored deep moral doubts about the bombings which were purportedly carried out under his leadership. When Arabs massacred the Jewish passengers of yet another vehicle traveling along a Galilee road, David Raziel responded by bombing the Arab market in Haifa, killing twenty-three Arabs and wounding eighty. In London, Jabotinsky angrily chided an *Irgun* agent over the devastating attack. "Life is sacred," he said. "How can you detonate bombs in Arab quarters at random, indiscriminately killing women and children? You must at least warn the Arabs in time to evacuate the places that you intend to attack." Jabotinsky wired David Raziel in Jerusalem, stating: "This should never happen again!" The local *Irgun* commander responded to his colleagues in distraught: "How can he tell us that? Should we also inform the Arabs of the exact time and place of our attacks, and give them the names and addresses of the attackers as well?!"

1938

Chapter Eleven
GOD BLESS AMERICA!

"What an incredible world!" Tevye reflected, as he gazed out the airplane window at the propellers which propelled the flying machine through the dark and turbulent sky. His grandfathers would never have dreamed that one day there would be flying machines that could whisk people from one side of the world to the other. As King David had declared, *"How manifold are Your works, O Lord. In wisdom You have made them all."*

Twenty-five-years ago in Anatevka, if a soothsayer had told Tevye that he was destined to shave off his beard and travel on an airplane to America to raise money to buy weapons for the secret Jewish Underground in *Eretz Yisrael*, the milkman would have called him a *"meshugene."* But lo and behold, here he was, clean-shaven and flying on an airplane to America!

Since the beginning of the flight, even before take-off, Tevye had reciting *"Tehillim,"* reading through the whole *Book of Psalms*, as his Mother and his cherished Golda often did, may their memories be for a blessing. All through the celestial voyage, he didn't stop praying that the Almighty keep the giant aircraft in the sky. After all, the airplane must have weighed a hundred tons. What kept it aloft in the air if not a miracle? The tiny propellers? "What foolishness! *A bubbe mayser!"* he mused in Yiddish. It was the will of the Almighty – as with everything else. The Master of Heaven and Earth wanted airplanes to fly, so He provided man with the technical knowledge to get the giant contraptions off the ground, but it was His will alone which kept them from tumbling through space back to Earth.

Tevye stared out at the stars which seemed close enough to touch. Once again, the words of the Psalmist formed on his lips. *"When I contemplate on Your heavens, the work of Your fingers, the moon and the stars, which You set in place, what is man that You take thought of him?"*

For the past several months, Tevye had sojourned in Warsaw, visiting his granddaughter's husband, "Yair" Avraham Stern, who was busy raising a Jewish army to invade Palestine and seize the country from the British. After the *Irgun* had split over the issue of *havlaga*, *Irgun* Commander, Avraham Tehomi, took the brunt of the group's leadership, and more than half of the rank and file, to the already established and semi-legal *Haganah*, which, under the Jewish Agency's control, championed restraint and political appeasement. Tehomi believed that by united the two quasi-armies, they would have more force if and when a Jewish State was formed. Stern opposed the merger, insisting that the Leftist leadership of the Jewish Agency was not interested in a true unification of forces, but rather sought to cripple the *Irgun* by placing it under its direction. Stern became one of the commanders of the underground *Irgun*. When David Raziel was appointed commander of military operations, Yair became the theoretician and visionary behind the curtains, inspiring a growing cadre of "Anonymous Soldiers" to enlist in the battle. While Raziel's forceful personality was no less charismatic than Stern's, and his erudition, certainly in Torah, even broader, Stern possessed an aura of mystery that drew people to follow him, with an almost blind allegiance, the way some people become disciples of spiritual mystics. Raziel was more down to earth. He had the outer appearance of a tough army general, confident in his know-how and accustomed to people following his commands. The two energetic idealists were the best of friends. Raziel admired the poet in Stern, and Stern admired the "born soldier" in Raziel. While they collaborated together to write a practical manual for the "Organization" on the use of weapons, David Raziel had the appearance of someone who knew how to use them. In contrast, Stern's demeanor was strikingly more elegant and refined, not needing a gun in his hand to project an image of being a very dangerous man. Their similarities and differences attracted them together, and eventually set them apart.

Stern found the Polish Government amendable to his plan. Upon his initiative, military training for young Polish Jews was organized under the supervision of Polish army officers. He purchased Polish weapons and arranged for their secret shipment to Haifa. Stern also started two *Irgun* newspapers in Warsaw, "*De Tat*," published in Yiddish, and, "*Free Jerusalem*," in Polish, to attract assimilated Jews to Zionism.

Stern's ideology was simple and straight to the point, attracting thousands of young Polish Jews who felt they had no future in the increasingly anti-Semitic country. To his way of thinking, since the Land of Israel was the Jewish Homeland, any foreign domination of the Land stood in the way of Jewish independence and freedom. Thus all foreign subjugation had to be challenged and removed. This, he maintained, would not be achieved through political diplomacy and petitions to world governments, but only through armed revolt. To Yair, this was the ultimate mission of the *Irgun*, the movement of national liberation of the Jewish People. The clock was ticking away. With the growth of Nazism, the survival of Jews throughout Europe was endangered. British control over Palestine, their pro-Arab policies, and their restrictions on immigration, threatened, not only the survival of the Jewish community in *Eretz Yisrael*, it also doomed millions of European Jews to Hitler's megalomaniacal whims. Now was the time to act!

Having no great love for the Jews, and viewing England as an enemy, the Polish Government agreed to assist the highly persuasive Stern in his plans. Polish leaders agreed to facilitate the evacuation of the Jews from Poland via Jewish immigration to Palestine. In addition, the Polish Government would provide vast amounts of weapons, and offer military training programs for Jews inside of Poland. As part of the agreement, the *Irgun* would receive 20,000 rifles and bayonets, 20 million rounds of ammunition, hundreds of machine guns, thousands of revolvers, tons of explosives, and crate-loads of grenades. Initial shipments were hidden in double-bottomed containers. Machine guns were packed on ships alongside construction equipment. Members of the *Irgun* awaited the arrival of the weapons in Haifa. The acquisition of the munitions sparked a wave of enthusiasm throughout the clandestine organization, but Germany's occupation of Czechoslovakia and Poland put an end to the project before an army of Jews could be recruited and trained.

On the long flight to America, the wing of the aircraft shook fragilely in the turbulence outside the window. Though Tevye had great faith in the Almighty, he squirmed in his seat. He had already walked up and down the aisle several times to stretch his back and legs. Having passed the age of sixty, he couldn't be called a spring chicken. If he sat too long, his spine began to lament, as if it were *Tisha B'Av*, the day of mourning over the destruction of the Holy Jerusalem Temple. The Sages were right when they said that sixty was the beginning of old age. Nonetheless, Tevye felt that his time hadn't come to be put out to pasture. Perhaps he was getting too old to be a soldier in the Jewish Underground in Palestine, but, as Rabbi Kook had predicted, he had other qualities he could call upon in serving the Jewish People, like life experience and the wisdom that evolves from it. Not that he was any kind of genius, but he could tell a horse from a jackass.

Once again, he passed a hand over his clean-shaven face. All of his life, like with Samson, a razor had never touched a single strand. But what could he do? When Tevye's revolver had jammed, Haj Amin al-Husseini had a chance to take a long look at his would-be, bearded assassin. Tevye had no choice but to shave.

His feet hurt in his new, tight-fitting shoes, and the tightness of his tie reminded him of his days in the Hebrew Brigade when the Turks captured him and tightened a hangman's noose around his neck, just before salvation arrived from Heaven. Although he felt like a clown in his double-breasted suit and Fedora hat, David Raziel told him that he had to play the part if he wanted to be taken seriously in America. The former milkman sighed a sigh of two-thousand years. He needed America like a *loch in kop* – a hole in the head. But, at least he would get to see his eldest daughter, Baylke, after a separation of almost thirty years, and, with a little *mazel*, he might even raise some needed *gelt* to buy guns for the "Organization."

The airplane landed safely at Idlewild Airport in New York. After collecting his suitcase, and after passing United

States Customs and Passport Clearance, Tevye walked into the hall for arriving passengers. He saw Baylke before she spotted him. He recognized her immediately. No longer a young woman, she had retained her striking looks. While his wife Golda had been a pretty woman, may her memory be for a blessing, she had possessed a modest, natural attractiveness that could have gone unnoticed in a crowd. In contrast, Baylke's beauty was more classic, almost chiseled like a statue – and sometimes just as cold. How well Tevye remembered that his eldest daughter's heart could be as frozen as a Russian winter, like the time when her wealthy husband, Pedhotzer, had offered Tevye money to move to Palestine, to get rid of his peasant of a father-in-law, with his muddy boots and barn-like smell. And all the time, Baylke had stood by her husband's side like an iceberg, not saying a single word. But that was the past, and the time had come to let bygones be bygones. Tevye's heart filled with joy when he saw her, dressed in elegant clothing, standing by her good-for-nothing husband. Overwhelmed by the rush of emotion surging in his heart, the sentimental father was prepared to forgive him too - not that a snake can grow legs. But through all of the years, Pedhotzer had cared for Tevye's daughter, and that's what counted the most, he realized, not his wounded honor.

Baylke knew she had a cold streak inside her, but now, eagerly awaiting her father's arrival, she felt nothing but warmth. Arriving passengers walked by, but she didn't see her *tata*. Funny, she mused. How long it had been since she thought of that word – *tata*. For three decades, she had been an orphan in the world without her mother or father. Yes, she had her husband, but it wasn't the same. Pedhotzer could never be her father. They were so different, like fire and water. While Pedhotzer had the scent of expensive cologne, her father smelled like mud and cows. But where was he, she wondered, not noticing that a man smartly dressed in the style of the times was standing by her side.

"Excuse me," he said. "Do you know someone named Baylke?"

The voice. That voice. It was the deep beloved voice of her father! Her mouth opened in surprise as she gazed at the clean-shaven figure before her. The same eyes. The same nose. The same glowing smile.

"*Pappa!*" she exclaimed. "*Pappa!*"

"Baylkile, my Baylkile!" Tevye cried, overwhelmed with emotion. "My daughter!"

Pedhotzer was as astonished as his wife. Could this distinguished looking gentleman in a smart double-breasted suit and Fedora hat be his father-in-law, the common milkman?!

Tevye gripped his long-lost daughter in a fatherly bear hug. A deep sob, both painful and joyous, shook his body. Never in his life had he experienced such great *simcha*. Not the joy at his wedding. Not even the joy he had felt at the birth of his son, Tzvi, after seven daughters. It was as if his Golda had come back to life. As if his Shprintza had arisen from the lake where she had drown. As if Bat Sheva and Hava had returned from the dead. In his inexpressible joy, born out of inexpressible pain, Tevye remember to thank the good Lord for His kindness, exclaiming out loud in Hebrew, "*Baruch atah Hashem elokanu melach haolam, mechayay hamatim!*" Blessed art Thou, O Lord, our God, King of the Universe, who returns the dead to life!"

"O, *Pappa*," Baylke cried.

Tears even formed in Pehotzer's eyes, like water from a stone. Gently, Tevye pushed his daughter away and turned to his son-in-law, a wealthy and successful businessman. Tevye gave him a hug.

"Tevye!" Baylke's normally emotionless husband exclaimed with an outburst of feeling.

"Pedhotzer!" Tevye uttered.

For a moment, like a still photograph captured in time, everyone in the airport lobby stopped in their tracks to watch the three sobbing people embrace. Then, like busy New Yorkers, they went about their business, as if the moment had never occurred.

Baylke removed a handkerchief from her shoulder bag and wiped away her tears.

"*Pappa*, why did you shave?"

"It's a long story," her father replied.

"Do you have all of your luggage?" Pedhotzer asked.

"Yes," Tevye answered. "Just this one piece."

"Fine, fine, let me take it," he said, reaching down to pick up the bag. "My car is outside. We'll talk on the way to the city. Let's go. I don't want to get a parking ticket."

Baylke smiled at her husband. For once, he was being a *mensch*. She knew that Pedhotzer didn't like her father, and that her father couldn't tolerate him. But all that seemed to be forgotten now. How wonderful! How wonderful! Thank the good Lord!

2.

Pedhotzer's bright yellow Lincoln Convertible Roadster stuck out from the other automobiles parked out on the street. There were other yellow cars – taxis – but they were smaller and shaped like shoeboxes, while the Lincoln had elegant, curving lines and no roof. Pedhotzer put Tevye's suitcase in the baggage compartment. Baylke sat in the rear seat, and Tevye sat in the spacious, leather upholstered seat up front. The dashboard had as many dials as an airplane. The driving wheel was made out of wood like the wheel of a ship. Pedhotzer honked the horn loudly as he guided the vehicle onto the road.

"What do you say about this baby?" he asked Tevye.

"Baby?" his father-in-law inquired.

"This automobile. It's a Lincoln."

"Very nice," Tevye said, not knowing much about cars. It was the first time he had ever ridden in a convertible, but since he had driven horse-drawn wagons all of his life, the open-air vehicle didn't impress him.

"The factory only produced thirty models like this," Pedhotzer announced proudly. "It's their top of the line, worth a small fortune."

"I didn't want my husband to buy it," Baylke said. "It's very pretty, especially at night, but with the country is suffering such a terrible financial Depression, and with so many people out of work, struggling to get along, I felt it would be too ostentatious to drive around in a car so expensive."

"It's our money," Pedhotzer said. "I work hard for it. What

business is it of anyone what I do with my earnings?" Then, glancing at Tevye, he explained, "You can get a standard Ford for five-hundred bucks. This beauty cost almost five thousand."

"What do you do when it rains?" the greenhorn asked.

"There's a sturdy cloth cover that unfolds from the rear with the press of a button, and which you can fold back down when you want to enjoy the sun."

"To me, a car like this is too cold in the winter," Baylke complained.

"The car has an excellent heater," her husband replied.

"Still, I feel cold all the same."

"I'll buy you another mink coat," he said with a laugh.

"She already has two."

"I'm sure my father isn't interested in your car, or in my mink coats. How is everyone, *Pappa*?" she asked.

Keeping his eyes on the unfamiliar scenery surrounding the highway, Tevye told them about the family in *Eretz Yisrael*.

"How is Hannie?" Baylke asked. "She's such a charming girl."

Tevye's granddaughter had lived with Baylke and Pedhotzer in their New York City townhouse for almost five years while she was attending Barnard College. "Fine," Tevye answered. "Happily married. She teaches and makes dresses on the side. Unfortunately, her husband travels a great deal, but Hannie is happy with her lot."

"She is a very nice girl, indeed," Pedhotzer said. "Very well mannered. Very serious. All the time she lived with us, she never dated men. I am happy she married the man she loved."

To Pedhotzer credit, he had displayed outstanding hospitality in allowing Tevye's granddaughter to live with them for such a long time. The *mitzvah* of hospitality, *hachnasat orachim*, was one of the fundamental principles of the Torah, stressing the importance of kindness, giving, and not living for oneself. When Pedhotzer had married Baylke, he had been a rich, young businessman, a builder of railways and roads. But in the upheaval of the Russian Revolution, he had lost his personal fortune. Seeing no future for individual enterprise, he journeyed with his wife to America. With his quick financial mind, he rapidly advanced from his job as a bank clerk to bank manager, to the director of a chain of New York banks. One of his clients was Meyer Lansky, head of the Jewish Mafia, who set up legal companies to launder monies made through extortion, racketeering, bootlegging, and gambling. When Lansky offered Pedhotzer a position with the "firm" as his chief financial advisor, Tevye's ambitious son-in-law seized the opportunity. Mastering the intricacies of American tax regulations, and working long hours, he managed to keep his boss out of trouble. To keep his wife happy, he gave her a generous allowance which she spent on clothes and jewelry, and luncheons with her friends. Now, to please the beautiful Baylke, who could be a tyrant to live with when she didn't get her way, he agreed to introduce her father to the powerful Mafia boss, who was known to have a warm spot in his heart for the plight of fellow Jews.

The expressway was filled with an endless flow of cars, traveling in both directions. The sky, Tevye noticed, was dismal and gray.

"How far away is New York City?" he asked.

"About another thirty minutes, if we don't run into traffic."

"How does it feel to be in America?" Baylke inquired.

"I don't know yet," her father answered. "I'm a little tired from the journey."

"Are you still a milkman?" Pedhotzer wanted to know.

"In a way. I help manage a milk company."

"Really?" Pedhotzer responded with almost a tone of respect in his voice.

"I'm dying of curiosity," Baylke said. "Why did you shave off your beard?"

In very general terms, Tevye described the situation in Palestine, the Arab violence, coupled with the policy of constant appeasement and restraint on the part of the Jewish Agency.

"Zionist leaders like Ben Gurion and Chaim Weizmann believe that the Jews can only win political concessions from the British by accepting the role of the victimized Jew, proving that we are a more moral people than our enemies. The Arabs take this as a sign of weakness and continue with their rampage and slaughter. While England promised in the Balfour Declaration to assist the Jewish People to establish a National Homeland in Palestine, they have reneged on their commitment a dozen times. A lot of Jews in the country have lost their patience with the policy of restraint and long to strike back at our enemies."

Pedhotzer was impressed to hear such a lucid presentation. Apparently, the former milkman had received some education in the past thirty years. "What is your personal opinion in the matter?" Pedhotzer asked.

"I agree that the time has come to fight fire with fire," Tevye responded.

"What does all this have to do with shaving your beard?" his daughter asked.

"Some Jews have begun to respond," Tevye answered. "The British believe I may be one of them."

"You mean you're in hiding? That's why you've come to America, and that's why you shaved off your beard?" Baylke asked in alarm.

Tevye turned toward his daughter. "My main reason for coming to America is to see you. If I can also help the situation of the Jews in *Eretz Yisrael* by finding people in America sympathetic to our cause, that will be an added *mitzvah*."

"We are trying our best to turn America into a Promised Land for the Jews," Pedhotzer noted.

"Let's hope they stay Jews. I am told that many marry out of the faith in order to be more American."

For a few noticeable seconds, both his daughter and her husband were silent.

"I may know some people who can help you," Pedhotzer said.

"You haven't murdered anyone, have you, *Tata*?" Baylke asked her father.

"If Arabs or British policemen are killed, it isn't murder. We are at war," Tevye replied.

"At war with the British?" Pedhotzer queried "I can

understand wanting to get even with the Arabs, but the thought of taking on the British Empire is absurd."

Tevye remained mysteriously silent.

"It seems to me to be an impossible situation," Pedhotzer concluding, priding himself on his intelligence and quick understanding. "The Arabs believe that Palestine is their country, just as the Jews feel it is theirs. The British undoubtedly are interested in Middle East oil and controlling the Suez Canal."

"That's why we need guns," Tevye said directly.

"*Tata,*" Baylke cried out. "How did you get yourself involved in all this?"

"In Anatevka, we wanted to live in peace, but the *goyim* wouldn't let us. The same thing is happening in *Eretz Yisrael*. How long can a person be a wanderer with no country of his own, getting hit over the head or killed just because he's a Jew? Enough is enough."

"You will like my friends," Pedhotzer remarked. "They are trying to make sure that the Jews in America don't get pushed around by the *goyim*."

"I hope my English is good enough to speak with them."

"You can speak with them in Yiddish," Pedhotzer assured him.

"Bugsy Siegel speaks Yiddish?" Baylke asked.

"Like a Rabbi."

"Tell me about my grandson, George," Tevye said. "Where is he? I am anxious to meet the grandson I have never met in my life."

Tevye noticed Pedhotzer glance up at the rear view mirror to look at his wife.

"I think we should tell him," Baylke said.

"We decided that we wouldn't," her husband answered.

"He'll find out sooner or later," she countered.

Pedhotzer shook his head in frustration. Suddenly, his eyes widened. The car in front of them on the highway came to an unexpected stop. Pedhotzer honked on the horn of the Lincoln and slammed on the brakes. Tevye and Balke lurched forward. Horns honked angrily behind them.

"Stupid idiot!" Pedhotzer cursed in Russian.

Everyone let out a deep breath of relief.

"Thank God the car wasn't hit," the angered driver exclaimed.

"The car!" Balke retorted. "Thank God that we weren't killed."

Tevye's neck hurt from the whiplash. After having sat for twenty hours on an airplane crossing the Atlantic, a twisted neck was the last thing he needed.

"I didn't buy collision insurance for the car," Pedhotzer disclosed. "It was too expensive."

Ahead of them, the roadway cleared, and the yellow convertible continued toward Manhattan.

"Keep your eyes on the road," Baylke told her husband.

"It wasn't my fault," he replied.

"What don't you want to tell me about my grandson?" Tevye inquired.

Again, Pedhotzer glanced sharply at his wife in the rear-view mirror.

"George has a girlfriend who isn't Jewish," his daughter confided.

"Oh, shit," Pedhotzer said. "It's not your father's business."

Tevye felt like he had been punched in the stomach. "Good God," he thought. "My grandson is in love with a *shicksa*!"

"He'll get over it," Baylke assured him. "It's just an infatuation. George has had a lot of girlfriends. He'll finish with this one as well."

For some reason, Tevye didn't feel reassured. Were women in America like disposable tissues, he wondered, that you could get rid of them so easily?

"Why should he finish with her?" her husband wanted to know. "She a decent girl. She has nice manners. She's studying law. Her parents are well-to-do people. Didn't one of your sisters run off with a *goy*?"

"He converted," Tevye said. "According to the full demands of Jewish Law."

"Don't worry, *Tata*," his daughter said. "Of course, if George decides to marry her, she'll be converted first."

"Why should she have to convert?" Pedhotzer asked.

"This is America, not Anatevka. Everyone is equal here. What does it matter whether he marries a Gentile or a Jew?"

"Easy, easy, Tevye," he heard his Golda say. Instinctively, he gazed up toward Heaven. There was an advantage to owning a convertible after all. "Don't get into a fight with him," Golda's calming voice advised him. "Pedhotzer is the boy's father, not you. In the merit of our righteous parents, may their memories be for a blessing, everything will turn out for the best. But if you start screaming about "TRADITION," Pedhotzer won't introduce you to his wealthy friends. So, for once in your life, instead of following your *kishkes*, follow your brain."

When a voice called out from Heaven, even a stubborn mule, like Bilam's ass, had sense enough to listen. Shouldn't Tevye as well? "When you speak to the boy in private," Golda told him, "you'll have the occasion to make him see the error of his ways. Arguing with Pedhotzer won't win you anything."

Golda was right – as always. Some things never change.

"Do you know Nathan Strauss Jr.?" Tevye asked, changing subjects. "His father was a big supporter of the Jewish causes in Palestine."

"Fathers are fathers, and sons are sons," the practical businessman answered. "If you don't have a personal connection, you'll just be another *shnorrer* from *Eretz Yisrael* looking for a hand-out."

"I have a personal letter of recommendation from Rabbi Kook."

"Never heard of him."

"He was the first Chief Rabbi," Tevye explained.

"Anyone can fake a letter of recommendation. It isn't worth the paper it's written on. New Yorkers aren't naïve."

Pedhotzer opened a drawer near the dashboard and pulled out a long cigar. "Want one?" he asked Tevye. "We import them from Cuba."

Tevye had never heard of Cuba, but he said, "Why not?"

"Do you have to smoke in the car?" Baylke asked her husband.

"It's a convertible," he answered.

"I hate the smell," his wife said.

"Hold your breath," he quipped with a laugh.

Handing a cigar to Tevye, he lit his own with the car lighter. "This car has everything," he said. "Too bad it can't cook."

"You're a real Jack Benny," his wife replied.

Tevye lit his cigar with the small, red-tipped lighter. Taking a puff, he coughed. He wasn't a smoker, but he could tell that the tobacco was fresh and strong.

"You're still religious?" Pedhotzer inquired.

"Of course," Tevye replied.

"What a shame."

"Leave my father alone," Baylke protested. "Just because you don't believe in anything, don't try to make my father an *apikorus* like you."

"*Tzitzit* and all?" his son-in-law asked, referring the four-cornered garment with strings which Tevye used to wear under his vest.

"Yes, of course. They're tucked into my trousers under my shirt."

"Keep them there," Pedhotzer advised.

"Judaism isn't something you part with like a broken wagon," Tevye noted.

"My father did," Pedhotzer said. "Lot's of Jews have discovered new ways. Do mean one favor. If you meet my employers, don't try to convert them. They are proud Jews. More than a few people have ended up with their throats slit for calling a Jew a '*kike*' in their presence. But if you start blabbering about religion, it will end the conversation before it begins. Understand?"

"Oh, stop frightening him," Baylke said.

Tevye was accustomed to being cursed by the Russians and British, but "*kike*" was a slur that he had never heard. Later, he learned that the derogatory expression originated on Ellis Island, home of the Statue of Liberty, the landing point for immigrants arriving in America, the land of equality and freedom. When Jews who didn't know how to write their names in English were told to sign entry forms with an X, they balked because the symbol X was associated with the Christian crucifix and cross. Instead, they signed the documents with a circle, called "*kikel*" in Yiddish. Soon, immigration officials began to call the Jews, "*kikes.*"

Up ahead in the distance, Tevye got his first glimpse of the towering skyline of Manhattan.

"Welcome to New York," Pedhotzer said to his guest as the convertible sped onto the Manhattan Bridge. A panoramic view of the city spread out before them. The driver pointed proudly to the sites: the Statue of Liberty on Ellis Island, where immigrant Jews landed on their way to the "golden shores of America," the Hudson River, Wall Street, the East River, the Brooklyn Bridge, Riker's Island, the Empire State Building, as tall as the Tower of Babel.

"Impressive, isn't it? What do you think?" Pedhotzer asked.

His question was answered by a loud grunt and a snore. The tired and travel-worn Tevye had fallen fast asleep.

3.

Meyer Lansky told Pedhotzer to take Tevye to the Joe Louis versus Max Schmeling heavyweight championship fight. Seventy-thousand spectators packed New York's Yankee Stadium to witness the highly-publicized battle which was taking place in an atmosphere of growing tension between the United States and Hitler's Third Reich. Tevye felt the great electricity in the air, even before the heralded boxing match began, as if some tremendous world event was about to take place. Baylke looked gorgeous in her flashy designer gown, as if she were attending a wedding. Lansky had given them front rows seats – the best in the house. Pedhotzer pointed out the famous people who were seated around them – the Mayor of New York City, Fiorello Henry La Guardia; FBI Chief, J. Edgar Hoover; actors Cary Grant, Douglas Fairbanks, and Gregory Peck, to name just a few. Shunning the limelight and the FBI, the Jewish Mafia boss preferred to listen to the bout on the radio.

A few days before the fight, Pedhotzer had asked Tevye how much money he had collected for the "cause."

"Maybe three hundred dollars," Tevye answered, feeling that he had failed in his mission. He wasn't much of a *shnorrer*. In addition, America had suffered a severe economic decline throughout the Great Depression.Most of the people whom Tevye met at the synagogues where he prayed were simple, hard-working Jews without extra money in their pockets. He had met a few successful businessmen and lawyers, but his spiel about the *Irgun* fell on deaf ears. "In God We Trust," was written on the dollar, and not many Americans wanted to part with their god. In a few instances, Jews who had already been approached by representatives of Ben Gurion's *Mapai* Party had been warned not to donate money to "Jabotinsky's gang of fascist hoodlums" whose reckless actions threatened to turn the British against the Zionist cause.

"Mr. Lansky advises you to bet all the money you have that Joe Louis will knockout Schmeling in the first round of the fight," Pedhotzer informed his father-in-law. "I'll add five-hundred dollars to what you have already. The odds of a first round knockout are twenty to one. You can turn your eight hundred into sixteen thousand without having to *shlep* off to *minyan* all over the city."

"Bet with who?" Tevye asked.

"With a betting syndicate, or with the bookie on the corner. They're all over town. I'll take care of it for you if you like."

Betting was gambling, and gambling was against the Torah. But betting on the outcome of a fight between two *goyim* didn't seem like such a big sin, especially if profits went to the cause of Jewish independence in the Land of Israel.

"It sounds like a good investment, but I don't know anything about boxing. Won't I be taking a risk?"

"Like they say, 'Life is a risk.' But when Mr. Lansky suggests something, it's smart to listen, if you want to keep on good terms. For instance, he wants you to fly out to the West Coast to meet Bugsy Siegel. Hollywood is loaded with Jews with big bucks. What do you say?"

Tevye hesitated. He didn't know that Lansky had sent a trusted worker, Moe Sedway, to speak with Schmeling, the former world heavyweight champion, to convince him to throw the fight for a hundred-thousand dollar pay-off. Even though the younger, reigning champion, Joe Louis, was favored to win the bout, Schmeling, in a masterful show of boxing skill, had knocked out the Negro American in the seventh round of their previous engagement. The very upright and principled German stubbornly refused the bride. Not about to give up so quickly, Lansky approached the New York State Athletic Commission. Lo and behold, three days before the fight, the Commission ruled that Schmeling's Jewish manager, Joe Jacobs, couldn't be at the encounter, in penalty for a past infraction. In addition, the prizefighter's regular coach at ringside suddenly announced that he was leaving the embattled pugilist, having received an offer from Lansky which he couldn't refuse. So when the German stepped into the ring to the thunderous boos of the patriotic American crowd, he did so without his familiar manager and corner man at his side.

Indeed, the highly-publicized match was no ordinary prizefight. The world heavyweight championship came to symbolize the ideology of Nazi German against the principle of equality upon which America was founded. Hitler had invaded Austria and made it a part of Germany called the "Anschluss." Increasing his diatribes against the Jews, he deported all Polish Jews from the country. A new law forced German Jews to have the letter "J" stamped on their passports. Next, the Fuhrer set his sights on Czechoslovakia. Meeting with Hitler, England's Prime Minister, Neville Chamberlain, agreed to Germany's latest foreign intrusion, provided that the aggression stop after capturing Prague. Returning to London, he declared that the meeting in Munich had achieved "peace in our time," assuring the British public that there would be no war in Europe. But the American media wasn't convinced.

With Joseph Goebbels and the Nazi propaganda machine using the German boxer, Max Schmeling, as proof of Aryan superiority, the heavyweight championship prizefight between the German and the Negro American took on mythological proportions. While Schmeling disliked the sensationalism surrounding the upcoming fight, he couldn't escape being casted as an evil German. Though proud of his German nationality, he was not a member of the Nazi Party.

"I am a boxer," he said, "not a politician. I am no Aryan
superman in any way." Nevertheless, a German publicist
assigned to Schmeling stated that no black man could defeat
the German prizefighter, and that Schmeling's winnings
from the fight would be used to purchase German tanks.
Hitler himself praised Schmeling and wished him a great
victory for the honor of the Reich. In turn, Joe Louis was
invited to the White House, and President Franklin Delano
Roosevelt told him, "Joe, we need muscles like yours to beat
Germany." Unlike his training for their first encounter,
when the "Brown Bomber" had made the mistake of playing
golf and chasing women, Louis trained seriously for the
championship battle, feeling that the black people in
America, and the country itself, were praying for his
triumph.

Even though it was night, huge light towers lit up the
gigantic stadium like the sun. Cigarette and cigar smoke
rose in the air like fumes rising from hell. Dozens of
photographers and TV cameramen surrounded the ring.
Flashbulbs flashed without respite. The cheers for Louis
were deafening as a powerful loudspeaker introduced him
to the crowd. Tevye was overwhelmed with the
extravaganza. To him, it was all *narrishkeit* and nonsense—
two human beings beating out each other's brains to the
roars of the crowd, a phenomenon recalling gladiator days
when Jews were thrown to the lions before a packed
amphitheater of bloodthirsty Romans. The eyes of the
spectators around Tevye shone with an animal gleam in
anticipation of the bell. The glow in his daughter's eyes was
just as excited. Only the tight-lipped FBI Chief looked
complacent and unfazed by the upcoming clash.

With the ring of the bell, Schmeling stalked forward with
the same upright stance that had troubled Louis in their
previous encounter. Keeping his right arm cocked, he
waited for his opponent to drop his left hand after a jab.
Louis charged forward, seeking an early kill. In far better
shape than in their first fight, in a barrage of stunning
punches, the "Brown Bomber" smashed through
Schmeling's defenses and landed a bombardment of hooks
to the German's head which left him wobbling. The referee

rushed between them and sent Louis to his corner to make sure the German still had his senses as he clutched onto the rope of the ring. When the action resumed, the heavyweight champ immediately connected with a vicious right hook to Schmeling's jaw, knocking him down to the canvas. The crowd roared in delight. The brave Schmeling rose to his feet, but after absorbing another three solid punches, his knees collapsed beneath him and he crashed to the floor of the ring. When the dizzy fighter rose to his feet, Tevye couldn't watch any more. Ten seconds later, the fight was over as the German crumpled to the canvas again, in the very first round, two minutes into the fight, to the thrill of seventy-thousand screaming Americans. Balke and Pedhotzer hugged joyfully in a rare display of emotion between them. Tevye was filled with disgust, but the *Irgun* was sixteen-thousand dollars richer.

A few days later, Tevye met Meyer Lansky for the first time on a pier by the Hudson River. Pedhotzer waited in his car. Accompanied by two bodyguards, the unassuming head of the "National Crime Syndicate" and America's wealthiest gangster, was attired in a regular business suit and hat. His most distinguishing feature was a big Jewish nose. Dock workers went about their work, loading and unloading the large ships docked alongside the piers.

"It's a pleasure to meet a pioneer *landsman* from *Eretz Yisroel*," he said in Yiddish, without the slightest trace of arrogance or conceit.

"Thank you for wanting to help us," Tevye replied.

"One day I hope to visit Jerusalem," the pleasant-faced mob leader confided.

"You are welcome to be my guest," Tevye told him. "We have a house-full of family, but we can always find room."

"That's very kind, but I prefer hotels when I travel. That way I don't get anyone into trouble. How was the prizefight?"

"I'm glad the German lost," Tevye told him.

"They should all drop dead, the Nazi bastards," the Jewish mobster said.

Tevye nodded his head. A large black sedan drove along

the pier and stopped some twenty yards away. Its front headlights flashed on and off like a signal.

"I want you to meet a friend," Lansky said. "He controls the waterfront and the longshoremen's union."

The two bodyguards led the way. A man wearing sunglasses emerged from the car and stood waiting as the Jews approached. A cigarette hung down from his lower lip. He wore a long black raincoat and his slickly combed silver hair shone with some kind of cream. To Tevye, he looked Italian, but he could have passed for a Jew. He shook hands with Lansky.

"Meyer," he said in greeting.

"Albert," Lansky replied.

Later Tevye learned that his name was Albert Anastasia, head of the largest Italian Costra Nosa family in the city.

"Arabs are killing Jews in Palestine, and the situation has gotten out of hand," Lansky told him.

"How can I help?" the man known as the "Godfather" asked in a rasping hoarse voice.

"When the next shipload of weapons destined for the Mediterranean leaves New York Harbor, I'd like the cargo delivered to my friends in Haifa by mistake."

The Italian crime boss glanced at Tevye.

"Who is he?" he asked.

"A friend from Jerusalem," Lansky told him.

"Ah, Jerusalem," he said, as if the city held memories for him like Sicily. "I'll see what I can do."

"Let me know how I can return the favor," Lansky told him.

The Italian nodded. "Regards to the family," he said.

4.

The taxi drove along the winding road of expensive Beverly Hills mansions and slowed to a stop before a high metal fence. Palm trees towered up from the grounds inside the private enclave. Tevye rang a bell by the gate and waited. In our previous volume, *Arise and Shine!*, we learned about the childhoods and exploits of Meyer (Suchowlañski) Lansky and Benjamin "Bugsy" Siegel, the feared founders of the Jewish Mafia in America. Suffice it to say that Pedhotzer had told Tevye a little about Bugsy Siegel, Meyer Lansky's childhood pal and partner in the first Jewish gang on the Lower East Side of New York. In the dog-eat-dog melting pot of the metropolis, immigrants had to fight to survive. Discovering that nothing was handed out to newcomers on a golden plate, the two tough, young Jews decided to bypass the years of hard work necessary to rise up the ladder of success in America and simply steal the golden plate. At first they offered protection to neighborhood Jewish merchants from the Italian thugs that bullied them into paying extortion fees; then the two fearless fellows expanding into the bootlegging business, selling whiskey during the years of Prohibition in America when alcohol was banned. Their organization, Murder Inc., became the most feared group in the city, putting the nice Jewish boys in competition with the top Italian Mafia families, who preferred to make alliances with them, rather than engage them in a bloody war. Lansky was known as the brains of the team, while Siegel was his wild and dangerous hitman. Arrested again and again on charges of murder, Siegel was never convicted after witnesses all mysteriously died or disappeared. The previous year, he had moved to California, capturing a large chunk of the revenue garnered from offshore gambling, wire betting on the horse races, prostitution, and the numbers racket. He muscled his way into the Hollywood movie unions, threatening to shut down studios that didn't agree to pay exorbitant extortion fees. Hearing about a small desert town in Nevada which was looking for a risk-taking developer, Siegel took a drive to Las Vegas to check-out its potential. While the Jews in Palestine were turning the desert into fruit groves and orchards, Siegel came up with the idea to turn the sleepy desert town into the biggest gambling emporium in the world. In a short time, he formed close relationships with politicians, businessmen, attorneys, and Hollywood celebrities, hosting lavish parties for the stars at his glamorous mansion in Beverly Hills.

Finally, a tiny window in the mansion gate slid open and two eyes appeared.

"Wadaya want?" a gruff voice asked with a strong New York accent.

"Mr. Meyer Lansky set up a meeting for me with Mr. Siegel," Tevye replied.

"Mr. Siegel is busy."

"This is the exact time I was told to come."

"What's your name?" the voice inquired.

"Tevye."

"Tevye what?"

"Just Tevye."

"Don't play games with me, old man," the owner of the two beady eyes warned in a threatening tone.

"Just tell Mr. Siegel that Mr. Lansky's friend, Tevye from Jerusalem is here for the meeting he scheduled."

"What's Jerusalem? The name of a race horse? A hotel? A movie company?"

Tevye wondered if the creature could possibly be Jewish.

"What's your name?" Tevye asked him.

"Who wants to know?"

"I do," Tevye ansered, flashing an impatient stare. Dressed in his double-breasted suit and Fedora hat, Tevye could have passed for a bigtime Mafia boss arriving for crucial powwow.

"Joe Joe," the doorman answered.

"If you prefer, I will return to my hotel and telephone Mr. Lansky to inform him that Joe Joe wouldn't let me see Mr. Siegel."

The eyes darted back and forth in thought. "Wade a minute," the cautious fellow said.

The hatch closed. Two minutes later, Tevye heard steps approach the gate. A motor sounded and the mechanical gate slid slowly open. A bodyguard built like a boxer stood beside the doorman, holding a sub-machine gun in his hands. It was a Thompson automatic, looking exactly like the less expensive replicas that Avraham Stern smuggled into Israel from Finland. The *Irgun* nicknamed the weapon, "Washington," after its American counterpart.

"Come inside," the doorman said, keeping a hand in his jacket pocket, as if he were clutching a revolver. With his free hand, he searched the visitor for weapons while his friend's Tommy gun casually pointed at Tevye's chest. With another mechanical whine, the gate of the compound slid shut.

The mansion was set back some thirty yards from the road. Carefully landscaped shrubs, palm trees, and gurgling pools decorated the spacious front lawn. A circular driveway led to the front door. Parked outside the small palace were several flashy and expensive automobiles. The bodyguard kept the Tommy gun raised as they walked along a pebbled pathway to the entrance porch. Tevye heard lively music coming from inside. The lobby of the house was all mirrors framed in gold. The doorman led Tevye into a large art-deco salon graced with long couches. The room was comfortably air-conditioned, a modern convenience which hadn't yet reached the Holy Land. Laughter and music came from the backyard. One wall of the salon was comprised of sliding glass doors looking out on the patio and swimming pool which sparkled in the bright Californian sunlight. Squinting through the glare, Tevye caught a glimpse of three young women in bathing suits before he averted his gaze. One of the glass doors slid open and Bugsy Siegel appeared wearing a bathing suit, drying his head with a towel. The doorman and the bodyguard retreated to the arched entrance of the salon, where they remained throughout the conversation.

"Welcome, Mr. Tevye," Siegel greeted in a happy, friendly tone. "Sorry to have kept you waiting."

"That's quite all right," Tevye replied. "Mr. Lansky sends his greetings."

"I invited him to come to L.A. for a vacation, but he doesn't know how to relax. All he knows is work, while I'm a man of work and play. Can I get you a drink? Scotch, bourbon, gin, champagne? We just popped opened a bottle of bubbly outside. Come out to the pool and join us."

"Thank you, but I'm allergic to sunshine," Tevye responding, making up an excuse.

"Keep your hat on. I'll introduce you to the girls. You can have anyone you want, or all three. Any friend of Meyer's is a friend of mine."

"It's comfortable here in the salon," Tevye insisted.

Though Siegel was trying his best to be hospitable, Tevye felt an aversion toward the man's obviously non-kosher lifestyle. But he hadn't come to his house to make friends. He had come to buy guns.

"I can lend you one of my bathing suits if you like," Siegel offered.

"I don't swim."

"You don't have to swim. Come say hello to the girls and have a glass of champagne."

"Thank you, but I have a wife."

"So do I," Siegel said. "Right now, she's in New York visiting her family."

"May I sit down?" Tevye asked.

"By all means. Be my guest. Feel at home."

Siegel was a handsome man with a trim, wiry build. In a way, he reminded Tevye of Avraham Stern. Both men projected a presence which attracted attention. Though Siegel was more naturally outgoing, Stern could be just as theatrical and entertaining when he chose. And, like Stern, who possessed a dark side, Siegel, the infamous hitman, undoubtedly possessed one too.

The women continued to giggle and frolic outside by the pool. Siegel sat down on the couch beside his guest.

"What can I do you for?" he asked, getting down to busy.

"I've come from Jerusalem," Tevye told him. "The Arabs have murdered several hundred Jews in the past two years. We need guns to fight back."

Siegel leaned closer. "The Jews in Palestine want to fight the Arabs?" he asked in interest and surprise.

"That's correct."

"Real fighting? Shooting and killing?"

Tevye nodded yes.

"You know how to use weapons?" the hitman asked.

"We've been training for almost four years."

"Training with what?"

"We have a few hand guns and rifles, and a few Thompson automatics made in Finland."

"Mickey, come here!" the gangster barked.

The bodyguard with the Tommy gun hurried forward.

"Put the Tommy on the table," Siegel commanded.

Mickey set the weapon on the coffee table by the sofa.

"Let's see you take it apart and reassemble it within a minute," Siegel said challengingly to his visitor to test him.

"With a blindfold or without?" Tevye asked.

"With," the gunman replied, glancing up at Mickey with a smile. He handed the towel on his shoulder to Mickey who wrapped it over Tevye's head. Tevye leaned forward and groped around till his hands rested on the weapon. Stripping the Thompson was an exercise he had practiced a few dozen times as part of his *Irgun* officer's training. Most of the time they didn't have bullets for target practice, so they endlessly repeated the dismantling of their guns.

"Ready?" Siegel asked.

"Ready."

"Go!"

With skilled and confident movements, Tevye took the gun apart. The stock, the barrel, the recoil spring, handle and trigger, drum magazine, bolt and sear. The two gangsters watched with admiration. Tevye managed to reassemble the pieces with a full ten seconds to spare. Mickey lifted the towel from his face.

"Very nice," Siegel said with a nod of his head. "You pass with flying colors. I'm on your team."

Siegel told Tevye to show up at the "Daily Planet Restaurant" in Hollywood in another two days and ask the manager, Mr. Murray, for the suitcase Mickey would leave there. Accompanying his guest across the front lawn to the gate, Siegel invited him to a party he was hosting at his house that evening.

"It's a chance for you to meet more people," he said. "I'll introduce you to my friends. A lot of actors and studio heads will be here. Louis Mayer, Jack Warner, George Raft, Clark Gable, Gary Cooper, Cary Grant, Jean Harlow, Greta Garbo, Vivian Leigh, Frank Sinatra, and a nice Jewish boy, Tony Curtis."

Tevye had never heard the names. "Thank you, Mr. Siegel."

"You can call me Bugsy. I used to hate the name. People called me that to imply that I was crazy. But I've gotten used to it."

Tevye nodded.

"Please come," the mobster said. "Kate Smith is going to sing her version of Irvin Berlin's 'God Bless America,' and we're gonna have a special private screening of the new Walt Disney film, 'Snow White and the Seven Dwarfs.' You'll have a great time."

"*Moshav latzim*," Tevye thought to himself – a gathering of clowns. But not wanting to jeopardize his standing with the influential fellow, he showed up for the bash. This time, he had no trouble getting past Joe Joe and Mickey. They both winked at him as if he were one of the gang. On the front lawn, two giant searchlights lit up the heavens above Los Angeles. There were almost as many stars around the pool as in the sky. The diamonds on the women glittered like the Milky Way. True to his word, the host of the party introduced Tevye to the two most powerful producers in Hollywood, Jake (Jacob) Warner, president of Warner Brothers Studios, and Louis B. Mayer (born Lazar Meir), co-founder of Metro-Goldwyn-Mayer.

"I told them to prepare a check for you," Siegel said, taking Tevye aside. "Ask Lansky who they should make out the check to, and you can cash them when you return to New York."

The popular songwriter, Irving Berlin, was also on hand with his Catholic wife, for whom he wrote the song, "Always," often played at American weddings. Born to the Beilin family in the Russian *shtetl* of Tolochin, his father, Moshe, was cantor of the *shul*. After Cossacks burnt their home to the ground, the family journeyed to America. There were so many cantors in New York, Irving's father found work in a kosher meat market on the Lower East Side until he died when Irving was only thirteen. Working to support his family at a variety of menial jobs for pennies, Irving became a waiter in a Bowery saloon. At night, after closing, he taught himself how to play the saloon's piano. Becoming a "singing waiter," it wasn't long before the songs which he wrote drew him recognition. With the lively, "Alexander's Ragtime Band," he became a star. A long list of other hits, including "White Christmas," made the Jewish musician America's most popular and successful composer.

"What else is new?" Tevye mused, not bothering to meet him. When a Jew used his talents to please the *goyim*, he was applauded with honor and riches. When he used them to boost Jewish pride, he was scorned.

By the pool, in front of a small orchestra and a line of American flags, Bugsy Siegel invited the singer, Kate Smith, to belt out America's popular new anthem.

"*Gevalt!*" Tevye thought. It was forbidden to listen to the singing of a woman! Inconspicuously, he slipped away from the backyard into the house, closing the salon's sliding glass doors to muffle her voice, but he could make out the words:

"While the storm clouds gather far across the sea,
Let us swear allegiance to a land that's free,
Let us all be grateful for a land so fair,
As we raise our voices in a solemn prayer."
God Bless America, land that I love.
Stand beside her, and guide her
Through the night with a light from above.
From the mountains, to the prairies,
To the oceans white with foam,
God bless America, My home sweet home.

"*Haval*," Tevye thought. What a shame! Across the ocean, in the real Promised Land, Jews were getting slaughtered in the struggle to be a free Jewish Nation in their own Jewish Land, and here, in Hollywood and New York, the Jews had fallen in love with America. Before his over-gracious host introduced him to some Hollywood starlet, Tevye decided to call it a night. Two days later, just as Siegel had promised, at the "Daily Planet Restaurant," a suitcase was waiting for him filled to the brim with fifty and one-hundred-dollar bills. The restaurant was named after the newspaper, *The Daily Planet*, featured in a popular new comic book called, "Superman," created, needless to say, by two talented Jews.

5.

Before leaving America, Tevye wanted to have a private talk with George, the grandson he hardly knew. Finding an opportunity when the young man was on vacation from

Harvard University, where he was studying for his Master Degree in Business, Tevye suggested they take a train ride to the Lower East Side of Manhattan, the bastion of Orthodox Judaism, where over a million Jews lived in row after row of brick tenement buildings. Born and bred in America, Tevye's grandson looked and dressed like his Gentile college classmates. Tevye wasn't a movie-goer, but he had seen enough movie billboards to know what his daughter, Baylke, was talking about when she said, "Isn't George handsome? Cary Grant or Clark Gable – take your pick." Indeed the youth was a fine-looking lad, with a calm and care-free aura. He could have fit in easily at the pool party in the home of Bugsy Siegel in Beverly Hills. To Tevye's chagrin, there wasn't any sign of *yiddishkeit* at all on the smiling, clean-shaven face.

"I haven't been to the Lower East Side since I was a small boy," he told his grandfather. "It will be like a trip down Memory Lane."

George had been born in the teeming hub of immigrant Jewish Life in New York City, but as soon as his father found financial security and success in the banking business, and began to work for Meyer Lansky, he moved his small family to a spacious townhouse on the Upper West Side, near Central Park, a far more elegant, and far less Jewish neighborhood. To put things bluntly, Pedhotzer raised his only son like a total *goy* – no *Shabbos*, no *shul*, no *kashrut*, no Hebrew or Yiddish, a symbolic piece of *matzah* on *Seder* Night, *Hanukah* candles on the living room table, not in the window, and no *mezuzah* on the door of the house so the *goyim* wouldn't know that Jews lived inside. "*Gornnisht m'gornisht*," Tevye thought. No Torah, no tradition, not even "*Shema Yisrael*." Did the boy have a *brit milah*? Tevye didn't dare to ask.

"I want to buy you a pair of *tefillin*," Tevye told him as they traveled downtown on the elevated subway above Third Avenue.

"*Tefillin*?" his grandson said in surprise. "Whatever for?"

"It's a Jewish tradition."

"If you haven't already noticed, there's a new generation

of Jews in America. I appreciate it, Grandpa, but you don't have to buy me a gift."

All during his time in America, Tevye felt he was visiting some other planet. But on the Lower East Side, a Jew could feel Jewish. A ghetto was a ghetto, whether in Warsaw, Russia, or the United States. On Essex Street, men weren't afraid to sport skullcaps, *peyes*, and *tzitzit*. Women dressed modestly from the neck to the ankle. Signs were written in Hebrew and Yiddish. Schimmel Knish Bakery, Katz's Delicatessen, Cohen's Appetizers, Ratner's Cafeteria, and Schapiro Wine Merchants. Pushcarts on the street were filled with latkes, knishes, blintzes, and smoked fish and herring, not to mention the aromatic barrels of sour pickles. Tevye bought four for a nickel – two for his grandson and two for himself.

"What was my grandmother like?" the boy asked.

"Like an angel," Tevye told him. "An angel on Earth. Not that she didn't get angry if I didn't do what she asked, or if I disagreed with her on this or that subject. She never went to school but she knew everything about everything. Golda was her name, just like her heart. She was devout as could be, praying all the time, and you could taste the blessing in her cooking. The finest hotels in our area bought her pastries and cakes, may her memory be for a blessing."

"Do you have a photograph of her?"

"A photograph?" Tevye asked. What did he need a photograph for? Her image was so imprinted on his mind, hardly a moment passed when he didn't see her face. "No. I don't have a photograph of your grandmother. No one in our village had a camera."

"What was the name of the town? I'm sure my Mom told me, but I've forgotten."

"Anatevka," Tevye told him, finding it hard to believe that his grandson didn't even know the name of the village his family came from. As the old saying goes, "When a tree has no roots, the first big wind will blow it down."

"How many cousins do I have?" George asked.

"I can't tell you about your father's side, but let's see… your aunt, Tzeitel, may she rest in peace, had Moishe and Hannie; Hava, may she rest in peace, had Akiva; Hodel had

Ben Zion with Perchik, and Ruth with Hillel, may their memories be for a blessing; your aunt, Ruchel, has David, Sarah, and Yehoshua; and I have three children from Carmel, my second wife, may she live a long life, Tzvi, Boaz, and Naomi."

"That's too many to count," George said with a chuckle.

"Why don't you come to Jerusalem and visit?" his grandfather suggested.

"One day, I'd like to. Maybe after I finish my Master's Degree."

"You will love it. It's the Land of the Jews."

"So is America," George said.

"America is the land of the Americans. God gave us our own Jewish Land."

"Jewish Land? What makes it Jewish? Does the Land keep the Sabbath?" he joked.

"As a matter of fact, it does," his grandfather told him. "It's called the '*Shmitta*' year, every seven years, when farmers have to let their fields lay fallow."

"America is good enough for me. I was born here."

"The first Jew, Avraham, was born in Babylonia, and the very first thing God told him was to go live in the Land of Israel. That is how the Almighty created the world. A fish lives in water, monkeys live in trees, and Jews are to live in the Holy Land, you see?"

"That's ancient history," George said.

"Want a knish?" Tevye asked, certain that all the *traf* the boy had eaten had poisoned his brain.

"No, thank you."

To his surprise, when Tevye looked around, they were no longer in the Jewish neighborhood. Little Chinamen scurried past them on the sidewalk, dressed in Chinese garb. George noticed his grandfather's astonishment.

"We're in Chinatown," he said. "It's adjacent to the Lower East Side. I come here a lot to eat."

"They were standing beside a Chinese restaurant. In a window display, behind the Chinese lettering, a few live lobsters were moving their feelers and claws.

"*Gevalt*," Tevye muttered.

"Have you ever eaten lobster? It's delicious."

Tevye shook his head no.

"Do you keep *kosher*?"

Tevye nodded, yes.

"There must be a *kosher* Chinese restaurant here. Do you want me to ask?"

"*Kosher* lobster?"

"Sure. Why not?" George asked. "America has everything."

Looking in the window, Tevye felt sick to his stomach. He turned away.

"When in Rome, do as the Romans do," his grandson said with a laugh.

"I hear you have a girlfriend," Tevye said, walking on down the bizarre Chinese-looking street.

"Who told you?"

"Your mother."

"What did she say?"

"She said she isn't Jewish."

"So what? Why does she have to be Jewish?"

"If a man's wife isn't Jewish, his children won't be Jewish," Tevye explained.

"That's nonsense," his grandson declared. "A baby isn't born Jewish. Judaism is a religion, not a race."

"Tell that to the Nazis," his grandfather replied.

"It's all a question of education and how a person is raised," George insisted.

"If you were raised your son as a Chinaman, would that make him Chinese?" Tevye asked.

George thought before answering. "Of course not," he said. "Chinese is a nationality."

"So is being a Jew."

"I'm afraid I don't follow you," the college student said.

"The name Jew started in the Diaspora. We are really '*Bnei Yisrael*' - the Children of Israel."

"Both you and my Mom can relax. I am not thinking of getting married. But when I do, if my girlfriend isn't Jewish, I'll have her convert to please you. OK?"

Tevye sensed that his grandson meant well, but that he didn't understand.

"Converting is no simple matter," he said. "A convert has

to study seriously about Judaism for a year and then make a commitment to observe the commandments of the Torah."

"We'll find some Rabbi who is willing to dispense with all that," George replied.

"A serious Rabbi won't agree," Tevye told him.

"So we'll find a Rabbi who isn't so serious. My Father will make him an offer he can't refuse."

You can buy everything in America, Tevye thought. Even Jewishness.

"Your parents are Jewish," he said. "You grandparents are Jewish, your great-grandparents, and your great-great-grandparents before them, for generation after generation, for thousands of years. If you break that chain by marrying a Gentile, all of those links will be lost, toppled like dominoes, generations of Jews cut off, a whole family line, lost, without a Jewish future."

"You're lucky you have a tribe of other grandchildren," George said lightly. "What does it hurt if there is one *goy* in the family? Anyway, I'm not getting married so fast. As my Father says, 'Why buy a cow when the milk is free?'"

Tevye had been a milkman all of his life, but it was the first time he had heard that expression. America!

Chapter Twelve
ANONYMOUS SOLDIERS

To better understand the intricacies of our saga, and to appreciate the true miracle of the rebirth of the Jewish State, during which the Jewish People were pitted, not only against vicious and powerful enemies, but also against themselves, we shall pause in the narrative to present a short summary of the political events leading up to the valiant underground rebellion which paved the way to Jewish independence in the Land of Israel.

In the spring of 1936, the Mufti of Jerusalem, Haj Amin al-Husseini, enlisted bands of mercenaries from Syria and Iraq in a violent uprising against the Jews of Palestine. The Arabs declared a general work strike, a boycott of Jewish products, and non-payment of taxes to the British Mandate Authority, while demanding an end to Jewish immigration, a cessation of land sales to Jews, and the establishment of a national Arab government in Palestine. In reaction, as we have already mentioned, the Zionist establishment, led by David Ben Gurion and Chaim Weizmann, advocated a policy of restraint. The military arm of the Jewish Agency ordered the *Haganah* to assume positions of defense only. Even Ze'ev Jabotinsky, head of the Revisionist Movement, ordered his followers not to strike back in revenge. When the Arab terrorists began attacking British soldiers, railways, and the Iraq-Haifa oil pipeline, the British deployed 20,000 troops to quell the attacks on British targets, leaving the Jews to fend for themselves. After over ninety Jews had been murdered throughout the country, livestock stolen, and Jewish agricultural fields and orchards torched, did a few young members of the underground *Irgun* strike back at the enemy, blowing up Arab markets, cafes, and buses in and around Jerusalem. Scores of Arabs were killed and wounded. The Jewish Agency denounced the bombings. In a most random fashion, the British rounded up and imprisoned known Revisionists and *Betar* recruits. As we recounted, in an assassination attempt on the Mufti, Tevye's pistol jammed as he held it just a meter from his head, causing the terrified *jihadist* to flee the country before the Jews tried again. Intimidated by the newfound valor of the Jews, the Arab violence in Jerusalem abated.

In the aftermath of the "Great Arab Revolt," the British sent a Royal Commission to Palestine, known as the Peel Commission, after its chairman, Lord Peel, to investigate the causes of the violence and to present operative conclusions. Invited to testify before the hearing committee of the Commission, Chaim Weizmann preached a policy of "parity" whereby Jews and Arabs would share equal political status, with Britain remaining the ultimate arbitrator. Next, the Peel Commission turned to David Ben Gurion for his opinion. Feeling that the Jewish community in Palestine lacked the economic stability and military posture for Jewish Statehood, in his address to the hearing committee, Ben Gurion also favored "parity," rejecting, for the time being, the possibility of a Jewish State as being politically unnecessary, morally undesirable, and against Jewish interests. Only Ze'ev Jabotinsky, presenting his testimony in London because of England's long-standing unwillingness to renew his visa to Palestine, demanded an immediate Jewish State, stating that England's inability to enforce stability in the country canceled its Mandate to rule in Palestine.

Setting forth his vision of "Greater Zionism," in an eloquent dissertation before the Peel Commission lasting an hour-and-a-half, Jabotinsky contended that the policies and opinions of the Jewish Agency did not represent the whole of the Jewish People. In conclusion, he stated, "If Great Britain is unable to fulfill its promises as set forth in the Balfour Declaration, we will bow to her decision, but then we shall expect Great Britain to give the Mandatory back, so that some other civilized nation can be appointed in its place."

Without mentioning the name of the High Commissioner of Palestine, Jabotinsky demanded that an official inquiring be conducted to determine who was responsible for the uncontrolled violence against the Jews:

"Someone is guilty for the ongoing slaughter, and I insist that the guilty party stand before a Royal Commission like this one, before a Judicial Committee, and I want him to answer for his mistaken conduct. Sometimes, even a simple man like myself has the right to say, *'J'accuse.'* Someone is guilty. Someone is guilty of commission, omission, neglect of duty, whatever name you give it. I believe it is guilt, and I accuse! And I believe that the person guilty should be punished, and that is what I humbly demand."

In declaring its findings, the Peel Commission recommended that the Mandate come to an end, and advised that the country be split into three parts. An Arab State, which would receive the largest chunk of territory, would be joined with Transjordan. The Jews would be awarded a tiny Jewish State along the Mediterranean coastline. Haifa and Jerusalem would be governed by the British, with a British ruled corridor from Jerusalem to Jaffa. As anyone with eyes could see, the low coastal plain awarded to the Jews would be at the mercy of the Arabs who dominated the hill country, thus vulnerable to constant Arab attack, while it had already been proven that the British wouldn't stand in the way.

Chaim Weizmann quickly approved the proposed partition. Living in England, cherishing his British passport, and accustomed to engaging in Zionist advocacy while wining and dining with the high society of London, he sided with the British. David Ben Gurion, second in influence in the official Zionist leadership, also agreed to the plan, believing it could be a first step in ultimately expanding the borders granted to the Jews. In contrast, Jabotinsky declared, "We have to fight against this scheme, though it is so unrealistic that nothing will come of it. But, indeed, it has one great positive feature – it contains an official stamp of British approval for the idea of a Jewish State."

The combined influence of Weizmann and Ben Gurion convinced the Zionist Congress to support the partition of Palestine, with the provision that the portion allotted to the Jews be eventually expanded. Members of the British House of Commons, who were sympathetic to the Zionist cause, did not comprehend the Zionist establishment's acceptance of the proposal, and they fought against it. After conferring with Jabotinsky, Winston Churchill managed to add a delaying amendment to the Government's plan, effectively derailing its implementation. All the while, the Arabs rejected the partition plan outright, demanding the exclusive formation of an Arab government to rule over Palestine. After nine months of cease fire, Arab leaders renewed their armed revolt with even more mercenaries, backed by widespread support from the local Arab population.

Not politically oriented by nature, Tevye's son, Tzvi, believed the Jews would win control over *Eretz Yisrael*, not through international negotiations, but through the convincing power of the sword. David Raziel, his friend and study partner in Rabbi Kook's yeshiva, was nearing that conclusion himself. Unlike other Revisionists and *Betarim* who viewed Weizmann and Ben Gurion with disdain for their fawning and acquiescent relationship with the British, Raziel strove to see the bigger picture, just as Rabbi Kook had taught, emphasizing that truth was the composite wholeness of all opinions and beliefs, and not the monopoly of one viewpoint alone. On that point, Avraham Stern disagreed with him, and, as we previously mentioned, he was in Poland raising an army of forty-thousand Jews to invade Palestine and seize the country by force.

And now, back to our story....

The sun had already disappeared below the rolling mountains of the Galilee, leaving a red glow in the sky. Tevye's twenty-four-year-old son, Tzvi, sat alongside Yitzhaq Ben-Ami in the passenger's seat of the Mack pick-up truck, one of the only trucks of its kind in the area. The right headlight of the vehicle was shattered, so Ben-Ami had to drive extra slowly around the winding, hillside curves. They were on their way back to Rosh Pina from Tiberias, where they had picked up supplies for the colony. Two-thousand years before in Rosh Pina, during a terrible draught, the holy *tzaddik*, Choni HaMa'agal, had drawn a circle in the sand and stood in its center, telling God that he wouldn't budge until He answered his prayers for rain. Nearby, in a cave in Meron, Rabbi Shimon bar Yochai had received the wisdom of the holy "*Zohar*" from the Biblical prophet, *Eliahu HaNavi*.

In mountainside glens, during the revolt against Rome, Rabbi Akiva had taught Torah to his twenty-four thousand students. The tombs of ancient Rabbis were everywhere, and the ground of the northern Galilee was steeped in the blood of defiant Jews who revolted against the vast legions of Vespasian and Titus. As a young *Betar* poet wrote, "The height will not be conquered, if no grave is on the slope." Generations later, in the town of Safed, the *Arizal* had unlocked the hidden mysteries of the *Kabbalah*. During cool dark nights, the scents of the forests perfumed the air with an aroma as pungent and soothing as the incense rising from the Altar of the Jerusalem Temple. While Tzvi wasn't a mystic, the quiet mountains of the *Galil* were an elixir to his soul.

The scholarly Ben-Ami was the commander of the Rosh Pina *"pluga,"* and an avid supporter of the project which sent young *Betar* immigrants to the hard-pressed settlements in the Galilee for two years of compulsory military training, guard duty, and agricultural work. *Pluga* meant a company of soldiers. For the mature and elderly residents of Rosh Pina, which had been founded in 1882 during the *"First Aliyah,"* the infusion of young strength and spirit was a blessing from Heaven. Because the new immigrants received the same low wages as Arab workers, the economically distressed settlement could replace the Arabs with Jews. Not belonging to the chain of socialist *kibbutzim* in the region, the embattled colony did not receive any funds from the Jewish Agency. Malaria still lingered in the area, the summers were hot, droughts in the winter often damaged the crops, and Arab poachers roamed the surrounding hillsides. In addition to military training and guard duty along the borders of the colony, the young, energetic men and women of the *plugot* rose at three in the morning, and after drinking a cup of tea and eating a piece of dark bread, sometimes with jam, they headed off to work in the colony's tobacco fields, olive groves, and quarry.

While the two year-long wave of Arab violence had abated in Jerusalem, ever since the *Irgun Tzvai Leumi* began to strike back with a vengeance, the bloodlust of the Arabs continued throughout the Galilee, which swarmed with mercenaries under the command of Fawzi El-Kaukji, an Iraqi officer in the employment of the Grand Mufti. Traveling along the serpentine roads of the Galilee became so dangerous, the Jews had to fasten wire grates over bus windows to repel rocks and grenades. The British did nothing to prevent the almost daily highway attacks. After blowing up a few Arab cafes, buses, and markets in Jerusalem, in retaliation for the killing of Jews, Tzvi decided that a stint up north in the Galilee with a *pluga* would spare him from the large-scale police round-ups and arrests of Jews associated with *Betar* and the Revisionists. He made his final decision after shooting at two Arab buses traveling along the hilly Motza-Jerusalem road, where Arabs had carried out a series of bloody ambushes on Jewish vehicles. The situation had become so dangerous, Jews avoided driving there at night. Since the road was the only direct way of reaching Tel Aviv, Jews compelled to travel at night had to make the hazardous journey in a convoy of cars accompanied by armed *Irgun* guards. Tzvi wanted to warn the Arabs that Jews could stage highways ambushes too. After shooting at the buses, the headlights of a third vehicle approached down the road. When it drew closer, Tzvi opened fire from his hiding place in the forest. It turned out to be an armored British police car with a mounted machine gun, which one of Tzvi's bullets put out of commission. Wanting to avoid a shootout, Tzvi fled through the forest on foot back to Jerusalem. The next day, he learned that one of his shots had killed an Arab riding on the first bus. The British set up a roadblock at the entrance to Jerusalem, searching every Jewish vehicle that entered or left the city. It was a good time, Tzvi reasoned, to journey up north before his *mazel* ran out.

For Tzvi, the forests of the *Galil*, and the quiet, pastoral, Old-World atmosphere surrounding the small wood cottages and tree-lined, cobblestone streets of Rosh Pina, acted like a calming retreat. His partner, Nachshon, decided to return to his home in Olat HaShachar until the wrath of the British subsided. Yaacov Eliav, the expert bomber, decided to remain underground and weather out the storm of arrests in Jerusalem.

Seeing two dark figures standing in the road up ahead,

Yitzhaq Ben-Ami slowed the truck to a stop. In the beam of the headlight, the two Jews could make out a man and woman dressed in the garbs of Arab peasants. The woman carried a child bundled in her arms. The man waved his arms excitedly, signaling the truck to halt.

"Maybe it's a trap," Tzvi said.

Roadside attacks occurred frequently in the region, leaving many Jews dead and wounded.

"Maybe. Maybe not," Ben-Ami replied. Though the young men were the same age, and equally devoted to the Zionist endeavor, their personalities and looks differed greatly. Marked by thoughtful intelligence, Ben-Ari had studied at Hebrew University before joining the *Betar* Youth Movement. In contrast, Tzvi was impulsive, motivated by his emotions. And while Tzvi had long twisted *peyes* hanging down from his ears to his shoulders, a skullcap that covered his head, and his mother's dark Yemenite complexion, the light-skinned and clean-shaven Ben-Ami looked like the educated class of *Ashkenazim* who sent their children to the secular Gymnasia High School in Tel Aviv. Unlike the "enlightened" socialist pioneers who rejected Judaism in principle, Ben-Ami respected the beliefs and traditions of his religious ancestors, though he didn't necessarily observe the commandments and rituals which gave the beliefs their fullest expression.

"She could be holding a bomb, and snipers could be waiting in the woods," Tzvi cautioned, not out of fear, which wasn't a part of his nature, but because highway attacks on Jews transpired all time.

"Keep me covered," the *pluga* commander said.

The two Jews got out of the car. As Ben-Ami approached the couple, Tzvi kept his hand on the revolver in his pocket. The husband ran forward.

"Help, please!" he begged in Arabic. "Please help us!"

Tzvi and Ben-Ami both understood the language.

"What's the matter?" Ben-Ami asked as the woman walked forward carrying her bundle.

"Our boy has been bitten by a snake!"

Ben-Ami could now clearly see that the Arab woman was carrying a child. Snake bites could be deadly. They Arabs gazed at the Jew with eyes pleading for compassion. The mother rolled the blanket away from the boy whose leg was swollen and blue.

"Climb in the back of the truck," Ben-Ami told them. "We'll take you to the hospital in Safed."

The decision didn't please Tzvi. He would have left them on the road for Arabs to help them. What was the point of rescuing a child who would probably grow up to be a killer of Jews? Arabs had slaughtered more Jews than Tzvi could remember, including his uncle, Hillel, and his sister, Hava. But Ben-Ami was the commander, so Tevye's son kept his mouth shut and lowered the back gate of the open pick-up.

On the drive to the hospitable, Ben-Ami felt a need to explain his decision.

"Not every Arab is an enemy," he said. "Most of them want to live their lives in peace. The Mufti and his agitators stir up the peasants with their incitement and lies. Their diatribes attract the hot-blooded and less intelligent of the lot. In my opinion, there is plenty of land in this country for everyone to live together in harmony."

"That's a dream that will never come to pass," Tzvi answered. "They simply don't want us here. The same way that we have national pride, so do the Arabs. You can't keep it from spreading. With them, it's a religious thing as well. Islam is against all infidels, especially the Jews."

"That's why we have to secure an international agreement which guarantees us sovereignty over the Land."

"You sound like Ben Gurion and Jabotinsky," Tzvi countered. "International politics won't get us anywhere. We have to conquer the Land with guns."

"You sound like Uri Zvi Greenberg and Avraham Stern," Yitzhaq replied.

After driving the Arabs to the small hospital in Safed, they drove back down the winding mountain road. When they reached Rosh Pina, a dozen of the colony's farmers were gathered in the town hall. Earlier in the evening, on his way home from the fields, a young worker, Shmuel Golden, had been stabbed to death by Arabs. The regional commander of the *Irgun* in the *Galil*, Joseph Duckler, who lived in Rosh Pina, presided over the emotion-packed meeting. Naturally, there were the usual differences of opinion over how to react. For the past year, Ben-Ami had taken over most of the veteran *Irgun* commander's work, because of weakening health.

"We are discussing how to react to the murder," Duckler told the newcomers.

"That's the problem," Tzvi commented. "Instead of discussing, we should strike back immediately."

"Your comment is out of line," Duckler replied in rebuke.

"This is an open forum, isn't it?"

"For the permanent residents of the colony."

"If volunteers aren't allowed to speak, why should we work here?" Tzvi responded belligerently.

"Believe me, young man, I have more experience than you do. The question is, should we do something out of the ordinary?"

"The ordinary is that we do nothing," Ben-Ami injected.

"It's obvious that the killers came from Ja'una," a Rosh Pina farmer said, accusing the nearby Arab village. "Why don't we go into their fields and teach some of their workers a lesson?"

"The Arabs don't do anything without the approval of their *Mukhtar*," Tzvi reminded the gathering. As head of the village, the *Mukhtar* ruled with an iron hand. "Why not blow up his house?"

"Explosives can be a problem. Why not just break into his house and shoot him?"

The voice belonged to a young member of the *pluga* named Shlomo ben Yosef, who had reached the shores of the Promised Land from Poland via the *Irgun's* "illegal" immigration program, the *Ha'apala*. Tzvi was surprised to hear the new *oleh* speak out. Normally, the recent immigrant was quiet and introspective, keeping his opinions to himself.

Duckler continued to chair the meeting, refusing to answer each of the strident comments directly.

"While the tracks of the assailants lead toward Ja'una, there is no proof that the murderers are residents of the village," he said. "For over a year, they have not troubled us. It may be that outsiders are guilty. Perhaps mercenaries have pressured the *Mukhtar* to give them sanctuary. While I

believe some retaliatory measure is in order, I am meeting
with the *Haganah* commander later this evening to discuss
our options."

That was interesting, Tzvi thought. Not that he believed
the *Haganah* would agree to strike back with a meaningful
response, but because the region's *Haganah* commander was
none other than his Aunt Hodel's son, Ben Zion, whom he
hadn't seen for three years, since the funeral of his murdered
father, Perchik Aronov.

"Discussing strategy with the *Haganah* will only lead to
more *havlaga*," Ben-Ami asserted. "People are fed up with
the official policy of restraint. Especially our young *Betar*
recruits. They want action."

Duckler answered with his usual air of authority. "Young
people allow their emotions to guide them. Older people
make use of their heads. That's why I am the general *Irgun*
commander of the region, and not you and your friends."

"Your meeting with *Haganah* will result in delivering a
warning to the *Mukhtar* and nothing more than that,"
Ben-Ami declared. "We need a strong response which all of
the Arabs in the area will understand. Some of our men
know how to use the 'Washington' Tommy gun, and Tzvi
worked with explosives."

"Very well," Duckler conceded. "In keeping with
democratic principles, I give you permission to formulate a
plan which will be considered by the security committee
after I meet with the *Haganah* commander. Is that acceptable
to you?"

"Yes, sir," Ben-Ami agreed, realizing it was the most he
could achieve at the moment.

"In the meantime, make sure to activate more guards,"
Duckler said, concluding the meeting.

Outside, while the residents returned to their homes, Tzvi
and Ben-Ami lingered to discuss the situation. Shlomo ben
Yosef joined them, along with a *pluga* member named
Itamar, who had worked in a quarry and knew a great deal
about explosives. Toward midnight, Duckler knocked on the
door of the small cottage, which the colony provided for the
commander of the *pluga*. Because many Rosh Pina residents
had abandoned the endangered settlement, there were

empty homes that served as barracks for the *plugot* trainees and workers. Duckler related that after his discussions with Ben Zion Aronov, the *Haganah* regional commander, and with Rosh Pina's security committee, the decision was made to place more guards around the colony, and to not allow Arabs from Ja'una to enter the settlement.

"More of the same nonsense," Ben-Ami exclaimed.

Duckler didn't appreciate the younger man's insubordination.

"For you enlightenment," he said. "What we do has international ramifications. If we act like the Arabs by carrying out some revenge action, we weaken our moral standing. When Lord Balfour expressed his willingness to help us establish a National Homeland, he did so, not only for political reasons, but on moral grounds as well. As it is, we don't know if villagers killed Golden, or whether the Mufti's mercenaries are responsible. We also don't know if they are waiting for us to walk into an ambush. And if that is the case, and a new wave of Arab violence breaks out because of it, then the entire Jewish *Yishuv* will be against us. We don't have a sufficient amount of weapons and ammunition to get ourselves tangled up in a war with all the Arab tribes in the *Galil*. In the end, I have to take responsibility for our decision, and its outcome – not you."

Ben-Ami didn't argue. But he realized that Duckler would never change his mind.

Earlier, when Ben Zion's meeting in Rosh Pina with Joseph Duckler had ended, the region's young *Haganah* commander was surprised to find his grandfather's son, Tzvi, waiting for him outside Duckler's home. Because Tzvi was his mother's half-brother, from Tevye's second wife, Tzvi was his uncle, even though they were practically the same age. When Hodel moved in with Tevye after her divorce from Perchik, the two boys grew up together. After his father's murder, Ben Zion never disclosed to anyone his father's dying confession that two Arabs had committed the crime. After the funeral, the guilt-ridden youth cut off all connection with his family and enlisted in the *Haganah*.

"Blessed be the Lord who brings the dead back to life," Tzvi said.

In a flash of seconds, Ben Zion's surprised expression turned to confusion, worry, displeasure, and finally unrepressed joy. For a moment, all of the angers, and conflicts, and guilt of the past disappeared. Suddenly, they were like brothers once again. For a minute, maybe less, politics and religion were forgotten. Like the best of old friends, they hugged, and laughed, and punched each other playfully, and hugged once again without any words.

"Tzvi!"

"Ben Zion!"

"My brother!"

"My brother!"

"I see you're growing a beard like your father," Ben Zion remarked, referring to the stubble on his uncle's chin.

"And I see you shaved your peyes."

"Ages ago."

Gazing at the broad-shouldered Ben Zion in his khaki uniform, a wide smile formed on Tzvi's face. "The *Haganah* commander! Who could have predicted?" he exclaimed.

"What are you doing here?" Ben Zion asked.

"Working in the fields and trying, not very successfully, to defend the settlement from its neighbors."

"With *Betar*?"

"For the past few months."

Tzvi didn't tell him about his activities in the *Irgun*, nor about the retaliation bombings which he had carried out in Jerusalem. As his father was fond of saying, quoting King Solomon, "*For birds of the sky will carry the utterance, and creatures with wings will disclose the matter.*" Silence, the Sages had taught, could be the greatest wisdom of all.

They stood in the after-midnight darkness of a small park. The only light came from a gas lamp on a pole. The windows of the colony's small houses were shuttered for the night. For several seconds, Ben Zion remained silent. Not only did he and Tzvi hold different religious beliefs, his uncle was a Revisionist, making them political rivals as well. Even though their ultimate goal was the same, and even though they had practically grown up together under the same roof, one was a follower of Ben Gurion, and the other a follower of the more militant disciples of Ze'ev Jabotinsky.

As Tevye would say, you can't make a wedding between a cat and a dog.

"How is my mother, and your father?" Ben Zion asked with a sudden coolness in his voice.

"Go visit them and find out for yourself," Tzvi answered bluntly, hinting at the pain that Ben Zion's disappearance had caused. "They don't love you any less because your beliefs are different than theirs," Tzvi told him. "Go see them. If you don't want to live like a Jew, at least act like a human being."

Tzvi's words of rebuke hit the mark. Suddenly Ben Zion recalled his painful separation from his family, through no fault of their own. He knew they still loved him. He knew that their religious beliefs weren't barriers that couldn't be breached. What prevented him from seeing them was his terrible feeling of betrayal and guilt in his having put politics ahead of morality. By his having kept silent during his father's murder investigation and trial, an innocent Jew had nearly been hung, and a terrible fraternal fire had raged throughout the Zionist world. The embers of brotherly hatred still glowed.

"Are they still living in the Old City?" Ben Zion inquired.

"No. In the wake of the Arab uprising, the British evacuated all of the Jews from the Western Wall Quarter. We moved outside the walls to the Bukharim neighborhood. My father's in America now, but your mother speaks about you every day."

"What is he doing?"

"Visiting Baylke," Tzvi answered. One of the rules of the *Irgun* was secrecy. Though the two young men were family, Tzvi's allegiance to the code of the Organization came first. "I suppose you convinced Duckler to respond to the latest murder by digging more graves, so we will be ready for the next batch of victims," he said with a clear dose of cynicism.

"What do you suggest?"

"I'd blow up the house of the local *Mukhtar* after making sure that he was inside. Only a campaign of retaliation, *"an eye-for-an-eye, and a tooth-for-a-tooth,"* will create the deterrence needed to end the Arab rampage against us. That's the strategy that worked in Jerusalem. The Arabs need to know that their acts of butchery will be met with their being butchered in return."

"And if your *'eye for an eye'* doesn't convince them, when all of the tribes in the region, and a horde of Fawzi El-Kaukji's mercenaries attack Rosh Pina, then what are you going to do? Pray to your God to save you?"

"My God? He isn't your God as well? You sound like the Wicked Son at the *Pesach Seder*."

"And you sound like the Simple Son. The problem with you and your friends is that act from your let your passions control you."

"And the problem with you and your friends is that you act from your heads, but instead of a *Yiddishe kop*, you think like the *goyim*."

Duckler emerged from his house, glanced at Tzvi and Ben Zion, and kept walking along the dark path.

"I don't have time to waste talking with a Revisionist," Ben Zion said. "I have more important things to do."

"Sure - running away from the truth like a dog with its tail between its legs. You're only inviting the next murder with your policy of weakness and fear."

"You should know. When it comes to murder, Revisionists are the experts" Ben Zion, replied accusingly.

"You still blame us for the murder of your father?"

"That's what the Criminal Court and the High Court of Appeals decided. They made it clear that the Revisionists were responsible for the murder."

"The Appeals Court freed Stavsky of all charges," Tzvi reminded him.

"On a legal technicality."

"If you socialists are such lovers of humanity, how is it that you were ready to let an innocent man go to the gallows just to achieve political gain?"

"The Chief Judge made it clear that they weren't reversing the findings of the High Criminal Court that Stavsky was one of the men who murdered my father."

"Everyone knows, from the Chief Police Investigator to the man in the street, that your father's wife lied when she altered her original testimony that Arabs had assaulted them on the beach."

"Good-bye," Ben Zion said, turning and striding away.

"God help you!" Tzvi shouted after him.

"I don't want anything to do with you or your God!" Ben Zion yelled back.

"God help you!" Tzvi screamed after him. "God help you!"

2.

A week later, the ban on the village was lifted. Arabs from Ju'ana once again entered the borders of Rosh Pina, using one of its main roads as a shortcut for their sheep and cattle on their way out to pasture. A few days later, another veteran settler of the colony was found murdered in his tobacco field.

Tzvi and his friend, Shlomo ben Yosef, were chopping wood when the colony's emergency bell sounded and Itamar came running with the distressing news.

"They killed Ben Gaon!" he exclaimed.

Everyone knew the good-natured old-timer who enjoyed telling stories to the *Betar plugot* recruits about the early, pioneering days of the colony.

"Where?" Tzvi asked.

"In his tobacco field."

"What difference does it make?" Ben Yosef asked angrily. "How many more Jews have to be killed before we teach the Arabs a lesson?"

Tzvi and Itamar didn't respond. Agreeing with the truth of his words, there was nothing to say. From all directions, men, women, and children hurried toward the town hall.

"Going to another meeting is a waste of time," Shlomo said. "Once again they'll decide not to retaliate. It's a *Chillul Hashem*. Did we return to Zion to be slaughtered like chickens? Is the *Betar* Movement all words and no action? Who needs another *Haganah* with different colored caps?"

"Let's wait and see," Tzvi advised.

"I'm tired of waiting," the passionate young man declared.

"Give me time to speak with Ben-Ami," Tzvi insisted.

"Speak to whomever you like. It's all empty talk. I understand why the Jews in Poland and Russia live in fear of every breeze. But here in our own Land? How can it be? What other nation would allow its people to be murdered without responding?!"

At the emergency meeting, Tzvi pulled Yitzhaq-Ben Ami aside. "If we don't respond," he told the local *Irgun* commander, "some of the fellows in the *pluga* surely will."

"Try to hold them in check," Ben-Ami answered. "I am going to Jerusalem tonight to speak with Moshe Rosenberg. He's the head of Irgun operations in the country. We need his approval."

"You'll be wasting your time. After we blew up some selected Arab targets in Jerusalem, Moshe Rosenberg ordered a succession of underground activity until the British ceased from their wide-scale round-up of Revisionists. "Speak with David Raziel instead," Tzvi advised. "He'll give us freedom of action."

"How do you know?" Ben-Ami asked.

"I know."

"Raziel is only the *Irgun* commander in Jerusalem," Ben-Ami countered. "We need the approval of Rosenberg to take action in the Galil."

"And he'll need the approval of Jabotinsky."

"We are a military organization, not cowboys from the Wild West," the disciplined army man said.

Tzvi felt the same sense of increasing frustration which Shlomo Ben Yosef had expressed so bluntly. For all of its militant slogans and odes to Jewish valor, Revisionist leadership refused to sound the trumpets of war and command its troops into action. At odds with Rosenberg's insistence that the Organization not deviate from the *Haganah's* policy of restraint, Raziel and Arvraham Stern had issued a clandestine proclamation to *Irgun* cells throughout the country following the stunning reprisal attacks in Jerusalem:

"Defensive actions alone can never succeed. The objective of war is to shatter the will of the enemy. This cannot be achieved without smashing their power. Purely defensive actions will never break the enemy's strength. He who does not wish to be defeated must attack. Our goal is not to oppress other people, but to insure our freedom and honor. We will not lay down arms until our enemies do the same."

For Tzvi and his friends, the proclamation was a clear call to war. But Raziel and Stern didn't head the Organization. To make a long story short, Moshe Rosenberg passed Ben-Ami's request to Jabotinsky in Paris, whose answer was to wait. Only when a telegram arrived signed "Mendelson" would *Irgun* commanders in *Eretz Yisrael* have permission to strike back at the Arabs.

While Ben Gaon's funeral still haunted everyone's thoughts, a Jewish taxi travelling along the Acco-Safed highway was ambushed by Arabs in broad daylight. The driver and three male passengers were brutally killed and dismembered. Two of them were *Haganah* soldiers heading for Kibbutz Degania on the shores of the Sea of Galilee. Two Jewish women from Rosh Pina were riding in the vehicle. They were raped in a ditch by the side of the road, then brutally hacked into pieces.

By the time Tzvi reached the gruesome site of the murder, Ben Zion Aronov had already arrived. The two exchanged glances. Tzvi didn't have to say a word. The massacre said everything. Yitzhak Ben-Ami covered the bodies with blankets. Two British policeman kept cars moving along the road. They ordered onlookers to keep their distance from the scene. A British police investigator walked around searching for clues. A British patrol car arrived at the scene, and a short, uniformed officer, sporting a very un-British beard and a pith helmet, opened the front door of the car and stepped out with an air of authority. He walked about in an official manner, observing the carnage. In one hand, he held a thick book which, to Tzvi, looked like a Bible in English. Two corpses lay in a ditch by the roadside. Lifting up a blanket, his face contorted at the sight of the blood-covered, half-naked females.

"What kind of animals would do this?" he said aloud, in a half-Scottish, half-British accent.

No one answered.

"Did you hear me?!" he asked in Hebrew, raising his voice. "What kind of animals behave in such a fashion?"

He lifting up another blanket covering the dismembered corpse of one of the passengers.

"*Vengeance and recompense are mine,*" he muttered, quoting a verse from the Bible. "*Vengeance and recompense are mine.*"

"Who are you, may I ask?" Ben-Ami inquired.

"Wingate. Captain Orde Wingate. British Army Intelligence. Though, I have to admit, there is nothing intelligent about the British Army if they allow massacres like this in their realm."

Everyone stared at the most atypical soldier.

"Who's in charge here?" he barked, striding over to the British police investigator.

"Not me, sir," the policeman responded timidly, unnerved by the authority that Wingate exuded. "I'm just a police investigator."

"Well then, let me tell you who is in charge here. The Ishmaelites are in charge. Do you hear me? They do what they damn please and nobody does anything to stop their barbaric savagery. I'm ashamed to be British. I am embarrassed to wear this uniform. England took it upon itself to help the Children of Israel rebuild their Homeland. This is the Land that the King of the Universe gave to them, just as it says right here in the Holy Bible – and the British are trying to wrest it away from them by letting the Ishmaelites slaughter the Jews."

Gazing at the massacre around him, he exclaimed, "This is how my dear country, England, is helping the Jews. By letting camel-eating savages hack them to pieces!"

The garrulous British army officer held up the Bible he was holding, like a minister delivering a sermon.

"This Holy Bible is their deed to this Land. God gave it to the Jews. He didn't give it to the British. He didn't give it to the sons of Yishmael. He gave it to the children of Abraham, Isaac, and Jacob. This book is their deed. The Lord gave the Arabs their own lands. If they don't like the situation here, let them live elsewhere!"

Everyone listened to his assertive words. The eccentric army captain took half an onion out from his uniform pocket and bit off a chunk. Tzvi noticed that an alarm clock was attached to his wrist.

"And who are you?" Wingate growled at Ben Zion.

"The regional *Haganah* commander," the young man replied, standing stiffly, as if he were facing his chief-of-staff.

"Scoundrel!" Wingate hollered. "You should be ashamed of yourself. A commander leads his troops into battle – he doesn't flee in fright. Do you enjoy seeing your people get slaughtered and raped?"

Wingate pointed again to the corpses on the ground. "Is this what you call *Haganah*? Defense? Is this how you defend your brothers and sisters, the People of God? You deserve to be court-martialed! If I were in charge here, no Arab would dare to lift up a hand against a Jew. In the Torah of Moses it states, '*Rise up and kill the enemy before he kills you.*' You don't have to be a military genius to figure it out. The Scripture doesn't mention "*Haganah.*" It doesn't preach defense. It says, attack and attack and attack, until you uproot and eradicate the evildoers from the Land. What is the matter with you people? Have you forgotten what the Torah teaches? Have you forgotten your brave heroes of old? Have you forgotten Joshua, Samson, Gideon, Deborah, King David? Have you forgotten the words of the Maccabee, 'The battle is not won by the many.' Where is your courage and pride?"

Wingate peered at Ben Zion, glaring at him with accusing eyes, as if he were responsible for the massacre on the road.

"I'm only a regional commander who follows orders," Ben Zion said. Tell it to Ben Gurion."

"Don't worry. I will. He is a traitor to his People. Why does the *Haganah* have guns if not to use them? Strike back! Tonight! Lead your men into every Arab village within ten miles and raise hell. Don't let them sleep at night for a month. Let the Ishmaelites be on the defense – not the Jews!"

Tzvi listened in amazement to hear from the lips of a Gentile the very words that the gamut of Zionist leaders feared to say.

"I'm probably the only British officer in Palestine who wants the Zionist dream to succeed, so take my advice. Don't wait for the British to save you. Save yourselves!"

Wingate took another bite out of his onion and strode back to his army vehicle. A British soldier stood at attention and opened a door of the car. Wingate paused and turned back to the Jews along the road.

"This cannot continue!" he declared. "I won't let it! Her Majesty's Government sent me here on a mission. I have a plan! *L'hitraot.* We shall meet once again!"

3.

Before Wingate could put his plan into operation, the day after the murderous attack on the Jewish taxi near Rosh Pina, three young "Anonymous Soldiers" decided to strike back on their own.

Shlomo Ben Yosef didn't discuss his decision with Tzvi or Yitzhak Ben-Ami, the *pluga* commander. "Borrowing" rifles and a grenade from the colony's cache, Ben Yosef and two friends set off to ambush an Arab bus on the Acre-Safed road. The twenty-five-year old *pluga* recruit had grown up as Shlomo Tabachnik in Lutzk, Poland. After receiving a religious education, he joined the *Betar* Youth Movement, and underwent *hachshara* agricultural training in preparation for *Aliyah.* Since the *Mapai*-dominated Jewish Agency didn't issue immigration certificates to followers of Jabotinsky, Ben Yosef came to *Eretz Yisrael* via the *Irgun's Ha'apala* immigration program, crossing borders illegally from country to country, and sailing stowed-away on a freighter from Greece. Arriving in the Promised Land, he Hebraized his name, wanting to shed off the pernicious influences of exile in foreign, Gentile lands. In Rosh Pina, in addition to his work alongside the colony's settlers, he underwent basic military training, in accord with *Betar's* vision of Jewish independence through military might. In the *pluga* barracks, on the wall beside his bunk, he pinned the solemn *Irgun* anthem, "Anonymous Soldiers," written by Avraham Stern.

> Anonymous Soldiers, we are here without uniforms
> Fear and the shadow of death surround us.
> We have all enlisted for life.
> Only death will release us from our duty.
> On the red days of pogroms and blood,
> On the dark nights of despair,

In cities and towns we will raise our flag
Emblazoned with defense and conquest!
We were not drafted with force, like so many slaves
To spill our blood on foreign lands.
Our desire is to be free men forever.
Our dream is to die for our Nation.

Filled with frustration and bitterness over the continuing Arab aggression against the Jews living in the *Galil*, Shlomo Ben Yosef's patience had come to an end. King Solomon had written, *"To everything there is a season, and a time to every purpose under the Heaven."* The time for revenge had come.

4.

The night before Shlomo Ben Yosef was hung, the Acco Prison guard passed by the condemned prisoner's cell several times to make sure he hadn't discovered a way to escape. On each occasion, the young man slept calmly, with a small smile on his lips. "How could it be?" the guard wondered. In the past, he had led several criminals to the gallows, Arabs convicted of murder. None of them had slept calmly on the eve of his execution.

When Shlomo Ben Yosef woke up, he washed, brushed his teeth, and calmly combed his hair. He removed the red prison outfit worn by prisoners condemned to death, glad that the moment had finally arrived after months of waiting.

"I asked for permission to wear my *Betar* uniform at the hanging, and the warden agreed," Ben Yosef protested when a Jewish guard arrived at his cell with a pair of civilian pants and a white shirt.

"I know," the guard said. "But this is what they gave me. Don't make an issue of it. If you want to demonstrate to the world that Jews aren't afraid to die in their struggle to free their Homeland, the message will be lost if we have to carry you kicking and screaming to the gallows because you weren't given your *Betar* uniform."

"I know you mean well, but if I am not given my uniform, they will have to lead a protesting Jew to the gallows, screaming out to all of the journalists on hand about the injustice of British rule in our Land."

"Very well," the guard said. "I will tell them."

Shlomo prayed the morning prayers which he knew by heart from his childhood. Then, on the limestone wall of his death-row cell, using a nail, he inscribed two messages in his rough Hebrew script: "It is good to die for one's country," echoing the valiant last words of Yosef Trumpeldor at Tel Chai; and, "With my end, may the *havlaga* end as well," expressing the hope that the Jews of the Holy Land would abandon the paralyzing policy of restraint and follow his example, rather than bow down to Arab terror and British subjugation.

Whistling a happy Zionist song, he wrote a short letter to his mother in Poland, telling her he loved her and not to be sad. "Be proud that your son is not going to die like a downtrodden Jew in the exile," he told her. His mother had sent a telegram to the British High Commissioner of Palestine, Sir Harold MacMichael, asking that the execution be postponed until she could come to Palestine and kiss her son farewell, but her request had been denied.

The previous evening, Ben Yosef had written several short letters and final reflections. To Ze'ev Jabotinsky, the founder and head of *Betar*, he wrote: "I am greatly honored to inform you that I go to my last sacred duty tomorrow as a soldier of *Betar* in *Eretz Yisrael*. I remain a faith-filled disciple of *Betar* until my last day."

In another note, he wrote, "To all my friends who bear the memory of Tel Hai in their hearts – do not be afraid! I shall die a proud *Betarist*, with the name of Ze'ev Jabotinsky on my lips. What is a Homeland? It is a land worth living for, fighting for, and dying for."

Although Ben Yosef's action had failed in an operative sense, and the hangman's noose was but an hour away, he didn't regret his decision to strike back at the Arabs after their repeated attacks on Rosh Pina. Enlisting two young friends from the *pluga*, Avraham Shein and Shalom Zuravin, who had just begun their military training, he outlined to them his plan. Securing weapons, they waited alongside the winding Safed-Rosh Pina road until an Arab bus drove by. "Now!" Ben Yosef commanded. He hurled a grenade, hoping the explosion would send the bus hurling down a ravine, but the explosion never sounded. The grenade didn't explode. His two comrades nervously fired their rifles as the vehicle sped by. None of the passengers were injured. Running away, the three young Jews decided to hide in an abandoned building not far from the road. An Arab shepherd saw the rifle-carrying figures enter the ruin. When British policemen arrived at the scene of the shooting, the shepherd told them what he had seen. Within an hour, British troops surrounded the ruin and arrested the three young Jews from Rosh Pina. A military tribunal in Haifa charged them with the illegal possession of weapons, and with the intention to harm and kill a large group of people - capital crimes. Although no one had been injured in the attack, British authorities decided to make the case an example in order to discourage other Jews from carrying out vigilante actions. At the conclusion of their speedy trial, Shalom Zuravin was declared clinically deranged and sentenced to incarceration in a mental institution. Avraham Shein and Shlomo Ben Yosef were condemned to "hang by the neck until they were dead." When it was subsequently proven that Shein was still a minor, his sentence was reduced to life imprisonment. Hearing the verdict, Shein and Ben Yosef shouted out in unison, "Long live the Kingdom of Israel on both banks of the Jordan!" Then, standing at attention, they sang out the *"HaTikvah"* anthem.

> As long as deep within the heart
> A Jewish soul stirs,
> And forward, to the ends of the East
> An eye looks out, towards Zion.
> Our hope is not yet lost
> The hope of two-thousand years
> To be a free people in our Land,
> The Land of Zion and Jerusalem.

"Mr. Ben Yosef, do you have anything to say?" the judge asked.

"Yes, I do."

"Very well."

"It is a poem by Ze'ev Jabotinsky."

"You want to recite a poem to the court?"

"Yes, sir," Ben Yosef responded, standing straight and fearless.

"Proceed."

Unfolding a piece of paper, the young Jewish soldier turned to face the onlookers and journalists assembled in the courtroom. In his unpolished Hebrew, he read, not a personal plea for clemency, but a political creed.

> "Just as a pillar in the center of a bridge
> And like a spine in the back of a man
> The middle of my country
> Is the holy Jordan River.
> There are two banks to the Jordan River;
> This in ours; and the other is ours as well.
> My country is small and desolate
> But she is mine from the top to the end.
> Spreading from the sea to the desert
> With the Jordan River in the middle.
> There are two banks to the Jordan River;
> This in ours; and the other is ours as well.
> Both my hands I have dedicated to you, my Homeland,
> Both my hands to the sickle and the shield.
> May my right hand be forgotten
> If I forget the left bank of the Jordan River.
> There are two banks to the Jordan River;
> This is ours; and the other is ours as well."

Two-weeks later, nail in hand, and now dressed in his *Betar* uniform, Shlomo Ben Yosef scratched another *Betar* teaching on the wall of his death-row cell. "You cannot conquer the heights of the mountain without leaving graves behind on the slope."

The Jewish guard reappeared with Tzvi. The condemned prisoner was allowed to see one last person before the execution, and Ben Yosef had chosen his friend from Rosh Pina.

"*Baruch haba!*" he greeted Tzvi with a confident smile. "Welcome. Welcome!"

Tzvi was surprised to see Shlomo dressed in his uniform,

as if were ready for a morning of military training. Tzvi managed a smile in order not to weaken his comrade's spirit. For Tevye's son, being in the famous Acco Prison was an unnerving experience. For one thing, he himself had killed enough Arabs to be escorted to the gallows. And, ironically, his father has been imprisoned in the old Turkish fortress years before, along with Ze'ev Jabotinsky and the very first fighters of the *Haganah*.

"How's everyone in the *pluga*?" Shlomo asked.

"Everyone is OK, except that we miss the three of you. How are you holding up?"

"Our friend, Shalom, went crazy. Maybe they tortured him. It could be that he wasn't one-hundred percent from the start. I probably shouldn't have taken him along. Thank God that Avraham is well. I'm glad he won't be joining me for the hanging party. After you chase the British back to England, when you free him from prison, he'll help you get rid of the Arabs as well."

Shlomo laughed. Tzvi's heart swelled with compassion, and with great admiration for the courageous *Betar* cadet before him.

"What about you?" he asked, adopting a light tone of voice, as if the hangman's noose wasn't being prepared just down the corridor. "How is the most famous prisoner in the world?"

"I don't care about being famous. If my death wakes up our brothers to fight for our Homeland, then my life has not passed in vain."

Shlomo grinned. His eyes showed no trace of fear. The opposite – he seemed exuberant, as if his life's dream was about to come true. Tzvi nodded. He had arrived at the prison prepared to cheer up his friend, when in fact, he was more worried and downcast than Shlomo. Tzvi glanced over his shoulder to make sure that the guard had left them alone. Though he had been thoroughly searched at the entrance to the prison by two British soldiers, the folded piece of paper in his pocket hadn't been confiscated.

"Listen to this," he said in a whisper. "Avraham Stern and David Raziel wrote it as a new manifesto for the *Irgun*. It's been sent to all *Etzel* commanders and posters have been pasted up all over the *Yishuv*. If you ask me, it's a declaration of war against the British."

Tzvi unfolded the paper and read:

"The *Etzel-Irgun* believes that the Hebrew State will not come about without an independent, national Hebrew army. In contrast, the Jewish Agency hopes to achieve a measure of national freedom by submitting to foreign rule and through a division of the Land. The *Etzel* stands at a crossroads - either we support the policy of appeasement and concession of the Jewish Agency, and, by doing so, submit to the foreign power; or we ready ourselves for greater sacrifice and danger. The willingness of our youth to sacrifice their lives in the struggle against our enemies will give rise to the Hebrew State."

"You, my dear friend, are the inspiration behind this proclamation," Tzvi told the condemned prisoner as his last minutes approached.

"What about *Rosh Betar*," Shlomo asked, referring to the head of the organization, Ze'ev Jabotinsky, to whom he felt devoted. "Does he agree with their words?"

"Apparently, his patience with the British is also coming to an end. A few days ago he sent a telegram to Raziel ordering him to 'invest heavily' if your sentence is carried out."

The telegram was signed, "Mendelson," the code word signaling that *Irgun* commanders in *Eretz Yisrael* had a green light to strike back without restraint.

A smile of peace and contentment graced Ben Yosef's young face. He nodded in satisfaction. "Please tell *Rosh Betar* that I went to the gallows with his name on my lips."

Tzvi trembled, feeling enormous respect for his friend's towering faith, and wondering if he, in the same situation, would act as courageously. Shlomo began to hum the solemn tune of the *"Betar* Song," which Jabotinsky had composed. As he began to sing the last stanza, *"Tagar,"* meaning, "Challenge," in his heavy Polish accent, Tzvi joined along.

Tagar
Despite every oppressor and enemy
Whether you rise or fall
With the torch of revolt
Carry a fire to ignite – do not fear!
Because silence is despicable.
We shall give up blood and soul
For the sake of the hidden glory
To die or conquer the mount.
Yodefet, Masada, Betar!

"Quiet!" the voice of an Arab prisoner shouted. "What the hell are you stinking Jews singing about?!"

The young friends laughed as if they were together in some pub, and not in the airless dungeon cell on death row in Acco Prison.

"Recite to me the end of the 'Flag Song'" Ben Yosef requested, as if hearing Jabotinsky's poem would bring him closer to the figure he so esteemed.

Not only was "*Rosh Betar*" an astute political leader and a daring military commander, he inspired a generation of young Jews with his brilliant orations, essays, articles, novels, and poems. Tzvi himself never possessed the gift of speech, but how could he say no to a man facing the gallows?

"At the time when the enemy is expelled
Then shall we rise and salute,
Long live the youth! Long live the sword!
Long live the blood of the Maccabee."

Unbeknownst to Tzvi and Shlomo, all through the night in London, Ze'ev Jabotinsky frantically tried to obtain a stay of execution, up to the very last hour. Ever since the arrest of the three young *Betarim*, the founder of the *Betar* Youth Movement exerted himself day and night on their behalf. He arranged for lawyers to represent them, and he would have come to Palestine himself to help prepare the defense, but the British had revoked his visa over fifteen years before, banning his re-entry into the country because of his strident activist work on behalf of the Jews.

The day after the three *Betarim* from Rosh Pina were sentenced, Jabotinsky spoke about the "outrageous situation in the Jewish Homeland" before a large crowd of Revisionists in London.

"For more than two years running, gangs of Arab hooligans have been terrorizing the country of our hopes and dreams," he exclaimed. "The Arabs go about freely, humiliating the Jews, and saying to them, in effect, 'You are dirt, this is not your country.' And then three young Jews, ages seventeen, nineteen, and twenty-five, went out and fired a volley of shots, killing no one. They were arrested, tried, and two of them were sentenced to death by a British Government that was either unable or unwilling to do something which any other government in its place would have done with a few battalions in a couple of weeks. I say to the Mandatory Government: It is no use sentencing Jews to death. You either have to stop the Arab terror by yourself, or allow our youth in Palestine to stop it. Don't let two boys pay the penalty for something which you have done, or omitted to do. I don't know what is going to happen to them, but from this podium, I send them my blessings, and I let the judges there know that if anything irreparable happens to them, tens of thousands of children will sit *shiva* in mourning for them, and their names will remain in the annuls of Jewish History as the names of martyrs and giants."

Jabotinsky waged a non-stop public campaign to save Shein and Ben Yosef from the gallows. He urged organizations throughout the world, Jewish and Gentile, to petition the British Government in protest. The office of Malcolm MacDonald, Britain's Secretary for the Colonies, was flooded with telegrams and phone calls, to no avail. While Stein's sentence was reduced to life imprisonment because of his youth, Shlomo Ben Yosef was to be hung in another ten days. Though Ben Yosef rejected the attempts to win clemency on his behalf, Jabotinsky pressed on in his campaign. Rising above political differences and scars, he urged David Ben Gurion, in his capacity as the head of the Zionist Executive, to speak with the British High Commissioner of Palestine, Sir Harold MacMichael.

Recalling the personal bond of respect they had previously forged in their unsuccessful attempt to unite their warring camps, Ben Gurion agreed. Leaving the humanitarian issue aside, Ben Gurion explained to the High Commissioner that, for the best interests of the Mandate Government, pardoning the condemned prisoner would be a prudent gesture. Otherwise, a thousand Ben Yosef's would rise up in moral anger against British rule and threaten its stability.

"Are you concerned for our stability, or for the stability of your Party?" the British High Commissioner shrewdly asked. "Certainly a skilled politician like yourself is aware that the sympathy of the masses is with Ben Yosef, and that his execution will increase the public's opposition to your policy of *havlaga* and appeasement. You are likely to be blamed for the young man's desperate and impetuous action, and for his death."

"That is a possibility, granted," Ben Gurion admitted. "Everyone stands to lose if he is hanged and turned into a martyr. The young man himself; the proponents of *havlaga*; and the British. I am sure you understand that."

"Indeed. However, I trust that you and the *Haganah* will find the means to quell any rebellious tendencies on the part of the Revisionists and keep young Maccabees like Ben Yosef under your control."

"Extremists like Ben Yosef do not listen to me."

"I am aware of that as well. But it is in your best interests to try to squash your ideological opponents. Nevertheless, I trust that Mr. Jabotinsky is wise enough to know that the British Empire is strong enough to crush any riffraff rebellion on his part against the Realm. Besides, even if I were to agree with your fears that Ben Yosef's execution will trigger an insurgency against our Administration, there are too many powerful people in London, and in the British Military, who are not as sensitive to the situation in Palestine as you are, and who do not share my views. Though I am High Commissioner, not everyone listens to me."

All the while, Jabotinsky did his best to strengthen the boy's hysterical mother. The day before the execution, Jabotinsky met with the Secretary for the Colonies, MacDonald, in London, but his appeals and warnings met deaf airs. The sentences, MacDonald explained were meant to "teach unruly elements a lesson and discourage further vigilante actions." Undaunted, Jabotinsky sent another delegation a few hours later to MacDonald, who remained rigid in his stance. At nine in the evening, one of the defense lawyers phoned Jabotinsky, telling him that he had discovered a precedent case from 1901, wherein an appeal to the Privy Council against a court martial verdict had been allowed. Once again, Jabotinsky arranged a late night meeting between a leading bannister sympathetic to the cause with MacDonald and with the Attorney General for the British Isles, asking for a stay of execution. At the same time, he received permission from the Librarian of the House of Commons to search for the arcane legal source in the stacks of the closed library. The needed document couldn't be found, and the meeting with MacDonald once again proved futile. In the middle of the night, a team of lawyers working around the clock discovered another precedent, this time of an Irish rebel, sentenced to death in 1920, who was granted a stay of execution and later a reprieve. Once again, the file couldn't be found. Unwilling to give up, at three o'clock in the morning, Jabotinsky, accompanied by two lawyers, rang the bell of the High Court. They explained to the startled High Court attendant who lived in the building that the matter was a question of life or death. Graciously, he led them to the basement where the records for 1920 were stored. Within a half hour, the file was found. Rushing to the home of MacDonald's personal secretary, they awakened him from bed. Receiving them in his slippers and sleeping robe, the courteous fellow didn't complain about the preposterous hour. Apologizing, he politely told them that he didn't know how to reach the Foreign Secretary at such an early hour. It was nearing dawn in London – too late to stop the hanging.

Tzvi and Shomo Ben Yosef heard the approaching footsteps. "Time to go," the prison guard said. The hooded hangman stood behind him. Two British soldiers stood holding rifles in the death-row corridor. The guard unlocked the cell door.

The condemned prisoner greeted them with a happy tone.

"Good morning, gentlemen!" he said with a broad smile. "*Shehechiyanu v'cheimanu v'higeanu l'zman hazeh*! Bless the Lord for having brought me to this moment."

He turned to Tzvi and gave him a hug. "Carry on, my friend," he said. "*Hazak v'amatz*! Be strong and filled with courage!"

Then, standing at attention, the twenty-five-year old gave Tzvi a *Betar* salute, as if saluting his commander. Tzvi saluted in return. "The Nation will always remember you," Tzvi told him in parting, stepping aside as the guard and hangman entered the cell.

The hooded executioner tied the prisoner's hands behind his back. Ben Yosef turned his head and gazed through the holes in the mask at the eyes of the executioner, causing the man to blink. They were the uncompassionate eyes of an Englishman. Ben Yosef sighed in relief. His only worry had been that the hangman be a Jew. Now he could go to his Maker in peace.

Once again, as he was led out the cell door, Ben Yosef began to sing the "*HaTikvah*" anthem. Tzvi joined in the singing as the guard and executioner led Ben Yosef away down the dungeon corridor, escorted by the two British soldiers. The words of the anthem echoed through the hallways of the prison. As they climbed the stairs to the main floor of the old fortress, they heard a chorus of loud voices singing along with them. All of the Jewish prisoners stood solemnly in the exercise yard, in the open courtyard of the prison. Seeing Ben Yosef, they straightened in attention, raising their hands to their brows in salute. Amplified by the open rotunda, the words of the song reached the upper floor of the prison. Not a prisoner, guard, prison official, or journalist failed to hear the stirring anthem of determination and hope.

Shlomo paused at the entrance to the execution chamber. Turning toward the Jewish prisoners in the courtyard, he called out, "Long live the Jewish State on both banks of the Jordan River! Long live Jabotinsky!"

The prisoners echoed his call. "Long live the Jewish State on both banks of the Jordan River! Long live Jabotinsky!"

The executioner pushed Ben Yosef into the stark, empty

room. In the middle of the chamber, a thick rope and hangman's noose hung motionlessly down from a wooden crossbeam. A wooden trap door waited underneath the rope on the bare stone floor. The door of the chamber closed. The Jewish prisoners continued to sing.

> "To be a free people in our Land,
> The Land of Zion and Jerusalem."

Chapter Thirteen
THE SQUEAKY DOOR

And now, dear Reader, allow me a brief hiatus from the events of this historical fiction or fictional history - in what we have termed a histortion or fictory in the introduction to our previous novel, *Arise and Shine!* – in order to present a bit of the intellectual, ideological, philosophical, and spiritual background out of which all of the subsequent action, self-sacrifice, and revolutionary struggle of this story is built, the saga of a few brave souls against the many to liberate the Land of Israel from alien, Gentile rule. After all, we are dealing with the Nation of Israel, and Jews are a very deep breed of people whose souls, set afire at Sinai, burn eternally throughout the chronicles of history in ever brighter flames. True, there are many Jewish souls, whose great spiritual fire is smothered in material trappings, like the souls of Meir Lansky and Bugsy Siegel, who were a product of material-minded America where ideological pursuits became constricted in the pursuit of power and wealth. Make no mistake – the freedom fighters of Israel weren't killers or gangsters, or Mafia-like gangs. True, not everyone was a deep philosopher like Yisrael Eldad, or a poet-warrior like Avraham Stern, but even the most simple soldiers and detonation experts, whether from the *Irgun*, *Lechi*, *Haganah*, or *Palmach*, were filled with a deep spiritual motivation and a passionate yearning for the Redemption of Israel. So, lest the Reader think that the scores of killings, bombings, assassinations, and intrigue that comprise the rest of our story are merely a Jewish copy of *The Godfather*, know that the most exalted goals of human existence are contained in the heroic epic of Israel's return to being a sovereign Nation in its own Promised Land.

As we mentioned in *Arise and Shine!* - the second volume of this pentalogy - the inner essence of the Zionist Movement was totally Divine. Very much like the Heavenly Decree, "*Let there be light,*" the Creator of Heaven and Earth decided that the time had arrived to return the exiled Jews to their Homeland. In accord with His unbounded humility, the Almighty set about this gigantic, world-shaking task, by hiding Himself in the seemingly natural events of history, such as the First World War, the Balfour Declaration, and the international treaties which followed. While the plethora of history books written about the era might not give God any credit, the Master of the World, operating incognito, decided that the time had come for the National Soul of the Jewish People to awaken from its almost two-thousand-year slumber in the graveyards of foreign lands, and for the *"dry bones"* of Ezekiel's prophecy to come to life and gather together in *Eretz Yisrael.* Needless to say, every Jew experienced the great new light according to his personal level and aspirations. For instance, when the light hit Theodore Herzl, it inspired him to write, *The Jewish State.* When it hit Eliezer Ben Yehuda, it motivated him to revive the Hebrew language. When the light of the inner, awakening soul of the Jewish People shone on Ze'ev Jabotinsky, it urged him to revitalize the military might of Israel's heroes of old, Joshua, Samson, King David, the Maccabees, and Bar Kochva. And when the light awakened in the giant, universal soul of Rabbi Kook, it led him to teach the Jewish People to see and understand that the light of God that was shining in the inner soul of the Zionist Movement, and in the souls of the pioneers who were returning to rebuild the desolate Land, even though they themselves were unaware of the deeply religious core of their actions.

Not every Jew became a Torah-quoting Zionist like Tevye. Other factors influenced the direction the light would take, things like upbringing, education, place of birth, and the root of one's soul. When the awakening light of Israel's Redemption hit some people, they became ardent socialists, or communists, or American businessmen. Even amongst religious Jews, if a person wasn't raised with the true nationalistic understanding of the Torah, whose underlying goal is to establish the Holy Jewish Nation in the Holy Jewish Land, then their orientation to the Torah became the truncated performance of personal commandments, like keeping *kosher* and observing *Shabbat*. Thus, many religious Jews rejected the Zionist Movement, especially when many of its proponents were scorners of the Torah. Upon Rabbi Kook's death, may the memory of a *Tzaddik* be for a blessing, the Jabotinskys, Ben Gurions, Menachem Begins, and Tevyes, were left to carry on in the darkness, without Rabbi Kook's all-encompassing vision and light. This too was the will of *Hashem*, in order that, with the removal of the great light, all of the smaller lights would arise and shine by themselves. And this is where Yisrael Eldad enters our story, along with other lights which we have already met, and still others whom we shall meet in upcoming chapters, and in the volumes to come. So remember, when Jewish Tommy guns start blasting away at British policemen and soldiers, and when British buildings and installations in Palestine get blown sky high in a cloud of awakened Hebrew wrath, it isn't only Menachem Begin and Avraham Stern giving the orders. It is the Holy One Blessed Be He, the "Master of Wars," working incognito, behind the scenes, in order to fulfill the promises He made in the Torah.

The life of twenty-eight-year old, Yisrael Eldad, born Scheib, was at a crossroads, as he traveled by train to the 1938 *Betar* World Conference in Warsaw. Indeed, the collective lives of the Jewish People were at a crossroads as well. In another few weeks, during "Kristallnacht" – the "Night of Broken Glass" – 267 synagogues throughout Germany would be torched and destroyed; 7,500 Jewish businesses would be looted and closed; 90 Jews murdered; and 30,000 Jews arrested and shipped off to "work camps". If anyone harbored doubts about Hitler's intentions until then, they would be shattered that night, like the windows of the great German *shuls*. In Soviet Russia, the tolerant attitude that had existed toward Yiddish culture in the early years of the Revolution had given way to a brutal repression of all expressions of national Jewish sentiment. In Poland, Lithuania, Latvia, Rumania, and Hungary, Jews faced official discrimination, daily physical attacks, unemployment, even starvation.

Scheib (which he Hebraized to Eldad after his *Aliyah* to Israel) was born in Galatia, a region spreading over the

Western Ukraine and Eastern Poland, which had a thriving Jewish community of some three million Jews – most of whom would perish in the Holocaust. His mother was a religious woman, and his father a Zionist. Refugees during World War One, they wandered from place to place for a year without a home. Not having candlesticks, Yisrael's father would stand the Sabbath candles upright in two halves of a potato. The family found residence in Lvov, where little Yisrael watched a funeral possession of Jews murdered in a pogrom. The boy was an avid reader, devouring Zionist literature and world classics like *Robinson Crusoe*. His father sent him to a Jewish high school which encouraged the study of Classic Literature and the Humanities. In his free time, he studied Judaism and Hebrew. At sixteen, he left home to continue his learning in Lodz where he attended a lecture of Ze'ev Jabotinsky. The stirring words of the passionate speaker forced Scheid-Eldad to confront his inner self for the first time in his life. Who was he? What was his purpose in life? Would he live for himself like the average man, or would he dedicate his life serving the Jewish People? The words of Jabotinsky, two months before Germany invaded Poland, rang in his ears:

"To my shame, the Jews are behaving as if their doom had been already sealed. I know nothing similar to it in all the history books which I have read; not even in novels have I ever encountered such submission to fate. Do you know what it resembles? It's as if twelve million educated, well-mannered people, were put in a wagon that was driven toward the edge of a cliff. What do they do? One weeps, one smokes a cigarette, one sings, but not a single person can be found to jump to his feet, grab the reins, and change the wagon's direction. That's the mood shared by everyone. They might as well have been chloroformed by their worst enemy."

Jabotinsky's metaphor disturbed Eldad profoundly. Less than a decade later, after the Holocaust, he realized that even before the Jews reached the crematories, they had already been gassed with a paralyzing inertia, a result of their absolute national impotence during their long centuries of exile in foreign lands.

Graduating from high school, the talented student entered the Rabbinical Academy of Vienna, where he studied Talmud, Torah, and Jewish Philosophy. In the afternoons, he enrolled in program of General Studies at the University of Vienna, eventually earning a doctorate in Philosophy.

Why am I telling you all this? First, because in the next volume of this literary quintet, Yisrael Eldad will become an important part of our story, offering us a deeper understanding of the dramatic events of our saga. Secondly, his life shows how greatly an individual, a movement, and a generation, can be influenced by the thinkers and writers of its age. This is especially true concerning the rebirth of the State of Israel. As Tevye was wont to say, "Thank the good Lord" for having raised up healthy Jewish souls in such a threatened generation, people like Rabbi Kook, Ze'ev Jabotinsky, Abba Ahimeir, Uri Zvi Greenberg, Avraham Stern, Menachem Begin, Yisrael Eldad, and others whose words and writings illuminated a path through the darkness on the road to Redemption.

Eldad possessed the soul of an artist. To him, literature contained more reality than life. No wonder that a novel called, *Samson*, written by Jabotinsky, opened a new page in his self-understanding. Its message was so brilliant, it taught him to see. The young and impressionable seeker could quote many of its passages by heart. In perhaps the most emotional scene, Samson, now blinded by enemies and captive on the Gaza shore, takes his leave from Hermesh, one of his soldiers who fought the Philistines. The Israelites need three things to rule over the Land, Samson tells him - weapons of iron, a national leader, and a joyous confidence in their ultimate victory, in order to preserve their spirits in times of defeat and despair:

"Shall I give our people a message from you?" Hermesh asks.

Samson thought for a while, then said slowly:

"Tell them two things in my name – two words. The first word is iron. They must acquire iron. They must give everything they have for iron – their silver and wheat, their oil, wine, and flocks, even their wives and daughters. All for iron! There is nothing in the world more valuable than iron. Will you tell them that?"

"I will. They will understand that."

"The second word they will not understand yet, but they must learn to understand it, and soon. The second word is this: a king! Say to Dan, Benjamin, Judah, Ephraim: a king! A man will give them the signal and all of a sudden, thousands will lift up their hands. So it is with the Philistines, and therefore the Philistines are lords of Canaan. Say it from Zorah to Hebron and Shechem, and farther even to Endor and Laish: a king!"

Then, in an afterthought, Samson added one other national foundation. "I have changed my mind," he said. "Tell them three things in my name, not two. They must get iron; they must choose a king; and they must learn to laugh."

Eldad, like so many other searching young Jews, discovered in the personage of Ze'ev Jabotinsky, not only a brilliant orator and literary master, but a "king" as well. He was the renowned founder of the Hebrew Brigade, the first commander of the *Haganah*, and the famous "prisoner of Acco." He possessed the bearing of a noble knight of old, an indefatigable crusader, always ready to venture forth for a noble cause, undaunted by obstacles, however towering they appeared. He was a gentleman's gentleman, living by a code of honor and proper behavior, which respected the rights of others, and championed the nobility of man, rich and poor, the famous and the unknown. A connoisseur of culture, literature, philosophy, and art, he encouraged higher learning and achievement. In his personal dress, he was immaculate, placing great importance on outward appearance and deportment. He walked erect at all times, like a soldier, with a bearing that proclaimed, "Jews! Walk erect and proud as true sons and soldiers of the kings of Israel of old!"

Yet, Jabotinsky himself suffered from deep frustrations. Gradually realizing that the England he so greatly respected was reneging on its promise to help the Jews, he began demanding a more militant Zionist stance to combat Britain's betrayal, only to be hostilely rejected by a Zionist establishment who didn't want to make waves. Stunned by the intransience of Weizmann and Ben Gurion to revamp the Zionist agenda in light of Britain's pro-Arab policies, Jabotinsky realized he would have to educate a new generation with a far bolder vision and spirit, to instill in Jewish youth the emotional and psychological fortitude needed to be rulers of their own Land, and not the ruled; to be conquerors and not the conquered; makers of their destiny, and not passive recipients of the crumbs granted them by the generosity of the Gentiles. He rightly sensed that if a more valiant banner of Zionism wasn't raised on high, young Jews would look elsewhere for salvation and meaning, and turn to the others "isms" sweeping through the world - Socialism, Communism, Pacifism, and Capitalism – abandoning the proud Hebrew Nationalism which they sought but couldn't find.

Eldad, along with myriads of young people possessed with powerful Jews souls, felt like a ship lost in a storm without a captain. They felt empty, dull of heart, longing for a great ideal they could embrace from the depths of their beings as their own. They yearned for a purpose in life that was pure and true to their own personal essence, as Jews, not something borrowed from others. A unique, Hebrew ideal is what Jabotinsky offered. He called for a Zionism without mixture and dross, not socialist-Zionism, or communist-Zionism, or Labor-Zionism, or an intellectual, universal-Zionism, but Zionism alone. He told the persecuted and downcast youth of the ghetto that they were the heirs of King David and the Maccabees, the progeny of the Prophets of Israel, bearers of a healing message for the world. History, he told them, was offering them the noblest of honors, and the most exalted responsibility - the re-establishing a Jewish State in Zion. He beckoned them to rise to the challenge. And they did.

In creating *Betar*, Jabotinsky hoped to transform his beliefs into practical expression. Chapter meetings offered the Jewish youth in Europe and America a wide range of social and cultural activities. Hebrew was taught, along with Jewish history and Zionist theory. Unlike other youth movements, *Betar* trained its recruits in military skills and self-defense. Jabotinsky wrote that he wanted "to see military training become as common among Jews as lighting Sabbath candles." He called upon Jewish parents to teach their children not only how to read, but "to shoot as well." The Zionist establishment, led by David Ben Gurion, vilified Jabotinsky for the new, militaristic tone he brought to the *Betar* Youth Movement, accusing him of irresponsibly filling the minds and hearts of Jewish youth with a "militaristic *dybbuk*" which was sure to backfire against the Jews. Jewish Agency leaders warned that Jabotinsky's "playing with sticks" would soon have the Zionist Movement facing British rifles and bayonets, turning their closest ally into a foe. Armored by his iron belief, *Rosh Betar*, as Jabotinsky was called, the *"Head of Betar,"* ignored personal insults, and pursued his vision, inwardly anguished by his inability to rally all the Jewish People into one, unified army dedicated to the conquest of Zion.

Appreciating the importance of physical might, the poet in Yisrael Eldad was also attracted to the accompanying noblesse of the *Betar* credo, *"Hadar,"* a Hebrew word whose meaning combines the character traits of dignity and honor, with the spiritual concepts of "majesty" and "splendor." Jabotinsky continually reminded Jews that they were the sons of prophets and kings, with a glorious ancestry which had shattered the primitive excesses of idolatry, while establishing the principles of justice and morality as the foundations of human existence. The concept of *Hadar* was intended to set the standard for a new Jewish society. It demanded that *Betar's* members be courteous at all times, conduct all of their activities with grace, permit women, elders, and small children to precede them in public places. And it taught the value of humor, when used in an uplifting manner. Jabotinsky exhorted Jews to act in an elevated and noble fashion, and to pursue unity and brotherhood in the task of reviving their lost, once glorious Kingdom.

Myriads of sensitive, young Jewish souls who were searching for their Jewish identity and their mission in life, discovered it in the teachings of Ze'ev Jabotinsky. But Jabotinsky alone didn't light the fire in the hearts of the Nation's youth. Their minds were awakened, and their dormant yearnings were also stirred by the Zionist poet and visionary, Uri Zvi Greenberg. His poems triggered an upheaval in their weltanschauung on the world. Greenberg wrote about the Jewish Savior who is ready to come, but the Jewish People are too occupied with their businesses and material concerns to care. The poem, "I'll Tell it to a Child," was addressed to children, the poet explained, because only children still retained the purity and innocence to truly believe.

Jewish children, in my house of lowly Zion.
Evening, darkness, bathed in the moon's full light.
I speak and you sit at my side.
To you, my dears, I will tell the story of the good
Mashiach
Who did not come.
To those who are older than you, I will not tell it.
Adults do not have eyes like yours, which shine with a
living flame.
Adults do not listen like you. The destiny of Zion has
passed from their hearts.
While the spirit of Mashiach departs from the Temple
Mount
In the form of an eagle in flight.

At the impressionable age of twenty-two, when Eldad heard that Greenberg would be giving a lecture, entitled, "The Land of Israel in Flames," he hurried to meet the famous poet who had fled the dark exile to live in the light-filled landscapes of *Eretz Yisrael*. Greenberg read excerpts from a long ballad, "Decay of the House of Israel," which expressed the lowliness of Zionists and a Zionism that abandoned the dream of renewing the ancient Israelite Kingdom, crowned with Torah, Holy Temple, and *Malkhut* – the holy Kingdom of God - replacing it with the dream of comfortable houses on *kibbutzim*.

"The arms of their ancestors reached out for God
But these have lost God and lost His Heavens.
They no longer offer their arms in prayer. They offer their
necks to any Arab

> Who flashes a knife, however feeble. Their lives they offer,
> out of fear."
> "Rise from the flames! Become a Burning Bush of wrath
> right here!
> Rise up from the blood! Be a Pillar of Glory spreading over
> the Land,
> Armed with the sword of lightening and the power of
> thunder!

Eldad, a lover of philosophy and literature, understood what the poem expressed. He understood that the *galut* – the exile of the Jews in foreign lands – would become their graveyard. The Torah and the Prophets of Israel had promised that the scattered Jews would return to their Homeland from the four corners of the globe, and the time had come. What could be a more meaningful destiny for him than to unite his life with this great historic plan? But to achieve their mission of being a beacon of light to world, it wasn't enough to build houses and plow fields, while Jewish blood flowed in the furrows. From another Greenberg poem, "One Truth and Not Two," Eldad learned that the Homeland wouldn't be conquered by merely purchasing property and building *kibbutzim*, but by taking up the sword against the country's usurpers.

> Your Rabbis taught: A land is bought with money
> You buy the land and work it with a hoe.
> And I say: A land is not bought with money.
> A land is conquered with blood.
> And only when conquered with blood is it hallowed to the
> people
> With the holiness of the blood.

But how could the weak and lowly remnant of Israel purge the mighty British Empire and the renegades of *Allah* from the Land? And what do you do with Jewish brothers who abandoned the dream of *Malkhut Yisrael*, the holy Kingdom of Israel, to be graced by the rebuilt Jerusalem Temple, the Sanhedrin, and a king from the House of David. The communists and socialists wanted to replace Israel's glory with a network of godless *kibbutzim*, whose roofs, the poet said, should be ripped off and scattered over the seas. What do you do with brothers willing to send an innocent Jew, Avraham Stavsky, to the gallows, just to defame Jews with opposing beliefs, and to hijack the Zionist Movement, in order to strip Judaism from the Jew and turn the Land of Israel into a worker's cooperative? What do you do with this strange mutant son of Israel who pens angry editorials condemning Jews who strike back at barbarous killers of Jewish women and children, and who hand fellow Jews over to the British Police in a wholesale fashion?

Could Eldad be like David Raziel who refused to be bullied by the priests of appeasement and *havlaga*. When Arabs continued to ambush Jews on the roads of the *Galil*, he ordered another bombing of the Arab market in Haifa which killed thirty-nine Arabs and wounded over fifty. In an exchange of bullets, an *Irgun* member dressed as an Arab was wounded. *Haganah* soldiers who raced to the scene found the wounded Jew and drove him to nearby *Haganah* headquarters. Fearing that the *Haganah* would hand him over to the British police, Raziel warned them by telephone that such an action would lead to the assassination of all the *Haganah* commanders in Haifa. The wounded man was immediately returned to the *Irgun*.

In Ben Yosef's memory, Raziel wrote an essay entitled, "Martyrs will Redeem the Homeland."

"No country," he wrote, "can be redeemed from foreign oppression except through harsh suffering. A struggle for National Freedom demands sacrifice, strife, and heroes who fall in battle. Nothing can stand against the spirit of National Sacrifice.

"A youth faced with death faces the loss of his future, physical pain, mental anguish at leaving his loved ones – these are all individual concerns. The eyes of an idealist, willing to die for his ideal, sees a different picture. He sees his nation sinking with no future in its cobwebbed state. He understands that his personal life alone is not the most valuable possession on earth, but rather the life of the Nation, National Liberty, and National Honor. If victory demands sacrifice and death – bring them on!

"The penetrating eyes of victory understand that spirit can

overcome the flesh. They know that a dead lion is better than a living dog. They see the cursed present transformed by the ideal of Redemption. The vision of these idealistic young men and women encompasses the hopes of the past and the dreams of a future coming real before them, for there is no mountain that cannot be conquered through sacrifice.

"The young heroes who have already died, and those who will follow in their footsteps, ready to conquer and ready to die, they call out to the Jewish Nation in a loud and proud voice, 'Rise up from the dust! Those who are dying shall redeem you!'"

Journeying to the *Betar* Conference, Eldad wondered if an academic like him who loved the serenity and peace of libraries, could become, like David Raziel, a soldier dedicated to liberating the Land of Israel through a war till the end. Could he make the jump from the library, yeshiva, and ghetto, to the battleground of Palestine and unite *Sefer* and *Safra*, the book and the sword?

Eldad gleaned the needed confidence from the pen of another poet, Avraham Stern. He also spoke about restoring *Malchut Yisrael*, but his poetry was the poetry of glorious self-sacrifice and underground warfare against the enemies of Israel.

> Yes, I am both a soldier and a poet!
> Today, I write with a pen – tomorrow with a sword.
> Today, I write with ink – tomorrow with blood.
> Today, on paper – tomorrow on flesh.
> Heaven gave the Book and the sword.
> Fate decreed – soldier and poet together.

His words were like bullets, his verses like grenades. Poetry to Stern was another weapon in the battle to liberate *Eretz Yisrael* from foreign rule. In memory of Shlomo Ben Yosef, hanged by the British, he wrote:

> "In a time of terrible strife in Israel
> When no one responds
> As bestial heathens murder our brethren
> And defile a daughter of Safed...

Jerusalem was like a woman disgraced
And Israel for a spoil.
Until there arose
Volunteers for the Nation
To retaliate and revenge
With blood.
The executed one didn't surrender
But gave up his soul to die
For Malkhut – the Kingdom of Israel.
And his aged mother, bereaved
For her son she silently weeps,
Her heart bound up in ropes of death.
She dreams, and behold the gallows.
And she awakens, and behold, a day shadowed in death.
They tested a heavy sack on a strong rope,
Between the walls of Acco prison, a strangling night...
And at eight o'clock in the morning
The hangman exchanged the sack for a man
Who ascended singing to the gallows.
Am Yisrael – Salute!!

Traveling on the train to the *Betar* convention in Warsaw, the young man who still called himself Scheib, wondered what could he do, a teacher of history, and a lover of philosophy and world literature, to play a part in the battle? True, he was the commander of a local *Betar* chapter, but he was an educator, not a soldier. But, as the poet declared, there was one truth, and not two. Could he, like Jabotinsky, Avraham Stern, and Uri Zvi Greenberg, use his spirit and his pen to provide fuel for the Hebrew revolution, to arouse and inspire the Anonymous Soldiers who would have to rise to the heights of self-sacrifice, like Shlomo Ben Yosef, in conquering the mountain?

It seemed to him that the *Betar* Youth Movement had come to a crossroads. For years, chapter commanders had been instilling the spirit of revolution in their young and eager members, but how long can you keep the bonfire burning when all you do is talk and practice military exercises with sticks? Instead of climbing up the mountain leading to Jerusalem, the Jewish youth of Europe loitered on the streets of Warsaw and Vilna, wasting their strength, squandering their passion, at best collecting coins for the Jewish National Fund, or attending Zionist Congresses and listening to endless speeches, but getting no closer to the mountain. And all the while, Arabs massacred Jews in the Holy Land, and the Zionist leadership shut their lips, and the Jews of the exile could already feel the fire under their feet as they waited for Salvation. Thousands of young people, men and women, waited and waited, their muscles still strong, not yet thinned by hunger and disease, their throats still filled with song, and not with the gas crematories, myriads waiting to be granted immigration certificates to Palestine, some of them turned away because the British had closed the gates; some because the Jewish Agency selected only those who fit the socialist agenda; others because they didn't have the 400 *zlotys* needed to secure passage on a clandestine *map'alim* ship organized by the *Irgun* or by the *Haganah*. Not finding an outlet for their nationalistic yearnings, many of the generation's squandered youth abandoned their Jewishness and joined the armies of Stalin, or any other revolutionary movement at hand.

Others, those poised for action, who flocked to the call of military training, had grown impatient with endless lectures and marching in formation. Hearing how the Jews in *Eretz Yisrael* were being slaughtered by Arabs without any reprisal, and smelling the ashes of Kristallnacht in the air, tens of thousands of restless *Betarim* youth yearned for armed struggle, not talk.

A great tension gripped the enormous crowd at the *Betar* Conference in Warsaw, as everyone looked to their cherished leader, *Rosh Betar*, Ze'ev Jabotinsky, to publically declare - further appeasement or war.

Wearing his *Betar* uniform, like almost everyone else in the large convention hall, Yisrael Eldad took a seat in the back of the auditorium. He only recognized three of the people sitting on the dais of the presidium in front of the packed and noisy crowd – Ze'ev Jabotinsky, the young Menachem Begin, and the poet, Uri Zvi Greenberg, his inspiration and mentor. Along with the blue-and-yellow flag of *Betar*, with its symbol of a *menorah*, long black banners hung in the hall, in memory of Shlomo Ben Yosef.

"Who is the man sitting to the left of *Rosh Betar*," Eldad asked the uniformed fellow sitting beside him.

"I don't know."

Eldad asked his other neighbor, but he didn't know either. How could he? With his clean-shaven face, Tevye, the man in civilian clothes on the dais, was a stranger to everyone except to Jabotinsky, whom he had faithfully served in the early days of the *Haganah*, and with whom he had spent months together in Acco Prison.

Glancing up toward the balcony, Eldad noticed a young, dapperly-dressed man, standing erect and rigid, like a cocked rifle, gazing down at the tension-filled gathering. His bearing and intense expression commanded Eldad's attention, even more than the figures on the stage. In the sea of uniformed *Betarim* cadets in the audience, his civilian suit and Fedora hat gave him an air of rank and distinction.

"Who is he?" he again asked the fellow sitting beside him, motioning toward the almost sinister observer in the balcony.

"Never seen him before. Maybe he's a reporter, or a *Mapai* spy."

The poet, Uri Zvi Greenberg, led off the convention, setting a strident tone with his poem, "Ode to the Nation," which described the great power and potential of the exiled generation, praising its ability to rebuild its Land and overcome its enemies, coupled with the frustrations and misdirected energies of its youth, whose talents were wasted in service of alien countries because their leaders lacked true Hebrew vision and courage. The young people in the packed convention hall greeted their beloved seer with a tumultuous enthusiasm, grateful to him for expressing the inner turmoil and revolutionary passions pulsing in their veins.

Mighty Nation! Even in exile, mounting to millions!
Your numerous sons, broad of shoulder and strong in
spirit,
Arms of iron, thighs of steel.

Sons equipped to work the soil and make homes,
To build houses and factories,
Bridges and tunnels, ports and highways.
Sons marching to battle against the enemy,
Striking the fear of their ancient race into his heart.
Sons to operate trains, ships, and planes,
To sing Hebrew ballads
In all the seaports of the world,
Wherever their ships dock with their cargoes,
Hues of sunset in their faces,
And the depth of the sea in their eyes.
Nation, your abundant daughters, lovely and sound,
Daughters to work in village and town,
Blessed to branch forth like trees,
Giving birth to a new generation
Healthy and beautiful and tanned by the sun.
And from them - prophets and scholars,
Men of action and daring,
Rulers to take command!
What shall they do here today,
Your sons and daughters,
In the fullness of their powers,
With the maelstrom of their pent-up fury,
The force of revolt within them?
What shall they do
With the fever of battle pounding in their blood?
Command them to conquer the Land,
To scale the peaks with standards flying,
Command them to go through fire,
To storm the walls of Titus, raze Bastilles.
As rebels they will go forth,
And you shall hear their song
Of freedom and conquest and Redemption,
Till the expansion of their borders and kingship- *Malchut*!
Command them to span the deepest chasms,
And they will turn their bodies into bridges.
Bid them tear down a building,
And they will break their bodies to smash it!
Therefore, O Nation,
Your sons and daughters are walking the earth in anger;

Hundreds, thousands, with rage in their blood,
Bitter of soul, grinding their teeth,
Blaspheming the Kingdom of David and blessing the
House of Stalin instead.
Trapped like tigers - so many dying unnoticed in prisons
In the spring of their youth,
Dragged off at sunrise to eternal sleep
In an alien land.
Can they be charged with betrayal?
No, it is not they who are guilty!
They are in need of leaders
Who like themselves are rebels in spirit
With rage in their blood.
They are in need of prophets
To march before them like Pillars of Fire
In their own generation, now!

The applause was thunderous, but it was nothing like the cheers for *Rosh Betar*. If Uri Zvi Greenberg personified the psalmist and poet of King David's all-encompassing personality, the "*Sweet Singer of Israel*," then Vladimir Ze'ev Jabotinsky personified the qualities of statesman and king. While he was also a distinguished writer, a persona of leadership radiated from his being, crowning him with an aura of royalty, which, like King David, he bore with no ostentation or pride. Nevertheless, while he had led soldiers on the battlefield, the fearless warrior side of King David's character was perhaps more concentrated in the young Menachem Begin, and with the mysterious man in the balcony, with David Raziel in Jerusalem, and in the hundreds of "Anonymous Soldiers" who were ready to face Goliath and risk their lives for *Am Yisrael*. Later, Yisrael Eldad came to realize that, in a literary sense, Jabotinsky was the tragic King Saul, while all of young *Betarim* in the convention hall contained sparks of the shepherd boy, David.

When Jabotinsky stood up to speak, a deafening applause filled the auditorium. Everyone rose to their feet. Tevye, Menachem Begin, Uri Zvi Greenberg, and the other *Betar* leaders on the stage, stood at attention, applauding. Truly, if there was a leader filled with the nobility and grandeur of Israel's Biblical heroes of the past, it was Ze'ev Jabotinsky. When he held up his hand, everyone sat down in diligent obedience, like soldiers before their commander. An absolute hush fell over the packed hall. It was as if you could hear the beating of ten-thousand hearts. What, they wanted to know, was the message to be derived from the clank of the trap doors and the snap of the rope, still echoing from the corridors of Acco Prison?

In hanging Ben Yosef, the British wanted to teach the Jews of a lesson, but they turned him into a hero instead. The day after the execution, *Betar* hung notices all over the country:

SHLOMO BEN YOSEF
Hero of the Israelite Nation, the first Jewish martyr in *Eretz Yisrael* executed by the ruling authorities since the days of Rabbi Akiva – a pillar of fire to a Nation fighting for its freedom, was hanged by the British in Acco Prison.

His example inspired young Jews throughout the world to yearn for national liberation and freedom from foreign oppressors. In *Eretz Yisrael,* his tomb became an altar. Throughout the Diaspora, in cities with large Jewish communities, windows of the British Consulates were shattered. Jews attached a black ribbon to their coats in mourning for the heroic young martyr who had been executed while crying out, "Long live Jabotinsky!"

In the wake of his execution, a searing resentment flared throughout the *Irgun* membership in Palestine against the organization's commander, Moshe Rosenberg. On his way to Poland, he received a telegram from Jabotinsky thanking him for his devoted work and relieving him of his position, to be replaced by David Raziel.

After Ben Yosef's hanging, a profoundly disturbed Jabotinsky had written a letter in Yiddish to the martyr's mother: "I do not merit that a noble soul like your son should die with my name on his lips. But as long as it is my lot to live, his name will live in my heart, and his disciples, more than mine, will be the trailblazers of the generation. It is not me who educated your son – it is he who taught me the meaning of Zionism."

Jabotinsky gazed out at the expectant and already electrified audience through his thick, round eyeglass frames, as if through binoculars. He knew that everyone was anxiously waiting to hear his official reaction to the policy of restraint and appeasement which both the Arabs and British perceived as weakness and surrender. While opposed to acts of reprisal against innocent people, he understood that the "*havlaga*" do-nothing policy of the Jewish Agency had turned the Jews in Palestine into a community of impotent cowards. But first he wanted to say something about Ben Yosef.

"I know that everyone is angry over the dastardly hanging of Shlomo Ben Yosef," he began. "I am angry too. We are angry at the crime committed against him and against the Jewish People, and we are angry at his murderers. Let not our anger blind us to the majesty of his heroism. Not his heroism in being ready to die for his country. Others have reached that great peak as well, and many others shall heroically do so in the future. The majesty of Ben Yosef lies in his perfect calmness in asking for a comb with which to properly coiffeur himself, that very same morning, as if he were beginning another ordinary day. Martyrdom for *Eretz Yisrael*, he taught us, is not some fantastic, out-of-the-ordinary expression of courage. Sacrifice for our Homeland is as natural as combing one's hair. This is the true meaning of Zionism."

The giant audience sat in spellbound silence.

"It is a fact that Shlomo Ben Yosef and his comrades undertook their action without asking for prior permission of the *Betar* leadership," he admitted, getting straight to the point.

"The three brave souls wanted to put an end to the disgrace whereby Jews are murdered with impunity, while Arabs remain free to commit their bloodthirsty deeds. Such an infamy must not be permitted!"

The crowd roared its approval. Raising his arm and magnifying his voice, he exclaimed, "If necessary, then post factum, I, as head of *Betar*, give you, Ben-Yosef and your two comrades, the order to go out onto the highway and do what you did!"

Once again, everyone in the hall rose to their feet in applause – everyone save the mysterious figure in the balcony, who stood by the railing, like a ship captain staring out at the horizon. What was going through his mind, Eldad wondered before turning his attention back to the stage. *Rosh Betar* motioned for the jubilant crowd to sit.

"There is a platitude that says it is immoral to punish the innocent in times of war," he said. "What superficial and hypocritical nonsense. In war, any war, this theory purports that the general populace is innocent. There are even those who say: the enemy soldier who fights me, who has been recruited against his will, what crime has he committed against me that I should kill him? Or what crime have I committed against him that he should kill me? But when a war breaks out, we unanimously demand that a sea blockade be imposed against the enemy to starve the population, including innocent women and children. And if London and Paris are hit by an air raid, we demand air strikes against Stuttgart and Milan, even though they are filled with innocent victims. There is no war which is not conducted against the innocent. War is accursed, but if you do not wish to harm the innocent, you will die. And if you do not wish to die – then shoot and stop prattling! This lesson was taught to me by my teacher, Ben Yosef!"

Once again, Yisrael Eldad rose to his feet with the cheering audience. If this wasn't a call to war – what was? Jabotinsky, the poet, acclaimed playwright and novelist, was like a skilled magician, revealing the mythic act hidden in the individual, heroic deed. Everyone in the hall knew the details of Ben Yosef's last morning and hanging, but the master orator was to prove that no one recognized its true depth and the soaring heights that his martyrdom had lifted the Jewish People on their path to Redemption.

Up on the dais, Tevye applauded whole-heartedly along with the enthusiastic masses. Mortified to be seated on stage with Jabotinsky and other *Betar* luminaries, his refusals had been overcome by *Rosh Betar's* emphatic insistence that he sit at his side. Caught up in the whirlwind of cheers and emotions accompanying the passionate speech, the milkman forgot about his embarrassment over being on the stage. Beside him, the young Menachem Begin, commander of *Betar's* military youth groups in Poland, clapped half-heartedly, waiting to hear the rest of the speech. Though he revered *Rosh Betar* with all of his being, the "enfant terrible" of the 100,000-strong, Polish *Betar* recruits, had grown impatient sitting in youth groups criticizing the Jewish Agency's submissive policy toward the British. His volcanic soul had grown restless with the Movement's endless military drills, without any clear orders from *Rosh Betar* to retaliate against the continuous slaughter of Jews. Was "Jabo's" de-facto approval of Ben Yosef's deed meant as operative command for the future, or were the stirring phrases merely an ear-pleasing eulogy to hide their leader's unwillingness to summon his troops into action?

"Everyone here is aware of the distressing situation in Palestine," Jabotinsky continued. "Since many of you undoubtedly have reservations about our policies, allow me to present a brief history, without going into detail, as a basis for clearheaded discussion. When the *Irgun Zvai Leumi* broke off from the *Haganah*, I had no official position of authority. Soon afterward, it was decided that my suggestions were to be followed concerning overall policy, and that I would have the authority to appoint the organization's commander in Palestine. However, since the British have barred me from returning to our country, all local decisions concerning activities in *Eretz Yisrael* are decided upon by the commanders on the scene. Meeting with the *Irgun* leadership in Egypt, we discussed what action should be taken in regards to the ongoing policy of *havlaga*. While understanding the desire for reprisal, I questioned the moral justification for such actions, since innocents not connected with the killing of Jews could be harmed in such forays. I questioned what public good would come of shooting an Arab peasant in the back on his way to sell vegetables in the market. After an unauthorized attempt to assassinate a certain Arab leader, now hiding in Lebanon, was attempted without success, the possibility was brought to my attention of eliminating him, for a certain sum of money, in light of the fact that he continues to direct terrorist attacks against the Jews in *Eretz Yisrael*."

Jabotinsky didn't turn toward Tevye when he said it, and Tevye's expression didn't change.

"I vetoed the proposal. 'Would we like to see our enemies assassinating people like Weizmann and Ben Gurion?' I asked. In addition, how could I authorize people to undertake such a dangerous mission when I sit comfortably in London and Paris?"

Yisrael Eldad, and all of the people surrounding him, listened in rapt attention. While everyone read newspaper articles about events in Palestine, the information was reported in a superficial manner, nothing like hearing an insider's in-depth explanation.

"When more and more innocent Jews were butchered in the unabated Arab uprising, and the demand to retaliate increased, I struggled day and night with the need to make a decision, tormented by the dilemma of ordering troops into life-risking actions when I myself couldn't share the dangers. On five different occasions, I wrote the awaited telegram with the code giving my approval, and five times I called the messenger back before he reached the post office. When Jews acted on their own, I was glad, but I still refrained from breaking the standing policy of restraint fostered by the Jewish Agency and the *Haganah*, hoping that if the British didn't crack down on the uprising, I could reach an agreement with the *Haganah* to combine forces and thus make our response much more unified and effective. Badgered by our comrade, Mr. Begin, and by local commanders in Palestine whose soldiers were foaming on the leash of *havlaga*, I told them, '*Men fregt nit dem Taten* - a son shouldn't always ask his father's permission.'"

His remark drew a response of laughter, temporarily breaking the heaviness of his words. Menachem Begin smiled broadly, showing an uneven front row of teeth.

"When bombs were planted in Arab markets and bus stations, the British demanded that all retaliations cease. They displayed their displeasure by rounding up dozens of known Revisionists and *Betar* activists. My son, Eri, one of the randomly arrested, is now being held under military detention in Acco Prison, where I had the dubious honor of living for many months, along with many dear comrades in arms. My son is incarcerated for being a Revisionist, and I am proud of him for that. The Jewish Agency called the reprisal attacks 'acts of terrorist aggression undermining the moral standing of the Jews of Palestine.' Eliahu Golomb, head of the *Haganah*, hurried to meet with me in London. While our politics differ, he is a soldier's soldier, with the interests of the people of Zion at heart. First, I told him, before any agreement can be reached, both in regard to a cease fire, and in regard to a pact between the *Irgun* and the *Haganah*, the Jewish Agency's reprehensible practice of providing the British Police with the names of Revisionists and *Betar* activists must come to an immediate end."

"No deals with informers!" came a loud cry from the balcony. Other *Betar* cadets surrounding the mysterious figure shouted catcalls of their own.

"Jewish traitors!"

"Remember the Stavsky trial!"

"It's time for action, not speeches!"

Uri Zvi Greenberg rose to his feet. "Like the brothers of Yosef, the disciples of Lenin and Marx will throw us into the dungeons of the British!" he declared.

Tevye wanted to add a ripe curse of his own, but who was he to voice an opinion before such a distinguished gathering?

Yisrael Eldad could not remain silent. "Uri Zvi Greenberg is right!" he shouted. "Making an agreement with the Jewish Agency is like throwing *Betar* into a pit with spiders and scorpions!"

Jabotinsky held up a silencing hand. "I told Golomb that I couldn't speak for the tens of thousands of frustrated Jews in Palestine, nor influence the decisions of local *Irgun* leaders who had grown tired of restraint and defense. For good or for bad, I explained that as the head of *Betar*, and the World Revisionist Movement, as well as Director of the New Zionist Organization, which are all legal bodies, in order to protect their official standing, I cannot associate myself with underground movements. Nonetheless, I told him, the urge of Jews to strike back at their murderers will not be crushed by arrests and imprisonment."

The crowd applauded, returning, for the moment, to Jabotinsky's corner. Israel Eldad was not swayed by the emotional appeal. He knew that after the spectacular "Black Friday" reprisals in Jerusalem, of which he had not been consulted, Jabotinsky refused to sanction further underground actions. While Jabotinsky presented a militant image in public, when it came to street bombings, he was inwardly riddled with moral doubts. Eldad sensed that the statesman in Jabotinsky continued to believe that the success of Zionism would come about through international negotiation and endeavor, and that the *Irgun* was to subordinate its local activism to the needs of the overall political scheme.

"Without a doubt, the message of 'Black Friday' brought a temporary end to the Arab terror in Jerusalem," Jabotinsky admitted. "After the fiasco of the Peel Commission, with the renewal of the Arab uprising, and the deed of Shlomo Ben Yosef and his friends, Golomb requested a meeting again in London, fearing that private Jewish militias would distance the British from the Zionist cause. He told me that he didn't want civil war to break out in Palestine, implying that the *Haganah* would be forced to wage war against militant Jewish forces in the *Yishuv* if they didn't agree to come under the *Haganah's* leadership. Golomb is a serious individual, and his threats need to be taken seriously. The Left is accustomed, in the tradition of the Bolsheviks, to deal violently with ideological opponents, as we have learned from the ignominious blood libel they waged surrounding Aronov's murder. Already they have handed over dozens of our followers to the British. But, to Golomb's credit, he is a wise and reasonable man, very aware of our strengths, as well as our joint national weakness. Because of this, we were able to reach an agreement."

The announcement was met with mix boos and cheers. Jabotinsky continued.

"It was decided that a commission composed of four members, with equal representation between the *Haganah* and the *Irgun*, would decide upon all military actions. Each organization would remain autonomous in its ideology, structure, and command. Furthermore, in every case where the *Haganah's* forces were awarded recognition by the Mandate Authorities as legal defense units, the *Irgun* would have a share. Unfortunately, as I expected, the agreement was sabotaged by Ben Gurion, who spends much of his time in London, battling Weizmann for control of the World Zionist Organization. Ben Gurion's correspondence with Golomb was intercepted by *Irgun* Intelligence. In his telegram, he wrote that Golomb's efforts to form a merger were a grave breach of discipline. 'If the agreement is not signed, don't sign it,' Ben Gurion ordered. 'If it is signed, then annul the signature!' In a subsequent wire, he wrote: 'Jabotinsky plans to blackmail the Zionist Organization, which we lead, to accept his breakaway group as an equal partner, by carrying out reprisal attacks in Palestine which we consider to be dangerous to our cause.' Thus, out of his paranoid fear of losing control of the Zionist Executive, Ben Gurion succeeded in preventing a union of forces which surely would have saved Jewish lives and strengthened the *Yishuv.* "

"To hell with Ben Gurion!" someone shouted.

"Life isn't so simple, my friend!" Jabotinsky shouted back. "The Cossacks in charge of *Mapai* are capable of throwing all of us into prison and throwing away the key. Once again their informants are collaborating with the British Police. You can be sure their double-agents are sitting in this auditorium today. Like the Bolsheviks they secretly admire, achieving domination and control justifies all means. To achieve their goals, they are capable of anything, even surrendering vast chunks of our Jewish Homeland to imposters who claim that our eternal inheritance belongs to them!"

"Traitors! Traitors! *Bogdim!*" voices called out.

"If they open fire on us, we will shoot back at them!" one of Eldad's neighbors shouted, waving a *Betar* flag in the air.

Menachem Begun jumped to his feet. "No!" he shouted. "Their way is not the way of *Betar*. There will be no civil war. Let us all march off to prison before we lift a hand against a brother!"

His outburst brought cheers from the audience. Jabotinsky waited until the applause for Begin ended. Nodding toward his young disciple, he turned back to face the energized crowd in the auditorium.

"Jews will no longer act like frightened mice!" he exclaimed, raising a fist with emotion.

"Today, a Jew in *Eretz Yisrael* cannot drive out of his *moshav* in the Galilee without risking his life. Attacks along the Jerusalem-Tel Aviv highway are just as frequent. Jews have to travel in convoys. After being shot at several times, if he hasn't been wounded or killed, a Jew thinks twice about traveling the roads of his country. Outside the confines of his house or community, his life is in danger. Often his wife pleads with him not to travel. 'Why be a hero?' she asks. Thus, in his very own Homeland, the Jew becomes like a trembling mouse in a cage, while the Arabs travels freely in absolute safety, like sultans in their palaces, even in Tel Aviv."

Eldad felt his blood boil. What was the matter with the Jews? Jabotinsky raised his voice.

"Why should the highway robbers refrain from killing when we turn the other cheek? I call them highway robbers, but they call themselves 'freedom fighters.' They are heralded as saviors by their people. Flowers are thrown at them in honor. Songs are written about them. Arab terrorists see themselves as national heroes.

"Two years ago, the Jews were the majority in the Old City of Jerusalem. Now most of them have fled in fear. Arabs have taken over their homes. The British assist the Arab cause by evacuating the Jews who remain. When we complain to the authorities, they answer, 'What do you want from us? The Jews are afraid to live there. We are protecting them by helping them move to another part of the city.'"

"This disgraceful situation must cease. *Havlaga* must be erased!" Jabotinsky finally cried out.

Cheering, aisle by aisle, everyone rose in approval. Jabotinsky paused once again until they were seated.

"The world must not be allowed to believe that Jews will let themselves be murdered without responding measure for measure!"

Eldad, who was standing far back from the stage, could see the fire in Jabotinsky's eyes.

"Today, a Jew who breaks the *havlaga* is considered a criminal in the eyes of the British, and in the eyes of the Jewish sycophants who control the *Yishuv*. Let some Englishman ask me who broke the *havlaga* in the defense and honor of his People – I will answer that I do not know. We are not obligated to supply names and addresses to the British, nor to Jews who incriminate their brothers.

"The *havlaga* in practice today in *Eretz Yisrael* must be broken. If we allow it to continue, the whole world will say that the Arabs are the landlords and that we are the encroachers, when exactly the opposite is true. Where is the morality in the situation where one side can murder and steal, and the other side is forbidden to react? If the British enact laws prohibiting Jews from safeguarding their lives, then these laws are immoral at their very foundation. I declare to you that the Supreme Conscience, the Divine Justice, demands that the *havlaga* be broken, and that anyone who does so is free of guilt. And if, wherever on this planet, there is a Jew who maintains that those who break the *havlaga* are guilty, than he is a cursed criminal, and his lowly betrayal of his People will be a lasting and unpardonable blemish in the history of the Jews."

The *Betarim* rose to their feet in a roar of consent.

"It turns out that we are our own greatest enemy in allowing this situation to persist. The Zionist establishment insists that, in the name of morality, Jews not employ the same violent paths of the Arabs. Where is the morality in this?! By letting ourselves be slaughtered, even the friends we have amongst the nations will say that if we are not willing to fight for our Homeland, it must not be ours.

"The truth is, the Jews in *Eretz Yisrael* are happy when the *havlaga* is broken. Unlike the leaders of the *Yishuv*, they still have common sense. Every day, they gaze at newspaper headlines, hoping to see news that Jews struck back against their oppressors. Believe me, even advocates of the *havlaga* don't believe in its effectiveness and justness, and only expound restraint and concession as a diplomatic means of maintaining their standing with the British. So if someone declares to you that he is a believer in the *havlaga*, tell him to go and tell his fairytales to his grandmother."

The jocular expression brought laughter and cheers from his listeners. Returning to Ben Yosef, he said:

"I have often spoken about '*Hadar*.' All of the distinguishing features of nobility, the nobility of the soul, valor, moral refinement, knightliness, the willingness for self-sacrifice for the Nation, all of these were contained in the heart of a young Jewish man from Rosh Pina who has become a symbol for all of us, a youth whose noblesse of spirit has captured the admiration of the world, and behold, he was a simple *Betar* cadet who God chose to elevate in the ranks. I am not worthy of speaking about him, but I can tell you that the British were stunned by the example he set, and they have begun to understand the meaning of '*Hadar*.' Shlomo Ben Yosef remained true to his oath to *Betar* and to our Nation. He wrote on the wall of his death cell: 'To die or to conquer the hill.'

"A Jewish guard who was on duty that morning in Acco Prison related that Ben Yosef guarded his nobility to the very last moment when the trapped doors opened beneath him and he descended into the abyss below with a smile on his lips. The policeman said that what separated Shlomo Ben Yosef from the doomed men whom he had accompanied to the gallows was the young man's utter peace of mind in the face of his imminent death. Other prisoners facing execution succumbed to despair, not caring how they looked, or about eating breakfast in the morning. But Ben Yosef calmly asked to wash and brush his teeth. Proudly, he dressed in his *Betar* uniform and left his cell singing, filled with one powerful faith in his heart and no other, graced with '*Hadar*,' and an exalted splendor, winning a great victory for all of us from the hands of his executioners."

Utter silence filled the large hall. Yisrael Eldad, who himself had a gift for words, sat in awe of *Rosh Betar* who was clearly infused with Divine Inspiration.

"A short time later, I visited Ben Shlomo's mother in Poland. She sobbed in my arms. I too wanted to weep, but following the example of her son, I did my best to strengthen her spirits, just as he has strengthened ours.

While I harbor a deep aversion in asking favors from the British overseers of Palestine, I wrote to Malcolm MacDonald, Secretary of State for the Colonies, with the request to intercede with the Palestine Authority in granting immigration certificates to Rachel Tabacznik, Shlomo's mother, along with the members of her family. I promised that we would provide her with a small house in Rosh Pina where her son is buried, and that we would provide for her financial well-being if necessary. 'Whatever the attitude of the British Government toward her son's actions,' I wrote, 'I trust that a nation known for its moral refinement will respect the pain of a mourning mother and sympathize with her wish to end her days near the place where he son was laid to rest.' I never received a response from my letter."

"Gentlemen," Jabotinsky concluded. "The goal before us is clear, and we recognize the foes and forces which stand in our way. I wish that God will grant you the power to fulfill your oath – your oath of allegiance to the Redemption of *Am Yisrael*."

A long round of applause met the conclusion of the speech, respectful, even awe-filled, but lacking the crowd's initial enthusiasm over Jabotinsky's opening words. Eldad himself was confused by the ambiguous messages. What was to be the official Revisionist policy – continued restraint, occasional retaliation, or outright revolt?

"Enough speeches!" a young voice called out from the balcony. "*An eye for an eye, a tooth for a tooth*! Enough Jewish blood has been spilled!"

The spontaneous call was followed by shouts of agreement. The main chorus of dissent came from the upper gallery. The mysterious figure had vanished. Later, Eldad discovered that he had organized the outbreaks against *Rosh Betar*.

"Blind revenge is neither practical nor politically expedient at the present time," the embattled leader called back.

"The hell with political expedience!" a voice in the crowd answered. "The blood of our brothers cries out from the earth!"

"It's time for armed resistance against the British!" another young, angry voice shouted. Jabotinsky shouted back at the heckler.

"It is utter nonsense to think that conditions exist in Palestine for a Garibaldi-like Jewish war of liberation against the British. As long as we lack the means to establish and sustain an independent Jewish State, it is incumbent upon Zionism to pursue policies that will enable it to appeal to the world's conscience."

Suddenly, Yisrael Eldad heard himself calling out, "When it comes to the Jews, the world has no conscience!"

The crowd stilled, waiting for "Jabo" to answer. Eldad felt his legs trembling.

"To say that conscience no longer exists – that is despair!" the besieged commander retorted. "Conscience rules the world. I respect it. It is forbidden to mock it."

Uri Zvi Greenberg rose, shook Jabotinsky's hand, and quietly walked off the stage. Could it be that he didn't want to be present to witness more arrows fired at the man who had revived Jewish pride and a rekindled a fighting spirit more than anyone else in the century? Or maybe he didn't want to speak out against Jabotinsky in public. Yisrael Eldad wanted to greet Uri Zvi Greenberg as the poet left the hall, but he remained in his seat, sensing that fireworks were about to explode.

It was Menachem Begin's turn to address the convention. Following Jabotinsky's example, the articulate spokesman for the youth of *Betar* had studied law, fashioning himself in his mentor's image, but because of his more passionate nature, the young *Betar* officer found it hard to adopt his teacher's sublime nobility and grace. Lacking Jabotinsky's political wisdom and experience, and holding no respect for the British Parliament, Begin had a tunnel vision which focused on the Jewish perspective alone, like a racehorse with blinders galloping straight toward the finish. The brazenness of youth rumbled in his veins. He spoke from the outpourings of his heart.

"With all due respect to our revered leader and commander, *Rosh Betar*," he began, "I come in the name of the youth of *Betar*."

A large gathering in the group around Eldad began to chant out, "Begin! Begin! Begin!"

Dressed in his *Betar* military uniform, the studious-looking and bespectacled activist held up a silencing hand.

"This gathering will not be turned into a circus!" he threatened. "And I repeat, with all respect and allegiance to our leader, the eyes of the Nation, I humbly report to this honored convention the feelings of our young people, the core of the *Betar* movement, as my position demands."

The crowd grew silent. Eldad listened in curious attention.

"Fellow Jews," Begin called out in his heavy Polish accent. "Brothers. Brothers in arms. It causes me great pain that at this time when the soil is burning under our feet on this wretched continent, and our blood is being spilled so cheaply in *Eretz Yisrael*, the *Betar* Movement has fallen into inertia and stagnation. There can be no doubt that if the present leadership here in Warsaw does not pull the wagon out of the mud of inaction which has led to its paralysis, the far more flamboyant *Irgun* in the Land of Israel will swallow us up. Our wonderful youth, the hope of our future, is tired of endless meetings and petitions decrying the policies of the Jewish Agency and its leaders, who bow down to the British at every opportunity, and who turn a blind eye as bloodthirsty Arabs slaughter innocent men, women, and children. The blessed Ben Yosef was the first sign of rebellion against the stagnant and rancid policy of the Zionist establishment, including, I am sorry to say, this distinguished body, honored representatives of World *Betar*. Ben Yosef acted on his own, without any orders, following the command of his own brave Jewish heart. In Poland, the bastion of *Betar's* strength, and in the Land of Israel, the number of Ben Yosefs are growing. Soon, hundreds will act on their own, ignoring a Revisionist Movement which fails to revise and lead. We all just heard the permission, defacto, which '*Rosh Betar*' gave to Ben Yosef. Was this inspiring declaration a one-time rejection of the hated *havlaga* and the endless Zionist policy of surrender and appeasement, or was it a clear '*get*' divorcing us from the impotency that has marked our wanderings in exile, an impotence which has now found its way to *Eretz Yisrael*?"

The audience sat in tense silence. Eldad held his breath. This was the first time, to his knowledge, that Jabotinsky had been publically challenged by one of his officers. Everyone knew of Begin's reverence and loyalty to the founder of the Movement. There was no personal motivation in his words, no stain of private ambition. He spoke a truth which everyone felt, and the truth, by itself, had the power to move mountains.

On the dais, Jabotinsky sat quietly, his hands clasped together on the table before him. Begin raised his voice. His hand gestured emphatically in the air. His body moved this way and that as the spirit of truth spoke through his lips, as if he were a *shofar* for every voice in the hall.

"*Betar* chapters are in a state of crisis!" he exclaimed. "Members openly scorn their commanders. Boredom and a lack of respect for their leaders are forcing our young people to look elsewhere for Salvation. The *Irgun*, with its atmosphere of secrecy and activism, is luring away the best of our recruits. If the *Betar* Movement fails to adopt a rejuvenated military posture, in deeds, not only in theory, it will surely fall apart."

Tevye glanced at Jabtotinsky, who betrayed no personal insult to Begin's critical remarks, nor any feeling of threat to his command of the organization. Indeed, he felt none. His attachment to *Am Yisrael*, and his dedication to the Jewish People, were so exalted, he had long ago transcended all thoughts of himself and considerations of ego. If he disagreed with his young disciple, it was on practical and political grounds alone, based on his knowledge of all of the complicated factors involved in the life-and-death puzzle surrounding the embattled Jewish Nation. Personally, he understood the frustration and anger throughout the ranks. He himself felt the terrible pent-up rage that was building into a conflagration that couldn't be contained. Hadn't his soul, the soul of a poet-warrior, expressed a dozen times over, his unrest with the status-quo and his glorification of rebellion and might? After all, it was his poems, his songs, his plays, his novel, *Samson*, his translations of *Spartacus* and *Faust* which had sparked the spirit of Hebrew rebellion at a time when Menachem Begin was still a child in britches.

Had he been a younger, less experience statesmen, he would have uttered the very same speech that his student was delivering now. So how could he feel anger or resentment toward Begin? Can a man resent his own son?

"We are poised on the threshold of a new stage of Zionism," Begin continued. "After the 'Practical Zionism' of Herzl which sought a practical solution to the 'Jewish Problem,' and the subsequent phase of 'Political Zionism,' when we endeavored to win political concessions from the nations of the world, we must now embark on the bold stage of 'Military Zionism.' In time, military and political policies will merge, but our Nation's salvation will only come through armed struggle. Incessantly appealing to the Gentiles for salvation won't help us. The world is indifferent to the fate of the Jews. Balfour no longer wields influence. The true anti-Semitic face of the Englishman has removed its mask. Gentiles sleep soundly at night, apathetic to our plight. The League of Nations is impotent. We cannot continue on this road to nowhere. The delegates in this hall want to fight! To win or to die!"

The roar was deafening now that someone had finally pulled the cork out from the neck of the bottle. The crowd, like a single organism, rose in unison. Yisrael Eldad rose with them and applauded with all of his might. Jabotinsky himself rose to his feet. Following his example, the notables on the stage stood up and applauded. Tevye felt overwhelmed by the power surging through the auditorium. The young faces in the crowd gleamed like small suns. Gradually, the cheering subsided.

"It is written in the *Betar* oath," the fearless spokesmen for Jewish youth declared to the charged gathering, "'I will raise my arm only in defense.' This restraint is destroying our Movement. The failure of this convention is certain if this oath remains. The time has come for a new oath, and we demand this change. The new oath shall be, **'I will raise my arm to defend my people and to conquer my Homeland!'**"

Another roar of approval shook the convention hall. Once again, everyone rose to their feet and applauded. This time, *Rosh Betar* and the others seated on the stage remained in their chairs. Tevye glanced at Jabotinsky whose expression was as stoic as a stone. Though the Revisionist leader agreed in his heart, his head, and his faith in the ultimate goodness of man, and in the noble traditions of British culture and civilization, told Jabotinsky that the time was not ripe for a Jewish revolution, especially when the weapons, the funding, and a fully-trained Jewish army were not yet available for a war against the armies of Edom and Yishmael. Passionate speeches had their place in keeping spirits strong, but the moment had not yet arrived for decisive action.

"We, the youth of *Betar*, demand a vote to change the wording!" Begin shouted, empowered by the backing of the crowd. "I will raise my arm to defend my people and to conquer my Homeland! I will raise my arm to defend my people and to conquer my Homeland!"

Eldad echoed the chant. The young uniformed *Betarim* around him stood up and joined in as well. Up on the stage, Begin kept shouting out the words until the whole audience was with him. **"I will raise my arm to defend my people and to conquer my Homeland! I will raise my arm to defend my people and to conquer my Homeland!"**

The chant became a deafening roar.

All the while, Begin dared not look at Jabotinsky, who had been much more than a mentor and role model for him. During his youth and his rise up the *Betar* ranks, Begin had deified the founder of the Movement. Each speech that Begin heard from the lips of Jabotinsky left him in awe. No other Jew spoke like he did, with such worldly erudition and passionate Jewish pride. And here Begin stood, the center of attention at the World *Betar* Convention in Warsaw, in the presence of *Rosh Betar*, criticizing his leadership. Begin himself was startled. He observed the scene, as if it were happening to someone else, as if he were seated in the audience and someone else was speaking on stage. Everyone present was as stunned as he was. This had never happened. No one in the Movement had ever publically challenged Jabotinsky before. Who was this young little upstart, Tevye wondered?

"Yes," Begin continued, unable to stop, as if driven on by a *dybbuk* inside him. He raised a hand to silence the huge crowd. "The time has come to command and to conquer. We can no longer look to the world to help us. Make no mistake, my friends, it is a world filled with wolves. And for too long the Jewish People have been sheep in their jaws."

Another ovation resounded throughout the hall. Begin had won the day. But he wasn't finished. Now, with a lower, calmer voice, he presented his *coup de grace*.

"Just a few months ago, Britain and France signed the Munich Agreement, conceding Czechoslovakia to Germany, on the stipulation that the Nazis agreed to cease further aggression. Conquered by Hitler's army, the people of Czechoslovakia appealed to the free nations of the West to come to their aid, but the champions of democracy turned a deaf ear and sacrificed Czechoslovakia to *Molech*. Yes, my friends. Let this be a lesson for us. The world is cruel arena, understanding sheer force alone. Britain won't save us. Not from the Arabs, and not from the Nazis! In the name of all the Jewish People, let the call go forth from this convention – the time has come for rebellion in *Eretz Yisrael*!"

The hall itself seemed to cheer, as if it had a voice of its own. Everyone in the audience rose to their feet in wild applause. Finally, someone had said what needed to be said. Flushed, and trembling inside, Begin resumed his seat. With his keen mind and scalpel-like insight, Yisrael Eldad tried to understand what had happened. Could it be that Begin had spoken for *Rosh Betar*, speaking words that Jabotinsky couldn't say because of his paralyzing respect for British culture and tradition, and because of the years he had served as a loyal British soldier in the Hebrew Brigade? Menachem Begin, in contrast, had never left Poland. The British Empire meant nothing to him. Raised in a sea of Polish anti-Semitism, and knowing nothing else, he harbored no endearment at all for the *goyim*. His thoughts and speech were free of the psychological shackles that constrained *Rosh Betar*, for all of his towering Jewish pride. And, to be fair, one also had to consider a factor that Jabotinsky himself had cited. As the head of official Zionist organizations, he couldn't make a public call for rebellion without setting those organizations in conflict with the law.

Perhaps Eldad's perception was correct. Perhaps

Jabotinsky was using Begin to voice his real feelings. The aging warrior asked to respond. Slowly, he walked to the podium, knowing that no ordinary speech or fancy rhetoric would win back the crowd. Once again, the dapper figure appeared in the balcony by the railing. When the noise and cheers subsided, Jabotinsky began.

"I hate three types of squeaks," he said, in a calm and almost jocular voice, capturing the crowd's attention immediately. "First, I dislike young calves that squeak and moo before dawn when a person is still asleep; but we must pardon them for the milk they provide. Also, I find the squeaking of factory machines and train wheels on their tracks most bothersome, but they too benefit man. One squeak, however, I loathe with all of my being, and for this, there is no forgiveness, for it serves no benefit or purpose – the squeaking of a door on its hinges. And your speech, Mr. Begin, is precisely such a squeaking door."

The anecdote drew some laughter, and some applause. Begin himself smiled. The tension in the hall seemed to ease.

"Gentlemen," Jabotinsky called out in a more serious tone. "I call upon you to consider the mathematics and the relative strengths of each side of the equation. To successfully engage our enemies in battle, we lack the numbers, the army, the weapons, and the accompanying means. Therefore, there is no justification in babbling about a revolt. Such prattle is merely a squeaky door."

When Jabotinsky glanced at Tevye, the clean-shaven milkman nodded. The expressions of the other dignitaries on the dais also revealed their assent.

A young *Betar* cadet in the audience jumped to his feet and yelled out in a cacophonous voice. "The Maccabees also lacked the numbers and the means. Numbers are important but they needn't be decisive. Mattityahu didn't delay the rebellion until he had a stockpile of weapons and more favorable odds. You have warned us again and again that the Jews have no future here on foreign soil. Will Hitler wait patiently for us while *Betar* trains and trains and trains us into a professional army?"

The young people sitting around him applauded his outburst. Jabotinsky stood calmly on the stage, ignoring the comment, as if it hadn't been spoken. The sheer force of his presence prevented pandemonium from breaking out in the hall.

"Allow me another parable," Jabotinsky said, continuing to administer emergency first-aid to his wounded authority. "Suppose tragedy strikes an area, a devastating fire with many victims, leaving children orphaned. Help is extended. Initially, the children are sent to different homes. As time passes, their charitable hosts grow weary of the burden. Bad feelings pollute the air. A wise person realizes that even a noble person doesn't want a stranger in his home forever. This is not a sign that the man is cruel. Rather his hospitality must be balanced with natural self-interest. A solution is found when everyone contributes to opening an orphanage. The children depart from the private homes, to the satisfaction of the owners, but they are not thrown into the street. The orphanage is waiting to take them in."

The crowd sat in silence, waiting for "Jabo" to explain.

"We can draw inference from this that the world is not as charitable as it maintains. No country, not even the most democratic, will allow all of the Jewish refugees to enter their borders. Yet mankind is not so cruel that it will refuse to help. The most noble amongst the nations will staunchly support the establishment of a Hebrew State, represented by the orphanage in our story. We must be patient until the orphanage is ready."

A voice rang out from the balcony. "*Eretz Yisrael* is not an orphanage! And we are not orphans in need of compassion! That is exile mentality!"

All heads rose toward the mysterious, dapper figure poised above the rotunda by the balcony railing.

"It's Yair," someone said.

"The name of our newspaper is *The Deed*," someone else called out in the main auditorium. "Not *The Voice*."

The remark drew a spattering of laughter.

"That is irrelevant!" Jabotinsky yelled back. "Without the voice, the deed has no meaning or value!"

His intensity silenced the crowd. Though Eldad sat a distance from the stage, he could feel the burning intensity of the speaker's eyes. *Rosh Betar* continued.

"The distinguished young gentleman in the audience maintains, 'We have no need for words, give us actions.' One thing he forgets is that speech is also an action - perhaps the most authentic and lasting of all other actions. Cities have been destroyed, and more will fall, but what was shouted in the wilderness thousands of years ago is alive and still relevant. The world was created by the Word. And it is the Word which will make the world a better place."

Rosh Betar held up his hand before the meeting erupted out of control.

"In conclusion, Mr. Begin," he said. "Not all Gentiles are wolves. If you, and your supporters in this assembly, do not believe that the world still has a moral conscience, then you have no choice but to step outside this auditorium and drown yourself in the Vistula River."

Eldad interpreted Jabotinsky's concluding remark as a call for restraint and submission to the *goyim*. Though Jabotinsky had brought a great burst of light into his personal life, illuminating the darkness of his personal exile, he rose to his feet, not intending to hurt him, Heaven forbid, but the greatness of the hour put the words in his mouth.

"With upmost respect for our cherished leader, I too probably sound like a squeaky door," he loudly exclaimed. "But an event in my life showed me that even a squeaky door can be useful. Once, a squeaky door awakened me from a deep slumber, saving me from the robbers who had opened it. When thieves threaten us in our home, and one's life is in danger, a squeaky door is welcome indeed!"

Just as a sprinkling of kerosene causes glimmering coals to burst into flame, Eldad's response ignited the fire in the hearts of the crowd. Understanding that he had substantiated Begin's call for action by refuting Jabotinsky's rebuttal, the youth of *Betar* reacted with thunderous applause.

Eldad felt astounded that the words had emerged from his mouth. Not because of the cleverness of his wit – he knew he was a witty fellow – but in uttering them in the presence of *Rosh Betar*. He was even more astounded by his mentor's reaction. Like Daniel in the lion's den, the noble figure on the podium seized victory from the jaws of defeat, teaching everyone present that the ideal of "*Hadar*" was not only an exalted credo, but an attainable reality.

Rather than sit down in anger, or stride off the stage in a rage, *Rosh Betar* smiled at Eldad's rebuttal, like a literature professor pleased with a student's playful juxtaposition of words. The elder statesman accepted his defeat good-naturedly, with the dignity and splendor that he preached. Like the picture of an English gentleman, dry and unruffled in a rainstorm, he applauded along with his cheering disciples, salvaging unity out of division. Even after the roar subsided, and the audience sat down in their seats, *Rosh Betar* remained clapping his hands longer than everyone. While Menachem Begin had commandeered the wheel of the ship, and Yisrael Eldad had swayed the direction of the rudder, Jabotinsky, the personification of "*Hadar*," remained upright and firm at the helm.

2.

Eldad hurried into the convention hall lobby, hoping to meet Uri Zvi Greenberg, but the poet had vanished. A half-hour recess had been announced before the convention would reconvene to vote on key issues. The lobby quickly filled up with animated, young *Betarim* who sensed that something unusual had transpired in the hall. A stranger approached Eldad with a serious expression.

"Mr. Scheib?"

"That's correct."

"Someone would like to speak with you upstairs on the fourth floor," he said.

"Who?" Eldad asked.

"I don't know," the messenger replied. "I was only given a room number."

Much later in his life, Eldad would write a book called, *First Tithe*, an autobiography written with the picturesque clarity of an Impressionist's canvas. This is how he described the encounter with the mysterious man who had stood on the balcony.

"I went upstairs and entered the long, narrow, calm room – strikingly calm in contrast to the noisy auditorium. Seated at a small table was a man, also calm, dressed unlike most everyone else at the conference, in a dark, civilian suit. His face was thin and calm. His fingers long, thin, calm. Even the calm was long and thin, like the room. Calmest of all was his dark, gray voice – like his eyes. He told me he had heard my words from the balcony. The words were well-spoken, words filled with obligation. What did I think should be done? Should *Betar* continue following along with the Jewish Agency's policy of restraint? Should we remain loyal to *Betar* come what may?"

Eldad realized that the strikingly calm man was Avraham Stern, an *Irgun* leader from *Eretz Yisrael* who was trying to raise a Jewish army in Poland, in order to wage war on the British usurpers of Zion. In Hebrew, his code name, "Yair," meant, "He will illumine." In Yiddish, the name Stern meant "star." Yair was also the name of the fearless Jewish commander who led the rebellion against the legions of Rome on the heights of Masada.

Eldad replied that, in his humble opinion, the organization deserved one more chance. If its leadership could be swayed toward genuine activism, why splinter it into factions?

"I will tell you why," Stern answered. "Your leader, the 'old man,' is tired. For years, he has battled all alone against windmills, and the great wind machines have exhausted his strength. Unable to topple them, he has been swayed by their illusions. Speeches and politics won't save us. The instruments of war are not newspaper articles and hollow declarations. What ultimately convinces are bayonets and bombs."

Eldad stood captivated by what he was hearing. There was no uncertainty in Stern's words. No doubts, nor fears.

"Last year, I met with Jabotinsky in Alexandria. When I demanded that we end the spineless *havlaga* policy of restraint, and commence a new policy of *hagava* – 'response' in *Eretz Yisrael* – your leader balked, tormented by twisted moral arguments and convoluted considerations, saying he would have to contemplate further on the matter, and that no acts of revenge were to be taken unless we received a telegram signed 'Mendelson.'"

Stern stared at Eldad with blue-grey eyes as deep and cold as the Black Sea in the heart of winter.

"Your leader stirs hearts when he speaks, but there is no clear direction in what he says. One moment he praises reprisal, then he condemns the killing of innocents. Perhaps, as Raziel has joked, we should notify the Arabs in advance regarding the exact time and location of our attacks. That way we will only blow up tables and chairs."

Eldad sensed that Stern was spreading his cards on the table, eager to hear his opinions before inviting him to be a comrade in arms. Probing eyes stared at him, waiting for a response.

"May I sit," Eldad asked.

"Of course. Please, have some biscuits. You must be hungry."

He pushed a plate of biscuits toward Eldad. "I was told that they are *kosher*. I myself try to keep *kosher* and observe *Shabbat*, and I join a prayer *minyan* when I can, though in our line of work, it is not always possible."

Eldad noted the words, "our line of work," as if he had already accepted him as part of the team.

"Do you speak Hebrew?" Yair asked.

"Yes."

"Yiddish?"

"Of course."

"Make a blessing if you like," Stern said in Yiddish with a smile. "I myself am lax in the matter, believing that the essence of belief itself is the main thing and not the ritual, but I respect those who have the strength to fulfill the letter of the Law, and I understand how doing so can be a fence against transgression."

"I tend to agree," the former Rabbinic student replied.

Once again, Stern referred to *Rosh Betar* as "your leader," implying that he himself did not place Jabotinsky on an exalted pedestal like his ordinary disciples.

"Your leader is still entrenched in the mud of politics. His love of literature and world philosophy has blurred his thinking. He mistakes British culture and civility for truth. Is he a genius? Yes. A righteous man? Indeed. His personal traits are impeccable, and his dedication to the Nation is unsurpassed. A lover of art and music as well. The true Renaissance man. But, like the Samson he wrote about so heroically, painting his noble character with such drama and pathos, Jabo's enamor for the seductive beauty of foreign cultures has blinded him to a higher ideal of, '*It is a Nation that shall dwell alone, and not be reckoned amongst the peoples.*'"

Eldad felt like a mountain climber, who, after reaching the summit, discovered there was still a higher peak ahead. Inspired in the past by Jabotinsky and Uri Zvi Greenberg, he felt his soul stirred anew by the warrior poet before him. But he wasn't sure he could scale the towering mountain before him.

"In Alexandria, I pressed upon the 'old man' the need to abandon his love affair with restraint. As you know, he has made the concept of '*Hadar*' into the *Betar* banner. In my opinion, he exaggerates the meaning of the term, turning it into a distorted, watered-down version of chivalry from the days of King Arthur and The Knights of the Round Table. I reminded him that David is our role model of a king, and not the mythological figure from Camelot. Regarding *Hadar*, King David says in his Psalms: '*Let the faithful exult in glory; let them sing upon their beds. Let the praises of God be in their mouth, and a double-edged sword in their hand to execute vengeance upon the nations, punishment upon peoples; to bind their kings with chains, and their nobles with fetters of iron; to execute upon them the written judgment. This is the **hadar** – the splendor – of all His faithful. Halleluya.*' Executing judgment on the enemies of Israel, this is the true splendor of a Jew!"

Suddenly, Stern banged his fist on the table and turned into an actor on stage, delivering an oration in Greek. When he finished, he looked at Eldad with a grin.

"As they say, 'It's Greek to me,'" Eldad remarked.

Yair translated the passage into Polish. "Fool, prate not to me about covenants. There can be no covenants between men and lions, wolves and lambs can never be of one mind, but they must surely hate each other through and through."

"Homer?" Eldad guessed, no stranger himself to Classic Literature.

"Excellent!" Stern exclaimed, as if pleased with the response of a student. "As he writes in the *Iliad* – with words that illuminate our war with the Arabs and British, 'There can be no understanding between you and me, nor may there be any covenants between us, till one or the other shall fall.'"

"Surely Jabotinsky will come to realize this himself."

This time, Yair spoke in English. "Love is blind, and lovers cannot see the petty follies that they themselves commit."

"That has to be Shakespeare."

Stern nodded. "You pass the test. A Renaissance man after the role model of your leader."

"Who, if I may ask, is your leader?"

"I am waiting for King David to return and lead the way. In the meantime, during my time in Poland, I have established a good many *Irgun* cells, who take their commands from us, not from *Rosh Betar*. In addition, we are publishing two newspapers in which Hindenberg has no share. "

Paul von Hindenberg was President of the German Reich before Adolf Hitler rose to power. As the Nazi Party grew increasingly influential, the former military hero became senile and obsolete. Stern's comparing him to Jabotinsky was shocking.

"Does David Raziel in Jerusalem feel the same as you?" Eldad asked regarding the militant *Irgun* commander in Jerusalem who Jabotinsky would soon appoint to head the organization throughout *Eretz Yisrael*.

"While David is a dear friend, and a military genius, he is still, unfortunately, under Jabo's spell. Together, we wrote a handbook about weaponry which is used in our training courses. He consults me on all decisions, and we compose the Organization's declarations together. I have learned a great deal from him during the course of our friendship, and I am indebted to him for persuading me to marry my wife. But I can foresee the day when our ways will part."

Once again, the probing gray eyes peered into Eldad's soul.

"Thank you for coming," Yair said, standing up, thin and tall. He held out a calm hand and a smile. "I am sure we will meet in the future," he said confidently.

Eldad returned to the auditorium, sensing that he had

come to a fork in the road. Two paths diverged before him. He remembered the Robert Frost poem: "Two roads diverged in a forest, and I – I took the one less traveled by, and that has made all the difference."

Despite Jabotinsky's objections, the convention voted with a resounding majority to approve Menachem Begin's proposal that the *Betar* oath be amended, not only to defend, but to conquer. Jabotinsky was unanimously re-elected to continue as the Movement's Supreme Commander. In appreciation, he sang a song he had written, what Yisrael Eldad felt was his Song of Ascent to the *Beit HaMikdash* in Jerusalem, a song glorifying the rebellion to free Zion, even in opposition to brothers who were willing to betray fellow Jews.

Not a single door squeaked in the hall.

Chapter Fourteen
HOMEWARD BOUND

On the fourth floor, in the long and narrow room above the convention hall, Yair stood up in respect when his wife's grandfather entered the room. Seeing the once-upon-a-time milkman clean-shaven and impeccably attired in a double-breasted suit and a stylish Fedora hat, Yair grinned. He couldn't get used to the new image.

Tevye knew what Hannie's husband was thinking. "I know," he said with a frown. "I can't get used to how I look myself."

"You look superb," the dapper Yair replied, unable to erase the smile on his face.

"Believe me, I'd rather go back to milking cows."

"Those days are over. I have a more important task for you."

Concluding his visit to America, Tevye had deposited the money he had raised in a special *Betar* bank account in New York, where it was transferred to Warsaw to pay for the weapons that Stern had purchased from the Polish Government.

"I want to go back home," Tevye said.

"You will," Yair answered. "By taking a group of four-hundred immigrants to Palestine with you."

"In my old wagon?" Tevye quipped.

"On a ship that we've hired – if we can get its engine to work."

"I get seasick," Tevye confided. "And I never learned how to swim." It was true. Although lakes and rivers abounded in Russia, Tevye had never learned to feel secure in water over his head. He remembered how Hevedke had saved him from downing when their ship had reached the Holy Land after they had to jump overboard into a turbulent sea. When Tevye lost hold of the rope leading to the shore, his future son-in-law came to his rescue. And a day didn't pass without his recalling sweet Shpritzer, his daughter, who had

drown in a pond near Anatevka after being jilted by a
callous suitor.

"Keep out of the water and you'll reach Jerusalem safe and
sound," Stern told him.

"Why me?" Tevye asked.

"You want to go home don't you? This way you won't
have problems with passport clearance. I doubt that anyone
is still looking for you, but some British Bobby might
recognize your nose. Plus you speak Russian, Polish,
Hebrew, Yiddish, *abisele* German, and English, and as head
of the group, you'll need them all. I want you to go to
Vienna where the *'ma'apilim'* immigrants will be waiting.
Yitzhaq Ben-Ami will meet you there to give you
instructions. For the last half year, he's been Tzvi's
commander with the *Betar plugot* in the *Galil*. We've
transferred him to oversee illegal immigration from Austria.
Raziel feels he is the right man for the job. Plus, he's been
arrested twice in Palestine for his *Betar* activity, and it has
become harder for him to work now that the British
Criminal Investigations Department is on his trail all the
time. The hiatus will do him good. He will introduce you to
the people you need to know, and while you're in Vienna,
you'll keep in contact with a representative of the Nazis to
arrange for further voyages."

"A representative of the Nazis?"

"They want to get rid of Germany's Jews, and we can be
of service by bringing them to Palestine."

"What's his name?" Tevye asked.

"Adolf Eichmann."

Tevye never heard of him. He sighed, unenthused about
the mission. "Another *mishegas*," he said.

"What can we do?" Stern responded. "Our lives are one
big, upside-down *mishegas*. The *mishegas* of saving the Jewish
People."

Tevye could offer no argument. He was a soldier now, not
a milkman. Once upon a time, his family had been his wife
and his daughters. Now he was married to all the Jews in
the world. "*Azoy gaytis*," he thought. What good would it do
to complain? The Almighty made the decisions, not him.

2.

Nearly 200,000 Jews lived in Vienna when Germany's 8th Army marched into Austria and annexed the country in what became known as the *Anschluss*. Almost immediately, violence against the well-to-do Jewish community became a daily occurrence. Jewish property was confiscated and Jews were denied all civil liberties. Jewish stores were looted and closed. Jewish organizations and institutions were outlawed. Jews were forced to wear yellow badges. On *Kristallnacht*, Vienna's 22 synagogues were torched, and Jewish factories were destroyed. That night 6,000 Jews were rounded up and sent to Dachau. The rhythmic clapping of Nazi boots marching through the streets rumbled throughout the city, with the guttural sound of soldiers singing the *Sturmabteilung* SA marching song, "*Dei Strassen Frei* – Make Way for Us!" Jews feared to venture outside lest they be beaten or arrested, never to be seen again. One day, seeing Nazi soldiers beat a young Jew unconscious with their clubs, Tevye instinctively ran over to help lift the bleeding victim from the road, only to be beaten himself. On another occasion, Tevye saw a group of Nazis drag an elderly Rabbi from a building and force him to polish their boots with his prayer shawl, spitting upon him with guffaws of laughter. When Tevye started to rush forward to help, Yitzhaq Ben-Ami grabbed his arm, stopping him.

"You'll only get beaten yourself," he said.

"*Rabono Shel Olam*," Tevye moaned. "Master of the World, have mercy."

The degradation of Jews was like a sport for the Germans. Often, they stopped young girls on the street and ordered them take to off their skirts and scrub the sidewalks while they looked on with glee. Jewish men were marched half-naked in the streets with top hats on their heads, with signs saying, "I'm a Jewish pig – hit me!"

When Tevye arrived in Vienna, Yitzhaq Ben-Ami had briefed him on the precarious situation, and on the background of the "illegal immigration" to Palestine. Ben-Ami, and Jabotinsky's son, Eri, the head of *Betar* in *Eretz Yisrael*, had spent months establishing the framework to receive the boats of Jewish immigrants they hoped would soon be coming. For the past four years, the Jewish Agency hadn't made any clandestine effort to bring more Jews into the country beyond the official British quota of sixteen-thousand immigrants per year. The number, the Mandate Government maintained, was the "absorptive capacity" of the *Yishuv*. In reality, the limit was enforced to placate the Arabs who threatened to revolt if the Jews were allowed to immigrate freely and take over the country. Both Chaim Weizmann and David Ben Gurion, leader of the dominant Labor Movement in the Zionist Congress, agreed to this policy, turning a blind eye to the growing Nazi threat, and turning a deaf ear to Jabotinsky's persistent cry that if the Jews didn't do away with the Diaspora, the Diaspora would do away with them.

As far back as 1932, Ben-Ami explained, Jabotinsky encouraged "illegal" immigration. In those days, before ships were hired to transport Jews lacking official immigration certificates to Palestine, Jews arriving in the country as tourists simply remained there after their visas had expired. But Jabotinsky went further, calling on young Jews to embrace a spirit of adventurism and dare to evade frontier patrols and cross borders without visas in order to reach Zion. He wrote:

"This adventure is no different from many other adventures. It has chances both of failure and of success. However, a nation, particularly its youth, should not bow its head and say with a sigh, 'In view of the fact that police have forbidden our salvation, we should resign ourselves and remain sitting at home obediently.' Rather, we must continue to fight for our freedom."

"If I were young," he wrote, "I would laugh at their visas and their restrictions. It is difficult, very difficult, but it is precisely this which constitutes that spirit of adventure which propels adventurers to climb mountains and not merely small hills. If I were young, I would buy myself a whistle, and buy whistles for all of my friends, so that we could whistle at the laws and restrictions of countries which try to prevent our reaching the shores of Zion!"

Ben Gurion and the Zionist establishment opposed the initial sea voyages, not wanting to irritate the British, but

Jabotinsky insisted that unauthorized *Aliyah* was the Nation's most urgent imperative. Thus the Revisionist Movement spearheaded large-scale illegal immigration called "*Aliyah Bet*" or "*Af-Al-Pe*," meaning, "In spite of everything." Now, since the *Betar* Youth Movement and the *Irgun* had grown in size and capability, secret night landings along the coast were possible every week. To encourage the effort, Jabotinsky wrote:

"The time has come to make 'illegal' immigration the national Jewish sport. Indeed, this sport has the noblest aim in the world. The national Jewish sport is intended to break through a barrier standing in the way of millions of destitute souls. It is helping to turn a homeless rabble into a Nation and to win them a country. While other sports are merely a game, our sport is sacredly serious."

Ben-Ami summarized the situation in his scholarly fashion. "Because of Ben Gurion's paranoia that the Revisionists will wrestle control of the Zionist Executive and the *Yishuv* away from him, the Jewish Agency refuses to grant *Betar* members immigration certificates, turning away all applicants who don't sign an oath of allegiance to the Labor Movement. The Jewish Agency sent sixty immigrations certificates to Vienna when a hundred-thousand Jews are clamoring to leave. Their representative threatened to report our names and aliases to the British if we don't stop our 'illegal' operations immediately. Before it is too late, we have to open the gates."

Tevye was no stranger to the "Jewish Wars." The fraternal strife surrounding the Aronov murder trial had badly weakened the entire settlement enterprise. Each time the fires of division and *machloket* appeared, his heart filled with chagrin. Just as the *Hashem* was one, the Jewish People were called upon to be one. Unity was the source of their strength.

"Now that the *Irgun* is more certain of its path as a movement of national liberation, we are free to ignore all quotas and restraints, and to determine policy on our own," Ben-Ami explained. "The fate of the Nation will be decided by the number of weapons we can bring to the Homeland, and by the number of Jews."

"How do you go about your work here without getting arrested?" Tevye wanted to know.

"First, my passport says that I am a university student from Palestine. Secondly, I am trying to evacuate the Jews from Austria, and that's exactly what the Germans want."

Tevye listened carefully.

"Your name here will be Zalman, a journalist from Jerusalem. We have set up a transport camp in a forest outside of the city. The first *ma'apilim* immigrants are from Poland and the Baltic states. A good number of young people from Vienna want to sail out on our first ship, but their parents refuse to give their consent to the voyage. No matter how bad things have become here, the Jews still don't want to believe the inevitable. Perhaps I can understand the wealthy, assimilated Jews here who think they are Austrians, but the religious are equally as blind. I can't explain it."

Neither could Tevye. Until he discovered the reason that evening.

Since Ben-Ami was taking the first group of *ma'apalim* to Israel in a matter of days, a young law student named Yonaton was to be Tevye's contact in Vienna, arranging for his living quarters, scheduling his meetings, and accompanying him on his visits to the transport camp, where Tevye had the task of preparing the immigrants for the clandestine and dangerous voyage. Ben-Ami said that young *Betar* cadet had the time to help since Jews were now barred from universities. Because the *Irgun* lacked the funds to pay the young man for his work, they agreed he could make the journey to the Holy Land for a third of the price. Though the rock-bottom fare of 400 *zloty* was certainly not a lot of money in regular times, a great many out-of-work, wishful emigrants couldn't afford the sum. Without telling his father, Yonaton was planning to travel on the "illegal immigration" freighter which Tevye would be accompanying to the Promised Land in another two weeks.

After their initial meeting, Yonaton invited Tevye for a *Shabbos Eve* dinner at his parents' apartment, in the *Haredi* neighborhood of the city. Tevye's young host explained that his uncle's family was now living with them in the cellar.

His uncle, a wealthy businessman, had watched helplessly as the Nazis burnt down his largest factory. Then the country's new rulers threw him and his family out of their spacious mansion, in order to house German troops.

They greeted the Sabbath in a basement since all but one *shul* in Vienna had been destroyed during *Kristallnacht*. It turned out that Yonaton's father was the Rabbi of the secret congregation. The *Litvak* liturgy differed somewhat from the *Galitzianer* style to which Tevye was accustomed, but a Jew was a Jew. The Nazis didn't differentiate between *Litvaks* and *Galitzianers*, so why should Tevye? Though the Jews prayed with fervor, Tevye felt the same emptiness he had experienced since leaving *Eretz Yisrael*. Nothing in the exile could compare with the sanctity of the Promised Land. In Jerusalem, the holy *kedusha* of *Shabbat* was so tangible, it literally saturated the air. That's why when Avraham first began to seek God in Ur Kasdin, where he was born, God told him, "*Lech lecha – get thee forth to the Land that I will show you.*" To become the father of a holy Nation, Avraham had to be in a unique holy place – the Holy Land. Tevye was no *Avraham Avinu*, but even to a simple Jew like him, the difference between the Diaspora and the Land of Israel was as clear as night and day. Whether it was the Lower East Side of New York, or the most Orthodox ghetto in Warsaw or Vienna, the familiar scent of chicken soup wafted through the neighborhood, but there was no holiness in the air.

When the evening prayer concluded, instead of chatting leisurely outside on the sidewalk, to *schmooze* and discuss the events of the week, the dark-coated Jews hurried away, afraid that a gang of goose-stepping Nazis might march out of some alley and beat them over the head with their clubs.

The Sabbath candles flickered in the large, cozy room which served as a kitchen, dining room, and salon. Everything was neatly arranged in honor of the *Shabbat*. Yonaton's mother and sisters, and his homeless aunt and female cousins, kept to the kitchen area. With the traditional authority of the master of the house, Yonatan's father led the singing of "*Shalom Aleichem*," and "*Eshet Chayil*," and blessed his children, holding his hands on their heads. Yonaton's mother remained in the background, hardly saying a word.

At first, Tevye felt that the tension in the room was a family matter, stemming from the father's strict and taciturn demeanor, characteristic of certain Ultra-Orthodox Rabbis from *Litvak* yeshivas, but after the *Kiddush* and *HaMotzei*, he realized that the presence of a guest from the Holy Land, on a mission to bring Jews on *Aliyah*, was the reason, exacerbating the conflict between the *Haredi* father and his Zionist son.

"I understand that you are from *Eretz Yisroel*," Yonaton's uncle said in *Litvak* Yiddish, pronouncing the "a" sound like and "o."

"*Baruch Hashem*," Tevye replied. "Thank the good Lord."

Tevye noticed Yonaton's father glance at him as he sipped at his soup. Tevye imagined that the Rabbi was trying to figure out where his clean-shaven and flashy-attired guest stood in the spectrum of Jewish observance, whether a despised free-thinker, or a practicing member of the club who shaved his beard to appear less Jewish. Outside of Tevye's black *yarmulke* and the fact that he spoke a fluent *Galitzianer* Yiddish, he bore no outward signs of *yirat Shamayim*, the fear of Heaven. True to his new image, he wore his *tzitzit* under his shirt. The fact that he spoke Yiddish was no sign either – many of the biggest heretics knew Yiddish from their youths.

"The minute I can arrange for the necessary papers, I'm on my way to America," the uncle said.

"*Am-a-reka*," Tevye said, changing the pronunciation and uttering the syllables slowly so that it meant, "the empty nation."

"Say what you will," the businessman said. "That fact is that a Jew can live in America like a human being and not a frightened dog."

"A person with faith is never afraid," the grey-bearded Rabbi answered. "*Though I walk through the valley of the shadow of death, I fear no evil.*"

"Lacking my brother's great faith, I became a businessman," the uncle explained to Tevye. "Today, I can't walk on the streets for fear that the Nazis will haul me away to some work camp. I can't stay downstairs in the cellar for fear of going insane. I am afraid to use the phone, speak to a friend, or go to my office. I hardly sleep. My bank accounts and property have been confiscated. Colleagues have vanished. At the American, British, and French consulates, I was told that receiving a visa would take over a year. Who knows what will be tomorrow? Who can live like a human being when any moment there could be a knock on the door?"

"What does our guest have to say?" the Rabbi asked.

Tevye smiled without responding, sensing that whatever he said could give birth to an argument.

Yonaton's sister spoke up, addressing her father from her place in the kitchen. "Doesn't the Torah state, *Tate*, that in the end of days, the persecuted Jews will find a refuge in Zion?"

"In the end of days," her father answered.

"It seems to me that the end of days has reached Vienna," Yonaton noted.

"It seems to you," his father said. "That's why we have Rabbis to teach us the proper understandings."

"I was just in America," Tevye reported.

"*Nu?*" the dispossessed merchant asked. "Tell us your impressions."

"In America, not all of the Jews are millionaires. They too have to struggle to survive."

"Struggle, yes. I am not afraid to struggle. But the *goyim* in America don't beat Jews with clubs and whips, and ship them off to Heaven knows where."

"I have a daughter in New York," Tevye informed them. "Her son is in love with a *shiksa*, may Heaven have mercy. In America, children are taught that everyone is equal, so why shouldn't a Jew marry a *goy*? That's what my grandson believes."

"A *shanda*," the Rabbi muttered.

"A curse on Columbus," his wife said from the kitchen.

"That doesn't happen in Israel," Tevye told them.

"There, the young people abandon the Torah," the Rabbi insisted. "It's the same thing."

"True, not everyone in the Holy Land is a righteous *Tzaddik*," Tevye agreed. "But as Rabbi Kook, of blessed memory, taught, even those who have strayed away from religion participate in the supreme *mitzvah* of resettling the Land."

Without saying anything, the Rabbi turned his head away from the table and spit toward the floor. Tevye didn't know if the expression of scorn was meant toward Rabbi Kook or the secular pioneers, but since he was a guest, he remained silent.

"I have made a final decision," Yonaton announced. "I am going to *Eretz Yisrael*."

His father glanced at him with angry eyes. "Why talk *nurrishkeit* at the *Shabbos* table? You know how I feel."

"Because I will be leaving with our guest, *Reb* Zalman, in another two weeks."

His father was silent. He glanced toward the kitchen at his wife. His gaze turned toward Tevye, as if he were a devil who had poisoned his son. Then he turned to his son.

"You want to turn your back on everything I have taught you and become a scorner who mocks the Torah?"

"The *mitzvah* of living in *Eretz Yisrael* is equal in weight to all of the commandments of the Torah," the youth argued.

"Who taught you that? Rabbi Jabotinsky?" his father asked cynically.

"Building the Jewish Nation in the Land of Israel is the ultimate goal of the Torah – not praying in a basement in Vienna and eating the Sabbath *seudah* in fear that the *goyim* will break into your house and beat out your brains."

Tevye kept silent. The women in the kitchen listened with open mouths.

"Plenty of Jews are getting slaughtered by the *goyim* in *Eretz Yisroel*," Yonaton's uncle reminded his agitated nephew.

"If all the Jews cowering in the foreign lands found the courage to return to our Homeland, the situation would be different," the passionate young Zionist countered, unwilling to back down.

His father banged a fist on the table, causing the *matzah* balls to jump in his soup bowl. "We will go when the Almighty tells us to go, when He sends the *Moshiach* to lead the way – not when pig-eaters like Ben Gurion wave a blue-and-white flag and whistle a Zionist tune."

"God is sending boats to take us there. Didn't you always teach me that God helps those who help themselves? Why remain here until the Germans kill us? Is that what God wants?"

"Enough!" the Rabbi shouted, banging his fist on the table again. "I will not tolerate heresy in this house!"

"It isn't heresy, *Tate*," his daughter protested. "We have no future here. I want to go to Palestine too!"

Their father stood up from the table. His body trembled, struggling to control his rage. "If you go, then you no longer have a father," he said. Then he turned away and strode out from the room.

Feeling ill at ease, as if he were the cause of the feud, Tevye stood up from the table. "I have to be going," he said.

"I'll come with you," Yonaton told him.

"So will I," his sister said.

Speechless by the eruption of emotion, their mother held a napkin to her mouth. The young people followed Tevye toward the door. "Where are you going?" the frightened woman asked.

"We are going home," Yonaton answered. "To the Land of Israel."

"You'll be better off in America," their uncle called after them.

Yonaton and his sister spent the night in a Jewish orphanage. After the Sabbath, they returned home and packed some clothes for the voyage. They never saw their father or mother again.

3.

The red Nazi flag with the black swastika flew from the façade of Vienna's City Hall. Since the German takeover of Austria a few months before, over forty thousand Austrians, Jews and non-Jews, had been arrested. It was risky to walk on the street without a swastika pin on your coat. Gestapo Headquarters were located in the center of the city in an elegant, nineteenth-century mansion once owned by the Rothschild Family. Two SS soldiers in black uniforms checked Tevye's passport at the gate.

"I have an appointment with Mr. Eichmann," Tevye informed them.

An armed escort came out and led Tevye to a small office, where he was told to wait. After some minutes, Adolf Eichmann strode into the room wearing an officer's cap, starched uniform, and polished boots. A leather whip stuck out from his belt. His face was long, thin, and pale, resembling a skeleton. Bowing cordially, he introduced himself, saying he was head of the Department of Jewish Affairs and Emigration.

"I understand you are here in Vienna to organize the transport of Jews to Palestine. I will be more than happy to help you," he said with a curt smile. He rushed on before Tevye could answer, as if he had to rush off to a more important meeting. "I will assign one my subordinates to assist you. We are prepared to approve emigration permits for as many Jews as you can transport to Palestine. I have been appraised of your organization's problems with the Jewish Agency. Since your budget is constricted, we will pay a modest sum for each passenger. My assistant will answer any questions you have. Good day."

The money, Tevye learned later, was from the nearly billion dollars which the Nazis stole from the Jews. With a slight bow, Eichmann strode to the door. Not finding his guards in the corridor, he began to scream. Within seconds, the poised military figure turned into a ranting maniac. Shouting hysterically, he pivoted to and fro, waving his hands, as if copying the raving gestures of the *Fuehrer*, whom Tevye had seen in a newsreel. Two SS men ran down the hallway. Standing at attention, they gave their commander a Nazi salute. Still yelling, Eichmann cursed them so fast, Tevye couldn't make out the words. Workers gathered in the hallway to see what was causing the loud commotion. Raising his whip, Eichmann smashed it down on the heads of the armed guards, calling them dogs. They weathered the blows without moving, afraid to offer resistance. Then, as quickly as the German's rage erupted, it ended, like the tail end of a storm. Returning his whip to his belt, Eichmann took a deep breath and stood straight, gazing around with a smile, as if nothing out of the ordinary had transpired.

Within the next six years, Eichmann would be responsible for overseeing the murder of millions of Jews by the Nazis. If Tevye had known what would be in the future, he would have found a way to kill him then and there. But no one, save perhaps Ze'ev Jabotinsky and Uri Zvi Greenberg, knew the full extent of the horror awaiting the Jewish People, so Tevye continued on with his work, organizing the clandestine sea voyage home.

4.

The world famous psychiatrist, Sigmund Freud, established his medical practice at 219 Berggasse Street in Vienna, in a new upper-class residential building erected on the ashes of the Ring Theater which had tragically burnt to the ground, taking the lives of more than six-hundred theater-goers. In granting a new building permit, the Austrian Government stipulated that a portion of the rental income from the reconstructed building be given to the orphaned children of the blaze. Thus, the building came to be known as, "The House of Atonement."

A servant answered the door and led Tevye into a spacious, richly-decorated apartment. Tevye followed her down a hallway to a very large study. "Dr. Freud will arrive shortly," she said, leaving him alone in the room. Immediately, Tevye felt like he had entered a completely different world. The study looked like a miniature museum, cluttered with literally dozens of primitive statues, religious icons, ancient artifacts, and masks. A heavy aroma of cigar smoke saturated the air. A high bookcase, neatly lined with books, spanned an entire wall. Resting on top of the bookcases were slabs of ancient tablets and other archeological relics. In the center of the eerie room was a worn leather armchair, facing a large wooden desk, which was also crowded with strange-looking figurines that Tevye had never seen in his life, some naked, some wearing headdresses like kings, others half-man, half-beast. The milkman from Anatevka didn't know if they were simple wood carvings or idols forbidden by Jewish Law. Tevye had an uncomfortable feeling that all of the tribal masks and shrunken heads were staring at him. Persian carpets covered the floor. A long, Roman-looking couch was situated not far from the psychiatrist's desk. On the wall above the ornate sofa was a framed painting of three towering Egyptian statues carved into the side of a cliff. A giant Greek urn stood in a corner, looking like a large milk container. Tevye's survey was interrupted by a dog who scurried into the study and hopped onto the chair behind the desk. Tevye didn't know about dog breeding and pedigrees, but the intelligent-looking animal wasn't the kind of dog that roamed the streets searching for edible garbage. Carefully combed and coiffured, the creature's jaw was graced with a trim white beard. The animal stared at the visitor with a serious gaze and barked. In the reflection of wall mirror behind the desk, Tevye could see himself waiting, surrounded by the strange collection of useless archeological *chazzerai* - junk.

Sigmund Freud entered the room slowly. Tall and stiff with age, his grey suit and black eyeglass-frames accentuated his snow-white hair and the paleness of his complexion. He glanced at Tevye with a stern, angry expression, like a father upset to discover a child in his study. His ruler straight lips and granite-like jaw were surrounded by a trim white goatee strikingly resembling his dog's. Upon the arrival of the famous psychiatrist, the canine hopped down from the chair and sat on its haunches to the side of the desk, staring at Tevye with the same dour look of disapproval which gripped the face of its master. Suffering from cancer of the mouth, numerous operations had locked Sigmund Freud's jaw into a constant angry expression.

When the gaunt physician sat down behind his desk, the light-filled window behind him cast his figure into a dark silhouette. Tevye found himself looking at his reflection in the mirror positioned beside the window. Was this a psychiatric technique, he wondered, to keep a patient focused on himself?

With his right hand, Freud grasped his chin and gave it a

push, as if to set his reconstructed jaw back into its proper place.

"Please, take off your hat and sit down," he said in a strained tone of voice. Assuming that Tevye was a resident of Vienna, he spoke in Austrian.

"Can we speak in Yiddish?" Tevye inquired.

"If I remember the language," the psychiatrist replied, switching to the vernacular known to most European Jews, no matter where they lived. "My parents spoke Yiddish at home, but not having occasion to use it, the language has become like a vestigial organ with me."

Again, with a small grimace, he held his jaw and gave it a push. The dog whimpered, as if feeling its master's discomfort.

"The creature sympathizes with my pain. Perhaps I should explain. My physicians like to hide the truth from me, but I seem to have a nasty cancer in my mouth. After more than a dozen operations, my speech is impaired and only cocaine and morphine grant me temporary relief from my sufferings."

He opened a desk drawer and removed what looked like a small snuff box. Opening its lid, he told the dog, "Come!"

"My need for the drug as a painkiller led me to discover cocaine's many medicinal properties."

The physician lowered the small box for the dog to take a few sniffs. Wagging its tail, it ran off and hopped up on the couch where it curled up with a contented smile on its face. Freud took a sniff himself. He held out the snuff box to his guest.

"No thank you," Tevye said.

"Have you ever tried?"

"No."

"How do you know you don't want it if you have never tried it?" the renowned doctor asked.

Tevye didn't have an answer.

"Most people are afraid of freedom," the silhouetted figure observed.

"I see that you like collecting relics and ancient artifacts," Tevye noted in a philosophical fashion. "Referring to the Two Tablets upon which God engraved the Ten

Commandments, the Sages of the Mishna, using a play on words, stated, 'Don't read the word *harut* as meaning engraved, but rather as *herut*, meaning freedom, for no man is free except the person who studies Torah.'"

"You're a practitioner of Judaism?" Freud asked.

"*Baruch Hashem*," Tevye answered.

"Religious doctrines are all illusions," the psychiatrist said in a bored voice. "They do not admit of proof, and therefore, no one can be compelled to consider them true, or to believe in them. While Judaism contains many lofty principles and teachings, the God of the Jews is as much of an illusion as the wooden figures on my desk. God does not exist. He is an invention of primitive man to help him cope with his primal fears by believing in a higher power who will take care of him. A father figure, if you will. Religion is a disavowal of reality, a tribal neurosis, the escapism of the masses, which will eventually pass from its primitive childhood stage to healthy maturity when mankind comes to embrace the teachings of science, and psychiatric theory, based upon my work."

"*Gevalt!*" Tevye thought to himself. No wonder the man has a cancer in his mouth, for spouting such heretical garbage.

Again, Freud took a sniff of the white powder in the snuff box. Then he lit a long cigar, leaned back in his chair, and inhaled deeply.

"Would you like to lie on the couch?" he asked.

"The couch?" Tevye muttered, glancing at the dog who seemed to be sleeping on the oriental-looking sofa, a contended smile spread across its face. "What for?"

"It's a technique I use in my therapy sessions," the psychiatrist said. "It enables the patient to enter a comforting, womb-like space, where he or she can feel safe. In addition, just between you and me, it also prevents me from having to look at depressed faces for hours on end. That alone can drive a sane man crazy. I can wake up the dog if you like."

"I'm comfortable in this chair," Tevye replied.

"Would you like to be hypnotized?"

"Hypnotized? What for?"

"To enter an uninhibited state where your hidden feelings can find free expression. That itself can liberate a person from crippling traumas of the past. Additionally, by bringing unconscious feelings to light, they can be treated like all other diseases and pathological states."

Tevye realized that the doctor thought he had come for a psychiatric consultation. Apparently, his secretary hadn't relayed the purpose of the visit.

"Do you suffer from depression, bouts of melancholy, anxiety, and outbursts of anger," Freud asked.

"When my daughter, Hava, was slaughtered by Arabs, I fell into a very deep mourning, but who has the luxury to dwell on one's problems? With work, and raising a family, and defending the neighborhood against Arab attack, and *schlepping* to America to raise money, and bringing Jews to Palestine in defiance of the British blockade, and *shachrit*, *mincha*, and *maariv* prayers, and learning Torah, who has time to be depressed?"

"I see," Freud said. "Perhaps you can tell me about some reoccurring dream you have."

"A reoccurring dream?"

"Yes. Everyone has them. Like Yosef and the Pharaoh. Dreams are the royal road to the unconscious."

Nothing came to Tevye's recollection. Once, he had a wild nightmare, after agreeing to a wedding match between his daughter, Tzeitl, and Lazar the wealthy butcher, that the butcher's dead wife, Fruma Sarah, returned to kill Tzeitl so her husband wouldn't remarry. Or maybe, Tevye had made up the dream to frighten Golda and convince her that their daughter should marry the bumbling tailor, Motel, instead. It was so long ago, Tevye couldn't remember.

"Don't be afraid," Dr. Freud said. "Feel free to tell me the first thing that comes into your mind."

The first thing that came into Tevye's mind was that the distinguished-looking man sitting behind the desk, surrounded by idols and voodoo masks, was a lunatic. The collector of shrunken heads glared at Tevye with a look so fierce, Tevye felt afraid not to answer.

"Sometimes I dream about being a rich man."

"What else? Something more bothersome."

"Now that you mention it, I do have a nightmare that repeats itself quite a bit. I am driving my milk wagon through a fierce Russian snowstorm when my horse falls ill, and I have to pull it and my wagon all the way home by myself."

"Ahha," Freud exclaimed, taking another long puff on his cigar and setting it carefully down on the ashtray. "Horses are sexual beasts, known for their lustful ways. The dream reveals your subconscious fears of sexual failure, stemming no doubt from a repressed Oedipus complex and suppressed anger toward your father."

"Angry at my father? Heaven forbid." Tevye said.

"Exactly. You are out of touch with your inmost feelings. That's why you are here – to free yourself from the shackles of your past which have imprisoned you in a dungeon of anger, fear, and guilt. Unexpressed emotions never die. They are buried alive during childhood and burst forth later in life in many destructive ways. While people complain about not feeling happy, when it comes to taking their neuroses away from them, they rise up in defense and denial like a lioness protecting her young."

"Actually," Tevye replied. "I came here because I was told that you are searching for a way to get out of Austria. I have come to offer a solution."

For a moment, Freud was silent. "Oh," he finally said. "I didn't realize. I assumed you were here for a consultation. No one told me."

He raised his cigar from an ashtray, where it was burning like incense on the Temple altar. Closing his eyes, the healer took another long drag. The aroma of the tobacco filled Tevye's head, making him feel a bit dizzy.

"My physicians tell me that smoking is killing me," Freud confided. "But what can I do? I am hopelessly addicted. A colleague once suggested that a cigar is a phallic symbol, and that my addiction to smoking expresses an unconscious search for my father whom I loved very much. I told him that sometimes a cigar is just a cigar. The truth is, I don't know how much longer I have left in this miserable world. If the Nazis don't burn me first, that large Greek urn in the corner of the room will soon house my ashes. My will is written and signed, with instructions that my body be cremated. Isn't that what your Bible teaches? *"For ashes you are, and to ashes you shall return."*

"I am not a Torah scholar, but I believe the verse is referring to dust, not to ashes. *'For dust you are, and to dust you shall return.'* Meaning that we are to be buried in the ground, not burned, God forbid, and sealed in a jar like pickled herring."

The ailing psychiatrist set his cigar in the ashtray and stood up from his desk with a groan. His dog raised its head, wondering if it were time for a walk.

"What is your proposition?" he asked, staring at Tevye with his fixed, stern expression.

"A ship is sailing to *Eretz Yisrael* in another week. I have been ordered to make room for you and your family if you would like to join us."

"Ordered by whom?"

"Ze'ev Jabotinsky."

"I see."

The Austrian physician stepped over to a table cluttered with more relics, statues, and stone heads. He rested a hand on a bust of himself for support.

"If I had a visa to exit the country, I could arrange transportation myself, but the Germans refuse to grant me one."

"The boat is filled with Jews without visas. We will be sailing clandestinely to Palestine."

"I prefer London," Freud said. "Even though the weather there is quite dreadful."

"You don't believe in Zionism?"

Freud paused before answering.

"On several occasions, Herzl lay on that couch when he was working as a journalist in Vienna. He was extremely troubled by bouts of depression and melancholy, stemming from a fierce tug of war between his libido, ego, and id. To escape, he allowed megalomaniacal fantasies to fill his head, like his Pied-Piper idea of leading the Jews to the Land of Israel to build a Jewish State. There are people who dream and immediately forget them. Others dream and remember them for an hour or two. Exceptional people dream and pursue their dreams in life. Theodore was one of them. His entire life was the pursuit of his dream. The acting out of dreams can lead to severe schizophrenia and mental disorder, but with Herzl, it was like a healing balm. I learned from him that dreams are most profound when they seem the most unattainable. Rather than continue psychiatric treatment, I dimmed it best that his psychosis remain intact. In fact, after I published my book, 'The Interpretation of Dreams,' I sent it to him to review in one of the newspapers he wrote for, the *Die Neue Freie Presse.* I included the inscription, 'To Theodore, in esteem for the poet and fighter who is dedicated to furthering the human rights of our People.'"

"Then you are a Zionist?"

"My thoughts regarding Zionism have changed over time. At first, perhaps through my friendship with Herzl, I thought it a splendid idea. Then after many years of research and study, as my understanding and formulation of psychiatry deepened, I came to the conclusion that religion and everything connected with it was pure neurotic fantasy. Even though Herzl didn't express his Zionism in religious terms, one cannot separate a return to the Land of Israel from its roots in Judaism, since the Torah and Hebrew prophets harp on the theme of Redemption via Israel's promised revival in its ancient Homeland. When the newly-found Hebrew University asked Albert Einstein and yours truly to join their faculty, I refused. Why? To tell you the truth, I was quite comfortable here. After World War One, everyone believed that mankind's insanity had spent itself, and that such psychotic bloodshed could never happen again. But on an individual level, the war left myriads of people horribly traumatized. My business was booming. In the year 1930, I was asked to sign a *Keren HaYesod* petition condemning the widespread Arab attacks against Jews. I wrote them a letter. Would you like to hear it?'

"By all means."

Freud stepped over to a bookcase. "I have already sent several crates of manuscripts and books to the London Psychiatric Society to be held in safekeeping, lest the Nazis confiscate them and burn them in a bonfire out on the street. What progress civilized man has made! In the Middle Ages, I myself would have been burned at the stake for my ideas. Now, for the time being, they are content to merely burn my books."

Freud selected a file from a shelf and found the letter.

"I have copies of my correspondences," he said.

The dog jumped to the floor when Freud sat down on the couch, taking its place. He read the epistle out loud, explaining his refusal to condemn the latest outbreak of Arab violence:

Letter to Dr. Chaim Koffler of the Jewish National Fund:

Vienna: 26 February 1930

Dear Sir,

I cannot do as you wish. I am unable to overcome my aversion to burdening the public with my name, and even the present critical time does not seem to me to warrant it. Whoever wants to influence the masses must give them something rousing and inflammatory and my sober judgement of Zionism does not permit this. I certainly sympathize with its goals, am proud of our Hebrew University in Jerusalem, and am delighted with our settlement's prosperity.

But, on the other hand, I do not think that Palestine could ever become a Jewish State, nor that the Christian and Islamic worlds would ever be prepared to have their holy places under Jewish care. It would have seemed more sensible to me to establish a Jewish Homeland on a less historically-burdened land. But I know that such a rational viewpoint would never have gained the enthusiasm of the masses and the financial support of the wealthy.

I concede with sorrow that the baseless fanaticism of our people is in part to be blamed for the awakening of Arab distrust. I can raise no sympathy at all for the misdirected piety which transforms a piece of a Herodian wall (the *Kotel*) into a national relic, thereby offending the feelings of the natives.

Now judge for yourself whether I, with such a critical point of view, am the right person to come forward as the consoling voice of a people deluded by unjustified hope.

> Your obedient servant,
> Freud

Exhausted, the psychiatrist lay down on the couch.

"Nevertheless," he continued, feeling a need to justify his decision to Tevye. "Ever since Hitler invaded Austria, followed by *Kristallnacht* and the clear sign of things to come, the Zionist solution seems to be the best alternative for the Jews. After all is said and done, the hysterical screaming of Mr. Jabotinsky has proven to be true prophecy. Poets like him are revolutionaries compared to ordinary men, because they drink at streams not yet accessible to science. Nonetheless, for selfish academic reasons, and in consideration of my faltering health, I prefer to spend my remaining days in London, which offers more sophisticated medical care."

"Jabotinsky knows many influential people in London," Tevye replied.

"My family and I would be indebted to you if you could intercede in our behalf."

"It may involve certain costs."

"The Nazis have seized my bank accounts in Austria, but funds can be provided by the Psychiatric Society in London if necessary."

Sigmund Freud closed his eyes. "Thank you for coming by," he said, cryptically adding, "Out of your vulnerabilities will come your strength."

Then he fell fast asleep on the couch.

5.

The voyage began back in Vienna. Under the cover of night, the crowd of motley *ma'apilim* boarded a Danube River ferry called the *Danube Dream,* which the *Irgun* had chartered for the first half of the journey to the Black Sea. It was the first time a clandestine rescue operation would sail down the Danube. Previous groups had traveled by train to

Italian to rendezvous with the transport ships to Palestine, until the British stopped a ship in the Mediterranean and sent it back to Italy. When the Germans refused to allow the Jewish refugees back into Austria or Germany, the Italians banned further transit permits, so an alternate route had to be found.

The Danube River was considered an international waterway. Traffic along the river had the "protected passage" status of the high seas. Even if passengers lacked visas to final destinations, international law maintained that refugees could not be detained. The Gestapo in Vienna agreed to this itinerary, but warned that the immigrants would not be allowed to return to German-ruled territory if ships were stopped by foreign powers.

An air of confusion and uncertainty surrounded the boarding. A squadron of S.S. Stormtroopers climbed out of trucks to oversee the midnight departure. The Nazis allowed the immigrants to take along only the possessions they could carry. Everyone was led through the Customs House and given a specially printed visa and "ticket" to Liberia. Gestapo agents searched through bags and pockets to make sure that no valuable objects were smuggled out of the country. Adolf Eichmann was present to supervise the operation. Tevye was in charge of the Jews, a mixed crowd of young and old, religious and not religious, all possessed by excitement and fear. Shouting out in Yiddish, the milkman turned refugee-smuggler herded them along the gangway onto the former, Danube River pleasure boat. When Tevye tried to board, an S.S. agent stopped him, demanding to see his papers.

"What is a journalist from Palestine doing on a ship of swine?" the German asked. Armed guards returned Tevye to the Customs House where he was stripped and searched. Observing the unexpected problem, Yonaton hurried to file a complaint with Eichmann who gave an order to free the group leader.

Just prior to departure, another truck arrived. German soldiers led a group of seven ghostlike figures toward the dock. They all wore striped prison uniforms. Their heads were shaved bald. The eldest was named Rabbi Novik. His relatives had paid a heavy ransom to secure his release from the Buchenwald work camp, along with six of his followers. A well-dressed woman on the dock called out, "Father!" She rushed forward, but a soldier held out his bayoneted rifle, not letting her pass. S.S. Stormtroopers shoved the emaciated skeletons up the ramp to the ship. The other passengers called them, "*glattkopfe*," meaning shaved heads. Their faces were gaunt and thin, with a look of fright in their eyes. They didn't speak, so no one knew what traumas they had endured. Their bellies were so shrunken, they could only nibble on bread and sip on tea. Whenever someone approached, they backed off, trembling. After the first day, passengers left them alone. Tevye wanted to speak with them, but with all of his chores, running between his human cargo and the crew, he didn't find time.

Sporting a large *swastika* painted on its hull, the *Danube Dream* was built to ferry eighty people on holiday trips along the Danube River. The captain of the vessel, an experienced Austrian seaman, immediately protested, refusing to set sail unless three-hundred people were sent back to shore. Though the Danube Steamship Company had agreed to transport the immigrants, the captain seized the opportunity to extract a little extortion *gelt* for his services.

"How much money do you want?" Tevye asked him.

"Four-hundred *zloty*," he replied.

"You'll get two-hundred when we rendezvous with the transport freighter."

"I want the whole four-hundred now."

"If you hold up our sailing, I will make sure that you get fired," Tevye told him with a no-nonsense expression. "Your employers are receiving a lot of money for the voyages we have chartered from the company. I'm sure they have other captains who can do the job."

The seaman stared at Tevye angrily, but Tevye didn't flinch. "A Jew is a Jew," he said. Then he strode away. Tevye sighed, sensing that the *Danube Dream* was going to be more like a *Danube Nightmare*. But having boarded the vessel, his passengers seemed greatly relieved, knowing they were on the way to the Promised Land. The trauma of leaving family behind soon gave way to a feeling of gaiety, even though the aging boat was overcrowded and the accommodations were uncomfortable and sparse. For Tevye, just waving goodbye to the Nazis on the dock was a reason to be thankful. In a few minutes, the ship was in the middle of the wide Danube River. The lights of Vienna soon disappeared. They were on the way, but what would be with the millions of Jews still stranded on shore? With a shortage of funds, and the opposition of the Jewish Agency, how could the *Irgun* rescue them all?

As Sholom Aleichem would say, to make a long story short, the *Danube Dream* sped slowly down the river along the verdant green shores of Slovakia. A steady column of smoke rose heavenward from the vessel's chimney, like the smoke of the sacrifices in the Jerusalem Temple of old. After a short stop in Bratislava to pick up more *ma'apilim*, the ship continued on its journey. Approaching towns and villages along the way, the Captain refrained from sounding the *Danube Dream's* horn, not wanting to attract any unnecessary attention. Hungarian troops, allied with the Germans, marched along the shore with their cavalry and canons. Docking in Budapest for the night, Tevye and Yonaton stood on the deck, listening to the strains of gypsy music while the passengers slept, some on the decks of the ship, others cramped in the quarters below. The excited youth was filled with questions. "What is the weather like in *Eretz Yisrael,*" he wanted to know. Did Tevye have a regular job? Was it easy to find work? Would the *Irgun* help the immigrants to start a new life? Did the Jews speak Yiddish or Hebrew? Did everyone have to spend two years in the *Betar plugot*, or could you study at the Hebrew University instead? Tevye answered all of his questions as if he were in charge of immigrant absorption in the country as well.

"What will be with my father and mother?" the youth finally asked.

"When the time came for the Jews to leave Egypt, four-fifths of them didn't want to go, even though they lived a life of hardship," Tevye answered. "They were comfortable with what they had. Why try something new? They had been slaves for so long, they had the mentality of slaves. Just like today. Some things don't change."

"You think they will all perish?"

"That's what Jabotinsky and Uri Zvi Greenberg have been warning, but people scoff at them and call them false prophets. *Hashem yirachem*. May God have mercy upon His People."

Twelve days after their departure from Vienna, the ferry reached the port of Sulina, where the Danube spilled into the Black Sea. The boat anchored in the middle of the river, waiting for the transport freighter which would carry them the rest of the way to Zion. After an anxious, day-long delay, a dirty and decrepit ship, no bigger than the *Danube Dream*, and bearing the name, *S.S. Odyssey*, chugged slowly toward the ferry, listing dangerously to its side. A torn Greek flag fluttered atop the vessel, alongside the soot-covered chimney. Instead of cheering at its arrival, the crowd on the deck of the *Danube Dream* became deathly silent.

"*Veyzmeer*," Tevye muttered. He knew it was his duty to rally the sunken spirits of his charges, but, crestfallen like them, he wondered how such a dilapidated freighter could make the ocean voyage. One-by-one, knapsacks were inspected, and the *ma'apilim* trekked across the plank joining the two boats. A tour of the vessel didn't lighten Tevye's concern. A ghost ship was better maintained. The airless and foul-smelling holds made the *Danube Dream* seem like a fancy hotel in comparison.

Escorted by two aides, Captain Papas extended a hand to Tevye. Built like a wrestler, the fellow leaned on a cane. He didn't wear an eye-patch, but he resembled a drunken pirate in every other way. The sweet smell of Ouzo oozed from his mouth when he spoke. Noticing Tevye's expression of worry, he laughed.

"Why such a long face?" he said in English. "I know this tub doesn't look like much, but either does my wife, and she's still a good, faithful women."

Laughing at his joke, he gave Tevye a good-natured slap on the back.

"Loosen up, mate. I've captained this bathtub all over the world, so don't you worry."

Then, he leaned closer with his foul-smelling breath and

whispered, "Just tell your people not to gather on the starboard side of ship, lest we capsize."

Then he straightened, adopting a more serious expression and captain-like voice. "If you need anything, tell my aids. They're top-notch sailors. This is their third time at this little game of cat and mouse. They can find the way by the stars if they have too. Any questions?"

Yonaton spoke up. "How long will the crossing take?"

"Depends on the weather. You Jews like to pray, right? So start praying. I won't bother in your prayers if you don't bother me in running the ship. May Zeus, or Christ, or the God of Moses be with us. If we have to, we can make room for all three."

"Charming fellow," Tevye thought. He inspired as much confidence as a wagon without any wheels.

Once again, to make a long story short, as they headed for Turkey in the open waters of the Black Sea, a smooth pathway, like the marble corridor of a palace, accompanied them on their journey. But, as the common expression goes, it was too good to be true. Just when the Jews thought they could close their eyes for a few serene hours of sleep, lightning bolts flashed, thunder shook the Heavens, and the sea rose up in anger, as if in revenge for having once allowed the Jews to pass through on their way out from Egypt. Tevye hurried topside to the bridge, only to find the Captain wobbling back and forth as unsteadily as the ship.

"There's a storm, sir!" Tevye reported.

"Well what do you know?!" the drunken seaman quipped, waving a bottle of Greek wine. "Look mates! We have a genuine Aristotle on board!"

Tevye glanced worriedly at the first-mate, who was battling with the helm. The ocean lifted the vessel like a toy. Everyone in the cabin tumbled toward the wall. Tevye fell down on his rump.

"Hold on, you fools!" the Captain shouted with a laugh, clutching the railing by the cabin window.

"Greed!" he cried. "Greed got me into this. For a few stinking gold coins I risked my ship and my crew to rescue a shipload of Christ-killers. For all I care, the sea can swallow them up!"

With the next sway of the vessel, the Captain let go of the railing and staggered forward, dropping down on his knees in front of Tevye, who sat with his back to a wall. His nose touched Tevye's when he spoke. His breath reeked of wine.

"Don't you worry, my friend," he said with a grin. "We've carried donkeys and pigs through more turbulent weather. Just tell your chattel to stay windward. Everyone windward! Is that clear?"

"Which way is windward?" Tevye asked.

"Toward the wind, Moses, toward the wind!"

"The wind is everywhere," Tevye muttered.

The muscular first-mate wrestled with the wheel. "The opposite side that we're tilting," he explained. "Take him below to the passengers," he commanded another seaman.

Fortunately, Yonaton and two of the crew had taken charge. In the overcrowded chambers in the belly of the vessel, in a hold of the ship that was used to transport crates of fertilizer, the *ma'apilim* huddled together against the windward wall, using their weight to keep the vessel's hull from flipping out of the water. Some faces were pale. Others were yellow. A gush of nausea rose in Tevye's throat, as if he too would fall seasick. Was this how Jonah felt, he wondered, in the belly of the whale? Many of the battered seafarers were ill and dehydrated. Food and water had to be rationed, and nursing mothers had run out of milk for their crying babies. A wealthy widow, who had boarded the freighter stylishly dressed and carrying a parasol, as if she were off to the opera, sat in a corner sobbing. The refined lady hardly slept during the three-week journey. For several days running, she had begged Tevye to let her off the boat, unwilling to accept the fact that they were in the middle of the sea. Once again, the woman appealed to him for mercy. "Please, captain," she begged. "Please get me off of this ship before I lose my mind and die."

Tevye found himself by Rabbi Novik, the released prisoner from Buchenwald, who looked strangely serene, his lips moving silently in prayer. "Even if the blade of an executioner's sword is poised above a person's neck, he shouldn't feel despair," the holy Jew said, continuing to pray.

Tevye headed for the next hold and its cargo of Jews. He stopped in a narrow corridor as dry heaves shook his body. Give him the reins of a horse and wagon and he could navigate through the darkest snowstorm, but shut him up inside the airless confines of a boat and his knees turned into jelly. Yonaton grasped his arm.

"Go up on deck for some air," the young man said. "I'll take care of the passengers."

When Tevye reached the deck, he got a glimpse of two lifeboats sailing gracefully away from the freighter atop two tall waves. Strong winds had broken the cranes which had held them in place. Then, gradually, the frothing sea turned calm, as if the crazed tantrum of some mythological sea god had abated.

"Poseidon be praised! Poseidon be praised," the Captain shouted from the deck, raising his wine bottle toward the heavens.

Clouds began to disperse. Rays of moonlight slanted down from the sky, lighting up a path through the dark ocean. Pale and exhausted passengers made their way to the deck for fresh air. When the ship reached Bosphorus, Turkish officials boarded in the morning to check the boat's documents before allowing the vessel to pass into the Bosphorus Strait, which divided the country in half. Seeing the jaundiced expressions of the refugees, and death-mask faces of the Buchenwald survivors, they hastily signed the clearance papers, warning the Captain not to unload his passengers in Turkey.

The Marmara Sea gave way to the Aegean Sea. As if reaching safe and familiar waters, the *Odyssey* sailed breezily past Greek Islands, toward the small port of Agios on the island of Crete, where a representative of the *Irgun* was to join them on the final leg of the voyage. Tevye was standing on deck, gazing up at the panorama of stars in the sky when the first-mate, a good-natured fellow named Adrian, strolled by, smoking a cigarette.

"Good evening," he said in greeting.

Instinctively, Tevye glanced up toward the navigator's cabin.

"I can't stand at the wheel all day and night," the Greek sailor said.

"I suppose not," Tevye answered.

"Did you know that most of the constellations are named after Greek gods?" the first-mate asked.

"I never really thought about it." Tevye replied. In the Talmud, the constellations had Hebrew names. The Hebrew expression, "*mazel tov*," meant, "You should have a good constellation." And in Yiddish, a "*shlimazel*" was a person with constant bad luck, like Tevye himself. Some Sages believed that constellations affected people's lives, and other maintained they didn't, saying that everything was controlled by the Creator. Still others explained that the mechanism that *Hashem* used in bringing everything about was via the constellations. One way or the other, Tevye prayed that their *mazel* remain favorable, affording them calm seas for the rest of the journey.

"Look," the Greek seafarer said. "You see the twinkling star where my finger is pointed and the circle of smaller stars around it?"

"I think so."

"That's 'Andromeda, the Princess.' She is the beautiful daughter of Queen Cassiopeia who was very vain, always bragging about her beauty, claiming that she was more beautiful than the sea nymphs. This angered Poseidon, the king of the sea. To pacify him, Cassiopeia chained her daughter to a boulder on the beach as a sacrifice to the sea monster, Cetus. The girl in distress was saved by her hero, Perseus, who slew Cetus by showing it the severed head of Medusa, turning the monster into stone."

"Do Greeks still believe in those legends and myths?" Tevye asked.

"Maybe when they're drunk," Adrian replied with a smile. "After a bottle or two, Captain Papas thinks he's Zeus himself."

"I haven't seen him all day."

"He sleeps a lot. He trusts us to do the sailing. Whenever there's a problem with the engine, we wake him up. He knows more about engines than all of us together. Like a mother with her baby, he senses when there is going to be a problem and fixes it before it occurs by giving it a kick in just the right place."

Tevye saw the gaunt, unworldly apparition of Rabbi Novik, still wearing his Buchenwald prisoner's uniform, pacing back and forth at the end of the deck by the aft of the ship.

"You see the bright star behind us?" the first-mate asked. "That's the North Star. It's as faithful a navigator as a compass. It's the highest of the seven stars which make up 'Stella Polaris' – the Little Bear."

"That's what we call, '*HaDlee HaKatan*' – the Little Dipper."

"Have a nice night," the sailor said. "We should reach Crete in another two hours."

After saying goodnight, Tevye strolled along the deck toward the aft of the ship, looking for Rabbi Novik, but he was nowhere in sight. Passengers who could no longer withstand the claustrophobic quarters below slept on the rear deck, one almost on top of the other. Circling back toward the bow, Tevye spotted the Rabbi standing against a wall, sheltered from the stiff sea breeze, gazing out toward the dark horizon. Though they had left the cold of Europe behind, his frail frame was shivering. During the week, the vacant, faraway look in his eyes had softened somewhat. But his gaunt features gave Tevye the chills. His white beard had a helter-skelter appearance, as if it had been snapped at with scissors or plucked. As Tevye approached, the Rabbi took a step away, as if the clean-shaven figure of authority might strike him.

"*Shalom Aleichem*," Tevye greeted, then added in Hebrew a few lines of the "*Nishmat*" prayer, "Were our mouth filled with song as the sea is with water, and our tongue with praise as the roaring waves; were our lips full of adoration like the wide expanse of the heavens, and our eyes as sparkling as the sun and the moon...."

"You should never know..." the Rabbi said in Yiddish.

His voice was little more than a whisper. Tevye guessed that they were about the same age, but the thin and trembling Rabbi looked ages older.

"When will we arrive, *bezrat Hashem*?" he asked.

"First we stop in Crete. Then the Holy Land. If there are no unexpected delays, maybe another three days and nights."

"Once I opposed Zionism," he confided. "When congregants asked me if they should go, I told them no. That is what our Rabbis taught us. 'Do not go up like a wall.' We had a tradition that the *Moshiach* would take us back to Zion. I understand now that their understanding of the matter was incorrect."

Tevye listened silently. Like a background symphony, the wind and the waves accompanied the Rabbi's tale.

"In spite of my opposition to Zionism, I spoke out against the Germans. Maybe that is why they arrested me. Maybe someone told them. They came during a class in the basement of the *shul*. We heard their boots marching down the stairs. They beat us with their clubs and dragged me and my students away. Who can fathom such ruthlessness? The worst of animals possess greater nobility. *Amalek*."

Rabbi Novik closed his eyes, but finding no respite there, he once again stared out at the black sea.

"In the camp, there were gunshots throughout the day. Prisoners disappeared. Other prisoners had to work. The lucky ones. We didn't work. The camp commander said he respected religion. Weren't the Jews, the Chosen People, he asked us? He wanted to see the God of the Jews protect His Chosen People. His officers nailed an old Jew to the wall of a barracks. They tore off his prison uniform, then smashed his groin with a board. Then they released Dobermans and let the dogs eat him alive. The camp commander laughed. We had to watch or be killed. One of my students couldn't bear it. He turned his gaze away. A soldier held a revolver to his head and shot him. 'Where is your God?' the Nazi devil asked. 'If you are the Chosen People, why doesn't He your God protect you?'"

Tevye couldn't speak. He wanted to comfort the man, but he couldn't find the words.

"For eight months, they fed us just enough to keep us alive. Every day, they forced us to witness a new atrocity. One day, they marched ten naked Jews to the edge of a pit and pushed them in with bayonets. Then a tractor buried them alive. We had to watch. 'Where is your God?' the commander repeated. Laughing, they pulled the hair out of our beards. They made us spend a night, standing outside in the rain. We were entertainment for them. They locked us into a black cell for two days with a dozen other prisoners. Some went insane. Others found some way to slit their wrists and bleed to death. One day, they marched us out to the cow stalls where they threw a Jew into a mound of manure. Each time he stood up, they pushed him back into the dung. 'Where is your God?' the commander screamed. When a student dared to shout out in protest, the commander ordered a guard to slice off his tongue with his knife. He's down below in the hold, still alive, but he can't tell you what he saw."

Tevye had heard enough. The question rang in his ears – "Where is your God? Why doesn't He protect you?" Rabbi Akiva had taught that everything that happened in life was for the good. But how could this horror be included? Tevye didn't understand. He couldn't.

"Do you want to know the worst thing?" the Rabbi asked. "I'm afraid that the horror is only just beginning."

Tevye's encounter with the Buchenwald survivor heightened the urgency of the mission. The 500 Jews on board the *Odyssey* were merely a drop in the bucket. They had to save millions before the Nazi war machine engulfed other countries and sent all of the Jews to death camps. If Tevye ever thought about returning to the milk business, he realized that those days were gone.

Reaching the small port of Agios, the freighter anchored in the picturesque harbor. As the hours passed, the crowd of passengers on the deck started to worry, and rumors began to spread that the *Irgun* liaison-man had been captured by the British and that the landing was delayed, or even canceled. Uncomfortable speaking to crowds, Tevye handed Yonaton a megaphone and asked him to assure the *ma'apilim* that everything was proceeding as planned. Sure enough, a ship appeared in the distance heading their way. People waited anxiously as the slow-moving freighter grew closer. It stopped a short distance away from the *Odyssey*, and a lifeboat was lowered into the water. Three men climbed down a rope ladder and entered the small go-between. It was only when the lifeboat drew closer to the immigrant ship that Tevye recognized the sailor who wasn't manning the oars. It was Tzvi, his eldest son! When the young man waved up at the *Odyssey* and called out, "*Shalom*," everyone cheered. Judging by their joyous reaction, you would have thought the *Mashiach* himself had arrived!

Tevye was waiting at the railing to embrace him. Father and son enjoyed a long and ardent hug.

"Surprised?" Tevye asked the swarthy, sunburnt lad. Dressed in short tan pants and a white t-shirt, he looked like a *sabra* pioneer, graced with rippling muscles and a confident grin.

"Ben-Ami informed me that you were awarded the honor of leading the group."

"Some big leader I am," Tevye replied, never seeking honor for himself. As the saying goes, "Honor is like a shadow – the more you run after it, the farther it runs away."

"Remember what you taught me? 'When there is no man, then be a man.'"

One of Tzvi's sidelocks fell out from his cap and he pushed it back into place.

"Where is Ben-Ami?" Tevye asked, glad to see that his son hadn't cut off his *peyes*, and exchanged the traditions of his forefathers for the fashions of modern times.

"He's already on his way back to Vienna to organize another voyage."

"What's the matter?" Tevye asked, seeing his son's amused expression.

"Nothing. I'm not used to seeing you without a beard, that's all. And instead of smelling like a farm, you smell like the sea."

"I've swallowed enough salt water on this trip to make *Kiddush* for a year," his father joked.

Tevye wanted to ask about his wife and his other children, about Hevedke and Nachman, about Hannie and Moishe and his other *eyniklech* – grandchildren - but who had the time for personal matters? "Is everything going as planned?" he asked.

"*Bezrat Hashem*, Tzvi reported. The British have increased their surveillance along the coast, but with Arabs striking British targets as well, the Brits are as shorthanded as we are. So far, all of our landings have met no resistance. But we don't take any chances."

The crowd around them shouted out a barrage of questions. Yonaton handed the megaphone to Tevye, who handed it to his son. Tzvi jumped up onto a platform beside coils of ropes and raised the bullhorn to his mouth. How the lad had matured, Tevye thought. In the six months since Tevye had left the Holy Land, the youth had become a *mench*! His aura of confidence immediately put the anxious crowd at ease.

"I come with greetings from *Eretz Yisrael*," he called out in his basic and rusty Yiddish. "We are very trained and experienced in these landings, so there is no need to fear. You can make our task easier by following orders and by staying calm whatever happens. In three more days you will reach your new home – the Promised Land."

Everyone cheered. Almost unanimously, everyone started singing the "*HaTikvah*." Rabbi Novik and his students joined in the singing. Seeing the strange group in their Buchenwald uniforms, with clean-shaven heads, Tzvi asked his father who they were.

"On the *Shabbos* of *Chol HaMoed Pesach*, we read the *haftarah* about Ezekiel and his vision of dry bones, which he commands to come back to life. There they are – the dry bones of the House of Israel," his father told him, nodding toward the emaciated group. "The Holy One Blessed Be He raised from them from the dead and is bringing them home to the Land of our life."

That night, in the dining cabin of the crew, when they were alone, Tzvi told his father a little about the family, whom he hardly saw now that he had become an underground soldier. When he finished the brief account, he updated him on the situation of the *Yishuv* and on events he had missed.

The biggest news was the death of Yaacov Raz, and the fact that "Yair" was back home for a visit.

"Yaacov Raz was assigned to Group 81 commanded by

Yaacov Eliav," Tzvi related. "His family immigrated to Israel from Afghanistan when he was fourteen. With his olive complexion, he looked like an Arab and knew all of their dialects. He worked in a grocery store to help support his destitute family. Yaacov bought his *Betar* uniform with the extra money he made by collecting empty bottles. He told his Jerusalem commander that the uniform was the most important thing in his life. When two Jews were stabbed to death while buying fruit in the Jaffa Gate plaza, Raziel ordered a reprisal attack. Immediately, Yaacov Raz volunteered to carry out the mission. Eliav worked on the bomb with Hevedke. Dressed like an Arab, Raz planted the device and fled. Several Arabs were killed and many wounded."

The way his son said it, Tevye could tell that he felt pleased with the operation's success. To the youth's way of thinking, the Arabs were an enemy. For slaughtering Jews, they deserved to die. He didn't believe, like Jabotinsky, that innocent lives had to be spared. The Arabs had declared war on the Jews without distinguishing between men, women, and children. According to their philosophy of war, everything was permitted. Tevye felt the same way.

Tzvi continued to recount what was to become the legend of Yaacov Raz.

"A week later, Raz was chosen to plant a powerful bomb in the Damascus Gate plaza. I worked on the plan with Eliav and David Raziel. This time, Raz dressed like an Arab porter. He carried the bomb in a large wicker basket strapped to his back and tied to his forehead. No one on our planning team knew that the Arab porters had called a work strike that morning. When Raz, a newcomer, showed up carrying the basket, he was yelled at and jostled for breaking the strike. As he set the basket down, one of the Arabs must have sensed something suspicious. He yelled out, 'He's a Jew! It's a bomb!' The Arabs attacked him, stabbing him with their knives. Thinking he was dead, they ran off. One of the Arabs alerted a policeman. The police blocked off the area, and a detonation expert arrived from the Criminal Investigations Department and dismantled the timer."

Tevye frowned. Not because the operation failed. What pained him was the fate of nineteen-year old, Yaacov Raz.

"Rav was in critical condition with thirteen knife wounds. The police brought him to the Government Hospital under heavy guard. The *Irgun* wanted to free him, but until he recovered, there was no chance of success. Doctors operated on him without using any aesthetics. Immediately after the surgery, the police started to interrogate him, wanting to know the names of everyone he knew in the *Irgun*. Agents from the Criminal Investigations Department never left his bedside. One of our sympathizers, a nurse in the hospital, witnessed the torture. The interrogators told Raz that they wouldn't give him a pain killer unless he cooperated with them and supplied them with names. He was conscious, but he refused to talk. At night, when he could no longer bear the pain, he waited till he was alone in the hospital room, then tore off all of his bandages. He bled to death without revealing anything. The *Irgun* pasted posters around the country, praising his great discipline, heroism, and self-sacrifice. It proclaimed, 'Step by step, victory will be attained with the blood of Anonymous Soldiers who go forth to battle to conquer or die, with an unquenchable willpower which cannot be broken by the threat of torture or force – not even by death.'"

Tevye listened in silence.

"A week later, we detonated a bomb in a crowded café adjacent to the site where Yaacov was stabbed. Ten Arabs were killed. Everyone understood the connection."

On other fronts, Tzvi reported, the *Haganah* had joined forces with the British in an all-out war against what was now called, "the Great Arab Revolt," which had claimed nearly five-hundred Jewish lives over the last three years. Extensive Arab attacks against key British installations, including bridges, trains, and the pipeline which brought oil from Iraqi petroleum fields to Haifa, finally forced the Mandate Government to crush the revolt. Ben Gurion named Tevye's grandson, Ben Zion, to be the *Haganah* liaison officer under the command of Orde Charles Wingate, the eccentric British soldier who was training "Special Night Squads" to raid mercenary camps and Arab villages with a ferocity that was snuffing out the coals of the rebellion. The *Irgun*, Tzvi related, had also done their share, conducting attacks and bombings against Arabs all over the country.

"During a planned attack in Haifa on a train filled with Arabs, a bomb was discovered under a seat and thrown out the train window," Tzvi told his father. "Two British police officers on the platform were accidently killed in the explosion. In retaliation, the police have stepped up their war against the *Irgun*. Yair has commanded everyone to go into hiding. There are no more meetings. He gives out orders one-by-one, or we come to him with plans and he approves them. That way, if someone is caught, he or she can't reveal information about the Organization. No one knows what anyone else is doing. The British have beefed up the Jewish Department of their anti-terror division, and a lot of our people have been arrested. Yair has become a main target. Unfortunately, it looks like he and David Raziel have come to a parting of ways. I met him for an hour at Hannie's place, but because of the crackdown, he doesn't sleep there at night. He's always on the run. He showed me a letter which Raziel wrote to Arthur Giles, Chief of the British Criminal Investigations Department. David explained that the *Irgun* had not intended to kill the British officers in Haifa, and he assured Giles that he was not an enemy of Great Britain in Palestine, stressing his admiration for English culture and for 'their noble effort to help the Jews.' Raziel stated that while he harbored criticism toward the British Administration for its increasingly pro-Arab policies, he and his comrades had no intention of uprooting Britain's rule in the country."

Tevye nodded. "*Haval*," he said. "It will be a pity if Stern and Raziel split up over this issue. I know that Avraham thinks differently about the British than David. I agree with him. Balfour was an extremely righteous individual. There may be another two or three honorable politicians like him in England, but behind their lofty airs and gentlemanly accents, the British have no great love for the Jews. As Rebbe Shimon Bar Yochai stated a long time ago, 'Esav hates Yaacov.' Why continue to stick our heads in the sand and pretend that the English have our best interests at heart?

They have fastened their clutches on Palestine, not to help us, but for their own selfish needs. "*Haval*," Tzvi's father repeated. "It's a shame that our two most dedicated people can't continue to work together. David is an excellent man, and a topnotch commander. We suffer from too much division already."

"Maybe you can meet with them to try to avoid a split," Tzvi suggested.

"Avraham is an *achshan*. More stubborn than a mule. I love him like a son, but when it comes to influencing his beliefs, *Gornisht helfn*, it's a waste of time, The fires of *Gehinom* will freeze over first. Besides, in advocating actions against the British, I believe that he's right. If we want this to be our country, it isn't enough to fight the Arabs alone."

"I've got good news for you, *Abba*," Tzvi said with a grin. "You can grow back your beard. Our people at British Police Headquarters say that since the Mufti fled the country, the search for his attempted assassin has ended. The British have had too much on their hands trying to quell the Arab Revolt and the countrywide retaliation bombings of the *Irgun*."

Tevye raised a hand to his chin. "Hmm," he remarked. "That's reassuring to know. Let's hope your mother agrees."

Calm weather accompanied the three-day sail through the Mediterranean Sea. On the eve of landing, well before dawn, Tevye went up to the deck to confer with the Captain. His snores filled the command room which smelled like a distillery. Adrian, the young first-mate, a noble Gentile if there was one, stood faithfully at the helm, steering the tilting, lopsided ship.

"Good morning," Tevye greeted him.

"It will be morning, Commander, in another hour," he said.

Tevye had already told had him ten times that he wasn't a commander, but the first-mate addressed him that way all the same.

"How far are we from shore?" Tevye asked.

"We should be able to see the coastline by the time the sun rises."

"Maybe we should turn off all lights, so we don't give the British a chance to spot us."

"Yes, sir, Commander, sir. On the double."

"Do you think we should wake the Captain?" Tevye asked.

"No reason to. I've done this before."

If everything went as planned, a specially-trained squad of *Betarim* would be waiting to bring them ashore.

"I'll be at the bow if you need me," Tevye told him. "At dawn I'll go below and get everyone ready."

"Good luck," the head sailor said.

"May God help us," Tevye responded.

"He will, Commander, don't you worry. God loves the Jews. Even though I'm a Christian, I know that Jews are God's chosen People. Since the beginning of time, everyone has been trying to kill you, and yet, you're still around. That's proof enough for me."

Indeed, Tevye reflected ironically. The Jews were God's Chosen People. The Almighty had chosen them to wander in exile without their own home for almost two-thousand years, and now that the dream of returning to Zion was in reach, an unpredictable sea, bands of marauding Arabs, and the British Empire were all doing their best to foil their efforts. Yes, the Jews were a Chosen People, but couldn't the good Lord occasionally choose someone else?

Grasping onto the railing of the deck, Tevye made his way to the bow and gazed out at the blackness, hoping to get a first glimpse of the Holy Land. Standing at the bow as it ascended and descended with the waves, the memory of his maiden voyage to the Promised Land flashed in his mind as clear as the rising sun. How could he ever forget how, at gunpoint, he had been forced to throw his beloved Golda's coffin overboard to appease a stormy sea and a wrathful captain who was convinced that the spreading plague and deaths aboard the endangered vessel were due to the fact that he was carrying a Jew's coffin in the hold of the ship. Tevye shivered from the memory.

Gripping onto the railing, Yonaton inched his way forward to the bow. "*Boker tov*," he said.

"It's early," Tevye told him.

"I couldn't sleep," the youth replied. "Any sign of land?"

"Not yet."

"I can't tell you how excited I feel." His eyes shone in the darkness. Joy flushed his face. He held a hand on his head so his kippah wouldn't blow away in the wind.

"You should wear a cap," Tevye told him.

"I forgot it down in the hold."

"When the Lord brought the exiles back to Zion, we were like those who dream," Tevye quoted from King David's Psalm.

"Our mouth was filled with laughter, and our tongues with ringing song," Yonaton continued.

The youth's enthusiasm returned Tevye to the present and to the miracle they were experiencing. Could there be a greater kindness than this – returning home to the Land of Israel? Could there be greater proof of the Almighty's faithfulness in fulfilling the promise he had made to Jews, that the day would come when He would remove their shackles and bring them back to their own Land? Although Tevye hadn't seen his wife, his daughters, and his sons for nearly half a year, his happiness over their imminent reunion was dwarfed by his joy in returning to *Eretz Yisrael*. He loved his family with a love beyond measure, but he loved the Land of Israel even more. Inspired by the overwhelming awareness that the dream of ages was coming true, Tevye recited the Psalm's final verses, forgetting the dangers which still lay ahead.

"Restore our fortunes, O Lord, like streams in the Negev. Those who are sowing in tears shall reap in joy. Sadly the farmer bears the bag of seed to the field; he shall come home with joy, bearing his sheaves."

"Your sheaves are the new immigrants down below," Yonaton said.

While Sigmund Freud had muttered a lot of nonsense during their meeting, the ailing doctor had said a wise thing when they spoke about Herzl. "A dream doesn't become reality through magic. It takes sweat, determination, and hard work," the psychiatrist said. When it came to the *mitzvah* of conquering *Eretz Yisrael*, you had to have *mesirut nefesh* – the willingness for self-sacrifice. The *ma'apilim* on the *S.S. Odyssey* were all prepared to risk their lives for the dream of reaching the Land of Israel, just like their ancestors of old. Tevye felt genuinely proud to have helped them on their journey.

6.

In another hour, when the coastline of *Eretz Yisrael* was sighted in the distance, a great cheer went up from the *ma'apilim* gathered on the deck of the *Odyssey*. Tevye felt an even greater thrill this time, due to the fact that his first sighting of the Promised Land had been shrouded in the anguish of having to throw Golda's coffin into the sea. "*Shecheyanu v'keyimanu, v'higeanu lazman hazeh!*" he said, thanking the good Lord for enabling him to reach this cherished moment. Passengers cried, unable to believe that they were about to fulfill a dream of two-thousand years. In place of the lifeless vacancy in Rabbi Novik's eyes, there was a shining glow. Still dressed in their striped Buchenwald uniforms, his students stood around him, unable to grasp the miracle that had raised them up from the valley of the shadow of death to bring them to what King David called, "*the Land of our life.*"

Tvzi stood on the bridge and announced that the journey hadn't ended. Their orders were to remain offshore, out of sight of the British, until a flag boat appeared to notify them of the point of arrival along the coast. A red flag meant Rishon L'Zion; a black flag meant the shore near Olat HaShachar; and a white flag meant Netanya.

Understanding that the worried passengers would feel calmer knowing all of the details, Tzvi outlined what lay ahead. He told them that a schooner would arrive after nightfall to ferry people to shore. The motorized vessel was built to accommodate fifty passengers, but since they had to avoid the British patrol boats in the area, the craft would take 250 and make two trips. People would have to stand in silence throughout the short trip, without lighting matches or flashlights to avoid detection.

"If British patrol boats try to seize us, there may be shooting," he warned, "so try to squat low and avoid panic. Unnecessary motion might cause the schooner to capsize.

Remain calm and follow instructions. I will travel with the first group, then return for the second. Remember, we have done this before without mishap, so trust in *Hashem*, have a little more patience, and He will bring us home in peace."

Tevye was impressed with the lad's coolness and leadership. Calmed by his words, the excited Jews waited like disciplined soldiers. A few hours later, a fishing boat appeared, a white flag hoisted on its mast. That meant Netanya was their goal, a half-day's sail away. Signaling the first-mate up in the cabin, Tzvi pointed northward.

The last leg of the journey was like a leisurely tourist excursion along the distant coastline. Passengers sat outside, enjoying the fresh air and sunshine, *kibbitzing* about the past and speculating about the future. Reaching the low buildings marking Netanya, Captain Papas extinguished the ship's engine. The *Odyssey* drifted quietly on the waves with a serenity that betrayed the pandemonium to come.

The small municipality of Netanya was named after Nathan Straus, the well-to-do Jew from New York who owned Macy's. Visiting Palestine with his brother in 1912, the millionaire was shocked by the rampart poverty of the Jewish community. Happy that he had the means to help the struggling *Yishuv*, he gave many generous contributions to a variety of charities and building projects. His brother and partner, Isidor, was far less enthused. After a few days surrounded by hardship and distress, he decided to return to England in time for the return voyage to America. Nathan (Natan in Hebrew) extended his stay in the Holy Land to continue his philanthropy, stumbling on a new coastal colony north of Tel Aviv, which came to be called *"Natan-Yah,"* or Netanya, which means "given by God," or "given by Natan." Consumed with his benevolent undertakings to help the Jews of Palestine, he literally "missed the boat" back to New York. The name of the ill-fated ocean liner was the *Titanic*. Straus's brother, Isidor, who fled from the miserable situation of the Jews of Palestine, went down with the ship.

With the onset of evening, the lights of the town flickered along the coastline. The boatful of immigrants slowly made its way toward shore. Anticipation increased. After a long, three-hour wait, a fishing schooner without lights appeared a short distance away. With a muffled hum, like a ghost ship, it slowly made its way alongside the *Odyssey*. Hebrew voices sounded from its direction. The crew of the freighter hurled ropes down to the much smaller craft. The schooner's sails were furled and tied down at the base of their masts. Its motor continued to hum.

Signal lights flashed onshore – three shorts bursts, followed by darkness, then another four flashes.

"That's our all-clear signal," Tzvi said. "Let's go."

He scaled down a rope ladder to the schooner with his father right behind him. Yonaton remained on the freighter with the passengers who would come to shore on the next sortie. Slowly, and miraculously as well, 250 *ma'aplim* squeezed onto the fishing boat. The blackness of night sheltered their being seen from the shore. With the weight of its passengers, the schooner sank into the water until it was literally surrounded by waves. Though the sea was reasonably calm, the offshore waves often rose above the heads of the disciplined but frightened immigrants. The pitch blackness, coupled with the rush of the wind and surf, caused all hearts to pound. Almost immediately, everyone was drenched. Tevye remembered that he never learned how to swim. Neither had many of the others. Everyone prayed fervently while the schooner brought them closer to Holy Land's shore. People were pressed so close together, there was no need to hold on. After some twenty minutes, more signal lights flashed from the coast. As if in pre-planned synchronization, a wave raised the fishing boat like a hand and sent it gliding toward the beach. Some twenty meters from shore, sand scraped the hull. Tzvi leapt into the water holding a rope. Trudging through the shallow water, he let out a sharp whistle and ran up the beach. Two figures raced out from the sand dunes and grabbed the long rescue line. Two horses galloped along the shore, their riders clutching rifles. Overcoming their desire to cheer, the new immigrants jumped off the schooner and waded to shore, clutching each other for safety. Grabbing onto the taut safety rope, fathers and mothers carried young children toward the beach. An arm grabbed Tevye. It belonged to Boaz, his twenty-year-old son. Young *plugot* cadets, men and women trained by *Betar*, dressed in khaki shorts, with shotguns slung over their shoulders, joined in the rescue effort. *Ma'apalim* – "climbers of mountains" – fell to their knees, not in exhaustion, but to kiss the sands of Zion.

On a ridge overlooking the beach, Avraham Stern stood observing the landing, attired in his usual suit and Stetson hat. Before anyone could celebrate, a roar of trucks filled the air. Surprised, Stern turned toward the road. The probing headlights of two British army trucks pierced the darkness. Calmly, he stepped toward the road, raised one of the Tommy guns that he had purchased in Finland, and released a blast of automatic fire at the windshield of the onrushing vehicle. The glass shattered. The driver collapsed over the steering wheel, and the lead truck swerved off the road, heading straight for Stern who dived out of the way. The truck sailed off the ridge and plummeted down toward the beach. Before Stern could stand, the second truck barreled by, followed by an open army jeep with a gunner. Machine gun fire burst in the air. Bullets whizzed by Stern on all sides. Undaunted, he stood up, but the vehicles were already beyond the range of his weapon.

At the bottom of the ridge, the lead truck had turned into a ball of flames. The British army jeep appeared at the top of a sand dune. Its powerful searchlight lit up the panic on the beach as the *ma'apilim* ran screaming in all directions. On horseback, Nachshon aimed his rifle, and with one shot, knocked out the jeep's searchlight. His next shot hit the helmeted gunner in the face. The Yemenite youth's horse-backed brother, Ariel, charged forward on his steed, heading for the second British Army truck like a knight in armor charging forward with his lance. As British soldiers jumped out from the canvas-covered vehicle, Nachshon opened fire. Ariel galloped forward and lobbed a grenade through the window of the driver's cabin. A powerful explosion blew the truck to smithereens. Tevye and Tzvi watched the fireworks from the beach as if they were watching a Hollywood war movie.

"Very impressive," Tevye said, proud of his wife's younger brothers.

The stunned British soldiers who hadn't been targeted by Nachshon, or killed in the grenade blast, began to fire haphazardly into the crowd on the beach. Appearing at the crest of a sand dune behind them, Stern triggered his "Washington" until the Brits lay dead along the dirt roadway. Once again quiet returned to the shore, with only the sound of wind and waves.

Brushing the dirt off his suit, Stern gazed out at the beach and waved toward Tevye.

"*Baruch haba*!" he shouted. "Welcome home!"

The signal officer ran over to Tzvi with his powerful flashlight.

"Signal the freighter to head up north," Tzvi ordered. "We can't take the chance of another landing here. We'll rendezvous with them in Hadera."

Kissing his father's cheek, the young *Irgun* officer ran back to the water and swam back to the schooner. The crew pushed it seaward, freeing its hull from the shallows. Tzvi hopped on board and the motor started, setting back off toward the *Odyssey*.

The young *Betarim* on shore began to march the new arrivals in rows of three along the beach. A trek through an orange grove would take them to a field where buses would transport them to Rosh Pina and other *moshavim* waiting to absorb them.

Ariel rode up to Tevye on his horse. He extended a hand to his much older brother-in-law, and Boaz helped boost his father onto the animal's back. Avraham Stern grabbed Nachshon's hand, and, without any additional help, mounted the steed borrowed from Olat HaShachar.

"How's my wife?" Tevye asked.

"She's waiting at Hannie's place to greet you with a hot bowl of soup," Ariel answered.

With a wide sweep of his arm, Stern shouted out, "*Yalla*! Let's go!"

Back by the dirt road, Rabbi Novik and his students stood near the twisted remains of the army truck, staring down at the dead British officers.

Lifting his gaze to the star-filled heavens, the Rabbi quoted a verse of *Tehillim*, "*Thou shall break them with a rod of iron. Thou shall shatter them into pieces like the urn of a potter.*"

Tevye instructed Ariel to ride over to the group of Buchenwald survivors.

"Come on, Rabbi," Tevye called. "You and your students have to join ranks with the others."

"Look," the frail man said, in a voice filled with wonder. "Gentiles can be gunned down, just like Jews."

Chapter Fifteen
WINGATE CRUSHES THE REVOLT

To David Ben Gurion, the British Intelligence Captain, Orde Charles Wingate, was "a pain in the arse." For several months, the Bible-toting Christian had badgered the Jewish and British leadership in Palestine, demanding they put an immediate end to the three-year-old "Great Arab Uprising" that was terrorizing Jewish and British targets alike. "If the British Army can't defeat ten-thousand, camel-eating *Ay-rabs*, then the Mandate Administration should pack up their bags and head home," he declared. The famed and eccentric militarist presented each official he met with a detailed proposal he had written, entitled: "Secret Appreciation of Possibilities of Night Movements by Armed Forces of the Crown, with Object of Putting an end to Terrorism in Palestine." He wrote:

"There is only one way to deal with the worsening situation - to persuade the Arab gangs that, in their predatory raids, there is every chance of their running into a government force which is determined to destroy them. The proposed special units will carry the offensive to the enemy, take away his initiative and keep him off-balance. They will operate at night and will surprise the enemy in their encampments and in the villages across the country where they seek shelter. The special force will be a mixed British-Jewish unit. The British have the formal training, the equipment and official support. The *Haganah* knows the land. Night operation will give the units the advantages of shock and surprise...."

Initially, as Arab attacks against British installations and personal increased, the Mandatory Government imposed martial law, arresting Arabs marauders without trial and sending them off to detention camps. British reinforcements arrived from Egypt and England, including the famous, 11th Hussar Division, supported by airplanes and Rolls-Royce armored cars with machine gun mounts. An explosives unit from the Royal Engineers joined the campaign.

When Britain continued to suffer heavy losses, Archibald Wavell, Commander of British Forces in Palestine, finally gave Wingate permission to organize the special units, remarking that the passionate soldier was more of a Zionist than Ben Gurion himself. Frustrated by the ongoing violence, and fearing that London would appoint a new Chief Commander if British losses continued, Wavell ordered the Jewish Agency to cooperate with Wingate. The Mandatory Government didn't officially recognize the *Haganah*, forbidding Jews to harbor more than a specific amount of weapons, lest a Jewish fighting force in Palestine become a threat to their rule. But Wingate insisted that the Jews would prove far better fighters than the soldiers of the Queen. In agreeing to the plan, the Mandate Authority hoped that by strengthening the *Haganah*, they could lessen the appeal of the *Irgun*, whose dramatic reprisal attacks were drawing more and more public favor amongst the Jews.

While Ben Gurion preached a policy of restraint in dealing with the ongoing Arab uprising, believing it would win, in the long run, political benefits for the *Yishuv*, he was secretly pleased with the plan. Not harboring any love for the Arabs, and frustrated by their militant leadership which rejected all proposals for peaceful co-existence, he also saw the British-*Haganah* cooperation as a path to bolstering the *Haganah's* dwindling popularity. People regarded it as a purely defensive force which had proved impotent in combatting Arab aggression. Wanting to move Perchik Aronov's son along in the ranks of the organization, he ordered *Haganah* commander, Yitzhak Sadeh, to appoint Ben Zion as Wingate's liaison officer.

Walking into the classroom in Ein Harod, Ben Zion was surprised to find Wingate playing with a gramophone. The contraption was a wooden box with a wide-mouthed horn rising above it like a trumpet-shaped flower. The record laying on the turntable rotated slowly as Wingate cranked up the handle which operated the spring-driven motor inside the box. Amazingly, the strident and bellicose chords of a symphony sounded from the contraption.

"Rossini's 'William Tell Overture,'" Wingate remarked with what looked like a proud smile, as if he had composed the symphony himself.

Ben Zion had spent two weeks recruiting the best *Haganah* soldiers for the project. He knew that he had been awarded the commission because he was the son of Perchik Aronov, and not for his own talents. Whether Ben Gurion had chosen him out of kindness, or to assuage guilt feelings left over from the Stavsky murder trial, or to win the favor of his step-mother, Sonia Aronov, Ben Zion didn't know. Thirty young candidates, looking fit and athletic in their khaki shirts and shorts, filed inside for their first meeting with the illustrious British commander who stood by a table at the front of the room, winding up the gramophone. An Old Testament Bible lay on every desk. When everyone was seated, the scraggly-bearded Wingate straightened and said, "Listen!"

No one moved a muscle. Trumpets and violins sounded. Cymbals crashed. Drums rumbled. Trombones raced to catch up to their furious beat. The trumpets blared, as if summoning troops to war. Wingate waved his arms like the conductor of an orchestra, ordering each instrument to join in the battle. With a quickening pace, he commanded his musical soldiers forward, each instrument in its place, musicians transformed into soldiers, drums into explosions, cellos into bombs, until the pounding of horses' hooves seemed to shake the earth. The rhythm quickened and the music grew louder and louder until it reached a thundering crescendo, climaxing, climaxing, climaxing until the enemy was utterly vanquished and victory achieved.

Finally, with the triumphant crescendo, the recruits stopped holding their breaths.

"That, gentlemen, is war," Wingate proclaimed in Hebrew. "The symphony of war. Keep it in your heads. Hear it over and over in your brains. Fill your hearts with its music. Think of nothing else. Hear the resounding rhythm ring in your ears. Hear the drums. Hear the violins. Let the echo of the trumpets blare in your heads. Do you all understand?" he shouted. "Do you?!"

"Yes, sir!" everyone called out in unison.

"No you don't!" Wingate yelled. "But you will. War is more than a science. War is a grand waltz to music. War is a celebration of life – not of death. The God of Israel is not a vengeful God. When He orders the Children of Israel to destroy the wicked and idol worshipping Canaanites, He is not advocating wanton slaughter. The goal is to uproot evil from the Earth in order to make the world a better place."

Ben Zion had heard something similar from Rabbi Kook who had spoken about war in a lecture that Ben Zion had attended in Jerusalem before he broke away from the shackles of religion and joined his father in Tel Aviv. Rabbi Kook said that the uprooting of tyrants purified and uplifted all of existence, preparing the way for *Mashiach* and world salvation. The wars of Israel, he taught, were the wars of *Hashem*, purging the world of the darkness of evil so that the light of God could appear in all of its benevolent goodness.

"Is what I am saying clear?" Wingate asked once more.

"Yes, commander!" everyone replied.

"Listen again!"

The out-of-the-ordinary Englishman cranked up the gramophone a second time, set the needle down in the middle of the record, and let them hear the bombastic symphony with its frenzied, unrestrained, ever-climaxing call to arms.

"Now do you understand?" he shouted. "A commander is like an orchestra conductor. His soldiers are his musicians. Their weapons are musical instruments. Rise up to the joy and beauty of the symphony of war! Rise up to the path of Heavenly Redemption! Cast aside all doubt and worry. Expel from your minds all weak-hearted notions of compassion and all misplaced feelings of mercy. We are facing the coldhearted killers of women and children. They don't merely murder – they hack their victims to pieces. They smash open their brains and stuff the bloodied white matter into their mouths. They rape women again and again, even after they've died. It is our job to conquer the enemy and to send these human devils to hell! Is that understood?!"

"Yes, sir!" his soldiers called back.

"Louder!"

"YES, SIR!"

"Very well," Wingate said, as if spent from some kind of religious ecstasy. He picked up a Bible from the table.

"This is to be our textbook," he said. "Our primer of Jewish military history."

Suddenly, his eyes narrowed and he stared keenly at one of the soldiers seated before him. His head flinched backwards in surprise.

"What is the meaning of this?!" he asked in stupefied wonder. "Can it be?" His glance turned inquiringly to Ben Zion who blushed.

"Good Lord," Wingate muttered, at a loss for words. Turning back to the soldier, he said, "If I am not mistaken, you are a woman."

"Yes, sir, Captain Wingate," she answered.

"On your feet!" he barked.

The young woman stood up. Shosh was her name. Ben Zion had chosen her because she could shoot a rifle more accurately than most men.

"At attention!" Wingate commanded.

The soldier straightened her back.

"You are a woman, indeed," the Englishman said.

A few soldiers couldn't stifle their giggles.

"Enough frivolity!" Wingate snapped. "There will be no improper behavior in this unit. There is a time and a place for everything. Levity will only tolerated at victory celebrations after the enemy has been destroyed."

"She is one of the best sharpshooters we have," Ben Zion explained, defending his decision to recruit women soldiers.

"I don't care if she can fly," Wingate answered. "Women do not have a place in the army."

Another short-haired soldier stood up. "I object," she said.

Wingate stared at her with a dumbfounded expression. He turned to Ben Zion. "What is the matter with you, sir? This is a commando unit, not a class in cooking."

"Women are an integral part of the *Haganah*. They fight alongside the men," Ben Zion informed him.

"This is not the *Haganah*. This a real army. Our mission is to seek out, attack, and eradicate the enemy, not to sit behind haystacks and wait for poachers to approach within shooting range. Mr. Ben Gurion may have other ideas about fighting, but if his way worked, I wouldn't be here. Our way is not through appeasement and concession, but through instilling terror and fear in the heart of our opponent. Compassion will be reserved for ourselves and for the people we are defending – not for the enemy. Is this clear?"

"We are not afraid to fight," one of the women declared.

Wingate frowned. Debating women was neither his custom nor his forte. "In this Holy Book, you won't find female warriors. In fact, in the Israelite tradition, it is forbidden for a women to even wear the uniform of a man. Jewelry are to be her ornaments, not arms."

"What about Devorah?" the other girl asked in a challenging voice.

"Devorah was a prophetess and judge, not a soldier. It was Barak who led the troops."

"And Yael?" the other asked.

"Yael killed Sisera by hammering a tent peg into his skull, a utensil used in the home, not in war. She too wasn't a soldier."

"What about Judith?" Ben Zion asked.

Wingate turned to him in annoyance, worried that such a lengthy debate with his recruits, over a matter so superficial, would lessen their respect and fear of him, qualities needed to lead soldiers into battle. While Judith did not appear in the *Tanach*, the scholarly militarist knew about her from having read extensively about Jewish military history, including the *Book of Judith* and *The Jewish Wars* of Josephus Flavius.

"Judith severed the head of Holofernes with his sword, not hers," he explained. "Perhaps, you could call her an undercover agent, not a soldier. Her weapons were her seductive beauty and strong wine. The Muslim mercenaries who Haj Amin al-Husseini has hired to lead the Great Arab Revolt do not drink wine. If you two ladies were to enter the tents of these soldiers of *Allah*, you would be raped and dismembered immediately and thrown outside as food for ravens and crows. And now, I bid you good day. If anyone objects, he is invited to leave as well. Time is short. The task is great, and I will not tolerate any further interruptions."

The men glanced around at one another, but no one stood up. Piqued by their dismissal, the girls threw back their heads haughtily and strut out from the classroom, adding a little feminine sway to their gait. A glow of laughter shined in the eyes of the men, but not a peep left their lips.

"Lest some of you harbor doubts or ill feelings about this most unnecessary and superfluous issue, while a woman may be an excellent sharpshooter, put a thirty kilo knapsack on her back, and have her run ten kilometers over mountains and rugged terrain. Her subsequent firing accuracy will be much poorer than a man's. And should she be needed to carry a wounded comrade on a stretcher over long distances, she will collapse under the burden. Plus," he concluded, holding up the Bible, "a woman's presence in a military camp leads to immorality, and, as the Torah states, the Israelite army camp must be kept holy at all times, and in all places, to insure God's deliverance in battle."

The *Haganah* soldiers sat quietly as Wingate lifted the record from the gramophone and slid it carefully into a large envelope.

"Please stand," he said.

Quickly, everyone jumped to their feet.

"Please sit," he ordered politely.

In unison, the soldiers all sat as one.

"Please stand."

"Please sit."

"Please stand."

"Please sit."

After the thirtieth time, the young soldiers began to feel tired and breathe heavily. Wingate wanted to return them to an army atmosphere of command and obedience, command and obedience, and to let them know that the fun and games were over.

"If you decide to continue in this unit, you will train and train and train, day and night, until you become serious soldiers. I don't know what you are used to, but here, we mean business. You will learn to live like animals in the wilderness. To defeat a cruel and ruthless enemy, you will learn to be crueler and more ruthless than he is. To fight a savage, you will become even more savage. Not out of a lust for killing, but out a love for goodness and truth. The Children of Israel were not a ruthless people, but they ruthlessly slaughtered the heathen nations in the Land because they knew that in obeying *Hashem's* command, they were cleansing the planet from barbaric idolatry and evil. Is that understood?"

"Yes, sir! Commander, sir," they shouted in unison.

"*Kayn HaMifaked*!" Wingate shouted back.

"*Kayn HaMifaked*!" they repeated.

"I count it as my privilege to help you fight your battle," Wingate told them. "I am not a Jew, but I know that God has chosen the Jewish People to lead the world out of the darkness of idolatry and the gamut of man-made credos which have led mankind astray. I also know that since I am a British officer, you view me with distrust, due to the fact that my Government has betrayed the historic mission which they took upon themselves in promising to help establish a Jewish Homeland in Palestine. May my efforts here be an atonement for their negligence, failure, and unwillingness to carry out their commission. And may our joint work together be an atonement for the falsehoods and betrayals of your own Jewish leaders, who have ingrained in your consciences that the Jewish People, even in their ancestral Homeland, must continue to be like sheep led to slaughter."

As the Englishman spoke, Ben Zion recalled voices from his youth and the fiery speeches of Moshe Segal, Abba Achemeir, Uri Zvi Greenberg, and Avraham Stern.

"In my humble opinion, the Jewish soldier can be the finest soldier in the world," Wingate declared. "The soldiers of Joshua ben Nun, King David, Yehuda the Maccabee, and Bar Kochva, have no equals in the history of warfare. It is no coincidence that we are gathered here, in the Jezreel Valley, in Ein Herod, to begin our training," Wingate said. "Who can tell me what happened here in days long past?"

No one answered.

"Please open your military textbooks to the '*Book of Judges*,' Chapter Seven, Verse One. What is your name?" he asked the first soldier in the first row.

"Moshe Dayan," the young man answered.

"Please read the verse aloud," Wingate requested.

"'*Then Yerubba'al, who is Gideon, and all the people who were with him, rose up early, and camped beside Ein Harod, so that the host of Midian was on the north side of them, by the Hill of Mor, in the valley*'."

"Thank you," Wingate said. "For seven years, the Midianites and Amalekites attacked the Israelites in consequence of their disobedience to God. The Israelite leaders turned to Gideon to lead the armies of Israel against their enemies. Twenty-two thousand soldiers volunteered to fight, but Hashem told Gideon to reduce the number, so that people would understand that his victory came, not from numbers, but from the hand of the Lord. Gideon reduced his troops to ten thousand, but the number was still too great. So with only three-hundred select soldiers, he led a Jewish commando force on a night attack against the Midianite camp. With shofars blaring, and with torches ablaze, the Jews sent the enemy running."

Ben Zion frowned. He knew that Wingate had a reputation for carrying out unorthodox military operations during his service in other British colonies, but he didn't expect that Bible Studies would be a part of the training.

"Can I have another volunteer, please," their new commander asked.

The *Haganah* recruit sitting beside Moshe Dayan raised his hand.

"Name, please."

"Yigal Allon."

"Please read aloud for us, in the '*First Book of Samuel*,' Chapter Fifteen, Verses One to Three."

The young fighter flipped through the pages of the thick book until he found the verses. He read them aloud in a deep bass voice which made the Biblical Hebrew echo through the pages of time. "*And Samuel said to Saul, 'The Lord sent me to anoint thee to be king over His People, over Israel. Now therefore hearken to the voice of the words of the Lord. Thus says the Lord of Hosts – I remember what Amalek did to Israel, how he ambushed him along the way, when he came up from Egypt. Now go and smite Amalek, and utterly destroy everything they have, and spare them not; rather slay both man and woman, infant and sucking, ox and sheep, camel and mules.'"*

Wingate continued down the line of recruits, asking each one to read a verse of two from the Bible:

"'Concerning the cities of the nations, which the Lord your God gives you for an inheritance, you shall not save alive anything that breathes, but you shall utterly annihilate them.'"

"'When the L-d your God shall deliver them before you, then you shall smite them and destroy them completely. You shall make no covenant with them, nor show mercy toward them.'"

"'And at that time, Joshua turned back and conquered Hazor, and slew its king with the sword. And they smote all the souls that were in it with the edge of the sword, utterly destroying them - there was not anything left that breathed. And he burnt Hazor with fire. And all of the cities of those kings, and all of their kings, did Joshua conquer and smite with the edge of the sword, and he completely laid waste to them, as Moses, the servant of the Lord, commanded.'"

"You can't turn verses from the Bible into military orders," one of the recruits protested.

Wingate answered in a dry, strait-forward fashion which made his meaning clear.

"As I previously stated, anyone who wants to pull out of this mission can do so now. I have a job to do, and I intend to accomplish it in quickest and most effective way possible. I am not looking to win a popularity contest, and I have no intention of entering politics. In other words, I don't give a damn what people say. I have a plan, and I have crystal-clear orders. How they need to be carried out are written down in this Holy Book."

Once again, Wingate held up the Bible. The young soldier looked around for support amongst his comrades, as if to say, "Let's get the hell out of here before this madmen gets us all court-martialed for war crimes against humanity." When no one rallied to his side, he stood up, and strode out of the classroom. Wingate faced his trainees with a stern expression. He thought for a moment, looked about the room as if he were waiting to hear a Voice out of Heaven, then stared at the *Haganah* candidates with small smile that was more like a grimace.

"Once again, gentlemen, let it be clear. We are fighting a savage enemy to whom everything is permissible. For them, morals do not exist. In their vocabulary, the word conscience is not to be found. Many of them are ruthless mercenaries from Syria and Iraq, hired by the Grand Mufti to wage war against the Jews. And against British targets as well. They get paid to kill, to maim, to slaughter, and to destroy. After they carry out their massacres, they hide like rats in the woods. It is our job to seek them out, to discover their hiding places, and to eradicate them from the face of the earth. They are paid killers. This is not their land. When we put the fear and terror of God in them, believe me, if they escape our swords, they will run back to their own countries in fear. Too many Jews have been butchered. Your brothers. The children of God. No more appeasement. No more *havlaga*. No more concession and surrender. If you follow me into battle, this 'Great Revolt' will be suppressed within in a month. You have my word."

The young Jews were silent. All of them had undergone extensive training, but no commander had ever spoken like the Bible-quoting Englishman.

"You are all familiar with the story of Purim, are you not?" he inquired. "The heroes of the tale are the beloved figures of Esther and Mordechai, who command the Jews *"to stand up for themselves and destroy, slay, and annihilate any armed force of any people or province that might assault them, with their little ones and women, and to plunder their goods."*

Wingate gazed dramatically around the room. "If I am not mistaken, Jews read the story twice on the holiday of *Purim*, when they read the *Megilla* – is that not correct?"

No one volunteered to answer.

"You are Jews, are you not?" Wingate asked with a tone of unmistaken derision. Everyone in the classroom remained silent.

"Can someone recite the first paragraph of *'Shema Yisrael?'*"

More silence. Ben Zion remembered all three paragraphs of the *Shema* by heart, but he kept quiet, not wanting his comrades to know that he had been raised in a religious home.

"I see," Wingate said with a frown. "It seems that before we can turn you into real soldiers, we will have to turn you into real Jews."

Ben Zion glanced around at his friends, certain that everyone must be angry with him for having selected them for the mission.

"Everyone has heard of King David, correct? Poet, warrior, king. Scion of the *Mashiach*. The '*Sweet Singer of Israel*.' Even the Christians revere his Psalms and base their liturgy on his words."

He turned to Ben Zion.

"Mr. Aronov. Could you please read for us Verse Twenty-Seven, from the '*First Book of Samuel*,' Chapter Eighteen?"

"What now?" Ben Zion thought, searching for the passage. Obediently, he read it aloud.

"'*Before time had passed, David arose and went, he and his soldiers, and slew two hundred Philistines. And David brought their foreskins and gave all of them to the king, that he might become the king's son-in-law*.'"

"A fitting gift for a king," Wingate said. "Believe me, as long as David was around, the Philistines ceased their aggression against the Jews."

Moshe Dayan raised his hand. "I have a question, Commander. Do you plan to cut off the foreskins of the mercenaries and send them to the Grand Mufti?"

A few of the soldiers couldn't contain their chuckles. Even Captain Wingate smiled.

"No," he replied. "I plan to castrate them completely and hang the trophies up on the branches of trees for the whole Arab world to see."

And that's just what he did.

2.

At the top of the hill, Captain Wingate peered through his pair of long binoculars, then handed them to Ben Zion for a look. Dark camouflage paint smeared their faces. Though the trainees had studied night surveillance, in the blackness of the Galilee forest, Ben Zion had trouble reading the woody landscape. Back and forth he searched, trying to spot the encampment of tents in the glade at the base of the hill.

"Just like the reconnaissance report read," Wingate said quietly. "I count nine tents. If there are six fighters in each tent - that totals fifty-four."

Finally, Ben Zion managed to locate the tents, whose sloping, canvas covers reflected the dim moonlight.

"Assuming there are guards, we'll be facing fifty-eight to sixty soldiers."

In the darkness, the commander's eyes were barely discernible under the brim of his pith helmet.

"We only number twenty-four," Ben Zion noted.

"We have the factor of surprise in our favor. Plus the fact that most of the Philistines are sleeping. When we strike at the camp, they'll be in shock."

The encampment of Arab terrorists was one of an estimated twenty that the mercenary leader, Fawzi el-Kaukji, has positioned throughout the *Galil*, in easy striking distance to Britain's Iraq-Haifa pipeline and the isolated Jewish colonies scattered along Palestine's northern border. The Tripoli-born el-Kaukji commanded a gang of one-thousand ruthless mercenaries, who killed for money, not in the name of Arab nationalism. From his hiding place in Damascus, Haj Amin al-Husseini had hired the powerful el-Kaukji to slaughter Jews at random and to strike at British installations, in his efforts to intimidate the British and win as much control of Palestine as he could.

"Bring the troops forward," Wingate told the Young *Haganah* fighter, not at all sure how Aronov, or the rest of the jelly-bellied Jews, would stand up to the test.

Ben Zion headed back down the hillside toward the waiting Special Night Squad, four of whom weren't soldiers at all - a British bugler, a Jewish violinist and trumpet player recruited from the Tel Aviv Symphony, and the stocky British cook who had been taught to crash cymbals together at climatic moments in the "William Tell Overture." All through their three weeks of rigorous, "guerilla warfare" training, the combined commando force of Jewish and British soldiers had listened to the strident symphony every day until its echo hardly ever left their ears. Drills were conducted at night in the forests of the Galilee. Wingate led the training himself. Night crawling, night camouflage, night navigating, night shooting, training with sabers, sticks, bayonets, and spears, marathon running over mountainous terrain, basic first aid, and survival skills. Soldiers with previous riding experience spent hours getting to know their steeds. Special scouts and Arab informers worked independently to prepare a list of targets. Wingate's strategy was simple – to eradicate as many enemy soldiers in the least amount of time, without losses to the SNS. Splitting the company in two, Wingate led the first group out on the day-long trek over the mountains to the mercenary encampment, while the second group finished preparations for an attack on an Arab village on the outskirts of Haifa.

Ben Zion brought the squad quietly up to the hilltop where Wingate waited, peering through his binoculars.

"Everyone will follow me down the hillside," he told them. "Before reaching the glen, we will halt and assume our positions, just as we practiced. No one is to cross the line until I give the signal. If anything happens to me, Ben Zion will give the command to advance. We are not here to capture terrorists. There will be no prisoners. These creatures are savages and ruthless killers. After a few lessons like this, their friends will flee from the country, believe me. Keep the music full volume in your ears and remember the words of King David."

Opening his Bible to the *Book of Psalms*, Wingate read out in a quiet voice:

"God of vengeance, Lord God of vengeance, appear! Arise, Thou Judge of the earth, render to the arrogant what they deserve. How long shall the wicked, O Lord, how long shall the wicked exult? They boast and speak arrogantly, the evildoers act insolently. They crush Thy People, O Lord, and afflict Thy heritage. The widow and the stranger they slay, and the fatherless they murder. And they think the Lord does not see, the God of Jacob does not observe."

Wingate faced his soldiers. "Gentleman, you are not merely soldiers of the Crown, or soldiers of the *Haganah*. You are now warriors of the Lord, God of Israel, King of Heaven and Earth. In His holy Name, we set upon the enemy to destroy them for the sake of justice, righteousness, and peace."

With a wave of his arm, he beckoned his troops forward, with a call that was to become the standard cry for all commanders in the armies of the modern State of Israel, "*Acharei*! After me!"

Occasional branches and twigs snapped under the boots of the soldiers as they followed their commander down the last stretch of the hillside. The Arabs felt so secure in their hide-out, they hadn't placed guards around the encampment. Until now, all British attacks had been staged in the daytime along the main roads, or in close proximity to British installations, while the Jews confined themselves to defense alone, almost never venturing beyond the boundaries of their settlements. Forty meters away from the clearing, Wingate raised a hand to stop their advance. Like the conductor of an orchestra, he pointed to his four musicians, then to his sharpshooters, then to his kerosene carrier, then to his arms-bearer who handed him and Ben Zion two-old fashioned bows and arrows whose heads were rapped with strips of cotton and cloth. Carefully, the Tel Aviv violinist removed his delicate instrument from its case. The trumpeter fingered his keys. The British bugler held his horn to his lips. The stocky cymbals player held his arms wide, prepared to strike the first blow.

For some reason, Ben Zion thought of his grandfather, Tevye. A Yiddish expression leapt into his head. "*Meshugener*," he thought, watching Wingate dip an arrow into the can of kerosene. The arms-bearer lit a match and held it to a torch which burst into flame. Wingate tilted his arrow into the torch and it too ignited with a muffled whooshing explosion.

With practiced skill, he fired the flaming arrow. It arced in the air and struck into a tent, whose dry canvas burst into flames.

"Now!" Wingate called out.

The bugle blared. The trumpeter trumpeted, and the violinist tilted his head to his instrument and commenced with the climax of the William Tell Overture with rapid thrusts of a horse-haired bow. "Da da da da - da da da da da da da. Da da da da - da da da da da da da...." The cymbal sounded with a loud clang that reverberated through the forest. Before Ben Zion could set an arrow into his bow, Wingate shot another flaming missile into the air. A second tent burst into flame. Screams filled the glen below.

"Don't fire until you see the whites of their eyes!" the shiny-eyed Wingate commanded.

Ben Zion pulled back the string of the bow until his fist reached his ear, then without flinching, he calmly released the end of the flaming arrow, just as he had practiced. Miraculously, the arrow streaked through the air and found its target. The tent caught fire. Its neighbor also started to burn with the arrival of Wingate's next arrow.

With the roar of the frenzied music baring in his ears, Ben Zion shot another flaming arrow into the air.

The first Arabs who ran screaming from the cones of fire were greeted by a blaze of rifle fire. One after another, the terrified mercenaries fell dead or wounded to the ground. Each fleeing Arab faced a barrage of angry bullets. Losing their wits in their panic, they all left their weapons inside the burning tents. Ignited by the fire, bullets exploded in all directions.

"Charge!" Wingate yelled.

Dropping his bow, he raced forward, raising his saber in the air.

"If it moves – kill it!" he shouted, as the outdoor symphony continued to play.

Following the orders of the well-rehearsed battle plan, the *Haganah* sharpshooters raced forward, firing on the run. Stopping in a line, they took aim and gunned down the helpless mercenaries. With nothing in his mind but the clash of the cymbals and the rapturous chords of the music, Ben Zion squeezed the trigger of his rifle, savoring the explosion and release of every bullet. His heart leapt in secret ecstasy as each mercenary crashed to the ground, as if he were the Arab who had shot and killed his father on the beach in Tel Aviv.

"Cease fire!" Wingate commanded. Then, holding up his sword, he called out, in a mix of English and Hebrew,

"Assault Squad 2! *Kadima*!" British troopers ran forward brandishing their sabers. In a wild charge, they chased after the mercenaries, striking them fatally with their swords. Wingate walked through the carnage on the ground, searching for survivors. Seeing the twitch of a finger, or hearing a groan, he aimed his pistol and fired, leaving no one alive. When he ran out of bullets, he drew his other pistol and continued to shoot at the bodies still breathing on the ground.

Then he raised his hand in the air. "Stop the music!" he shouted.

Silence fell over the glen. Only the burning tents crackled. Soldiers panted with heavy breaths. A few Arabs ran off alive into the woods.

"Dayan; Allon!" Wingate barked. "After them!"

The two Jews sprinted off. In less than a minute, a roar of gunshots shattered the forest stillness once again.

Wingate stared around at the slaughter. "What are you waiting for?!" he yelled. "Dismember them all!"

No one responded.

"Dismember them!" I said. "That's what they do to their victims!"

Ben Zion glanced around at the faces of his comrades. No one volunteered.

Wingate turned toward the Jews. "Do you want to win this war?!" he shouted. "I am doing this for you! Do you want the mercenaries of the Mufti to murder and rape more of your women?! Do you?!"

With a wild anger in his eyes, he glared at the *Haganah* soldiers.

"Have you forgotten King David?!" he shouted. "He was a Jew! He knew how to deal with the enemy! Are *Haganah* soldiers holier than he was?! I command you to dismember them now!"

"*Yalla*," said one of the Jews. Stepping forward, he drew his sword from its sheath.

"*Yalla*!" Wingate yelled, turning toward the British soldiers.

"*Yalla*!" they called out, banishing their sabers.

""*Halleluyah, halleluyah!*" the eccentric commander shouted. "*Blessed be those who come in the Name of the Lord!*"

3.

Wingate was only beginning. Leading each foray of the Special Night Squads himself, he ruthlessly attacked as many targets as he could, one after another, knowing that the British Government would, sooner or later, cave in to Arab complaints and expediently transfer the "unorthodox and uncontrollable troublemaker" and "Zionist sympathizer" to lead a troop of pardoned convicts against some native uprising in the jungles of Africa, or in the rice paddies of India, where Mahatma Ghandi's non-violent opposition to British colonization was gaining millions of followers every month.

In a series of anti-British attacks, Arab marauders had blown up the Iraqi-Haifa pipeline in several unguarded places, damaged British railway lines with mines, and bombed a bus transporting British soldiers. The same gang regularly ambushed Jewish cars and buses along the road leading from Acre to Tiberias. Learning that the band of Fawzi el-Kaukji mercenaries was hiding in an Arab village in the mountains overlooking the highway, Wingate transported his counter-insurgency troops to the area.

In a briefing with Ben Zion, Moshe Dayan, and Yigal Allon, before setting out from Ein Harod, Wingate revealed his plan to massacre the entire village. At first, the stunned Ben Zion reacted with silence.

"How can you do that?" he finally asked.

"Using the same principle of surprise we used against the mercenaries," Wingate nonchalantly replied.

"Morally," Ben Zion said.

"Excuse me?" asked the onion-chewing commander, not understanding the question.

"How can you kill innocent people?"

"What innocent people?" Dayan interjected. "The villagers give shelter to the mercenaries. They know who they are and provide them with a base for their acts of terror."

"Woman and children?" Ben Zion responded. "What do they have to do with anything?"

"You should know, my noble friend," Dayan said, "that women are not always innocent bystanders. They hear what their men discuss, and they often take a part in their actions. In a small Arab village, everyone knows who is who, and if the women go along with harboring the marauders, then they are guilty too."

"Indeed," Wingate concurred. "One of the Seven Commandments beholden upon all Children of Noah, including the Arabs, is to establish courts of justice. For instance, when the people of Shechem failed to protest when the king's son kidnapped and raped Dina, the sons of Jacob, Shimon and Levy, were justified in slaying all of the inhabitants of the city for their having consented to the crime."

"First of all," Ben Zion protested, "they only killed the males in the city, and secondly, Jacob, their father condemned them for their violent deed."

"The fact remains that after their decisive action, no one in the Land of Canaan dared to rise up against the Jews in battle."

"You can't be serious," Ben Zion replied. "Then was then, and now is now."

Wingate gazed back at him with a cold, unflinching stare. "What is the difference?" he asked.

"Today there are newspapers and radios, and news is spread to all of the world."

"Let is spread. Let the nations of the world begin to fear the Jews."

"Our men won't take a part in killing children," Allon declared.

"Children who grow up with pictures of the hero, Fawzi el-Kaukji, on the walls of their homes, are likely to grow up to be terrorists like him," Dayan argued.

"We have not returned to our Homeland to be as morally corrupt as the Arabs," Allon shot back.

"Morals have nothing to do with this," Wingate said. "These savages are at war with us. They have no morals or qualms about butchering innocent Jews. How many women and children have they already slaughtered? Without hesitation, they attack hospitals and orphanages to kill and maim children and old people alike. In a war, if you hold on to a higher standard, you can be sure you will lose. You cannot snuff out evil with a compassionate heart. Those who are kind to the cruel are cruel to the kind in the end."

"The Torah says otherwise," Ben Zion asserted. "Look in your Bible. Before going to war against the Canaanites, Joshua sent a letter offering them a chance to flee, or to surrender and live in peace."

"To live in peace under Israelite rule," the Bible enthusiast amended. "The Canaanites didn't agree back then, and the Arabs in Palestine won't agree today to such a condition. The only remaining option is war."

"You can't decide that for yourself," Ben Zion argued, unwilling to back down.

"Very well," Wingate said. "When we reach the village, you and I shall go to the house of the local *mukhtar*, and you can ask him to turn over the mercenaries hiding in his village - or else, he will be responsible for the consequences."

"Maybe we can kidnap him and bring him to us," Dayan suggested. "Why should you place yourselves in danger by entering the village?"

"That's a more prudent plan," Allon agreed.

"Still, someone will have to enter the village and bring the *mukhtar* to us," Wingate noted.

"If it will avoid a wholesale massacre, I volunteer," Ben Zion declared.

Both Ben Zion and Wingate left the meeting with troubled minds. Ben Zion felt it was his duty as a moral human being to prevent the massacre of innocent people, while the British commander felt his duty was to terminate the "Great Arab Revolt," which had already taken the lives of five-hundred Jews. In addition, British policemen had been shot, a British magistrate assassinated in the Galilee, and Arab attacks on the British pipeline, British installations, and lines of communications in Palestine had caused extensive financial loss. Furthermore, the honor of the British Empire had been badly damaged by Britain's impotence in quelling the rebellion, fueling the spirit of Arab nationalism which could easily spread throughout other British colonies in the region, and British territories around the globe.

Two days before the raid, Ben Zion traveled to the British military garrison in Haifa with a British officer in the Secret Night Squads unit to secure two Lewis machine guns to be used in the operation. Under the pretense of making a phone call to *Haganah* headquarters in Jerusalem, he phoned David Ben Gurion, whom he luckily found at home.

"He's sleeping," Ben Gurion's wife told the caller. In fact, her husband was reading in his study, but since he was so seldom at home, she watched over him like a dragon guarding a treasure, not letting anything or anybody intrude on their rare time together.

"It's an emergency," Ben Zion told her.

"I'm sorry. You will have to call back later."

"People's lives are at stake."

"Call back later, please."

"He won't be at home later..." Ben Zion began to argue, but the line was disconnected.

"Who was it?" Ben Gurion asked, gazing up from the book he was reading on the history of the American Revolution. In his free moments at home, in their small apartment in Tel Aviv, Ben Gurion chose to relax with his children and read, his one great personal pleasure. If he didn't finish at least one book at day, he literally couldn't fall asleep at night. His study was filled with thousands of books, perhaps the largest private collection of books in the country. His thirst for knowledge was unquenchable, exactly opposite the passion he felt for his wife. Katherine watched over his health, making sure he brushed his teeth and combed the cluster of hair that stuck out from the sides of his balding head like wings. Never caring about his outward appearance, Ben Gurion was grateful that he had someone who kept his clothes clean and ironed. Whatever love he felt towards her was a platonic endeavor, far dryer than the stimulation he received from his books. Feelings of emotional love were locked away in the vaults of his childhood memories. Physical love he found elsewhere.

"It was a journalist on the phone," his wife answered.

Ben Gurion returned to his reading. Journalists didn't

interest him. While he appreciated their power in shaping public opinion, he also needed time to himself. His goal in life was not to be famous, but to shape the future of the Jewish People according to his vision, which he had fashioned to a great extent from his prodigal reading. Interviews were important, but he knew that the world wouldn't come to an end if David Ben Gurion wasn't in the news every day.

Again the telephone rang. This time, Katherine ignored it. The ringing continued persistently, disturbing Ben Gurion's concentration.

"Why don't you answer it?" he asked his wife.

"It's probably the same pest," she replied, preparing him something healthy to eat in the apartment's small kitchen.

"Answer it anyway," he told her.

Dutifully, she obeyed. This time, Ben Zion used some *"protectzia,"* knowing the power of his father's name. Plus, Ben Gurion had told him personally on several occasions to call him whenever he needed assistance.

"Please tell your husband that Ben Zion Aronov is calling," he said.

Katherine covered the mouthpiece of the telephone in her hand. "It's the son of Perchik Aronov," she informed her husband.

Immediately, he set the book down on the arm of his easy chair and walked to breakfront where his wife stood holding the phone.

"Shalom," he answered. "I hope you are well."

"Shalom," Ben Zion said. "Yes. Thank you. I am fine, but I have something to tell you."

"I'm listening."

Ben Zion gazed around the busy garrison office to make sure no one was ease-dropping on the conversation.

"Captain Wingate is planning an attack on an Arab village in the Galilee where a gang of mercenaries has been hiding out. He intends to raze the entire village to the ground in order to teach the Arabs a lesson."

"He's in charge of the unit," Ben Gurion replied.

"He intends to massacre everyone."

"He's the commander."

"Even innocent villagers, men, women, and children."

"I find that hard to believe," Ben Gurion responded. "Nevertheless, the special unit which Wingate has mustered is under his command with the full authority of the British Army. The *Haganah* is only a supplementary force aiding the British. Any operations carried out by Wingate and the unit are the responsibility of the British Government, not ours."

Ben Zion grasped the receiver of the phone without answering. He hadn't expected such a response.

"Anything else?" Ben Gurion asked.

"But there are moral factors involved," Ben Zion stammered.

"The British are very moral people," Ben Gurion replied. "Let them deal with the matter. If Wingate thinks he's found the way to end the killing of Jews, more power to him. Thank you for calling, and please keep me informed."

Ben Gurion hung up the phone.

"How do you want me to make your eggs?" his wife asked him.

"The way I like them," he said.

"I make them for you in several ways. With the yokes intact, scrambled, flipped, as an omelet with cheese or vegetables, or *shakshouka*, with tomatoes, chili peppers, and onions, the way the *Sefardim* like them."

"I never noticed the difference," her husband said, going back to his book. "Whatever you prefer."

When Ben Zion returned to Ein Harod with the canon-like, long-cylindered machine guns, Yigal Allon informed him that Captain Wingate had transferred him to the surveillance team which was gathering information for future operations. Ben Zion stiffened, as if he had received a slap in the face. His cheeks turned crimson.

"He didn't give me a reason," Allon said. "But I think he doesn't want your excessive moral concerns to interfere in the operation and possibly endanger our own men."

"I am prepared to put my personal opinions aside and follow orders," Ben Zion replied.

"Tell him that. He makes the decisions, not me."

Ben Zion searched the base, but couldn't find Wingate anywhere. Outside of the Commander's quarters, a soldier pointed toward a hill overlooking the valley. Ben Zion made out a figure positioned half-way up the rocky incline. Making his way up the slope, Ben Zion heard the vibrating sound of a violin. He discovered Wingate dressed only in a loincloth, standing with his arms outstretched over his head, his palms pressed together, his eyes closed in deep meditation. On a flat boulder beside him, a record on the gramophone played the haunting strains of Hindu music. Soft, high-pitched voices cried out in the background, as if calling from some beckoning, far-off world. Ben Zion stood quietly observing the bizarre scene. The squad's near-naked commander inhaled deeply, holding his breath for half a minute. Finally, he released the air and any built-up tensions trapped in his wiry but muscular body.

"Mountain Pose," he explained, without opening his eyes, as if sensing that someone was there.

Then, his limbs gracefully flowed into another position, one hand touching his lower leg, while he twisted his torso to gaze up at his other raised arm.

"Triangle Pose," he said, holding the contorted angle for more than a minute.

Ben Zion gazed down the slope at the valley and at the small military base below. How vulnerable to an Arab ambush, he thought.

Slowly exhaling the air in his lungs, Wingate raised a foot and bent it to his thigh, until he balanced himself on one leg, with his palms pressed together by his chest in a praying position. "Tree Pose," he said, briefly glancing at his visitor. When his body started to quiver and waver, he set his foot back on the ground, well in front of him. Stretching his other foot behind him, he gazed up at his arms raised over his head. "Warrior Pose," he explained. "I try to practice yoga at least twice a week to help strengthen my concentration and nerves. But I don't experiment with mantras lest I become like Mahatma Ghandi and disavow all military endeavor."

He lowered his arms to shoulder level and held them straight out to the sides in a pose reminiscent of a Greek javelin thrower. "Warrior Pose 2," he said. When he finished the exercise, he stood with his feet together and gazed out over the valley. "My inner *karma* tells me that I have lived in this country, in several reincarnations, throughout all of my life."

Once again, Ben Zion heard his grandfather's voice in his head. "*Meshugener*" Tevye said.

The music came to an end. Wingate bent down to lift the needle from the record to prevent the final chords from repeating over and over.

"Did you bring the machine guns?" he asked.

"Yes, *HaMifaked*."

"Excellent."

Ben Zion kept his gaze focused on Wingate's face, to avoid seeing him nearly naked. "I request to know why I've been transferred," he said.

"I need a deep thinker like you on our surveillance team."

"Regarding our previous discussion, I have altered my thinking," Ben Zion told him.

"Dismissed," Wingate curtly replied.

"I have come to appreciate your point of view," Ben Zion continued.

"Dismissed," the Special Night Squad commander repeated.

"But, sir, please *HaMifaked*, I.…."

"Mr. Aronov," Wingate interrupted, raising his tone. "One Mahatma Ghandi in the world is more than sufficient. From today on, if you choose to continue with this elite unit, you will serve as a member of its surveillance team, and that is a final decision. Understood?"

"Yes, sir," Ben Zion said. Unhappily, he turned away and walked down the hill back to the base.

To make a long story short - the Arab village overlooking the Acre-Rosh Pina road was completely destroyed - the mercenary terrorists who hid there, along with the villagers who provided them refuge, including the elderly, women, and children. Using all of the SNS soldiers except Perchik, Wingate surrounded the village, cutting it off from the world. Escapees were shot. Arabs were loaded onto buses and forced to drive over land mines. Flame-throwing braziers were used to burn down the houses. You can read about the details in history books. No one was spared. When the news spread throughout Palestine, Arabs thought twice before waging attacks against the British and the Jews. The great Arab folk-hero, Fawzi el-Kaukji, gathered his dwindled gangs of hired killers and snuck out of the country. Other mercenary bands hired by the Grand Mufti kept staging random attacks, but it didn't take Wingate long to hunt them down and wipe them off the map. When the Mufti lodged formal complaints with governments all over the world, the British honored Wingate with a Distinguished Service Order and called him back to England, mission accomplished. The Great Revolt was over.

1939

Chapter Sixteen
REBELLION AT LAST

Tevye followed Yaacov Eliav into the small tailor shop of Mazliah Nimrodi in the always busy Mahane Yehuda open market. The young *Irgun* bomb expert approached the Sephardi tailor with an unusual request. He wanted Nimrodi to make him a special overcoat lined with explosives. When Eliav explained that the coat's detonation was to be a symbolic response to the recent "White Paper" which the British Colonial Secretary, Malcolm MacDonald, had formulated, the tailor was happy to lend his talents to the "*mitzvah*."

"Me?" Tevye asked when Eliav chose him for the assignment. "Why me?"

"We can make you to look like a distinguished Englishman. You can fake a British accent if you have to. And I need someone bulky enough to wear a large overcoat without its attracting suspicion."

Tevye stared at the young *Irgun* special-operations commander. The lad was no more than twenty – younger than Tevye's son, Tzvi, and almost twenty years younger than Tevye's older daughters. After his initial hesitation, he agreed to take part in the bombing for the sake of his children, and for their children, and for all of the Jewish children in the Holy Land and throughout the world, so that they would all have a place on Earth where they could live a life of Jewish independence and honor.

According to the new reassessment of British policy, the National Jewish Revival in Palestine was to be terminated. In the coming five years, the last 75,000 Jewish immigrants would be allowed into the country. Sale of land to Jews would be curtailed. After ten years, an independent Palestine State would be formed with an Arab majority. Although several important British members of Parliament opposed the plan as being both impractical and a betrayal of England's national obligations, MacDonald turned a deaf ear. The Jews reacted with indignation and fury. Even Ben Gurion lambasted the new policy statement, speaking for the first time about a military struggle against the British.

The reaction of Ze'ev Jabotinsky to the "White Paper" was even more forceful. He issued a statement warning: "If Britain should attempt to destroy Zionism by its present proposal, the conflict in Palestine must assume the form of armed struggle. If an attempt is made to establish an Arab Government in Palestine, there will be a bitter fight in all parts of the country, commencing with Jerusalem. Jews will surrender nothing peacefully. Jews must not only proclaim their readiness for armed struggle, but must also prepare for it through the militarization of the entire *Yishuv*."

"Words," Yair Stern told Eliav when he read Jabotinsky's belligerent response. "More words without the willingness to act on them."

Eliav was in Poland at the time, completing the course in army officer training which Stern had organized in full cooperation with the Government of Poland.

Jabotinsky followed this announcement with a plan for an armed Jewish revolt in Palestine, which he sent to *Irgun* High Command, in six coded communications. He proposed that he and a boatload of fighters would arrive in Tel Aviv in October. The *Irgun* would facilitate the landing by whatever means necessary. They and a force of *Irgun* soldiers would then occupy strategic centers of British power in Palestine, including the Government House in Jerusalem. Raising the Jewish national flag, they would fend off the British for at least 24 hours, no matter how many lives were lost. Zionist leaders in Western Europe and the United States would then declare an independent Jewish State and would function as a provisional government-in-exile. While *Irgun* commanders gave serious consideration to the plan, they balked over the heavy losses which such a coup involved.

Stern's plan was to raise a Jewish army of 40,000 well-trained soldiers and to conquer Palestine by force from its alien occupier. Poland was ready to arm the troops and ship massive amounts of armaments to Palestine to insure the project's success. Top Polish Army officers enthusiastically led the four-months of thorough and rigorous training. Facing their own upcoming confrontation with the Germans, the Poles received inspiration from the spirit and resolve of the young Jewish trainees who flocked to the forest training camp to join the Hebrew resistance and the struggle for national liberation. Eliav used the opportunity to enhance his knowledge of explosives and land mines. At the conclusion of the training program, before returning to Jerusalem, Stern gave him a green light to carry out any underground operation he felt would be effective, even if his local commanders didn't agree. While Eliav was sailing back to *Eretz Yisrael*, the Nazis invaded Czechoslovakia, and set their sights on Poland, overrunning the country before Stern could put his grand plan into action.

A week after their first visit to the tailor, Mazliah Nimrodi returned from his back room with the coat he had fashioned according to Tevye's measurements and Eliav's sketch. The tailor had started from scratch, sewing the material together so the coat couldn't be traced. After Nimrodi locked the door of the shop, he held up his creation for their inspection, then draped the long coat over a sewing table. Eliav stuffed the pocketed shoulders with blasting gelatin instead shoulder pads, shaping the sensitive material like modeling clay. Then he lined the coat's inside pockets with more blasting gelatin and added ten sticks of dynamite. The timer was installed in a small secret pocket. Two wires led from the timer to an electronic firing device by the cuff of the sleeve. Four hidden batteries supplied the power.

As the tailor and Tevye looked on, Eliav checked the electrical system and tried the timer with a test lamp. When everything was in place, Nimrodi covered Eliav's handiwork with a second cloth lining. His deft fingers finished the stitching in no time. The tailor held up the overcoat for Tevye, who carefully slipped his arms through the sleeves.

"A perfect fit!" Nimrodi declared in satisfaction.

Eliav rubbed his hand over the material. "Beautiful," he said. "Not the slightest bulge."

The tailor smiled and bowed his head at the compliment. "I am proud to be of help," he said.

Tevye stood stiffly, afraid to move lest the overcoat explode.

"You can relax, Zalman," Eliav told him, calling Tevye by his code name. "Until the timer is set, the system remains inactive."

After synchronizing Tevye's watch with the timer and repeating his instructions, Eliav led Tevye out to the street. The target was the Rex Cinema just off Jaffa Road, located in the British Government Office Compound, known as the "Triangle," where the Mandatory Courts, the National Police Headquarters, and the Criminal Investigation Division were situated. British officials and well-to-do Arabs frequented the movie house. Avraham Stern had suggested the popular place of entertainment in the list of possible targets he had discussed with Eliav at the end of his training in Poland. Because the cinema was in the middle of the British Government Compound, attacking it would be a direct blow to the Mandate Authority, showing that the Jewish Underground was capable of penetrating its very heart and turning British life in Palestine into a "bloody hell," as the British were fond of saying. Eliav had conducted extensive reconnaissance, using Jews who looked like Arabs and spoke Arabic fluently. He sent them to see the currently playing film to determine the exact time of the showing and the layout of the theater, dressing them in suits with the colorful handkerchiefs that Arabs liked to sport in their breast pocket, and grooming them with hair lotion and cologne. Carrying Arab identification cards forged by the *Irgun* Documentation Division, they aroused no suspicion as they surreptitiously carried out their surveillance.

The theater had two entrances, front and back. One led to the orchestra, and the other to the balcony. The orchestra was guarded by ushers who frisked moviegoers as they entered the hall and checked packages and bags. Because the balcony was frequented by dignitaries and their wives, or mistresses, no search was conducted.

Tevye wasn't alone in the mission. Three "Arab" couples would sit by the railing of the balcony. The women would carry explosives in their handbags, hidden in a boxes of chocolates. Fittingly, the chocolates were imported English *bonbonnieres*. With Hevedke's assistance, Eliav removed the sweets from their wrappers and replaced them with explosive gelatin. Under a false cardboard bottom, he filled the box with nails and dynamite to heighten the impact of the explosion. The wires attached to the battery-powered detonator were hidden under the long ribbons fastened around the box, complete with a decorative bow. After tying the ribbons to the balcony railing, when the disguised couples in the balcony heard the first explosion, they were to thrown the boxes down toward the orchestra. When the ribbon reached its end, just above the heads in the audience, the jerk would trigger the bomb. Outside the theater, across the street, sharpshooters would be waiting behind the stone wall of the small Mamilla Cemetery. After the explosions, when movie-goers fled from the theater, the sharpshooters would open fire with submachine guns. Because of the secrecy of the operation, and to conceal the identity of the *Irgunists* carrying out the attack, in the invent that someone was captured, as Tevye headed apprehensively toward the Rex Cinema in his exploding overcoat, he didn't know that one of the young couples in the balcony would be his nineteen-year-old twins, Boaz and Naomi. With their dark Yemenite complexions, and "out-on-the-town" clothing, they had no trouble passing for the college-age children of wealthy Arabs.

Tevye could feel his heart beating rapidly as he approached the theater, accompanied by Yaacov Eliav. The coat frightened him more than the mission. After all, Eliav was the youngest commander in the *Irgun*. He knew that the plan had been meticulously planned, and that Eliav was a well-trained craftsman when it came to making bombs. But still, something could go wrong. Time bombs were known to explode prematurely. Life didn't come with any guarantees. That's why the Torah instructed a Jew to safeguard his life very carefully. But, he reasoned, war was different. Military encounter involved danger. When a Jewish soldier set off to battle, the Torah commanded him to forget about his wife and children, and every selfish concern, and concentrate all of his thoughts and efforts on the mission at hand. Tevye's feet kept walking, even though apprehensions troubled his thoughts. "*Azoy gaytis*," he ruminated with a sigh of surrender. What could he do? Destiny was destiny. He walked on toward the cinema building, trusting that God would look after him. And if his hour had come to say farewell to this world, so be it. The Lord gives and the Lord takes away. Blessed be the Name of the Lord.

"Good evening, good evening," he repeated under his breath, rehearsing his English. "Quite a lovely evening, isn't it?"

As they neared the Rex Cinema, he glanced around the street, checking to see if his overcoat caught people's attention. After all, the winter had passed, and though Jerusalem enjoyed cool evenings, most Jerusalemites had hung their overcoats away in their closets. Eliav strode beside him, as if to make certain that his lead bomber didn't run away. Across the street from the movie-house, Eliav reached his hand into a pocket of the overcoat and activated the timer. Then he slipped the timer into one of his own pockets, so that Tevye's pockets would be empty when he was searched at the entrance to the theater.

"Don't become absorbed in the movie," Eliav said. "Keep your eyes on your watch. At eight-thirty, the bomb is set to explode." Then Eliav continued walking along the street, as if they weren't together, leaving Tevye alone to carry out the assignment. In the meantime, Eliav lingered across the street, as if he were waiting for someone.

Tevye felt the weight of the coat as he stepped up to the ticket booth and purchased a ticket. "One, please," he said in his finest English accent. The cashier didn't even bother to look up at him. He waited by the entrance for a crowd to gather, then melted in with the other moviegoers as inconspicuously as he could, holding his head stiffly in the style of English officials. An usher at the door patted the pockets of the coat and let Tevye enter the lobby. Groups of Arabs stood by the posters of the "Tarzan" movie that was currently playing. Their hands gestured in animated conversation, as if they were anticipating a fun time in the jungles of Africa. Another usher in the lobby glanced at Tevye and waved him into the dark auditorium, without a search. Clusters of British viewers and Arabs sat in distinctly separate rows. His heartbeat racing, Tevye chose an aisle filled with Englishmen. A noisy newsreel was showing on the large screen at the front of the hall, depicting the advance of German troops in Czechoslovakia. Tevye excused himself as he moved down the row of seats, brushing against people's knees. All eyes remained focused on the screen. Sitting down, he glanced up at the balcony. In the semi-darkness, he could make out the outline of three couples sitting along the railing. Nervously, he glanced at his watch. Another eight minutes and his coat would explode. Standing up, he carefully took off the heavy garment and draped it gently over the empty seat in front of him. "Popcorn," he said to the person in the neighboring chair, disturbing the man's view as he edged along the row of occupied seats. "Popcorn," he repeated as he made his way toward the aisle. "Popcorn," he explained to the usher standing by the door of the hall. Luckily, the usher in the lobby and the guard by the entrance were busy checking last-minute arrivals. Quickening his pace, Tevye hurried out from the theater.

In the balcony of the movie house, Tevye's daughter, Naomi, tied the ribbon of the box of chocolates to the railing. Her brother, Boaz, held the box steadily in his hands. Further along the railing of the gallery, the other two couples were preparing their bombs as well. No one paid any attention to them as goose-stepping Nazis paraded noisily across the silver screen below.

When the newsreel ended, the theater's lights dimmed. Latecomers settled into their seats. A crescendo of music filled the dark auditorium, announcing the start of the movie. At precisely 8:30, the MGM lion appeared on the screen and opened its jaws, and the coat-bomb exploded, drowning out the lion's roar. Shockwaves caused the building to shake. The *Irgun* agents in the balcony threw the boxes of dynamite down toward the main hall, where they exploded just above the heads of the screaming moviegoers. All through the pandemonium, the movie continued to play.

Panicked survivors rushed for the exit, trampling people in their way. Bodies remained slumped over chairs. Boaz and Naomi acted like everyone else as they rushed down the stairs. Following instructions, they hurried toward the lobby. People escaping out the back door were met with gunfire and exploding grenades. "Keep calm! Keep calm!" an usher shouted in the jammed lobby as terrified people pushed forward to reach the narrow exit. An Arab shoved his way between Boaz and Naomi. "Wait for me!" Naomi called to her brother in Hebrew. Immediately, she knew she had made a mistake. She felt a hand grab her as she reached the door. "Come with me," a theater guard commanded, dragging her away. Outside, Boaz searched for his sister, but she was gone. Assuming she was lost in the crowd, he hurried off to the rendezvous site, expecting to find her there. But she never showed up. The British Police had arrested her along with a few other suspects, not knowing they had apprehended one of the *Irgun* bombers.

2.

In the dark basement of an elementary school on the border of the Geula neighborhood in Jerusalem, Tevye sat in tense silence, listening to Eliav's summary of the Rex Cinema operation. The emergency meeting of the Jerusalem *Irgun* command had been summoned to decide how to respond to Naomi's arrest. As a rule, the command avoided meeting together, lest British Police capture the leadership of the Organization in one swoop. In response to increasing Jewish reprisals, a Jewish Department of the Criminal Investigation Division had been established in British Police Headquarters located in the Russian Compound, and its leaders worked overtime trying to figure out the who's-who of the clandestine "Jewish terror" organization. Paid informers helped them in their efforts, and the Jewish Agency and *Haganah* supplied them with the names of suspected Revisionist and *Betar* activists, in order to keep on good terms with the Mandate Authority and to weaken the military wing of Jabotinsky's Revisionist Movement which threatened Ben Gurion's control of the Zionist establishment.

The attack on the movie house in the heart of the British Government center in Jerusalem had been, not only a strategic and military success, the deadly bombing had also dealt a profound psychological blow to all British officials in Palestine, shattering their feeling of invincibility and security. The stunning attack let the British know that the Jewish Underground could reach them anywhere, even in the bastion of their Government center, meters away from their Police and Army Headquarters, even in their cafes and places of leisure.

"At the moment, we know of five dead and over twenty seriously wounded," Eliav concluded.

"We can expect a wave of arrests in response," David Raziel said. "No doubt they're in a panic."

"It's about time," Stern observed.

"Everyone involved in the attack will have to go into hiding," Binyamin Zeroni, commander of the Jerusalem district, said in a quiet voice. He sat hunched over, a shadow of his former self, like someone who had returned from hell.

"You did a superlative job, Yaacov," Raziel said, commending Eliav.

If there was ever an example of a military officer, it was Raziel, a deeply religious individual who had studied years in yeshiva before learning at Hebrew University. After the Ben Yosef execution, Jabotinsky had appointed him head of *Irgun* operations throughout the country. "I want to hear your ideas for follow-up operations," he told twenty-year-old Eliav. "In my opinion, we can't rest on our laurels. We have to keep the pressure on the British till they drastically alter their policies."

"We have to keep pressure on the British until they depart from our Land," Stern remarked, back in the country on the eve of the Nazi takeover of Poland, a "*fait accompli*" which was merely a matter of time, ending his dream of organizing an army of Polish Jews to oust the British from Palestine. Until Zeroni's wounds were healed, Yair was chosen to be the acting *Irgun* commander of Jerusalem.

"An all-out war on the British isn't advisable now," Raziel

countered. Although the two friends were like brothers, differences in political outlook and strategy were beginning to pull them apart. "In a very short time, the British may find themselves at war with Hitler. Say what you will about Britain's betrayal of their Mandate to help us, Germany is a far greater threat to the Jews. If Britain goes to war against the Nazis, we have to support them - not open another front against them behind their backs."

"Excuse me for thinking otherwise," Stern argued. "As long as the German's are willing to help us bring Jews to Palestine, they are our allies. And as long as the British prevent further immigration, they are our enemies. It is as simple as that."

"What about my daughter?" Tevye asked, getting down to the point. "She's in a cage with animals who, for all of their pompous manners and ways, have as few moral feelings as the Germans. They are *vilda chayas* with fancy English accents, that's all. They are no more civilized than the Arabs. We have to free her as fast as we can."

There was a moment of silence. Everyone knew the truths of his words. Tzvi and Boaz, listened tensely, not daring to voice their opinions in the presence of their commanders. They had been invited to the meeting only because they were the captured girl's brothers, and because Boaz had participated in the attack on the cinema building.

It was common knowledge to the *Irgun* that the British employed torture in their investigations. After Tzvi's attack on the Arab bus destined for Hevron, one of the *Irgun's* Jerusalem district commanders, Yosef Hakim, was arrested and severely tortured by the Criminal Investigation Division, headed by malevolent Ralph Cairns. After Hakim stubbornly refused to reveal any information about the Organization, or to mention any names, he was released and expelled from the country. To shatter the myth of British gentility and allegiance to international law, the *Irgun* distributed a poster around the country, detailing some of the methods employed by the CID:

"Suspects are beaten with rubber sticks all over their bodies. They are hung up by their thumbs and their feet, and their privates are pulverized. The torturers pull out their hair and their beards. They burn the Jews with cigarettes, and pour water into their stomachs and lungs until they choke."

Cairns supervised the torture during the investigations, often delivering the blows on his own. He took pleasure in torturing women, abusing them in unspeakable fashions.

Eliav himself had been arrested in a round-up of *Irgun* operators. While it soon became clear to him that the police had no concrete evidence linking him to any specific attack, they threatened to torture him if he didn't confess to his wrongdoings and supply them with the names of his collaborators.

Eliav smiled at Cairns with a laughing, scorn-filled expression. "Since you seem to think that my friends and I masterminded several murderous attacks, if you torture me, my friends will even the score. They will hunt you down and kill you wherever you flee."

"Is that a threat?" Cairns snared.

"No. It's a promise."

Without the slightest fear, and with eyes as cold as ice, Eliav stared at the torturer until he turned away unnerved. Cairns ordered police guards to return the suspect to his dungeon cell. Six other young *Irgun* soldiers were crowded inside.

"Did they torture you," a youth with *peyes* asked.

"No," Eliav answered.

"I don't know what I will do if they torture me," the frightened prisoner said.

"Trust in God," Eliav told him. "*Hashem* protects those who revere him."

Later, after enduring several days of torture, the young religious boy told Eliav that he hadn't revealed anything about the *Irgun*. Cairns stuck burning cigarettes in his ears and inserted sharp bamboo sticks underneath his fingernails, a favorite torture technique of the Turks. When he refused to cooperate, Cairns had him locked in a tiny isolation cell for eleven days, warning him that he would suffer further punishment if he told anyone that he had been tortured.

Back in the darkened school basement, Tevye was running

out of patience. "I will lead any mission to free my daughter, at whatever risk," he told the group.

"We all want to rescue the girl," Raziel assured him, "But we can't try to free her until we know where she is. I can't send men into the police station or jail with tommy guns blazing. Chances are they wouldn't come out alive."

"David is right," said Binyamin Zeroni. "No matter how much personal pain we feel about your daughter's wellbeing, we can't act in an irresponsible fashion."

Tevye wanted to stand up and argue, but he knew they were right. Binyamin Zeroni had personally experienced the cruelty of the CID investigations. Just months before, he had been stopped by police while driving in Jerusalem. Entering his car with guns drawn, two policemen ordered him to drive to the Russian Compound. Surrounded by British detectives, and with guns cocked and pointed at his head, he refused to give a statement of any kind until he was allowed to meet with a lawyer. Now, for the newcomers in the room, and to emphasize the inhumanity of the foe they were facing, he told them, in capsule form, what had transpired, during his long and brutal investigation.

"After my arrest, when I refused to talk and asked for a lawyer, they handcuffed me, chained my legs, and took me to the cellar to be investigated by Ralph Cairns who was sitting behind a table. Cairn stood up and began to strike me on the head and the neck. Then he slapped my ears simultaneously for fifteen minutes until a ringing pain filled my brain and my body convulsed in shock. I collapsed to the floor, but policemen raised me back to the chair so that Cairns could continue the torture. 'Who are your friends?' he asked again and again. 'Tell us the names of your friends, you dirty Jew bastard, or we will torture you until you die.' After I collapsed to the floor once again, they carried me to a small empty cell and dumped me there for the night."

Everyone sat in silent suspense. Tevye could hardly bear to listen, worried over the fate of his daughter. Instinctively, Eliav squeezed his hands into a fist. Tzvi's head became dizzy with anger and thoughts of revenge. Raziel, who had already heard the story, listened with a rising tension that he forced himself to control.

"In the morning, they brought me back to the torture chamber. Cairns pulled me by the hair. Again and again, he pounded my head against the wall till I felt dizzy. 'Do you want to die?' he asked. 'We will torture you morning, noon, and night.' When I told him that my friends would kill him, he held his pistol to my chin and quoted the Psalms, '*Though I walk through the valley of the shadow of death I fear no evil for Thou art with me.*' Then he ordered the guards to strip me. They held me down naked on a table, facing the ceiling. Guards tied my hands and feet and my underpants were stuffed into my mouth. Giles, the head of the CID, and his deputy, Shaw, came into the room to watch. Cairns put on rubber gloves, then began to squeeze my privates. The pain was so intense it traveled up and down my body. He continued to squeeze and squeeze until I lost all sense of time. Then with a flat leather slab, he began to whip the soles of my feet. I managed to free a hand and pull the cloth from my mouth. I screamed as loud as I could until a guard slapped me and shoved the underwear back in my mouth. 'You bloody Jew! You filthy dog!' Cairns cursed me. 'Start to talk!' The torture continued until I passed out. I awoke naked in the bare cell. I wasn't able to walk."

Tevye stood up from his chair. He walked away from the group, pacing along the walls of the basement like a lion in a cage.

"They next morning, they had to carry me back to the torture chamber. Cairns showed me a photograph of my girlfriend that they found in my apartment. 'You see this picture?' he says. 'What a beautiful lassy. We will find her and bring her here. Do you know what we will do to her, you stinking Jew bastard? We will strip her naked and rape her in front of your eyes. It will be my pleasure. Then we will torture her like we did to you. Do you think we have finished with you? We have only started. So be a smart Jew and tell us the names of your friends.'"

"He's a dead man," Stern said.

Tevye could hardly breathe.

"When I refused to speak, Cairns ordered two Arabs to carry me into another room. Again he attacked my private parts with a fiendish relish."

The tortured man began to describe the ordeal in the present tense, as if the living nightmare was still taking place before his eyes.

"My head is pressed into a vice, and my hands and feet are tied. Cairns wraps a cloth around my nose and fastens it with a clothespin. I can't breathe through my nose, so I have to open my mouth. With a smile, Cairns starts to pour water down my throat. I try to close my mouth but I can't breathe. When I open my mouth, he fills it with water. I have no choice but to swallow it. My lungs filled with water."

Zeroni paused. His head slumped down on his chest. Then he raised it. With a look of death in his eyes, he continued

"My belly started to swell. My heart was about to burst. All the time, Cairns keeps talking. 'Ready to give us the information, or do you want more torture? We have plenty of water. Why be stupid? Life is good. Your friends are enjoying themselves on the beach in Tel Aviv, eating ice cream and hugging girls. We will keep torturing you, Ben, until you give us their names.' They poured seven, eight, nine kettles down my throat until vomit gushed out of my mouth and my nose. Cairns orders Arabs to carry me into another room, where they hang me up by my thumbs. 'After we capture all of the Jewish pigs, we'll send them back to Hitler who knows how to deal with them,' Cairns vows. Pictures of my life flash before my eyes. Again, he beats me in the groin. My body goes limp. The monster checks my pulse to see if I am still living. He orders the guards to lower me to the floor. They use smelling salts to revive me. Then they tie a rope around my feet and hang me upside down from the ceiling. With a wet whip, Cairns beats me all over my body. By now, my body is numb with pain. Luckily, I lose consciousness. When I awake, I am back in the foul-smelling cell, naked on the concrete floor. I haven't eaten in three days. I cannot stand or walk. I can barely speak. Every muscle in my body aches whenever I try to move."

The door of the room opened. Everyone looked up. Tevye strode out of the dark basement, closing the door behind him.

Raziel turned to Tzvi. "Tell your father not to go home. If the police discover your sister's identity, they will try to arrest him as well. Warn your mother, if the police haven't been there already. Boaz, you have to go underground too."

Tzvi and Boaz hurried after their father.

"Let me take care of Cairns," Eliav said.

"Agreed," Raziel answered.

"I will find out about the girl from our people at the station," Stern said.

Zeroni continued the story, as if he had to exorcise the lingering trauma by speaking. "The torture continued for another two days. In addition to the physical abuse, they wouldn't let me sleep. At night, I was forced to lie on my back with my eyes open, staring at the light bulb by the ceiling. Guards were changed every two hours to make sure I stayed awake. Every time I closed my eyes, someone kicked me. I nearly lost my mind. On the fifth day, they left me alone. They started to feed me. When I asked to be moved to a cleaner cell where I could breathe, they agreed."

To make a long story short, Zeroni escaped. Three-quarters dead, but somewhat strengthened from the food he had eaten, he decided to take the risk. When his guards were sleeping, he stood up and walked back and forth in his cell to get used to walking again. Using the bars of the cell door like a ladder, he climbed up and hoisted himself up to the top of the wall, where a wire net separated the cell from the guard room. Using a sharp piece of glass he found on the wall, he scraped away at the bottom of the net for an hour until it broke free from the concrete. It took him another hour to squeeze his way under the sharp spikes of the wire. With dawn approaching, he quietly lowered himself down in the guard room, where two Arab guards slept soundly on their cots. One stirred, sat up, then lay back down, pulling a blanket over his head. A master skeleton key rested on the table. The loud snoring of the guards covered the click of the door lock. Suddenly fresh air filled his lungs. He found himself standing outdoors in one of the courtyards of the jail. Using the little strength he had left, he grabbed a drain pipe and shimmied up the pipe to the shards of sharp glass and barb wire at the top of the wall. Rolling over the glass and the barb wire, he dropped down to another narrow jail courtyard where privileged prisoners were allowed to smoke cigarettes. Lights shone in the upper-floor windows of buildings across the street. With the glimmer of dawn in the sky, he had only one more wall to scale to be free. Grabbing a small table used for playing checkers, he dragged it to the outer prison wall and climbed up to more coils of barbwire. With bloody scratches all over his body, he dropped down to the street. He was free!

3.

Filled with rage, Tevye strode through the dark streets of Jerusalem, not knowing where he was headed. He knew that it was forbidden to question the ways of the Almighty. After all, the Creator of Heaven and Earth wasn't bound by the limits of human intelligence and logic. Given all of the wondrous workings and ordered perfection of the universe, from the movement of the planets to the beating of the human heart, and the ability to see, who was Tevye to criticize the *Rabono Shel Olam,* the Master of the World, or to protest His doings? But what had his young daughter ever done wrong to deserve such a cruel and horrid fate? And if her imprisonment was to punish him for his sins, why must his daughter suffer? Why? Why?

Without knowing how he got there, Tevye found himself outside the Russian Compound Prison, where Naomi was imprisoned. Vacantly, he stared at the wall and wire fence surrounding the jail. Seeing a policeman heading his way, Tevye grasped the revolver in his pocket. His arm twitched. The noise, he thought. The noise of the gunshot would alert the police in the station. He was no longer young enough to flee from pursuers. As the policeman passed under a streetlamp, Tevye could make out his English-looking features. In his pocket, his finger rested on the trigger of the gun. Tevye's thoughts raced in his head. Perhaps, he could kill him and disappear into a nearby alley. Just then, in the distance, two other policemen walked out of the police-station compound.

"Why are you standing here?" the Bobby asked roughly.

"Is there a law against standing?" Tevye replied.

"Around police stations there is. Move on."

Casually joking with one another, the other policemen headed their way.

"I told you to move it, Moses!" the copper in front of him barked.

Tevye could feel his hand tremble.

"I'm going," he said.

Turning away from the prison, and mumbling curses under his breath, Tevye headed back down the incline toward Jaffa Road.

In an interrogation room of the British Police Headquarters in Jerusalem, Ralph Cairns, head of the Criminal Investigation Division, slapped Naomi in the face.

"Admit that you're a Jewess!" he demanded.

The young woman refused to answer him, or even to look at his round, piggish face.

"What a pity," Cairns said.

Back home in Manchester, Cairns had been a mediocre police detective, who enjoyed beating and torturing suspects before bringing them to the station for booking. Married to a Catholic woman who never missed going to church on Sunday, he himself was no great believer, but, just to be on the safe side, he went to confession once a month and told the priest about the sins he committed at a local brothel on his beat. His excessive roughness with the women led one of them to complain to a frequent visitor of the brothel, the assistant mayor of the city. Cairns was harshly reprimanded by his commander and transferred to a different district. When friends on the force received promotions, he was passed by. Rumors of his misbehavior spread about until his wife demanded they take up residence elsewhere. Learning that the British Police Department was recruiting policemen for stints of service in Palestine, assignments which promised better wages and career advancement, Cairns signed up. For his wife, Jerusalem held a spiritual and historical attraction, while for him, it was a chance to see the world and flee from his disgraced reputation. Upon his arrival in the country, his understanding of the political situation was minimal. Everyone knew that Jews had crucified Jesus, and that was enough reason to hate them. In Manchester, he had never encountered an Arab, but in Palestine, everyone in the department regarded them as scum, so he did as well. After two years of distinguished service, treating Arabs and Jews with equal disdain and derision, Police Commissioner Giles appointed him to head the Jewish Division of the Criminal Investigations Department, not because Cairns was a wizard detective, but because he needed a ruthless individual to deal with a small Jewish uprising.

"Don't be foolish, little girl," Cairns told Naomi. "I know you are a Jewess. Be smart and nothing will happen to you. To avoid unnecessary unpleasantness, tell me who you are, and the name of people who were with you in the cinema, and we will let you go home. No one likes to see young girls in prison."

Naomi didn't answer. She had taken an oath of secrecy to the Organization that she would never betray. She had sworn on the Bible. Even more - how could she betray her own father and brothers? She was ready to die and not tell the British one word.

"Jews can be more stubborn than mules," Cairns quipped, turning to a colleague on the force, a Jewish officer named Blakely.

"Maybe she doesn't understand the consequences," Blakely said. He turned to the golden-skinned girl and smiled. She was a good-looker, with a nice figure.

"This isn't a pleasant place," he said to her in Hebrew. "The people here have a job to do, and they get results in whatever way they can. Though police are in charge of keeping the law on the streets, in here, there is no law. So, if you want to see your father and mother again, and one day get married and have a family of your own, it's best to cooperate. So tell us your name."

The girl remained silent.

Born in London, Blakely had grown up in a Jewish family that believed assimilation was the answer to the "Jewish Problem." Because of his bossy nature and quick temper, he was always getting into fights in high school, until he was expelled for unruly behavior. A stint in the army didn't help to refine him, and he was soon dismissed for insubordination. Not caring about his dismal military record, the British Foreign Legion agreed to sign him on, sending him to the colony of Sudan, where he took his frustrations out on the natives. When his two-year contract ended, he returned to London and married a bar girl of ill repute. During a bar brawl, a policeman gave him a whack on the head with his club. The blow had a positive effect on his senses, making him understand that it was preferable to be the bloke who held the baton, and not the poor slob getting clubbed. So he joined the London Police Force, became an obedient officer, and after four years of service in Britain's penal system, he signed up for a transfer to Palestine, leaving his pregnant wife in London with two babies. He signed up for a course in Hebrew, and worked on his homework diligently. At the end of the year, he spoke well enough to communicate – albeit with a heavy Cockney accent - and to understand what people were saying. In the meantime, he proved to be a capable prison guard, with a clear animosity toward the Jews. Cairns put him in charge of gathering information about the *Irgun*. With a modest expense allowance from the Mandate coffers which he used to pay Jewish informers willing to cooperate, and to hire prostitutes for himself, he succeeded in establishing an effective intelligence network which led to many arrests. He was always happy to participate in a torture session or two, in order to glean whatever extra information he could in his march up the ranks. If he had a Jewish conscience somewhere in his being, it didn't show.

"Pretty little bitch, isn't she?" Cairns said, staring at Naomi. "In my experience, the surest way to tell whether a woman is Jewish or not is when you rape them. The Jewesses cry. The Arab women seem to take it for granted."

Naomi knew enough English to understand the gist of his words. Inwardly, she trembled, but she wouldn't let them see her fear.

Dear Reader, at this point we will pass over the details of what followed. While the popular fashion today is to describe everything in the name of art and freedom of expression, we learned in Volume Two of this pentalogy that while Rabbi Kook praised the positive value of art, he warned that all of the arts, including literature, must keep within the strict framework of Jewish Law and not fall prey to the drunkenness which art and artists are prone. Matters which add pollution to the world, and which soil the imagination - rather than uplifting humanity and ennobling the mind and spirit - are better left buried.

Let it simply be recorded that for refusing to cooperate with the Criminal Investigation Division of the British Mandate Police Force, Tevye's daughter was assaulted and raped, by Ralph Cairns and Lieutenant Blakely in a dungeon cell of the Russian Compound, behind a sealed iron door through which no screams could be heard. Broken in body but not in spirit, she admitted she was Jewish, but she refused to reveal her name, or mention the name of anyone she knew. Convinced that the girl's resistance would collapse after a stint in confinement, Cairns put her under military detention, and without ever seeing a lawyer or a judge, Tevye's daughter, Naomi, was transferred to the Bethlehem Prison for Women.

4.

Ever since *Seder* Night a decade before, when the dapperly-dressed Avraham Stern had knocked on their door unexpectedly, Tevye had experienced a lot of ups and downs with the eccentric intellectual who had finally married his granddaughter, Hannie, after a long, rollercoaster courtship. A day after the meeting in the school basement, Tevye received a note to wait outside a small Yemenite synagogue on Agripas Street by the Machane Yehuda market. Yair, as he called himself now, didn't have to say anything for Tevye to understand that the news about Naomi wasn't good. His dead serious expression conveyed everything. It was Friday afternoon, and the market was crowded with shoppers taking advantage of the lowered prices of fruits, vegetables, and fresh fish from Tel Aviv which would spoil if not cooked before the onset of *Shabbat*. The information about Naomi had been gleaned from a telephone operator at the Russian Compound jail who was a secret member of the *Irgun*.

Stern motioned Tevye to follow him down an alleyway into the Even Yisrael neighborhood where he had a hide-out in a basement wine cellar, located in the house of an *Irgun* sympathizer who ran a wine store in the "*shuk*," as the market was called. The small religious neighborhoods bordering Machane Yehuda were strongholds of the secret organization, where "Anonymous Soldiers" who were forced to go underground could find refuge and something to eat in the small, stone houses clustered along a labyrinth of cobblestone paths. In their daily prayers, devout Jews pray, "Let there be no hope for informers," and indeed, the religious neighborhoods proved loyal havens for Jews who had to hide from the British Police. Tzvi and Boaz had found quarters in the Sephardi Orphanage. David Raziel often hid out in the Ashkenazi Synagogue of Mishkenot Yisrael. Binyamin Zeroni spent time recuperating from his torture wounds in the large, two-story home of a benevolent doctor who worked in the Bikur Holim Hospital. Hevedke had moved his glass-blowing and shofar-drilling studio to the Succat Shalom neighborhood, where he lived in a one-room flat with his son, Akiva. And to avoid getting his parents into trouble with the police, Yaacov Eliav was a common boarder in the Batei Rand Courtyard, where a large group of immigrants from Galatia, Poland had settled.

"Did they torture her?" Tevye asked, when they were seated in the cramped and humid basement, surrounded by kegs of wine. Tevye guessed that the mat on the stone floor was Stern's bed. This was one of the reasons why Tevye had opposed Stern's romance with his granddaughter, Hannie. He knew that if they married, the girl would hardly see her headstrong revolutionist of a husband.

Stern didn't answer his question.

"Worse?" Tevye wanted to know.

Stern returned his worried gaze with a cold and emotionless stare.

"They raped her?"

"The British have been raping us for the last twenty years," Stern answered.

"I'm talking about my daughter."

"The rape of our People and the rape of our Land overshadows all private concerns, no matter how painful."

"My daughter," Tevye repeated.

"She is like my daughter as well. Your pain and rage is no greater than mine. All of our soldiers are brothers, sisters, and sons. When each of us swore allegiance to the Organization, we all knew what could be. To die alone in a dungeon. To be shot dead in an alley. To have our bodies blown into irretrievable pieces. We swore allegiance to the cause knowing there is something greater than our individual lives – *Malchut Yisrael* – and the life of the Nation. I don't have to quote verses to you. '*I passed by you and saw you weltering in your blood. Live through you blood, I said to you, live through your blood.*'"

Tevye knew that for Stern, the speech he had just delivered wasn't mere words. He believed the things he said with all of his soul. He felt connected to the Jewish People with all of his being. Perhaps, Tevye thought, his love for the Nation was so complete because he didn't yet have a child of his own. Tevye loved the Jewish People too, but he also loved his family. To Tevye, Naomi wasn't another "Anonymous Soldier." She was his flesh and blood. To help any Jew, Tevye would do whatever he could, but to save his daughter, he would gladly hurl himself into a raging fire without a moment's hesitation and give up his life to save her.

"She's been transferred to the Bethlehem Prison for Women," Stern told him. "She didn't tell them anything. For now, you can go back to your home. Because of her valor, we can continue to fight. The Organization has friends who work in the prison. When we learn her daily schedule, we will save her."

"How?" Tevye asked.

"With God's help, we will find the right way."

"When?"

"As soon as we can."

Tevye gazed vacantly at the barrels of wine in the basement. If he had to, he would drive a wagon-load of barrels filled with dynamite into the courtyard of the

Bethlehem Prison and blow up the building to rescue his daughter.

5.

Before the Secret Night Squads of Charles Wingate, and the reprisals of the *Irgun* succeeded in crushing the Great Arab Revolt, the Jews still living in the Old City of Jerusalem either fled from their homes, or found themselves evacuated by the British who refused to protect them. Tevye's family moved to the Geula neighborhood, outside the Old City walls. Since the attack on the Rex Cinema, and Naomi's capture, fearing that his home was under surveillance, either by the British Police or their informers, Tevye kept a safe distance away, meeting his wife and daughters in secret rendezvous places around the city. He found temporary quarters in the home of his old friend, Rabbi Moshe Segal, the world famous *shofar* blower, whose *Yom Kippur* blasts at the *Kotel*, in defiance of the British ban, were heard around the world. That *Shabbat* evening, after hearing the grim news from Stern about Naomi, he surprised his wife, Carmel, when he showed up at their door.

"Tevye!" she said in happy surprise. Instinctively, her eyes darted behind him to make sure there was no one watching in the courtyard below.

"It's all right," he reassured her. "She didn't tell them anything."

"How is she?" his wife worriedly asked. Naomi had inherited her dark, Yemenite features from her mother, and the same hazel-brown eyes.

"She is fine," he answered.

"They didn't torture her?"

"No."

Carmel breathed in relief. Realizing they were still standing in the doorway, she took her husband's hand and pulled him inside. The family was seated around the long table in the center of the salon.

"*Zaide*!" "*Saba*!" "*Pappa*!" "Tevye!" voices called out.

Like on many holiday nights, even the *kinder* who had homes of their own gathered together to eat the Sabbath meal with the *Pappa* of the tribe. That's the way it had been for the Jews of Anatevka, and that's the way it had been for Jewish families for the last two-thousand years in all the lands of their dispersion. As the saying goes – "More than the Jews kept the *Shabbat* – the *Shabbat* kept the Jews." That was the beauty and blessing of tradition.

"How good to be home," Tevye thought, as he touched the *mezuzah* on the door post with his hand. First, his daughters, Hodel and Ruchel, came running to hug their father. Then the grandchildren, all in their young twenties, Ruth, David, Sarah, Yehoshua, and Akiva, the son of Hevedke and Hava, may her murder be avenged.

"Where's Moishe?" Tevye asked, noticing that the son of Tzeitl was missing, may her memory be for a blessing as well.

"At his yeshiva," Carmel replied.

While Moishe had enrolled in the training courses of *Betar* and the *Irgun*, like all the others, David Raziel insisted he remain in yeshiva, saying that the Nation needed Torah scholars just as much as it needed soldiers. His sons-in-law, Rabbi Nachman, Ruchel's husband, and the one-armed Hevedke, waited their turn to greet him. As the saying goes, "There is joy in the port when the ships return to the harbor!" The door opened, and, Tevye's sons, Tzvi and Boaz, appeared. Everyone cried out with pleasure to welcome the warriors home. Carmel hugged them with a motherly squeeze. Placing his hands on their heads, Tevye blessed his offspring with the traditional priestly blessing from the Torah. With a small sigh he remembered his daughters who were no longer living – Tzeitl, who had died of pneumonia; Shpritzer who had drowned in Anatevka; Bat Sheva who had succumbed to malaria while draining the swamps of the Holy Land; and Hava who had been butchered by Arabs in Hevron, may their memories be for a blessing, and may the murderers of Hava be avenged. Far away, his daughter, Baylke, was in America, along with her son, George, but at least, thank the good Lord, they were healthy. His granddaughter, Hannie, was spending a secluded *Shabbat* at home with her husband, Yair. Only one other person was missing, his youngest daughter, Naomi, who was spending the holy Sabbath incarcerated in the Bethlehem Prison for Women. Closing his eyes, Tevye blessed her as well. *"May the Lord bless you and protect you; may the Lord shine His countenance upon you and be gracious unto you; may the Lord favor you and grant you peace."*

6.

A closed police van transported Naomi to the infamous women's prison in Bethlehem, where Arab murderers and criminals were jailed. Only recently, after the three-year Great Arab Revolt had been quelled, a corridor had been opened for Jewish women, mostly members of the Jewish Underground, who, until then, had been jailed in a former maternity hospital near the Russian Compound. After her horrible ordeal, Tevye's daughter hardly spoke. Her eyes remained fixed in a faraway glance. She reacted to common sights with a frightened jerk, as if expecting to be hurt. Often, she sat hunched over, trembling, seeming to sob, but no tears fell on her cheeks. Inside her head, her mind was blank. Not wanting to think about what they had done to her, her mind stopped to think. The doctor whom Cairns summoned to examine her, to see if he could continue with the "investigation," concluded that the young woman was in a state of extreme trauma and shock. Suspecting the *Irgun* had informers within the Police Department, and not wanting his methods of investigation to become a public outcry, Cairns decided to ship the girl off to a penal asylum until she agreed to talk.

The police van drove by Rachel's Tomb on the way to Bethlehem. In the past, accompanied by her family, Naomi had traveled to the famous burial site to pray for the welfare of her family, for the welfare of the Jews in the Holy Land, and for the welfare of all the children of Rachel scattered around the world. Rachel, the only Matriarch not buried in the *Maharat HaMachpela* in Hevron, had *"died on the way,"* as recorded in the Torah. Over the generations, at her domed roadside tomb, Jews prayed that their supplications would join Rachel's Heavenly tears, and evoke mercy on her offspring, the Children of Israel, beseeching God to safeguard the exiled and wandering Jews, and to bring them home to the Land of Israel, as the Prophet, Jeremiah, consoled:

"Thus says the Lord: A voice was heard in Rama weeping, lamentation and bitter weeping, Rachel weeping for her children. She refused to be comforted because they are gone. Thus says the Lord: Keep thy voice from weeping, and thy eyes from tears, for thy work shall be rewarded, says the Lord, and thy children shall come back again to their own border."

A serpentine road led up a hill to the prison which looked like a medieval castle. A tall stone wall, topped with barb wire, encircled the fortress-like building. A towering iron gate guarded the entrance from which no one escaped. Across the road, the bell of a monastery chimed on the hour, reminding prisoners that time still existed outside the walls of their cells.

The policeman driving the van tugged on a metal bar protruding from the gate. A bell rang inside the compound. Two dogs began to bark – large bloodhounds chained up in the back yard, ready to track down any escapee, but no one ever escaped from the netherworld of Bethlehem Prison. After a minute, an armed Arab guard opened a latch and peered out. "We have a new guest for you," the driver joked. The guard inserted a large, oversized skeleton key into the lock. Slowly, with a loud screech of protest, the heavy gate swung open. The foreboding edifice was three-stories high. A pleasant courtyard bordered by blossoming frangipani trees, and landscaped with bushes and flowering shrubs, disguised the grim reality of house of horrors within the thick stone walls. Naomi hardly gazed around. An Arab woman guard, built like a man, with an ugly scar on her face, took the new inmate's file and dragged Naomi by her sleeve through a door which the guard opened with a smaller master key. Like the other guards in the prison, she wore gray pants and a tight-fitting gray shirt with white buttons and a high, starched collar.

"Walk down the hall," she ordered, chewing a wad of gum.

When Naomi didn't respond, the mannish woman kicked her hard in the rear.

"Walk down the hall I ordered!" she yelled.

Naomi continued to stare vacantly into space. Grabbing the girl's arm with a twist, the guard pulled her along the corridor to the admission office, where a British policeman sat at a desk reading a magazine. Dressed in an immaculate uniform and shiny helmet, he looked completely out of place in the dingy room. Stacks of papers and dossiers were piled on his desk, waiting for somebody to process them.

"What new treasure have you brought us today, Pigeon?" he asked, looking Naomi up and down in an unsavory manner.

"She's deaf and dumb," the guard called Pigeon responded.

The admission's officer accepted the file and scanned the first page.

"No name?" he said. "Then that's what we'll call her. 'No Name.' Put her in the cage with the other crazies."

The policeman flipped the file to the edge of his desk and continued reading his London gazette, giving Naomi another look as the guard pushed her out from the room. Pigeon shoved Naomi across the corridor to another room, furnished with only a table and chair. Closing the door, she ordered Naomi to strip. When the girl didn't respond, she punched her hard in the chest. "Jewish dog," she said. Continuing to curse her in Arabic, the muscular guard pulled off the new prisoner's clothes and gave her an invasive body search, laughing as she abused her. Naomi instinctively swung her arms in protest, but the guard was much stronger. She held her down against the table, twisting her arm painfully behind her back. Deep in her soul, Tevye's daughter silently asked, "God, where are You?" And her own voice silently answered, *"Though I walk through the valley of the shadow of death, I shall fear no evil, for You are with me."* But her conscious mind remained switched off to what was happening, unable to deal with the continuing torment.

When the search was concluded, the guard ordered Naomi to put on her clothes. Slowly, with the cumbersome movements of a *golem*, the young girl obeyed, as if to salvage some crumb of human dignity.

"So you are not all gone after all," the gruff matron noted as Naomi dressed. "Sit down and put on your shoes."

Without bothering to straighten her clothes, Naomi sat down and slowly put on her shoes. Tears streamed from her eyes.

"Crying won't help you here, you miserable wench."

When Naomi finished dressing, Pigeon ordered her to take a blanket and a *borsh* from the pile on the floor. The *borsh* was a thin mat made by the prisoners out of pieces of cloth. Like a little girl, Naomi clutched the lice-filled blanket to her body, as if it could offer her protection and human warmth from a world turned cold and cruel. "*Yalla,*" Pigeon shouted, pushing her out the door as if she were an animal. She dragged her down the corridor to a gate of bars leading up a narrow stone stairway. A strong smell of Arab cooking came from the prison kitchen. Further down the corridor, two prisoners squatted by the floor scrubbing the cobblestones with soapy rags. A male attendant in a white shirt supervised their work. A wooden club with a leather strap dangled from his hand, swaying back and forth in a threatening manner. Pigeon grabbed the large key hanging on a nail on the wall, turned it in the lock, and swung open the gate. "*Yalla,*" she barked again, shoving the new prisoner up the stairs to another gate with iron bars.

"Anybody home?" Pigeon called out. Another matron appeared on the landing, as masculine looking as her comrade. Her hair was short, parted on the side and combed back like a man's. She wore the same tight-fitting uniform and sucked on an unlit cigarette. Taking another key off a hook, she opened the creaky gate.

"Another one for the crazy ward," Pigeon informed her.

There were two rooms on the landing. The door of one room was opened. A young Jewish woman sat ironing staff uniforms. Looking up at the new arrival, her eyes shone with kindness. Her name was Rachel Ohevet Ami. Not all of Eliav's operations proved successful. Rachel had volunteered to dress up as an Arab woman and bring a large basket of fruit to the Arab visitor's section of the Jerusalem Prison. Because of its heaviness, she asked an Arab passerby to carry the basket for her up the incline to the jail.

Suspicious by the weight of the basket, the man set it down to check it contents and discovered the bomb that Eliav had hidden under a top layer of fruit. Because of her age, instead of a death sentence, the young Jewish girl was sentenced to life in prison. Seeing Naomi, whom she recognized from an *Irgun* training course, Rachel stood up. Instinctively, she set her iron down and stepped away from the ironing table to greet her and say a comforting word, but the guard held out a hand. "*Mamnua!*" she snapped in Arabic. "It's forbidden!" Rachel frowned sadly as the prison guard pushed Naomi down the corridor. "Please, *Hashem*, help the girl," she prayed. "Help all of us. Help all of Your children." Powerless to assist a sister imprisoned for the cause, she sat down and continued with her ironing.

The other room along the hallway belonged to the Arab warden. His name was Bashar, a former police captain from Jaffa. The guard knocked on the door. She opened it when Bashar called out, granting permission.

"A new prisoner for the asylum," the guard informed him.

Basher looked at young Jewess. "Bring her to me for an interview at the end of the day, after I read her file."

"Come on, princess," the guard said, pulling Naomi further down the corridor to another short flight of stairs leading to another gate of bars, which another female guard unlocked. A foul stench filled the air. Screams and animal-like howls rang out from a more distant part of the ghoulish building. On one side of the corridor was a barred cell, as large as a ballroom, where Arab women prisoners were jailed - a mixture of petty criminals, murderers, and whores. Some slept on the floor without mats. Small infants in orange crates cried for attention. A new mother paced back and forth along the wall by the small barred windows, carrying her prison-born baby in a cloth sling tied around her neck. Some prisoners crowded around a radio, listening to an Arabic announcer. Others played *sheshbesh* on the floor.

Further down the corridor, five young women from the *Irgun* were locked behind bars in a room where political prisoners were kept. The room was far cleaner, smelling of strong disinfectant, and the prisoners seemed to take interest in how they dressed and combed their hair. Looking fed and healthy, they all stared at Naomi with compassion as the guard paused to display her like a slave being sold at market.

"Here's another Jewish ...," the guard said, using a vulgar expression. "I'm taking her upstairs to your sisters. She doesn't have a name, but who needs one here? If you meet her, explain to her that it doesn't pay to play dumb. If she wants to be treated like a human being and join you in your fancy suite, convince her to talk."

Outside the prison, the bell of the monastery chimed three times with loud echoing dongs. The guard dragged Naomi to the end of the hall and up another narrow flight of stone stairs leading to another locked gate and a dark, dungeon-like garret where the mentally ill were sequestered behind a solid iron door. Shrieks and animal-like cries sounded from the rancid-smelling cell. A policeman's club hung from a nail in the wall. Wrapping the strap around her hand, the guard opened the lock with the large master key. Many of the women inside the cave-like hall were Jewish. They looked like ghouls - pale, gaunt, with their hair unkempt. One stood facing the wall with a catatonic expression on her face. Another walked across the large room as if she were sleepwalking. Two prisoners sat slumped against the wall as if they were drugged. They never saw doctors, received a minimum of food and water, wore the same clothes for weeks, and were showered by a guard once a month with the kind of hard brushes used to scrub horses. Many died without ever breathing fresh air or seeing the light of day. The guard shoved Naomi into the chamber.

"Enjoy your stay," she said, locking the iron door behind her.

7.

Avraham Stern gave Yaacov Eliav a homework assignment – to think up a plan of action that would put the British Mandate Authority in Palestine on the defense, at the same time, keep Cairns and his sidekick, Blakely, distracted until *Irgun* intelligence could map out their daily routine as precisely as possible, in preparation for their elimination. "I want every British official in this country to think twice about remaining in Palestine," Stern said.

Eliav reported back with a bank of targets, concentrating mainly on British communications, including the telephone and postal systems. Working with Hevedke and Akiva, the industrious Eliav designed simple time bombs that would give the bomb squads ten minutes to plant the explosive device and vacate the targeted site. While the bombs were being made, information was gathered regarding the location of telephone junction boxes and the lines that serviced Arab neighborhoods and British Government facilities. To carry out the bombings, *Irgun* volunteers dressed up as telephone repair workers. The "telephone repair teams" arrived at the sites, which were generally situated at large intersections, and set to work uncovering the telephone boxes buried in the ground by the sidewalk, sealed with a metal lid. The "telephone workers" spread a tent over the underground box in order to work undisturbed, while other "workers" stood guard. Each team had a trained detonations expert familiar with the timing and wiring mechanisms. On a sunny day in early June, Eliav's army of saboteurs blew up three telephone junction boxes in Jerusalem situated on King George Street; another near the Eden Hotel off Ben Yehuda; and one by the Russian Compound. Some 2000 phones were disconnected by the explosions, including lines serving the British Army and Police. Follow-up attacks in Tel Aviv knocked out most of the phone lines serving British facilities. They next day, 23 targets were hit in Jerusalem. At sunset, powerful explosions resounded all over the city. In several locations, fires erupted. The sirens and alarms of police cars, ambulances, and fire trucks clanged for hours, as if the city had suffered an aerial attack. British soldiers and policemen ran in helter-skelter panic like chickens who had lost their heads. "The Irish are coming! The Irish are coming!" they screamed, shouting out the code name for a major attack. All of Eliav's men returned safely from their missions. In retaliation, the Government imposed a curfew on Jewish neighborhoods, searching for the bomb factory of the Jews. In the meantime, *Irgun* intelligence assembled hour-by-hour reports on the comings and goings of Cairns and Blakely, and other top CID personnel.

Stage two of Eliav's plan was already underway. As a test, a mail box was chosen in a British neighborhood that had a phone booth nearby. Wanting to taste some "action" on the street, rather than sitting all day in his father's workshop, carefully passing wires through sensitive gelatin explosives and TNT, Akiva volunteered to plant one of the bombs. Tevye's grandsons, David and Yehoshua joined him as co-bomber and lookout. Two other young *Irgun* cadets guarded the bicycles which the bombers used to flee the site. After Akiva hid a small explosive in the phone booth, David came by and slipped a thick envelope into the cast-iron mail box. The detonation in the phone booth attracted a crowd. When two policemen arrived, the bomb in the mail box exploded. The two "Bobbies" were killed, along with two Englishmen. Encouraged by the success, and given a green light by Stern, Eliav set his sights on the Central Post Office, which was located adjacent to CID Headquarters, home of the Jewish Underground Department of Britain's Secret Police. Eliav hoped that the explosion would attract the attention of Fred Clark, the CID explosives expert, who had successfully dismantled several *Irgun* bombs in the past. Eliav and Hevedke prepared four thick envelopes stuffed with powerful explosives, an electronic detonator, battery, and wrist watch. One of the envelopes was rigged especially for Clark's arrival with a double wire. If the Englishman tried to dismantle the bomb by cutting the visible wire, when the cutting knife or scissor merely touched the second wire, it would close the circuit, triggering the explosion. Late in the evening, when the post office was closed and the mail already collected, so that no Jewish mail collector be harmed, Akiva rode by on his bicycle and slid the four thick envelopes into the four mailboxes on the outside portico of the building. The powerful explosions of the first three bombs created a gaping hole in the wall of the post office. Two British policemen and two Arab guards were wounded. The fourth envelope with the booby-trapped wiring purposely didn't explode - just as planned. In the morning, when the debris was being cleared from the building, a postal worker discovered the suspicious envelope. Fred Clark was summoned immediately. The moment he cut the top wire, the bomb detonated. His head was severed from his body. It flew up to the ceiling of the lobby where it stuck to the wall, its eyes gazing down below. Any British official who saw the gory sight had to think twice about remaining in Palestine.

8.

The British weren't about to let a few bombs chase them out of Palestine with its strategic proximity to the Suez Canal and close proximity to vast oil resources. In the past, the British Empire had faced insurgencies throughout colonies around the globe, and its iron-fist policies had dealt with the disturbances in a most competent manner. Decision-makers in London and Jerusalem felt certain that the handful of rebellious Jews in Palestine would give up their struggle in the face of death, imprisonment, and exile. But the British underestimated the spirit of the Jews which had awakened with the return of the Children of Israel to their Land.

The day after the bombing at the Central Post Office adjacent to the British Government Center in Jerusalem, the British Police surrounded religious neighborhoods where they suspected that members of the *Etzel-Irgun* were hiding. A curfew was imposed. Soldiers with machine guns kept watch on the roofs, while others conducted house-to-house searches. Suspects were arrested and imprisoned. Some were tortured and released. *Irgun* members found guilty in speedy trials received long terms of incarceration. Many were deported to British labor camps in Africa. When police knocked on the door, looking for Tevye, Carmel told them that her husband was in America. Hannie said that her husband was in Poland. Undaunted by the crackdown, Stern pressed for more attacks. The police ransacked the flat Eliav had rented, discovering some drawings of bombs which he had neglected to destroy, but they couldn't find him.

Knowing that his apartment was being watched, he remained underground in a basement near Machane Yehuda, where he continued to fabricate bombs in Hevedke's glass-blowing workshop. Ordering another exploding coat from the tailor, Mazliah, he converted large, British-Government envelopes into letter bombs, with six sticks of dynamite in each official-looking package. A member of the *Irgun*, named Meir, worked in the *Kol Yerushalayim* Radio Station run by the Government. Swayed by Stern's magnetism, he agreed to plant the explosives in the building on Melisande Street. Since Meir worked there as a technician, he had no difficulty passing the guard in the lobby without being searched. He hung up the TNT-packed coat in the control room and placed the envelopes in the studios. Then he walked to a distant wing of the building where his office was located. Eliav was waiting outside by the bandstand near the Russian Compound, where musical bands played for the public on Wednesdays, in accord with English tradition. At the pre-arranged time, the music was interrupted by tremendous explosions. To make a long story short, the Government building suffered great damage, and all radio broadcasts ceased. Four people were killed in the blasts, including a Jewish announcer who was not supposed to have been near the studios. Broadcasts were only renewed weeks later in Ramallah. The following week, Meir was summoned for questioning, along with other Jews who worked in the building. Lacking any substantial evidence, the court sentenced him to a year of administrative arrest. Later, his incarceration was extended, and he was exiled to a British internment camp in Sudan.

It was time for Ralph Cairn to leave the planet.

9.

Stern and Raziel decided to first eliminate Cairns' sidekick, Lieutenant Blakely. The assimilated English Jew had established a network of Jewish informers who presented a daily danger to the *Irgun*. Many people didn't have steady employment, and the easy money that the CID offered for information about *Irgun* members was a powerful temptation. Other informers, including *Histadrut* workers and *Haganah* soldiers, informed on their brethren for ideological reasons, or because of orders they received from above.

Irgun intelligence provided Stern with a detailed report of Blakely's weekly schedule, including where he lived, what time he left his home in the morning, his route to and from work, when he returned, where he liked to dine, and how he spent his free time. Since he often left Police Headquarters during the day at unpredictable hours, whenever he was needed in the field, Stern narrowed the hit to three options. On Tuesday nights, he left his home in the German Colony around nine in the evening to frequent a brothel in the Talpiot neighborhood. A driver picked him up in a police car, waited outside while Blakely was in the brothel, then drove him home. On Fridays, after leaving Police Headquarters in the Russian Compound, he took a haircut and shave in an Arab barbershop across the street from the Old City, bought a bottle of spirits in a wine shop nearby, and purchased a bouquet of flowers for his latest mistress. The other possibility was to lure him to a café on the pretense of meeting a new informer and to shoot him in the presence of all the customers.

Stern met with Yaacov Eliav and Tevye in Hevedke's glassblowing workshop to discuss the possibilities.

"Take your pick," Stern told them.

Eliav offered his opinion first. "If we summon him to a meeting in a pub frequented by British policemen and British army personal, there is no reason for him to be suspicious. And we can kill several birds with one stone. Our man can be waiting in the café with a briefcase. During the course of their conversation, he can excuse himself to go to the bathroom. On his way out the back exit, he can trigger the bomb. Goodbye Blakely and all of the Brits around him."

Stern shook his head. "Let's save that plan for another occasion. I'd rather just kill Blakely so that everyone will know that we marked him specifically. That way all the upper brass will be on warning. If others are eliminated with him, people will think it was just an unlucky coincidence that Blakely was there as well."

"There's also a possibility that the briefcase will be checked and the bomb discovered before Blakely arrives," Hevedke noted, carefully coloring a delicate glass figurine with a thin painter's brush. "Or Blakely himself might get suspicious when he sees the briefcase under the table."

"I don't know how suspicious he will be," Eliav replied. "This is first time we are targeting a high-ranking CID officer. They probably think we are too afraid to go after them."

"It sounds like a messy operation," Tevye remarked.

"What do you suggest?" Stern asked.

"Whatever you people decide. I just want to be a part of the team to avenge what the devil did to my daughter."

"There's something poetic about killing the son-of-a-bitch when he's indulging himself in a brothel," Stern said. "Measure for measure."

"You want to blow up a brothel?" Eliav asked.

"No," Stern said. "Just him. We could plant one of our girls there by paying off the madam, or pay one of the regular prostitutes to make sure Blakely gets drunk, then shoot him when he leaves the place."

"His driver may mess things up," Eliav noted.

"Why not shoot him when he getting a shave?" Tevye suggested. "On Fridays, after finishing work, he doesn't have a bodyguard or driver. All the gunman has to do is walk into the barbershop and pull the trigger. A getaway car outside will be ready to whisk him away."

"You learned something from your friends in America," Stern quipped.

"When they saw that I could assemble the parts of a Thompson with my eyes blindfolded, they offered me a job."

For a moment, their banter eased the tension in Hevedke's glassblowing studio.

"I volunteer for the job," Akiva said, standing in the doorway to the back room, holding a shofar in hand. When the youth wasn't making bombs, he bore the cartilage out of shofars for his father after boiling them for five hours in a large, water-filled pot.

"You look too *Ashkenazic* to be hanging around the Arab

shuk opposite the Old City," Tevye said. "My son, Tzvi, will do it."

"We can dress him as an Arab and have him selling newspapers," Eliav advised.

"Sounds good to me," Stern said. "But what if a policeman happens to stroll by?"

"We can dress someone else as an Arab to stand guard outside the barbershop," Eliav suggested. "He can warn Tzvi. If he has to, he'll kill the policeman. After Blakely is terminated, the guard on watch and Tzvi will flee in a getaway car."

"This time no automatic revolver," Tevye insisted. "I learned that lesson when I had a chance to kill the Mufti, but the automatic cartridge jammed."

"It sounds like I won't be needed for this one," Eliav, the bomb expert, said. "It will leave me time to concentrate of Cairns."

"After his buddy, Blakely, is eliminated, Cairns will be a lot more precautious. It won't be easy to get to him," Tevye observed.

Stern stared at Tevye with a cold expression. "No one is impossible to kill," he said, "if the assassin is ready to die."

On a Friday afternoon after work, Blakely set nonchalantly off on his weekend routine, planning to get a shave and a haircut, and buy a bottle of imported wine and a bouquet of flowers for his most recent darling. As always, the Arab barber treated him like royalty, bowing in respect as he entered the small shop. "*Ahlan wa sahlan*," he greeted in welcome. "*Ahlan wa sahlan*." Turning off the radio which was playing loud Arab music, the shop's proprietor hurried to the waiting barber's chair, which he brushed with a great display of care, as if to remove any stray hairs on the seat. With a gracious gesture of his arm, the barber invited the honored police lieutenant to sit. Then he swung a clean sheet over Blakely and fastened it behind his neck. Not suspecting that his life was in danger, the CID detective didn't bother to remove his revolver from his shoulder holster. The barber swirled the chair so that Blakely could have a better look at himself in the mirror on the wall. As he began to spatter shaving lather on Blakely's face, another customer entered the shop. "Sit, please, sit," the barber told him in English, motioning to a small wooden chair by the door. In the mirror, Blakely saw the man take a seat. He was a cop on the force, named Phillips, without his uniform.

"Hallo!" he said in surprise, recognizing his superior in the barber chair. He stood up in attention, as if they were on duty. "Lieutenant Blakely, sir, how are you? I didn't recognize you at first with all that foam on your chin. My lucky fortune meeting you here, isn't it? I'm on my way to the precinct and thought I'd tidy up a bit before my shift."

"Relax," Blakely said. "Sit down. We're just getting started."

"Pour yourself a cup of black coffee," the proprietor told him.

Outside on the crowded sidewalk, dressed in a long, white, Arab *thwab* and carrying a small stack of newspapers, Tzvi was surprised when an Englishman in civilian dress entered the barber shop and sat down to wait his turn. That wasn't a part of the plan, but the trained *Irgun* soldier didn't lose his cool. Undaunted, he decided to go ahead with the mission. He nodded at Nachshon who stood by the street, also garbed as an Arab, waiting to signal the driver of the getaway car parked down the road by a bus station.

Entering the barber shop, Tzvi called out in practiced Arabic, "*Nyuz*. Newspapers. Today's newspaper." The Englishman in the chair was pouring himself a cup of aromatic Turkish coffee from a shiny brass *dallah*. Passing by, Tzvi noticed that he was wearing the shoes worn by British policemen.

"Newspapers," Tzvi repeated, approaching the barber chair.

"No. No. Get out!" the barber snapped, flicking the newspaper vendor away with his hand.

Tzvi slid his revolver out from under the papers. "Policemen shouldn't harm young Jewish girls," he said in Hebrew, as Blakely turned to look his way. Tevye's son let the newspapers drop to the floor. Raising the gun opposite Blakely's face, the calm hitman fired a bullet between his startled eyes. The shot rang out loudly. The barber fell backwards in fright. His cup of shaving foam flew out of his hand. In the mirror, Tzvi saw the startled off-duty copper drop his cup of coffee and fumble for his gun. Turning, Tevye's son stood in a balanced position and fired two shots into the policeman's chest. Then he strode quickly out of the barber shop.

When Nachshon heard the first shot, he held up his hand, signaling the driver. Pedestrians on the sidewalk reacted in commotion. As people hurried out from neighboring shops, Nachshon pulled a revolver from his *jalabiyyah* and sprayed two storefronts, warning people to stay away. The crowd dropped down to the ground as Tzvi ran to the street. The getaway car braked to a halt and Nachshon and Tzvi hopped inside. The car screeched away. Within seconds, the barbershop was far behind. To their *mazel*, the light at the intersection was green. Before British Police could react, the assassins had vanished. When Ralph Cairns arrived on the scene and saw the gaping bullet hole between Blakely's eyes, and half his skull missing, he instinctively knew that he was next in line.

10.

Once upon a time in Florence, Avraham Stern had been studying for a doctorate in Ancient Greek Literature when, like the sweet-singing Sirens in the saga of Odysseus, a more enticing mission called him away. And just as Oedipus and Achilles met their downfall through hubris, Ralph Cairns was killed by his overgrown arrogance as well. The Chief British Police Investigator of the CID could have requested a transfer to some other remote spot on the globe, or retired from the police force and found an executive's job in a security firm in London, but he wasn't going to let a bunch of stinking Jewish thugs chase him out of town. He was the commander of a team who had been appointed by the British Government to maintain law and order in Palestine, and that's exactly what he would do. Danger and risk came with the job. He wasn't afraid. But he wasn't some innocent rookie either. Haunted by the memory of Blakely's blood-drenched face, he became extremely cautious and always on the lookout, making sure that his handgun was in good working condition. He carried it with him everywhere. Whenever he was outside of British Police Headquarters, he kept his right hand in his coat pocket, clutching the gun. He started to wear a bulletproof vest, and a bodyguard accompanied him on all of his outings.

Cairns lived in a building in Gan Rehavia, on the corner of Shmuel HaNagid and Narkiss, by the Bezalel Art School. Returning to his apartment from work, he would take a shortcut through an open construction site. Eliav decided to plant the bomb there. He made sure the blast would bury Cairns in a deep crater, fitting his stature and prestige. Two nights before the carefully-planned assassination, the bomb team transferred the heavy can of explosives to an abandoned warehouse near the site where two apartment buildings were being constructed, hiding it in the ground for safekeeping. On the night before the operation, two workers were sent to bring the bomb from the ruin to the target area, where two other team members had prepared a hole along the path that Cairns always walked. Working in darkness in the middle of the night, they silently poured gravel into the small pit to hold the bomb firmly in place. Covering the powerful land mine with dirt, they smoothed it down with their shoes until it looked like every other section of the pathway. Hevedke's son, Akiva, attached the thin detonator wires they had left sticking out from the ground with a long wire that he unrolled as he walked backwards toward a stonecutter's hut, some forty meters away. The clandestine workers covered the wire with dirt and gravel so that it couldn't be seen. Finally, Akiva placed a stone over the end of the wire as a marker.

The next day, the team took turns strolling by the construction site to make sure that nothing had been disturbed. In the late afternoon, after the construction workers had quit for the day, Eliav arrived wearing the uniform of an auxiliary policeman. He carried a lunch box containing the batteries which would power the charge. A lookout stood at a bus station across the street. His job was to signal Eliav when Cairns appeared. In the stone-cutter's hut, the skilled bomber removed the stone from the end of the wire and carefully hooked up the batteries, switch, and plug. When the time came, he would complete the circuit by hooking up the socket with the wire. Now, there was nothing more to do but wait and pray. The few people who passed by the site saw a uniformed guard reading a newspaper. After dark had fallen, the stakeout, who was standing under a streetlight by the bus station, raised up his hand when Cairns approached with his bodyguard. Eliav crouched in the hut. Deft and confident fingers made final twists of the wires. The younger bomber's hand hovered over the switch. Two typically-dressed Englishmen strolled down the path. When they came directly in line with the tree which paralleled the mine, Eliav pressed on the switch. The forceful explosion shook the heavens and earth. Rocks rattled on the sheet-metal roof of the flimsy shack where Eliav lay prostrate on the ground. When he looked out the doorway, all he could see was dust. Wiping his fingerprints off the batteries and switch, he placed them in the hole he had already dug and covered them up. Taking the lunch box, he hurried toward the street where people were beginning to gather. No one paid attention to him. The cloud of dust began to disperse over the construction site. Peering into the darkness, everyone wanted to know what happened. In another five minutes, Eliav was back in Machane Yehuda where Tevye, Raziel, and Stern were waiting. They had heard the great explosion and knew all was well when they saw the smile on Eliav's face. Cairns and his bodyguard had been blown to smithereens. An arm here, a foot there. Some teeth and bones. Nothing else remained.

11.

To make a long story short, as Sholom Aleichem would say, Tevye asked Rabbi Aryeh Levine to visit Naomi in the prison. The saintly Rabbi was known as the "Rabbi of the Prisoners." Now that Jewish women were incarcerated in the women's prison in Bethlehem, he made a point of visiting them twice a month, always stopping on the way to pray at Rachel's Tomb. And always, he carried messages to them from the *Irgun* and from their families. His warmth, spirit, and optimism had a strengthening effect on the downcast prisoners, and his visits were known to save despairing souls from depression and even suicide.

Without touching Naomi, the holy Rabbi succeeded in warming her frozen heart with the elixir of concern in his eyes. "Don't give up hope," he told the young woman. "God will save you. Right down the road, our mother, Rachel, is pleading for your welfare, along with the welfare of all of her children. Trust in *Hashem*. Pray to Him, and purge all the anger from your heart. His ways are not our ways. His thoughts are not like ours. We cannot fathom His doings. But all of his paths are just, and all his ways are kindness. Do not blame Him for the evildoing of men. King David, the most saintly of God's servants, who was born here in Bethlehem, didn't he also suffer from the deeds of the wicked, and even from the righteous Saul who sought to slay him? Yet he never complained. Who are we to question *Hashem's* doings? Always remember, '*The Lord is near to the broken hearted, and saves those who are crushed in spirit. A good person may have many ills, but the Lord delivers him from them all.*'"

Reb Aryeh arranged for Naomi to be transferred to the cell for political prisoners. There, the Jewish women lovingly nursed the traumatized girl back to health, gradually restoring her confidence in life. Though everyone had a sad tale of their own, they all gathered around her side to rescue her from her pit of depression. Their faith and optimism were like a healing balm. The Rabbi returned the same week to learn how Tevye's daughter was progressing. Naomi grew stronger each day. One morning, a flicker of light appeared in her vacant glance. One afternoon, she smiled. She began to speak. Urged by her friends, she even sang along with them, singing Zionist songs while a guard in the hallway shouted, "*Mamnua*! It's forbidden!" Their love returned the young woman to life. Though hesitant and still fragile, she even joined them in dancing a lively *hora*. Finally, Naomi allowed herself to cry in the arms of Rachel Ohevet Ami, who had become a friend, a sister, and a mother to her. She wept and wept until her tears could have irrigated a dry, unfertile wasteland, transforming it into a verdant valley yielding bushels of fruit.

Naomi made up her mind – she was going to escape. When she confided her decision to her cellmates, everyone tried to dissuade her. No one escaped from Bethlehem Prison. Any attempt was dangerous. If she wasn't killed, she would be caught and punished. Guards were posted on the roof at night. During the day, policemen patrolled the perimeter. And if a prisoner managed to somehow sneak out from the compound, the territory back to Jerusalem was filled with hilly terrain and hostile Arabs. Willful young girl that she was, Naomi wouldn't back down. She gathered all the information she could. During her daily walk in the yard, she observed all of the guard posts and barb-wire fences. She learned the times the sentries changed their watches. She stared at the stones of the five-meter-high wall, as if her eyes could bore through rock to freedom. In a corner of the yard, the old wall had been weathered by streams of winter rainwater flooding down from a hill directly behind the building. Some of the large stones had been slightly dislodged. Here and there, they jutted from the wall, making ideal hand and foot holds. Naomi felt certain she could scale the high wall at nighttime when guards often left their stations to chat with each other, while others slept, never dreaming that a prisoner would try to escape. At the top of the wall was a two-meter-high fence of barb wire, and coils of barb wire waited below in the ditch on the other side of the wall to greet anyone who was crazy enough to jump to the ground.

A lawyer for the *Irgun* came to visit the prisoners. He told Naomi that they were going to disclose her identity and request a trial. As a mere accomplice, she would receive a few years in jail, no more, and a way would be found to free her while she was taken to or from court. Naomi refused. She didn't want to jeopardize her family. "Anyway," she informed the lawyer, "I am planning to escape on my own tomorrow night."

"Does anyone know?" the surprised lawyer asked.

"No," Naomi answered. "Beside my friends here, I haven't told anyone."

"Don't you think you should ask the advice of the Organization?"

"No," the determined girl replied. "I am doing this on my own."

That afternoon, her cellmates wrapped strips of blankets and floor mats around her arms and legs, her chest and her waist. For added protection, she wore long johns and a pair of gym shorts. Under her prison uniform, she wore her street clothes. When dinner ended, after her shift cleaning the kitchen, she hid in a supply closet. Taking out a roll of bandage, she wrapped the cloth again and again around her hands, to buffer the spikes of barb wire. Upstairs in the prison corridor, the night count was lackadaisical as usual, and when Naomi's turn to call out her number arrived, Rachel said it. When Naomi heard the monastery bells chime nine, she hurried out from the closet and lifted a chair onto the kitchen counter under a small window that was always left open for ventilation. Shoulder after shoulder, she squeezed through the frame and dropped to the ground. The yard was dark, but she knew every meter by heart. Running to the back corner where the wall could be climbed, she thanked God that the footholds held firm. Within seconds, she reached the top of the wall. The guard tower was deserted. Before the new guard arrived to begin his shift, she grabbed ahold of the barb wire and scaled the fence, shutting her mind to the pain. Opposite her, the bell tower of the monastery rose up in the darkness. Down the hill, the lights of Bethlehem shone in the night, and in the far distance the twinkling lights of Jerusalem. Grabbing the bar at the top of the fence, Naomi scrambled up and over the merciless spikes. She thought of the martyrdom of Rabbi Akiva, how the Romans flayed off his skin with sharpened iron combs, and how the body was just the vessel which housed the soul. Instead of leaping blindly to freedom, she froze when she glanced down at the coils of barb wire awaiting her on the ground. The height of the fall scared her less than the thought of the pain. But if she hesitated any longer, the sweep of the guard-tower searchlight would expose her for sure. "Trust in *Hashem*," she thought. "Trust in *Hashem*," she repeated and jumped. Bracing her head in her arms, a miracle occurred. Instead of ripping her flesh to pieces, the coils of wire cushioned her fall like a spring, as if an angel had reached out its arms and caught her. The spikes of the wire cut into her skin wherever there was no bandage or extra clothing, but none of her bones felt broken. Sheltering her face in her arms, she rolled over and over on the buoyant coils of wire until she was free.

"Halt!" a British voice called out.

Without glancing back, Naomi scrambled to her feet and started to run. A rifle fired. The bullet made a whooshing sound over her head. The prison bloodhounds started to bark. Heart racing, she ran down the hill, stumbled, fell, got up and kept running as fast as she could. Leaving the winding road, she dashed down a dark alley, but met a dead end. Retracing her tracks, and losing valuable time, she heard the roar of a truck engine in the distance and the loud clanging of the prison's emergency bell. Another gunshot sounded. The wild barking of dogs came closer. Naomi raced off down the road. A volley of gunshots rang out. Making an impulsive decision, she ran into a grove of olive trees in the direction she hoped was Jerusalem. Leaving the grove, she came to the main road, bordered by a few houses and shops which were sealed for the night. Crossing the deserted road, she ran toward the hills in the distance. Another olive grove afforded her some shelter, but the roar of a truck sounded behind her, along with the frantic barking of the bloodhounds and more gunshots. The bullets tore through the branches of the ancient olives trees which dated back to the time of King David.

"Please *Hashem*," she prayed in her mind, too out of breath to speak. "In the merit of our matriarch Rachel, please save me. In the merit of King David, come to my aid."

The frantic barking of the hounds grew closer. Realizing that the slope up the hill was slowing her progress, she veered back down toward the road. Reaching a terraced hillside, she ran and ran, tripping over rocks, rising and running again. Footsteps pounded the earth behind her. Gunshots roared in the night. A bullet slammed into her thigh. "I'm finished," she thought, still running, dragging her wounded leg behind her. The bloodhounds howled, smelling her blood. Her vision began to blur. Up ahead, Naomi saw the dome of Rachel's Tomb. She ran toward the holy site, summoning all of her remaining strength. At least, if she had to die, she would die in Rachel's embrace. Out of breath, she reached the stone building.

"Halt!" a voice called out. "Halt or we'll shoot!"

Naomi turned to face her pursuers. In surrender, she held up her hands. The bloodhounds barked furiously, tugging at their leashes, ready to tear her to shreds. Five soldiers pointed rifles her way. The headlamps of a truck shone in her eyes. The dark figures of policemen appeared. Another vehicle screeched to a stop. Exhausted, she fell back against the wall of the tomb. Suddenly, an angry volley of gunshots resounded over the hillsides where the Maccabees had battled the Greeks, and where the army of Bar Kochba had ambushed Romans legions. Naomi closed her eyes, expecting to die, but none of the bullets hit her. The headlights of a truck went black. Another roar of gunshots exploded around the tomb like thunder. A grenade shook the earth. A truck exploded. One after the other, the soldiers facing her spun around in a twisted dances of death. Grunting, they crumbled to the ground. The bloodhounds whelped. After another blaze of automatic fire, a sudden stillness filled the air. Then she heard a cheer and running footsteps. Her brothers, Tzvi and Boaz ran to greet her, their rifles held up victoriously in the air. Then she saw Avraham Stern and Nachshon, Akiva and Yaacov Eliav. Behind them she saw her father, running toward her with outstretched arms. "*Abba!*" she shouted, running to him and collapsing in his embrace. "*Abba!*"

"My little lioness," Tevye said. Naomi fainted in exhaustion. Tevye lifted the bleeding girl in his arms.

"Let's go!" Stern shouted.

Surrounding Tevye and his daughter like a squad of angels, the fighters of the *Irgun* led the way to two sedans parked on the road. A police siren sounded in the night and a police car sped toward them, its red light flashing. Eliav loaded a grenade on a special launcher he had fashioned and aimed the weapon at the road. With a squeeze of the trigger, he fired the missile. A moment later, a great explosion sent the police car tumbling off the road in a tower of flames. "*Yalla*," Stern called out. Gently, Tevye set his daughter in the back seat of a car.

"Thank the good Lord," Tevye said.

His daughter slept on his shoulder all of the way back to Jerusalem.

To Be Continued

Acknowledgements

While this novel is a work of fiction, in painting the historical background, I relied on a palette of many sources which I would like to acknowledge. Readers who would like a more complete and factual account of the events of the period and the personages involved, will experience many hours of enjoyable and edifying reading in the following list of books, some in English and others in Hebrew. There are hundreds of books about modern Zionism, and these are little more than a shelf's worth, but they are filled with inspiration and a plethora of important information.

Ben Gurion, Prophet of Fire, by Dan Kurzman; a Touchstone Book, Simon and Schuster, Inc. New York, 1984.

The Life and Times of Vladimir Jabotinsky, Fighter and Prophet, by Joseph B. Schechtman; Volumes One and Two, Eshel Books, Silver Spring, Maryland, 1956.

An Angel Among Men, Impressions from the Life of Rav Avraham Yitzhak HaKohen Kook, by Simcha Raz, English translation by Moshe D. Lichtman; Kol Mevaser Publications, Jerusalem, 2003.

The Wandering Jew has Arrived, by Albert Londres, translated from the French by Helga Abraham; Gefen Publishing House, Jerusalem, 2017.

Years of Wrath, Days of Glory, by Yitshaq Ben-Ami, Memoirs from the Irgun; Robert Speller and Sons Publishers, New York, 1982.

Days of Fire, the Secret Story of the Making of Israel, by Shmuel Katz; Steimatzky's Agency Ltd. Jerusalem, 1966.

Free Jerusalem, Heroes, Heroines, and Rogues who Created the State of Israel, by Zev Golan; Devora Publishing Company, Jerusalem, 2003.

Stern: The Man and His Gang, by Zev Golan; Yair Publishing, Tel Aviv, 2011.

Wanted, by Yaacov Eliav, translated from the Hebrew by Mordecai Schreiber; Shengold Publishers, Inc. New York, 1984.

Weizmann, His Life and Times, by H.M. Blumberg; Yad Weizmann, Israel, 1975.

דמע ונגה, דם וזהב, עיונים בשירת אורי צבי גרינברג, ע״י ישראל אלדד, הוצאת שוקן, ירושלים ותל אביב, 2003

המשפט, ע״י אב״א אחימאיר, הועד להוצאת כתבי אחימאיר, תל אביב, 1968

העלילה הגדולה, לפני רצח ארלוזורוב ולאחריו, ח. בן ירוחם, הוצאת מכון זיבוטינסקי, 1982

לחישה רועמת, סיפורו של הרב קוק, ע״י רזיאל ממט, יד יצחק בן-צבי ועם עובד, 2006

ברגמן, חייו של יאיר אברהם שטרן, ע״י עדה אמיכל-ייבין, הדר הוצאת ספרים בע״מ, תל אביב, 1986

בדמי לעד תחיי, שירים, יאיר אברהם שטרן, הוצאת יאיר ע״ש אברהם שטרן, תל אביב, 1983

מכתבים לרוני, אברהם שטרן – יאיר, הוצאת יאיר ע״ש אברהם שטרן, תל אביב, 2000

ספורה של לוחמה, גאולה כהן, הוצאת ספרים קרני בע״מ, תל אביב, 1961

I would also like to acknowledge the background impressions which I gleaned from visiting the National Library of Israel, the Menachem Begin Heritage Center, and the Central Zionist Archives in Jerusalem; and from the *Haganah* Museum, the *Etzel* Museum, the *Lechi* Museum, and the Jabotinsky Institute in Tel Aviv. For people who don't like to leave their homes, there are many Internet websites which detail the years of Modern Zionism, and a treasure of material can be found on Wikipedia. Needless to say, every article, book, and museum has its own point of view, and the best general background can be obtained by creating a mosaic from them all. Thanks to Moshe Kaplan for preparing the book for printing, and to Yisrael Medad for guiding me through the background research, and for his encyclopedic overview and understanding of the era. Finally, I would like to thank Mrs. Cherna Moskowitz and the Cherna Moskowitz Foundation for their help in publishing the book.

Glossary

Abba: father

Abisele: a little

Achshan: a stubborn person

Afikomen: one of the matzahs eaten at the Passover Seder

Aliyah: moving to Israel. Literally, an ascent

Allah: Arabic word for God

Am HaAretz: a person who hasn't learned Torah; an ignorant fellow

Am Yisrael: the Nation of Israel

Apikorus: a non-believer

Apikorsut: heresy

Aron HaKodesh: the ark in the synagogue where the Torah scrolls are kept

Ashkenazim: Jews whose ancestors in the Diaspora lived in ancient Rome, Germany, Russia, and Eastern Europe

Avinu: our father

Azoy gaytis: that's the way it goes

Baal tshuva: a Jew who returns to religious observance

Balabusta: an old-fashion homemaker

B'Aretz: in the Land of Israel

Baruch haba: welcome

Beit HaMikdash: the Holy Jerusalem Temple

Beit Knesset: synagogue

Beit Midrash: study hall

Bershert: a marriage partner sent from God

Betarim: members of the Betar organization

Bezrat Hashem: with the help of God

Bimah: pulpit

Birionim: a group of zealot freedom-fighters against Rome's conquest of Israel, and the name of an underground Jewish organization against the British.

Bittul Torah: wasted time not studying Torah

B'kitzor: in short

Boged: traitor

Boker tov: good morning

Brit: covenant

Brit milah: Jewish circumcision ceremony

Busha: a scandal or shame

B'vakasha: please

Casbah: a roofed Arab market

Chabora: a group with a set goal, like in baking matzot before Passover

Chazzer: a pig

Chazzerai: junk; an assortment of unimportant things

Chevre Kadisha: the Jewish burial society

Chillul Hashem: a desecration of God

Chol HaMoed: the intermediary days of a week-long Jewish Festival

Cholent: a popular dish with meat, potatoes, vegetables, and hard-boiled eggs

Chuppah: wedding canopy

Chutzpah: bold arrogance

Clal Yisrael: the entire Nation of Israel, past, present, and future

Dafka: precisely

Daven: to pray

Dayan: a judge of Jewish Law

Dunam: a measure of land

Dvar Torah: a teaching of Torah

Ema: mother

Eretz Yisrael: the Land of Israel

Eshes chayil: a woman of valor

Etrog: a fruit connected with the holiday of Sukkot

Etzel: another name for the "Irgun"

Eyniklech: grandchildren

Fellahin: Arab peasant laborers

Fertummelt: a mixed-up person

Frum: religiously observant

Gabai: the beacon of a synagogue, or a Rabbi's helper

Galil: the Galilee

Galitzianer: a Jew from Galacia, often a disciple of the Hasidic movement

Galut: the Diaspora outside the Land of Israel; exile

Gan Eden: the Garden of Eden, or Heaven

Gashash: someone expert in following footprint tracks
Gehinom: hell
Gelt: money
Gemara: the Talmud
Geula: Redemption; the return of the Jews to the Land of Israel
Gevalt: an expression of apprehension or surprise
Gingee: redheaded
Gornisht helfn: beyond help; no help from there
Gornisht mit gornisht: a whole lot of nothing
Goy: a non-Jew
Goyisha: pertaining to the Gentiles
Grantze mitzeya: a disparaging expression meaning, a big bargain!
Haftarah: a portion of Scripture read on Shabbat
Haganah: defense; the name of the semi-official Jewish defense force in Palestine
Haggadah: the traditional story and prayers recited during the Passover meal
Halacha: Jewish law
Halav: milk
Hallel: Psalms praising God
Haluka: charity fund
HaMifaked: the commander
Hamisha: homey, family-style
HaMotzei: the blessing over bread recited at the beginning of a meal
Haredi: an ultra-Orthodox Jew, often anti-Zionist
HaRav: term of respect for a Rabbi
Hashem: God; literally, The Name
Hashem yirachem: may God have mercy
Has v'shalom: an expression meaning, Heaven forbid
Hatan: groom
Haval: what a pity; what a waste
Havlaga: a passive policy of restraint and appeasement
Heder: Torah school for very young boys
Heder Yichud: a room where a bride and groom can be alone after their wedding
Irgun: organization; the name of the secret Jewish Underground in Palestine

Jihad: the Muslim expression for war against all disbelievers and non-Muslims

Kaddish: the mourner's prayer

Kadima: forward!

Kaftan: an Arab robe

Kayn: yes

Kedusha: holiness

Keffiyeh: an Arab headdress

Kibbitz: light banter

Kibbitzer: someone who gives unasked-for advice

Kibbutznik: a member of a kibbutz

Kiddush: the Sabbath or Festival meal blessing recited over wine

Kike: a derogatory racial slur similar to "dirty Jew"

Kinder: children

Kippah: skullcap

Kishkes: entrails; gut emotions

Kittel: a white gown used in Jewish prayer and religious ceremonies

Kohen: a member of the Jewish priestly clan

Kosher: permissible according to Jewish law

Kotel: the Wailing Wall; the Western Wall; also known as the Wall – the outer wall of the Second Temple

Kvetch: complain; a complainer

Lamdan: a wise scholar

L'Azazel: to hell; or to hell with it

L'Chaim: to life!

Lehi: a breakaway group from the Irgun, more radically anti-British, also known as the Stern Gang

L'havdil: to make a distinction between two things

Litvaks: Ashkenazic, non-Hasidic Jews from Lithuania

Lo aleynu: it shouldn't happen to us

Lokshen: silliness; a falsehood

Lulav: the branch of a date palm connected with the holiday of Sukkot

Ma'apilim: immigrants to Israel arriving on "illegal" refugee boats

Machloket: argument; disagreement; disunity

Malkhut: Kingship

Malkhut Yisrael: the Kingdom of Israel

Mamash: exactly

Mame loshn: mother tongue

Manna: the bread-like substance that fell from Heaven in the Wilderness

Mashiach (also pronounced Moshiach): the prophesized Jewish savior

Mazel: luck; good or bad fortune; also written, mazal

Mazel tov: a blessing of congratulations; a wish for good luck!

Melamed: teacher

Mensch: a respectable man; a reliable person

Meshugener: a crazy person or idea

Mishegas: craziness; insanity

Mezuzah: verses of the "Shema" from the Torah, set in a casing and fastened to the doorpost of a Jewish home

Metsiye: a bargain; a fortunate discovery

Mifaked: commander

Mikveh: ritual purity bath

Minyan: a group of ten Jews

Mishna: the teachings of the Sages which form the basis of the Oral Law and Talmud

Misnaged: a religious Jew who opposes the Hasidic movement and its teachings

Mizrachnik: a follower of the Mizrachi movement of religious and Zionist Jews

Moishe Rabanu: Moses, our teacher

Moshav: a farming and agricultural collective and settlement

Motzei Shabbat: the evening at the end of the Sabbath

Mukhtar: an Arab village leader

Muzzein: an Arab call to prayer usually situated in a mosque tower

Natlah: a vessel used for the ritual washing of hands

Narrishkeit: nonsense

Nedunia: wedding dowry

Nu: an expression meaning, what's new?

Olim: new immigrants to Israel (plural for Oleh)

Orot: lights; the name of a book by Rabbi Kook

Oy vey's mir: an expression of worry or exasperation

Pamalia: a group escorting a distinguished person

Parnassa: livelihood

Parve: neutral; neither a milk or meat product

Pashkevil: a street poster in the Ultra-Orthodox community

Pesach: the holiday of Passover

Pesach Seder: the traditional evening meal on the first night of Passover

Peyes: side-locks of hair

Pish: urine; to urinate; pisher means, something small

Plotz: to fall down or pass out

Protectzia: influence; protection

Pushke: a small charity box

Rasha: a wicked person

Reb: a term of respect like Mister

Rebbetzin: the wife of a Rabbi

Ribono Shel Olam: the Master of the World; God

Rosh Betar: the head of the Betar Movement, Ze'ev Jabotinsky

Rosh Yeshiva: the head of a yeshiva

Saba: grandfather

Sabalim: porters

Savlanut: patience

Sefardim: Jews whose ancestors in the Diaspora lived in North Africa and Middle Eastern countries

Sefer: book

Seudah: meal

Shabbat: the Jewish Sabbath and day of prayer and rest

Shabbos: an alternative pronunciation for Shabbat; the Sabbath

Shachrit: the morning prayer

Shadchan: matchmaker

Shalom: peace; hello

Shamash: a Rabbi's secretary or assistant

Shar Shechem: the Shechem Gate of the Old City, also called the Damascus Gate

Shaygetz: a non-Jewish man

Shechinah: the Divine Presence

Sheikh: a Muslim clergyman

Shema: the fundamental prayer of Jewish belief from the Torah

Shicksa: a Gentile woman

Shidduch: an arranged meeting or date; a marriage match

Shikker: a drunk
Shlep: to carry a heavy burden; a long trek
Shiva: the first seven days of mourning following burial
Shlimazel: a person of consistently bad luck; a bumbler
Shnorrer: a person who asks for a handout; a money raiser
Shomerim: guards
Shvitzer: an arrogant boaster
Shul: synagogue
Shtetl: a Jewish village in Russia and Eastern Europe
Shtreimel: a round, distinguished fur hat worn by certain
    religious Jews on the Sabbath and holidays
Shtuyot: foolishness
Simcha: joy
Spodik: a high, distinguished fur hat worn by certain
    religious Jews
Stender: a stand used to support a Talmudic text or prayer
    book
Tallit katan: a four-cornered prayer garment with ritual
    fringes
Talmud Torah: the study of Torah; a Torah school for young
    boys
Tanach: the Jewish Bible
Tefillah: prayer
Tehillim: Psalms
Tefillin: phylacteries worn on the arm and upper forehead
Tikun: rectification
Todah: thanks
Torat Eretz Yisrael: the original understanding of Torah
    which focuses on the establishment of a holy,
    independent, Israelite Nationhood in the Land of Israel
    for all of the Jewish People.
Traf: not kosher
Tzaddik: a holy and righteous person
Tzitzit: ritual fringes worn on a four-cornered prayer
    garment or shawl
Tzuris: trouble
Vaad: committee
Vatikan: the early morning prayer at dawn
Yerushalayim: Jerusalem
Yidden: Jews

Yishuv: a settlement; also, when capitalized, used to designate the entire Jewish community in Palestine - the Old Yishuv for the Ultra-Orthodox community, and the New Yishuv for the modern secular Zionists

Zaide: grandfather

ABOUT THE AUTHOR

Tzvi Fishman was born in Syracuse, New York. He attended Phillips Andover Academy in Massachusetts, and graduated from the New York University School of Film and Television. While commuting between New York and Hollywood, he sold four originals screenplays and published his first novel with Dell Publishers. In addition to his writing, he taught screenwriting at NYU. After moving to Jerusalem, where he lives with his wife and seven children, he served in the Israel Defense Forces. He has published nearly twenty novels and books on a wide range of Jewish themes, some of which are available at Amazon Books. He is the recipient of the Israel Ministry of Education Award for Creativity and Jewish Culture. Recently, he produced and directed the feature film, "Stories of Rebbe Nachman" starring Israel's popular actor, Yehuda Barkan. Presently, he is working on Volume Four of the *Tevye in the Promised Land* Series.

If you enjoyed *The Lion's Roar*, you are sure to love:

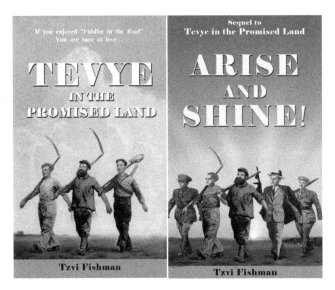

"The *Tevye in the Promised Land* Series is a wonderful achievement. For adults and young people alike, these historical novels about the rebirth of the Jewish People in the Land of Israel are powerful tools, inviting people to enjoy once again the almost lost art of reading. The incredible drama of Modern Zionism, along with the towering personalities which dominated the era, their heroism and great ideals, come alive in the pages of this fun-reading saga. If the next two volumes of the series possess the same passion and charm, then Mr. Fishman has created a literary treasure for the Jewish People."

> Yisrael Medad, Menachem Begin Heritage Center

All three volumes of the *Tevye in the Promised Land* Series are available at Amazon Books, and, in Israel, at Sifriyat Bet-El Publishers Ltd, Jerusalem - www.beitel.co.il

For more information: www.tzvifishmanbooks.com

TEVYE
IN THE PROMISED LAND

"The Jews of Anatevka have three days to clear out of the area."

Thus begins Tevye's unforgettable journey to the Promised Land. Tzvi Fishman's stirring family saga of the continuing adventures of Sholom Aleichem's beloved character, Tevye the Milkman, immortalized in "Fiddler on the Roof," takes up where the original stories left off. This dramatic story of the Jewish People's love for their eternal Homeland is the first part of the *Tevye in the Promised Land* Series.

At a crossroads at the outskirts of their Anatevka village, Tevye and his daughters meet up with a troupe of Zionists headed for Palestine. Just then, as if the Almighty is pointing the way, the Anatevka mailman comes running with a letter from Tevye's long-lost daughter, Hodel. Her communist husband, Perchik, has been exiled from Russia, and they are living in the Holy Land on a non-religious kibbutz!

Clinging to the Bible and the tradition he loves, Tevye has to defend his daughters, not only against the modern lifestyle of the Zionist pioneers, but against malaria-infested swamps, deadly plagues, swarms of locusts, Turkish prisons, and Arab marauders. With steadfast determination and faith, Tevye perseveres through trials and hardships in rebuilding the Jewish homeland. While trying to do his best as a father in marrying off his daughter's to suitable husbands, Tevye himself finds a new bride to take the place of his deeply-missed Golda. Finally, as World War One threatens to destroy the Jewish settlements in Palestine, Tevye joins the first Jewish fighting brigade since the days of Bar Kochba and Rabbi Akiva. In a daring secret mission, he helps the British rout the Turks.

Filled with laughter, heartbreak, and joy, *Tevye in the Promised Land* is the compelling story of a people's rebirth, and a triumph of inspiration and faith.

Volume Two in the *Tevye in the Promised Land* Series

ARISE AND SHINE!

When Rabbi Kook arrives in Jerusalem in 1919, Tevye joins the fanfare at the railway depot to greet him. Rabbi Kook reminds the simple milkman from Anatevka that at this great time in Jewish history, as the Nation of Israel rises to rebirth in its ancient and eternal Homeland, a far greater destiny awaits him. Indeed, when the colony of Tel Hai and its heroic commander, Yosef Trumpeldor, fall under Arab siege, Perchik enlists Tevye to lead a daring rescue mission. When Arab riots break out in Jerusalem, Tevye joins Ze'ev Jabotinsky's group of Jewish defenders, the *Haganah*, for which he is imprisoned in the infamous Acco Prison. Meanwhile, the ambitious David Ben Gurion is building a powerful worker's union and seizing control of the *Yishuv* in Palestine. One *Pesach* Night, Tevye's granddaughter, Hannie, brings a surprise guest to the *Seder*, a charismatic young man named Avraham Stern, future leader of the "Stern Gang." Angered by their romance, and by Stern's unwillingness to marry the innocent girl, Tevye sends his granddaughter off to live in America with her aunt Baylke, whose husband, Pedhotzer, has become the financial advisor of the notorious Jewish gangsters, Meyer Lansky and Bugsy Siegel. Tevye's grandson, Ben Zion, rejects the sacred traditions of Judaism and abandons Jerusalem to live in Tel Aviv with his communist father, Perchik, who has become Ben Gurion's most ardent disciple. Little by little, the British renounce the Balfour Declaration and encourage the Arabs to declare war against further Jewish settlement. While Rabbi Kook battles for the rights of Jews to pray at the *Kotel*, the bloodthirsty Arab pogroms of 1929 lead to the widespread slaughter of Jews, including Tevye's daughter, Hava. Grief-struck and exasperated by the official Jewish Agency policy of constraint and appeasement, Tevye decides to strike back singlehandedly, igniting the sparks of a future rebellion which is destined to burst into a towering flame, leading the Jews to Redemption and Independence in their Land.

Tevye in the Promised Land Series
COMING - AUTUMN 2019
Volume Four
ANONYMOUS SOLDIERS

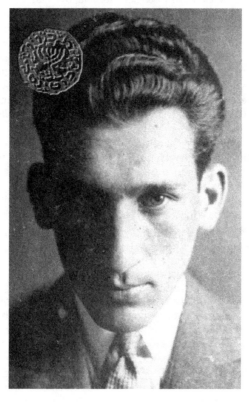

WANTED!